I0831318

THE COMPLETE HEIMSKRINGLA
KING HARALD'S SAGA

The Complete Heimskringla
Sturluson, Snorri c. 1179 – 1241
Written c.1225 – 1230
Translated by Samuel Laing
Translation pubiblished by Longman in 1844
Laing, Samuel 1780 – 1868

Cover design by: A.R. Roumanis

Text set in Minion Pro. Chapter headings set in News Gothic Standard.

ISBN: 978-1-77878-544-3

FIRST EDITION / FIRST PRINTING

Many classics were originally published with inconsistent spellings of the same word, spelling errors, and printer errors. The text of our titles have been edited to give readers the best possible reading experience. Sometimes we can make mistakes, which is why we post "first edition" in all of our titles. This is a standard notice that is historically used by publishers. The above edition notice refers to our edition of this title. If changes are made to correct an error in the text, we will change the wording to "second edition." If we change printers but the text remains the same, the wording will change to "second printing."

LIBRARY AND ARCHIVES CANADA CATALOGUING IN PUBLICATION

Title: The complete Heimskringla : King Harald's saga / Snorri Sturluson ; translated by Samuel Laing.

Other titles: Heimskringla. English (Laing)

Names: Snorri Sturluson, 1179?-1241, author. | Laing, Samuel, 1780-1868, translator.

Description: First edition. | "Translation published by Longman in 1844"--Copyright page.

Identifiers: Canadiana 20240369165 | ISBN 9781778785443 (hardcover)

Subjects: LCGFT: Poetry.

Classification: LCC PT7277 .E5 2024 | DDC 839/.61—DC23

THE COMPLETE HEIMSKRINGLA
KING HARALD'S SAGA

SNORRI STURLUSON

Translated by Samuel Laing

VANCOUVER:
ROYAL CLASSICS
2024

CONTENTS

Preface 7

1 Halfdan the Black Saga 11

2 Harald Harfager's Saga 18

3 Hakon the Good's Saga 52

4 Saga of King Harald Grafeld and of Earl Hakon Son of Sigurd 83

5 King Olaf Trygvason's Saga 99

6 Saga of Olaf Haraldson (St. Olaf) 195

7 Saga of Magnus the Good 474

8 Saga of Harald Hardrade 513

9 Saga of Olaf Kyrre 598

10 Magnus Barefoot's Saga 607

11 Saga of Sigurd the Crusader and his Brothers Eystein and Olaf 634

12 Saga of Magnus the Blind and of Harald Gille 675

13 Saga of Sigurd, Inge, and Eystein, the Sons of Harald 695

14 Saga of Hakon Herdebreid ("Hakon the Broad-Shouldered") 726

15 Magnus Erlingson's Saga 745

Preface

In this book I have had old stories written down, as I have heard them told by intelligent people, concerning chiefs who have have held dominion in the northern countries, and who spoke the Danish tongue; and also concerning some of their family branches, according to what has been told me. Some of this is found in ancient family registers, in which the pedigrees of kings and other personages of high birth are reckoned up, and part is written down after old songs and ballads which our forefathers had for their amusement. Now, although we cannot just say what truth there may be in these, yet we have the certainty that old and wise men held them to be true.

Thjodolf of Hvin was the skald of Harald Harfager, and he composed a poem for King Rognvald the Mountain-high, which is called "Ynglingatal." This Rognvald was a son of Olaf Geirstadalf, the brother of King Halfdan the Black. In this poem thirty of his forefathers are reckoned up, and the death and burial-place of each are given. He begins with Fjolner, a son of Yngvefrey, whom the Swedes, long after his time, worshipped and sacrificed to, and from whom the race or family of the Ynglings take their name.

Eyvind Skaldaspiller also reckoned up the ancestors of Earl Hakon the Great in a poem called "Haleygjatal", composed about Hakon; and therein he mentions Saeming, a son of Yngvefrey, and he likewise tells of the death and funeral rites of each. The lives and times of the Yngling race were written from Thjodolf's relation enlarged afterwards by the accounts of intelligent people.

As to funeral rites, the earliest age is called the Age of Burning; because all the dead were consumed by fire, and over their ashes were raised standing stones. But after Frey was buried under a cairn at Upsala, many chiefs raised cairns, as commonly as stones, to the memory of their relatives.

The Age of Cairns began properly in Denmark after Dan Milkillate had raised for himself a burial cairn, and ordered that he should be buried in it on his death, with his royal ornaments and armour, his horse and saddle-furniture, and other valuable goods; and many of his descendants followed his example. But the burning of the dead continued, long after that time, to be the custom of the Swedes and Northmen. Iceland was occupied in the time that Harald Harfager was the King of Norway. There were skalds in Harald's court whose poems the people know by heart even at the present day, together with all the songs about the kings who have ruled in Norway since his time; and we rest the foundations of our story principally upon the songs which were sung in the presence of the chiefs themselves or of their sons, and take all to be true that is found in such poems about their feats and battles: for although it be the fashion with skalds to praise most those in whose presence they are standing, yet no one would dare to relete to a chief what he, and all those who heard it, knew to be a false and imaginary, not a true account of his deeds; because that would be mockery, not praise.

OF THE PRIEST ARE FRODE

The priest Are Frode (the learned), a son of Thorgils the son of Geller, was the first man in this country who wrote down in the Norse language narratives of events both old and new. In the beginning of his book he wrote principally about the first settlements in Iceland, the laws and government, and next of the lagmen, and how long each had administered the law; and he reckoned the years at first, until the time when Christianity was introduced into Iceland, and afterwards reckoned from that to his own times. To this he added many other subjects, such as the lives and times of kings of Norway and Denmark, and also of England; beside accounts of great events which have taken place in this country itself. His narratives are considered by many men of knowledge to be the most remarkable of all; because he was a man of good understanding, and so old that his birth was as far back as the year after Harald Sigurdson's fall. He wrote, as he himself says, the lives and times of the kings of Norway from the report of Od Kolson, a grandson of Hal of Sida. Od again took his information from Thorgeir Afradskol, who was an intelligent man, and so old that when Earl Hakon the Great was killed he was dwelling at Nidarnes–the same place at which King Olaf Trygvason afterwards laid the foundation of the merchant town of Nidaros (i.e., Throndhjem) which is now there. The priest Are came, when seven years old, to Haukadal to Hal Thorarinson, and was there fourteen years. Hal was a man of great knowledge and of excellent memory; and he could even remember being baptized, when he was three years old, by the priest Thanghrand, the year before Christianity was established by law in Iceland. Are was twelve years of age when Bishop Isleif died, and at his death eighty years had elapsed since the fall of Olaf Trygvason. Hal died nine years later than Bishop Isleif, and had attained nearly the age of ninety-four years. Hal had traded between the two countries, and had enjoyed intercourse with King Olaf the Saint, by which he had gained greatly in reputation, and he had become well acquainted with the kingdom of Norway. He had fixed his residence in Haukadal when he was thirty years of age, and he had dwelt there sixty-four years, as Are tells us. Teit, a son of Bishop Isleif, was fostered in the house of Hal at Haukadal, and afterwards dwelt there himself. He taught Are the priest, and gave him information about many circumstances which Are afterwards wrote down. Are also got many a piece of information from Thurid, a daughter of the gode Snorre. She was wise and intelligent, and remembered her father Snorre, who was nearly thirty-five years of age when Christianity was introduced into Iceland, and died a year after King Olaf the Saint's fall. So it is not wonderful that Are the priest had good information about ancient events both here in Iceland, and abroad, being a man anxious for information, intelligent and of excellent memory, and having besides learned much from old intelligent persons. But the songs seem to me most reliable if they are sung correctly, and judiciously interpreted.

BOOK ONE

Halfdan the Black Saga

PRELIMINARY REMARKS

OF THIS SAGA there are other versions found in "Fagrskinna" and in "Flateyjarbok". The "Flateyjarbok" version is to a great extent a copy of Snorre. The story about Halfdan's dream is found both in "Fagrskinna" and in "Flateyjarbok". The probability is that both Snorre and the author of "Fagrskinna" must have transcribed the same original text.–Ed.

1. HALFDAN FIGHTS WITH GANDALF AND SIGTRYG

HALFDAN WAS A year old when his father was killed, and his mother Asa set off immediately with him westwards to Agder, and set herself there in the kingdom which her father Harald had possessed. Halfdan grew up there, and soon became stout and strong; and, by reason of his black hair, was called Halfdan the Black. When he was eighteen years old he took his kingdom in Agder, and went immediately to Vestfold, where he divided that kingdom, as before related, with his brother Olaf. The same autumn he went with an army to Vingulmark against King Gandalf. They had many battles, and sometimes one, sometimes the other gained the victory; but at last they agreed that Halfdan should have half of Vingulmark, as his father Gudrod had had it before. Then King Halfdan proceeded to Raumarike, and subdued it. King Sigtryg, son of King Eystein, who then had his residence in Hedemark, and who had subdued Raumarike before, having heard of this, came out with his army against King Halfdan, and there was great battle, in which King

Halfdan was victorious; and just as King Sigtryg and his troops were turning about to fly, an arrow struck him under the left arm, and he fell dead. Halfdan then laid the whole of Raumarike under his power. King Eystein's second son, King Sigtryg's brother, was also called Eystein, and was then king in Hedemark. As soon as Halfdan had returned to Vestfold, King Eystein went out with his army to Raumarike, and laid the whole country in subjection to him.

2. BATTLE BETWEEN HALFDAN AND EYSTEIN

When King Halfdan heard of these disturbances in Raumarike, he again gathered his army together; and went out against King Eystein. A battle took place between them, and Halfdan gained the victory, and Eystein fled up to Hedemark, pursued by Halfdan. Another battle took place, in which Halfdan was again victorious; and Eystein fled northwards, up into the Dales to the herse Gudbrand. There he was strengthened with new people, and in winter he went towards Hedemark, and met Halfdan the Black upon a large island which lies in the Mjosen lake. There a great battle was fought, and many people on both sides were slain, but Halfdan won the victory. There fell Guthorm, the son of the herse Gudbrand, who was one of the finest men in the Uplands. Then Eystein fled north up the valley, and sent his relation Halvard Skalk to King Halfdan to beg for peace. On consideration of their relationship, King Halfdan gave King Eystein half of Hedemark, which he and his relations had held before; but kept to himself Thoten, and the district called Land. He likewise appropriated to himself Hadeland, and thus became a mighty king.

3. HALFDAN'S MARRIAGE

Halfdan the Black got a wife called Ragnhild, a daughter of Harald Gulskeg (Goldbeard), who was a king in Sogn. They had a son, to whom Harald gave his own name; and the boy was brought up in Sogn, by his mother's father, King Harald. Now when this Harald had lived out his days nearly, and was become weak, having no son, he gave his dominions to his daughter's son Harald, and gave him his title of king; and he died soon after. The same winter his daughter Ragnhild died; and the following spring the young Harald fell sick and died at ten years of age. As soon as Halfdan the Black heard of his son's death, he took the road northwards to Sogn with a great force, and was well received. He claimed the heritage and dominion after his son; and no opposition being made, he took the whole kingdom. Earl Atle Mjove (the Slender), who was a friend of King Halfdan, came to him from Gaular; and the king set him over the Sogn district, to judge in the country according to the country's laws, and collect scat upon the king's account. Thereafter King Halfdan proceeded to his kingdom in the Uplands.

4. HALFDAN'S STRIFE WITH GANDALF'S SONS.

In autumn, King Halfdan proceeded to Vingulmark. One night when he was there in guest quarters, it happened that about midnight a man came to him who had been on the watch on horseback, and told him a war force was come near to the house. The king instantly got up, ordered his men to arm themselves, and went out of the house and drew them up in battle order. At the same moment, Gandalf's sons, Hysing and Helsing, made their appearance with a large army. There was a great battle; but Halfdan being overpowered by the numbers of people fled to the forest, leaving many of his men on this spot. His foster-father, Olver Spake (the Wise), fell here. The people now came in swarms to King Halfdan, and he advanced to seek Gandalf's sons. They met at Eid, near Lake Oieren, and fought there. Hysing and Helsing fell, and their brother Hake saved himself by flight. King Halfdan then took possession of the whole of Vingulmark, and Hake fled to Alfheimar.

5. HALFDAN'S MARRIAGE WITH HJORT'S DAUGHTER.

Sigurd Hjort was the name of a king in Ringerike, who was stouter and stronger than any other man, and his equal could not be seen for a handsome appearance. His father was Helge Hvasse (the Sharp); and his mother was Aslaug, a daughter of Sigurd the worm-eyed, who again was a son of Ragnar Lodbrok. It is told of Sigurd that when he was only twelve years old he killed in single combat the berserk Hildebrand, and eleven others of his comrades; and many are the deeds of manhood told of him in a long saga about his feats. Sigurd had two children, one of whom was a daughter, called Ragnhild, then twenty years of age, and an excellent brisk girl. Her brother Guthorm was a youth. It is related in regard to Sigurd's death that he had a custom of riding out quite alone in the uninhabited forest to hunt the wild beasts that are hurtful to man, and he was always very eager at this sport. One day he rode out into the forest as usual, and when he had ridden a long way he came out at a piece of cleared land near to Hadeland. There the berserk Hake came against him with thirty men, and they fought. Sigurd Hjort fell there, after killing twelve of Hake's men; and Hake himself lost one hand, and had three other wounds. Then Hake and his men rode to Sigurd's house, where they took his daughter Ragnhild and her brother Guthorm, and carried them, with much property and valuable articles, home to Hadeland, where Hake had many great farms. He ordered a feast to be prepared, intending to hold his wedding with Ragnhild; but the time passed on account of his wounds, which healed slowly; and the berserk Hake of Hadeland had to keep his bed, on account of his wounds, all the autumn and beginning of winter. Now King Halfdan was in Hedemark at the Yule entertainments when he heard this news; and one morning early, when the king was dressed, he called to him Harek Gand, and told him to go over to Hadeland, and bring him Ragnhild, Sigurd Hjort's daughter. Harek got ready with a hundred men, and made his journey so that they came over the lake to Hake's house in the grey of the morning, and beset all the doors and stairs of the places where the house-servants slept. Then they broke into the sleeping-room where Hake slept, took Ragnhild, with her brother Guthorm, and all the goods that were there, and set fire to the house-servants' place, and burnt all the people in it. Then they covered over a magnificent waggon, placed Ragnhild and Guthorm in it, and drove down upon the ice. Hake got up and went after them a while; but when he came to the ice on the lake, he turned his sword-hilt to the ground and let himself fall upon the point, so that the sword went through him. He was buried under a mound on the banks of the lake. When King Halfdan, who was very quick of sight, saw the party returning over the frozen lake, and with a covered waggon, he knew that their errand was accomplished according to his desire. Thereupon he ordered the tables to be set out, and sent people all round in the neighbourhood to invite plenty of guests; and the same day there was a good feast which was also Halfdan's marriage-feast with Ragnhild, who became a great queen. Ragnhild's mother was Thorny, a daughter of Klakharald king in Jutland, and a sister of Thrye Dannebod who was married to the Danish king, Gorm the Old, who then ruled over the Danish dominions.

6. OF RAGNHILD'S DREAM.

Ragnhild, who was wise and intelligent, dreamt great dreams. She dreamt, for one, that she was standing out in her herb-garden, and she took a thorn out of her shift; but while she was holding the thorn in her hand it grew so that it became a great tree, one end of which struck itself down into the earth, and it became firmly rooted; and the other end of the tree raised itself so high in the air that she could scarcely see over it, and it became also wonderfully thick. The under part of the tree was red with blood, but the stem upwards was beautifully green and the branches white as snow. There were many and great limbs to the tree, some high up, others low down; and so vast were the tree's branches that they seemed to her to cover all Norway, and even much more.

7. OF HALFDAN'S DREAM.

King Halfdan never had dreams, which appeared to him an extraordinary circumstance; and he told it to a man called Thorleif Spake (the Wise), and asked him what his advice was about it. Thorleif said that what he himself did, when he wanted to have any revelation by dream, was to take his sleep in a swine-sty, and then it never failed that he had dreams. The king did so, and the following dream was revealed to him. He thought he had the most beautiful hair, which was all in ringlets; some so long as to fall upon the ground, some reaching to the middle of his legs, some to his knees, some to his loins or the middle of his sides, some to his neck, and some were only as knots springing from his head. These ringlets were of various colours; but one ringlet surpassed all the others in beauty, lustre, and size. This dream he told to Thorleif, who interpreted it thus:–There should be a great posterity from him, and his descendants should rule over countries with great, but not all with equally great, honour; but one of his race should be more celebrated than all the others. It was the opinion of people that this ringlet betokened King Olaf the Saint.

King Halfdan was a wise man, a man of truth and uprightness–who made laws, observed them himself, and obliged others to observe them. And that violence should not come in place of the laws, he himself fixed the number of criminal acts in law, and the compensations, mulcts, or penalties, for each case, according to every one's birth and dignity[1].

1 The penalty, compensation, or manbod for every injury, due the

Queen Ragnhild gave birth to a son, and water was poured over him, and the name of Harald given him, and he soon grew stout and remarkably handsome. As he grew up he became very expert at all feats, and showed also a good understanding. He was much beloved by his mother, but less so by his father.

8. HALFDAN'S MEAT VANISHES AT A FEAST

King Halfdan was at a Yule-feast in Hadeland, where a wonderful thing happened one Yule evening. When the great number of guests assembled were going to sit down to table, all the meat and all the ale disappeared from the table. The king sat alone very confused in mind; all the others set off, each to his home, in consternation. That the king might come to some certainty about what had occasioned this event, he ordered a Fin to be seized who was particularly knowing, and tried to force him to disclose the truth; but however much he tortured the man, he got nothing out of him. The Fin sought help particularly from Harald, the king's son, and Harald begged for mercy for him, but in vain. Then Harald let him escape against the king's will, and accompanied the man himself. On their journey they came to a place where the man's chief had a great feast, and it appears they were well received there. When they had been there until spring, the chief said, "Thy father took it much amiss that in winter I took some provisions from him,–now I will repay it to thee by a joyful piece of news: thy father is dead; and now thou shalt return home, and take possession of the whole kingdom which he had, and with it thou shalt lay the whole kingdom of Norway under thee."

---

party injured, or to his family and next of kin if the injury was the death or premeditated murder of the party, appears to have been fixed for every rank and condition, from the murder of the king down to the maiming or beating a man's cattle or his slave. A man for whom no compensation was due was a dishonored person, or an outlaw. It appears to have been optional with the injured party, or his kin if he had been killed, to take the mulct or compensation, or to refuse it, and wait for an opportunity of taking vengeance for the injury on the party who inflicted it, or on his kin. A part of each mulct or compensation was due to the king; and, these fines or penalties appear to have constituted a great proportion of the king's revenues, and to have been settled in the Things held in every district for administering the law with the lagman.–L.

9. HALFDAN'S DEATH.

Halfdan the Black was driving from a feast in Hadeland, and it so happened that his road lay over the lake called Rand. It was in spring, and there was a great thaw. They drove across the bight called Rykinsvik, where in winter there had been a pond broken in the ice for cattle to drink at, and where the dung had fallen upon the ice the thaw had eaten it into holes. Now as the king drove over it the ice broke, and King Halfdan and many with him perished. He was then forty years old. He had been one of the most fortunate kings in respect of good seasons. The people thought so much of him, that when his death was known and his body was floated to Ringerike to bury it there, the people of most consequence from Raumarike, Vestfold, and Hedemark came to meet it. All desired to take the body with them to bury it in their own district, and they thought that those who got it would have good crops to expect. At last it was agreed to divide the body into four parts. The head was laid in a mound at Stein in Ringerike, and each of the others took his part home and laid it in a mound; and these have since been called Halfdan's Mounds.

BOOK TWO

Harald Harfager's Saga

1. HARALD'S STRIFE WITH HAKE AND HIS FATHER GANDALF.

HARALD[2] WAS BUT TEN years old when he succeeded his father (Halfdan the Black). He became a stout, strong, and comely man, and withal prudent and manly. His mother's brother, Guthorm, was leader of the hird, at the head of the government, and commander ('hertogi') of the army. After Halfdan the Black's death, many chiefs coveted the dominions he had left. Among these King Gandalf was the first; then Hogne and Frode, sons of Eystein, king of Hedemark; and also Hogne Karuson came from Ringerike. Hake, the son of Gandalf, began with an expedition of 300 men against Vestfold, marched by the main road through some valleys, and expected to come suddenly upon King Harald; while his father Gandalf sat at home with his army, and prepared to cross over the fiord into Vestfold. When Duke Guthorm heard of this he gathered an army, and marched up the country with King Harald against Hake. They met in a valley, in which they fought a great battle, and King Harald was victorious; and there fell King Hake and most of his people. The place has since been called Hakadale. Then King Harald and Duke Guthorm turned back, but they found

2 The first twenty chapters of this saga refer to Harald's youth and his conquest of Norway. This portion of the saga is of great importance to the Icelanders, as the settlement of their Isle was a result of Harald's wars. The second part of the saga (chaps. 21-46) treats of the disputes between Harald's sons, of the jarls of Orkney, and of the jarls of More. With this saga we enter the domain of history.–Ed.

King Gandalf had come to Vestfold. The two armies marched against each other, and met, and had a great battle; and it ended in King Gandalf flying, after leaving most of his men dead on the spot, and in that state he came back to his kingdom. Now when the sons of King Eystein in Hedemark heard the news, they expected the war would come upon them, and they sent a message to Hogne Karuson and to Herse Gudbrand, and appointed a meeting with them at Ringsaker in Hedemark.

2. KING HARALD OVERCOMES FIVE KINGS.

AFTER THE BATTLE KING Harald and Guthorm turned back, and went with all the men they could gather through the forests towards the Uplands. They found out where the Upland kings had appointed their meeting-place, and came there about the time of midnight, without the watchmen observing them until their army was before the door of the house in which Hogne Karuson was, as well as that in which Gudbrand slept. They set fire to both houses; but King Eystein's two sons slipped out with their men, and fought for a while, until both Hogne and Frode fell. After the fall of these four chiefs, King Harald, by his relation Guthorm's success and powers, subdued Hedemark, Ringerike, Gudbrandsdal, Hadeland, Thoten, Raumarike, and the whole northern part of Vingulmark. King Harald and Guthorm had thereafter war with King Gandalf, and fought several battles with him; and in the last of them King Gandalf was slain, and King Harald took the whole of his kingdom as far south as the river Raum.

3. OF GYDA, DAUGHTER OF EIRIE.

KING HARALD SENT HIS men to a girl called Gyda, daughter of King Eirik of Hordaland, who was brought up as foster-child in the house of a great bonde in Valdres. The king wanted her for his concubine; for she was a remarkably handsome girl, but of high spirit withal. Now when the messengers came there, and delivered their errand to the girl, she answered, that she would not throw herself away even to take a king for her husband, who had no greater kingdom to rule over than a few districts. "And methinks," said she, "it is wonderful that no king here in Norway will make the whole country subject to him, in the same way as Gorm the Old did in Denmark, or Eirik at Upsala." The messengers thought her answer was dreadfully haughty, and asked what she thought would come of such an answer; for Harald was so mighty a man, that his invitation was good enough for her. But although she had replied to their errand differently from what they wished, they saw no chance, on this occasion, of taking her with them against her will; so they prepared to return. When they were ready, and the people followed them out, Gyda said to the messengers, "Now tell to King Harald these my words. I will only agree to be his lawful wife upon the condition that he shall first, for my sake, subject to himself the whole of Norway, so that he may rule over that kingdom as freely and fully as King Eirik over the Swedish dominions, or King Gorm over Denmark; for only then, methinks, can he be called the king of a people."

4. KING HARALD'S VOW.

Now came the messengers back to King Harald, bringing him the words of the girl, and saying she was so bold and foolish that she well deserved that the king should send a greater troop of people for her, and inflict on her some disgrace. Then answered the king, "This girl has not spoken or done so much amiss that she should be punished, but rather she should be thanked for her words. She has reminded me," said he, "of something which it appears to me wonderful I did not think of before. And now," added he, "I make the solemn vow, and take God to witness, who made me and rules over all things, that never shall I clip or comb my hair until I have subdued the whole of Norway, with scat[3], and duties, and domains; or if not, have died in the attempt." Guthorm thanked the king warmly for his vow; adding, that it was royal work to fulfil royal words.

5. THE BATTLE IN ORKADAL.

After this the two relations gather together a great force, and prepare for an expedition to the Uplands, and northwards up the valley (Gudbrandsdal), and north over Dovrefjeld; and when the king came down to the inhabited land he ordered all the men to be killed, and everything wide around to be delivered to the flames. And when the people came to know this, they fled every one where he could; some

3 (1) Scat was a land-tax, paid to the king in money, malt, meal, or flesh-meat, from all lands, and was adjudged by the Thing to each king upon his accession, and being proposed and accepted as king.

down the country to Orkadal, some to Gaulardal, some to the forests. But some begged for peace, and obtained it, on condition of joining the king and becoming his men. He met no opposition until he came to Orkadal. There a crowd of people had assembled, and he had his first battle with a king called Gryting. Harald won the victory, and King Gryting was made prisoner, and most of his people killed. He took service himself under the king, and swore fidelity to him. Thereafter all the people in Orkadal district went under King Harald, and became his men.

6. KING HARALD S LAWS FOR LAND PROPERTY.

King Harald made this law over all the lands he conquered, that all the udal property should belong to him; and that the bondes, both great and small, should pay him land dues for their possessions. Over every district he set an earl to judge according to the law of the land and to justice, and also to collect the land dues and the fines; and for this each earl received a third part of the dues, and services, and fines, for the support of his table and other expenses. Each earl had under him four or more herses, each of whom had an estate of twenty marks yearly income bestowed on him and was bound to support twenty men-at-arms, and the earl sixty men, at their own expenses. The king had increased the land dues and burdens so much, that each of his earls had greater power and income than the kings had before; and when that became known at Throndhjem, many great men joined the king and took his service.

7. BATTLE IN GAULARDAL.

It is told that Earl Hakon Grjotgardson came to King Harald from Yrjar, and brought a great crowd of men to his service. Then King Harald went into Gaulardal, and had a great battle, in which he slew two kings, and conquered their dominions; and these were Gaulardal district and Strind district. He gave Earl Hakon Strind district to rule over as earl. King Harald then proceeded to Stjoradal, and had a third battle, in which he gained the victory, and took that district also. There upon the Throndhjem people assembled, and four kings met together with their troops. The one ruled over Veradal, the second over Skaun, third over the Sparbyggja district, and the fourth over Eyin Idre (Inderoen);

and this latter had also Eyna district. These four kings marched with their men against King Harald, but he won the battle; and some of these kings fell, and some fled. In all, King Harald fought at the least eight battles, and slew eight kings, in the Throndhjem district, and laid the whole of it under him.

8. HARALD SEIZES NAUMUDAL DISTRICT.

North in Naumudal were two brothers, kings,–Herlaug and Hrollaug; and they had been for three summers raising a mound or tomb of stone and lime and of wood. Just as the work was finished, the brothers got the news that King Harald was coming upon them with his army. Then King Herlaug had a great quantity of meat and drink brought into the mound, and went into it himself, with eleven companions, and ordered the mound to be covered up. King Hrollaug, on the contrary, went upon the summit of the mound, on which the kings were wont to sit, and made a throne to be erected, upon which he seated himself. Then he ordered feather-beds to be laid upon the bench below, on which the earls were wont to be seated, and threw himself down from his high seat or throne into the earl's seat, giving himself the title of earl. Now Hrollaug went to meet King Harald, gave up to him his whole kingdom, offered to enter into his service, and told him his whole proceeding. Then took King Harald a sword, fastened it to Hrollaug's belt, bound a shield to his neck, and made him thereupon an earl, and led him to his earl's seat; and therewith gave him the district Naumudal, and set him as earl over it ((A.D. 866)).[4]

9. KING HARALD'S HOME AFFAIRS.

King Harald then returned to Throndhjem, where he dwelt during the winter, and always afterwards called it his home. He fixed here his head residence, which is called Lade. This winter he took to wife Asa, a daughter of Earl Hakon Grjotgardson, who then stood in great favour and honour with the king. In spring the king fitted out his

4 Before writing was in general use, this symbolical way of performing all important legal acts appears to have entered into the jurisprudence of all savage nations; and according to Gibbon, chap. 44, "the jurisprudence of the first Romans exhibited the scenes of a pantomime; the words were adapted to the gestures, and the slightest error or neglect in the forms of proceeding was sufficient to annul the substance of the fairest claims."–Ed.

ships. In winter he had caused a great frigate (a dragon) to be built, and had it fitted-out in the most splendid way, and brought his house-troops and his berserks on board. The forecastle men were picked men, for they had the king's banner. From the stem to the mid-hold was called rausn, or the fore-defence; and there were the berserks. Such men only were received into King Harald's house-troop as were remarkable for strength, courage, and all kinds of dexterity; and they alone got place in his ship, for he had a good choice of house-troops from the best men of every district. King Harald had a great army, many large ships, and many men of might followed him. Hornklofe, in his poem called "Glymdrapa", tells of this; and also that King Harald had a battle with the people of Orkadal, at Opdal forest, before he went upon this expedition.

"O'er the broad heath the bowstrings twang,
While high in air the arrows sang.
The iron shower drives to flight
The foeman from the bloody fight.
The warder of great Odin's shrine,
The fair-haired son of Odin's line,
Raises the voice which gives the cheer,
First in the track of wolf or bear.
His master voice drives them along
To Hel–a destined, trembling throng;
And Nokve's ship, with glancing sides,
Must fly to the wild ocean's tides.–
Must fly before the king who leads
Norse axe-men on their ocean steeds."

10. BATTLE AT SOLSKEL

King Harald moved out with his army from Throndhjem, and went southwards to More. Hunthiof was the name of the king who ruled over the district of More. Solve Klofe was the name of his son, and both were great warriors. King Nokve, who ruled over Raumsdal, was the brother of Solve's mother. Those chiefs gathered a great force when they heard of King Harald, and came against him. They met at Solskel, and there was a great battle, which was gained by King Harald (A.D. 867). Hornklofe tells of this battle:–

"Thus did the hero known to fame,
The leader of the shields, whose name
Strikes every heart with dire dismay,
Launch forth his war-ships to the fray.
Two kings he fought; but little strife
Was needed to cut short their life.
A clang of arms by the sea-shore,–
And the shields' sound was heard no more."

The two kings were slain, but Solve escaped by flight; and King Harald laid both districts under his power. He stayed here long in summer to establish law and order for the country people, and set men to rule them, and keep them faithful to him; and in autumn he prepared to return northwards to Throndhjem. Ragnvald Earl of More, a son of Eystein Glumra, had the summer before become one of Harald's men; and the king set him as chief over these two districts, North More and Raumsdal; strengthened him both with men of might and bondes, and gave him the help of ships to defend the coast against enemies. He was called Ragnvald the Mighty, or the Wise; and people say both names suited him well. King Harald came back to Throndhjem about winter.

11. FALL OF KINGS ARNVID AND AUDBJORN.

The following spring (A.D. 868) King Harald raised a great force in Throndhjem, and gave out that he would proceed to South More. Solve Klofe had passed the winter in his ships of war, plundering in North More, and had killed many of King Harald's men; pillaging some places, burning others, and making great ravage; but sometimes he had been, during the winter, with his friend King Arnvid in South More. Now when he heard that King Harald was come with ships and a great army, he gathered people, and was strong in men-at-arms; for many thought they had to take vengeance of King Harald. Solve Klofe went southwards to Firdafylke (the Fjord district), which King Audbjorn ruled over, to ask him to help, and join his force to King Arnvid's and his own. "For," said he, "it is now clear that we all have but one course to take; and that is to rise, all as one man, against King Harald, for we have strength enough, and fate must decide the victory; for as to the other condition of becoming his servants, that is no condition for us, who are not less noble than Harald. My father thought it better to fall in battle for his kingdom, than to go willingly into

King Harald's service, or not to abide the chance of weapons like the Naumudal kings." King Solve's speech was such that King Audbjorn promised his help, and gathered a great force together and went with it to King Arnvid, and they had a great army. Now, they got news that King Harald was come from the north, and they met within Solskel. And it was the custom to lash the ships together, stem to stem; so it was done now. King Harald laid his ship against King Arnvid's, and there was the sharpest fight, and many men fell on both sides. At last King Harald was raging with anger, and went forward to the fore-deck, and slew so dreadfully that all the forecastle men of Arnvid's ship were driven aft of the mast, and some fell. Thereupon Harald boarded the ship, and King Arnvid's men tried to save themselves by flight, and he himself was slain in his ship. King Audbjorn also fell; but Solve fled. So says Hornklofe:–

"Against the hero's shield in vain
The arrow-storm fierce pours its rain.
The king stands on the blood-stained deck,
Trampling on many a stout foe's neck;
And high above the dinning stound
Of helm and axe, and ringing sound
Of blade and shield, and raven's cry,
Is heard his shout of 'Victory!'"

Of King Harald's men, fell his earls Asgaut and Asbjorn, together with his brothers-in-law, Grjotgard and Herlaug, the sons of Earl Hakon of Lade. Solve became afterwards a great sea-king, and often did great damage in King Harald's dominions.

12. KING VEMUND BURNT TO DEATH.

After this battle (A.D. 868) King Harald subdued South More; but Vemund, King Audbjorn's brother, still had Firdafylke. It was now late in harvest, and King Harald's men gave him the counsel not to proceed south-wards round Stad. Then King Harald set Earl Ragnvald over South and North More and also Raumsdal, and he had many people about him. King Harald returned to Throndhjem. The same winter (A.D. 869) Ragnvald went over Eid, and southwards to the Fjord district. There he heard news of King Vemund, and came by night to a place called Naustdal, where King Vemund was living in guest-quarters. Earl Ragnvald surrounded the house in which they were quartered, and burnt the king in it, together with ninety men. The came Berdlukare to Earl Ragnvald with a complete armed long-ship, and they both returned to More. The earl took all the ships Vemund had, and all the goods he could get hold of. Berdlukare proceeded north to Throndhjem to King Harald, and became his man; and dreadful berserk he was.

13. DEATH OF EARLS HAKON, AND ATLE MJOVE.

The following spring (A.D. 869) King Harald went southwards with his fleet along the coast, and subdued Firdafylke. Then he sailed eastward along the land until he came to Vik; but he left Earl Hakon Grjotgardson behind, and set him over the Fjord district. Earl Hakon sent word to Earl Atle Mjove that he should leave Sogn district, and be earl over Gaular district, as he had been before, alleging that King Harald had given Sogn district to him. Earl Atle sent word that he would keep both Sogn district and Gaular district, until he met King Harald. The two earls quarreled about this so long, that both gathered troops. They met at Fialar, in Stavanger fiord, and had a great battle, in which Earl Hakon fell, and Earl Atle got a mortal wound, and his men carried him to the island of Atley, where he died. So says Eyvind Skaldaspiller:–

"He who stood a rooted oak,
Unshaken by the swordsman's stroke,
Amidst the whiz of arrows slain,
Has fallen upon Fjalar's plain.
There, by the ocean's rocky shore,
The waves are stained with the red gore
Of stout Earl Hakon Grjotgard's son,
And of brave warriors many a one."

14. HARALD AND THE SWEDISH KING EIRIK.

King Harald came with his fleet eastward to Viken and landed at Tunsberg, which was then a trading town. He had then been four years in Throndhjem, and in all that time had not been in Viken. Here he heard the news that Eirik Eymundson, king of Sweden, had laid under him Vermaland, and was taking scat or land-tax from all the forest settlers; and also that he called the whole country north to Svinasund, and west along the sea, West Gautland; and which altogether he reckoned to his kingdom, and took land-tax from it. Over this country he had set an earl, by name Hrane Gauzke, who had the earldom between Svinasund and the Gaut river, and was a mighty earl. And it was told to King Harald that the Swedish king said he would not rest until he had as great a kingdom in Viken as Sigurd Hring, or his son Ragnar Lodbrok, had possessed; and that was Raumarike and Vestfold, all the way to the isle Grenmar, and also Vingulmark, and all that lay south of it. In all these districts many chiefs, and many other people, had given obedience to the Swedish king. King Harald was very angry at this, and summoned the bondes to a Thing at Fold, where he laid an accusation against them for treason towards him. Some bondes defended themselves from the accusation, some paid fines, some were punished. He went thus through the whole district during the summer, and in harvest he did the same in Raumarike, and laid the two districts under his power. Towards winter he heard that Eirik king of Sweden was, with his court, going about in Vermaland in guest-quarters.

15. HARALD AT A FEAST OF THE PEASANT AKE.

King Harald takes his way across the Eid forest eastward, and comes out in Vermaland, where he also orders feasts to be prepared for himself. There was a man by name Ake, who was the greatest of the bondes of Vermaland, very rich, and at that time very aged. He sent men to King Harald, and invited him to a feast, and the king promised to come on the day appointed. Ake invited also King Eirik to a feast, and appointed the same day. Ake had a great feasting hall, but it was old; and he made a new hall, not less than the old one, and had it ornamented in the most splendid way. The new hall he had hung with new hangings, but the old had only its old ornaments. Now when the kings came to the feast, King Eirik with his court was taken into the old hall; but Harald with his followers into the new. The same difference was in all the table furniture, and King Eirik and his men had the old-fashioned vessels and horns, but all gilded and splendid; while King Harald and his men had entirely new vessels and horns adorned with gold, all with carved figures, and shining like glass; and both companies had the best of liquor. Ake the bonde had formerly been King Halfdan the Black s man. Now when daylight came, and the feast was quite ended, and the kings made themselves ready for their journey, and the horses were saddled, came Ake before King Harald, leading in his hand his son Ubbe, a boy of twelve years of age, and said, "If the goodwill I have shown to thee, sire, in my feast, be worth thy friendship, show it hereafter to my son. I give him to thee now for thy service." The king thanked him with many agreeable words for his friendly entertainment, and promised him his full friendship in return. Then Ake brought out great presents, which he gave to the king, and they gave each other thereafter the parting kiss. Ake went next to the Swedish king, who was dressed and ready for the road, but not in the best humour. Ake gave to him also good and valuable gifts; but the king answered only with few words, and mounted his horse. Ake followed the king on the road and talked with him. The road led through a wood which was near to the house; and when Ake came to the wood, the king said to him, "How was it that thou madest such a difference between me and King Harald as to give him the best of everything, although thou knowest thou art my man?" "I think" answered Ake, "that there failed in it nothing, king, either to you or to your attendants, in friendly entertainment at this feast. But that all the utensils for your drinking were old, was because you are now old; but King Harald is in the bloom of youth, and therefore I gave him the new things. And as to my being thy man, thou art just as much my man." On this the king out with his sword, and gave Ake his deathwound. King Harald was ready now also to mount his horse, and desired that Ake should be called. The people went to seek him; and some ran up the road that King Eirik had taken, and found Ake there dead. They came back, and told the news to King Harald, and he bids his men to be up, and avenge Ake the bonde. And away rode he and his men the way King Eirik had taken, until they came in sight of each other. Each for himself rode as hard as he could, until Eirik came into the wood which divides Gautland and Vermaland. There King Harald wheels about, and returns to Vermaland, and lays the country under him, and kills King Eirik's men wheresoever he can find them. In winter King Harald returned to Raumarike, and dwelt there a while.

16. HARALD'S JOURNEY TO TUNSBERG.

King Harald went out in winter to his ships at Tunsberg, rigged them, and sailed away eastward over the fiord, and subjected all Vingulmark to his dominion. All winter he was out with his ships, and marauded in Ranrike; so says Thorbjorn Hornklofe:–

"The Norseman's king is on the sea,
Tho' bitter wintry cold it be.–
On the wild waves his Yule keeps he.
When our brisk king can get his way,
He'll no more by the fireside stay
Than the young sun; he makes us play
The game of the bright sun-god Frey.
But the soft Swede loves well the fire
The well-stuffed couch, the doway glove,
And from the hearth-seat will not move."

The Gautlanders gathered people together all over the country.

17. THE BATTLE IN GAUTLAND.

In spring, when the ice was breaking up, the Gautlanders drove stakes into the Gaut river to hinder King Harald with his ships from coming to the land. But King Harald laid his ships alongside the stakes, and plundered the country, and burnt all around; so says Horn klofe:–

"The king who finds a dainty feast,
For battle-bird and prowling beast,
Has won in war the southern land
That lies along the ocean's strand.
The leader of the helmets, he
Who leads his ships o'er the dark sea,
Harald, whose high-rigged masts appear
Like antlered fronts of the wild deer,
Has laid his ships close alongside
Of the foe's piles with daring pride."

Afterwards the Gautlanders came down to the strand with a great army, and gave battle to King Harald, and great was the fall of men. But it was King Harald who gained the day. Thus says Hornklofe:–

"Whistles the battle-axe in its swing
O'er head the whizzing javelins sing,
Helmet and shield and hauberk ring;
The air-song of the lance is loud,

The arrows pipe in darkening cloud;
Through helm and mail the foemen feel
The blue edge of our king's good steel
Who can withstand our gallant king?
The Gautland men their flight must wing."

18. HRANE GAUZKE'S DEATH.

King Harald went far and wide through Gautland, and many were the battles he fought there on both sides of the river, and in general he was victorious. In one of these battles fell Hrane Gauzke; and then the king took his whole land north of the river and west of the Veneren, and also Vermaland. And after he turned back there-from, he set Duke Guthorm as chief to defend the country, and left a great force with him. King Harald himself went first to the Uplands, where he remained a while, and then proceeded northwards over the Dovrefjeld to Throndhjem, where he dwelt for a long time. Harald began to have children. By Asa he had four sons. The eldest was Guthorm. Halfdan the Black and Halfdan the White were twins. Sigfrod was the fourth. They were all brought up in Throndhjem with all honour.

19. BATTLE IN HAFERSFJORD.

News came in from the south land that the people of Hordaland and Rogaland, Agder and Thelemark, were gathering, and bringing together ships and weapons, and a great body of men. The leaders of this were Eirik king of Hordaland; Sulke king of Rogaland, and his brother Earl Sote: Kjotve the Rich, king of Agder, and his son Thor Haklang; and from Thelemark two brothers, Hroald Hryg and Had the Hard. Now when Harald got certain news of this, he assembled his forces, set his ships on the water, made himself ready with his men, and set out southwards along the coast, gathering many people from every district. King Eirik heard of this when he same south of Stad; and having assembled all the men he could expect, he proceeded southwards to meet the force which he knew was coming to his help from the east. The whole met together north of Jadar, and went into Hafersfjord, where King Harald was waiting with his forces. A great battle began, which was both hard and long; but at last King Harald gained the day. There King Eirik fell, and King Sulke, with his brother Earl Sote. Thor Haklang, who was a great berserk, had laid his ship against King Harald's, and there was above all measure a desperate attack, until Thor Haklang fell, and his whole ship was cleared of men. Then King Kjotve fled to a little isle outside, on which there was a good place of strength. Thereafter all his men fled, some to their ships, some up to the land; and the latter ran southwards over the country of Jadar. So says Hornklofe, viz.:–

"Has the news reached you?–have you heard
Of the great fight at Hafersfjord,
Between our noble king brave Harald
And King Kjotve rich in gold?
The foeman came from out the East,
Keen for the fray as for a feast.
A gallant sight it was to see
Their fleet sweep o'er the dark-blue sea:
Each war-ship, with its threatening throat
Of dragon fierce or ravenous brute[1]
Grim gaping from the prow; its wales
Glittering with burnished shields,[2] *like scales*
Its crew of udal men of war,
Whose snow-white targets shone from far
And many a mailed spearman stout
From the West countries round about,
English and Scotch, a foreign host,
And swordamen from the far French coast.
And as the foemen's ships drew near,
The dreadful din you well might hear
Savage berserks roaring mad,
And champions fierce in wolf-skins clad,[3]
Howling like wolves; and clanking jar
Of many a mail-clad man of war.
Thus the foe came; but our brave king
Taught them to fly as fast again.
For when he saw their force come o'er,

---

1 The war-ships were called dragons, from being decorated with the head of a dragon, serpent, or other wild animal; and the word "draco" was adopted in the Latin of the Middle Ages to denote a ship of war of the larger class. The snekke was the cutter or smaller war-ship.–L.

2 The shields were hung over the side-rails of the ships.–L.

3 The wolf-skin pelts were nearly as good as armour against the sword. The wolf-skin pelts were nearly as good as armour against the sword.

He launched his war-ships from the shore.
On the deep sea he launched his fleet
And boldly rowed the foe to meet.
Fierce was the shock, and loud the clang
Of shields, until the fierce Haklang,
The foeman's famous berserk, fell.
Then from our men burst forth the yell
Of victory, and the King of Gold
Could not withstand our Harald bold,
But fled before his flaky locks
For shelter to the island rocks.
All in the bottom of the ships
The wounded lay, in ghastly heaps;
Backs up and faces down they lay
Under the row-seats stowed away;
And many a warrior's shield, I ween
Might on the warrior's back be seen,
To shield him as he fled amain
From the fierce stone-storm's pelting rain.
The mountain-folk, as I've heard say,
Ne'er stopped as they ran from the fray,
Till they had crossed the Jadar sea,
And reached their homes–so keen each soul
To drown his fright in the mead bowl."

20. HARALD SUPREME SOVEREIGN IN NORWAY.

After this battle King Harald met no opposition in Norway, for all his opponents and greatest enemies were cut off. But some, and they were a great multitude, fled out of the country, and thereby great districts were peopled. Jemtaland and Helsingjaland were peopled then, although some Norwegians had already set up their habitation there. In the discontent that King Harald seized on the lands of Norway, the out-countries of Iceland and the Farey Isles were discovered and peopled. The Northmen had also a great resort to Hjaltland (Shetland Isles) and many men left Norway, flying the country on account of King Harald, and went on viking cruises into the West sea. In winter they were in the Orkney Islands and Hebrides; but marauded in summer in Norway, and did great damage. Many, however, were the mighty men who took service under King Harald, and became his men, and dwelt in the land with him.

21. HARALD'S MARRIAGE AND HIS CHILDREN.

WHEN KING HARALD HAD now become sole king over all Norway, he remembered what that proud girl had said to him; so he sent men to her, and had her brought to him, and took her to his bed. And these were their children: Alof–she was the eldest; then was their son Hrorek; then Sigtryg, Frode, and Thorgils. King Harald had many wives and many children. Among them he had one wife, who was called Ragnhild the Mighty, a daughter of King Eirik, from Jutland; and by her he had a son, Eirik Blood-axe. He was also married to Svanhild, a daughter of Earl Eystein; and their sons were Olaf Geirstadaalf, Bjorn and Ragnar Rykkil. Lastly, King Harald married Ashild, a daughter of Hring Dagson, up in Ringerike; and their children were, Dag, Hring, Gudrod Skiria, and Ingigerd. It is told that King Harald put away nine wives when he married Ragnhild the Mighty. So says Hornklofe:–

"Harald, of noblest race the head,
A Danish wife took to his bed;
And out of doors nine wives he thrust,–
The mothers of the princes first.
Who 'mong Holmrygians hold command,
And those who rule in Hordaland.
And then he packed from out the place
The children born of Holge's race."

King Harald's children were all fostered and brought up by their relations on the mother's side. Guthorm the Duke had poured water over King Harald's eldest son and had given him his own name. He set the child upon his knee, and was his foster-father, and took him with himself eastward to Viken, and there he was brought up in the house of Guthorm. Guthorm ruled the whole land in Viken and the Uplands, when King Harald was absent.

22. KING HARALD'S VOYAGE TO THE WEST.

KING HARALD HEARD THAT the vikings, who were in the West sea in winter, plundered far and wide in the middle part of Norway; and therefore every summer he made an expedition to search the isles and outskerries[4]

4 *Skerries are the uninhabited dry or halt-tide rocks of a coast.–L.*

on the coast. Wheresoever the vikings heard of him they all took to flight, and most of them out into the open ocean. At last the king grew weary of this work, and therefore one summer he sailed with his fleet right out into the West sea. First he came to Hjaltland (Shetland), and he slew all the vikings who could not save themselves by flight. Then King Harald sailed southwards, to the Orkney Islands, and cleared them all of vikings. Thereafter he proceeded to the Sudreys (Hebrides), plundered there, and slew many vikings who formerly had had men-at-arms under them. Many a battle was fought, and King Harald was always victorious. He then plundered far and wide in Scotland itself, and had a battle there. When he was come westward as far as the Isle of Man, the report of his exploits on the land had gone before him; for all the inhabitants had fled over to Scotland, and the island was left entirely bare both of people and goods, so that King Harald and his men made no booty when they landed. So says Hornklofe:-

"The wise, the noble king, great
Whose hand so freely scatters gold,
Led many a northern shield to war
Against the town upon the shore.
The wolves soon gathered on the sand
Of that sea-shore; for Harald's hand
The Scottish army drove away,
And on the coast left wolves a prey."

In this war fell Ivar, a son of Ragnvald, Earl of More; and King Harald gave Ragnvald, as a compensation for the loss, the Orkney and Shetland isles, when he sailed from the West; but Ragnvald immediately gave both these countries to his brother Sigurd, who remained behind them; and King Harald, before sailing eastward, gave Sigurd the earldom of them. Thorstein the Red, a son of Olaf the White and of Aud the Wealthy, entered into partnership with him; and after plundering in Scotland, they subdued Caithness and Sutherland, as far as Ekkjalsbakke. Earl Sigurd killed Melbridge Tooth, a Scotch earl, and hung his head to his stirrup-leather; but the calf of his leg were scratched by the teeth, which were sticking out from the head, and the wound caused inflammation in his leg, of which the earl died, and he was laid in a mound at Ekkjalsbakke. His son Guthorm ruled over these countries for about a year thereafter, and died without children. Many vikings, both Danes and Northmen, set themselves down then in those countries.

23. HARALD HAS HIS HAIR CLIPPED.

After King Harald had subdued the whole land, he was one day at a feast in More, given by Earl Ragnvald. Then King Harald went into a bath, and had his hair dressed. Earl Ragnvald now cut his hair, which had been uncut and uncombed for ten years; and therefore the king had been called Lufa (i.e., with rough matted hair). But then Earl Ragnvald gave him the distinguishing name–Harald Harfager (i.e., fair hair); and all who saw him agreed that there was the greatest truth in the surname, for he had the most beautiful and abundant head of hair.

24. ROLF GANGER DRIVEN INTO BANISHMENT.

Earl Ragnvald was King Harald's dearest friend, and the king had the greatest regard for him. He was married to Hild, a daughter of Rolf Nefia, and their sons were Rolf and Thorer. Earl Ragnvald had also three sons by concubines,–the one called Hallad, the second Einar, the third Hrollaug; and all three were grown men when their brothers born in marriage were still children Rolf became a great viking, and was of so stout a growth that no horse could carry him, and wheresoever he went he must go on foot; and therefore he was called Rolf Ganger. He plundered much in the East sea. One summer, as he was coming from the eastward on a viking's expedition to the coast of Viken, he landed there and made a cattle foray. As King Harald happened, just at that time, to be in Viken, he heard of it, and was in a great rage; for he had forbid, by the greatest punishment, the plundering within the bounds of the country. The king assembled a Thing, and had Rolf declared an outlaw over all Norway. When Rolf's mother, Hild heard of it she hastened to the king, and entreated peace for Rolf; but the king was so enraged that here entreaty was of no avail. Then Hild spake these lines:–

"Think'st thou, King Harald, in thy anger,
To drive away my brave Rolf Ganger
Like a mad wolf, from out the land?
Why, Harald, raise thy mighty hand?
Why banish Nefia's gallant name-son,
The brother of brave udal-men?
Why is thy cruelty so fell?
Bethink thee, monarch, it is ill
With such a wolf at wolf to play,

Who, driven to the wild woods away
May make the king's best deer his prey."

Rolf Ganger went afterwards over sea to the West to the Hebrides, or Sudreys; and at last farther west to Valland, where he plundered and subdued for himself a great earldom, which he peopled with Northmen, from which that land is called Normandy. Rolf Ganger's son was William, father to Richard, and grandfather to another Richard, who was the father of Robert Longspear, and grandfather of William the Bastard, from whom all the following English kings are descended. From Rolf Ganger also are descended the earls in Normandy. Queen Ragnhild the Mighty lived three years after she came to Norway; and, after her death, her son and King Harald's was taken to the herse Thorer Hroaldson, and Eirik was fostered by him.

25. OF THE FIN SVASE AND KING HARALD.

King Harald, one winter, went about in guest-quarters in the Uplands, and had ordered a Christmas feast to be prepared for him at the farm Thoptar. On Christmas eve came Svase to the door, just as the king went to table, and sent a message to the king to ask if he would go out with him. The king was angry at such a message, and the man who had brought it in took out with him a reply of the king's displeasure. But Svase, notwithstanding, desired that his message should be delivered a second time; adding to it, that he was the Fin whose hut the king had promised to visit, and which stood on the other side of the ridge. Now the king went out, and promised to go with him, and went over the ridge to his hut, although some of his men dissuaded him. There stood Snaefrid, the daughter of Svase, a most beautiful girl; and she filled a cup of mead for the king. But he took hold both of the cup and of her hand. Immediately it was as if a hot fire went through his body; and he wanted that very night to take her to his bed. But Svase said that should not be unless by main force, if he did not first make her his lawful wife. Now King Harald made Snaefrid his lawful wife, and loved her so passionately that he forgot his kingdom, and all that belonged to his high dignity. They had four sons: the one was Sigurd Hrise; the others Halfdan Haleg, Gudrod Ljome and Ragnvald Rettilbeine. Thereafter Snaefrid died; but her corpse never changed, but was as fresh and red as when she lived. The king sat always beside her, and thought she would come to life again. And so it went on for three years that he was sorrowing over her death, and the people over his delusion. At last Thorleif the Wise succeeded, by his prudence, in curing him of his delusion by accosting him thus:–"It is nowise wonderful, king, that thou grievest over so beautiful and noble a wife, and bestowest costly coverlets and beds of down on her corpse, as she desired; but these honours fall short of what is due, as she still lies in the same clothes. It would be more suitable to raise her, and change her dress." As soon as the body was raised in the bed all sorts of corruption and foul smells came from it, and it was necessary in all haste to gather a pile of wood and burn it; but before this could be done the body turned blue, and worms, toads, newts, paddocks, and all sorts of ugly reptiles came out of it, and it sank into ashes. Now the king came to his understanding again, threw the madness out of his mind, and after that day ruled his kingdom as before. He was strengthened and made joyful by his subjects, and his subjects by him and the country by both.

26. OF THJODOLF OF HVIN, THE SKALD.

After King Harald had experienced the cunning of the Fin woman, he was so angry that he drove from him the sons he had with her, and would not suffer them before his eyes. But one of them, Gudrod Ljome, went to his foster-father Thjodolf of Hvin, and asked him to go to the king, who was then in the Uplands; for Thjodolf was a great friend of the king. And so they went, and came to the king's house late in the evening, and sat down together unnoticed near the door. The king walked up and down the floor casting his eye along the benches; for he had a feast in the house, and the mead was just mixed. The king then murmured out these lines:–

"Tell me, ye aged gray-haired heroes,
Who have come here to seek repose,
Wherefore must I so many keep
Of such a set, who, one and all,
Right dearly love their souls to steep,
From morn till night, in the mead-bowl?"

Then Thjodolf replies:–

"A certain wealthy chief, I think,
Would gladly have had more to drink

With him, upon one bloody day,
When crowns were cracked in our sword-play."

Thjodolf then took off his hat, and the king recognised him, and gave him a friendly reception. Thjodolf then begged the king not to cast off his sons; "for they would with great pleasure have taken a better family descent upon the mother's side, if the king had given it to them." The king assented, and told him to take Gudrod with him as formerly; and he sent Halfdan and Sigurd to Ringerike, and Ragnvald to Hadaland, and all was done as the king ordered. They grew up to be very clever men, very expert in all exercises. In these times King Harald sat in peace in the land, and the land enjoyed quietness and good crops.

27. OF EARL TORFEINAR'S OBTAINING ORKNEY.

When Earl Ragnvald in More heard of the death of his brother Earl Sigurd, and that the vikings were in possession of the country, he sent his son Hallad westward, who took the title of earl to begin with, and had many men-at-arms with him. When he arrived at the Orkney Islands, he established himself in the country; but both in harvest, winter, and spring, the vikings cruised about the isles plundering the headlands, and committing depredations on the coast. Then Earl Hallad grew tired of the business, resigned his earldom, took up again his rights as an allodial owner, and afterwards returned eastward into Norway. When Earl Ragnvald heard of this he was ill pleased with Hallad, and said his son were very unlike their ancestors. Then said Einar, "I have enjoyed but little honour among you, and have little affection here to lose: now if you will give me force enough, I will go west to the islands, and promise you what at any rate will please you–that you shall never see me again." Earl Ragnvald replied, that he would be glad if he never came back; "For there is little hope," said he, "that thou will ever be an honour to thy friends, as all thy kin on thy mother's side are born slaves." Earl Ragnvald gave Einar a vessel completely equipped, and he sailed with it into the West sea in harvest. When he came to the Orkney Isles, two vikings, Thorer Treskeg and Kalf Skurfa, were in his way with two vessels. He attacked them instantly, gained the battle, and slew the two vikings. Then this was sung:–

"Then gave he Treskeg to the trolls,
Torfeinar slew Skurfa."

He was called Torfeinar, because he cut peat for fuel, there being no firewood, as in Orkney there are no woods. He afterwards was earl over the islands, and was a mighty man. He was ugly, and blind of an eye, yet very sharp-sighted withal.

28. KING EIRIK EYMUNDSON'S DEATH.

Duke Guthorm dwelt principally at Tunsberg, and governed the whole of Viken when the king was not there. He defended the land, which, at that time, was much plundered by the vikings. There were disturbances also up in Gautland as long as King Eirik Eymundson lived; but he died when King Harald Harfager had been ten years king of all Norway.

29. GUTHORM'S DEATH IN TUNSBERG.

After Eirik, his son Bjorn was king of Svithjod for fifty years. He was father of Eirik the Victorious, and of Olaf the father of Styrbjorn. Guthorm died on a bed of sickness at Tunsberg, and King Harald gave his son Guthorm the government of that part of his dominions and made him chief of it.

30. EARL RAGNVALD BURNT IN HIS HOUSE.

When King Harald was forty years of age many of his sons were well advanced, and indeed they all came early to strength and manhood. And now they began to take it ill that the king would not give them any part of the kingdom, but put earls into every district; for they thought earls were of inferior birth to them. Then Halfdan Haleg and Gudrod Ljome set off one spring with a great force, and came suddenly upon Earl Ragnvald, earl of More, and surrounded the house in which he was, and burnt him and sixty men in it. Thereafter Halfdan took three long-ships, and fitted them out, and sailed into the West sea; but Gudrod set himself down in the land which Ragnvald formerly had. Now when King Harald heard this he set out with a great force against Gudrod, who had no other way left but to surrender, and he was sent to Agder. King Harald then set Earl

Ragnvald's son Thorer over More, and gave him his daughter Alof, called Arbot, in marriage. Earl Thorer, called the Silent, got the same territory his father Earl Ragnvald had possessed.

31. HALFDAN HALEG'S DEATH.

Halfdan Haleg came very unexpectedly to Orkney, and Earl Einar immediately fled; but came back soon after about harvest time, unnoticed by Halfdan. They met and after a short battle Halfdan fled the same night. Einar and his men lay all night without tents, and when it was light in the morning they searched the whole island and killed every man they could lay hold of. Then Einar said "What is that I see upon the isle of Rinansey? Is it a man or a bird? Sometimes it raises itself up, and sometimes lies down again." They went to it, and found it was Halfdan Haleg, and took him prisoner.

Earl Einar sang the following song the evening before he went into this battle:–

"Where is the spear of Hrollaug? where
Is stout Rolf Ganger's bloody spear!
I see them not; yet never fear,
For Einar will not vengeance spare
Against his father's murderers, though
Hrollaug and Rolf are somewhat slow,
And silent Thorer sits add dreams
At home, beside the mead-bowl's streams."

Thereafter Earl Einar went up to Halfdan, and cut a spread eagle upon his back, by striking his sword through his back into his belly, dividing his ribs from the backbone down to his loins, and tearing out his lungs; and so Halfdan was killed. Einar then sang:–

"For Ragnvald's death my sword is red:
Of vengeance it cannot be said
That Einar's share is left unsped.
So now, brave boys, let's raise a mound,–
Heap stones and gravel on the ground
O'er Halfdan's corpse: this is the way
We Norsemen our scat duties pay."

Then Earl Einar took possession of the Orkney Isles as before. Now when these tidings came to Norway, Halfdan's brothers took it much to heart, and thought that his death demanded vengeance; and many were of the same opinion. When Einar heard this, he sang:–

"Many a stout udal-man, I know,
Has cause to wish my head laid low;
And many an angry udal knife
Would gladly drink of Eina's life.
But ere they lay Earl Einar low,–
Ere this stout heart betrays its cause,
Full many a heart will writhe, we know,
In the wolf's fangs, or eagle's claws."

32. HARALD AND EINAR RECONCILED.

King Harald now ordered a levy, and gathered a great force, with which he proceeded westward to Orkney; and when Earl Einar heard that King Harald was come, he fled over to Caithness. He made the following verses on this occasion:–

"Many a bearded man must roam,
An exile from his house and home,
For cow or horse; but Halfdan's gore
Is red on Rinansey's wild shore.
A nobler deed–on Harald's shield
The arm of one who ne'er will yield
Has left a scar. Let peasants dread
The vengeance of the Norsemen's head:
I reck not of his wrath, but sing,
'Do thy worst!–I defy thee, king!–'"

Men and messages, however, passed between the king and the earl, and at last it came to a conference; and when they met the earl submitted the case altogether to the king's decision, and the king condemned the earl Einar and the Orkney people to pay a fine of sixty marks of gold. As the bondes thought this was too heavy for them to pay, the earl offered to pay the whole if they would surrender their udal lands to him. This they all agreed to do: the poor because they had but little pieces of land; the rich because they could redeem their udal rights again when they liked. Thus the earl paid the whole fine to the king, who returned in harvest to Norway. The earls for a long time afterwards possessed all the udal lands in Orkney, until Sigurd son of Hlodver gave back the udal rights.

33. DEATH OF GUTHORM AND HALFDAN THE WHITE.

While King Harald's son Guthorm had the defence of Viken, he sailed outside of the islands on the coast, and came in by one of the mouths of the tributaries of the Gaut river. When he lay there Solve Klofe came upon him, and immediately gave him battle, and Guthorm fell. Halfdan the White and Halfdan the Black went out on an expedition, and plundered in the East sea, and had a battle in Eistland, where Halfdan the White fell.

34. MARRIAGE OF EIRIK.

Eirik, Harald's son, was fostered in the house of the herse Thorer, son of Hroald, in the Fjord district. He was the most beloved and honoured by King Harald of all his sons. When Eirik was twelve years old, King Harald gave him five long-ships, with which he went on an expedition,–first in the Baltic; then southwards to Denmark, Friesland, and Saxland; on which expedition he passed four years. He then sailed out into the West sea and plundered in Scotland, Bretland, Ireland, and Valland, and passed four years more in this way. Then he sailed north to Finmark, and all the way to Bjarmaland, where he had many a battle, and won many a victory. When he came back to Finmark, his men found a girl in a Lapland hut, whose equal for beauty they never had seen. She said her name was Gunhild, and that her father dwelt in Halogaland, and was called Ozur Tote. "I am here," she said, "to learn sorcery from two of the most knowing Fins in all Finmark, who are now out hunting. They both want me in marriage. They are so skilful that they can hunt out traces either upon the frozen or the thawed earth, like dogs; and they can run so swiftly on skees that neither man nor beast can come near them in speed. They hit whatever they take aim at, and thus kill every man who comes near them. When they are angry the very earth turns away in terror, and whatever living thing they look upon then falls dead. Now ye must not come in their way; but I will hide you here in the hut, and ye must try to get them killed." They agreed to it, and she hid them, and then took a leather bag, in which they thought there were ashes which she took in her hand, and strewed both outside and inside of the hut. Shortly after the Fins came home, and asked who had been there; and she answered, "Nobody has been here." "That is wonderful," said they, "we followed the traces close to the hut, and can find none after that." Then they kindled a fire, and made ready their meat, and Gunhild prepared her bed. It had so happened that Gunhild had slept the three nights before, but the Fins had watched the one upon the other, being jealous of each other. "Now," she said to the Fins, "come here, and lie down one on each side of me." On which they were very glad to do so. She laid an arm round the neck of each and they went to sleep directly. She roused them up; but they fell to sleep again instantly, and so soundly the she scarcely could waken them. She even raised them up in the bed, and still they slept. Thereupon she too two great seal-skin bags, and put their heads in them, and tied them fast under their arms; and then she gave a wink to the king's men. They run forth with their weapons, kill the two Fins, and drag them out of the hut. That same night came such a dreadful thunder-storm that the could not stir. Next morning they came to the ship, taking Gunhild with them, and presented her to Eirik. Eirik and his followers then sailed southwards to Halogaland and he sent word to Ozur Tote, the girl's father, to meet him. Eirik said he would take his daughter in marriage, to which Ozur Tote consented, and Eirik took Gunhild and went southwards with her (A.D. 922).

35. HARALD DIVIDES HIS KINGDOM.

WHEN KING HARALD WAS fifty years of age many of his sons were grown up, and some were dead. Many of them committed acts of great violence in the country, and were in discord among themselves. They drove some of the king's earls out of their properties, and even killed some of them. Then the king called together a numerous Thing in the south part of the country, and summoned to it all the people of the Uplands. At this Thing he gave to all his sons the title of king, and made a law that his descendants in the male line should each succeed to the kingly title and dignity; but his descendants by the female side only to that of earl. And he divided the country among them thus:–Vingulmark, Raumarike, Vestfold and Thelamark, he bestowed on Olaf, Bjorn, Sigtryg, Frode, and Thorgils. Hedemark and Gudbrandsdal he gave to Dag, Hring, and Ragnar. To Snaefrid's sons he gave Ringerike, Hadeland, Thoten, and the lands thereto belonging. His son Guthorm, as before mentioned, he had set over the country from Glommen to Svinasund and Ranrike. He had set him to defend the country to the East, as before has been written. King Harald himself generally dwelt in the middle of the country, and Hrorek and Gudrod were generally with his court, and had great estates in Hordaland and in Sogn. King Eirik was also with his father King Harald; and the king loved and regarded him the most of all his sons, and gave him Halogaland and North More, and Raumsdal. North in Throndhjem he gave Halfdan the Black, Halfdan the White, and Sigrod land to rule over. In each of these districts he gave his sons the one half of his revenues, together with the right to sit on a high-seat,–a step higher than earls, but a step lower than his own high-seat. His king's seat each of his sons wanted for himself after his death, but he himself destined it for Eirik. The Throndhjem people wanted Halfdan the Black to succeed to it. The people of Viken, and the Uplands, wanted those under whom they lived. And thereupon new quarrels arose among the brothers; and because they thought their dominions too little, they drove about in piratical expeditions. In this way, as before related, Guthorm fell at the mouth of the Gaut river, slain by Solve Klofe; upon which Olaf took the kingdom he had possessed. Halfdan the White fell in Eistland, Halfdan Haleg in Orkney. King Harald gave ships of war to Thorgils and Frode, with which they went westward on a viking cruise, and plundered in Scotland, Ireland, and Bretland. They were the first of the Northmen who took Dublin. It is said that Frode got poisoned drink there; but Thorgils was a long time king over Dublin, until he fell into a snare of the Irish, and was killed.

36. DEATH OF RAGNVALD RETTILBEINE.

Eirik Blood-axe expected to be head king over all his brothers and King Harald intended he should be so; and the father and son lived long together. Ragnvald Rettilbeine governed Hadaland, and allowed himself to be instructed in the arts of witchcraft, and became an area warlock. Now King Harald was a hater of all witchcraft. There was a warlock in Hordaland called Vitgeir; and when the king sent a message to him that he should give up his art of witchcraft, he replied in this verse:–

"The danger surely is not great
From wizards born of mean estate,
When Harald's son in Hadeland,
King Ragnvald, to the art lays hand."

But when King Harald heard this, King Eirik Blood-axe went by his orders to the Uplands, and came to Hadeland and burned his brother Ragnvald in a house, along with eighty other warlocks; which work was much praised.

37. DEATH OF GUDROD LJOME.

Gudrod Ljome was in winter on a friendly visit to his foster-father Thjodolf in Hvin, and had a well-manned ship, with which he wanted to go north to Rogaland. It was blowing a heavy storm at the time; but Gudrod was bent on sailing, and would not consent to wait. Thjodolf sang thus:–

"Wait, Gudrod, till the storm is past,–
Loose not thy long-ship while the blast
Howls over-head so furiously,–
Trust not thy long-ship to the sea,–
Loose not thy long-ship from the shore;
Hark to the ocean's angry roar!
See how the very stones are tost
By raging waves high on the coast!
Stay, Gudrod, till the tempest's o'er–
Deep runs the sea off the Jadar's shore."

Gudrod set off in spite of what Thjodolf could say: and when they came off the Jadar the vessel sunk with them, and all on board were lost.

38. KING BJORN KAUPMAN'S DEATH.

King Harald's son, Bjorn, ruled over Vestfold at that time, and generally lived at Tunsberg, and went but little on war expeditions. Tunsberg at that time was much frequented by merchant vessels, both from Viken and the north country, and also from the south, from Denmark, and Saxland. King Bjorn had also merchant ships on voyages to other lands, by which he procured for himself costly articles, and such things as he thought needful; and therefore his brothers called him Farman (the Seaman), and Kaupman (the Chapman). Bjorn was a man of sense and understanding, and promised to become a good ruler. He made a good and suitable marriage, and had a son by his wife, who was named

Gudrod. Eirik Blood-axe came from his Baltic cruise with ships of war, and a great force, and required his brother Bjorn to deliver to him King Harald's share of the scat and incomes of Vestfold. But it had always been the custom before, that Bjorn himself either delivered the money into the king's hands, or sent men of his own with it; and therefore he would continue with the old custom, and would not deliver the money. Eirik again wanted provisions, tents, and liquor. The brothers quarrelled about this; but Eirik got nothing and left the town. Bjorn went also out of the town towards evening up to Saeheim. In the night Eirik came back after Bjorn, and came to Saeheim just as Bjorn and his men were seated at table drinking. Eirik surrounded the house in which they were; but Bjorn with his men went out and fought. Bjorn, and many men with him, fell. Eirik, on the other hand, got a great booty, and proceeded northwards. But this work was taken very ill by the people of Viken, and Eirik was much disliked for it; and the report went that King Olaf would avenge his brother Bjorn, whenever opportunity offered. King Bjorn lies in the mound of Farmanshaug at Saeheim.

39. RECONCILIATION OF THE KINGS.

King Eirik went in winter northwards to More, and was at a feast in Solve, within the point Agdanes; and when Halfdan the Black heard of it he set out with his men, and surrounded the house in which they were. Eirik slept in a room which stood detached by itself, and he escaped into the forest with four others; but Halfdan and his men burnt the main house, with all the people who were in it. With this news Eirik came to King Harald, who was very wroth at it, and assembled a great force against the Throndhjem people. When Halfdan the Black heard this he levied ships and men, so that he had a great force, and proceeded with it to Stad, within Thorsbjerg. King Harald lay with his men at Reinsletta. Now people went between them, and among others a clever man called Guthorm Sindre, who was then in Halfdan the Black's army, but had been formerly in the service of King Harald, and was a great friend of both. Guthorm was a great skald, and had once composed a song both about the father and the son, for which they had offered him a reward. But he would take nothing; but only asked that, some day or other, they should grant him any request he should make, which they promised to do. Now he presented himself to King Harald, brought words of peace between them, and made the request to them both that they should be reconciled. So highly did the king esteem him, that in consequence of his request they were reconciled. Many other able men promoted this business as well as he; and it was so settled that Halfdan should retain the whole of his kingdom as he had it before, and should let his brother Eirik sit in peace. After this event Jorun, the skald-maid, composed some verses in "Sendibit" ("The Biting Message"):–

> *"I know that Harald Fairhair*
> *Knew the dark deed of Halfdan.*
> *To Harald Halfdan seemed*
> *Angry and cruel."*

40. BIRTH OF HAKON THE GOOD.

Earl Hakon Grjotgardson of Hlader had the whole rule over Throndhjem when King Harald was anywhere away in the country; and Hakon stood higher with the king than any in the country of Throndhjem. After Hakon's death his son Sigurd succeeded to his power in Throndhjem, and was the earl, and had his mansion at Hlader. King Harald's sons, Halfdan the Black and Sigrod, who had been before in the house of his father Earl Hakon, continued to be brought up in his house. The sons of Harald and Sigurd were about the same age. Earl Sigurd was one of the wisest men of his time, and married Bergljot, a daughter of Earl Thorer the Silent; and her mother was Alof Arbot, a daughter of Harald Harfager. When King Harald began to grow old he generally dwelt on some of his great farms in Hordaland; namely, Alreksstader or Saeheim, Fitjar, Utstein, or Ogvaldsnes in the island Kormt. When Harald was seventy years of age he begat a son with a girl called Thora Mosterstang, because her family came from Moster. She was descended from good people, being connected with Kare (Aslakson) of Hordaland; and was moreover a very stout and remarkably handsome girl. She was called the king's servant-girl; for at that time many were subject to service to the king who were of good birth, both men and women. Then it was the custom, with people of consideration, to choose with great care the man who should pour water over their children, and give them a name. Now when the time came that Thora, who was then at Moster, expected her confinement, she would to King Harald, who was then living at Saeheim; and she went northwards in a ship belonging to Earl Sigurd. They lay at night close to the land; and there Thora brought forth a child upon the land, up among the rocks, close to the ship's gangway, and it was a man child. Earl Sigurd poured water over him, and called him Hakon, after his own father, Hakon earl of Hlader. The boy soon grew handsome, large in size, and very like his father King Harald. King Harald let him follow his mother, and they were both in the king's house as long as he was an infant.

41. KING ATHELSTAN'S MESSAGE

At this time a king called Aethelstan had taken the Kingdom of England. He was called victorious and faithful. He sent men to Norway to King Harald, with the errand that the messengers should present him with a sword, with the hilt and handle gilt, and also the whole sheath adorned with gold and silver, and set with precious jewels. The ambassador presented the sword-hilt to the king, saying, "Here is a sword which King Athelstan sends thee, with the request that thou wilt accept it." The king took the sword by the handle; whereupon the ambassador said, "Now thou hast taken the sword according to our king's desire, and therefore art thou his subject as thou hast taken his sword." King Harald saw now that this was an insult, for he would be subject to no man. But he remembered it was his rule, whenever anything raised his anger, to collect himself, and let his passion run off, and then take the matter into consideration coolly. Now he did so, and consulted his friends, who all gave him the advice to let the ambassadors, in the first place, go home in safety.

42. HAUK'S JOURNEY TO ENGLAND.

The following summer King Harald sent a ship westward to England, and gave the command of it to Hauk Habrok. He was a great warrior, and very dear to the king. Into his hands he gave his son Hakon. Hank proceeded westward in England, and found King Athelstan in London, where there was just at the time a great feast and entertainment. When they came to the hall, Hauk told his men how they should conduct themselves; namely, that he who went first in should go last out, and all should stand in a row at the table, at equal distance from each other; and each should have his sword at his left side, but should fasten his cloak so that his sword should not be seen. Then they went into the hall, thirty in number. Hauk went up to the king and saluted him, and the king bade him welcome. Then Hauk took the child Hakon, and set it on the king's knee. The king looks at the boy, and asks Hauk what the meaning of this is. Hauk replies, "Herald the king bids thee foster his servant-girl's child." The king was in great anger, and seized a sword which lay beside him, and drew it, as if he was going to kill the child. Hauk says, "Thou hast borne him on thy knee, and thou canst murder him if thou wilt; but thou wilt not make an end of all King Harald's sons by so doing." On that Hauk went out with all his men, and took the way direct to his ship, and put to sea,–for they were ready,–and came back to King Harald. The king was highly pleased with this; for it is the common observation of all people, that the man who fosters another's children is of less consideration than the other. From these transactions between the two kings, it appears that each wanted to be held greater than the other; but in truth there was no injury, to the dignity of either, for each was the upper king in his own kingdom till his dying day.

43. HAKON, THE FOSTER-SON OF ATHELSTAN, IS BAPTIZED.

King Athelstan had Hakon baptized, and brought up in the right faith, and in good habits, and all sorts of good manners, and he loved Hakon above all his relations; and Hakon was beloved by all men. He was henceforth called Athelstan's foster-son. He was an accomplished skald, and he was larger, stronger and more beautiful than other men; he was a man of understanding and eloquence, and also a good Christian. King Athelstan gave Hakon a sword, of which the hilt and handle were gold, and the blade still better; for with it Hakon cut down a mill-stone to the centre eye, and the sword thereafter was called the Quernbite[5]. Better sword never came into Norway, and Hakon carried it to his dying day.

44. EIRIK BROUGHT TO THE SOVEREIGNTY.

When King Harald was eighty years of age (A.D. 930) he became very heavy, and unable to travel through the country, or do the business of a king. Then he brought his son Eirik to his high-seat, and gave

5 Quern is the name of the small hand mill-stones still found. in use among the cottars in Orkney, Shetland, and the Hebrides. This sword is mentioned in the Younger Edda. There were many excellent swords in the olden time, and many of them had proper names.

him the power and command over the whole land. Now when King Harald's other sons heard this, King Halfdan the Black also took a king's high-seat, and took all Throndhjem land, with the consent of all the people, under his rule as upper king. After the death of Bjorn the Chapman, his brother Olaf took the command over Vestfold, and took Bjorn's son, Gudrod, as his foster-child. Olaf's son was called Trygve; and the two foster-brothers were about the same age, and were hopeful and clever. Trygve, especially, was remarkable as a stout and strong man. Now when the people of Viken heard that those of Hordaland had taken Eirik as upper king, they did the same, and made Olaf the upper king in Viken, which kingdom he retained. Eirik did not like this at all. Two years after this, Halfdan the Black died suddenly at a feast in Throndhjem and the general report was that Gunhild had bribed a witch to give him a death-drink. Thereafter the Throndhjem people took Sigrod to be their king.

45. KING HARALD'S DEATH.

King Harald lived three years after he gave Eirik the supreme authority over his kingdom, and lived mostly on his great farms which he possessed, some in Rogaland, and some in Hordaland. Eirik and Gunhild had a son on whom King Harald poured water, and gave him his own name, and the promise that he should be king after his father Eirik. King Harald married most of his daughters within the country to his earls, and from them many great families are descended. Harald died on a bed of sickness in Hogaland (A.D. 933), and was buried under a mound at Haugar in Karmtsund. In Haugesund is a church, now standing; and not far from the churchyard, at the north-west side, is King Harald Harfager's mound; but his grave-stone stands west of the church, and is thirteen feet and a half high, and two ells broad. One stone was set at head and one at the feet; on the top lay the slab, and below on both sides were laid small stones. The grave, mound, and stone, are there to the present day. Harald Harfager was, according to the report of men of knowledge, or remarkably handsome appearance, great and strong, and very generous and affable to his men. He was a great warrior in his youth; and people think that this was foretold by his mother's dream before his birth, as the lowest part of the tree she dreamt of was red as blood. The stem again was green and beautiful, which betokened his flourishing kingdom; and that the tree was white at the top showed that he should reach a grey-haired old age. The branches and twigs showed forth his posterity, spread over the whole land; for of his race, ever since. Norway has always had kings.

46. THE DEATH OF OLAF AND OF SIGROD.

King Eirik took all the revenues (A.D. 934), which the king had in the middle of the country, the next winter after King Harald's decease. But Olaf took all the revenues eastward in Viken, and their brother Sigrod all that of the Throndhjem country. Eirik was very ill pleased with this; and the report went that he would attempt with force to get the sole sovereignty over the country, in the same way as his father had given it to him. Now when Olaf and Sigrod heard this, messengers passed between them; and after appointing a meeting place, Sigrod went eastward in spring to Viken, and he and his brother Olaf met at Tunsberg, and remained there a while. The same spring (A.D. 934), King Eirik levied a great force, and ships and steered towards Viken. He got such a strong steady gale that he sailed night and day, and came faster than the news of him. When he came to Tunsberg, Olaf and Sigrod, with their forces, went out of the town a little eastward to a ridge, where they drew up their men in battle order; but as Eirik had many more men he won the battle. Both brothers, Olaf and Sigrod, fell there; and both their grave-mounds are upon the ridge where they fell. Then King Eirik went through Viken, and subdued it, and remained far into summer. Gudrod and Trygve fled to the Uplands. Eirik was a stout handsome man, strong, and very manly,–a great and fortunate man of war; but bad-minded, gruff, unfriendly, and silent. Gunhild, his wife, was the most beautiful of women,–clever, with much knowledge, and lively; but a very false person, and very cruel in disposition. The children of King Eirik and Gunhild were, Gamle, the oldest; then Guthorm, Harald, Ragnfrod, Ragnhild, Erling, Gudrod, and Sigurd Sleva. All were handsome, and of manly appearance[6].

6 Of Eirik, his wife, and children, see the following sagas.

BOOK THREE

Hakon the Good's Saga

PRELIMINARY REMARKS.

Of Eirik Blood-axe's five years' reign Snorre has no separate saga. He appears not to have been beloved by the people and his queen Gunhild seems to have had a bad influence on him.

Other accounts of Hakon may be found in "Fagrskinna" (chaps. 25-34), "Agrip", "Historia", "Norvegiae", and in "Thjodrek" (chap. 4).

The reader is also referred to "Saxo", "Egla", "Laxdaela", "Kormaks Saga", "Gisle Surssons Saga", "Halfred's Saga", "Floamanna Saga", "Viga Glum's Saga", and to "Landnamabok".

Skald mentioned in this Saga are:–Glum Geirason, Thord Sjarekson, Guthorm Sindre, Kormak Ogmundson, and Eyvind Skaldaspiller. In the "Egla" are found many poems belonging to this epoch by Egil Skallagrimson.

In "Fagrskinna" is found a poem (not given by Snorre) which Gunhild (his wife) had made on King Eirik after his death, telling how Odin welcomed him to Valhal. The author or skald who composed it is not known, but it is considered to be one of the gems of old Norse poetry, and we here quote it in Vigfusson's translation in his "Corpus Poeticum", vol. i. pp. 260, 261. Gudbrand Vigfusson has filled up a few gaps from "Hakonarmat", the poem at the end of this Saga. We have changed Vigfusson's orthography of names, and brought them into harmony with the spelling used in this work:–Ed.

"Odin wakes in the morning and cries, as he opens his eyes, with his dream still fresh in his mind:–'What dreams are these? I thought I arose before daybreak to make Valhal ready for a host of slain. I woke up the host of the chosen. I bade them ride up to strew the benches, and to till up the beer-vats, and I bade valkyries to bear the wine, as if a king were coming. I look for the coming of some noble chiefs from the earth, wherefore my heart is glad.'

"Brage, Odin's counsellor, now wakes, as a great din is heard without, and calls out:–'What is that thundering? as if a thousand men or some great host were tramping on–the walls and the benches are creaking withal–as if Balder was coming back to the ball of Odin?'

"Odin answers:–'Surely thou speakest foolishly, good Brage, although thou art very wise. It thunders for Eirik the king, that is coming to the hall of Odin.'

"Then turning to his heroes, he cries:–'Sigmund and Sinfjotle, rise in haste and go forth to meet the prince! Bid him in if it be Eirik, for it is he whom I look for.'

"Sigmund answers:–'Why lookest thou more for Eirik, the king, to Odin's hall, than for other kings?'

"Odin answers:–'Because he has reddened his brand, and borne his bloody sword in many a land.'

"Quoth Sigmund:–'Why didst thou rob him, the chosen king of victory then, seeing thou thoughtest him so brave?'

"Odin answered:–'Because it is not surely to be known, when the grey wolf shall come upon the seat of the god.'

SECOND SCENE.–Without Valhal. Sigmund and Sinfjotle go outside the hall and meet Eirik.

"Quoth Sigmund:–'Hail to thee, Eirik, be welcome here, and come into the hall, thou gallant king! Now I will ask thee, what kings are these that follow thee from the clash of the sword edges?'

"Eirik answers:–'They are five kings; I will tell thee all their names; I myself am the sixth (the names followed in the song, whereof the rest is lost.)

"Fagrskinna" says "Hakonarmal" was the model of this poem.

1. HAKON CHOSEN KING.

HAKON, ATHELSTAN'S FOSTER-SON, was in England at the time (A.D. 934) he heard of his father King Harald's death, and he immediately made himself ready to depart. King Athelstan gave him men, and a choice of good ships, and fitted him out for his journey most excellently. In harvest time he came to Norway, where he heard of the death of his brothers, and that King Eirik was then in Viken. Then Hakon sailed northwards to Throndhjem, where he went to Sigurd earl of Hlader who was the ablest man in Norway. He gave Hakon a good reception; and they made a league with each other, by which Hakon promised great power to Sigurd if he was made king. They assembled then a numerous Thing, and Sigurd the earl recommended Hakon's cause to the Thing, and proposed him to the bondes as king. Then Hakon himself stood up and spoke; and the people said to each other, two and two, as they heard him, "Herald Harfager is come again, grown and young." The beginning of Hakon's speech was, that he offered himself to the bondes as king, and desired from them the title of king, and aid and forces to defend the kingdom. He promised, on the other hand, to make all the bondes udal-holders, and give every man udal rights to the land he lived on. This speech met such joyful applause, that the whole public cried and shouted that they would take him to be king. And so it was that the Throndhjem people took Hakon, who was then fifteen years old, for king; and he took a court or bodyguard, and servants, and proceeded through the country. The news reached the Uplands that the people in Throndhjem had taken to themselves a king, who in every respect was like King Harald Harfager,–with the difference, that Harald had made all the people of the land vassals, and unfree; but this Hakon wished well to every man, and offered the bondes to give them their udal rights again, which Harald had taken from them. All were rejoiced at this news, and it passed from mouth to mouth,–it flew, like fire in dry grass, through the whole land, and eastward to the land's end. Many bondes came from the Uplands to meet King Hakon. Some sent messengers, some tokens; and all to the same effect–that his men they would be: and the king received all thankfully.

2. KING HAKON'S PROGRESS THROUGH THE COUNTRY.

Early in winter (935), the king went to the Uplands, and summoned the people to a Thing; and there streamed all to him who could come. He was proclaimed king at every Thing; and then he proceeded eastward to Viken, where his brother's sons, Trygve and Gudrod, and many others, came unto him, and complained of the sorrow and evil his brother Eirik had wrought. The hatred to King Eirik grew more and more, the more liking all men took to King Hakon; and they got more boldness to say what they thought. King Hakon gave Trygve and Gudrod the title of kings, and the dominions which King Harald had bestowed on their fathers. Trygve got Ranrike and Vingulmark, and Gudrod, Vestfold; but as they were young, and in the years of childhood, he appointed able men to rule the land for them. He gave them the country on the same conditions as it had been given before,–that they should have half of the scat and revenues with him. Towards spring King Hakon returned north, over the Uplands, to Throndhjem.

3. EIRIK'S DEPARTURE FROM THE COUNTRY.

King Hakon, early in spring, collected a great army at Throndhjem, and fitted out ships. The people of Viken also had a great force on foot, and intended to join Hakon. King Eirik also levied people in the middle of the country; but it went badly with him to gather people, for the leading men left him, and went over to Hakon. As he saw himself not nearly strong enough to oppose Hakon, he sailed (A.D. 935) out to the West sea with such men as would follow him. He first sailed to Orkney, and took many people with him from that country; and then went south towards England, plundering in Scotland, and in the north parts of England, wherever he could land. Athelstan, the king of England, sent a message to Eirik, offering him dominions under him in England; saying that King Harald his father was a good friend of King Athelstan, and therefore he would do kindly towards his sons. Messengers passed between the two kings; and it came to an agreement that King Eirik should take Northumberland as a fief from King Athelstan, and which land he should defend against the Danes or other vikings. Eirik should let himself be baptized, together with his wife and children, and all the people who had followed him. Eirik accepted this offer, and was baptized, and adopted the right faith. Northumberland is called a fifth part of England. Eirik had his residence at York, where Lodbrok's sons, it was said, had formerly been, and Northumberland was principally inhabited by Northmen. Since Lodbrok's sons had taken the country, Danes and Northmen often plundered there, when the power of the land was out of their hands. Many names of places in the country are Norwegian; as Grimsby, Haukfliot, and many others.

4. EIRIK'S DEATH.

King Eirik had many people about him, for he kept many Northmen who had come with him from the East; and also many of his friends had joined him from Norway. But as he had little land, he went on a cruise every summer, and plundered in Scotland, the Hebrides, Ireland, and Bretland, by which he gathered property. King Athelstan died on a sick bed, after a reign of fourteen years, eight weeds, and three days. After him his brother Jatmund was king of England, and he was no friend to the Northmen. King Eirik, also, was in no great favour with him; and the word went about that King Jatmund would set another chief over Northumberland. Now when King Eirik heard this, he set off on a viking cruise to the westward; and from the Orkneys took with him the Earls Arnkel and Erlend, the sons of Earl Torfeinar. Then he sailed to the Hebrides, where there were many vikings and troop-kings, who joined their men to his. With all this force he steered to Ireland first, where he took with him all the men he could, and then to Bretland, and plundered; and sailed thereafter south to England, and marauded there as elsewhere. The people fled before him wherever he appeared. As King Eirik was a bold warrior, and had a great force, he trusted so much to his people that he penetrated far inland in the country, following and plundering the fugitives. King Jatmund had set a king, who was called Olaf, to defend the land; and he gathered an innumerable mass of people, with whom he marched against King Eirik. A dreadful battle ensued, in which many Englishmen fell; but for one who fell came three in his place out of the country behind, and when evening came on the loss of men turned on the side of the Northmen, and many people fell. Towards the end of the day, King Eirik and five kings with him fell. Three of them were Guthorm and his two sons, Ivar and Harek: there fell, also, Sigurd and Ragnvald; and with them Torfeinar's two sons, Arnkel and Erlend. Besides these, there was a great slaughter of Northmen; and those who escaped went to Northumberland, and brought the news to Gunhild and her sons (A.D. 941).

5. GUNHILD AND HER SONS.

When Gunhild and her sons knew for certain that King Eirik had fallen, after having plundered the land of the King of England, they thought there was no peace to be expected for them; and they made themselves ready to depart from Northumberland, with all the ships King Eirik had left, and all the men who would go with them. They took also all the loose property, and goods which they had gathered partly as taxes in England, partly as booty on their expeditions. With their army they first steered northward to Orkney, where Thorfin Hausakljufer was earl, a son of Torfeinar, and took up their station there for a time. Eirik's sons subdued these islands and Hjaltland, took scat for themselves, and staid there all the winter; but went on viking cruises in summer to the West, and plundered in Scotland and Ireland. About this Glum Geirason sings:–

"The hero who knows well to ride
The sea-horse o'er the foamingtide,–
He who in boyhood wild rode o'er
The seaman's horse to Skanea's shore.
And showed the Danes his galley's bow,
Right nobly scours the ocean now.
On Scotland's coast he lights the brand
Of flaming war; with conquering hand
Drives many a Scottish warrior tall
To the bright seats in Odin's hall.
The fire-spark, by the fiend of war
Fanned to a flame, soon spreads afar.
Crowds trembling fly,–the southern foes
Fall thick beneath the hero's blows:
The hero's blade drips red with gore,
Staining the green sward on the shore."

6. BATTLE IN JUTLAND.

WHEN KING EIRIK HAD left the country, King Hakon, Athelstan's foster-son, subdued the whole of Norway. The first winter (A.D. 936) he visited the western parts, and then went north, and settled in Throndhjem. But as no peace could be reasonably looked for so long as King Eirik with his forces could come to Norway from the West sea, he set himself with his men-at-arms in the middle of the country,–in the Fjord district, or in Sogn, or Hordaland, or Rogaland. Hakon placed Sigurd earl of Hlader over the whole Throradhjem district, as he and his father had before had it under Harald Harfager. When King Hakon heard of his brother Eirik's death, and also that his sons had no footing in England, he thought there was not much to fear from them, and he went with his troops one summer eastward to Viken. At that time the Danes plundered often in Viken, and wrought much evil there; but when they heard that King Hakon was come with a great army, they got out of the way, to Halland; and those who were nearest to King Hakon went out to sea, and over to Jotland (Jutland). When the king heard of this, he sailed after them with all his army. On arriving in Jutland he plundered all round; and when the country people heard of it, they assembled in a great body, and determined to defend their land, and fight. There was a great battle; and King Hakon fought so boldly, that he went forward before his banner without helmet or coat of mail. King Hakon won the victory, and drove the fugitives far up the country. So says Guthorm Sindre, in his song of Hakon:–

"Furrowing the deep-blue sea with oars,
The king pursues to Jutland's shores.
They met; and in the battle storm
Of clashing shields, full many a form
Of goodly warrior on the plain,
Full many a corpse by Hakon slain,
Glutted the ravens, who from far,
Scenting the banquet-feast of war,
Came in black flocks to Jutland's plains
To drink the blood-wine from the veins."

7. BATTLE IN EYRARSUND (THE SOUND).

Then Hakon steered southwards with his fleet to seek the vikings, and so on to Sealand. He rowed with two cutters into the Eyrarsund, where he found eleven viking ships, and instantly attacked them. It ended in his gaining the victory, and clearing the viking ships of all their men. So says Guthorm Sindre:–

"Hakon the Brave, whose skill all know
To bend in battle storm the bow,
Rushed o'er the waves to Sealand's tongue,
His two war-ships with gilt shields hung,
And cleared the decks with his blue sword
That rules the fate of war, on board
Eleven ships of the Vindland men.–
Famous is Hakon's name since then."

8. KING HAKON'S EXPEDITION TO DENMARK.

Thereafter King Hakon carried war far and wide in Sealand; plundering some, slaying others, taking some prisoners of war, taking ransom from others, and all without opposition. Then Hakon proceeded along the coast of Skane, pillaging everywhere, levying taxes and ransome from the country, and killing all vikings, both Danish and Vindish. He then went eastwards to the district of Gautland, marauded there, and took great ransom from the country. So says Guthorm Sindre:-

"Hakon, who midst the battle shock
Stands like a firmly-rooted oak,
Subdued all Sealand with the sword:
From Vindland vikings the sea-bord
Of Scania swept; and, with the shield
Of Odin clad, made Gautland yield
A ransom of the ruddy gold,
Which Hakon to his war-men bold
Gave with free hand, who in his feud
Against the arrow-storm had stood."

King Hakon returned back in autumn with his army and an immense booty; and remained all the winter (A.D. 946) in Viken to defend it against the Danes and Gautlanders, if they should attack it.

9. OF KING TRYGVE.

IN THE SAME WINTER King Trygve Olafson returned from a viking cruise in the West sea, having before ravaged in Ireland and Scotland. In spring (A.D. 946) King Hakon went north, and set his brother's son, King Trygve, over Viken to defend that country against enemies. He gave him also in property all that he could reconquer of the country in Denmark, which the summer before King Hakon had subjected to payment of scat to him. So says Guthorm:-

"King Hakon, whose sharp sword dyes red
The bright steel cap on many a head,
Has set a warrior brave and stout
The foreign foeman to keep out,-
To keep that green land safe from war
Which black Night bore to dwarf Annar[7].

7 The dwarf Annar was the husband of Night, and Earth was their daughter.-L.

For many a carle whose trade's to wield
The battle-axe, and swing the shield,
On the swan's ocean-skates has come,
In white-winged ships, across the foam,–
Across the sea, from far Ireland,
To war against the Norseman's land."

10. OF GUNHILD S SONS.

King Harald Gormson ruled over Denmark at that time. He took it much amiss that King Hakon had made war in his dominions, and the report went that he would take revenge; but this did not take place so soon. When Gunhild and her sons heard there was enmity between Denmark and Norway, they began to turn their course from the West. They married King Eirik's daughter, Ragnhild, to Arnfin, a son of Thorfin Hausakljufer; and as soon as Eirik's sons went away, Thorfin took the earldom again over the Orkney Islands. Gamle Eirikson was somewhat older than the other brothers, but still he was not a grown man. When Gunhild and her sons came from the westward to Denmark, they were well received by King Harald. He gave them great fiefs in his kingdom, so that they could maintain themselves and their men very well. He also took Harald Eirikson to be his foster-son, set him on his knee, and thereafter he was brought up at the Danish king's court. Some of Eirik's sons went out on viking expeditions as soon as they were old enough, and gathered property, ravaging all around in the East sea. They grew up quickly to be handsome men, and far beyond their years in strength and perfection. Glum Geirason tells of one of them in the Grafeld song:–

"I've heard that, on the Eastland coast,
Great victories were won and lost.
The king, whose hand is ever graced
With gift to skald, his banner placed
On, and still on; while, midst the play
Of swords, sung sharp his good sword's sway
As strong in arm as free of gold,
He thinn'd the ranks of warriors bold."

Then Eirik's sons turned northwards with their troops to Viken and marauded there; but King Trygve kept troops on foot with which he met them, and they had many a battle, in which the victory was sometimes on one side, and sometimes on the other. Sometimes Eirik's sons plundered in Viken, and sometimes Trygve in Sealand and Halland.

11. KING HAKON AS A LAW-GIVER.

As long as Hakon was king in Norway, there was good peace between the bondes and merchants; so that none did harm either to the life or goods of the other. Good seasons also there were, both by sea and land. King Hakon was of a remarkably cheerful disposition, clever in words, and very condescending. He was a man of great understanding also, and bestowed attention on law-giving. He gave out the Gula-thing's laws on the advice of Thorleif Spake (the Wise); also the Frosta-thing's laws on the advice of Earl Sigurd, and of other Throndhjem men of wisdom. Eidsiva-thing laws were first established in the country by Halfdan the Black, as has before been written.

12. THE BIRTH OF EARL HAKON THE GREAT.

King Hakon kept Yule at Throndhjem, and Earl Sigurd had made a feast for him at Hlader. The night of the first day of Yule the earl's wife, Bergljot, was brought to bed of a boy-child, which afterwards King Hakon poured water over, and gave him his own name. The boy grew up, and became in his day a mighty and able man, and was earl after his father, who was King Hakon's dearest friend.

13. OF EYSTEIN THE BAD.

Eystein, a king of the Uplands, whom some called the Great, and some the Bad, once on a time made war in Throndhjem, and subdued Eyna district and Sparbyggia district, and set his own son Onund over them; but the Throndhjem people killed him. Then King Eystein made another inroad into Throndhjem, and ravaged the land far and wide, and subdued it. He then offered the people either his slave, who was called Thorer Faxe, or his dog, whose name was Saur, to be their king. They preferred the dog, as they thought they would sooner get rid of him. Now the dog was, by witchcraft, gifted with three men's wisdom; and when he barked, he spoke one word and barked two. A collar and chain of gold and silver were made for him, and his courtiers carried him on their shoulders when the weather or ways were foul. A throne was erected for him, and he sat upon a high place, as kings are used to sit. He dwelt on Eyin Idre (Idre Isle), and had his mansion in a place now called Saurshaug. It is told that the occasion of his death was that the wolves one day broke into his fold, and his courtiers stirred him up to defend his cattle; but when he ran down from his mound, and attacked the wolves, they tore him into pieces. Many other extraordinary things were done by this King Eystein against the Throndhjem people, and in consequence of this persecution and trouble, many chiefs and people fled and left their udal properties.

14. JAMTALAND AND HELSINGJALAND.

Ketil Jamte, a son of Earl Onund of Sparabu, went eastward across the mountain ridge, and with him a great multitude, who took all their farm-stock and goods with them. They cleared the woods, and established large farms, and settled the country afterwards called Jamtaland. Thorer Helsing, Ketil's grandson, on account of a murder, ran away from Jamtaland and fled eastward through the forest, and settled there. Many people followed, and that country, which extends eastward down to the seacoast, was called Helsingjaland; and its eastern parts are inhabited by Swedes. Now when Harald Harfager took possession of the whole country many people fled before him, both people of Throndhjem and of Naumudal districts; and thus new settlers came to Jamtaland, and some all the way to Helsingjaland. The Helsingjaland people travelled into Svithiod for their merchandise, and thus became altogether subjects of that country. The Jamtaland people, again, were in a manner between the two countries; and nobody cared about them, until Hakon entered into friendly intercourse with Jamtaland, and made friends of the more powerful people. Then they resorted to him, and promised him obedience and payment of taxes, and became his subjects; for they saw nothing but what was good in him, and being of Norwegian race they would rather stand under his royal authority than under the king of Sweden: and he gave them laws, and rights to their land. All the people of Helsingjaland did the same,–that is, all who were of Norwegian race, from the other side of the great mountain ridge.

15. HAKON SPREADS CHRISTIANITY.

King Hakon was a good Christian when he came to Norway; but as the whole country was heathen, with much heathenish sacrifice, and as many great people, as well as the favour of the common people, were to be conciliated, he resolved to practice his Christianity in private. But he kept Sundays, and the Friday fasts, and some token of the greatest holy-days. He made a law that the festival of Yule should begin at the same time as Christian people held it, and that every man, under penalty, should brew a meal of malt into ale, and therewith keep the Yule holy as long as it lasted. Before him, the beginning of Yule, or the slaughter night, was the night of mid-winter (Dec. 14), and Yule was kept for three days thereafter. It was his intent, as soon as he had set himself fast in the land, and had subjected the whole to his power, to introduce Christianity. He went to work first by enticing to Christianity the men who were dearest to him; and many, out of friendship to him, allowed themselves to be baptized, and some laid aside sacrifices. He dwelt long in the Throndhjem district, for the strength of the country lay there; and when he thought that, by the support of some powerful people there, he could set up Christianity he sent a message to England for a bishop and other teachers; and when they arrived in Norway, Hakon made it known that he would proclaim Christianity over all the land. The people of More and Raumsdal referred the matter to the people of Throndhjem. King Hakon then had several churches consecrated, and put priests into them; and when he came to Throndhjem he summoned the bondes to a Thing, and invited them to accept Christianity. They gave an answer to the effect that they would defer the matter until the Frosta-thing, at which there would be men from every district of the Throndhjem country, and then they would give their determination upon this difficult matter.

16. ABOUT SACRIFICES.

Sigurd, earl of Hlader, was one of the greatest men for sacrifices, and so had Hakon his father been; and Sigurd always presided on account of the king at all the festivals of sacrifice in the Throndhjem country. It was an old custom, that when there was to be sacrifice all the bondes should come to the spot where the temple stood and bring with them all that they required while the festival of the sacrifice lasted. To this festival all the men brought ale with them; and all kinds of cattle, as well as horses, were slaughtered, and all the blood that came from them was called "hlaut", and the vessels in which it was collected were called hlaut-vessels. Hlaut-staves were made, like sprinkling brushes, with which the whole of the altars and the temple walls, both outside and inside, were sprinkled over, and also the people were sprinkled with the blood; but the flesh was boiled into savoury meat for those present. The fire was in the middle of the floor of the temple, and over it hung the kettles, and the full goblets were handed across the fire; and he who made the feast, and was a chief, blessed the full goblets, and all the meat of the sacrifice. And first Odin's goblet was emptied for victory and power to his king; thereafter, Niord's and Freyja's goblets for peace and a good season. Then it was the custom of many to empty the brage-goblet[8]; and then the guests emptied a goblet to the memory of departed friends, called the remembrance goblet. Sigurd the earl was an open-handed man, who did what was very much celebrated; namely, he made a great sacrifice festival at Hlader of which he paid all the expenses. Kormak Ogmundson sings of it in his ballad of Sigurd:–

"Of cup or platter need has none
The guest who seeks the generous one,–
Sigurd the Generous, who can trace
His lineage from the giant race;
For Sigurd's hand is bounteous, free,–
The guardian of the temples he.
He loves the gods, his liberal hand
Scatters his sword's gains o'er the land–"

17. THE FROSTA-THING.

King Hakon came to the Frosta-thing, at which a vast multitude of people were assembled. And when the Thing was seated, the king spoke to the people, and began his speech with saying,–it was his message and entreaty to the bondes and householding men, both great and small, and to the whole public in general, young and old, rich and poor, women as well as men, that they should all allow themselves to be baptized, and should believe in one God, and in Christ the son of Mary and refrain from all sacrifices and heathen gods; and should keep holy the seventh day, and abstain from all work on it, and keep a fast on the

8 The brage-goblet, over which vows were made.–L.

seventh day. As soon as the king had proposed this to the bondes, great was the murmur and noise among the crowd. They complained that the king wanted to take their labour and their old faith from them, and the land could not be cultivated in that way. The labouring men and slaves thought that they could not work if they did not get meat; and they said it was the character of King Hakon, and his father, and all the family, to be generous enough with their money, but sparing with their diet. Asbjorn of Medalhus in the Gaulardal stood up, and answered thus to the king's proposal:–

"We bondes, King Hakon, when we elected thee to be our king, and got back our udal rights at the Thing held in Throndhjem, thought we had got into heaven; but now we don't know whether we have really got back our freedom, or whether thou wishest to make vassals of us again by this extraordinary proposal that we should abandon the ancient faith which our fathers and forefathers have held from the oldest times, in the times when the dead were burnt, as well as since that they are laid under mounds, and which, although they were braver than the people of our days, has served us as a faith to the present time. We have also held thee so dear, that we have allowed thee to rule and give law and right to all the country. And even now we bondes will unanimously hold by the law which thou givest us here in the Frosta-thing, and to which we have also given our assent; and we will follow thee, and have thee for our king, as long as there is a living man among us bondes here in this Thing assembled. But thou, king, must use some moderation towards us, and only require from us such things as we can obey thee in, and are not impossible for us. If, however, thou wilt take up this matter with a high hand, and wilt try thy power and strength against us, we bondes have resolved among ourselves to part with thee, and to take to ourselves some other chief, who will so conduct himself towards us that we can freely and safely enjoy that faith that suits our own inclinations. Now, king, thou must choose one or other of these conditions before the Thing is ended."

The bondes gave loud applause to this speech, and said it expressed their will, and they would stand or fall by what had been spoken. When silence was again restored, Earl Sigurd said, "It is King Hakon's will to give way to you, the bondes, and never to separate himself from your friendship." The bondes replied, that it was their desire that the king should offer a sacrifice for peace and a good year, as his father was want to do; and thereupon the noise and tumult ceased, and the Thing was concluded. Earl Sigurd spoke to the king afterwards, and advised him not to refuse altogether to do as the people desired, saying there was nothing else for it but to give way to the will of the bondes; "for it is, as thou hast heard thyself, the will and earnest desire of the head-people, as well as of the multitude. Hereafter we may find a good way to manage it." And in this resolution the king and earl agreed (A.D. 950).

18. KING HAKON OFFERS SACRIFICES.

THE HARVEST THEREAFTER, towards the winter season, there was a festival of sacrifice at Hlader, and the king came to it. It had always been his custom before, when he was present at a place where there was sacrifice, to take his meals in a little house by himself, or with some few of his men; but the bondes grumbled that he did not seat himself in his high-seat at these the most joyous of the meetings of the people. The earl said that the king should do so this time. The king accordingly sat upon his high-seat. Now when the first full goblet was filled, Earl Sigurd spoke some words over it, blessed it in Odin's name, and drank to the king out of the horn; and the king then took it, and made the sign of the cross over it. Then said Kar of Gryting, "What does the king mean by doing so? Will he not sacrifice?" Earl Sigurd replies, "The king is doing what all of you do, who trust to your power and strength. He is blessing the full goblet in the name of Thor, by making the sign of his hammer over it before he drinks it." On this there was quietness for the evening. The next day, when the people sat down to table, the bondes pressed the king strongly to eat of horse-flesh[9]; and as he would on no account do so, they wanted him to drink of the soup; and as he would not do this, they insisted he should at least taste the gravy; and on his refusal they were going to lay hands on him. Earl Sigurd came and made peace among them, by asking the king to hold his mouth over the handle of the kettle, upon which the fat smoke of the boiled horse-flesh had settled itself; and the king first laid a linen cloth over the handle, and then gaped over it, and returned to the high-seat; but neither party was satisfied with this.

---

9 This eating of horse-flesh at these religious festivals was considered the most direct proof of paganism in the following times, and was punished by death or mutilation by Saint Olaf. It was a ceremony apparently commemorative of their Asiatic origin and ancestors.

19. FEAST OF THE SACRIFICE AT MORE.

The winter thereafter the king prepared a Yule feast in More, and eight chiefs resolved with each other to meet at it. Four of them were from without the Throndhjem district–namely, Kar of Gryting, Asbjorn of Medalhus, Thorberg of Varnes, and Orm from Ljoxa; and from the Throndhjem district, Botolf of Olvishaug, Narfe of Staf in Veradal, Thrand Hak from Egg, and Thorer Skeg from Husaby in Eyin Idre. These eight men bound themselves, the four first to root out Christianity in Norway, and the four others to oblige the king to offer sacrifice to the gods. The four first went in four ships southwards to More, and killed three priests, and burnt three churches, and then they returned. Now, when King Hakon and Earl Sigurd came to More with their court, the bondes assembled in great numbers; and immediately, on the first day of the feast, the bondes insisted hard with the king that he should offer sacrifice, and threatened him with violence if he refused. Earl Sigurd tried to make peace between them, and brought it so far that the king took some bits of horse-liver, and emptied all the goblets the bondes filled for him without the sign of the cross; but as soon as the feast was over, the king and the earl returned to Hlader. The king was very ill pleased, and made himself ready to leave Throndhjem forthwith with all his people; saying that the next time he came to Throndhjem, he would come with such strength of men-at-arms that he would repay the bondes for their enmity towards him. Earl Sigurd entreated the king not to take it amiss of the bondes; adding, that it was not wise to threaten them, or to make war upon the people within the country, and especially in the Throndhjem district, where the strength of the land lay; but the king was so enraged that he would not listen to a word from anybody. He went out from Throndhjem, and proceeded south to More, where he remained the rest of the winter, and on to the spring season (A.D. 950); and when summer came he assembled men, and the report was that he intended with this army to attack the Throndhjem people.

20. BATTLE AT OGVALDSNES.

But just as the king had embarked with a great force of troops, the news was brought him from the south of the country, that King Eirik's sons had come from Denmark to Viken and had driven King Trygve Olafson from his ships at Sotanes, and then had plundered far and wide around in Viken, and that many had submitted to them. Now when King Hakon heard this news, he thought that help was needed; and he sent word to Earl Sigurd, and to the other chiefs from whom he could expect help, to hasten to his assistance. Sigurd the earl came accordingly with a great body of men, among whom were all the Throndhjem people who had set upon him the hardest to offer sacrifice; and all made their peace with the king, by the earl's persuasion. Now King Hakon sailed south along the coast; and when he came south as far as Stad, he heard that Eirik's sons were come to North Agder. Then they advanced against each other, and met at Kormt. Both parties left their ships there, and gave battle at Ogvaldsnes. Both parties had a great force, and it was a great battle. King Hakon went forward bravely, and King Guthorm Eirikson met him with his troop, and they exchanged blows with each other. Guthorm fell, and his standard was cut down. Many people fell around him. The army of Eirik's sons then took flight to their ships and rowed away with the loss of many a man. So says Guthorm Sindre:–

"The king's voice waked the silent host
Who slept beside the wild sea-coast,
And bade the song of spear and sword
Over the battle plain be heard.
Where heroes' shields the loudest rang,
Where loudest was the sword-blade's clang,
By the sea-shore at Kormt Sound,
Hakon felled Guthorm to the ground."

Now King Hakon returned to his ships, and pursued Gunhild's sons. And both parties sailed all they could sail, until they came to East Adger, from whence Eirik's sons set out to sea, and southwards for Jutland (A.D. 950). Guthorm Sindre speaks of it in his song:–

"And Guthorm's brothers too, who know
So skilfully to bend the bow,
The conquering hand must also feel
Of Hakon, god of the bright steel,–
The sun-god, whose bright rays, that dart
Flame-like, are swords that pierce the heart.
Well I remember how the King
Hakon, the battle's life and spring,
O'er the wide ocean cleared away

Eirik's brave sons. They durst not stay,
But round their ships' sides hung their shields
And fled across the blue sea-fields."

King Hakon returned then northwards to Norway, but Eirik's sons remained a long time in Denmark.

21. KING HAKON'S LAWS.

King Hakon after this battle made a law, that all inhabited land over the whole country along the sea-coast, and as far back from it as the salmon swims up in the rivers, should be divided into ship-raths according to the districts; and it was fixed by law how many ships there should be from each district, and how great each should be, when the whole people were called out on service. For this outfit the whole inhabitants should be bound whenever a foreign army came to the country. With this came also the order that beacons should be erected upon the hills, so that every man could see from the one to the other; and it is told that a war-signal could thus be given in seven days, from the most southerly beacon to the most northerly Thing-seat in Halogaland

22. CONCERNING EIRIK'S SONS.

Eirik's sons plundered much on the Baltic coasts and sometimes, as before related, in Norway; but so long as Hakon ruled over Norway there was in general good peace, and good seasons, and he was the most beloved of kings. When Hakon had reigned about twenty years in Norway (A.D. 954), Eirik's sons came from Denmark with a powerful army, of which a great part consisted of the people who had followed them on their expeditions; but a still greater army of Danes had been placed at their disposal by King Harald Gormson. They sailed with a fair wind from Vendil, and came to Agder; and then sailed northwards, night and day, along the coast. But the beacons were not fired, because it had been usual to look for them lighted from the east onwards, and nobody had observed them from the east coast; and besides King Hakon had set heavy penalties for giving false alarm, by lighting the beacons without occasion. The reason of this was, that ships of war and vikings cruised about and plundered among the outlying islands, and the country people took them for Eirik's sons, and lighted the beacons, and set the whole country in trouble and dread of war. Sometimes, no doubt, the sons of Eirik were there; but having only their own troops, and no Danish army with them, they returned to Denmark; and sometimes these were other vikings. King Hakon was very angry at this, because it cost both trouble and money to no purpose. The bondes also suffered by these false alarms when they were given uselessly; and thus it happened that no news of this expedition of Eirik's sons circulated through the land until they had come as far north as Ulfasund, where they lay for seven days. Then spies set off across Eid and northwards to More. King Hakon was at that time in the island Frede, in North More, at a place called Birkistrand, where he had a dwelling-house, and had no troops with him, only his bodyguard or court, and the neighbouring bondes he had invited to his house.

23. OF EGIL ULSERK.

The spies came to King Hakon, and told him that Eirik's sons, with a great army, lay just to the south of Stad. Then he called together the most understanding of the men about him, and asked their opinion, whether he should fight with Eirik's sons, although they had such a great multitude with them, or should set off northwards to gather together more men. Now there was a bonde there, by name Egil Ulserk, who was a very old man, but in former days had been strong and stout beyond most men, and a hardy man-at-arms withal, having long carried King Harald Harfager's banner. Egil answered thus to the king's speech,–"I was in several battles with thy father Harald the king, and he gave battle sometimes with many, sometimes with few people; but he always came off with victory. Never did I hear him ask counsel of his friends whether he should fly–and neither shalt thou get any such counsel from us, king; but as we know we have a brave leader, thou shalt get a trusty following from us." Many others agreed with this speech, and the king himself declared he was most inclined to fight with such strength as they could gather. It was so determined. The king split up a war-arrow, which he sent off in all directions, and by that token a number of men was collected in all haste. Then said Egil Ulserk,–"At one time the peace had lasted so long I was afraid I might come to die the death of old age[10], within doors upon a bed of straw, although I would

10 In all the sagas of this pagan time, the dying on a bed of sickness is mentioned as a kind of derogatory end of a man of any celebrity.–L.

rather fall in battle following my chief. And now it may so turn out in the end as I wished it to be."

24. BATTLE AT FREDARBERG.

Eirik's sons sailed northwards around Stad; as soon as the wind suited; and when they had passed it, and heard where King Hakon was, they sailed to meet him. King Hakon had nine ships, with which he lay under Fredarberg in Feeysund; and Eirik's sons had twenty ships, with which they brought up on the south side of the same cape, in Feeysund. King Hakon sent them a message, asking them to go upon the land; and telling them that he had hedged in with hazel boughs a place of combat at Rastarkalf, where there is a flat large field, at the foot of a long and rather low ridge. Then Eirik's sons left their ships, and went northwards over the neck of land within Fredarberg, and onward to Rastarkalf. Then Egil asked King Hakon to give him ten men with ten banners, and the king did so. Then Egil went with his men under the ridge; but King Hakon went out upon the open field with his army, and set up his banner, and drew up his army, saying, "Let us draw up in a long line, that they may not surround us, as they have the most men." And so it was done; and there was a severe battle, and a very sharp attack. Then Egil Ulserk set up the ten banners he had with him, and placed the men who carried them so that they should go as near the summit of the ridge as possible, and leaving a space between each of them. They went so near the summit that the banners could be seen over it, and moved on as if they were coming behind the army of Eirik's sons. Now when the men who stood uppermost in the line of the troops of Eirik's sons saw so many flying banners advancing high over the edge of the ridge, they supposed a great force must be following, who would come behind their army, and between them and their ships. They made each other acquainted with what was going on in a loud shout, and the whole took to flight; and when the king saw it, they fled with the rest. King Hakon now pushes on briskly with his people, pursuing the flying, and killing many.

25. OF KING GAMLE.

When Gamle Eirikson came up the ridge of the hill he turned round, and he observed that not more people were following than his men had been engaged with already, and he saw it was but a stratagem of war; so he ordered the war-horns to be blown, his banner to be set up, and he put his men in battle order. On this, all his Northmen stood, and turned with him, but the Danes fled to the ships; and when King Hakon and his men came thither, there was again sharp conflict; but now Hakon had most people. At last the Eirik's sons' force fled, and took the road south about the hill; but a part of their army retreated upon the hill southwards, followed by King Hakon. There is a flat field east of the ridge which runs westward along the range of hills, and is bounded on its west side by a steep ridge. Gamle's men retreated towards this ground; but Hakon followed so closely that he killed some, and others ran west over the ridge, and were killed on that side of it. King Hakon did not part with them till the last man of them was killed.

26. KING GAMLE AND ULSERK FALL.

Gamle Eirikson fled from the ridge down upon the plain to the south of the hill. There he turned himself again, and waited until more people gathered to him. All his brothers, and many troops of their men, assembled there. Egil Ulserk was in front, and in advance of Hakon's men, and made a stout attack. He and King Gamle exchanged blows with each other, and King Gamle got a grievous wound; but Egil fell, and many people with him. Then came Hakon the king with the troops which had followed him, and a new battle began. King Hakon pushed on, cutting down men on both sides of him, and killing the one upon the top of the other. So sings Guthorm Sindre:–

"Scared by the sharp sword's singing sound,
Brandished in air, the foe gave ground.
The boldest warrior cannot stand
Before King Hakon's conquering hand;
And the king's banner ever dies
Where the spear-forests thickest rise.
Altho' the king had gained of old
Enough of Freyja's tears of gold[11]*,*

11 Freyja's husband was Od; and her tears, when she wept at the long absence of her husband, were tears of gold. Od's wife's tears is the skald's expression here for gold– understood, no doubt, as readily as any allusion to Plutus would convey the equivalent meaning in modern poetry.–L.

He spared himself no more than tho'
He'd had no well-filled purse to show."

When Eirik's sons saw their men falling all round, they turned and fled to their ships; but those who had sought the ships before had pushed off some of them from the land, while some of them were still hauled up and on the strand. Now the sons of Eirik and their men plunged into the sea, and betook themselves to swimming. Gamle Eirikson was drowned; but the other sons of Eirik reached their ships, and set sail with what men remained. They steered southwards to Denmark, where they stopped a while, very ill satisfied with their expedition.

27. EGIL ULSERK'S BURIAL-GROUND.

King Hakon took all the ships of the sons of Eirik that had been left upon the strand, and had them drawn quite up, and brought on the land. Then he ordered that Egil Ulserk, and all the men of his army who had fallen, should be laid in the ships, and covered entirely over with earth and stones. King Hakon made many of the ships to be drawn up to the field of battle, and the hillocks over them are to be seen to the present day a little to the south of Fredarberg. At the time when King Hakon was killed, when Glum Geirason, in his song, boasted of King Hakon's fall, Eyvind Skaldaspiller composed these verses on this battle:–

"Our dauntless king with Gamle's gore
Sprinkled his bright sword o'er and o'er:
Sprinkled the gag that holds the mouth
Of the fell demon Fenriswolf[12].
Proud swelled our warriors' hearts when he
Drove Eirik's sons out to the sea,
With all their Guatland host: but now
Our warriors weep–Hakon lies low!"

High standing stones mark Egil Uslerk s grave.

12 The Fenriswolf, one of the children of Loke, begotten with a giantess, was chained to a rock, and gagged by a sword placed in his mouth, to prevent him devouring mankind. Fenriswolf's gag is a skaldic expression for a sword.–L.

28. NEWS OF WAR COMES TO KING HAKON.

When King Hakon, Athelstan's foster-son, had been king for twenty-six years after his brother Eirik had left the country, it happened (A.D. 960) that he was at a feast in Hordaland in the house at Fitjar on the island Stord, and he had with him at the feast his court and many of the peasants. And just as the king was seated at the supper-table, his watchmen who were outside observed many ships coming sailing along from the south, and not very far from the island. Now, said the one to the other, they should inform the king that they thought an armed force was coming against them; but none thought it advisable to be the bearer of an alarm of war to the king, as he had set heavy penalties on those who raised such alarms falsely, yet they thought it unsuitable that the king should remain in ignorance of what they saw. Then one of them went into the room and asked Eyvind Finson to come out as fast as possible, for it was very needful. Eyvind immediately came out and went to where he could see the ships, and saw directly that a great army was on the way; and he returned in all haste into the room, and, placing himself before the kind, said, "Short is the hour for acting, and long the hour for feasting." The king cast his eyes upon him, and said, "What now is in the way?" Eyvind said–

"Up king! the avengers are at hand!
Eirik's bold sons approach the land!
The Judgment of the sword they crave
Against their foe. Thy wrath I brave;
Tho' well I know 'tis no light thing
To bring war-tidings to the king
And tell him 'tis no time to rest.
Up! gird your armour to your breast:
Thy honour's dearer than my life;
Therefore I say, up to the strife!"

Then said the king, "Thou art too brave a fellow, Eyvind, to bring us any false alarm of war." The others all said it was a true report. The king ordered the tables to be removed, and then he went out to look at the ships; and when it could be clearly seen that these were ships of war, the king asked his men what resolution they should take–whether to give battle with the men they had, or go on board ship and sail away northwards along the land. "For it is easy to see," said he, "that we must now fight against a much greater force than we ever had against us before; although we thought just the same the last time we fought against

Gunhild's sons." No one was in a hurry to give an answer to the king; but at last Eyvind replied to the king's speech:–

"Thou who in the battle-plain
Hast often poured the sharp spear-rain!
Ill it beseems our warriors brave
To fly upon the ocean wave:
To fly upon the blue wave north,
When Harald from the south comes forth,
With many a ship riding in pride
Upon the foaming ocean-tide;
With many a ship and southern viking,–
Let us take shield in hand, brave king!"

The king replied, "Thy counsel, Eyvind, is manly, and after my own heart; but I will hear the opinion of others upon this matter." Now as the king's men thought they discerned what way the king was inclined to take, they answered that they would rather fall bravely and like men, than fly before the Danes; adding, that they had often gained the victory against greater odds of numbers. The king thanked them for their resolution, and bade them arm themselves; and all the men did so. The king put on his armour, and girded on his sword Kvernbit, and put a gilt helmet upon his head, and took a spear (Kesja) in his hand, and a shield by his side. He then drew up his courtmen and the bondes in one body, and set up his banner.

29. THE ARMAMENT OF EIRIK'S SONS.

AFTER GAMLE'S DEATH King Harald, Eirik's son, was the chief of the brothers, and he had a great army with him from Denmark. In their army were also their mother's brothers,–Eyvind Skreyja, and Alf Askman, both strong and able men, and great man slayers. The sons of Eirik brought up with their ships off the island, and it is said that their force was not less than six to one,–so much stronger in men were Eirik's sons.

30. KING HAKON'S BATTLE ARRAY.

When King Hakon had drawn up his men, it is told of him that he threw off his armour before the battle began. So sings Eyvind Skaldaspiller, in Hakmarmal:–

"They found Blorn's brother bold
Under his banner as of old,
Ready for battle. Foes advance,-
The front rank raise the shining lance:
And now begins the bloody fray!
Now! now begins Hild's wild play!
Our noble king, whose name strikes fear
Into each Danish heart,-whose spear
Has single-handed spilt the blood
Of many a Danish noble,-stood
Beneath his helmet's eagle wing
Amidst his guards; but the brave king
Scorned to wear armour, while his men
Bared naked breasts against the rain
Of spear and arrow, his breast-plate rung
Against the stones; and, blithe and gay,
He rushed into the thickest fray.
With golden helm, and naked breast,
Brave Hakon played at slaughter's feast."

King Hakon selected willingly such men for his guard or court-men as were distinguished for their strength and bravery, as his father King Harald also used to do; and among these was Thoralf Skolmson the Strong, who went on one side of the king. He had helmet and shield, spear and sword; and his sword was called by the name of Footbreadth. It was said that Thoralf and King Hakon were equal in strength. Thord Sjarekson speaks of it in the poem he composed concerning Thoralf:-

"The king's men went with merry words
To the sharp clash of shields and flame swords,
When these wild rovers of the sea
At Fitlar fought. Stout Thoralf he
Next to the Northmen's hero came,
Scattering wide round the battle flame
For in the storm of shields not one
Ventured like him with brave Hakon."

When both lines met there was a hard combat, and much bloodshed. The combatants threw their spears and then drew their swords. Then King Hakon, and Thoralf with him, went in advance of the banner, cutting down on both sides of them. So says Eyvind Skaldaspiller:-

"The body-coats of naked steel,
The woven iron coats of mail,
Like water fly before the swing
Of Hakon's sword–the champion-king.
About each Gotland war-man's head
Helm splits, like ice beneath the tread,
Cloven by the axe or sharp swordblade,
The brave king, foremost in the fight,
Dyes crimson-red the spotless white
Of his bright shield with foemen's gore.–
Amidst the battle's wild uproar,
Wild pealing round from shore to shore."

31. FALL OF SKREYJA AND ASKMAN.

King Hakon was very conspicuous among other men, and also when the sun shone his helmet glanced, and thereby many weapons were directed at him. Then Eyvind Finson took a hat and put it over the king's helmet. Now Eyvind Skreyja called out, "Does the king of the Norsemen hide himself, or has he fled? Where is now the golden helmet?" Then Eyvind, and his brother Alf with him, pushed on like fools or madmen. King Hakon shouted to Eyvind, "Come on as thou art coming, and thou shalt find the king of the Norsemen." So says Eyvind Skaldaspiller:–

"The raiser of the storm of shields,
The conqueror in battle fields,–
Hakon the brave, the warrior's friend,
Who scatters gold with liberal hand,
Heard Skreyja's taunt, and saw him rush,
Amidst the sharp spears' thickest push,
And loudly shouted in reply–
'If thou wilt for the victory try,
The Norseman's king thou soon shall find!
Hold onwards, friend! Hast thou a mind!"

It was also but a short space of time before Eyvind did come up swinging his sword, and made a cut at the king; but Thoralf thrust his shield so hard against Eyvind that he tottered with the shock. Now the king takes his sword Kvernbit with both hands, and hewed Eyvind through helm and head, and clove him down to the shoulders. Thoralf also slew Alf Askman. So says Eyvind Skaldaspiller:–

"With both his hands the gallant king
Swung round his sword, and to the chin
Clove Eyvind down: his faithless mail
Against it could no more avail,
Than the thin plank against the shock
When the ship's side beats on the rock.
By his bright sword with golden haft
Thro' helm, and head, and hair, was cleft
The Danish champion; and amain,
With terror smitten, fled his men."

After this fall of the two brothers, King Hakon pressed on so hard that all men gave way before his assault. Now fear came over the army of Eirik's sons, and the men began to fly; and King Hakon, who was at the head of his men, pressed on the flying, and hewed down oft and hard. Then flew an arrow, one of the kind called "flein", into Hakon's arm, into the muscles below the shoulder; and it is said by many people that Gunhild's shoe-boy, whose name was Kisping, ran out and forwards amidst the confusion of arms, called out "Make room for the king-killer," and shot King Hakon with the flein. Others again say that nobody could tell who shot the king, which is indeed the most likely; for spears, arrows, and all kinds of missiles flew as thick as a snow-drift. Many of the people of Eirik's sons were killed, both on the field of battle and on the way to the ships, and also on the strand, and many threw themselves into the water. Many also, among whom were Eirik's sons, got on board their ships, and rowed away as fast as they could, and Hakon's men after them. So says Thord Sjarekson:–

"The wolf, the murderer, and the thief,
Fled from before the people's chief:
Few breakers of the peace grew old
Under the Northmen's king so bold.
When gallant Hakon lost his life
Black was the day, and dire the strife.
It was bad work for Gunhild's sons,
Leading their pack of Hungry Danes
From out the south, to have to fly,
And many a bonde leave to die,

Leaning his heavy wounded head
On the oar-bench for feather-bed.
Thoralf was nearest to the side
Of gallant Hakon in the tide
Of battle; his the sword that best
Carved out the raven's bloody feast:
Amidst the heaps of foemen slain
He was named bravest on the plain."

32. HAKON'S DEATH.

WHEN KING HAKON CAME out to his ship he had his wound bound up; but the blood ran from it so much and so constantly, that it could not be stopped; and when the day was drawing to an end his strength began to leave him. Then he told his men that he wanted to go northwards to his house at Alreksstader; but when he came north, as far as Hakonarhella Hill, they put in towards the land, for by this time the king was almost lifeless. Then he called his friends around him, and told them what he wished to be done with regard to his kingdom. He had only one child, a daughter, called Thora, and had no son. Now he told them to send a message to Eirik's sons, that they should be kings over the country; but asked them to hold his friends in respect and honour. "And if fate," added he, "should prolong my life, I will, at any rate, leave the country, and go to a Christian land, and do penance for what I have done against God; but should I die in heathen land, give me any burial you think fit." Shortly afterwards Hakon expired, at the little hill on the shore-side at which he was born. So great was the sorrow over Hakon's death, that he was lamented both by friends and enemies; and they said that never again would Norway see such a king. His friends removed his body to Saeheim, in North Hordaland, and made a great mound, in which they laid the king in full armour and in his best clothes, but with no other goods. They spoke over his grave, as heathen people are used to do, and wished him in Valhal. Eyvind Skaldaspiller composed a poem on the death of King Hakon, and on how well he was received in Valhal. The poem is called "Hakonarmal":–

"In Odin's hall an empty place
Stands for a king of Yngve's race;
'Go, my valkyries,' Odin said,
'Go forth, my angels of the dead,

Gondul and Skogul, to the plain
Drenched with the battle's bloody rain,
And to the dying Hakon tell,
Here in Valhal shall he dwell.'

"At Stord, so late a lonely shore,
Was heard the battle's wild uproar;
The lightning of the flashing sword
Burned fiercely at the shore of Stord.
From levelled halberd and spearhead
Life-blood was dropping fast and red;
And the keen arrows' biting sleet
Upon the shore at Stord fast beat.

"Upon the thundering cloud of shield
Flashed bright the sword-storm o'er the field;
And on the plate-mail rattled loud
The arrow-shower's rushing cloud,
In Odin's tempest-weather, there
Swift whistling through the angry air;
And the spear-torrents swept away
Ranks of brave men from light of day.

"With batter'd shield, and blood-smear'd sword
Slits one beside the shore of Stord,
With armour crushed and gashed sits he,
A grim and ghastly sight to see;
And round about in sorrow stand
The warriors of his gallant band:
Because the king of Dags' old race
In Odin's hall must fill a place.

"Then up spake Gondul, standing near
Resting upon her long ash spear,–
'Hakon! the gods' cause prospers well,
And thou in Odin's halls shalt dwell!'
The king beside the shore of Stord
The speech of the valkyrie heard,
Who sat there on his coal-black steed,
With shield on arm and helm on head.

"Thoughtful, said Hakon, 'Tell me why
Ruler of battles, victory
Is so dealt out on Stord's red plain?
Have we not well deserved to gain?'
'And is it not as well dealt out?'
Said Gondul. 'Hearest thou not the shout?
The field is cleared–the foemen run–
The day is ours–the battle won!'

"Then Skogul said, 'My coal-black steed,
Home to the gods I now must speed,
To their green home, to tell the tiding
That Hakon's self is thither riding.'
To Hermod and to Brage then
Said Odin, 'Here, the first of men,
Brave Hakon comes, the Norsemen's king,–
Go forth, my welcome to him bring.'

"Fresh from the battle-field came in,
Dripping with blood, the Norsemen'a king.
'Methinks,' said he, great Odin's will
Is harsh, and bodes me further ill;
Thy son from off the field to-day
From victory to snatch away!'
But Odin said, 'Be thine the joy
Valhal gives, my own brave boy!'

"And Brage said, 'Eight brothers here
Welcome thee to Valhal's cheer,
To drain the cup, or fights repeat
Where Hakon Eirik's earls beat.'
Quoth the stout king, 'And shall my gear,
Helm, sword, and mail-coat, axe and spear,
Be still at hand! 'Tis good to hold
Fast by our trusty friends of old.'

"Well was it seen that Hakon still
Had saved the temples from all ill[13]*;*

13 Hakon, although a Christian, appears to have favoured the old religion, and spared the temples of Odin, and therefore a place in Valhal is assigned him.–L.

For the whole council of the gods
Welcomed the king to their abodes.
Happy the day when men are born
Like Hakon, who all base things scorn.–
Win from the brave and honoured name,
And die amidst an endless fame.

"Sooner shall Fenriswolf devour
The race of man from shore to shore,
Than such a grace to kingly crown
As gallant Hakon want renown.
Life, land, friends, riches, all will fly,
And we in slavery shall sigh.
But Hakon in the blessed abodes
For ever lives with the bright gods."

BOOK FOUR

Saga of King Harald Grafeld and of Earl Hakon Son of Sigurd

PRELIMINARY REMARKS

This saga might be called Gunhild's Saga, as she is the chief person in it. The reign of King Harald and Earl Hakon is more fully described in the next saga, that is, Olaf Trygvason's. Other literature on this epoch:

"Agrip" (chap. 8), "Historia Norvegia", (p. 12), "Thjodrek" (chap. 5), "Saxo" (pp. 479-482), "Egla" (chaps. 81, 82), "Floamanna" (chap. 12), "Fareyinga" (chaps. 2, 4, 10), "Halfred's Saga" (chap. 2), "Hord Grimkelsons Saga" (chaps. 13, 18), "Kormak" (chaps. 19-27), "Laxdaela" (chaps. 19-21), "Njala" (chaps, 3-6).

The skalds of this saga are:–Glum Geirason, Kormak Agmundson, Eyvind Skaldaspiller, and Einar Helgason Skalaglam.

1. GOVERNMENT OF THE SONS OF EIRIK.

When King Hakon was killed, the sons of Eirik took the sovereignty of Norway. Harald, who was the oldest of the living brothers, was over them in dignity. Their mother Gunhild, who was called the King-mother, mixed herself much in the affairs of the country. There were many chiefs in the land at that time. There was Trygve Olafson in the Eastland, Gudrod Bjornson in Vestfold, Sigurd earl of Hlader in the Throndhjem land; but Gunhild's sons held the middle of the country the first winter. There went messages and ambassadors between Gunhild's sons and Trygve and Gudrod, and all was settled upon the footing that they should hold from Gunhild's sons the same part of the country which they formerly had held under King Hakon. A man called Glum Geirason, who was King Harald's skald, and was a very brave man, made this song upon King Hakon's death:–

"Gamle is avenged by Harald!
Great is thy deed, thou champion bold!
The rumour of it came to me
In distant lands beyond the sea,
How Harald gave King Hakon's blood
To Odin's ravens for their food."

This song was much favoured. When Eyvind Finson heard of it he composed the song which was given before, viz.:–

"Our dauntless king with Gamle's gore
Sprinkled his bright sword o'er and o'er," &c.

This song also was much favoured, and was spread widely abroad; and when King Harald came to hear of it, he laid a charge against Evyind affecting his life; but friends made up the quarrel, on the condition that Eyvind should in future be Harald's skald, as he had formerly been King Hakon's. There was also some relationship between them, as Gunhild, Eyvind's mother, was a daughter of Earl Halfdan, and her mother was Ingibjorg, a daughter of Harald Harfager. Thereafter Eyvind made a song about King Harald:–

"Guardian of Norway, well we know
Thy heart failed not when from the bow
The piercing arrow-hail sharp rang
On shield and breast-plate, and the clang
Of sword resounded in the press
Of battle, like the splitting ice;
For Harald, wild wolf of the wood,
Must drink his fill of foeman's blood."

Gunhild's sons resided mostly in the middle of the country, for they did not think it safe for them to dwell among the people of Throndhjem or of Viken, where King Hakon's best friends lived; and also in both places there were many powerful men. Proposals of agreement then passed between Gunhild's sons and Earl Sigurd, .or they got no scat from the Throndhjem country; and at last an agreement was concluded between the kings and the earl, and confirmed by oath. Earl Sigurd was to get the same power in the Throndhjem land which he had possessed under King Hakon, and on that they considered themselves at peace. All Gunhild's sons had the character of being penurious; and it was said they hid their money in the ground. Eyvind Skaldaspiller made a song about this:–

"Main-mast of battle! Harald bold!
In Hakon's days the skald wore gold
Upon his falcon's seat; he wore
Rolf Krake's seed, the yellow ore
Sown by him as he fled away,
The avenger Adils' speed to stay.
The gold crop grows upon the plain;
But Frode's girls so gay[14] *in vain*
Grind out the golden meal, while those
Who rule o'er Norway's realm like foes,
In mother earth's old bosom hide
The wealth which Hakon far and wide
Scattered with generous hand: the sun
Shone in the days of that great one,
On the gold band of Fulla's brow,[15]
On gold-ringed hands that bend the bow,
On the skald's hand; but of the ray
Of bright gold, glancing like the spray
Of sun-lit waves, no skald now sings–
Buried are golden chains and rings."

Now when King Harald heard this song, he sent a message to Eyvind to come to him, and when Eyvind came made a charge against him of being unfaithful. "And it ill becomes thee," said the king, "to be my enemy, as thou hast entered into my service." Eyvind then made these verses:–

---

14 Menja and Fenja were strong girls of the giant race, whom Frode bought in Sweden to grind gold and good luck to him; and their meal means gold.–L.

15 Fulla was one of Frig's attendants, who wore a gold band on the forehead, and the figure means gold,–that the sun shone on gold rings on the hands of the skalds in Hakon's days.–L.

"One lord I had before thee, Harald!
One dear-loved lord! Now am I old,
And do not wish to change again,–
To that loved lord, through strife and pain,
Faithful I stood; still true to Hakon,–
To my good king, and him alone.
But now I'm old and useless grown,
My hands are empty, wealth is flown;
I am but fir for a short space
In thy court-hall to fill a place."

But King Harald forced Eyvind to submit himself to his clemency. Eyvind had a great gold ring, which was called Molde, that had been dug up out of the earth long since. This ring the King said he must have as the mulet for the offence; and there was no help for it. Then Eyvind sang:–

"I go across the ocean-foam,
Swift skating to my Iceland home
Upon the ocean-skates, fast driven
By gales by Thurse's witch fire given.
For from the falcon-bearing hand
Harald has plucked the gold snake band
My father wore–by lawless might
Has taken what is mine by right."

Eyvind went home; but it is not told that he ever came near the king again.

2. CHRISTIANITY OF GUNHILD'S SONS.

Gunhild's sons embraced Christianity in England, as told before; but when they came to rule over Norway they made no progress in spreading Christianity–only they pulled down the temples of the idols, and cast away the sacrifices where they had it in their power, and raised great animosity by doing so. The good crops of the country were soon wasted in their days, because there were many kings, and each had his court about him. They had therefore great expenses, and were very greedy. Besides, they only observed those laws of King Hakon which suited themselves. They were, however, all of them remarkably handsome men–stout, strong, and expert in all exercises. So says Glum Geirason, in the verses he composed about Harald, Gunhild's son:–

"The foeman's terror, Harald bold,
Had gained enough of yellow gold;
Had Heimdal's teeth[16] *enough in store,*
And understood twelve arts or more."

The brothers sometimes went out on expeditions together, and sometimes each on his own account. They were fierce, but brave and active; and great warriors, and very successful.

3. COUNCILS BY GUNHILD AND HER SONS.

GUNHILD THE KING-MOTHER, and her sons, often met, and talked together upon the government of the country. Once Gunhild asked her sons what they intended to do with their kingdom of Throndhjem. "Ye have the title of king, as your forefathers had before you; but ye have little land or people, and there are many to divide with. In the East, at Viken, there are Trygve and Gudrod; and they have some right, from relationship, to their governments. There is besides Earl Sigurd ruling over the whole Throndhjem country; and no reason can I see why ye let so large a kingdom be ruled by an earl, and not by yourselves. It appears wonderful to me that ye go every summer upon viking cruises against other lands, and allow an earl within the country to take your father's heritage from you. Your grandfather, whose name you bear, King Harald, thought it but a small matter to take an earl's life and land when he subdued all Norway, and held it under him to old age."

Harald replied, "It is not so easy, mother, to cut off Earl Sigurd as to slay a kid or a calf. Earl Sigurd is of high birth, powerful in relations, popular, and prudent; and I think if the Throndhjem people knew for certain there was enmity between us, they would all take his side, and we could expect only evil from them. I don't think it would be safe for any of us brothers to fall into the hands of the Throndhjem people."

Then said Gunhild, "We shall go to work another way, and not put ourselves forward. Harald and Erling shall come in harvest to North

16 Heimdal was one of the gods, whose horse was called Gold-top; and the horse's teeth were of gold.

More, and there I shall meet you, and we shall consult together what is to be done." This was done.

4. GUNHILD'S SONS AND GRJOTGARD.

Earl Sigurd had a brother called Grjotgard, who was much younger, and much less respected; in fact, was held in no title of honour. He had many people, however, about him, and in summer went on viking cruises, and gathered to himself property. Now King Harald sent messengers to Throndhjem with offers of friendship, and with presents. The messengers declared that King Harald was willing to be on the same friendly terms with the earl that King Hakon had been; adding, that they wished the earl to come to King Harald, that their friendship might be put on a firm footing. The Earl Sigurd received well the king's messengers and friendly message, but said that on account of his many affairs he could not come to the king. He sent many friendly gifts, and many glad and grateful words to the king, in return for his friendship. With this reply the messengers set off, and went to Grjotgard, for whom they had the same message, and brought him good presents, and offered him King Harald's friendship, and invited him to visit the king. Grjotgard promised to come and at the appointed time he paid a visit to King Harald and Gunhild, and was received in the most friendly manner. They treated him on the most intimate footing, so that Grjotgard had access to their private consultations and secret councils. At last the conversation, by an understanding between the king and queen, was turned upon Earl Sigurd; and they spoke to Grjotgard about the earl having kept him so long in obscurity, and asked him if he would not join the king's brothers in an attack on the earl. If he would join with them, the king promised Grjotgard that he should be his earl, and have the same government that Sigurd had. It came so far that a secret agreement was made between them, that Grjotgard should spy out the most favourable opportunity of attacking by surprise Earl Sigurd, and should give King Harald notice of it. After this agreement Grjotgard returned home with many good presents from the king.

5. SIGURD BURNT IN A HOUSE IN STJORADAL

Earl Sigurd went in harvest into Stjoradal to guest-quarters, and from thence went to Oglo to a feast. The earl usually had many people about him, for he did not trust the king; but now, after friendly messages had passed between the king and him, he had no great following of people with him. Then Grjotgard sent word to the king that he could never expect a better opportunity to fall upon Earl Sigurd; and immediately, that very evening, Harald and Erling sailed into Throndhjem fjord with several ships and many people. They sailed all night by starlight, and Grjotgard came out to meet them. Late in the night they came to Oglo, where Earl Sigurd was at the feast, and set fire to the house; and burnt the house, the earl, and all his men. As soon as it was daylight, they set out through the fjord, and south to More, where they remained a long time.

6. HISTORY OF HAKON, SIGURD'S SON.

HAKON, THE SON OF Earl Sigurd, was up in the interior of the Throndhjem country when he heard this news. Great was the tumult through all the Throndhjem land, and every vessel that could swim was put into the water; and as soon as the people were gathered together they took Earl Sigurd's son Hakon to be their earl and the leader of the troops, and the whole body steered out of Throndhjem fjord. When Gunhild's sons heard of this, they set off southwards to Raumsdal and South More; and both parties kept eye on each other by their spies. Earl Sigurd was killed two years after the fall of King Hakon (A.D. 962). So says Eyvind Skaldaspiller in the "Haleygjatal":–

"At Oglo, as I've heard, Earl Sigurd
Was burnt to death by Norway's lord,–
Sigurd, who once on Hadding's grave
A feast to Odin's ravens gave.
In Oglo's hall, amidst the feast,
When bowls went round and ale flowed fast,
He perished: Harald lit the fire
Which burnt to death the son of Tyr."

Earl Hakan, with the help of his friends, maintained himself in the Throndhjem country for three years; and during that time (A.D. 963-965) Gunhild's sons got no revenues from it. Hakon had many a battle with Gunhild's sons, and many a man lost his life on both sides. Of this Einar Skalaglam speaks in his lay, called "Vellekla," which he composed about Earl Hakon:–

"The sharp bow-shooter on the sea
Spread wide his fleet, for well loved he
The battle storm: well loved the earl
His battle-banner to unfurl,
O'er the well-trampled battle-field
He raised the red-moon of his shield;
And often dared King Eirik's son
To try the fray with the Earl Hakon."

And he also says:–

"Who is the man who'll dare to say
That Sigurd's son avoids the fray?
He gluts the raven–he ne'er fears
The arrow's song or flight of spears,
With thundering sword he storms in war,
As Odin dreadful; or from far
He makes the arrow-shower fly
To swell the sail of victory.
The victory was dearly bought,
And many a viking-fight was fought
Before the swinger of the sword
Was of the eastern country lord."

And Einar tells also how Earl Hakon avenged his father's murderer:–

"I praise the man, my hero he,
Who in his good ship roves the sea,
Like bird of prey, intent to win
Red vengeance for his slaughtered kin.
From his blue sword the iron rain
That freezes life poured down amain
On him who took his father's life,
On him and his men in the strife.
To Odin many a soul was driven,–
To Odin many a rich gift given.
Loud raged the storm on battle-field–
Axe rang on helm, and sword on shield."

The friends on both sides at last laid themselves between, and brought proposals of peace; for the bondes suffered by this strife and war in the land. At last it was brought to this, by the advice of prudent men, that Earl Hakon should have the same power in the Throndhjem land which his father Earl Sigurd had enjoyed; and the kings, on the other hand, should have the same dominion as King Hakon had: and this agreement was settled with the fullest promises of fidelity to it. Afterwards a great friendship arose between Earl Hakon and Gunhild, although they sometimes attempted to deceive each other. And thus matters stood for three years longer (A.D. 966-968), in which time Earl Hakon sat quietly in his dominions.

7. OF HARALD GRAFELD.

King Hakon had generally his seat in Hordaland and Rogaland, and also his brothers; but very often, also, they went to Hardanger. One summer it happened that a vessel came from Iceland belonging to Icelanders, and loaded with skins and peltry. They sailed to Hardanger, where they heard the greatest number of people assembled; but when the folks came to deal with them, nobody would buy their skins. Then the steersman went to King Harald, whom he had been acquainted with before, and complained of his ill luck. The king promised to visit him, and did so. King Harald was very condescending, and full of fun. He came with a fully manned boat, looked at the skins, and then said to the steersman, "Wilt thou give me a present of one of these gray-skins?" "Willingly," said the steersman, "if it were ever so many." On this the king wrapped himself up in a gray-skin, and went back to his boat; but before they rowed away from the ship, every man in his suite bought such another skin as the king wore for himself. In a few days so many people came to buy skins, that not half of them could be served with what they wanted; and thereafter the king was called Harald Grafeld (Grayskin).

8. EARL EIRIK'S BIRTH.

Earl Hakon came one winter to the Uplands to a feast, and it so happened that he had intercourse with a girl of mean birth. Some time after the girl had to prepare for her confinement, and she bore a child, a boy, who had water poured on him, and was named Eirik. The mother carried the boy to Earl Hakon, and said that he was the father. The earl placed him to be brought up with a man called Thorleif the Wise, who dwelt in Medaldal, and was a rich and powerful man, and a great friend of the earl. Eirik gave hopes very early that he would become an able man, was handsome in countenance, and stout and strong for a child; but the earl did not pay much attention to him. The earl himself was one of the handsomest men in countenance,–not tall, but very strong, and well practised in all kinds of exercises; and withal prudent, of good understanding, and a deadly man at arms.

9. KING TRYGVE OLAFSON'S MURDER.

It happened one harvest (A.D. 962) that Earl Hakon, on a journey in the Uplands, came to Hedemark; and King Trygve Olafson and King Gudrod Bjornson met him there, and Dale-Gudbrand also came to the meeting. They had agreed to meet, and they talked together long by themselves; but so much only was known of their business, that they were to be friends of each other. They parted, and each went home to his own kingdom. Gunhild and her sons came to hear of this meeting, and they suspected it must have been to lay a treasonable plot against the kings; and they often talked of this among themselves. When spring (A.D. 963) began to set in, King Harald and his brother King Gudrod proclaimed that they were to make a viking cruise, as usual, either in the West sea, or the Baltic. The people accordingly assembled, launched the ships into the sea, and made themselves ready to sail. When they were drinking the farewell ale,–and they drank bravely,–much and many things were talked over at the drink-table, and, among other things, were comparisons between different men, and at last between the kings themselves. One said that King Harald excelled his brothers by far, and in every way. On this King Gudrod was very angry, and said that he was in no respect behind Harald, and was ready to prove it. Instantly both parties were so inflamed that they challenged each other to battle, and ran to their arms. But some of the guests who were less drunk, and had more understanding, came between them, and quieted them; and each went to his ship, but nobody expected that they would all sail together. Gudrod sailed east ward along the land, and Harald went out to sea, saying he would go to the westward; but when he came outside of the islands he steered east along the coast, outside of the rocks and isles. Gudrod, again, sailed inside, through the usual channel, to Viken, and eastwards to Folden. He then sent a message to King Trygve to meet him, that they might make a cruise together in summer in the Baltic to plunder. Trygve accepted willingly, and as a friend, the invitation;

and as heard King Gudrod had but few people with him, he came to meet him with a single boat. They met at Veggen, to the east of Sotanes; but just as they were come to the meeting place, Gudrod's men ran up and killed King Trygve and twelve men. He lies buried at a place called Trygve's Cairn (A.D. 963).

10. KING GUDROD'S FALL.

King Harald sailed far outside of the rocks and isles; but set his course to Viken, and came in the night-time to Tunsberg, and heard that Gudrod Bjornson was at a feast a little way up the country. Then King Harald set out immediately with his followers, came in the night, and surrounded the house. King Gudrod Bjornson went out with his people; but after a short resistance he fell, and many men with him. Then King Harald joined his brother King Gudrod, and they subdued all Viken.

11. OF HARALD GRENSKE.

King Gudrod Bjornson had made a good and suitable marriage, and had by his wife a son called Harald, who had been sent to be fostered to Grenland to a lenderman called Hroe the White. Hroe's son, called Hrane Vidforle (the Far-travelled), was Harald's foster-brother, and about the same age. After his father Gudrod's fall, Harald, who was called Grenske, fled to the Uplands, and with him his foster-brother Hrane, and a few people. Harald staid a while there among his relations; but as Eirik's sons sought after every man who interfered with them, and especially those who might oppose them, Harald Grenske's friends and relations advised him to leave the country. Harald therefore went eastward into Svithjod, and sought shipmates, that he might enter into company with those who went out a cruising to gather property. Harald became in this way a remarkably able man. There was a man in Svithjod at that time called Toste, one of the most powerful and clever in the land among those who had no high name or dignity; and he was a great warrior, who had been often in battle, and was therefore called Skoglar-Toste. Harald Grenske came into his company, and cruised with Toste in summer; and wherever Harald came he was well thought of by every one. In the winter Harald, after passing two years in the Uplands, took up his abode with Toste, and lived five years with him. Toste had a daughter, who was both young and handsome, but she was proud and high-minded. She was called Sigrid, and was afterwards married to the Swedish king, Eirik the Victorious, and had a son by him, called Olaf the Swede, who was afterwards king of Svithjod. King Eirik died in a sick-bed at Upsala ten years after the death of Styrbjorn.

12. EARL HAKON'S FEUDS.

Gunhild's sons levied a great army in Viken (A.D. 963), and sailed along the land northwards, collecting people and ships on the way out of every district. They then made known their intent, to proceed northwards with their army against Earl Hakon in Throndhjem. When Earl Hakon heard this news, he also collected men, and fitted out ships; and when he heard what an overwhelming force Gunhild's sons had with them, he steered south with his fleet to More, pillaging wherever he came, and killing many people. He then sent the whole of the bonde army back to Throndhjem; but he himself, with his men-at-arms, proceeded by both the districts of More and Raumsdal, and had his spies out to the south of Stad to spy the army of Gunhild's sons; and when he heard they were come into the Fjords, and were waiting for a fair wind to sail northwards round Stad, Earl Hakon set out to sea from the north side of Stad, so far that his sails could not be seen from the land, and then sailed eastward on a line with the coast, and came to Denmark, from whence he sailed into the Baltic, and pillaged there during the summer. Gunhild's sons conducted their army north to Throndhjem, and remained there the whole summer collecting the scat and duties. But when summer was advanced they left Sigurd Slefa and Gudron behind; and the other brothers returned eastward with the levied army they had taken up in summer.

13. OF EARL HAKON AND GUNHILD'S SONS.

Earl Hakon, towards harvest (A.D. 963), sailed into the Bothnian Gulf to Helsingjaland, drew his ships up there on the beach, and took the land-ways through Helsingjaland and Jamtaland, and so eastwards round the dividing ridge (the Kjol, or keel of the country), and down into the Throndhjem district. Many people streamed towards him, and he fitted out ships. When the sons of Gunhild heard of this they got on board their ships, and sailed out of the Fjord; and Earl Hakon came to his seat at Hlader, and remained there all winter. The sons of Gunhild, on the other hand, occupied More; and they and the earl attacked each other in turns, killing each other's people. Earl Hakon kept his dominions of Throndhjem, and was there generally in the winter; but in summer he sometimes went to Helsingjaland, where he went on board of his ships and sailed with them down into the Baltic, and plundered there; and sometimes he remained in Throndhjem, and kept an army on foot, so that Gunhild's sons could get no hold northwards of Stad.

14. SIGURD SLEFA'S MURDER.

One summer Harald Grayskin with his troops went north to Bjarmaland, where be forayed, and fought a great battle with the inhabitants on the banks of the Vina (Dwina). King Harald gained the victory, killed many people, plundered and wasted and burned far and wide in the land, and made enormous booty. Glum Geirason tells of it thus:–

"I saw the hero Harald chase
With bloody sword Bjarme's race:
They fly before him through the night,
All by their burning city's light.
On Dwina's bank, at Harald's word,
Arose the storm of spear and sword.
In such a wild war-cruise as this,
Great would he be who could bring peace."

King Sigurd Slefa came to the Herse Klyp's house. Klyp was a son of Thord, and a grandson of Hordakare, and was a man of power and great family. He was not at home; but his wife Alof give a good reception to the king, and made a great feast at which there was much drinking. Alof was a daughter of Asbjorn, and sister to Jarnskegge, north in Yrjar. Asbjorn's brother was called Hreidar, who was father to Styrkar, whose son was Eindride, father of Einar Tambaskielfer. In the night the king went to bed to Alof against her will, and then set out on his journey. The harvest thereafter, King Harald and his brother King Sigurd Slefa went to Vors, and summoned the bondes to a Thing. There the bondes fell on them, and would have killed them, but they escaped and took different roads. King Harald went to Hardanger, but King Sigurd to Alrekstader. Now when the Herse Klyp heard of this, he and his relations assembled to attack the king; and Vemund Volubrjot[17] was chief of their troop. Now when they came to the house they attacked the king, and Herse Klyp, it is said, ran him through with his sword and killed him; but instantly Klyp was killed on the spot by Erling Gamle (A.D. 965).

15. GRJOTGARD'S FALL.

King Harald Grafeld and his brother King Gudrod gathered together a great army in the east country, with which they set out northwards to Throndhjem (A.D. 968). When Earl Hakon heard of it he collected men, and set out to More, where he plundered. There his father's brother, Grjotgard, had the command and defence of the country on account of Gunhild's sons, and he assembled an army by order of the kings. Earl Hakon advanced to meet him, and gave him battle; and there fell Grjotgard and two other earls, and many a man besides. So says Einar Skalaglam:–

"The helm-crown'd Hakon, brave as stout,
Again has put his foes to rout.
The bowl runs o'er with Odin's mead,[18]
That fires the skald when mighty deed
Has to be sung. Earl Hakon's sword,
In single combat, as I've heard,
Three sons of earls from this one fray
To dwell with Odin drove away."[19]

Thereafter Earl Hakon went out to sea, and sailed outside the coast, and came to Denmark. He went to the Danish King, Harald Gormson, and was well received by him, and staid with him all winter (A.D. 969). At that time there was also with the Danish king a man called Harald, a son of Knut Gormson, and a brother's son of King Harald. He was lately come home from a long viking cruise, on which he had gathered great riches, and therefore he was called Gold Harald. He thought he had a good chance of coming to the Danish kingdom.

---

17 Volubrjotr.–Literally "the one who breaks the vala", that is, breaks the skulls of witches.

18 Odin's mead, called Bodn, was the blood or mead the sons of Brage, the god of poets, drank to inspire them.–L.

19 To dwell with Odin,–viz. slew them.–L.

16. KING ERLING'S FALL.

King Harald Grafeld and his brothers proceeded northwards to Throndhjem, where they met no opposition. They levied the scat-duties, and all other revenues, and laid heavy penalties upon the bondes; for the kings had for a long time received but little income from Throndhjem, because Earl Hakon was there with many troops, and was at variance with these kings. In autumn (A.D. 968) King Harald went south with the greater part of the men-at-arms, but King Erlin remained behind with his men. He raised great contributions from the bondes, and pressed severely on them; at which the bondes murmured greatly, and submitted to their losses with impatience. In winter they gathered together in a great force to go against King Erling, just as he was at a feast; and they gave battle to him, and he with the most of his men fell (A.D. 969).

17. THE SEASONS IN NORWAY AT THIS TIME.

While Gunhild's sons reigned in Norway the seasons were always bad, and the longer they reigned the worse were the crops; and the bondes laid the blame on them. They were very greedy, and used the bondes harshly. It came at length to be so bad that fish, as well as corn, were wanting. In Halogaland there was the greatest famine and distress; for scarcely any corn grew, and even snow was lying, and the cattle were bound in the byres[20] all over the country until midsummer. Eyvind Skaldaspiller describes it in his poem, as he came outside of his house and found a thick snowdrift at that season:–

"Tis midsummer, yet deep snows rest
On Odin's mother's frozen breast:
Like Laplanders, our cattle-kind
In stall or stable we must bind."

18. THE ICELANDERS AND EYVIND THE SKALD.

Eyvind composed a poem about the people of Iceland, for which they rewarded him by each bonde giving him three silver pennies, of full

20 Byres = gards or farms.

weight and white in the fracture. And when the silver was brought together at the Althing, the people resolved to have it purified, and made into a row of clasps; and after the workmanship of the silver was paid, the row of clasps was valued at fifty marks. This they sent to Eyvind; but Eyvind was obliged to separate the clasps from each other, and sell them to buy food for his household. But the same spring a shoal of herrings set in upon the fishing ground beyond the coast-side, and Eyvind manned a ship's boat with his house servants and cottars, and rowed to where the herrings were come, and sang:–

"Now let the steed of ocean bound
O'er the North Sea with dashing sound:
Let nimble tern and screaming gull
Fly round and round–our net is full.
Fain would I know if Fortune sends
A like provision to my friends.
Welcome provision 'tis, I wot,
That the whale drives to our cook's pot."

So entirely were his movable goods exhausted, that he was obliged to sell his arrows to buy herrings, or other meat for his table:–

"Our arms and ornaments of gold
To buy us food we gladly sold:
The arrows of the bow gave we
For the bright arrows of the sea."[21]

21 Herrings, from their swift darting along, are called the arrows of the sea.

BOOK FIVE

King Olaf Trygvason's Saga

PRELIMINARY REMARKS.

HITHERTO THE NARRATIVE HAS been more or less fragmentary. With Olaf Trygvason's Saga reliable history begins, and the narration is full and connected. The story of Hakon the earl is incorporated in this saga.

Accounts of Olaf Trygvason may be found in Od the Monk's legendary saga, in parts of "Agrip", "Historia Norvegiae", and in Thjodrek. Icelandic works on this epoch are:

"Egla", "Eyrbyggja", "Finboga", "Floamanna", "Faereyinga", "Hallfredar Saga", "Havardar Saga", "Are's Islendinga-bok", "Kristni Saga", "Laxdaela", "Ljosvetninga", "Njala", "Orkneyinga", "Viga Glums Saga", and "Viga Styrs Saga".

The skalds quoted are: Glum Geirason, Eyvind Finson, Skaldaspiller, Einar Skalaglam, Tind Halkelson, Eyjolf Dadaskald, Hallarstein, Halfred Vandraedaskald, Haldor Ukristne, Skule Thorsteinson, and Thord Kolbeinson.

1. OLAF TRYGVASON'S BIRTH.

KING TRYGVE OLAFSON HAD married a wife who was called Astrid. She was a daughter of Eirik Bjodaskalle, a great man, who dwelt at Oprustader. But after Trygve's death (A.D. 963) Astrid fled, and privately took with her all the loose property she could. Her foster-father, Thorolf Lusarskeg, followed her, and never left her; and others of her faithful followers spied about to discover her enemies, and where they were. Astrid was pregnant with a child of King Trygve, and she went to a lake, and concealed herself in a holm or small island in it with a few men. Here her child was born, and it was a boy; and water was poured over it, and it was called Olaf after the grandfather. Astrid remained all summer here in concealment; but when the nights became dark, and the day began to shorten and the weather to be cold, she was obliged to take to the land, along with Thorolf and a few other men. They did not seek for houses unless in the night-time, when they came to them secretly; and they spoke to nobody. One evening, towards dark, they came to Oprustader, where Astrid's father Eirik dwelt, and privately sent a man to Eirik to tell him; and Eirik took them to an out-house, and spread a table for them with the best of food. When Astrid had been here a short time her travelling attendants left her, and none remained, behind with her but two servant girls, her child Olaf, Thorolf Lusarskeg, and his son Thorgils, who was six years old; and they remained all winter (A.D. 964).

2. OF GUNHILD S SONS.

After Trygve Olafson's murder, Harald Grafeld and his brother Gudrod went to the farm which he owned; but Astrid was gone, and they could learn no tidings of her. A loose report came to their ears that she was pregnant to King Trygve; but they soon went away northwards, as before related. As soon as they met their mother Gunhild they told her all that had taken place. She inquired particularly about Astrid, and they told her the report they had heard; but as Gunhild's sons the same harvest and winter after had bickerings with Earl Hakon, as before related, they did not seek after Astrid and her son that winter.

3. ASTRID'S JOURNEY.

The spring after (A.D. 964) Gunhild sent spies to the Uplands, and all the way down to Viken, to spy what they could about Astrid; and her men came back, and could only tell her that Astrid must be with her father Eirik, and it was probable was bringing up her infant, the son of Trygve. Then Gunhild, without delay, sent off men well furnished with arms and horses, and in all a troop of thirty; and as their leader she sent a particular friend of her own, a powerful man called Hakon. Her orders were to go to Oprustader, to Eirik, and take King Trygve's son from thence, and bring the child to her; and with these orders the men went out. Now when they were come to the neighbourhood of Oprustader, some of Eirik's friends observed the troop of travellers, and about the close of the day brought him word of their approach. Eirik immediately, in the night, made preparation for Astrid's flight, gave her good guides, and send her away eastward to Svithjod, to his good friend Hakon Gamle, who was a powerful man there. Long before day they departed, and towards evening they reached a domain called Skaun. Here they saw a large mansion, towards which they went, and begged a night's lodging. For the sake of concealment they were clad in mean clothing. There dwelt here a bonde called Bjorn Eiterkveisa, who was very rich, but very inhospitable. He drove them away; and therefore, towards dark, they went to another domain close by that was called Vidar. Thorstein was the name of the bonde; and he gave them lodging, and took good care of them, so that they slept well, and were well entertained. Early that morning Gunhild's men had come to Oprustader, and inquired for Astrid and her son. As Eirik told them she was not there, they searched the whole house, and remained till late in the day before they got any news of Astrid. Then they rode after her the way she had taken, and late at night they came to Bjorn Eiterkveisa in Skaun, and took up their quarters there. Hakon asked Bjorn if he knew anything about Astrid, and he said some people had been there in the evening wanting lodgings; "but I drove them away, and I suppose they have gone to some of the neighbouring houses." Thorstein's labourer was coming from the forest, having left his work at nightfall, and called in at Bjorn's house because it was in his way; and finding there were guests come to the house, and learning their business, he comes to Thorstein and tells him of it. As about a third part of the night was still remaining, Thorstein wakens his guests and orders them in an angry voice to go about their business; but as soon as they were out of the house upon the road, Thorstein tells them that Gunhild's messengers were at Bjorn's house, and are upon the trace of them. They entreat of him to help them, and he gave them a guide and some provisions. He conducted them through a forest to a lake, in which there was an islet overgrown with reeds. They waded out to the islet, and hid themselves among the reeds. Early in the morning Hakon rode away from Bjorn's into the township, and wherever he came he asked after Astrid; and when he came to Thorstein's he asked if she had been there. He said that some people had been there; but as soon as it was daylight they had set off again, eastwards, to the forest. Hakon made Thorstein go along with them, as he knew all the roads and hiding-places. Thorstein went with them; but when they were come into the woods, he led them right across the way Astrid had taken. They went about and about the whole day to no purpose, as they could find no trace of her, so they turned back to tell Gunhild the end of their travel. Astrid and her friends proceeded on their journey, and came to Svithjod, to Hakon Gamle (the Old), where she and her son remained a long time, and had friendly welcome.

4. HAKON'S EMBASSY TO SWEDEN.

When Gunhild, the mother of the kings, heard that Astrid and her son Olaf were in the kingdom of Svithjod, she again sent Hakon, with a good attendance, eastward, to Eirik king of Sweden, with presents and messages of friendship. The ambassadors were well received and well treated. Hakon, after a time, disclosed his errand to the king, saying that Gunhild had sent him with the request that the king would assist him in getting hold of Olaf Trygvason, to conduct him to Norway, where Gunhild would bring him up. The king gave Hakon people with him, and he rode with them to Hakon the Old, where Hakon desired, with many friendly expressions, that Olaf should go with him. Hakon the Old returned a friendly answer, saying that it depended entirely upon Olaf's mother. But Astrid would on no account listen to the proposal; and the messengers had to return as they came, and to tell King Eirik how the matter stood. The ambassadors then prepared to return home, and asked the king for some assistance to take the boy, whether Hakon the Old would or not. The king gave them again some attendants; and when they came to Hakon the Old, they again asked for the boy, and on his refusal to deliver him they used high words and threatened violence. But one of the slaves, Buste by name, attacked Hakon, and was going to kill him; and they barely escaped from the thralls without a cudgelling, and proceeded home to Norway to tell Gunhild their ill success, and that they had only seen Olaf.

5. OF SIGURD EIRIKSON.

Astrid had a brother called Sigurd, a son of Eirik Bjodaskalle, who had long been abroad in Gardarike (Russia) with King Valdemar, and was there in great consideration. Astrid had now a great inclination to travel to her brother there. Hakon the Old gave her good attendants, and what was needful for the journey, and she set out with some merchants. She had then been two years (A.D. 965-966) with Hakon the Old, and Olaf was three years of age. As they sailed out into the Baltic, they were captured by vikings of Eistland, who made booty both of the people and goods, killing some, and dividing others as slaves. Olaf was separated from his mother, and an Eistland man called Klerkon got him as his share along with Thorolf and Thorgils. Klerkon thought that Thorolf was too old for a slave, and that there was not much work to be got out of him, so he killed him; but took the boys with him, and sold them to a man called Klerk for a stout and good ram. A third man, called Reas, bought Olaf for a good cloak. Reas had a wife called Rekon, and a son by her whose name was Rekone. Olaf was long with them, was treated well, and was much beloved by the people. Olaf was six years in Eistland in this banishment (A.D. 987-972).

6. OLAF IS SET FREE IN EISTLAND.

Sigurd, the son of Eirik (Astrid's brother), came into Eistland from Novgorod, on King Valdemar's business to collect the king's taxes and rents. Sigurd came as a man of consequence, with many followers and great magnificence. In the market-place he happened to observe a remarkably handsome boy; and as he could distinguish that he was a foreigner, he asked him his name and family. He answered him, that his name was Olaf; that he was a son of Trygve Olafson; and Astrid, a daughter of Eirik Bjodaskalle, was his mother. Then Sigurd knew that the boy was his sister's son, and asked him how he came there. Olaf told him minutely all his adventures, and Sigurd told him to follow him to the peasant Reas. When he came there he bought both the boys, Olaf and Thorgils, and took them with him to Holmgard. But, for the first, he made nothing known of Olaf's relationship to him, but treated him well.

7. KLERKON KILLED BY OLAF.

Olaf Trygvason was one day in the market-place, where there was a great number of people. He recognized Klerkon again, who had killed his foster-father Thorolf Lusarskeg. Olaf had a little axe in his hand, and with it he clove Klerkon's skull down to the brain, and ran home to his lodging, and told his friend Sigurd what he had done. Sigurd immediately took Olaf to Queen Allogia's house, told her what had happened, and begged her to protect the boy. She replied, that the boy appeared far too comely to allow him to be slain; and she ordered her people to be drawn out fully armed. In Holmgard the sacredness of peace is so respected, that it is law there to slay whoever puts a man to death except by judgment of law; and, according to this law and usage, the whole people stormed and sought after the boy. It was reported that he was in the Queen's house, and that there was a number of armed men there. When this was told to the king, he went there with his people, but would allow no bloodshed. It was settled at last in peace, that the king should name the fine for the murder; and the queen paid it. Olaf remained afterwards with the queen, and was much beloved. It is a law at Holmgard, that no man of royal descent shall stay there without the king's permission. Sigurd therefore told the queen of what family Olaf was, and for what reason he had come to Russia; namely, that he could not remain with safety in his own country: and begged her to speak to the king about it. She did so, and begged the king to help a king's son whose fate had been so hard; and in consequence of her entreaty the king promised to assist him, and accordingly he received Olaf into his court, and treated him nobly, and as a king's son. Olaf was nine years old when he came to Russia, and he remained nine years more (A.D. 978-981) with King Valdemar. Olaf was the handsomest of men, very stout and strong, and in all bodily exercises he excelled every Northman that ever was heard of.

8. OF HAKON EARL OF HLADER.

Earl Hakon, Sigurd's son, was with the Danish king, Harald Gormson, the winter after he had fled from Norway before Gunhild's sons. During the winter (A.D. 969) the earl had so much care and sorrow that he took to bed, and passed many sleepless nights, and ate and drank no more than was needful to support his strength. Then he sent a private message to his friends north in Throndhjem, and proposed to them that they should kill King Erling, if they had an opportunity; adding, that he would come to them in summer. The same winter the Throndhjem people accordingly, as before related, killed King Erling. There was great friendship between Earl Hakon and Gold Harald, and Harald told Hakon all his intentions. He told him that he was tired of a ship-life, and wanted to settle on the land; and asked Hakon if he thought his brother King Harald would agree to divide the kingdom with him if he asked it. "I think," replied Hakon, "that the Danish king would not deny thy right; but the best way to know is to speak to the king himself. I know for certain so much, that you will not get a kingdom if you don't ask for it." Soon after this conversation Gold Harald spoke to the king about the matter, in the presence of many great men who were friends to both; and Gold Harald asked King Harald to divide the kingdom with him in two equal parts, to which his royal birth and the custom of the Danish monarchy gave him right. The king was highly incensed at this demand, and said that no man had asked his father Gorm to be king over half of Denmark, nor yet his grandfather King Hordaknut, or Sigurd Orm, or Ragnar Lodbrok; and he was so exasperated and angry, that nobody ventured to speak of it to him.

9. OF GOLD HARALD.

GOLD HARALD WAS NOW worse off than before; for he had got no kingdom, and had got the king's anger by proposing it. He went as usual to his friend Hakon, and complained to him of his fate, and asked for good advice, and if he could help him to get his share of the kingdom; saying that he would rather try force, and the chance of war, than give it up.

Hakon advised him not to speak to any man so that this should be known; "for," said he, "it concerns thy life: and rather consider with thyself what thou art man enough to undertake; for to accomplish such a purpose requires a bold and firm man, who will neither stick at good nor evil to do that which is intended; for to take up great resolutions, and then to lay them aside, would only end in dishonour."

Gold Harald replies–"I will so carry on what I begin, that I will not hesitate to kill Harald with my own hands, if I can come thereby to the kingdom he denies me, and which is mine by right." And so they separated.

Now King Harald comes also to Earl Hakon, and tells him the demand on his kingdom which Gold Harald had made, and also his answer, and that he would upon no account consent to diminish his kingdom. "And if Gold Harald persists in his demand, I will have no hesitation in having him killed; for I will not trust him if he does not renounce it."

The earl answered,–"My thoughts are, that Harald has carried his demand so far that he cannot now let it drop, and I expect nothing but war in the land; and that he will be able to gather a great force, because his father was so beloved. And then it would be a great enormity if you were to kill your relation; for, as things now stand, all men would say that he was innocent. But I am far from saying, or advising, that you should make yourself a smaller king than your father Gorm was, who in many ways enlarged, but never diminished his kingdom."

The king replies,–"What then is your advice,–if I am neither to divide my kingdom, nor to get rid of my fright and danger?"

"Let us meet again in a few days," said Earl Hakon, "and I will then have considered the matter well, and will give you my advice upon it."

The king then went away with his people.

10. COUNCILS HELD BY HAKON AND HARALD.

Earl Hakon had now great reflection, and many opinions to weigh, and he let only very few be in the house with him. In a few days King Harald came again to the earl to speak with him, and ask if he had yet considered fully the matter they had been talking of.

"I have," said the earl, "considered it night and day ever since, and find it most advisable that you retain and rule over the whole of your kingdom just as your father left it; but that you obtain for your relation Harald another kingdom, that he also may enjoy honour and dignity."

"What kind of kingdom is that," said the king, "which I can give to Harald, that I may possess Denmark entire?"

"It is Norway," said the earl. "The kings who are there are oppressive to the people of the country, so that every man is against them who has tax or service to pay."

The king replies,–"Norway is a large country, and the people fierce, and not good to attack with a foreign army. We found that sufficiently when Hakon defended that country; for we lost many people, and gained no victory. Besides, Harald the son of Eirik is my foster-son, and has sat on my knee."

The earl answers, "I have long known that you have helped Gunhild's sons with your force, and a bad return you have got for it; but we shall get at Norway much more easily than by fighting for it with all the Danish force. Send a message to your foster-son Harald, Eirik's son, and offer him the lands and fiefs which Gunhild's sons held before in Denmark. Appoint him a meeting, and Gold Harald will soon conquer for himself a kingdom in Norway from Harald Grafeld."

The king replies, that it would be called a bad business to deceive his own foster-son.

"The Danes," answered the earl, "will rather say that it was better to kill a Norwegian viking than a Danish, and your own brother's son."

They spoke so long over the matter, that they agreed on it.

11. HARALD GORMSON'S MESSAGE TO NORWAY.

Thereafter Gold Harald had a conference with Earl Hakon; and the earl told him he had now advanced his business so far, that there was hope a kingdom might stand open for him in Norway. "We can then continue," said he, "our ancient friendship, and I can be of the greatest use to you in Norway. Take first that kingdom. King Harald is now very old, and has but one son, and cares but little about him, as he is but the son of a concubine."

The Earl talked so long to Gold Harald that the project pleased him well; and the king, the earl, and Gold Harald often talked over the business together. The Danish king then sent messengers north to Norway to Harald Grafeld, and fitted them out magnificently for their journey. They were well received by Harald. The messengers told him that Earl Hakon was in Denmark, but was lying dangerously sick, and almost out of his senses. They then delivered from Harald, the Danish king, the invitation to Harald Grafeld, his foster-son, to come to him and receive investiture of the fiefs he and his brothers before him had formerly held in Denmark; and appointing a meeting in Jutland. Harald Grafeld laid the matter before his mother and other friends. Their opinions were divided. Some thought that the expedition was not without its danger, on account of the men with whom they had to deal; but the most were in haste to begin the journey, for at that time there was such a famine in Norway that the kings could scarcely feed their men-at-arms; and on this account the Fjord, on which the kings resided, usually got the name of Hardanger (Hardacre). In Denmark, on the other hand, there had been tolerably good crops; so that people thought that if King Harald got fiefs, and something to rule over there they would get some assistance. It was therefore concluded, before the messengers returned, that Harald should travel to Denmark to the Danish king in summer, and accept the conditions King Harald offered.

12. TREACHERY OF HARALD AND HAKON.

Harald Grafeld went to Denmark in the summer (A.D. 969) with three long-ships; and Herse Arinbjorn, from the Fjord district, commanded one of them. King Harald sailed from Viken over to Limfjord in Jutland, and landed at the narrow neck of land where the Danish king was expected. Now when Gold Harald heard of this, he sailed there with nine ships which he had fitted out before for a viking cruise. Earl Hakon had also his war force on foot; namely, twelve large ships, all ready, with which he proposed to make an expedition. When Gold Harald had departed Earl Hakon says to the king, "Now I don't know if we are not sailing on an expedition, and yet are to pay the penalty of not having joined it. Gold Harald may kill Harald Grafeld, and get the kingdom of Norway; but you must not think he will be true to you, although you do help him to so much power, for he told me in winter that he would take your life if he could find opportunity to do so. Now I will win Norway for you, and kill Gold Harald, if you will promise me a good condition under you. I will be your earl; swear an oath of fidelity to you, and, with your help, conquer all Norway for you; hold the country under your rule; pay you the scat and taxes; and you will be a greater king than your father, as you will have two kingdoms under you." The king and the earl agreed upon this, and Hakon set off to seek Gold Harald.

13. DEATH OF HARALD GRAFELD.

Gold Harald came to the neck of land at Limfjord, and immediately challenged Harald Grafeld to battle; and although Harald had fewer men, he went immediately on the land, prepared for battle, and drew up his troops. Before the lines came together Harald Grafeld urged on his men, and told them to draw their swords. He himself advanced the foremost of the troop, hewing down on each side. So says Glum Geirason, in Grafeld's lay:–

"Brave were thy words in battlefield,
Thou stainer of the snow-white shield!–
Thou gallant war-god! With thy voice
Thou couldst the dying man rejoice:
The cheer of Harald could impart
Courage and life to every heart.
While swinging high the blood-smeared sword,
By arm and voice we knew our lord."

There fell Harald Grafeld. So says Glum Geirason:–

"On Limfjord's strand, by the tide's flow,
Stern Fate has laid King Harald low;
The gallant viking-cruiser–he

Who loved the isle-encircling sea.
The generous ruler of the land
Fell at the narrow Limfjord strand.
Enticed by Hakon's cunning speech
To his death-bed on Limfjord's beach."

The most of King Harald's men fell with him. There also fell Herse Arinbjorn.

This happened fifteen years after the death of Hakon, Athelstan's foster-son, and thirteen years after that of Sigurd earl of Hlader. The priest Are Frode says that Earl Hakon was thirteen years earl over his father's dominions in Throndhjem district before the fall of Harald Grafeld; but, for the last six years of Harald Grafeld's life, Are Frode says the Earl Hakon and Gunhild's sons fought against each other, and drove each other out of the land by turns.

14. GOLD HARALD'S DEATH.

SOON AFTER HARALD GRAFELD's fall, Earl Hakon came up to Gold Harald, and the earl immediately gave battle to Harald. Hakon gained the victory, and Harald was made prisoner; but Hakon had him immediately hanged on a gallows. Hakon then went to the Danish king, and no doubt easily settled with him for the killing his relative Gold Harald.

15. DIVISION OF THE COUNTRY.

SOON AFTER KING HARALD Gormson ordered a levy of men over all his kingdom, and sailed with 600 ships[22]. There were with him Earl Hakon, Harald Grenske, a son of King Gudrod, and many other great men who had fled from their udal estates in Norway on account of Gunhild's sons. The Danish king sailed with his fleet from the south to Viken, where all the people of the country surrendered to him. When he came to Tunsberg swarms of people joined him; and King Harald gave to Earl Hakon the command of all the men who came to him in Norway, and gave him the government over Rogaland, Hordaland, Sogn, Fjord-district, South More, Raumsdal, and North More. These seven districts gave King Harald to Earl Hakon to rule over, with the

22 i.e., 720 ships, as they were counted by long hundreds, 100=120.

same rights as Harald Harfager gave with them to his sons; only with the difference, that Hakon should there, as well as in Throndhjem, have the king's land-estates and land-tax, and use the king's money and goods according to his necessities whenever there was war in the country. King Harald also gave Harald Grenske Vingulmark, Vestfold, and Agder all the way to Lidandisnes (the Naze), together with the title of king; and let him have these dominions with the same rights as his family in former times had held them, and as Harald Harfager had given with them to his sons. Harald Grenske was then eighteen years old, and he became afterwards a celebrated man. Harald king of Denmark returned home thereafter with all his army.

16. GUNHILD'S SONS LEAVE THE COUNTRY.

Earl Hakon proceeded northwards along the coast with his force; and when Gunhild and her sons got the tidings they proceeded to gather troops, but were ill off for men. Then they took the same resolution as before, to sail out to sea with such men as would follow them away to the westward (A.D. 969). They came first to the Orkney Islands, and remained there a while. There were in Orkney then the Earls Hlodver. Arnfid, Ljot, and Skule, the sons of Thorfin Hausakljufer.

Earl Hakon now brought all the country under him, and remained all winter (A.D. 970) in Throndhjem. Einar Skalaglam speaks of his conquests in "Vellekla":–

"Norway's great watchman, Harald, now
May bind the silk snood on his brow–
Seven provinces he seized. The realm
Prospers with Hakon at the helm."

As Hakon the earl proceeded this summer along the coast subjecting all the people to him, he ordered that over all his dominions the temples and sacrifices should be restored, and continued as of old. So it is said in the "Vellekla":–

"Hakon the earl, so good and wise,
Let all the ancient temples rise;–
Thor's temples raised with fostering hand
That had been ruined through the land.
His valiant champions, who were slain

On battle-fields across the main,
To Thor, the thunder-god, may tell
How for the gods all turns out well.
The hardy warrior now once more
Offers the sacrifice of gore;
The shield-bearer in Loke's game
Invokes once more great Odin's name.
The green earth gladly yields her store,
As she was wont in days of yore,
Since the brave breaker of the spears
The holy shrines again uprears.
The earl has conquered with strong hand
All that lies north of Viken land:
In battle storm, and iron rain
Hakon spreads wide his sword's domain."

The first winter that Hakon ruled over Norway the herrings set in everywhere through the fjords to the land, and the seasons ripened to a good crop all that had been sown. The people, therefore, laid in seed for the next year, and got their lands sowed, and had hope of good times.

17. HAKON'S BATTLE WITH RAGNFRED.

King Ragnfred and King Gudrod, both sons of Gunhild and Eirik, were now the only sons of Gunhild remaining in life. So says Glum Geirason in Grafeld's lay:–

"When in the battle's bloody strife
The sword took noble Harald's life,
Half of my fortunes with him fell:
But his two brothers, I know well,
My loss would soon repair, should they
Again in Norway bear the sway,
And to their promises should stand,
If they return to rule the land."

Ragnfred began his course in the spring after he had been a year in the Orkney Islands. He sailed from thence to Norway, and had with him fine troops, and large ships. When he came to Norway he learnt that Earl Hakon was in Throndhjem; therefore he steered northwards around Stad, and plundered in South More. Some people submitted to him; for it often happens, when parties of armed men scour over a country, that those who are nearest the danger seek help where they think it may be expected. As soon as Earl Hakon heard the news of disturbance in More, he fitted out ships, sent the war-token through the land, made ready in all haste, and proceeded out of the fjord. He had no difficulty in assembling men. Ragnfred and Earl Hakon met at the north corner of More; and Hakon, who had most men, but fewer ships, began the battle. The combat was severe, but heaviest on Hakon's side; and as the custom then was, they fought bow to bow, and there was a current in the sound which drove all the ships in upon the land. The earl ordered to row with the oars to the land where landing seemed easiest. When the ships were all grounded, the earl with all his men left them, and drew them up so far that the enemy might not launch them down again, and then drew up his men on a grass-field, and challenged Ragnfred to land. Ragnfred and his men laid their vessels in along the land, and they shot at each other a long time; but upon the land Ragnfred would not venture: and so they separated. Ragnfred sailed with his fleet southwards around Stad; for he was much afraid the whole forces of the country would swarm around Hakon. Hakon, on his part, was not inclined to try again a battle, for he thought the difference between their ships in size was too great; so in harvest he went north to Throndhjem, and staid there all winter (A.D. 971). King Ragnfred consequently had all the country south of Stad at his mercy; namely, Fjord district, Hordaland, Sogn, Rogaland; and he had many people about him all winter. When spring approached he ordered out the people and collected a large force. By going about the districts he got many men, ships, and warlike stores sent as he required.

18. BATTLE BETWEEN HAKON AND RAGNFRED.

Towards spring Earl Hakon ordered out all the men north in the country; and got many people from Halogaland and Naumudal; so that from Bryda to Stad he had men from all the sea-coast. People flocked to him from all the Throndhjem district and from Raumsdal. It was said for certain that he had men from four great districts, and that seven earls followed him, and a matchless number of men. So it is said in the "Vellekla":-

"Hakon, defender of the land,
Armed in the North his warrior-band
To Sogn's old shore his force he led,
And from all quarters thither sped
War-ships and men; and haste was made
By the young god of the sword-blade,
The hero-viking of the wave,
His wide domain from foes to save.
With shining keels seven kings sailed on
To meet this raven-feeding one.
When the clash came, the stunning sound
Was heard in Norway's farthest bound;
And sea-borne corpses, floating far,
Brought round the Naze news from the war."

Earl Hakon sailed then with his fleet southwards around Stad; and when he heard that King Ragnfred with his army had gone towards Sogn, he turned there also with his men to meet him: and there Ragnfred and Hakon met. Hakon came to the land with his ships, marked out a battle-field with hazel branches for King Ragnfred, and took ground for his own men in it. So it is told in the "Vellekla":–

"In the fierce battle Ragnfred then
Met the grim foe of Vindland men;
And many a hero of great name
Fell in the sharp sword's bloody game.
The wielder of fell Narve's weapon,
The conquering hero, valiant Hakon
Had laid his war-ships on the strand,
And ranged his warriors on the land."

There was a great battle; but Earl Hakon, having by far the most people, gained the victory. It took place on the Thinganes, where Sogn and Hordaland meet.

King Rangfred fled to his ships, after 300 of his men had fallen. So it is said in the "Vellekla":–

"Sharp was the battle-strife, I ween,–
Deadly and close it must have been,
Before, upon the bloody plain,
Three hundred corpses of the slain

Were stretched for the black raven's prey;
And when the conquerors took their way
To the sea-shore, they had to tread
O'er piled-up heaps of foemen dead."

After this battle King Ragnfred fled from Norway; but Earl Hakon restored peace to the country, and allowed the great army which had followed him in summer to return home to the north country, and he himself remained in the south that harvest and winter (A.D. 972).

19. EARL HAKON'S MARRIAGE.

Earl Hakon married a girl called Thora, a daughter of the powerful Skage Skoptason, and very beautiful she was. They had two sons, Svein and Heming, and a daughter called Bergljot who was afterwards married to Einar Tambaskielfer. Earl Hakon was much addicted to women, and had many children; among others a daughter Ragnhild, whom he married to Skopte Skagason, a brother of Thora. The Earl loved Thora so much that he held Thora's family in higher respect than any other people, and Skopte his brother-in-law in particular; and he gave him many great fiefs in More. Whenever they were on a cruise together, Skopte must lay his ship nearest to the earl's, and no other ship was allowed to come in between.

20. DEATH OF SKOPTE.

One summer that Earl Hakon was on a cruise, there was a ship with him of which Thorleif Spake (the Wise) was steersman. In it was also Eirik, Earl Hakon's son, then about ten or eleven years old. Now in the evenings, as they came into harbour, Eirik would not allow any ship but his to lie nearest to the earl's. But when they came to the south, to More, they met Skopte the earl's brother-in-law, with a well-manned ship; and as they rowed towards the fleet, Skopte called out that Thorleif should move out of the harbour to make room for him, and should go to the roadstead. Eirik in haste took up the matter, and ordered Skopte to go himself to the roadstead. When Earl Hakon heard that his son thought himself too great to give place to Skopte, he called to them immediately that they should haul out from their berth, threatening them with chastisement if they did not. When Thorleif heard this, he ordered his men to slip their land-cable, and they did so; and Skopte laid his vessel next to the earl's as he used to do. When they came together, Skopte brought the earl all the news he had gathered, and the earl communicated to Skopte all the news he had heard; and Skopte was therefore called Tidindaskopte (the Newsman Skopte). The winter after (A.D. 973) Eirik was with his foster-father Thorleif, and early in spring he gathered a crew of followers, and Thorleif gave him a boat of fifteen benches of rowers, with ship furniture, tents, and ship provisions; and Eirik set out from the fjord, and southwards to More. Tidindaskopte happened also to be going with a fully manned boat of fifteen rowers' benches from one of his farms to another, and Eirik went against him to have a battle. Skopte was slain, but Eirik granted life to those of his men who were still on their legs. So says Eyjolf Dadaskald in the "Banda Lay":–

"At eve the youth went out
To meet the warrior stout–
To meet stout Skopte–he
Whose war-ship roves the sea
Like force was on each side,
But in the whirling tide
The young wolf Eirik slew
Skopte, and all his crew
And he was a gallant one,
Dear to the Earl Hakon.
Up, youth of steel-hard breast–
No time hast thou to rest!
Thy ocean wings spread wide–
Speed o'er the foaming tide!
Speed on–speed on thy way!
For here thou canst not stay."

Eirik sailed along the land and came to Denmark, and went to King Harald Gormson, and staid with him all winter (A.D. 974). In spring the Danish king sent him north to Norway, and gave him an earldom, and the government of Vingulmark and Raumarike, on the same terms as the small scat-paying kings had formerly held these domains. So says Eyjolf Dadaskald:–

"South through ocean's spray
His dragon flew away
To Gormson's hall renowned.

Where the bowl goes bravely round.
And the Danish king did place
This youth of noble race
Where, shield and sword in hand,
He would aye defend his land."

Eirik became afterwards a great chief.

21. OLAF TRYGVASON'S JOURNEY FROM RUSSIA.

All this time Olaf Trygvason was in Gardarike (Russia), and highly esteemed by King Valdemar, and beloved by the queen. King Valdemar made him chief over the men-at-arms whom he sent out to defend the land. So says Hallarsteid:–

"The hater of the niggard band,
The chief who loves the Northman's land,
Was only twelve years old when he
His Russian war-ships put to sea.
The wain that ploughs the sea was then
Loaded with war-gear by his men–
With swords, and spears, and helms: and deep
Out to the sea his good ships sweep."

Olaf had several battles, and was lucky as a leader of troops. He himself kept a great many men-at-arms at his own expense out of the pay the king gave him. Olaf was very generous to his men, and therefore very popular. But then it came to pass, what so often happens when a foreigner is raised to higher power and dignity than men of the country, that many envied him because he was so favoured by the king, and also not less so by the queen. They hinted to the king that he should take care not to make Olaf too powerful,–"for such a man may be dangerous to you, if he were to allow himself to be used for the purpose of doing you or your kingdom harm; for he is extremely expert in all exercises and feats, and very popular. We do not, indeed, know what it is he can have to talk of so often with the queen." It was then the custom among great monarchs that the queen should have half of the court attendants, and she supported them at her own expense out of the scat and revenue provided for her for that purpose. It was so also at the court of King Valdemar that the queen had an attendance as large as the king, and they vied with each other about the finest men, each wanting to have such in their own service. It so fell out that the king listened to such speeches, and became somewhat silent and blunt towards Olaf. When Olaf observed this, he told it to the queen; and also that he had a great desire to travel to the Northern land, where his family formerly had power and kingdoms, and where it was most likely he would advance himself. The queen wished him a prosperous journey, and said he would be found a brave man wherever he might be. Olaf then made ready, went on board, and set out to sea in the Baltic.

As he was coming from the east he made the island of Borgundarholm (Bornholm), where he landed and plundered. The country people hastened down to the strand, and gave him battle; but Olaf gained the victory, and a large booty.

22. OLAF TRYGVASON'S MARRIAGE.

WHILE OLAF LAY AT Borgundarholm there came on bad weather, storm, and a heavy sea, so that his ships could not lie there; and he sailed southwards under Vindland, where they found a good harbour. They conducted themselves very peacefully, and remained some time. In Vindland there was then a king called Burizleif, who had three daughters,–Geira, Gunhild, and Astrid. The king's daughter Geira had the power and government in that part where Olaf and his people landed, and Dixen was the name of the man who most usually advised Queen Geira. Now when they heard that unknown people were came to the country, who were of distinguished appearance, and conducted themselves peaceably, Dixen repaired to them with a message from Queen Geira, inviting the strangers to take up their winter abode with her; for the summer was almost spent, and the weather was severe and stormy. Now when Dixen came to the place he soon saw that the leader was a distinguished man, both from family and personal appearance, and he told Olaf the queen's invitation with the most kindly message. Olaf willingly accepted the invitation, and went in harvest (A.D. 982) to Queen Geira. They liked each other exceedingly, and Olaf courted Queen Geira; and it was so settled that Olaf married her the same winter, and was ruler, along with Queen Geira, over her dominions. Halfred Vandredaskald tells of these matters in the lay he composed about King Olaf:–

"Why should the deeds the hero did
In Bornholm and the East be hid?

His deadly weapon Olaf bold
Dyed red: why should not this be told?"

23. EARL HAKON PAYS NO SCAT.

Earl Hakon ruled over Norway, and paid no scat; because the Danish king gave him all the scat revenue that belonged to the king in Norway, for the expense and trouble he had in defending the country against Gunhild's sons.

24. HARALD OPPOSES CHRISTIANITY.

The Emperor Otta (Otto) was at that time in the Saxon country, and sent a message to King Harald, the Danish king, that he must take on the true faith and be baptized, he and all his people whom he ruled; "otherwise," says the emperor, "we will march against him with an army." The Danish king ordered the land defence to be fitted out, Danavirke[23] (the Danish wall) to be well fortified, and his ships of war rigged out. He sent a message also to Earl Hakon in Norway to come to him early in spring, and with as many men as he could possibly raise. In spring (A.D. 975) Earl Hakon levied an army over the whole country which was very numerous, and with it he sailed to meet the Danish king. The king received him in the most honourable manner. Many other chiefs also joined the Danish king with their men, so that he had gathered a very large army.

25. OLAF TRYGVASON'S WAR EXPEDITION.

Olaf Trygvason had been all winter (A.D. 980) in Vindland, as before related, and went the same winter to the baronies in Vindland which had formerly been under Queen Geira, but had withdrawn themselves from obedience and payment of taxes. There Olaf made war, killed many people, burnt out others, took much property, and laid all of them under subjection to him, and then went back to his castle.

23 Danavirke. The Danish work was a wall of earth, stones, and wood, with a deep ditch in front, and a castle at every hundred fathoms, between the rivers Eider and Slien, constructed by Harald Blatand (Bluetooth) to oppose the progress of Charlemagne. Some traces of it still exist. –L.

Early in spring Olaf rigged out his ships and set off to sea. He sailed to Skane and made a landing. The people of the country assembled, and gave him battle; but King Olaf conquered, and made a great booty. He then sailed eastward to the island of Gotland, where he captured a merchant vessel belonging to the people of Jamtaland. They made a brave defence; but the end of it was that Olaf cleared the deck, killed many of the men, and took all the goods. He had a third battle in Gotland, in which he also gained the victory, and made a great booty. So says Halfred Vandredaskald:–

"The king, so fierce in battle-fray,
First made the Vindland men give way:
The Gotlanders must tremble next;
And Scania's shores are sorely vexed
By the sharp pelting arrow shower
The hero and his warriors pour;
And then the Jamtaland men must fly,
Scared by his well-known battle-cry."

26. OTTA AND HAKON IN BATTLE.

The Emperor Otta assembled a great army from Saxland, Frakland, Frisland, and Vindland. King Burizleif followed him with a large army, and in it was his son-in-law, Olaf Trygvason. The emperor had a great body of horsemen, and still greater of foot people, and a great army from Holstein. Harald, the Danish king, sent Earl Hakon with the army of Northmen that followed him southwards to Danavirke, to defend his kingdom on that side. So it is told in the "Vellekla":–

"Over the foaming salt sea spray
The Norse sea-horses took their way,
Racing across the ocean-plain
Southwards to Denmark's green domain.
The gallant chief of Hordaland
Sat at the helm with steady hand,
In casque and shield, his men to bring
From Dovre to his friend the king.
He steered his war-ships o'er the wave
To help the Danish king to save
Mordalf, who, with a gallant band

Was hastening from the Jutes' wild land,
Across the forest frontier rude,
With toil and pain through the thick wood.
Glad was the Danish king, I trow,
When he saw Hakon's galley's prow.
The monarch straightway gave command
To Hakon, with a steel-clad band,
To man the Dane-work's rampart stout,
And keep the foreign foemen out."

The Emperor Otta came with his army from the south to Danavirke, but Earl Hakon defended the rampart with his men. The Dane-work (Danavirke) was constructed in this way:–Two fjords run into the land, one on each side; and in the farthest bight of these fjords the Danes had made a great wall of stone, turf, and timber, and dug a deep and broad ditch in front of it, and had also built a castle over each gate of it. There was a hard battle there, of which the "Vellekla" speaks:–

"Thick the storm of arrows flew,
Loud was the din, black was the view
Of close array of shield and spear
Of Vind, and Frank, and Saxon there.
But little recked our gallant men;
And loud the cry might be heard then
Of Norway's brave sea-roving son–
'On 'gainst the foe! On! Lead us on!"

Earl Hakon drew up his people in ranks upon all the gate-towers of the wall, but the greater part of them he kept marching along the wall to make a defence wheresoever an attack was threatened. Many of the emperor's people fell without making any impression on the fortification, so the emperor turned back without farther attempt at an assault on it. So it is said in the "Vellekla":–

"They who the eagle's feast provide
In ranked line fought side by side,
'Gainst lines of war-men under shields
Close packed together on the fields,
Earl Hakon drive by daring deeds
The Saxons to their ocean-steeds;

And the young hero saves from fall
The Danavirke–the people's wall."

After this battle Earl Hakon went back to his ships, and intended to sail home to Norway; but he did not get a favourable wind, and lay for some time outside at Limafjord.

27. HARALD AND HAKON ARE BAPTIZED.

THE EMPEROR OTTA TURNED back with his troops to Slesvik, collected his ships of war, and crossed the fjord of Sle into Jutland. As soon as the Danish king heard of this he marched his army against him, and there was a battle, in which the emperor at last got the victory. The Danish king fled to Limafjord and took refuge in the island Marsey. By the help of mediators who went between the king and the emperor, a truce and a meeting between them were agreed on. The Emperor Otta and the Danish king met upon Marsey. There Bishop Poppo instructed King Harald in the holy faith; he bore red hot irons in his hands, and exhibited his unscorched hands to the king. Thereafter King Harald allowed himself to be baptized, and also the whole Danish army. King Harald, while he was in Marsey, had sent a message to Hakon that he should come to his succour; and the earl had just reached the island when the king had received baptism. The king sends word to the earl to come to him, and when they met the king forced the earl to allow himself also to be baptized. So Earl Hakon and all the men who were with him were baptized; and the king gave them priests and other learned men with them, and ordered that the earl should make all the people in Norway be baptized. On that they separated; and the earl went out to sea, there to wait for a wind.

28. HAKON RENOUNCES CHRISTIANITY.

WHEN A WIND CAME with which he thought he could get clear out to sea, he put all the learned men on shore again, and set off to the ocean; but as the wind came round to the south-west, and at last to west, he sailed eastward, out through Eyrarsund, ravaging the land on both sides. He then sailed eastward along Skane, plundering the country wherever he came. When he got east to the skerries of East Gautland, he ran in and landed, and made a great blood-sacrifice. There came two ravens flying which croaked loudly; and now, thought the earl, the blood-offering has been accepted by Odin, and he thought good luck would be with him any day he liked to go to battle. Then he set fire to his ships, landed his men, and went over all the country with armed hand. Earl Ottar, who ruled over Gautland, came against him, and they held a great battle with each other; but Earl Hakon gained the day, and Earl Ottar and a great part of his men were killed. Earl Hakon now drove with fire and sword over both the Gautlands, until he came into Norway; and then he proceeded by land all the way north to Throndhjem. The "Vellekla" tells about this:–

"On the silent battle-field,
In viking garb, with axe and shield,
The warrior, striding o'er the slain,
Asks of the gods 'What days will gain?'
Two ravens, flying from the east,
Come croaking to the bloody feast:
The warrior knows what they foreshow–
The days when Gautland blood will flow.
A viking-feast Earl Hakon kept,
The land with viking fury swept,
Harrying the land far from the shore
Where foray ne'er was known before.
Leaving the barren cold coast side,
He raged through Gautland far and wide,–
Led many a gold-decked viking shield
O'er many a peaceful inland field.
Bodies on bodies Odin found
Heaped high upon each battle ground:
The moor, as if by witchcraft's power,
Grows green, enriched by bloody shower.
No wonder that the gods delight
To give such luck in every fight
To Hakon's men–for he restores
Their temples on our Norway shores."

29. THE EMPEROR OTTA RETURNS HOME.

The Emperor Otta went back to his kingdom in the Saxon land, and parted in friendship with the Danish king. It is said that the Emperor Otta stood godfather to Svein, King Harald's son, and gave him his name; so that he was baptized Otta Svein. King Harald held fast by his Christianity to his dying day.

King Burizleif went to Vindland, and his son-in-law King Olaf went with him. This battle is related also by Halfred Vandredaskald in his song on Olaf:–

"He who through the foaming surges
His white-winged ocean-coursers urges,
Hewed from the Danes, in armour dressed,
The iron bark off mail-clad breast."

30. OLAF'S JOURNEY FROM VINDLAND.

Olaf Trygvason was three years in Vindland (A.D. 982-984) when Geira his queen fell sick, and she died of her illness. Olaf felt his loss so great that he had no pleasure in Vindland after it. He provided himself, therefore, with warships, and went out again a plundering, and plundered first in Frisland, next in Saxland, and then all the way to Flaemingjaland (Flanders). So says Halfred Vandredaskald:–

"Olaf's broad axe of shining steel
For the shy wolf left many a meal.
The ill-shaped Saxon corpses lay
Heaped up, the witch-wife's horses' [24] *prey.*
She rides by night: at pools of blood.
Where Frisland men in daylight stood,
Her horses slake their thirst, and fly
On to the field where Flemings lie.
The raven-friend in Odin's dress–
Olaf, who foes can well repress,
Left Flemish flesh for many a meal
With his broad axe of shining steel."

31. KING OLAF'S FORAYS.

Thereafter Olaf Trygvason sailed to England, and ravaged wide around in the land. He sailed all the way north to Northumberland,

24 Ravens were the witches' horses.–L.

where he plundered; and thence to Scotland, where he marauded far and wide. Then he went to the Hebrides, where he fought some battles; and then southwards to Man, where he also fought. He ravaged far around in Ireland, and thence steered to Bretland, which he laid waste with fire and sword, and all the district called Cumberland. He sailed westward from thence to Valland, and marauded there. When he left the west, intending to sail to England, he came to the islands called the Scilly Isles, lying westward from England in the ocean. Thus tells Halfred Vandraskald of these events:–

The brave young king, who ne'er retreats,
The Englishman in England beats.
Death through Northumberland is spread
From battleaxe and broad spearhead.
Through Scotland with his spears he rides;
To Man his glancing ships he guides:
Feeding the wolves where'er he came,
The young king drove a bloody game.
The gallant bowmen in the isles
Slew foemen, who lay heaped in piles.
The Irish fled at Olaf's name–
Fled from a young king seeking fame.
In Bretland, and in Cumberland,
People against him could not stand:
Thick on the fields their corpses lay,
To ravens and howling wolves a prey."

Olaf Trygvason had been four years on this cruise (A.D. 985-988), from the time he left Vindland till he came to the Scilly Islands.

32. KING OLAF IS BAPTIZED.

While Olaf Trygvason lay in the Scilly Isles he heard of a seer, or fortune-teller, on the islands, who could tell beforehand things not yet done, and what he foretold many believed was really fulfilled. Olaf became curious to try this man's gift of prophecy. He therefore sent one of his men, who was the handsomest and strongest, clothed him magnificently, and bade him say he was the king; for Olaf was known in all countries as handsomer, stronger, and braver than all others, although, after he had left Russia, he retained no more of his name than that he was called Ole, and was Russian. Now when the messenger came to the fortune-teller, and gave himself out for the king, he got the answer, "Thou art not the king, but I advise thee to be faithful to thy king." And more he would not say to that man. The man returned, and told Olaf, and his desire to meet the fortune-teller was increased; and now he had no doubt of his being really a fortune-teller. Olaf repaired himself to him, and, entering into conversation, asked him if he could foresee how it would go with him with regard to his kingdom, or of any other fortune he was to have. The hermit replies in a holy spirit of prophecy, "Thou wilt become a renowned king, and do celebrated deeds. Many men wilt thou bring to faith and baptism, and both to thy own and others' good; and that thou mayst have no doubt of the truth of this answer, listen to these tokens: When thou comest to thy ships many of thy people will conspire against thee, and then a battle will follow in which many of thy men will fall, and thou wilt be wounded almost to death, and carried upon a shield to thy ship; yet after seven days thou shalt be well of thy wounds, and immediately thou shalt let thyself be baptized." Soon after Olaf went down to his ships, where he met some mutineers and people who would destroy him and his men. A fight took place, and the result was what the hermit had predicted, that Olaf was wounded, and carried upon a shield to his ship, and that his wound was healed in seven days. Then Olaf perceived that the man had spoken truth, that he was a true fortune-teller, and had the gift of prophecy. Olaf went once more to the hermit, and asked particularly how he came to have such wisdom in foreseeing things to be. The hermit replied, that the Christian God himself let him know all that he desired; and he brought before Olaf many great proofs of the power of the Almighty. In consequence of this encouragement Olaf agreed to let himself be baptized, and he and all his followers were baptized forthwith. He remained here a long time, took the true faith, and got with him priests and other learned men.

33. OLAF MARRIES GYDA.

In autumn (A.D. 988) Olaf sailed from Scilly to England, where he put into a harbour, but proceeded in a friendly way; for England was Christian, and he himself had become Christian. At this time a summons to a Thing went through the country, that all men should come to hold a Thing. Now when the Thing was assembled a queen called Gyda came to it, a sister of Olaf Kvaran, who was king of Dublin in Ireland. She had been married to a great earl in England, and after his death she was at the head of his dominions. In her territory there was a man called Alfvine, who was a great champion and single-combat man. He had paid his addresses to her; but she gave for answer, that she herself would choose whom of the men in her dominions she would take in marriage; and on that account the Thing was assembled, that she might choose a husband. Alfvine came there dressed out in his best clothes, and there were many well-dressed men at the meeting. Olaf had come there also; but had on his bad-weather clothes, and a coarse over-garment, and stood with his people apart from the rest of the crowd. Gyda went round and looked at each, to see if any appeared to her a suitable man. Now when she came to where Olaf stood she looked at him straight in the face, and asked "what sort of man he was?"

He said, "I am called Ole; and I am a stranger here."

Gyda replies, "Wilt thou have me if I choose thee?"

"I will not say no to that," answered he; and he asked what her name was, and her family, and descent.

"I am called Gyda," said she; "and am daughter of the king of Ireland, and was married in this country to an earl who ruled over this territory. Since his death I have ruled over it, and many have courted me, but none to whom I would choose to be married."

She was a young and handsome woman. They afterwards talked over the matter together, and agreed, and Olaf and Gyda were betrothed.

34. KING OLAF AND ALFVINE'S DUEL.

Alfvine was very ill pleased with this. It was the custom then in England, if two strove for anything, to settle the matter by single combat[25]; and now Alfvine challenges Olaf Trygvason to fight about this business. The time and place for the combat were settled, and that each should have twelve men with him. When they met, Olaf told his men to do exactly as they saw him do. He had a large axe; and when Alfvine was going to cut at him with his sword he hewed away the sword out of his hand, and with the next blow struck down Alfvine himself. He then bound him fast. It went in the same way with all Alfvine's men. They were beaten down, bound, and carried to Olaf's lodging. Thereupon he ordered Alfvine to quit the country, and never appear in it again; and Olaf took all his prop-

25 Holm-gang: so called because the combatants went to a holm or uninhabited isle to fight in Norway.–L.

erty. Olaf in this way got Gyda in marriage, and lived sometimes in England, and sometimes in Ireland.

35. KING OLAF GETS HIS DOG VIGE.

WHILE OLAF WAS IN Ireland he was once on an expedition which went by sea. As they required to make a foray for provisions on the coast, some of his men landed, and drove down a large herd of cattle to the strand. Now a peasant came up, and entreated Olaf to give him back the cows that belonged to him. Olaf told him to take his cows, if he could distinguish them; "but don't delay our march." The peasant had with him a large house-dog, which he put in among the herd of cattle, in which many hundred head of beasts were driven together. The dog ran into the herd, and drove out exactly the number which the peasant had said he wanted; and all were marked with the same mark, which showed that the dog knew the right beasts, and was very sagacious. Olaf then asked the peasant if he would sell him the dog. "I would rather give him to you," said the peasant. Olaf immediately presented him with a gold ring in return, and promised him his friendship in future. This dog was called Vige, and was the very best of dogs, and Olaf owned him long afterwards.

36. HARALD GORMSON SAILS AGAINST ICELAND.

THE DANISH KING, Harald Gormson, heard that Earl Hakon had thrown off Christianity, and had plundered far and wide in the Danish land. The Danish king levied an army, with which he went to Norway; and when he came to the country which Earl Hakon had to rule over he laid waste the whole land, and came with his fleet to some islands called Solunder. Only five houses were left standing in Laeradal; but all the people fled up to the mountains, and into the forest, taking with them all the moveable goods they could carry with them. Then the Danish king proposed to sail with his fleet to Iceland, to avenge the mockery and scorn all the Icelanders had shown towards him; for they had made a law in Iceland, that they should make as many lampoons against the Danish king as there were headlands in his country; and the reason was, because a vessel which belonged to certain Icelanders was stranded in Denmark, and the Danes took all the property, and called it wreck. One of the king's bailiffs called Birger was to blame for this; but the lampoons were made against both. In the lampoons were the following lines:–

"The gallant Harald in the field
Between his legs lets drop his shield;
Into a pony he was changed.
And kicked his shield, and safely ranged.
And Birger, he who dwells in halls
For safety built with four stone walls,
That these might be a worthy pair,
Was changed into a pony mare."

37. HARALD SENDS A WARLOCK TO ICELAND.

King Harald told a warlock to hie to Iceland in some altered shape, and to try what he could learn there to tell him: and he set out in the shape of a whale. And when he came near to the land he went to the west side of Iceland, north around the land, where he saw all the mountains and hills full of guardian-spirits, some great, some small. When he came to Vapnafjord he went in towards the land, intending to go on shore; but a huge dragon rushed down the dale against him with a train of serpents, paddocks, and toads, that blew poison towards him. Then he turned to go westward around the land as far as Eyjafjord, and he went into the fjord. Then a bird flew against him, which was so great that its wings stretched over the mountains on either side of the fjord, and many birds, great and small, with it. Then he swam farther west, and then south into Breidafjord. When he came into the fjord a large grey bull ran against him, wading into the sea, and bellowing fearfully, and he was followed by a crowd of land-spirits. From thence he went round by Reykjanes, and wanted to land at Vikarsskeid, but there came down a hill-giant against him with an iron staff in his hands. He was a head higher than the mountains, and many other giants followed him. He then swam eastward along the land, and there was nothing to see, he said, but sand and vast deserts, and, without the skerries, high-breaking surf; and the ocean between the countries was so wide that a long-ship could not cross it. At that time Brodhelge dwelt in Vapnafjord, Eyjolf Valgerdson in Eyjafjord, Thord Geller in Breidafjord, and Thorod Gode in Olfus. Then the Danish king turned about with his fleet, and sailed back to Denmark.

Hakon the earl settled habitations again in the country that had been laid waste, and paid no scat as long as he lived to Denmark.

38. HARALD GORMSON'S DEATH.

Svein, King Harald's son, who afterwards was called Tjuguskeg (forked beard), asked his father King Harald for a part of his kingdom; but now, as before, Harald would not listen to dividing the Danish dominions, and giving him a kingdom. Svein collected ships of war, and gave out that he was going on a viking cruise; but when all his men were assembled, and the Jomsborg viking Palnatoke had come to his assistance he ran into Sealand to Isafjord, where his father had been for some time with his ships ready to proceed on an expedition. Svein instantly gave battle, and the combat was severe. So many people flew to assist King Harald, that Svein was overpowered by numbers, and fled. But King Harald received a wound which ended in his death: and Svein was chosen King of Denmark. At this time Sigvalde was earl over Jomsborg in Vindland. He was a son of King Strutharald, who had ruled over Skane. Heming, and Thorkel the Tall, were Sigvalde's brothers. Bue the Thick from Bornholm, and Sigurd his brother, were also chiefs among the Jomsborg vikings: and also Vagn, a son of Ake and Thorgunna, and a sister's son of Bue and Sigurd. Earl Sigvalde had taken King Svein prisoner, and carried him to Vindland, to Jomsborg, where he had forced him to make peace with Burizleif, the king of the Vinds, and to take him as the peace-maker between them. Earl Sigvalde was married to Astrid, a daughter of King Burizleif; and told King Svein that if he did not accept of his terms, he would deliver him into the hands of the Vinds. The king knew that they would torture him to death, and therefore agreed to accept the earl's mediation. The earl delivered this judgment between them–that King Svein should marry Gunhild, King Burizleif's daughter; and King Burizleif again Thyre, a daughter of Harald, and King Svein's sister; but that each party should retain their own dominions, and there should be peace between the countries. Then King Svein returned home to Denmark with his wife Gunhild. Their sons were Harald and Knut (Canute) the Great. At that time the Danes threatened much to bring an army into Norway against Earl Hakon.

39. VOW OF THE JOMSBORG VIKINGS.

King Svein made a magnificent feast, to which he invited all the chiefs in his dominions; for he would give the succession-feast, or the heirship-ale, after his father Harald. A short time before, Strutharald in Skane, and Vesete in Bornholm, father to Bue the Thick and to Sigurd, had died; and King Svein sent word to the Jomsborg vikings that Earl Sigvalde and Bue, and their brothers, should come to him, and drink the funeral-ale for their fathers in the same feast the king was giving. The Jomsborg vikings came to the festival with their bravest men, forty ships of them from Vindland, and twenty ships from Skane. Great was the multitude of people assembled. The first day of the feast, before King Svein went up into his father's high-seat, he drank the bowl to his father's memory, and made the solemn vow, that before three winters were past he would go over with his army to England, and either kill King Adalrad (Ethelred), or chase him out of the country. This heirship bowl all who were at the feast drank. Thereafter for the chiefs of the Jomsborg vikings was filled and drunk the largest horn to be found, and of the strongest drink. When that bowl was emptied, all men drank Christ's health; and again the fullest measure and the strongest drink were handed to the Jomsborg vikings. The third bowl was to the memory of Saint Michael, which was drunk by all. Thereafter Earl Sigvalde emptied a remembrance bowl to his father's honour, and made the solemn vow, that before three winters came to an end he would go to Norway, and either kill Earl Hakon, or chase him out of the country. Thereupon Thorkel the Tall, his brother, made a solemn vow to follow his brother Sigvalde to Norway, and not flinch from the battle so long as Sigvalde would fight there. Then Bue the Thick vowed to follow them to Norway, and not flinch so long as the other Jomsborg vikings fought. At last Vagn Akason vowed that he would go with them to Norway, and not return until he had slain Thorkel Leira, and gone to bed to his daughter Ingebjorg without her friends' consent. Many other chiefs made solemn vows about different things. Thus was the heirship-ale drunk that day, but the next morning, when the Jomsborg vikings had slept off their drink, they thought they had spoken more than enough. They held a meeting to consult how they should proceed with their undertaking, and they determined to fit out as speedily as possible for the expedition; and without delay ships and men-at-arms were prepared, and the news spread quickly.

40. EIRIK AND HAKON MAKE A WAR LEVY.

When Earl Eirik, the son of Hakon, who at that time was in Raumarike, heard the tidings, he immediately gathered troops, and went to the Uplands, and thence over the mountains to Throndhjem, and joined his father Earl Hakon. Thord Kolbeinson speaks of this in the lay of Eirik:–

"News from the south are flying round;
The bonde comes with look profound,
Bad news of bloody battles bringing,
Of steel-clad men, of weapons ringing.
I hear that in the Danish land
Long-sided ships slide down the strand,
And, floating with the rising tide,
The ocean-coursers soon will ride."

The earls Hakon and Eirik had war-arrows split up and sent round the Throndhjem country; and despatched messages to both the Mores, North More and South More, and to Raumsdal, and also north to Naumudal and Halogaland. They summoned all the country to provide both men and ships. So it is said in Eirik's lay:

"The skald must now a war-song raise,
The gallant active youth must praise,
Who o'er the ocean's field spreads forth
Ships, cutters, boats, from the far north.
His mighty fleet comes sailing by,–
The people run to see them glide,
Mast after mast, by the coast-side."

Earl Hakon set out immediately to the south, to More, to reconnoitre and gather people; and Earl Eirik gathered an army from the north to follow.

41. EXPEDITION OF THE JOMSBORG VIKINGS.

THE JOMSBORG VIKINGS ASSEMBLED their fleet in Limafjord, from whence they went to sea with sixty sail of vessels. When they came under the coast of Agder, they steered northwards to Rogaland with their fleet, and began to plunder when they came into the earl's territory; and so they sailed north along the coast, plundering and burning. A man, by name Geirmund, sailed in a light boat with a few men northwards to More, and there he fell in with Earl Hakon, stood before his dinner table, and told the earl the tidings of an army from Denmark having come to the south end of the land. The earl asked if he had any certainty of it. Then Geirmund stretched forth one arm, from which the hand was cut off, and said, "Here is the token that the enemy is in the land." Then the earl questioned him particularly about this army. Geirmund says it consists of Jomsborg vikings, who have killed many people, and plundered all around. "And hastily and hotly they pushed on," says he "and I expect it will not be long before they are upon you." On this the earl rode into every fjord, going in along the one side of the land and out at the other, collecting men; and thus he drove along night and day. He sent spies out upon the upper ridges, and also southwards into the Fjords; and he proceeded north to meet Eirik with his men. This appears from Eirik's lay:–

"The earl, well skilled in war to speed
O'er the wild wave the viking-steed,
Now launched the high stems from the shore,
Which death to Sigvalde's vikings bore.
Rollers beneath the ships' keels crash,
Oar-blades loud in the grey sea splash,
And they who give the ravens food
Row fearless through the curling flood."

Eirik hastened southwards with his forces the shortest way he could.

42. OF THE JOMSBORG VIKINGS.

Earl Sigvalde steered with his fleet northwards around Stad, and came to the land at the Herey Isles. Although the vikings fell in with the country people, the people never told the truth about what the earl was doing; and the vikings went on pillaging and laying waste. They laid to their vessels at the outer end of Hod Island, landed, plundered, and drove both men and cattle down to the ships, killing all the men able to bear arms.

As they were going back to their ships, came a bonde, walking near to Bue's troop, who said to them, "Ye are not doing like true warriors, to be driving cows and calves down to the strand, while ye should be giving chase to the bear, since ye are coming near to the bear's den."

"What says the old man?" asked some. "Can he tell us anything about Earl Hakon?"

The peasant replies, "The earl went yesterday into the Hjorundarfjord with one or two ships, certainly not more than three, and then he had no news about you."

Bue ran now with his people in all haste down to the ships, leaving all the booty behind. Bue said, "Let us avail ourselves now of this news we have got of the earl, and be the first to the victory." When they came to their ships they rode off from the land. Earl Sigvalde called to them, and asked what they were about. They replied, "The earl is in the fjord;" on which Earl Sigvalde with the whole fleet set off, and rowed north about the island Hod.

43. BATTLE WITH THE JOMSBORG VIKINGS.

THE EARLS HAKON AND Eirik lay in Halkelsvik, where all their forces were assembled. They had 150 ships, and they had heard that the Jomsborg vikings had come in from sea, and lay at the island Hod; and they, in consequence, rowed out to seek them. When they reached a place called Hjorungavag they met each other, and both sides drew up their ships in line for an attack. Earl Sigvalde's banner was displayed in the midst of his army, and right against it Earl Hakon arranged his force for attack. Earl Sigvalde himself had 20 ships, but Earl Hakon had 60. In Earl's army were these chiefs,–Thorer Hjort from Halogaland, and Styrkar from Gimsar. In the wing of the opposite array of the Jomsborg vikings was Bue the Thick, and his brother Sigurd, with 20 ships. Against him Earl Eirik laid himself with 60 ships; and with him were these chiefs,–Gudbrand Hvite from the Uplands, and Thorkel Leira from Viken. In the other wing of the Jomsborg vikings' array was Vagn Akason with 20 ships; and against him stood Svein the son of Hakon, in whose division was Skegge of Yrjar at Uphaug, and Rognvald of Aervik at Stad, with 60 ships. It is told in the Eirik's lay thus:–

"The bonde's ships along the coast
Sailed on to meet the foemen's host;
The stout earl's ships, with eagle flight,
Rushed on the Danes in bloody fight.
The Danish ships, of court-men full,
Were cleared of men,–and many a hull
Was driving empty on the main,
With the warm corpses of the slain."

Eyvind Skaldaspiller says also in the "Haleygja-tal":–

"Twas at the peep of day,–
Our brave earl led the way;
His ocean horses bounding–

His war-horns loudly sounding!
No joyful morn arose
For Yngve Frey's base foes
These Christian island-men
Wished themselves home again."

Then the fleets came together, and one of the sharpest of conflicts began. Many fell on both sides, but the most by far on Hakon's side; for the Jomsborg vikings fought desperately, sharply, and murderously, and shot right through the shields. So many spears were thrown against Earl Hakon that his armour was altogether split asunder, and he threw it off. So says Tind Halkelson:–

"The ring-linked coat of strongest mail
Could not withstand the iron hail,
Though sewed with care and elbow bent,
By Norn[26]*, on its strength intent.*
The fire of battle raged around,–
Odin's steel shirt flew all unbound!
The earl his ring-mail from him flung,
Its steel rings on the wet deck rung;
Part of it fell into the sea,–
A part was kept, a proof to be
How sharp and thick the arrow-flight
Among the sea-steeds in this fight."

44. EARL SIGVALDE'S FLIGHT.

THE JOMSBORG VIKINGS HAD larger and higher-sided ships; and both parties fought desperately. Vagn Akason laid his ship on board of Svein Earl Hakon's son's ship, and Svein allowed his ship to give way, and was on the point of flying. Then Earl Eirik came up, and laid his ship alongside of Vagn, and then Vagn gave way, and the ships came to lie in the same position as before. Thereupon Eirik goes to the other wing, which had gone back a little, and Bue had cut the ropes, intending to pursue them. Then Eirik laid himself, board to board, alongside of Bue's ship,

26 Norn, one of the Fates, stands here for women, whose business it was to sew the rings of iron upon the cloth which made these ring-mail coats or shirts. The needles, although some of them were of gold, appear to have been without eyes, and used like shoemaker's awls.–L.

and there was a severe combat hand to hand. Two or three of Eirik's ships then laid themselves upon Bue's single vessel. A thunder-storm came on at this moment, and such a heavy hail-storm that every hailstone weighed a pennyweight. The Earl Sigvalde cut his cable, turned his ship round, and took flight. Vagn Akason called to him not to fly; but as Earl Sigvalde paid no attention to what he said, Vagn threw his spear at him, and hit the man at the helm. Earl Sigvalde rowed away with 35 ships, leaving 25 of his fleet behind.

45. BUE THROWS HIMSELF OVERBOARD.

THEN EARL HAKON LAID his ship on the other side of Bue's ship, and now came heavy blows on Bue's men. Vigfus, a son of Vigaglum, took up an anvil with a sharp end, which lay upon the deck, and on which a man had welded the hilt to his sword just before, and being a very strong man cast the anvil with both hands at the head of Aslak Holmskalle, and the end of it went into his brains. Before this no weapon could wound this Aslak, who was Bue's foster-brother, and forecastle commander, although he could wound right and left. Another man among the strongest and bravest was Havard Hoggande. In this attack Eirik's men boarded Bue's ship, and went aft to the quarter-deck where Bue stood. There Thorstein Midlang cut at Bue across his nose, so that the nosepiece of his helmet was cut in two, and he got a great wound; but Bue, in turn, cut at Thorstein's side, so that the sword cut the man through. Then Bue lifted up two chests full of gold, and called aloud, "Overboard all Bue s men," and threw himself overboard with his two chests. Many of his people sprang overboard with him. Some fell in the ship, for it was of no use to call for quarter. Bue's ship was cleared of people from stem to stern, and afterwards all the others, the one after the other.

46. VIKINGS BOUND TOGETHER IN ONE CHAIN.

EARL EIRIK THEN LAID himself alongside of Vagn's ship, and there was a brave defence; but at last this ship too was cleared, and Vagn and thirty men were taken prisoners, and bound, and brought to land. Then came up Thorkel Leira, and said, "Thou madest a solemn vow, Vagn, to kill me, but now it seems more likely that I will kill thee." Vagn and his men sat all upon a log of wood together. Thorkel had an axe in his hands, with which he cut at him who sat outmost on the log. Vagn and the other prisoners were bound so that a rope was fastened on their feet, but they had their hands free. One of them said, "I will stick this cloak-pin that I have in my hand into the earth, if it be so that I know anything, after my head is cut off." His head was cut off, but the cloak-pin fell from his hand. There sat also a very handsome man with long hair, who twisted his hair over his head, put out his neck, and said, "Don't make my hair bloody." A man took the hair in his hands and held it fast. Thorkel hewed with his axe; but the viking twitched his head so strongly that he who was holding his hair fell forwards, and the axe cut off both his hands, and stuck fast in the earth. Then Earl Eirik came up, and asked, "Who is that handsome man?"

He replies, "I am called Sigurd, and am Bue's son. But are all the Jomsborg vikings dead?"

Eirik says, "Thou art certainly Boe's son. Wilt thou now take life and peace?"

"That depends," says he, "upon who it is that offers it."

"He offers who has the power to do it–Earl Eirik."

"That will I," says he, "from his hands." And now the rope was loosened from him.

Then said Thorkel Leira, "Although thou should give all these men life and peace, earl, Vagn Akason shall never come from this with life." And he ran at him with uplifted axe; but the viking Skarde swung himself in the rope, and let himself fall just before Thorkel's feet, so that Thorkel .ell over him, and Vagn caught the axe and gave Thorkel a death-wound. Then said the earl, "Vagn, wilt thou accept life?"

"That I will," says he, "if you give it to all of us."

"Loose them from the rope," said the earl, and it was done. Eighteen were killed, and twelve got their lives.

47. DEATH OF GISSUR OF VALDERS.

Earl Hakon, and many with him, were sitting upon a piece of wood, and a bow-string twanged from Bue's ship, and the arrow struck Gissur from Valders, who was sitting next the earl, and was clothed splendidly. Thereupon the people went on board, and found Havard Hoggande standing on his knees at the ship's railing, for his feet had been cut off[27],

27 This traditionary tale of a warrior fighting on his knees after his legs were cut off, appears to have been a popular idea among the Northmen, and is

and he had a bow in his hand. When they came on board the ship Havard asked, "Who fell by that shaft?"

They answered, "A man called Gissur."

"Then my luck was less than I thought," said he.

"Great enough was the misfortune," replied they; "but thou shalt not make it greater." And they killed him on the spot.

The dead were then ransacked, and the booty brought all together to be divided; and there were twenty-five ships of the Jomsborg vikings in the booty. So says Tind:

"Many a viking's body lay
Dead on the deck this bloody day,
Before they cut their sun-dried ropes,
And in quick flight put all their hopes.
He whom the ravens know afar
Cleared five-and-twenty ships of war:
A proof that in the furious fight
None can withstand the Norsemen's might."

Then the army dispersed. Earl Hakon went to Throndhjem, and was much displeased that Earl Eirik had given quarter to Vagn Akason. It was said that at this battle Earl Hakon had sacrificed for victory his son, young Erling, to the gods; and instantly came the hailstorm, and the defeat and slaughter of the Jomsborg vikings.

Earl Eirik went to the Uplands, and eastward by that route to his own kingdom, taking Vagn Akason with him. Earl Eirik married Vagn to Ingebjorg, a daughter of Thorkel Leira, and gave him a good ship of war and all belonging to it, and a crew; and they parted the best of friends. Then Vagn went home south to Denmark, and became afterwards a man of great consideration, and many great people are descended from him.

48. KING HARALD GRENSKE'S DEATH.

Harald Grenske, as before related, was king in Vestfold, and was married to Asta, a daughter of Gudbrand Kula. One summer (A.D. 994) Harald Grenske made an expedition to the Baltic to gather property, and he came to Svithjod. Olaf the Swede was king there, a son of Eirik

related by their descendants in the ballad o. Chevy Chase.–L.

the Victorious, and Sigrid, a daughter of Skoglartoste. Sigrid was then a widow, and had many and great estates in Svithjod. When she heard that her foster-brother was come to the country a short distance from her, she sent men to him to invite him to a feast. He did not neglect the invitation, but came to her with a great attendance of his followers, and was received in the most friendly way. He and the queen sat in the high-seat, and drank together towards the evening, and all his men were entertained in the most hospitable manner. At night, when the king went to rest, a bed was put up for him with a hanging of fine linen around it, and with costly bedclothes; but in the lodging-house there were few men. When the king was undressed, and had gone to bed, the queen came to him, filled a bowl herself for him to drink, and was very gay, and pressed to drink. The king was drunk above measure, and, indeed, so were they both. Then he slept, and the queen went away, and laid herself down also. Sigrid was a woman of the greatest understanding, and clever in many things. In the morning there was also the most excellent entertainment; but then it went on as usual when people have drunk too much, that next day they take care not to exceed. The queen was very gay, and she and the king talked of many things with each other; among other things she valued her property, and the dominions she had in Svithjod, as nothing less than his property in Norway. With that observation the king was nowise pleased, and he found no pleasure in anything after that, but made himself ready for his journey in an ill humor. On the other hand, the queen was remarkably gay, and made him many presents, and followed him out to the road. Now Harald returned about harvest to Norway, and was at home all winter; but was very silent and cast down. In summer he went once more to the Baltic with his ships, and steered to Svithjod. He sent a message to Queen Sigrid that he wished to have a meeting with her and she rode down to meet him. They talked together and he soon brought out the proposal that she should marry him. She replied, that this was foolish talk for him, who was so well married already that he might think himself well off. Harald says, "Asta is a good and clever woman; but she is not so well born as I am." Sigrid replies, "It may be that thou art of higher birth, but I think she is now pregnant with both your fortunes." They exchanged but few words more before the queen rode away. King Harald was now depressed in mind, and prepared himself again to ride up the country to meet Queen Sigrid. Many of his people dissuaded him; but nevertheless he set off with a great attendance, and came to the house in which the queen dwelt. The same evening came another king, called Vissavald, from Gardarike (Russia), likewise to pay his addresses to Queen Sigrid. Lodging was given to both the kings, and to all their people, in a great old room of an out-building, and all the furniture was of the same character; but there was no want of drink in the evening, and that so strong that all were drunk, and the watch, both inside and outside, fell fast asleep. Then Queen Sigrid ordered an attack on them in the night, both with fire and sword. The house was burnt, with all who were in it and those who slipped out were put to the sword. Sigrid said that she would make these small kings tired of coming to court her. She was afterwards called Sigrid the Haughty (Storrada).

49. BIRTH OF OLAF, SON OF HARALD GRENSKE.

THIS HAPPENED THE WINTER after the battle of the Jomsborg vikings at Hjorungavag. When Harald went up the country after Sigrid, he left Hrane behind with the ships to look after the men. Now when Hrane heard that Harald was cut off, he returned to Norway the shortest way he could, and told the news. He repaired first to Asta, and related to her all that had happened on the journey, and also on what errand Harald had visited Queen Sigrid. When Asta got these tidings she set off directly to her father in the Uplands, who received her well; but both were enraged at the design which had been laid in Svithjod, and that King Harald had intended to set her in a single condition. In summer (A.D. 995) Asta, Gudbrand's daughter, was confined, and had a boy child, who had water poured over him, and was called Olaf. Hrane himself poured water over him, and the child was brought up at first in the house of Gudbrand and his mother Asta.

50. ABOUT EARL HAKON.

EARL HAKON RULED OVER the whole outer part of Norway that lies on the sea, and had thus sixteen districts under his sway. The arrangement introduced by Harald Harfager, that there should be an earl in each district, was afterward continued for a long time; and thus Earl Hakon had sixteen earls under him. So says the "Vellekla":–

"Who before has ever known
Sixteen earls subdued by one?

Who has seen all Norway's land
Conquered by one brave hero's hand?
It will be long in memory held,
How Hakon ruled by sword and shield.
When tales at the viking's mast go round,
His praise will every mouth resound."

While Earl Hakon ruled over Norway there were good crops in the land, and peace was well preserved in the country among the bondes. The Earl, for the greater part of his lifetime, was therefore much beloved by the bondes; but it happened, in the longer course of time, that the earl became very intemperate in his intercourse with women, and even carried it so far that he made the daughters of people of consideration be carried away and brought home to him; and after keeping them a week or two as concubines, he sent them home. He drew upon himself the indignation of me relations of these girls; and the bondes began to murmur loudly, as the Throndhjem people have the custom of doing when anything goes against their judgment.

51. THORER KLAKKA'S JOURNEY.

Earl Hakon, in the mean time, hears some whisper that to the westward, over the Nor.h sea, was a man called Ole, who was looked upon as a king. From the conversation of some people, he fell upon the suspicion that he must be of the royal race of Norway. It was, indeed, said that this Ole was from Russia; but the earl had heard that Trygve Olafson had had a son called Olaf, who in his infancy had gone east to Gardarike, and had been brought up by King Valdemar. The earl had carefully inquired about this man, and had his suspicion that he must be the same person who had now come to these western countries. The earl had a very good friend called Thorer Klakka, who had been long upon viking expeditions, sometimes also upon merchant voyages; so that he was well acquainted all around. This Thorer Earl Hakon sends over the North sea, and told him to make a merchant voyage to Dublin, many were in the habit of doing, and carefully to discover who this Ole was. Provided he got any certainty that he was Olaf Trygvason, or any other of the Norwegian royal race, then Thorer should endeavor to ensnare him by some deceit, and bring him into the earl's power.

52. OLAF TRYGVASON COMES TO NORWAY.

On this Thorer sails westward to Ireland, and hears that Ole is in Dublin with his wife's father King Olaf Kvaran. Thorer, who was a plausible man, immediately got acquainted with Ole; and as they often met, and had long conversations together, Ole began to inquire about news from Norway, and above all of the Upland kings and great people,– which of them were in life, and what dominations they now had. He asked also about Earl Hakon, and if he was much liked in the country. Thorer replies, that the earl is such a powerful man that no one dares to speak otherwise than he would like; but that comes from there being nobody else in the country to look to. "Yet, to say the truth, I know it to be the mind of many brave men, and of whole communities, that they would much rather see a king of Harald Harfager's race come to the kingdom. But we know of no one suited for this, especially now that it is proved how vain every attack on Earl Hakon must be." As they often talked together in the same strain, Olaf disclosed to Thorer his name and family, and asked him his opinion, and whether he thought the bondes would take him for their king if he were to appear in Norway. Thorer encouraged him very eagerly to the enterprise, and praised him and his talents highly. Then Olaf's inclination to go to the heritage of his ancestors became strong. Olaf sailed accordingly, accompanied by Thorer, with five ships; first to the Hebrides, and from thence to the Orkneys. At that time Earl Sigurd, Hlodver's son, lay in Osmundswall, in the island South Ronaldsa, with a ship of war, on his way to Caithness. Just at the same time Olaf was sailing with his fleet from the westward to the islands, and ran into the same harbour, because Pentland Firth was not to be passed at that tide. When the king was informed that the earl was there, he made him be called; and when the earl came on board to speak with the king, after a few words only had passed between them, the king says the earl must allow himself to be baptized, and all the people of the country also, or he should be put to death directly; and he assured the earl he would lay waste the islands with fire and sword, if the people did not adopt Christianity. In the position the earl found himself, he preferred becoming Christian, and he and all who were with him were baptized. Afterwards the earl took an oath to the king, went into his service, and gave him his son, whose name was Hvelp (Whelp), or Hunde (Dog), as an hostage; and the king took Hvelp to Norway with him. Thereafter Olaf went out to sea to the eastward, and made the land at Morster Island, where he first touched the ground of Norway. He had high mass sung in a tent, and afterwards on the spot a church was built. Thorer Klakka said now to the king, that the best plan for him would be not to make it known who he was, or to let any report about him get abroad; but to seek out Earl Hakon as fast as possible and fall upon him by surprise. King Olaf did so, sailing northward day and night, when wind permitted, and did not let the people of the country know who it was that was sailing in such haste. When he came north to Agdanes, he heard that the earl was in the fjord, and was in discord with the bondes. On hearing this, Thorer saw that things were going in a very different way from what he expected; for after the battle with the Jomsborg vikings all men in Norway were the most sincere friends of the earl on account of the victory he had gained, and of the peace and security he had given to the country; and now it unfortunately turns out that a great chief has come to the country at a time when the bondes are in arms against the earl.

53. EARL HAKON'S FLIGHT.

Earl Hakon was at a feast in Medalhus in Gaulardal and his ships lay out by Viggja. There was a powerful bonde, by name Orm Lyrgja, who dwelt in Bunes, who had a wife called Gudrun, a daughter of Bergthor of Lundar. She was called the Lundasol; for she was the most-beautiful of women. The earl sent his slaves to Orm, with the errand that they should bring Orm's wife, Gudrun, to the earl. The thralls tell their errand, and Orm bids them first seat themselves to supper; but before they had done eating, many people from the neighbourhood, to whom Orm had sent notice, had gathered together: and now Orm declared he would not send Gudrun with the messengers. Gudrun told the thralls to tell the earl that she would not come to him, unless he sent Thora of Rimul after her. Thora was a woman of great influence, and one of the earl's best beloved. The thralls say that they will come another time, and both the bonde and his wife would be made to repent of it; and they departed with many threats. Orm, on the other hand, sent out a message-token to all the neighbouring country, and with it the message to attack Earl Hakon with weapons and kill him. He sent also a message to Haldor in Skerdingsstedja, who also sent out his message-token. A short time before, the earl had taken away the wife of a man called Brynjolf, and there had very nearly been an insurrection about that business. Having now again got this message-token, the people made a general revolt, and set out all to Medalhus. When the earl heard of this, he left the house with his followers, and concealed himself in a deep glen, now called Jarlsdal (Earl's Dale). Later in the day, the earl got news of the bondes' army. They had beset all the roads; but believed the earl had escaped to his ships, which his son Erlend, a remarkably handsome and hopeful young man, had the command of. When night came the earl dispersed his people, and ordered them to go through the forest roads into Orkadal; "for nobody will molest you," said he, "when I am not with you. Send a message to Erlend to sail out of the fjord, and meet me in More. In the mean time I will conceal myself from the bondes." Then the earl went his way with one thrall or slave, called Kark, attending him. There was ice upon the Gaul (the river of Gaulardal), and the earl drove his horse upon it, and left his coat lying upon the ice. They then went to a hole, since called Jarlshella (the Earl's Hole), where they slept. When Kark awoke he told his dream,–that a black threatening mad had come into the hole, and was angry that people should have entered it; and that the man had said, "Ulle is dead." The earl said that his son Erlend must be killed. Kark slept again and was again disturbed in his sleep; and when he awoke he told his dream,–that the same man had again appeared to him, and bade him tell the earl that all the sounds were closed. From this dream the earl began to suspect that it betokened a short life to him. They stood up, and went to the house of Rimul. The earl now sends Kark to Thora, and begs of her to come secretly to him. She did so and received the earl kindly and he begged her to conceal him for a few nights until the army of the bondes had dispersed. "Here about my house," said she, "you will be hunted after, both inside and outside; for many know that I would willingly help you if I can. There is but one place about the house where they could never expect to find such a man as you, and that is the swine-stye." When they came there the earl said, "Well, let it be made ready for us; as to save our life is the first and foremost concern." The slave dug a great hole in it, bore away the earth that he dug out, and laid wood over it. Thora brought the tidings to the earl that Olaf Trygvason had come from sea into the fjord, and had killed his son Erlend. Then the earl and Kark both went into the hole. Thora covered it with wood, and threw earth and dung over it, and drove the swine upon the top of it. The swine-style was under a great stone.

54. ERLEND'S DEATH.

Olaf Trygvason came from sea into the fjord with five long-ships, and Erlend, Hakon's son, rowed towards him with three ships. When the vessels came near to each other, Erlend suspected they might be enemies, and turned towards the land. When Olaf and his followers saw long-ships coming in haste out of the fjord, and rowing towards them, they thought Earl Hakon must be here; and they put out all oars to follow them. As soon as Erlend and his ships got near the land they rowed aground instantly, jumped overboard, and took to the land; but at the same instant Olaf's ship came up with them. Olaf saw a remarkably handsome man swimming in the water, and laid hold of a tiller and threw it at him. The tiller struck Erlend, the son of Hakon the earl, on the head, and clove it to the brain; and there left Erlend his life. Olaf and his people killed many; but some escaped, and some were made prisoners, and got life and freedom that they might go and tell what had happened. They learned then that the bondes had driven away Earl Hakon, and that he had fled, and his troops were all dispersed.

55. EARL HAKON'S DEATH.

The bondes then met Olaf, to the joy of both, and they made an agreement together. The bondes took Olaf to be their king, and resolved, one and all, to seek out Earl Hakon. They went up Gaulardal; for it seemed to them likely that if the earl was concealed in any house it must be at Rimul, for Thora was his dearest friend in that valley. They come up, therefore, and search everywhere, outside and inside the house, but could not find him. Then Olaf held a House Thing (trusting), or council out in the yard, and stood upon a great stone which lay beside the swine-stye, and made a speech to the people, in which he promised to enrich the man with rewards and honours who should kill the earl. This speech was heard by the earl and the thrall Kark. They had a light in their room.

"Why art thou so pale," says the earl, "and now again black as earth? Thou hast not the intention to betray me?"

"By no means," replies Kark.

"We were born on the same night," says the earl, "and the time will be short between our deaths."

King Olaf went away in the evening. When night came the earl kept himself awake but Kark slept, and was disturbed in his sleep. The earl woke him, and asked him "what he was dreaming of?"

He answered, "I was at Hlader and Olaf Trygvason was laying a gold ring about my neck."

The earl says, "It will be a red ring Olaf will lay about thy neck if he catches thee. Take care of that! From me thou shalt enjoy all that is good, therefore betray me not."

They then kept themselves awake both; the one, as it were, watching upon the other. But towards day the earl suddenly dropped asleep; but his sleep was so unquiet that he drew his heels under him, and raised his neck, as if going to rise, and screamed dreadfully high. On this Kark, dreadfully alarmed, drew a large knife out of his belt, stuck it in the earl's throat, and cut it across, and killed Earl Hakon. Then Kark cut off the earl's head, and ran away. Late in the day he came to Hlader, where he delivered the earl's head to King Olaf, and told all these circumstances of his own and Earl Hakon's doings. Olaf had him taken out and beheaded.

56. EARL HAKON'S HEAD.

King Olaf, and a vast number of bondes with him, then went out to Nidarholm, and had with him the heads of Earl Hakon and Kark. This holm was used then for a place of execution of thieves and ill-doers, and there stood a gallows on it. He had the heads of the earl and of Kark hung upon it, and the whole army of the bondes cast stones at them, screaming and shouting that the one worthless fellow had followed the other. They then sent up to Gaulardal for the earl's dead body. So great was the enmity of the Throndhjem people against Earl Hakon, that no man could venture to call him by any other name than Hakon the Bad; and he was so called long after those days. Yet, sooth to say of Earl Hakon, he was in many respects fitted to be a chief: first, because he was descended from a high race; then because he had understanding and knowledge to direct a government; also manly courage in battle to gain victories, and good luck in killing his enemies. So says Thorleif Raudfeldson:–

"In Norway's land was never known
A braver earl than the brave Hakon.
At sea, beneath the clear moon's light,
No braver man e'er sought to fight.
Nine kings to Odin's wide domain
Were sent, by Hakon's right hand slain!
So well the raven-flocks were fed–
So well the wolves were filled with dead!"

Earl Hakon was very generous; but the greatest misfortunes attended even such a chief at the end of his days: and the great cause of this was that the time was come when heathen sacrifices and idolatrous worship were doomed to fall, and the holy faith and good customs to come in their place.

57. OLAF TRYGVASON ELECTED KING.

Olaf Trvgvason was chosen at Throndhjem by the General Thing to be the king over the whole country, as Harald Harfager had been. The whole public and the people throughout all the land would listen to nothing else than that Olaf Trygvason should be king. Then Olaf went round the whole country, and brought it under his rule, and all the people of Norway gave in their submission; and also the chiefs in the Uplands and in Viken, who before had held their lands as fiefs from the Danish king, now became King Olaf's men, and held their hands from him. He went thus through the whole country during the first winter (A.D. 996) and the following summer. Earl Eirik, the son of Earl Hakon, his brother Svein, and their friends and relations, fled out of the country, and went east to Sweden to King Olaf the Swede, who gave them a good reception. So says Thord Kolbeinson:–

"O thou whom bad men drove away,
After the bondes by foul play,
Took Hakon's life! Fate will pursue
These bloody wolves, and make them rue.
When the host came from out the West,
Like some tall stately war-ship's mast,
I saw the son of Trygve stand,
Surveying proud his native land."

And again,–

"Eirik has more upon his mind,
Against the new Norse king designed,
Than by his words he seems to show–
And truly it may well be so.
Stubborn and stiff are Throndhjem men,
But Throndhjem's earl may come again;
In Swedish land he knows no rest–
Fierce wrath is gathering in his breast."

58. LODIN'S MARRIAGE

LODIN WAS THE NAME of a man from Viken who was rich and of good family. He went often on merchant voyages, and sometimes on viking cruises. It happened one summer that he went on a merchant voyage with much merchandise in a ship of his own. He directed his course first to Eistland, and was there at a market in summer. To the place at which the market was held many merchant goods were brought, and also many thralls or slaves for sale. There Lodin saw a woman who was to be sold as a slave: and on looking at her he knew her to be Astrid Eirik's daughter, who had been married to King Trygve. But now she was altogether unlike what she had been when he last saw her; for now she was pale, meagre in countenance, and ill clad. He went up to her, and asked her how matters stood with her. She replied, "It is heavy to be told; for I have been sold as a slave, and now again I am brought here for sale." After speaking together a little Astrid knew him, and begged him to buy her; and bring her home to her friends. "On this condition," said he, "I will bring thee home tn Norway, that thou wilt marry me." Now as Astrid stood in great need, and moreover knew that Lodin was a man of high birth, rich, and brave, she promised to do so for her ransom. Lodin accordingly bought Astrid, took her home to Norway with him, and married her with her friends' consent. Their children were Thorkel Nefia, Ingerid, and Ingegerd. Ingebjorg and Astrid were daughters of Astrid by King Trygve. Eirik Bjodaskalle's sons were Sigird, Karlshofud, Jostein, and Thorkel Dydril, who were all rich and brave people who had estates east in the country. In Viken in the east dwelt two brothers, rich and of good descent; one called Thorgeir, and the other Hyrning; and they married Lodin and Astrid's daughters, Ingerid and Ingegerd.

59. OLAF BAPTIZES THE COUNTRY OF VIKEN.

WHEN HARALD GORMSON, king of Denmark, had adopted Christianity, he sent a message over all his kingdom that all people should be baptized, and converted to the true faith. He himself followed his message, and used power and violence where nothing else would do. He sent two earls, Urguthrjot and Brimilskjar, with many people to Norway, to proclaim Christianity there. In Viken, which stood directly under the king's power, this succeeded, and many were baptized of the country folk. But when Svein Forked-beard, immediately after his father King

Harald's death, went out on war expeditions in Saxland, Frisland, and at last in England, the Northmen who had taken up Christianity returned back to heathen sacrifices, just as before; and the people in the north of the country did the same. But now that Olaf Trygvason was king of Norway, he remained long during the summer (A.D. 996) in Viken, where many of his relatives and some of his brothers-in-law were settled, and also many who had been great friends of his father; so that he was received with the greatest affection. Olaf called together his mother's brothers, his stepfather Lodin, and his brothers-in-law Thorgeir and Hyrning, to speak with them, and to disclose with the greatest care the business which he desired they themselves should approve of, and support with all their power; namely, the proclaiming Christianity over all his kingdom. He would, he declared, either bring it to this, that all Norway should be Christian, or die. "I shall make you all," said he, "great and mighty men in promoting this work; for I trust to you most, as blood relations or brothers-in-law." All agreed to do what he asked, and to follow him in what he desired. King Olaf immediately made it known to the public that he recommended Christianity to all the people in his kingdom, which message was well received and approved of by those who had before given him their promise; and these being the most powerful among the people assembled, the others followed their example, and all the inhabitants of the east part of Viken allowed themselves to be baptized. The king then went to the north part of Viken and invited every man to accept Christianity; and those who opposed him he punished severely, killing some, mutilating others, and driving some into banishment. At length he brought it so far, that all the kingdom which his father King Trvgve had ruled over, and also that of his relation Harald Grenske, accepted of Christianity; and during that summer (A.D. 996) and the following winter (A.D. 997) all Viken was made Christian.

60. OF THE HORDALAND PEOPLE.

Early in spring (A.D. 997) King Olaf set out from Viken with a great force northwards to Agder, and proclaimed that every man should be baptized. And thus the people received Christianity, for nobody dared oppose the king's will, wheresoever he came. In Hordaland, however, were many bold and great men of Hordakare's race. He, namely, had left four sons,–the first Thorleif Spake; the second, Ogmund, father of Thorolf Skialg, who was father of Erling of Sole; the third was Thord father of the Herse Klyp who killed King Sigurd Slefa, Gunhild's son; and lastly, Olmod, father of Askel, whose son was Aslak Fitjaskalle; and that family branch was the greatest and most considered in Hordaland. Now when this family heard the bad tidings, that the king was coming along the country from the eastward with a great force, and was breaking the ancient law of the people, and imposing punishment and hard conditions on all who opposed him, the relatives appointed a meeting to take counsel with each other, for they knew the king would come down upon them at once: and they all resolved to appear in force at the Gula-Thing, there to hold a conference with King Olaf Trygvason.

61. ROGALAND BAPTIZED.

When King Olaf came to Rogaland, he immediately summoned the people to a Thing; and when the bondes received the message-token for a Thing, they assembled in great numbers well armed. After they had come together, they resolved to choose three men, the best speakers of the whole, who should answer King Olaf, and argue with the king; and especially should decline to accept of anything against the old law, even if the king should require it of them. Now when the bondes came to the Thing, and the Thing was formed, King Olaf arose, and at first spoke good-humoredly to the people; but they observed he wanted them to accept Christianity, with all his fine words: and in the conclusion he let them know that those who should speak against him, and not submit to his proposal, must expect his displeasure and punishment, and all the ill that it was in his power to inflict. When he had ended his speech, one of the bondes stood up, who was considered the most eloquent, and who had been chosen as the first who should reply to King Olaf. But when he would begin to speak such a cough seized him, and such a difficulty of breathing, that he could not bring out a word, and had to sit down again. Then another bonde stood up, resolved not to let an answer be wanting, although it had gone so ill with the former: but he stammered so that he could not get a word uttered, and all present set up a laughter, amid which the bonde sat down again. And now the third stood up to make a speech against King Olaf's; but when he began he became so hoarse and husky in his throat, that nobody could hear a word he said, and he also had to sit down. There was none of the bondes now to speak against the king, and as nobody answered him there was no opposition; and it came to this, that all agreed to what the king had proposed. All the people of the Thing accordingly were baptized before the Thing was dissolved.

62. ERLING SKJALGSON'S WOOING.

King Olaf went with his men-at-arms to the Gula-Thing; for the bondes had sent him word that they would reply there to his speech. When both parties had come to the Thing, the king desired first to have a conference with the chief people of the country; and when the meeting was numerous the king set forth his errand,–that he desired them, according to his proposal, to allow themselves to be baptized. Then said Olmod the Old, "We relations have considered together this matter, and have come to one resolution. If thou thinkest, king, to force us who are related together to such things as to break our old law, or to bring us under thyself by any sort of violence, then will we stand against thee with all our might: and be the victory to him to whom fate ordains it. But if thou, king, wilt advance our relations' fortunes, then thou shalt have leave to do as thou desirest, and we will all serve thee with zeal in thy purpose."

The king replies, "What do you propose for obtaining this agreement?"

Then answers Olmod, "The first is, that thou wilt give thy sister Astrid in marriage to Erling Skjalgson, our relation, whom we look upon as the most hopeful young man in all Norway."

King Olaf replied, that this marriage appeared to him also very suitable; "as Erling is a man of good birth, and a good-looking man in appearance: but Astrid herself must answer to this proposal."

Thereupon the king spoke to his sister. She said, "It is but of little use that I am a king's sister, and a king's daughter, if I must marry a man who has no high dignity or office. I will rather wait a few years for a better match." Thus ended this conference.

63. HORDALAND BAPTIZED.

King Olaf took a falcon that belonged to Astrid, plucked off all its feathers, and then sent it to her. Then said Astrid, "Angry is my brother." And she stood up, and went to the king, who received her kindly, and she said that she left it to the king to determine her marriage. "I think," said the king, "that I must have power enough in this land to raise any man I please to high dignity." Then the king ordered Olmod and Erling to be called to a conference, and all their relations; and the marriage was determined upon, and Astrid betrothed to Erling. Thereafter the king held the Thing, and recommended Christianity to the bondes; and as Olmod, and Erling, and all their relations, took upon themselves the most active part in forwarding the king's desire, nobody dared to speak against it; and all the people were baptized, and adopted Christianity.

64. ERLING SKJALGSON'S WEDDING.

Erling Skjalgson had his wedding in summer, and a great many people were assembled at it. King Olaf was also there, and offered Erling an earldom. Erling replied thus: "All my relations have been herses only, and I will take no higher title than they have; but this I will accept from thee, king, that thou makest me the greatest of that title in the country." The king consented; and at his departure the king invested his brother-in law Erling with all the land north of the Sognefjord, and east to the Lidandisnes, on the same terms as Harald Harfager had given land to his sons, as before related.

65. RAUMSDAL AND FJORD-DISTRICTS BAPTIZED.

The same harvest King Olaf summoned the bondes to a Thing of the four districts at Dragseid, in Stad: and there the people from Sogn, the Fjord-districts, South More, and Raumsdal, were summoned to meet. King Olaf came there with a great many people who had followed him from the eastward, and also with those who had joined him from Rogaland and Hordaland. When the king came to the Thing, he proposed to them there, as elsewhere, Christianity; and as the king had such a powerful host with him, they were frightened. The king offered them two conditions,–either to accept Christianity, or to fight. But the bondes saw they were in no condition to fight the king, and resolved, therefore, that all the people should agree to be baptized. The king proceeded afterwards to North More, and baptized all that district. He then sailed to Hlader, in Throndhjem; had the temple there razed to the ground; took all the ornaments and all property out of the temple, and from the gods in it; and among other things the great gold ring which Earl Hakon had ordered to be made, and which hung in the door of the temple; and then had the temple burnt. But when the bondes heard of this, they sent out a war-arrow as a token through the whole district, ordering out a warlike force, and intended to meet the king with it. In the meantime King Olaf sailed with a war force out of the fjord along the coast northward, intending to proceed to Halogaland, and baptize there. When he came north to Bjarnaurar, he heard from Halogaland that a force was assembled there to defend the country against the king. The chiefs of this force were Harek of Thjotta, Thorer Hjort from Vagar, and Eyvind Kinrifa. Now when King Olaf heard this, he turned about and sailed southwards along the land; and when he got south of Stad proceeded at his leisure, and came early in winter (A.D. 998) all the way east to Viken.

66. OLAF PROPOSES MARRIAGE TO QUEEN SIGRID.

Queen Sigrid in Svithjod, who had for surname the Haughty, sat in her mansion, and during the same winter messengers went between King Olaf and Sigrid to propose his courtship to her, and she had no objection; and the matter was fully and fast resolved upon. Thereupon King Olaf sent to Queen Sigrid the great gold ring he had taken from the temple door of Hlader, which was considered a distinguished ornament. The meeting for concluding the business was appointed to be in spring on the frontier, at the Gaut river. Now the ring which King Olaf had sent Queen Sigrid was highly prized by all men; yet the queen's gold-smiths, two brothers, who took the ring in their hands, and weighed it, spoke quietly to each other about it, and in a manner that made the queen call them to her, and ask "what they smiled at?" But they would not say a word, and she commanded them to say what it was they had discovered. Then they said the ring is false. Upon this she ordered the ring to be broken into pieces, and it was found to be copper inside. Then the queen was enraged, and said that Olaf would deceive her in more ways than this one. In the same year (A.D. 998) King Olaf went into Ringenke, and there the people also were baptized.

67. OLAF HARALDSON BAPTIZED.

Asta, the daughter of Gudbrand, soon after the fall of Harald Grenske married again a man who was called Sigurd Syr, who was a king in Ringerike. Sigurd was a son of Halfdan, and grandson of Sigurd Hrise, who was a son of Harald Harfager. Olaf, the son of Asta and Harald Grenske, lived with Asta, and was brought up from childhood in the house of his stepfather, Sigurd Syr. Now when King Olaf Trygvason came to Ringerike to spread Christianity, Sigurd Syr and his wife allowed themselves to be baptized, along with Olaf her son; and Olaf Trygvason was godfather to Olaf, the stepson of Harald Grenske. Olaf was then three years old. Olaf returned from thence to Viken, where he remained all winter. He had now been three years king in Norway (A.D. 998).

68. MEETING OF OLAF AND SIGRID.

Early in spring (A.D. 998) King Olaf went eastwards to Konungahella to the meeting with Queen Sigrid; and when they met the business was considered about which the winter before they had held communication, namely, their marriage; and the business seemed likely to be concluded. But when Olaf insisted that Sigrid should let herself be baptized, she answered thus:–"I must not part from the faith which I have held, and my forefathers before me; and, on the other hand, I shall make no objection to your believing in the god that pleases you best." Then King Olaf was enraged, and answered in a passion, "Why should I care to have thee, an old faded woman, and a heathen jade?" and therewith struck her in the face with his glove which he held in his hands, rose up, and they parted. Sigrid said, "This may some day be thy death." The king set off to Viken, the queen to Svithjod.

69. THE BURNING OF WARLOCKS.

Then the king proceeded to Tunsberg, and held a Thing, at which he declared in a speech that all the men of whom it should be known to a certainty that they dealt with evil spirits, or in witchcraft, or were sorcerers, should be banished forth of the land. Thereafter the king had all the neighborhood ransacked after such people, and called them all before him; and when they were brought to the Thing there was a man among them called Eyvind Kelda, a grandson of Ragnvald Rettilbeine, Harald Harfager's son. Eyvind was a sorcerer, and particularly knowing in witchcraft. The king let all these men be seated in one room, which was well adorned, and made a great feast for them, and gave them strong drink in plenty. Now when they were all very drunk, he ordered the house be set on fire, and it and all the people within it were consumed, all but Eyvind Kelda, who contrived to escape by the smoke-hole in the roof. And when he had got a long way off, he met some people on the road going to the king, and he told them to tell the king that Eyvind Kelda had slipped away from the fire, and would never come again in King Olaf's power, but would carry on his arts of witchcraft as much as ever. When the people came to the king with such a message from Eyvind, the king was ill pleased that Eyvind had escaped death.

70. EYVIND KELDA'S DEATH.

When spring (A.D. 998) came King Olaf went out to Viken, and was on visits to his great farms. He sent notice over all Viken that he would call out an army in summer, and proceed to the north parts of the country. Then he went north to Agder; and when Easter was approaching he took the road to Rogaland with 300 (=360) men, and came on Easter evening north to Ogvaldsnes, in Kormt Island, where an Easter feast was prepared for him. That same night came Eyvind Kelda to the island with a well-manned long-ship, of which the whole crew consisted of sorcerers and other dealers with evil spirits. Eyvind went from his ship to the land with his followers, and there they played many of their pranks of witchcraft. Eyvind clothed them with caps of darkness, and so thick a mist that the king and his men could see nothing of them; but when they came near to the house at Ogvaldsnes, it became clear day. Then it went differently from what Eyvind had intended: for now there came just such a darkness over him and his comrades in witchcraft as they had made before, so that they could see no more from their eyes than from the back of their heads but went round and round in a circle upon the island. When the king's watchman saw them going about, without knowing what people these were, they told the king. Thereupon he rose up with his people, put on his clothes, and when he saw Eyvind with his men wandering about he ordered his men to arm, and examine what folk these were. The king's men discovered it was Eyvind, took him and all his company prisoners, and brought them to the king. Eyvind now told all he had done on his journey. Then the king ordered these all to be taken out to a skerry which was under water in flood tide, and there to be left bound. Eyvind and all with him left their lives on this rock, and the skerry is still called Skrattasker.

71. OLAF AND ODIN'S APPARITION.

It is related that once on a time King Olaf was at a feast at this Ogvaldsnes, and one eventide there came to him an old man very gifted in words, and with a broad-brimmed hat upon his head. He was one-eyed, and had something to tell of every land. He entered into conversation with the king; and as the king found much pleasure in the guest's speech, he asked him concerning many things, to which the guest gave good answers: and the king sat up late in the evening. Among other things, the king asked him if he knew who the Ogvald had been who had given his name both to the ness and to the house. The guest replied, that this Ogvald was a king, and a very valiant man, and that he made great sacrifices to a cow which he had with him wherever he went, and considered it good for his health to drink her milk. This same King Ogvald had a battle with a king called Varin, in which battle Ogvald fell. He was buried under a mound close to the house; "and there stands his stone over him, and close to it his cow also is laid." Such and many other things, and ancient events, the king inquired after. Now, when the king had sat late into the night, the bishop reminded him that it was time to go to bed, and the king did so. But after the king was undressed, and had laid himself in bed, the guest sat upon the foot-stool before the bed, and still spoke long with the king; for after one tale was ended, he still wanted a new one. Then the bishop observed to the king, it was time to go to sleep, and the king did so; and the guest went out. Soon after the king awoke, asked for the guest, and ordered him to be called, but the guest was not to be found. The morning after, the king ordered his cook and cellar-master to be called, and asked if any strange person had been with them. They said, that as they were making ready the meat a man came to them, and observed that they were cooking very poor meat for the king's table; whereupon he gave them two thick and fat pieces of beef, which they boiled with the rest of the meat. Then the king ordered that all the meat should be thrown away, and said this man can be no other than the Odin whom the heathens have so long worshipped; and added, "but Odin shall not deceive us."

72. THE THING IN THRONDHJEM.

King Olaf collected a great army in the east of the country towards summer, and sailed with it north to Nidaros in the Throndhjem country. From thence he sent a message-token over all the fjord, calling the people of eight different districts to a Thing; but the bondes changed the Thing-token into a war-token; and called together all men, free and unfree, in all the Throndhjem land. Now when the king met the Thing, the whole people came fully armed. After the Thing was seated, the king spoke, and invited them to adopt Christianity; but he had only spoken a short time when the bondes called out to him to be silent, or they would attack him and drive him away. "We did so," said they, "with Hakon foster-son of Athelstan, when he brought us the same message, and we held him in quite as much respect as we hold thee." When King Olaf saw how incensed the bondes were, and that they had such a war force that he could make no resistance, he turned his speech as if he would give way to the bondes, and said, "I wish only to be in a good understanding with you as of old; and I will come to where ye hold your greatest sacrifice-festival, and see your customs, and thereafter we shall consider which to hold by." And in this all agreed; and as the king spoke mildly and friendly with the bondes, their answer was appeased, and their conference with the king went off peacefully. At the close of it a midsummer sacrifice was fixed to take place in Maeren, and all chiefs and great bondes to attend it as usual. The king was to be at it.

73. JARNSKEGGE OR IRON BEARD.

There was a great bonde called Skegge, and sometimes Jarnskegge, or Iron Beard, who dwelt in Uphaug in Yrjar. He spoke first at the Thing to Olaf; and was the foremost man of the bondes in speaking against Christianity. The Thing was concluded in this way for that time,–the bondes returned home, and the king went to Hlader.

74. THE FEAST AT HLADER.

King Olaf lay with his ships in the river Nid, and had thirty vessels, which were manned with many brave people; but the king himself was often at Hlader, with his court attendants. As the time now was approaching at which the sacrifices should be made at Maeren, the king prepared a great feast at Hlader, and sent a message to the districts of Strind, Gaulardal, and out to Orkadal, to invite the chiefs and other great bondes. When the feast was ready, and the chiefs assembled, there was a handsome entertainment the first evening, at which plenty of liquor went round, and the guests were made very drunk. The night after they all slept in peace. The following morning, when the king was dressed, he had the early mass sung before him; and when the mass was over, ordered to sound the trumpets for a House Thing: upon which all his men left the ships to come up to the Thing. When the Thing was seated, the king stood up, and spoke thus: "We held a Thing at Frosta, and there I invited the bondes to allow themselves to be baptized; but they, on the other hand, invited me to offer sacrifice to their gods, as King Hakon, Athelstan's foster-son, had done; and thereafter it was agreed upon between us that we should meet at Maerin, and there make a great sacrifice. Now if I, along with you, shall turn again to making sacrifice, then will I make the greatest of sacrifices that are in use; and I will sacrifice men. But I will not select slaves or malefactors for this, but will take the greatest men only to be offered to the gods; and for this I select Orm Lygra of Medalhus, Styrkar of Gimsar, Kar of Gryting, Asbjorn Thorbergson of Varnes, Orm of Lyxa, Haldor of Skerdingsstedja;" and besides these he named five others of the principal men. All these, he said, he would offer in sacrifice to the gods for peace and a fruitful season; and ordered them to be laid hold of immediately. Now when the bondes saw that they were not strong enough to make head against the king, they asked for peace, and submitted wholly to the king's pleasure. So it was settled that all the bondes who had come there should be baptized, and should take an oath to the king to hold by the right faith, and to renounce sacrifice to the gods. The king then kept all these men as hostages who came to his feast, until they sent him their sons, brothers, or other near relations.

75. OF THE THING IN THRONDHJEM.

King Olaf went in with all his forces into the Throndhjem country; and when he came to Maeren all among the chiefs of the Throndhjem people who were most opposed to Christianity were assembled, and had with them all the great bondes who had before made sacrifice at that place. There was thus a greater multitude of bondes than there had been at the Frosta-Thing. Now the king let the people be summoned to the Thing, where both parties met armed; and when the Thing was seated the king made a speech, in which he told the people to go over to Christianity. Jarnskegge replies on the part of the bondes, and says that the will of the bondes is now, as formerly, that the king should not break their laws. "We want, king," said he, "that thou shouldst offer sacrifice, as other kings before thee have done." All the bondes applauded his speech with a loud shout, and said they would have all things according to what Skegge said. Then the king said he would go into the temple of their gods with them, and see what the practices were when they sacrificed. The bondes thought well of this proceeding, and both parties went to the temple.

76. THE THRONDHJEM PEOPLE BAPTIZED.

Now King Olaf entered into the temple with some few of his men and a few bondes; and when the king came to where their gods were, Thor, as the most considered among their gods, sat there adorned with gold and silver. The king lifted up his gold-inlaid axe which he carried in his hands, and struck Thor so that the image rolled down from its seat. Then the king's men turned to and threw down all the gods from their seats; and while the king was in the temple, Jarnskegge was killed outside of the temple doors, and the king's men did it. When the king came forth out of the temple he offered the bondes two conditions,–that all should accept of Christianity forthwith, or that they should fight with him. But as Skegge was killed, there was no leader in the bondes' army to raise the banner against King Olaf; so they took the other condition, to surrender to the king's will and obey his order. Then King Olaf had all the people present baptized, and took hostages from them for their remaining true to Christianity; and he sent his men round to every district, and no man in the Throndhjem country opposed Christianity, but all people took baptism.

77. A TOWN IN THE THRONDHJEM COUNTRY.

King Olaf with his people went out to Nidaros, and made houses on the flat side of the river Nid, which he raised to be a merchant town, and gave people ground to build houses upon. The king's house he had built just opposite Skipakrok; and he transported thither, in harvest, all that was necessary for his winter residence, and had many people about him there.

78. KING OLAF'S MARRIAGE.

King Olaf appointed a meeting with the relations of Jarnskegge, and offered them the compensation or penalty for his bloodshed; for there were many bold men who had an interest in that business. Jarnskegge had a daughter called Gudrun; and at last it was agreed upon between the parties that the king should take her in marriage. When the wedding day came King Olaf and Gudrun went to bed together. As soon as Gudrun, the first night they lay together, thought the king was asleep, she drew a knife, with which she intended to run him through; but the king saw it, took the knife from her, got out of bed, and went to his men, and told them what had happened. Gudrun also took her clothes, and went away along with all her men who had followed her thither. Gudrun never came into the king's bed again.

79. BUILDING OF THE SHIP CRANE.

THE SAME AUTUMN (A.D. 998) King Olaf laid the keel of a great longship out on the strand at the river Nid. It was a snekkja; and he employed many carpenters upon her, so that early in winter the vessel was ready. It had thirty benches for rowers, was high in stem and stern, but was not broad. The king called this ship Tranen (the Crane). After Jarnskegge's death his body was carried to Yrjar, and lies there in the Skegge mound on Austrat.

80. THANGBRAND THE PRIEST GOES TO ICELAND.

WHEN KING OLAF TRYGVASON had been two years king of Norway (A.D. 997), there was a Saxon priest in his house who was called Thangbrand, a passionate, ungovernable man, and a great man-slayer; but he was a good scholar, and a clever man. The king would not have him in his house upon account of his misdeeds; but gave him the errand to go to Iceland, and bring that land to the Christian faith. The king gave him a merchant vessel: and, as far as we know of this voyage of his, he landed first in Iceland at Austfjord in the southern Alptfjord, and passed the winter in the house of Hal of Sida. Thangbrand proclaimed Christianity in Iceland, and on his persuasion Hal and all his house people, and many other chiefs, allowed themselves to be baptized; but there were many more who spoke against it. Thorvald Veile and Veterlide the skald composed a satire about Thangbrand; but he killed them both outright. Thangbrand was two years in Iceland, and was the death of three men before he left it.

81. OF SIGURD AND HAUK.

There was a man called Sigurd, and another called Hauk, both of Halogaland, who often made merchant voyages. One summer (A.D. 998) they had made a voyage westward to England; and when they came back to Norway they sailed northwards along the coast, and at North More they met King Olaf's people. When it was told the king that some Halogaland people were come who were heathen, he ordered the steersmen to be brought to him, and he asked them if they would consent to be baptized; to which they replied, no. The king spoke with them in many ways, but to no purpose. He then threatened them with death and torture: but they would not allow themselves to be moved. He then had them laid in irons, and kept them in chains in his house for some time, and often conversed with them, but in vain. At last one night they disappeared, without any man being able to conjecture how they got away. But about harvest they came north to Harek of Thjotta, who received them kindly, and with whom they stopped all winter (A.D. 999), and were hospitably entertained.

82. OF HAREK OF THJOTTA.

It happened one good-weather day in spring (A.D. 999) that Harek was at home in his house with only few people, and time hung heavy on his hands. Sigurd asked him if he would row a little for amusement. Harek was willing; and they went to the shore, and drew down a six-oared skiff; and Sigurd took the mast and rigging belonging to the boat out of the boat-house, for they often used to sail when they went for amusement on the water. Harek went out into the boat to hang the rudder. The brothers Sigurd and Hauk, who were very strong men, were fully armed, as they were used to go about at home among the peasants. Before they went out to the boat they threw into her some butter-kits and a bread-chest, and carried between them a great keg of ale. When they had rowed a short way from the island the brothers hoisted the sail, while Harek was seated at the helm; and they sailed away from the island. Then the two brothers went aft to where Harek the bonde was sitting; and Sigurd says to him, "Now thou must choose one of these conditions,–first, that we brothers direct this voyage; or, if not, that we bind thee fast and take the command; or, third, that we kill thee." Harek saw how matters stood with him. As a single man, he was not better than one of those brothers, even if he had been as well armed; so it appeared to him wisest to let them determine the course to steer, and bound himself by oath to abide by this condition. On this Sigurd took the helm, and steered south along the land, the brothers taking particular care that they did not encounter people. The wind was very favourable; and they held on sailing along until they came south to Throndhjem and to Nidaros, where they found the king. Then the king called Harek to him, and in a conference desired him to be baptized. Harek made objections; and although the king and Harek talked over it many times, sometimes in the presence of other people, and sometimes alone, they could not agree upon it. At last the king says to Harek, "Now thou mayst return home, and I will do thee no injury; partly because we are related together, and partly that thou mayst not have it to say that I caught thee by a trick: but know for certain that I intend to come north next summer to visit you Halogalanders, and ye shall then see if I am not able to punish those who reject Christianity." Harek was well pleased to get away as fast as he could. King Olaf gave Harek a good boat of ten or twelve pair of oars, and let it be fitted out with the best of everything needful; and besides he gave Harek thirty men, all lads of mettle, and well appointed.

83. EYVIND KINRIFA'S DEATH.

Harek of Thjotta went away from the town as fast as he could; but Hauk and Sigurd remained in the king's house, and both took baptism. Harek pursued his voyage until he came to Thjotta. He sent immediately a message to his friend Eyvind Kinrifa, with the word that he had been with King Olaf; but would not let himself be cowed down to accept Christianity. The message at the same time informed him that King Olaf intended coming to the north in summer against them, and they must be at their posts to defend themselves; it also begged Eyvind to come and visit him, the sooner the better. When this message was delivered to Eyvind, he saw how very necessary it was to devise some counsel to avoid falling into the king's hands. He set out, therefore, in a light vessel with a few hands as fast as he could. When he came to Thjotta he was received by Harek in the most friendly way, and they immediately entered into conversation with each other behind the house. When they had spoken together but a short time, King Olaf's men, who had secretly followed Harek to the north, came up, and took Eyvind prisoner, and carried him away to their ship. They did not halt on their voyage until they came to Throndhjem, and presented themselves to

King Olaf at Nidaros. Then Eyvind was brought up to a conference with the king, who asked him to allow himself to be baptized, like other people; but Eyvind decidedly answered he would not. The king still, with persuasive words, urged him to accept Christianity, and both he and the bishop used many suitable arguments; but Eyvind would not allow himself to be moved. The king offered him gifts and great fiefs, but Eyvind refused all. Then the king threatened him with tortures and death, but Eyvind was steadfast. Then the king ordered a pan of glowing coals to be placed upon Eyvind's belly, which burst asunder. Eyvind cried, "Take away the pan, and I will say something before I die," which also was done. The king said, "Wilt thou now, Eyvind, believe in Christ?" "No," said Eyvind, "I can take no baptism; for I am an evil spirit put into a man's body by the sorcery of Fins because in no other way could my father and mother have a child." With that died Eyvind, who had been one of the greatest sorcerers.

84. HALOGALAND MADE CHRISTIAN.

The spring after (A.D. 999) King Olaf fitted out and manned his ships, and commanded himself his ship the Crane. He had many and smart people with him; and when he was ready, he sailed northwards with his fleet past Bryda, and to Halogaland. Wheresoever he came to the land, or to the islands, he held a Thing, and told the people to accept the right faith, and to be baptized. No man dared to say anything against it, and the whole country he passed through was made Christian. King Olaf was a guest in the house of Harek of Thjotta, who was baptized with all his people. At parting the king gave Harek good presents; and he entered into the king's service, and got fiefs, and the privileges of lendsman from the king.

85. THORER HJORT'S DEATH.

There was a bonde, by name Raud the Strong, who dwelt in Godey in Salten fjord. Raud was a very rich man, who had many house servants; and likewise was a powerful man, who had many Fins in his service when he wanted them. Raud was a great idolater, and very skillful in witchcraft, and was a great friend of Thorer Hjort, before spoken of. Both were great chiefs. Now when they heard that King Olaf was coming with a great force from the south to Halogaland, they gathered together an army, ordered out ships, and they too had a great force on foot. Raud had a large ship with a gilded head formed like a dragon, which ship had thirty rowing benches, and even for that kind of ship was very large. Thorer Hjort had also a large ship. These men sailed southwards with their ships against King Olaf, and as soon as they met gave battle. A great battle there was, and a great fall of men; but principally on the side of the Halogalanders, whose ships were cleared of men, so that a great terror came upon them. Raud rode with his dragon out to sea, and set sail. Raud had always a fair wind wheresoever he wished to sail, which came from his arts of witchcraft; and, to make a short story, he came home to Godey. Thorer Hjort fled from the ships up to the land: but King Olaf landed people, followed those who fled, and killed them. Usually the king was the foremost in such skirmishes, and was so now. When the king saw where Thorer Hjort, who was quicker on foot than any man, was running to, he ran after him with his dog Vige. The king said, "Vige! Vige! Catch the deer." Vige ran straight in upon him; on which Thorer halted, and the king threw a spear at him. Thorer struck with his sword at the dog, and gave him a great wound; but at the same moment the king's spear flew under Thorer's arm, and went through and through him, and came out at his other-side. There Thorer left his life; but Vige was carried to the ships.

86. KING OLAF'S VOYAGE TO GODEY.

King Olaf gave life and freedom to all the men who asked it and agreed to become Christian. King Olaf sailed with his fleet northwards along the coast, and baptized all the people among whom he came; and when he came north to Salten fjord, he intended to sail into it to look for Raud, but a dreadful tempest and storm was raging in the fjord. They lay there a whole week, in which the same weather was raging within the fjord, while without there was a fine brisk wind only, fair for proceeding north along the land. Then the king continued his voyage north to Omd, where all the people submitted to Christianity. Then the king turned about and sailed to the south again; but when he came to the north side of Salten fjord, the same tempest was blowing, and the sea ran high out from the fjord, and the same kind of storm prevailed for several days while the king was lying there. Then the king applied to Bishop Sigurd, and asked him if he knew any counsel about it; and the bishop said he would try if God would give him power to conquer these arts of the Devil.

87. OF RAUD'S BEING TORTURED.

Bishop Sigurd took all his mass robes and went forward to the bow of the king's ship; ordered tapers to be lighted, and incense to be brought out. Then he set the crucifix upon the stem of the vessel, read the Evangelist and many prayers, besprinkled the whole ship with holy water, and then ordered the ship-tent to be stowed away, and to row into the fjord. The king ordered all the other ships to follow him. Now when all was ready on board the Crane to row, she went into the fjord without the rowers finding any wind; and the sea was curled about their keel track like as in a calm, so quiet and still was the water; yet on each side of them the waves were lashing up so high that they hid the sight of the mountains. And so the one ship followed the other in the smooth sea track; and they proceeded this way the whole day and night, until they reached Godey. Now when they came to Raud's house his great ship, the dragon, was afloat close to the land. King Olaf went up to the house immediately with his people; made an attack on the loft in which Raud was sleeping, and broke it open. The men rushed in: Raud was taken and bound, and of the people with him some were killed and some made prisoners. Then the king's men went to a lodging in which Raud's house servants slept, and killed some, bound others, and beat others. Then the king ordered Raud to be brought before him, and offered him baptism. "And," says the king, "I will not take thy property from thee, but rather be thy friend, if thou wilt make thyself worthy to be so." Raud exclaimed with all his might against the proposal, saying he would never believe in Christ, and making his scoff of God. Then the king was wroth, and said Raud should die the worst of deaths. And the king ordered him to be bound to a beam of wood, with his face uppermost, and a round pin of wood set between his teeth to force his mouth open. Then the king ordered an adder to be stuck into the mouth of him; but the serpent would not go into his mouth, but shrunk back when Raud breathed against it. Now the king ordered a hollow branch of an angelica root to be stuck into Raud's mouth; others say the king put his horn into his mouth, and forced the serpent to go in by holding a red-hot iron before the opening. So the serpent crept into the mouth of Raud and down his throat, and gnawed its way out of his side; and thus Raud perished. King Olaf took here much gold and silver, and other property of weapons, and many sorts of precious effects; and all the men who were with Raud he either had baptized, or if they refused had them killed or tortured. Then the king took the dragonship which Raud had owned, and steered it himself; for it was a much larger and handsomer vessel than the Crane. In front it had a dragon's head, and aft a crook, which turned up, and ended with the figure of the dragon's tail. The carved work on each side of the stem and stern was gilded. This ship the king called the Serpent. When the sails were hoisted they represented, as it were, the dragon's wings; and the ship was the handsomest in all Norway. The islands on which Raud dwelt were called Gylling and Haering; but the whole islands together were called Godey Isles, and the current between the isles and the mainland the Godey Stream. King Olaf baptized the whole people of the fjord, and then sailed southwards along the land; and on this voyage happened much and various things, which are set down in tales and sagas,–namely, how witches and evil spirits tormented his men, and sometimes himself; but we will rather write about what occurred when King Olaf made Norway Christian, or in the other countries in which he advanced Christianity. The same autumn Olaf with his fleet returned to Throndhjem, and landed at Nidaros, where he took up his winter abode. What I am now going to write about concerns the Icelanders.

88. OF THE ICELANDERS.

Kjartan Olafson, a son's son of Hoskuld, and a daughter's son of Egil Skallagrimson, came the same autumn (A.D. 999) from Iceland to Nidaros, and he was considered to be the most agreeable and hopeful man of any born in Iceland. There was also Haldor, a son of Gudmund of Modruveller; and Kolbein, a son of Thord, Frey's gode, and a brother's son of Brennuflose; together with Sverting, a son of the gode Runolf. All these were heathens; and besides them there were many more,–some men of power, others common men of no property. There came also from Iceland considerable people, who, by Thangbrand's help, had been made Christians; namely, Gissur the white, a son of Teit Ketilbjornson; and his mother was Alof, daughter of herse Bodvar, who was the son of Vikingakare. Bodvar's brother was Sigurd, father of Eirik Bjodaskalle, whose daughter Astrid was King Olaf's mother. Hjalte Skeggjason was the name of another Iceland man, who was married to Vilborg, Gissur the White's daughter. Hjalte was also a Christian; and King Olaf was very friendly to his relations Gissur and Hjalte, who live with him. But the Iceland men who directed the ships, and were heathens, tried to sail away as soon as the king came to the town of Nidaros, for they were told the king forced all men to become Christians; but the wind came stiff against them, and drove them back to Nidarholm. They who directed the ships were Thorarin Nefjulson, the skald Halfred Ottarson, Brand the Generous, and

Thorleik, Brand's son. It was told the king that there were Icelanders with ships there, and all were heathen, and wanted to fly from a meeting with the king. Then the king sent them a message forbidding them to sail, and ordering them to bring their ships up to the town, which they did, but without discharging the cargoes.

(They carried on their dealings and held a market at the king's pier. In spring they tried three times to slip away, but never succeeded; so they continued lying at the king's pier. It happened one fine day that many set out to swim for amusement, and among them was a man who distinguished himself above the others in all bodily exercises. Kjartan challenged Halfred Vandredaskald to try himself in swimming against this man, but he declined it. "Then will I make a trial," said Kjartan, casting off his clothes, and springing into the water. Then he set after the man, seizes hold of his foot, and dives with him under water. They come up again, and without speaking a word dive again, and are much longer under water than the first time. They come up again, and without saying a word dive a third time, until Kjartan thought it was time to come up again, which, however, he could in no way accomplish, which showed sufficiently the difference in their strength. They were under water so long that Kjartan was almost drowned. They then came up, and swam to land. This Northman asked what the Icelander's name was. Kjartan tells his name.

He says, "Thou art a good swimmer; but art thou expert also in other exercises?"

Kjartan replied, that such expertness was of no great value.

The Northman asks, "Why dost thou not inquire of me such things as I have asked thee about?"

Kjartan replies, "It is all one to me who thou art, or what thy name is."

"Then will I," says he, "tell thee: I am Olaf Trygvason."

He asked Kjartan much about Iceland, which he answered generally, and wanted to withdraw as hastily as he could; but the king said, "Here is a cloak which I will give thee, Kjartan." And Kjartan took the cloak with many thanks.)[28]

89. BAPTISM OF THE ICELANDERS.

When Michaelmas came, the king had high mass sung with great splendour. The Icelanders went there, listening to the fine singing and the

28 The part included in parenthesis is not found in the original text of "Heimskringla", but taken from "Codex Frisianus".

sound of the bells; and when they came back to their ships every man told his opinion of the Christian man's worship. Kjartan expressed his pleasure at it, but most of the others scoffed at it; and it went according to the proverb, "the king had many ears," for this was told to the king. He sent immediately that very day a message to Kjartan to come to him. Kjartan went with some men, and the king received him kindly. Kjartan was a very stout and handsome man, and of ready and agreeable speech. After the king and Kjartan had conversed a little, the king asked him to adopt Christianity. Kjartan replies, that he would not say no to that, if he thereby obtained the king's friendship; and as the king promised him the fullest friendship, they were soon agreed. The next day Kjartan was baptized, together with his relation Bolle Thorlakson, and all their fellow-travelers. Kjartan and Bolle were the king's guests as long as they were in their white baptismal clothes, and the king had much kindness for them. Wherever they came they were looked upon as people of distinction.

90. HALFRED VANDREDASKALD BAPTIZED.

As King Olaf one day was walking in the street some men met him, and he who went the foremost saluted the king. The king asked the man his name, and he called himself Halfred.

"Art thou the skald?" said the king.

"I can compose poetry," replied he.

"Wilt thou then adopt Christianity, and come into my service?" asked the king.

"If I am baptized," replies he, "it must be on one condition,–that thou thyself art my godfather; for no other will I have."

The king replies, "That I will do." And Halfred was baptized, the king holding him during the baptism.

Afterwards the king said, "Wilt thou enter into my service?"

Halfred replied, "I was formerly in Earl Hakon's court; but now I will neither enter into thine nor into any other service, unless thou promise me it shall never be my lot to be driven away from thee."

"It has been reported to me," said the king, "that thou are neither so prudent nor so obedient as to fulfil my commands."

"In that case," replied Halfred, "put me to death."

"Thou art a skald who composes difficulties," says the king; "but into my service, Halfred, thou shalt be received."

Halfred says, "if I am to be named the composer of difficulties, what cost thou give me, king, on my name-day?"

The king gave him a sword without a scabbard, and said, "Now compose me a song upon this sword, and let the word sword be in every line of the strophe." Halfred sang thus:

"This sword of swords is my reward.
For him who knows to wield a sword,
And with his sword to serve his lord,
Yet wants a sword, his lot is hard.
I would I had my good lord's leave
For this good sword a sheath to choose:
I'm worth three swords when men use,
But for the sword-sheath now I grieve."

Then the king gave him the scabbard, observing that the word sword was wanting in one line of his strophe. "But there instead are three swords in one of the lines," says Halfred. "That is true," replies the king.–Out of Halfred's lays we have taken the most of the true and faithful accounts that are here related about Olaf Trygvason.

91. THANGBRAND RETURNS FROM ICELAND.

The same harvest (A.D. 999) Thangbrand the priest came back from Iceland to King Olaf, and told the ill success of his journey; namely, that the Icelanders had made lampoons about him; and that some even sought to kill him, and there was little hope of that country ever being made Christian. King Olaf was so enraged at this, that he ordered all the Icelanders to be assembled by sound of horn, and was going to kill all who were in the town, but Kjartan, Gissur, and Hjalte, with the other Icelanders who had become Christians, went to him, and said, "King, thou must not fail from thy word–that however much any man may irritate thee, thou wilt forgive him if he turn from heathenism and become Christian. All the Icelanders here are willing to be baptized; and through them we may find means to bring Christianity into Iceland: for there are many amongst them, sons of considerable people in Iceland, whose friends can advance the cause; but the priest Thangbrand proceeded there as he did here in the court, with violence and manslaughter, and such conduct the people there would not submit to." The king harkened to those remonstrances; and all the Iceland men who were there were baptized.

92. OF KING OLAF'S FEATS.

King Olaf was more expert in all exercises than any man in Norway whose memory is preserved to us in sagas; and he was stronger and more agile than most men, and many stories are written down about it. One is that he ascended the Smalsarhorn, and fixed his shield upon the very peak. Another is, that one of his followers had climbed up the peak after him, until he came to where he could neither get up nor down; but the king came to his help, climbed up to him, took him under his arm, and bore him to the flat ground. King Olaf could run across the oars outside of the vessel while his men were rowing the Serpent. He could play with three daggers, so that one was always in the air, and he took the one falling by the handle. He could walk all round upon the ship's rails, could strike and cut equally well with both hands, and could cast two spears at once. King Olaf was a very merry frolicsome man; gay and social; was very violent in all respects; was very generous; was very finical in his dress, but in battle he exceeded all in bravery. He was distinguished for cruelty when he was enraged, and tortured many of his enemies. Some he burnt in fire; some he had torn in pieces by mad dogs; some he had mutilated, or cast down from high precipices. On this account his friends were attached to him warmly, and his enemies feared him greatly; and thus he made such a fortunate advance in his undertakings, for some obeyed his will out of the friendliest zeal, and others out of dread.

93. BAPTISM OF LEIF EIRIKSON.

Leif, a son of Eirik the Red, who first settled in Greenland, came this summer (A.D. 999) from Greenland to Norway; and as he met King Olaf he adopted Christianity, and passed the winter (A.D. 1000) with the king.

94. FALL OF KING GUDROD.

Gudrod, a son of Eirik Bloodaxe and Gunhild, had been ravaging in the west countries ever since he fled from Norway before the Earl Hakon. But the summer before mentioned (A.D. 999), where King Olaf Trygvason had ruled four years over Norway, Gudrod came to the country, and had many ships of war with him. He had sailed from

England; and when he thought himself near to the Norway coast, he steered south along the land, to the quarter where it was least likely King Olaf would be. Gudrod sailed in this way south to Viken; and as soon as he came to the land he began to plunder, to subject the people to him, and to demand that they should accept of him as king. Now as the country people saw that a great army was come upon them, they desired peace and terms. They offered King Gudrod to send a Thing-message over all the country, and to accept of him at the Thing as king, rather than suffer from his army; but they desired delay until a fixed day, while the token of the Thing's assembling was going round through the land. The king demanded maintenance during the time this delay lasted. The bondes preferred entertaining the king as a guest, by turns, as long as he required it; and the king accepted of the proposal to go about with some of his men as a guest from place to place in the land, while others of his men remained to guard the ships. When King Olaf's relations, Hyrning and Thorgeir, heard of this, they gathered men, fitted out ships, and went northwards to Viken. They came in the night with their men to a place at which King Gudrod was living as a guest, and attacked him with fire and weapons; and there King Gudrod fell, and most of his followers. Of those who were with his ships some were killed, some slipped away and fled to great distances; and now were all the sons of Eirik and Gunhild dead.

95. BUILDING OF THE SHIP LONG SERPENT.

The winter after, King Olaf came from Halogaland (A.D. 1000), he had a great vessel built at Hladhamrar, which was larger than any ship in the country, and of which the beam-knees are still to be seen. The length of keel that rested upon the grass was seventy-four ells. Thorberg Skafhog was the man's name who was the master-builder of the ship; but there were many others besides,–some to fell wood, some to shape it, some to make nails, some to carry timber; and all that was used was of the best. The ship was both long and broad and high-sided, and strongly timbered.

While they were planking the ship, it happened that Thorberg had to go home to his farm upon some urgent business; and as he remained there a long time, the ship was planked up on both sides when he came back. In the evening the king went out, and Thorberg with him, to see how the vessel looked, and everybody said that never was seen so large and so beautiful a ship of war. Then the king returned to the town. Early next morning the king returns again to the ship, and Thorberg with him. The carpenters were there before them, but all were standing idle with their arms across. The king asked, "what was the matter?" They said the ship was destroyed; for somebody had gone from, stem to stern, and cut one deep notch after the other down the one side of the planking. When the king came nearer he saw it was so, and said, with an oath, "The man shall die who has thus destroyed the vessel out of envy, if he can be discovered, and I shall bestow a great reward on whoever finds him out."

"I can tell you, king," said Thorberg, "who has done this piece of work."–

"I don't think," replies the king, "that any one is so likely to find it out as thou art."

Thorberg says, "I will tell you, king, who did it. I did it myself."

The king says, "Thou must restore it all to the same condition as before, or thy life shall pay for it."

Then Thorberg went and chipped the planks until the deep notches were all smoothed and made even with the rest; and the king and all present declared that the ship was much handsomer on the side of the hull which Thorberg, had chipped, and bade him shape the other side in the same way; and gave him great thanks for the improvement. Afterwards Thorberg was the master builder of the ship until she was entirely finished. The ship was a dragon, built after the one the king had captured in Halogaland; but this ship was far larger, and more carefully put together in all her parts. The king called this ship Serpent the Long, and the other Serpent the Short. The long Serpent had thirty-four benches for rowers. The head and the arched tail were both gilt, and the bulwarks were as high as in sea-going ships. This ship was the best and most costly ship ever made in Norway.

96. EARL EIRIK, THE SON OF HAKON.

Earl Eirik, the son of Earl Hakon, and his brothers, with many other valiant men their relations, had left the country after Earl Hakon's fall. Earl Eirik went eastwards to Svithjod, to Olaf, the Swedish king, and he and his people were well received. King Olaf gave the earl peace and freedom in the land, and great fiefs; so that he could support himself and his men well. Thord Kolbeinson speaks of this in the verses before given. Many people who fled from the country on account of King Olaf Trygvason came out of Norway to Earl Eirik; and the earl resolved to fit out ships and go a-cruising, in order to get property for himself and his people. First he steered to Gotland, and lay there long in summer watching for merchant vessels sailing towards the land, or for vikings. Sometimes he landed and ravaged all round upon the sea-coasts. So it is told in the "Banda-drapa":–

"Eirik, as we have lately heard,
Has waked the song of shield and sword–
Has waked the slumbering storm of shields
Upon the vikings' water-fields:
From Gotland's lonely shore has gone
Far up the land, and battles won:
And o'er the sea his name is spread,
To friends a shield, to foes a dread."

Afterwards Earl Eirik sailed south to Vindland, and at Stauren found some viking ships, and gave them battle. Eirik gained the victory, and slew the vikings. So it is told in the "Banda-drapa":–

"Earl Eirik, he who stoutly wields
The battle-axe in storm of shields,
With his long ships surprised the foe
At Stauren, and their strength laid low
Many a corpse floats round the shore;
The strand with dead is studded o'er:
The raven tears their sea-bleached skins–
The land thrives well when Eirik wins."

97. EIRIK'S FORAY ON THE BALTIC COASTS.

Earl Eirik sailed back to Sweden in autumn, and staid there all winter (A.D. 997); but in the spring fitted out his war force again, and sailed up the Baltic. When he came to Valdemar's dominions he began to plunder and kill the inhabitants, and burn the dwellings everywhere as he came along, and to lay waste the country. He came to Aldeigiuburg, and besieged it until he took the castle; and he killed many people, broke down and burned the castle, and then carried destruction all around far and wide in Gardarike. So it is told in the "Banda-drapa":–

"The generous earl, brave and bold,
Who scatters his bright shining gold,

Eirik with fire-scattering hand,
Wasted the Russian monarch's land,–
With arrow-shower, and storm of war,
Wasted the land of Valdemar.
Aldeiga burns, and Eirik's might
Scours through all Russia by its light."

Earl Eirik was five years in all on this foray; and when he returned from Gardarike he ravaged all Adalsysla and Eysysla, and took there four viking ships from the Danes and killed every man on board. So it is told in the "Banda-drapa":–

"Among the isles flies round the word,
That Eirik's blood-devouring sword
Has flashed like fire in the sound,
And wasted all the land around.
And Eirik too, the bold in fight,
Has broken down the robber-might
Of four great vikings, and has slain
All of the crew–nor spared one Dane.
In Gautland he has seized the town,
In Syssels harried up and down;
And all the people in dismay
Fled to the forests far away.
By land or sea, in field or wave,
What can withstand this earl brave?
All fly before his fiery hand–
God save the earl, and keep the land."

When Eirik had been a year in Sweden he went over to Denmark (A.D. 996) to King Svein Tjuguskeg, the Danish king, and courted his daughter Gyda. The proposal was accepted, and Earl Eirik married Gyda; and a year after (A.D. 997) they had a son, who was called Hakon. Earl Eirik was in the winter in Denmark, or sometimes in Sweden; but in summer he went a-cruising.

98. KING SVEIN'S MARRIAGE.

THE DANISH KING, Svein Tjuguskeg, was married to Gunhild, a daughter of Burizleif, king of the Vinds. But in the times we have just been speaking of it happened that Queen Gunhild fell sick and died. Soon after King Svein married Sigrid the Haughty, a daughter of Skoglartoste, and mother of the Swedish king Olaf; and by means of this relationship there was great friendship between the kings and Earl Eirik, Hakon's son.

99. KING BURIZLEIF'S MARRIAGE.

Burizleif, the king of the Vinds, complained to his relation Earl Sigvalde, that the agreement was broken which Sigvalde had made between King Svein and King Burizleif, by which Burizleif was to get in marriage Thyre, Harald's daughter, a sister of King Svein: but that marriage had not proceeded, for Thyre had given positive no to the proposal to marry her to an old and heathen king. "Now," said King Burizleif to Earl Sigvalde, "I must have the promise fulfilled." And he told Earl Sigvalde to go to Denmark, and bring him Thyre as his queen. Earl Sigvalde loses no time, but goes to King Svein of Denmark, explains to him the case; and brings it so far by his persuasion, that the king delivered his sister Thyre into his hands. With her went some female attendants, and her foster-father, by name Ozur Agason, a man of great power, and some other people. In the agreement between the king and the earl, it was settled that Thyre should have in property the possessions which Queen Gunhild had enjoyed in Vindland, besides other great properties as bride-gifts. Thyre wept sorely, and went very unwillingly. When the earl came to Vindland, Burizleif held his wedding with Queen Thyre, and received her in marriage; bus as long as she was among heathens she would neither eat nor drink with them, and this lasted for seven days.

100. OLAF GETS THYRE IN MARRIAGE.

It happened one night that Queen Thyre and Ozur ran away in the dark, and into the woods, and, to be short in our story, came at last to Denmark. But here Thyre did not dare to remain, knowing that if her brother King Svein heard of her, he would send her back directly to Vindland. She went on, therefore, secretly to Norway, and never stayed her journey until she fell in with King Olaf, by whom she was kindly received. Thyre related to the king her sorrows, and entreated his advice in her need, and protection in his kingdom. Thyre was a well-spoken woman, and the king had pleasure in her conversation. He saw she was a handsome woman, and it came into his mind that she would be a good match; so he turns the conversation that way, and asks if she will marry him. Now, as she saw that her situation was such that she could not help herself, and considered what a luck it was for her to marry so celebrated a man, she bade him to dispose himself of her hand and fate; and, after nearer conversation, King Olaf took Thyre in marriage. This wedding was held in harvest after the king returned from Halogaland (A.D. 999), and King Olaf and Queen Thyre remained all winter (A.D. 1000) at Nidaros.

The following spring Queen Thyre complained often to King Olaf, and wept bitterly over it, that she who had so great property in Vindland had no goods or possessions here in the country that were suitable for a queen; and sometimes she would entreat the king with fine words to get her property restored to her, and saying that King Burizleif was so great a friend of King Olaf that he would not deny King Olaf anything if they were to meet. But when King Olaf's friends heard of such speeches, they dissuaded him from any such expedition. It is related at the king one day early in spring was walking in the street, and met a man in the market with many, and, for that early season, remarkably large angelica roots. The king took a great stalk of the angelica in his hand, and went home to Queen Thyre's lodging. Thyre sat in her room weeping as the king came in. The king said, "Set here, queen, is a great angelica stalk, which I give thee." She threw it away, and said, "A greater present Harald Gormson gave to my mother; and he was not afraid to go out of the land and take his own. That was shown when he came here to Norway, and laid waste the greater part of the land, and seized on all the scat and revenues; and thou darest not go across the Danish dominions for this brother of mine, King Svein." As she spoke thus, King Olaf sprang up, and answered with loud oath, "Never did I fear thy brother King Svein; and if we meet he shall give way before me!"

101. OLAF'S LEVY FOR WAR.

Soon after the king convoked a Thing in the town, and proclaimed to all the public, that in summer would go abroad upon an expedition out of the country, and would raise both ships and men from every district; and at the same time fixed how many ships would have from the whole Throndhjem fjord. Then he sent his message-token south and north, both along the sea-coast and up in the interior of the country, to let an army be gathered. The king ordered the Long Serpent to be put into the water, along with all his other ships both small and great. He himself steered the Long Serpent. When the crews were taken out for the ships, they were so carefully selected that no man on board the Long Serpent was older than sixty or younger than twenty years, and all were men distinguished for strength and courage. Those who were Olaf's bodyguard were in particular chosen men, both of the natives and of foreigners, and the boldest and strongest.

102. CREW ON BOARD OF THE LONG SERPENT.

Ulf the Red was the name of the man who bore King Olaf's banner, and was in the forecastle of the Long Serpent; and with him was Kolbjorn the marshal, Thorstein Uxafot, and Vikar of Tiundaland, a brother of Arnliot Gelline. By the bulkhead next the forecastle were Vak Raumason from Gaut River, Berse the Strong, An Skyte from Jamtaland, Thrand the Strong from Thelamork, and his brother Uthyrmer. Besides these were, of Halogaland men, Thrand Skjalge and Ogmund Sande, Hlodver Lange from Saltvik, and Harek Hvasse; together with these Throndhjem men–Ketil the High, Thorfin Eisle, Havard and his brothers from Orkadal. The following were in the fore-hold: Bjorn from Studla, Bork from the fjords. Thorgrim Thjodolfson from Hvin, Asbjorn and Orm, Thord from Njardarlog, Thorstein the White from Oprustadar, Arnor from More, Halstein and Hauk from the Fjord district, Eyvind Snak, Bergthor Bestil, Halkel from Fialer, Olaf Dreng, Arnfin from Sogn, Sigurd Bild, Einar from Hordaland, and Fin, and Ketil from Rogaland and Grjotgard the Brisk. The following were in the hold next the mast: Einar Tambaskelfer, who was not reckoned as fully experienced, being only eighteen years old; Thorstein Hlifarson, Thorolf, Ivar Smetta, and Orm Skogarnef. Many other valiant men were in the Serpent, although we cannot tell all their names. In every half division of the hold were eight men, and each and all chosen men; and in the fore-hold were thirty men. It was a common saying among people, that the Long Serpent's crew was as distinguished for bravery, strength, and daring, among other men, as the Long Serpent was distinguished among other ships. Thorkel Nefja, the king's brother, commanded the Short Serpent; and Thorkel Dydril and Jostein, the king's mother's brothers, had the Crane; and both these ships were well manned. King Olaf had eleven large ships from Throndhjem, besides vessels with twenty rowers' benches, smaller vessels, and provision-vessels.

103. ICELAND BAPTIZED.

WHEN KING OLAF HAD nearly rigged out his fleet in Nidaros, he appointed men over the Throndhjem country in all districts and communities. He also sent to Iceland Gissur the White and Hjalte Skeggjason, to proclaim Christianity there; and sent with them a priest called Thormod, along with several men in holy orders. But he retained with him, as hostages, four Icelanders whom he thought the most important; namely, Kjartan Olafson, Haldor Gudmundson, Kolbein Thordson, and Sverting Runolfson. Of Gissur and Hjalte's progress, it is related that they came to Iceland before the Althing, and went to the Thing; and in that Thing Christianity was introduced by law into Iceland, and in the course of the summer all the people were baptized (A.D. 1000).

104. GREENLAND BAPTIZED

THE SAME SPRING King Olaf also sent Leif Eirikson (A.D. 1000) to Greenland to proclaim Christianity there, and Leif went there that summer. In the ocean he took up the crew of a ship which had been lost, and who were clinging to the wreck. He also found Vinland the Good; arrived about harvest in Greenland; and had with him for it a priest and other teachers, with whom he went to Brattahild to lodge with his father Eirik. People called him afterwards Leif the Lucky: but his father Eirik said that his luck and ill luck balanced each other; for if Leif had saved a wreck in the ocean, he had brought a hurtful person with him to Greenland, and that was the priest.

105. RAGNVALD SENDS MESSENGERS TO OLAF.

THE WINTER AFTER King Olaf had baptized Halogaland, he and Queen Thyre were in Nidaros; and the summer before Queen Thyre had brought King Olaf a boy child, which was both stout and promising, and was called Harald, after its mother's father. The king and queen loved the infant exceedingly, and rejoiced in the hope that it would grow up and inherit after its father; but it lived barely a year after its birth, which both took much to heart. In that winter were many Icelanders and other clever men in King Olaf's house, as before related. His sister Ingebjorg, Trygve's daughter, King Olaf's sister, was also at the court at that time. She was beautiful in appearance, modest and frank with the people, had a steady manly judgment, and was beloved of all. She was very fond of the Icelanders who were there, but most of Kjartan Olafson, for he had been longer than the others in the king's house; and he found it always amusing to converse with her, for she had both understanding and cleverness in talk. The king was always gay and full of mirth in his intercourse with people; and often asked about the manners of the great men and chiefs in the neighbouring countries, when strangers from Denmark or Sweden came to see him. The summer before Halfred Vandredaskald had come from Gautland, where he had been with Earl Ragnvald, Ulf's son, who had lately come to the government of West Gautland. Ulf, Ragnvald's father, was a brother of Sigurd the Haughty; so that King Olaf the Swede and Earl Ragnvald were brother's and sister's children. Halfred told Olaf many things about the earl: he said he was an able chief, excellently fitted for governing, generous with money, brave and steady in friendship. Halfred said also the earl desired much the friendship of King Olaf, and had spoken of making court Ingebjorg, Trygve's daughter. The same winter came ambassadors from Gautland, and fell in with King Olaf in the north, in Nidaros, and brought the message which Halfred had spoken of,–that the earl desired to be King Olaf's entire friend, and wished to become his brother-in-law by obtaining his sister Ingebjorg in marriage. Therewith the ambassadors laid before the king sufficient tokens in proof that in reality they came from the earl on this errand. The king listened with approbation to their speech; but said that Ingebjorg must determine on his assent to the marriage. The king then talked to his sister about the matter, and asked her opinion about it. She answered to this effect,– "I have been with you for some time, and you have shown brotherly care and tender respect for me ever since you came to the country. I will agree therefore to your proposal about my marriage, provided that you do not marry me to a heathen man." The king said it should be as she wished. The king then spoke to the ambassadors; and it was settled before they departed that in summer Earl Ragnvald should meet the king in the east parts of the country, to enter into the fullest friendship with each other, and when they met they would settle about the marriage. With this reply the earl's messengers went westward, and King Olaf remained all winter in Nidaros in great splendour, and with many people about him.

106. OLAF SENDS EXPEDITION TO VINDLAND.

King Olaf proceeded in summer with his ships and men southwards along the land (and past Stad. With him were Queen Thyre and Ingebjorg, Trygveis daughter, the king's sister). Many of his friends also joined him, and other persons of consequence who had prepared themselves to travel with the king. The first man among these was his brother-in-law, Erling Skjalgson, who had with him a large ship of thirty benches of rowers, and which was in every respect well equipt. His brothers-in-law Hyrning and Thorgeir also joined him, each of whom for himself steered a large vessel; and many other powerful men besides followed him. (With all this war-force he sailed southwards along the land; but when he came south as far as Rogaland he stopped there, for Erling Skjalgson had prepared for him a splendid feast at Sole. There Earl Ragnvald, Ulf's son, from Gautland, came to meet the king, and to settle the business which had been proposed in winter in the messages between them, namely, the marriage with Ingebjorg the king's sister. Olaf received him kindly; and when the matter came to be spoken of, the king said he would keep his word, and marry his sister Ingebjorg to him, provided he would accept the true faith, and make all his subjects he ruled over in his land be baptized; The earl agreed to this, and he and all his followers were baptized. Now was the feast enlarged that Erling had prepared, for the earl held his wedding there with Ingebjorg the king's sister. King Olaf had now married off all his sisters. The earl, with Ingebjorg, set out on his way home; and the king sent learned men with him to baptize the people in Gautland, and to teach them the right faith and morals. The king and the earl parted in the greatest friendship.)

107. OLAF'S EXPEDITION VINDLAND.

(After his sister Ingebjorg's wedding, the king made ready in all haste to leave the country with his army, which was both great and made up of fine men.) When he left the land and sailed southwards he had sixty ships of war, with which he sailed past Denmark, and in through the Sound, and on to Vindland. He appointed a meeting with King Burizleif; and when the kings met, they spoke about the property which King Olaf demanded, and the conference went off peaceably, as a good account was given of the properties which King Olaf thought himself entitled to there. He passed here much of the summer, and found many of his old friends.

108. CONSPIRACY AGAINST KING OLAF.

The Danish king, Svein Tjuguskeg, was married, as before related, to Sigrid the Haughty. Sigrid was King Olaf Trygvason's greatest enemy; the cause of which, as before said, was that King Olaf had broken off with her, and had struck her in the face. She urged King Svein much to give battle to King Olaf Trygvason; saying that he had reason enough, as Olaf had married his sister Thyre without his leave, "and that your predecessors would not have submitted to." Such persuasions Sigrid had often in her mouth; and at last she brought it so far that Svein resolved firmly on doing so. Early in spring King Svein sent messengers eastward into Svithjod, to his son-in-law Olaf, the Swedish king, and to Earl Eirik; and informed them that King Olaf of Norway was levying men for an expedition, and intended in summer to go to Vindland. To this news the Danish king added an invitation to the Swedish king and Earl Eirik to meet King Svein with an army, so that all together they might make an attack; on King Olaf Trygvason. The Swedish king and Earl Eirik were ready enough for this, and immediately assembled a great fleet and an army through all Svithjod, with which they sailed southwards to Denmark, and arrived there after King Olaf Trygvason had sailed to the eastward. Haldor the Unchristian tells of this in his lay on Earl Eirik:–

"The king-subduer raised a host
Of warriors on the Swedish coast.
The brave went southwards to the fight,
Who love the sword-storm's gleaming light;
The brave, who fill the wild wolf's mouth,
Followed bold Eirik to the south;
The brave, who sport in blood–each one
With the bold earl to sea is gone."

The Swedish king and Earl Eirik sailed to meet the Danish king, and they had all, when together, an immense force.

109. EARL SIGVALDE'S TREACHEROUS PLANS.

AT THE SAME TIME that king Svein sent a message to Svithjod for an army, he sent Earl Sigvalde to Vindland to spy out King Olaf Trygvason's proceedings, and to bring it about by cunning devices that King Svein and King Olaf should fall in with each other. So Sigvalde sets out to go to Vindland. First, he came to Jomsborg, and then he sought out King Olaf Trygvason. There was much friendship in their conversation, and the earl got himself into great favour with the king. Astrid, the Earl's wife, King Burizleif's daughter, was a great friend of King Olaf Trygvason, particularly on account of the connection which had been between them when Olaf was married to her sister Geira. Earl Sigvalde was a prudent, ready-minded man; and as he had got a voice in King Olaf's council, he put him off much from sailing homewards, finding various reasons for delay. Olaf's people were in the highest degree dissatisfied with this; for the men were anxious to get home, and they lay ready to sail, waiting only for a wind. At last Earl Sigvalde got a secret message from Denmark that the Swedish king's army was arrived from the east, and that Earl Eirik's also was ready; and that all these chiefs had resolved to sail eastwards to Vindland, and wait for King Olaf at an island which is called Svold. They also desired the earl to contrive matters so that they should meet King Olaf there.

110. KING OLAF'S VOYAGE FROM VINDLAND.

THERE CAME FIRST A flying report to Vindland that the Danish king, Svein, had fitted out an army; and it was soon whispered that he intended to attack King Olaf. But Earl Sigvalde says to King Olaf, "It never can be King Svein's intention to venture with the Danish force alone, to give battle to thee with such a powerful army; but if thou hast any suspicion that evil is on foot, I will follow thee with my force (at that time it was considered a great matter to have Jomsborg vikings with an army), and I will give thee eleven well-manned ships." The king accepted this offer; and as the light breeze of wind that came was favourable, he ordered the ships to get under weigh, and the war-horns to sound the departure. The sails were hoisted and all the small vessels, sailing fastest, got out to sea before the others. The earl, who sailed nearest to the king's ship, called to those on board to tell the king to sail in his keel-track: "For I know where the water is deepest between the islands and in the sounds, and these large ships require the deepest." Then the earl sailed first with his eleven ships, and the king followed with his large ships, also eleven in number; but the whole of the rest of the fleet sailed out to sea. Now when Earl Sigvalde came sailing close under the island Svold, a skiff rowed out to inform the earl that the Danish king's army was lying in the harbour before them. Then the earl ordered the sails of his vessels to be struck, and they rowed in under the island. Haldor the Unchristian says:–

"From out the south bold Trygve's son
With one-and-seventy ships came on,
To dye his sword in bloody fight,
Against the Danish foeman's might.
But the false earl the king betrayed;
And treacherous Sigvalde, it is said,
Deserted from King Olaf's fleet,
And basely fled, the Danes to meet."

It is said here that King Olaf and Earl Sigvalde had seventy sail of vessels: and one more, when they sailed from the south.

111. CONSULTATION OF THE KINGS.

The Danish King Svein, the Swedish King Olaf, and Earl Eirik, were there with all their forces (1000). The weather being fine and clear sunshine, all these chiefs, with a great suite, went out on the isle to see the vessels sailing out at sea, and many of them crowded together; and they saw among them one large and glancing ship. The two kings said, "That is a large and very beautiful vessel: that will be the Long Serpent."

Earl Eirik replied, "That is not the Long Serpent." And he was right; for it was the ship belonging to Eindride of Gimsar.

Soon after they saw another vessel coming sailing along much larger than the first; then says King Svein, "Olaf Trygvason must be afraid, for he does not venture to sail with the figure-head of the dragon upon his ship."

Says Earl Eirik, "That is not the king's ship yet; for I know that ship by the coloured stripes of cloth in her sail. That is Erling Skialgson's. Let him sail; for it is the better for us that the ship is away from Olaf's fleet, so well equipt as she is."

Soon after they saw and knew Earl Sigvalde's ships, which turned in and laid themselves under the island. Then they saw three ships coming along under sail, and one of them very large. King Svein ordered his men to go to their ships, "for there comes the Long Serpent."

Earl Eirik says, "Many other great and stately vessels have they besides the Long Serpent. Let us wait a little."

Then said many, "Earl Eirik will not fight and avenge his father; and it is a great shame that it should be told that we lay here with so great a force, and allowed King Olaf to sail out to sea before our eyes."

But when they had spoken thus for a short time, they saw four ships coming sailing along, of which one had a large dragon-head richly gilt. Then King Svein stood up and said, "That dragon shall carry me this evening high, for I shall steer it."

Then said many, "The Long Serpent is indeed a wonderfully large and beautiful vessel, and it shows a great mind to have built such a ship."

Earl Eirik said so loud that several persons heard him, "If King Olaf had no ether vessels but only that one, King Svein would never take it from him with the Danish force alone."

Thereafter all the people rushed on board their ships, took down the tents, and in all haste made ready for battle.

While the chiefs were speaking among themselves as above related, they saw three very large ships coming sailing along, and at last after them a fourth, and that was the Long Serpent. Of the large ships which had gone before, and which they had taken for the Long Serpent, the first was the Crane; the one after that was the Short Serpent; and when they really, saw the Long Serpent, all knew, and nobody had a word to say against it, that it must be Olaf Trygvason who was sailing in such a vessel; and they went to their ships to arm for the fight.

An agreement had been concluded among the chiefs, King Svein, King Olaf the Swede, and Earl Eirik, that they should divide Norway among them in three parts, in case they succeeded against Olaf Trygvason; but that he of the chiefs who should first board the Serpent should have her, and all the booty found in her, and each should have the ships he cleared for himself. Earl Eirik had a large ship of war which he used upon his viking expeditions; and there was an iron beard or comb above on both sides of the stem, and below it a thick iron plate as broad as the combs, which went down quite to the gunnel.

112. OF KING OLAF'S PEOPLE.

When Earl Sigvalde with his vessels rowed in under the island, Thorkel Dydril of the Crane, and the other ship commanders who sailed with him, saw that he turned his ships towards the isle, and thereupon let fall the sails, and rowed after him, calling out, and asking why he sailed that way. The Earl answered, that he was waiting for king Olaf, as he feared there were enemies in the water. They lay upon their oars until Thorkel Nefia came up with the Short Serpent and the three ships which followed him. When they told them the same they too struck sail, and let the ships drive, waiting for king Olaf. But when the king sailed in towards the isle, the whole enemies' fleet came rowing within them out to the Sound. When they saw this they begged the king to hold on his way, and not risk battle with so great a force. The king replied, high on the quarter-deck where he stood, "Strike the sails; never shall men of mine think of flight. I never fled from battle. Let God dispose of my life, but flight I shall never take." It was done as the king commanded. Halfred tells of it thus:–

"And far and wide the saying bold
Of the brave warrior shall be told.
The king, in many a fray well tried,
To his brave champions round him cried,
'My men shall never learn from me
From the dark weapon-cloud to flee.'
Nor were the brave words spoken then
Forgotten by his faithful men."

113. OLAF'S SHIPS PREPARED FOR BATTLE.

King Olaf ordered the war-horns to sound for all his ships to close up to each other. The king's ship lay in the middle of the line, and on one side lay the Little Serpent, and on the other the Crane; and as they made fast the stems together[29], the Long Serpent's stem and the short Serpent's were made fast together; but when the king saw it he called out to his

29 The mode of fighting in sea battles appears, from this and many other descriptions, to have been for each party to bind together the stems and sterns of their own ships, forming them thus into a compact body as soon as the fleets came within fighting distance, or within spears' throw. They appear to have fought principally from the forecastles; and to have used grappling irons for dragging a vessel out of the line, or within boarding distance.–L.

men, and ordered them to lay the larger ship more in advance, so that its stern should not lie so far behind in the fleet.

Then says Ulf the Red, "If the Long Serpent is to lie as much more ahead of the other ships as she is longer than them, we shall have hard work of it here on the forecastle."

The king replies, "I did not think I had a forecastle man afraid as well as red."

Says Ulf, "Defend thou the quarterdeck as I shall the forecastle."

The king had a bow in his hands, and laid an arrow on the string, and aimed at Ulf.

Ulf said, "Shoot another way, king, where it is more needful: my work is thy gain."

114. OF KING OLAF.

King Olaf stood on the Serpent's quarterdeck, high over the others. He had a gilt shield, and a helmet inlaid with gold; over his armour he had a short red coat, and was easy to be distinguished from other men. When King Olaf saw that the scattered forces of the enemy gathered themselves together under the banners of their ships, he asked, "Who is the chief of the force right opposite to us?"

He was answered, that it was King Svein with the Danish army.

The king replies, "We are not afraid of these soft Danes, for there is no bravery in them; but who are the troops on the right of the Danes?"

He was answered, that it was King Olaf with the Swedish forces.

"Better it were," says King Olaf, "for these Swedes to be sitting at home killing their sacrifices, than to be venturing under our weapons from the Long Serpent. But who owns the large ships on the larboard side of the Danes?"

"That is Earl Eirik Hakonson," say they.

The king replies, "He, methinks, has good reason for meeting us; and we may expect the sharpest conflict with these men, for they are Norsemen like ourselves."

115. THE BATTLE BEGINS.

The kings now laid out their oars, and prepared to attack (A.D. 1000). King Svein laid his ship against the Long Serpent. Outside of him Olaf the Swede laid himself, and set his ship's stern against the outermost ship of King Olaf's line; and on the other side lay Earl Eirik. Then a hard combat began. Earl Sigvalde held back with the oars on his ships, and did not join the fray. So says Skule Thorsteinson, who at that time was with Earl Eirik:–

"I followed Sigvalde in my youth,
And gallant Eirik, and in truth
The' now I am grown stiff and old,
In the spear-song I once was bold.
Where arrows whistled on the shore
Of Svold fjord my shield I bore,
And stood amidst the loudest clash
When swords on shields made fearful crash."

And Halfred also sings thus:–

"In truth I think the gallant king,
Midst such a foemen's gathering,
Would be the better of some score
Of his tight Throndhjem lads, or more;
For many a chief has run away,
And left our brave king in the fray,
Two great kings' power to withstand,
And one great earl's, with his small band,
The king who dares such mighty deed
A hero for his skald would need."

116. FLIGHT OF SVEIN AND OLAF THE SWEDE.

This battle was one of the severest told of, and many were the people slain. The forecastle men of the Long Serpent, the Little Serpent, and the Crane, threw grapplings and stem chains into King Svein's ship, and used their weapons well against the people standing below them, for they cleared the decks of all the ships they could lay fast hold of; and King Svein, and all the men who escaped, fled to other vessels, and laid themselves out of bow-shot. It went with this force just as King Olaf Trygvason had foreseen. Then King Olaf the Swede laid himself in their place; but when he came near the great ships it went with him as with them, for he lost many men and some ships, and was obliged to get away. But Earl Eirik laid his ship side by side with the outermost of King Olaf's ships, thinned it of men, cut the cables, and let it drive. Then he laid alongside of the next, and fought until he had cleared it of men also. Now all the people who were in the smaller ships began to run into the larger, and the earl cut them loose as fast as he cleared them of men. The Danes and Swedes laid themselves now out of shooting distance all around Olaf's ship; but Earl Eirik lay always close alongside of the ships, and used hid swords and battle-axes, and as fast as people fell in his vessel others, Danes and Swedes, came in their place. So says Haldor, the Unchristian:-

"Sharp was the clang of shield and sword,
And shrill the song of spears on board,
And whistling arrows thickly flew
Against the Serpent's gallant crew.
And still fresh foemen, it is said,
Earl Eirik to her long side led;
Whole armies of his Danes and Swedes,
Wielding on high their blue sword-blades."

Then the fight became most severe, and many people fell. But at last it came to this, that all King Olaf Trygvason's ships were cleared of men except the Long Serpent, on board of which all who could still carry their arms were gathered. Then Earl Eirik lay with his ship by the side of the Serpent, and the fight went on with battle-axe and sword. So says Haldor:-

"Hard pressed on every side by foes,
The Serpent reels beneath the blows;
Crash go the shields around the bow!
Breast-plates and breasts pierced thro' and thro!
In the sword-storm the Holm beside,
The earl's ship lay alongside
The king's Long Serpent of the sea-
Fate gave the earl the victory."

117. OF EARL EIRIK.

Earl Eirik was in the forehold of his ship, where a cover of shields[30] had been set up. In the fight, both hewing weapons, sword, and axe, and the thrust of spears had been used; and all that could be used as weapon for casting was cast. Some used bows, some threw spears with the hand. So many weapons were cast into the Serpent, and so thick flew spears and arrows, that the shields could scarcely receive them, for on all sides the Serpent was surrounded by war-ships. Then King Olaf's men became so mad with rage, that they ran on board of the enemies ships, to get at the people with stroke of sword and kill them; but many did not lay themselves so near the Serpent, in order to escape the close encounter with battle-axe or sword; and thus the most of Olaf's men went overboard and sank under their weapons, thinking they were fighting on plain ground. So says Halfred:–

"The daring lads shrink not from death;–
O'erboard they leap, and sink beneath
The Serpent's keel: all armed they leap,
And down they sink five fathoms deep.
The foe was daunted at the cheers;
The king, who still the Serpent steers,
In such a strait–beset with foes–
Wanted but some more lads like those."

118. OF EINAR TAMBARSKELVER.

Einar Tambarskelver, one of the sharpest of bowshooters, stood by the mast, and shot with his bow. Einar shot an arrow at Earl Eirik, which hit the tiller end just above the earl's head so hard that it entered the wood up to the arrow-shaft. The earl looked that way, and asked if they knew who had shot; and at the same moment another arrow flew between his hand and his side, and into the stuffing of the chief's stool, so that the barb stood far out on the other side. Then said the earl to a man called Fin,–but some say he was of Fin (Laplander) race, and was

30 Both in land and sea fights the commanders appear to have been protected from missile weapons,–stones, arrows, spears,–by a shieldburg: that is, by a party of men bearing shields surrounding them in such a way that the shields were a parapet, covering those within the circle. The Romans had a similar military arrangement of shields in sieges–the testudo.–L.

a superior archer,–"Shoot that tall man by the mast." Fin shot; and the arrow hit the middle of Einar's bow just at the moment that Einar was drawing it, and the bow was split in two parts.

"What is that," cried King Olaf, "that broke with such a noise?"

"Norway, king, from thy hands," cried Einar.

"No! not quite so much as that," says the king; "take my bow, and shoot," flinging the bow to him.

Einar took the bow, and drew it over the head of the arrow. "Too weak, too weak," said he, "for the bow of a mighty king!" and, throwing the bow aside, he took sword and shield, and fought Valiantly.

119. OLAF GIVES HIS MEN SHARP SWORDS.

The king stood on the gangways of the Long Serpent, and shot the greater part of the day; sometimes with the bow, sometimes with the spear, and always throwing two spears at once. He looked down over the ship's sides, and saw that his men struck briskly with their swords, and yet wounded but seldom. Then he called aloud, "Why do ye strike so gently that ye seldom cut?" One among the people answered, "The swords are blunt and full of notches." Then the king went down into the forehold, opened the chest under the throne, and took out many sharp swords, which he handed to his men; but as he stretched down his right hand with them, some observed that blood was running down under his steel glove, but no one knew where he was wounded.

120. THE SERPENT BOARDED.

Desperate was the defence in the Serpent, and there was the heaviest destruction of men done by the forecastle crew, and those of the forehold, for in both places the men were chosen men, and the ship was highest, but in the middle of the ship the people were thinned. Now when Earl Eirik saw there were but few people remaining beside the ship's mast, he determined to board; and he entered the Serpent with four others. Then came Hyrning, the king's brother-in-law, and some others against him, and there was the most severe combat; and at last the earl was forced to leap back on board his own ship again, and some who had accompanied him were killed, and others wounded. Thord Kolbeinson alludes to this:–

"On Odin's deck, all wet with blood,
The helm-adorned hero stood;
And gallant Hyrning honour gained,
Clearing all round with sword deep stained.
The high mountain peaks shall fall,
Ere men forget this to recall."

Now the fight became hot indeed, and many men fell on board the Serpent; and the men on board of her began to be thinned off, and the defence to be weaker. The earl resolved to board the Serpent again, and again he met with a warm reception. When the forecastle men of the Serpent saw what he was doing, they went aft and made a desperate fight; but so many men of the Serpent had fallen, that the ship's sides were in many places quite bare of defenders; and the earl's men poured in all around into the vessel, and all the men who were still able to defend the ship crowded aft to the king, and arrayed themselves for his defence. So says Haldor the Unchristian:–

"Eirik cheers on his men,–
'On to the charge again!'
The gallant few
Of Olaf's crew
Must refuge take
On the quarter-deck.
Around the king
They stand in ring;
Their shields enclose
The king from foes,
And the few who still remain
Fight madly, but in vain.
Eirik cheers on his men–
'On to the charge again!'"

121. THE SERPENT'S DECKS CLEARED.

Kolbjorn the marshal, who had on clothes and arms like the kings, and was a remarkably stout and handsome man, went up to king on the quarter-deck. The battle was still going on fiercely even in the forehold[31].

31 From the occasional descriptions of vessels in this and other battles, it

But as many of the earl's men had now got into the Serpent as could find room, and his ships lay all round her, and few were the people left in the Serpent for defence against so great a force; and in a short time most of the Serpent's men fell, brave and stout though they were. King Olaf and Kolbjorn the marshal both sprang overboard, each on his own side of the ship; but the earl's men had laid out boats around the Serpent, and killed those who leaped overboard. Now when the king had sprung overboard, they tried to seize him with their hands, and bring him to Earl Eirik; but King Olaf threw his shield over his head, and sank beneath the waters. Kolbjorn held his shield behind him to protect himself from the spears cast at him from the ships which lay round the Serpent, and he fell so upon his shield that it came under him, so that he could not sink so quickly. He was thus taken and brought into a boat, and they supposed he was the king. He was brought before the earl; and when the earl saw it was Kolbjorn, and not the king, he gave him his life. At the same moment all of King Olaf's men who were in life sprang overboard from the Serpent; and Thorkel Nefia, the king's brother, was the last of all the men who sprang overboard. It is thus told concerning the king by Halfred:–

"The Serpent and the Crane
Lay wrecks upon the main.
On his sword he cast a glance,–
With it he saw no chance.
To his marshal, who of yore
Many a war-chance had come o'er,
He spoke a word–then drew in breath,
And sprang to his deep-sea death."

122. REPORT AMONG THE PEOPLE.

Earl Sigvalde, as before related, came from Vindland, in company with King Olaf, with ten ships; but the eleventh ship was manned with the men of Astrid, the king's daughter, the wife of Earl Sigvalde. Now when King Olaf sprang overboard, the whole army raised a shout of victory; and then Earl Sigvalde and his men put their oars in the water and rowed towards the battle. Haldor the Unchristian tells of it thus:–

may be inferred that even the Long Serpent, described in the 95th chapter as of 150 feet of keel was only docked fore and aft; the thirty-four benches for rowers occupying the open area in the middle, and probably gangways running along the side for communicating from the quarter-deck to the forcastle.–L.

"Then first the Vindland vessels came
Into the fight with little fame;
The fight still lingered on the wave,
Tho' hope was gone with Olaf brave.
War, like a full-fed ravenous beast,
Still oped her grim jaws for the feast.
The few who stood now quickly fled,
When the shout told–'Olaf is dead!'"

But the Vindland cutter, in which Astrid's men were, rowed back to Vindland; and the report went immediately abroad and was told by many, that King Olaf had cast off his coat-of-mail under water, and had swum, diving under the longships, until he came to the Vindland cutter, and that Astrid's men had conveyed him to Vindland: and many tales have been made since about the adventures of Olaf the king. Halfred speaks thus about it:–

"Does Olaf live? or is he dead?
Has he the hungry ravens fed?
I scarcely know what I should say,
For many tell the tale each way.
This I can say, nor fear to lie,
That he was wounded grievously–
So wounded in this bloody strife,
He scarce could come away with life."

But however this may have been, King Olaf Trygvason never came back again to his kingdom of Norway. Halfred Vandredaskald speaks also thus about it:

"The witness who reports this thing
Of Trygvason, our gallant king,
Once served the king, and truth should tell,
For Olaf hated lies like hell.
If Olaf 'scaped from this sword-thing,
Worse fate, I fear, befel our king
Than people guess, or e'er can know,
For he was hemm'd in by the foe.
From the far east some news is rife
Of king sore wounded saving life;
His death, too sure, leaves me no care

For cobweb rumours in the air.
It never was the will of fate
That Olaf from such perilous strait
Should 'scape with life! this truth may grieve–
'What people wish they soon believe.'"

123. OF EARL EIRIK, THE SON OF HAKON.

By this victory Earl Eirik Hakonson became owner of the Long Serpent, and made a great booty besides; and he steered the Serpent from the battle. So says Haldor:–

"Olaf, with glittering helmet crowned,
Had steered the Serpent through the Sound;
And people dressed their boats, and cheered
As Olaf's fleet in splendour steered.
But the descendent of great Heming,
Whose race tells many a gallant sea-king,
His blue sword in red life-blood stained,
And bravely Olaf's long ship gained."

Svein, a son of Earl Hakon, and Earl Eirik's brother, was engaged at this time to marry Holmfrid, a daughter of King Olaf the Swedish king. Now when Svein the Danish king, Olaf the Swedish king, and Earl Eirik divided the kingdom of Norway between them, King Olaf got four districts in the Throndhjem country, and also the districts of More and Raumsdal; and in the east part of the land he got Ranrike, from the Gaut river to Svinasund. Olaf gave these dominions into Earl Svein's hands, on the same conditions as the sub kings or earls had held them formerly from the upper-king of the country. Earl Eirik got four districts in the Throndhjem country, and Halogaland, Naumudal, the Fjord districts, Sogn, Hordaland, Rogaland, and North Agder, all the way to the Naze. So says Thord Kolbeinson:–

"All chiefs within our land
On Eirik's side now stand:
Erling alone, I know
Remains Earl Eirik's foe.
All praise our generous earl,–
He gives, and is no churl:

All men are well content
Fate such a chief has sent.
From Veiga to Agder they,
Well pleased, the earl obey;
And all will by him stand,
To guard the Norsemen's land.
And now the news is spread
That mighty Svein is dead,
And luck is gone from those
Who were the Norsemen's foes."

The Danish king Svein retained Viken as he had held it before, but he gave Raumarike and Hedemark to Earl Eirik. Svein Hakonson got the title of earl from Olaf the Swedish king. Svein was one of the handsomest men ever seen. The earls Eirik and Svein both allowed themselves to be baptized, and took up the true faith; but as long as they ruled in Norway they allowed every one to do as he pleased in holding by his Christianity. But, on the other hand, they held fast by the old laws, and all the old rights and customs of the land, and were excellent men and good rulers. Earl Eirik had most to say of the two brothers in all matters of government.

BOOK SIX

Saga of Olaf Haraldson[32]

PRELIMINARY REMARKS.

OLAF HARALDSON THE Saint's Saga is the longest, the most important, and the most finished of all the sagas in "Heimskringla". The life of Olaf will be found treated more or less freely in "Agrip", in "Historia Norvegiae", in "Thjodrek the Monk", in the legendary saga, and in "Fagrskinna". Other old Norse literature relating to this epoch:

Are's "Islendingabok", "Landnama", "Kristni Saga", "Biskupasogur", "Njala", "Gunlaugs Saga", "Ormstungu", "Bjarnar Saga Hitdaelakappa", "Hallfredar Thattr Vandraedaskalde", "Eyrbyggia", "Viga Styrs Saga", "Laxdaela", "Fostbraedra", "Gretla", "Liosvetninga", "Faereyinga", "Orkneyinga".

Olaf Haraldson was born 995, went as a viking at the age of twelve, 1007; visited England, one summer and three winters, 1009-1012; in France two summers and one winter, 1012-1013; spent the winter in Normandy, 1014; returned to Norway and was recognized as King, April 3, 1015; fled from Norway the winter of 1028-1029; fell at Stiklestad, July 29 (or August 31), 1030.

Skalds quoted in this saga are:–Ottar Svarte, Sigvat Skald, Thord Kolbeinson, Berse Torfason, Brynjolf, Arnor Jarlaskald, Thord Siarekson, Harek, Thorarin Loftunga, Halvard Hareksblese, Bjarne Gulbraskald, Jokul Bardson, Thormod Kolbrunarskald, Gissur, Thorfin Mun, Hofgardaref.

32 King Olaf the Saint reigned from about the year 1015 to 1030. The death of King Olaf Trygvason was in the year 1000: and Earl Eirik held the government for the Danish and Swedish kings about fifteen years.–L.

1. OF SAINT OLAF'S BRINGING UP.

Olaf, Harald Grenske's son, was brought up by his stepfather Sigurd Syr and his mother Asta. Hrane the Far-travelled lived in the house of Asta, and fostered this Olaf Haraldson. Olaf came early to manhood, was handsome in countenance, middle-sized in growth, and was even when very young of good understanding and ready speech. Sigurd his stepfather was a careful householder, who kept his people closely to their work, and often went about himself to inspect his corn-rigs and meadowland, the cattle, and also the smith-work, or whatsoever his people had on hand to do.

2. OF OLAF AND KING SIGURD SYR.

It happened one day that King Sigurd wanted to ride from home, but there was nobody about the house; so he told his stepson Olaf to saddle his horse. Olaf went to the goats' pen, took out the he-goat that was the largest, led him forth, and put the king's saddle on him, and then went in and told King Sigurd he had saddled his riding horse. Now when King Sigurd came out and saw what Olaf had done, he said "It is easy to see that thou wilt little regard my orders; and thy mother will think it right that I order thee to do nothing that is against thy own inclination. I see well enough that we are of different dispositions, and that thou art far more proud than I am." Olaf answered little, but went his way laughing.

3. OF RING OLAF'S ACCOMPLISHMENTS.

When Olaf Haraldson grew up he was not tall, but middle-sized in height, although very thick, and of good strength. He had light brown hair, and a broad face, which was white and red. He had particularly fine eyes, which were beautiful and piercing, so that one was afraid to look him in the face when he was angry. Olaf was very expert in all bodily exercises, understood well to handle his bow, and was distinguished particularly in throwing his spear by hand: he was a great swimmer, and very handy, and very exact and knowing in all kinds of smithwork, whether he himself or others made the thing. He was distinct and acute in conversation, and was soon perfect in understanding and strength. He was beloved by his friends and acquaintances, eager in his amusements, and one who always liked to be the first, as it was suitable he should be from his birth and dignity. He was called Olaf the Great.

4. KING OLAF'S WAR EXPEDITION.

Olaf Haraldson was twelve years old when he, for the first time, went on board a ship of war (A.D. 1007). His mother Asta got Hrane, who was called the foster-father of kings, to command a ship of war and take Olaf under his charge; for Hrane had often been on war expeditions. When Olaf in this way got a ship and men, the crew gave him the title of king; for it was the custom that those commanders of troops who were of kingly descent, on going out upon a viking cruise, received the title of king immediately although they had no land or kingdom. Hrane sat at the helm; and some say that Olaf himself was but a common rower, although he was king of the men-at-arms. They steered east along the land, and came first to Denmark. So says Ottar Svarte, in his lay which he made about King Olaf:–

"Young was the king when from his home
He first began in ships to roam,
His ocean-steed to ride
To Denmark o'er the tide.
Well exercised art thou in truth–
In manhood's earnest work, brave youth!
Out from the distant north
Mighty hast thou come forth."

Towards autumn he sailed eastward to the Swedish dominions, and there harried and burnt all the country round; for he thought he had good cause of hostility against the Swedes, as they killed his father Harald. Ottar Svarte says distinctly that he came from the east, out by way of Denmark:–

"Thy ship from shore to shore,
With many a well-plied car,
Across the Baltic foam is dancing.–
Shields, and spears, and helms glancing!
Hoist high the swelling sail
To catch the freshening gale!
There's food for the raven-flight

Where thy sail-winged ship shall light;
Thy landing-tread
The people dread;
And the wolf howls for a feast
On the shore-side in the east."

5. OLAF'S FIRST BATTLE.

The same autumn Olaf had his first battle at Sotasker, which lies in the Swedish skerry circle. He fought there with some vikings, whose leader was Sote. Olaf had much fewer men, but his ships were larger, and he had his ships between some blind rocks, which made it difficult for the vikings to get alongside; and Olaf's men threw grappling irons into the ships which came nearest, drew them up to their own vessels, and cleared them of men. The vikings took to flight after losing many men. Sigvat the skald tells of this fight in the lay in which he reckons up King Olaf's battles:–

"They launch his ship where waves are foaming–
To the sea shore
Both mast and oar,
And sent his o'er the seas a-roaming.
Where did the sea-king first draw blood?
In the battle shock
At Sote's rock;
The wolves howl over their fresh food."

6. FORAY IN SVITHJOD.

King Olaf steered thereafter eastwards to Svithjod, and into the Lag (the Maelar lake), and ravaged the land on both sides. He sailed all the way up to Sigtuna, and laid his ships close to the old Sigtuna. The Swedes say the stone-heaps are still to be seen which Olaf had laid under the ends of the gangways from the shore to the ships. When autumn was advanced, Olaf Haraldson heard that Olaf the Swedish king was assembling an army, and also that he had laid iron chains across Stoksund (the channel between the Maelar lake and the sea), and had laid troops there; for the Swedish king thought that Olaf Haraldson would be kept in there till frost came, and he thought little of Olaf's force knowing he had but few people. Now when King Olaf Haraldson came to Stoksund he could not get through, as there was a castle west of the sound, and men-at-arms lay on the south; and he heard that the Swedish king was come there with a great army and many ships. He therefore dug a canal across the flat land Agnafit out to the sea. Over all Svithjod all the running waters fall into the Maelar lake; but the only outlet of it to the sea is so small that many rivers are wider, and when much rain or snow falls the water rushes in a great cataract out by Stoksund, and the lake rises high and floods the land. It fell heavy rain just at this time; and as the canal was dug out to the sea, the water and stream rushed into it. Then Olaf had all the rudders unshipped and hoisted all sail aloft. It was blowing a strong breeze astern, and they steered with their oars, and the ships came in a rush over all the shallows, and got into the sea without any damage. Now went the Swedes to their king, Olaf, and told him that Olaf the Great had slipped out to sea; on which the king was enraged against those who should have watched that Olaf did not get away. This passage has since been called King's Sound; but large vessels cannot pass through it, unless the waters are very high. Some relate that the Swedes were aware that Olaf had cut across the tongue of land, and that the water was falling out that way; and they flocked to it with the intention to hinder Olaf from getting away, but the water undermined the banks on each side so that they fell in with the people, and many were drowned: but the Swedes contradict this as a false report, and deny the loss of people. The king sailed to Gotland in harvest, and prepared to plunder; but the Gotlanders assembled, and sent men to the king, offering him a scat. The king found this would suit him, and he received the scat, and remained there all winter. So says Ottar Svarte:–

"Thou seaman-prince! thy men are paid:
The scat on Gotlanders is laid;
Young man or old
To our seamen bold
Must pay, to save his head:
The Yngling princes fled,
Eysvssel people bled;
Who can't defend the wealth they have
Must die, or share with the rover brave."

7. THE SECOND BATTLE.

It is related here that King Olaf, when spring set in, sailed east to Eysyssel, and landed and plundered; the Eysyssel men came down to the strand and grave him battle. King Olaf gained the victory, pursued those who fled, and laid waste the land with fire and sword. It is told that when King Olaf first came to Eysvssel they offered him scat, and when the scat was to be brought down to the strand the king came to meet it with an armed force, and that was not what the bondes there expected; for they had brought no scat, but only their weapons with which they fought against the king, as before related. So says Sigvat the skald:–

"With much deceit and bustle
To the heath of Eysyssel
The bondes brought the king,
To get scat at their weapon-thing.
But Olaf was too wise
To be taken by surprise;
Their legs scarce bore them off
O'er the common test enough."

8. THE THIRD BATTLE.

After this they sailed to Finland and plundered there, and went up the country. All the people fled to the forest, and they had emptied their houses of all household goods. The king went far up the country, and through some woods, and came to some dwellings in a valley called Herdaler,–where, however, they made but small booty, and saw no people; and as it was getting late in the day, the king turned back to his ships. Now when they came into the woods again people rushed upon them from all quarters, and made a severe attack. The king told his men to cover themselves with their shields, but before they got out of the woods he lost many people, and many were wounded; but at last, late in the evening, he got to the ships. The Finlanders conjured up in the night, by their witchcraft, a dreadful storm and bad weather on the sea; but the king ordered the anchors to be weighed and sail hoisted, and beat off all night to the outside of the land. The king's luck prevailed more than the Finlanders' witchcraft; for he had the luck to beat round the Balagard's side in the night, and so got out to sea. But the Finnish army proceeded on land, making the same progress as the king made with his ships. So says Sigvat:–

"The third fight was at Herdaler, where
The men of Finland met in war
The hero of the royal race,
With ringing sword-blades face to face.
Off Balagard's shore the waves
Ran hollow; but the sea-king saves
His hard-pressed ship, and gains the lee
Of the east coast through the wild sea."

9. THE FOURTH BATTLE IN SUDERVIK.

King Olaf sailed from thence to Denmark, where he met Thorkel the Tall, brother of Earl Sigvalde, and went into partnership with him; for he was just ready to set out on a cruise. They sailed southwards to the Jutland coast, to a place called Sudervik, where they overcame many viking ships. The vikings, who usually have many people to command, give themselves the title of kings, although they have no lands to rule over. King Olaf went into battle with them, and it was severe; but King Olaf gained the victory, and a great booty. So says Sigvat:–

"Hark! hark! The war-shout
Through Sudervik rings,
And the vikings bring out
To fight the two kings.
Great honour, I'm told,
Won these vikings so bold:
But their bold fight was vain,
For the two brave kings gain."

10. THE FIFTH BATTLE IN FRIESLAND.

King Olaf sailed from thence south to Friesland, and lay under the strand of Kinlima in dreadful weather. The king landed with his men; but the people of the country rode down to the strand against them, and he fought them. So says Sigvat:–

"Under Kinlima's cliff,
This battle is the fifth.
The brave sea-rovers stand
All on the glittering sand;
And down the horsemen ride
To the edge of the rippling tide:
But Olaf taught the peasant band
To know the weight of a viking's hand."

11. DEATH OF KING SVEIN FORKED BEARD.

The king sailed from thence westward to England. It was then the case that the Danish king, Svein Forked Beard, was at that time in England with a Danish army, and had been fixed there for some time, and had seized upon King Ethelred's kingdom. The Danes had spread themselves so widely over England, that it was come so far that King Ethelred had departed from the country, and had gone south to Valland. The same autumn that King Olaf came to England, it happened that King Svein died suddenly in the night in his bed; and it is said by Englishmen that Edmund the Saint killed him, in the same way that the holy Mercurius had killed the apostate Julian. When Ethelred, the king of the English, heard this in Flanders, he returned directly to England; and no sooner was he come back, than he sent an invitation to all the men who would enter into his pay, to join him in recovering the country. Then many people flocked to him; and among others, came King Olaf with a great troop of Northmen to his aid. They steered first to London, and sailed into the Thames with their fleet; but the Danes had a castle within. On the other side of the river is a great trading place, which is called Sudvirke. There the Danes had raised a great work, dug large ditches, and within had built a bulwark of stone, timber, and turf, where they had stationed a strong army. King Ethelred ordered a great assault; but the Danes defended themselves bravely, and King Ethelred could make nothing of it. Between the castle and Southwark (Sudvirke) there was a bridge, so broad that two wagons could pass each other upon it. On the bridge were raised barricades, both towers and wooden parapets, in the direction of the river, which were nearly breast high; and under the bridge were piles driven into the bottom of the river. Now when the attack was made the troops stood on the bridge everywhere, and defended themselves. King Ethelred was very anxious to get possession of the bridge, and he called together all the chiefs to consult how they should get the bridge broken down. Then said King Olaf he would attempt to lay his fleet alongside of it, if the other ships would do the same. It was then determined in this council that they should lay their war forces under the bridge; and each made himself ready with ships and men.

12. THE SIXTH BATTLE.

King Olaf ordered great platforms of floating wood to be tied together with hazel bands, and for this he took down old houses; and with these, as a roof, he covered over his ships so widely, that it reached over the ships' sides. Under this screen he set pillars so high and stout, that there both was room for swinging their swords, and the roofs were strong enough to withstand the stones cast down upon them. Now when the fleet and men were ready, they rode up along the river; but when they came near the bridge, there were cast down upon them so many stones and missile weapons, such as arrows and spears, that neither helmet nor shield could hold out against it; and the ships themselves were so greatly damaged, that many retreated out of it. But King Olaf, and the Northmen's fleet with him, rowed quite up under the bridge, laid their cables around the piles which supported it, and then rowed off with all the ships as hard as they could down the stream. The piles were thus shaken in the bottom, and were loosened under the bridge. Now as the armed troops stood thick of men upon the bridge, and there were likewise many heaps of stones and other weapons upon it, and the piles under it being loosened and broken, the bridge gave way; and a great part of the men upon it fell into the river, and all the ethers fled, some into the castle, some into Southwark. Thereafter Southwark was stormed and taken. Now when the people in the castle saw that the river Thames was mastered, and that they could not hinder the passage of ships up into the country, they became afraid, surrendered the tower, and took Ethelred to be their king. So says Ottar Svarte:–

"London Bridge is broken down.–
Gold is won, and bright renown.
Shields resounding,
War-horns sounding,
Hild is shouting in the din!
Arrows singing,
Mail-coats ringing–

Odin makes our Olaf win!"

And he also composed these:–

"King Ethelred has found a friend:
Brave Olaf will his throne defend–
In bloody fight
Maintain his right,
Win back his land
With blood-red hand,
And Edmund's son upon his throne replace–
Edmund, the star of every royal race!"

Sigvat also relates as follows:–

"At London Bridge stout Olaf gave
Odin's law to his war-men brave–
'To win or die!'
And their foemen fly.
Some by the dyke-side refuge gain–
Some in their tents on Southwark plain!
The sixth attack
Brought victory back."

13. THE SEVENTH BATTLE.

King Olaf passed all the winter with King Ethelred, and had a great battle at Hringmara Heath in Ulfkel's land, the domain which Ulfkel Snilling at that time held; and here again the king was victorious. So says Sigvat the skald:–

"To Ulfkel's land came Olaf bold,
A seventh sword-thing he would hold.
The race of Ella filled the plain–
Few of them slept at home again!
Hringmara heath
Was a bed of death:
Harfager's heir
Dealt slaughter there."

And Ottar sings of this battle thus:–

"From Hringmara field
The chime of war,

Sword striking shield,
Rings from afar.
The living fly;
The dead piled high
The moor enrich;
Red runs the ditch."

The country far around was then brought in subjection to King Ethelred: but the Thingmen[33] and the Danes held many castles, besides a great part of the country.

14. EIGHTH AND NINTH BATTLES OF OLAF.

King Olaf was commander of all the forces when they went against Canterbury; and they fought there until they took the town, killing many people and burning the castle. So says Ottar Svarte:–

"All in the grey of morn
Broad Canterbury's forced.
Black smoke from house-roofs borne
Hides fire that does its worst;
And many a man laid low
By the battle-axe's blow,
Waked by the Norsemen's cries,
Scarce had time to rub his eyes."

Sigvat reckons this King Olaf's eighth battle:–

"Of this eighth battle I can tell
How it was fought, and what befell,
The castle tower
With all his power
He could not take,
Nor would forsake.
The Perthmen fought,
Nor quarter sought;

33 *Thing-men were hired men-at-arms; called Thing-men probably from being men above the class of thralls or unfree men, and entitled to appear at Things, as being udal-born to land at home.*

By death or flight
They left the fight.
Olaf could not this earl stout
From Canterbury quite drive out."

At this time King Olaf was entrusted with the whole land defence of England, and he sailed round the land with his ships of War. He laid his ships at land at Nyjamoda, where the troops of the Thingmen were, and gave them battle and gained the victory. So says Sigvat the skald:-

"The youthful king stained red the hair
Of Angeln men, and dyed his spear
At Newport in their hearts' dark blood:
And where the Danes the thickest stood-
Where the shrill storm round Olaf's head
Of spear and arrow thickest fled.
There thickest lay the Thingmen dead!
Nine battles now of Olaf bold,
Battle by battle, I have told."

King Olaf then scoured all over the country, taking scat of the people and plundering where it was refused. So says Ottar:-

"The English race could not resist thee,
With money thou madest them assist thee;
Unsparingly thou madest them pay
A scat to thee in every way;
Money, if money could be got-
Goods, cattle, household gear, if not.
Thy gathered spoil, borne to the strand,
Was the best wealth of English land."

Olaf remained here for three years (A.D. 1010-1012).

15. THE TENTH BATTLE.

The third year King Ethelred died, and his sons Edmund and Edward took the government (A.D. 1012). Then Olaf sailed southwards out to sea, and had a battle at Hringsfjord, and took a castle situated at Holar, where vikings resorted, and burnt the castle. So says Sigvat the skald:-

"Of the tenth battle now I tell,
Where it was fought, and what befell.
Up on the hill in Hringsfjord fair
A robber nest hung in the air:
The people followed our brave chief,
And razed the tower of the viking thief.
Such rock and tower, such roosting-place,
Was ne'er since held by the roving race."

16. ELEVENTH, TWELFTH AND THIRTEENTH BATTLES.

Then King Olaf proceeded westwards to Grislupollar, and fought there with vikings at Williamsby; and there also King Olaf gained the victory. So says Sigvat:–

"The eleventh battle now I tell,
Where it was fought, and what befell.
At Grislupol our young fir's name
O'ertopped the forest trees in fame:
Brave Olaf's name–nought else was heard
But Olaf's name, and arm, and sword.
Of three great earls, I have heard say,
His sword crushed helm and head that day."

Next he fought westward on Fetlafjord, as Sigvat tells:–

"The twelfth fight was at Fetlafjord,
Where Olaf's honour-seeking sword
Gave the wild wolf's devouring teeth
A feast of warriors doomed to death."

From thence King Olaf sailed southwards to Seljupollar, where he had a battle. He took there a castle called Gunvaldsborg, which was very large and old. He also made prisoner the earl who ruled over the castle and who was called Geirfin. After a conference with the men of the castle, he laid a scat upon the town and earl, as ransom, of twelve thousand gold shillings: which was also paid by those on whom it was imposed. So says Sigvat:–

"The thirteenth battle now I tell,
Where it was fought, and what befell.

In Seljupol was fought the fray,
And many did not survive the day.
The king went early to the shore,
To Gunvaldsborg's old castle-tower;
And a rich earl was taken there,
Whose name was Geridin, I am sure."

17. FOURTEENTH BATTLE AND OLAF'S DREAM.

Thereafter King Olaf steered with his fleet westward to Karlsar, and tarried there and had a fight. And while King Olaf was lying in Karlsa river waiting a wind, and intending to sail up to Norvasund, and then on to the land of Jerusalem, he dreamt a remarkable dream–that there came to him a great and important man, but of a terrible appearance withal, who spoke to him, and told him to give up his purpose of proceeding to that land. "Return back to thy udal, for thou shalt be king over Norway for ever." He interpreted this dream to mean that he should be king over the country, and his posterity after him for a long time.

18. FIFTEENTH BATTLE.

After this appearance to him he turned about, and came to Poitou, where he plundered and burnt a merchant town called Varrande. Of this Ottar speaks:–

"Our young king, blythe and gay,
Is foremost in the fray:
Poitou he plunders, Tuskland burns,–
He fights and wins where'er he turns."

And also Sigvat says:–

"The Norsemen's king is on his cruise,
His blue steel staining,
Rich booty gaining,
And all men trembling at the news.
The Norsemen's kings up on the Loire:
Rich Partheney

In ashes lay;
Far inland reached the Norsemen's spear."

19. OF THE EARLS OF ROUEN.

King Olaf had been two summers and one winter in the west in Valland on this cruise; and thirteen years had now passed since the fall of King Olaf Trygvason. During this time earls had ruled over Norway; first Hakon's sons Eirik and Svein, and afterwards Eirik's sons Hakon and Svein. Hakon was a sister's son of King Canute, the son of Svein. During this time there were two earls in Valland, William and Robert; their father was Richard earl of Rouen. They ruled over Normandy. Their sister was Queen Emma, whom the English king Ethelred had married; and their sons were Edmund, Edward the Good, Edwy, and Edgar. Richard the earl of Rouen was a son of Richard the son of William Long Spear, who was the son of Rolf Ganger, the earl who first conquered Normandy; and he again was a son of Ragnvald the Mighty, earl of More, as before related. From Rolf Ganger are descended the earls of Rouen, who have long reckoned themselves of kin to the chiefs in Norway, and hold them in such respect that they always were the greatest friends of the Northmen; and every Northman found a friendly country in Normandy, if he required it. To Normandy King Olaf came in autumn (A.D. 1013), and remained all winter (A.D. 1014) in the river Seine in good peace and quiet.

20. OF EINAR TAMBASKELFER.

After Olaf Trygvason's fall, Earl Eirik gave peace to Einar Tambaskelfer, the son of Eindride Styrkarson; and Einar went north with the earl to Norway. It is said that Einar was the strongest man and the best archer that ever was in Norway. His shooting was sharp beyond all others; for with a blunt arrow he shot through a raw, soft oxhide, hanging over a beam. He was better than any man at running on snow-shoes, was a great man at all exercises, was of high family, and rich. The earls Eirik and Svein married their sister Bergliot to Einar. Their son was named Eindride. The earls gave Einar great fiefs in Orkadal, so that he was one of the most powerful and able men in the Throndhjem country, and was also a great friend of the earls, and a great support and aid to them.

21. OF ERLING SKIALGSON.

When Olaf Trygvason ruled over Norway, he gave his brother-in-law Erling half of the land scat, and royal revenues between the Naze and Sogn. His other sister he married to the Earl Ragnvald Ulfson, who long ruled over West Gautland. Ragnvald's father, Ulf, was a brother of Sigrid the Haughty, the mother of Olaf the Swedish king. Earl Eirik was ill pleased that Erling Skialgson had so large a dominion, and he took to himself all the king's estates, which King Olaf had given to Erling. But Erling levied, as before, all the land scat in Rogaland; and thus the inhabitants had often to pay him the land scat, otherwise he laid waste their land. The earl made little of the business, for no bailiff of his could live there, and the earl could only come there in guest-quarters, when he had a great many people with him. So says Sigvat:–

"Olaf the king
Thought the bonde Erling
A man who would grace
His own royal race.
One sister the king
Gave the bonde Erling;
And one to an earl,
And she saved him in peril."

Earl Eirik did not venture to fight with Erling, because he had very powerful and very many friends, and was himself rich and popular, and kept always as many retainers about him as if he held a king's court. Erling was often out in summer on plundering expeditions, and procured for himself means of living; for he continued his usual way of high and splendid living, although now he had fewer and less convenient fiefs than in the time of his brother-in-law King Olaf Trygvason. Erling was one of the handsomest, largest, and strongest men; a better warrior than any other; and in all exercises he was like King Olaf himself. He was, besides, a man of understanding, jealous in everything he undertook, and a deadly man at arms. Sigvat talks thus of him:–

"No earl or baron, young or old,
Match with this bonde brave can hold.
Mild was brave Erling, all men say,
When not engaged in bloody fray:

His courage he kept hid until
The fight began, then foremost still
Erling was seen in war's wild game,
And famous still is Erling's name."

It was a common saying among the people, that Erling had been the most valiant who ever held lands under a king in Norway. Erlings and Astrid s children were these–Aslak, Skialg, Sigurd, Lodin, Thorer, and Ragnhild, who was married to Thorberg Arnason. Erling had always with him ninety free-born men or more, and both winter and summer it was the custom in his house to drink at the mid-day meal according to a measure[34], but at the night meal there was no measure in drinking. When the earl was in the neighbourhood he had 200[35] men or more. He never went to sea with less than a fully-manned ship of twenty benches of rowers. Erling had also a ship of thirty-two benches of rowers, which was besides, very large for that size, and which he used in viking cruises, or on an expedition; and in it there were 200 men at the very least.

22. OF THE HERSE ERLING SKIALGSON.

ERLING HAD ALWAYS AT home on his farm thirty slaves, besides other serving-people. He gave his slaves a certain day's work; but after it he gave them leisure, and leave that each should work in the twilight and at night for himself, and as he pleased. He gave them arable land to sow corn in, and let them apply their crops to their own use. He laid upon each a certain quantity of labour to work themselves free by doing it; and there were many who bought their freedom in this way in one year, or in the second year, and all who had any luck could make themselves free within three years. With this money he bought other slaves: and to some of his freed people he showed how to work in the herring-fishery, to others he showed some useful handicraft; and some cleared his outfields and set up houses. He helped all to prosperity.

34 There were silver-studs in a row from the rim to the bottom of the drinking born or cup; and as it went round each drank till the stud appeared above the liquor. This was drinking by measure.–L.

35 I.e., 240.

23. OF EARL EIRIK.

When Earl Eirik had ruled over Norway for twelve years, there came a message to him from his brother-in-law King Canute, the Danish king, that he should go with him on an expedition westward to England; for Eirik was very celebrated for his campaigns, as he had gained the victory in the two hardest engagements which had ever been fought in the north countries. The one was that in which the Earls Hakon and Eirik fought with the Jomsborg vikings; the other that in which Earl Eirik fought with King Olaf Trygvason. Thord Kolbeinson speaks of this:–

"A song of praise
Again I raise.
To the earl bold
The word is told,
That Knut the Brave
His aid would crave;
The earl, I knew,
To friend stands true."

The earl would not sleep upon the message of the king, but sailed immediately out of the country, leaving behind his son Earl Hakon to take care of Norway; and, as he was but seventeen years of age, Einar Tambaskelfer was to be at his hand to rule the country for him.

Eirik met King Canute in England, and was with him when he took the castle of London. Earl Eirik had a battle also to the westward of the castle of London, and killed Ulfkel Snilling. So says Thord Kolbeinson:–

"West of London town we passed,
And our ocean-steeds made fast,
And a bloody fight begin,
England's lands to lose or win.
Blue sword and shining spear
Laid Ulfkel's dead corpse there,
Our Thingmen hear the war-shower sounding
Our grey arrows from their shields rebounding."

Earl Eirik was a winter in England, and had many battles there. The following autumn he intended to make a pilgrimage to Rome, but he died in England of a bloody flux.

24. THE MURDER OF EDMUND.

King Canute came to England the summer that King Ethelred died, and had many battles with Ethelred's sons, in which the victory was sometimes on one side, sometimes on the other. Then King Canute took Queen Emma in marriage; and their children were Harald, Hardacanute, and Gunhild. King Canute then made an agreement with King Edmund, that each of them should have a half of England. In the same month Henry Strion murdered King Edmund. King Canute then drove all Ethelred's sons out of England. So says Sigvat:–

"Now all the sons of Ethelred
Were either fallen, or had fled:
Some slain by Canute,–some they say,
To save their lives had run away."

25. OLAF AND ETHELRED'S SONS.

King Ethelred's sons came to Rouen in Valland from England, to their mother's brother, the same summer that King Olaf Haraldson came from the west from his viking cruise, and they were all during the winter in Normandy together. They made an agreement with each other that King Olaf should have Northumberland, if they could succeed in taking England from the Danes. Therefore about harvest, Olaf sent his foster-father Hrane to England to collect men-at-arms; and Ethelred's sons sent tokens to their friends and relations with him. King Olaf, besides, gave him much money with him to attract people to them. Hrane was all winter in England, and got promises from many powerful men of fidelity, as the people of the country would rather have native kings over them; but the Danish power had become so great in England, that all the people were brought under their dominion.

26. BATTLE OF KING OLAF.

In spring (A.D. 1014) King Olaf and King Ethelred's sons set out together to the west, and came to a place in England called Jungufurda, where they landed with their army and moved forward against the castle. Many men were there who had promised them their aid. They took the castle; and killed many people. Now when King Canute's men heard of this they assembled an army, and were soon in such force that Ethelred's sons could not stand against it; and they saw no other way left but to return to Rouen. Then King Olaf separated from them, and would not go back to Valland, but sailed northwards along England, all the way to Northumberland, where he put into a haven at a place called Valde; and in a battle there with the townspeople and merchants he gained the victory, and a great booty.

27. OLAF'S EXPEDITION TO NORWAY.

King Olaf left his long-ships there behind, but made ready two ships of burden; and had with him 220 men in them, well-armed, and chosen people. He sailed out to sea northwards in harvest, but encountered a tremendous storm and they were in danger of being lost; but as they had a chosen crew, and the king s luck with them, all went on well. So says Ottar:–

"Olaf, great stem of kings, is brave–
Bold in the fight, bold on the wave.
No thought of fear
Thy heart comes near.
Undaunted, 'midst the roaring flood,
Firm at his post each shipman stood;
And thy two ships stout
The gale stood out."

And further he says:–

"Thou able chief! with thy fearless crew
Thou meetest, with skill and courage true,
The wild sea's wrath
On thy ocean path.
Though waves mast-high were breaking round.
Thou findest the middle of Norway's ground,
With helm in hand
On Saela's strand."

It is related here that King Olaf came from the sea to the very middle of Norway; and the isle is called Saela where they landed, and is outside of Stad. King Olaf said he thought it must be a lucky day for them, since they had landed at Saela in Norway; and observed it was a good omen that it so happened. As they were going up in the isle, the king slipped with one foot in a place where there was clay, but supported himself with the other foot. Then said he "The king falls." "Nay," replies Hrane, "thou didst not fall, king, but set fast foot in the soil." The king laughed thereat, and said, "It may be so if God will." They went down again thereafter to their ships, and sailed to Ulfasund, where they heard that Earl Hakon was south in Sogn, and was expected north as soon as wind allowed with a single ship.

28. HAKON TAKEN PRISONER BY OLAF.

King Olaf steered his ships within the ordinary ships' course when he came abreast of Fjaler district, and ran into Saudungssund. There he laid his two vessels one on each side of the sound with a thick cable between them. At the same moment Hakon, Earl Eirik's son, came rowing into the sound with a manned ship; and as they thought these were but two merchant-vessels that were lying in the sound, they rowed between them. Then Olaf and his men draw the cable up right under Hakon's ship's keel and wind it up with the capstan. As soon as the vessel's course was stopped her stern was lifted up, and her bow plunged down; so that the water came in at her fore-end and over both sides, and she upset. King Olaf's people took Earl Hakon and all his men whom they could get hold of out of the water, and made them prisoners; but some they killed with stones and other weapons, and some were drowned. So says Ottar:–

"The black ravens wade
In the blood from thy blade.
Young Hakon so gay,
With his ship, is thy prey:
His ship, with its gear,
Thou hast ta'en; and art here,
Thy forefather's land
From the earl to demand."

Earl Hakon was led up to the king's ship. He was the handsomest man that could be seen. He had long hair, as fine as silk, bound about his bead with a gold ornament.

When he sat down in the fore-hold, the king said to him, "It is not false what is said of your family, that ye are handsome people to look at; but now your luck has deserted you."

Hakon the earl replied, "It has always been the case that success is changeable; and there is no luck in the matter. It has gone with your family as with mine, to have by turns the better lot. I am little beyond childhood in years; and at any rate we could not have defended ourselves, as we did not expect any attack on the way. It may turn out better with us another time."

Then said King Olaf, "Dost thou not apprehend that thou art in that condition that, hereafter, there can be neither victory nor defeat for thee?"

The earl replies, "That is what thou only canst determine, king, according to thy pleasure."

Olaf says, "What wilt thou give me, earl, if for this time I let thee go, whole and unhurt?"

The earl asks what he would take.

"Nothing," says the king, "except that thou shalt leave the country, give up thy kingdom, and take an oath that thou shalt never go into battle against me."

The earl answered, that he would do so. And now Earl Hakon took the oath that he would never fight against Olaf, or seek to defend Norway against him, or attack him; and King Olaf thereupon gave him and all his men life and peace. The earl got back the ship which had brought him there, and he and his men rowed their way. Thus says Sigvat of him:–

"In old Saudungs sound
The king Earl Hakon found,
Who little thought that there
A foeman was so near.
The best and fairest youth
Earl Hakon was in truth,
That speaks the Danish tongue,
And of the race of great Hakon."

29. HAKON'S DEPARTURE FROM NORWAY.

After this (A.D. 1014) the earl made ready as fast as possible to leave the country and sail over to England. He met King Canute, his mother's brother, there, and told him all that had taken place between him and King Olaf. King Canute received him remarkably well, placed him in his court in his own house, and gave him great power in his kingdom. Earl Hakon dwelt a long time with King Canute. During the time Svein and Hakon ruled over Norway, a reconciliation with Erling Skialgson was effected, and secured by Aslak, Erling's son, marrying Gunhild, Earl Svein's daughter; and the father and son, Erling and Aslak, retained all the fiefs which King Olaf Trygvason had given to Erling. Thus Erling became a firm friend of the earl's, and their mutual friendship was confirmed by oath.

30. ASTA RECEIVES HER SON OLAF.

King Olaf went now eastward along the land, holding Things with the bondes all over the country. Many went willingly with him; but some, who were Earl Svein's friends or relations, spoke against him. Therefore King Olaf sailed in all haste eastward to Viken; went in there with his ships; set them on the land; and proceeded up the country, in order to meet his stepfather, Sigurd Syr. When he came to Vestfold he was received in a friendly way by many who had been his father's friends or acquaintances; and also there and in Folden were many of his family. In autumn (A.D. 1014) he proceeded up the country to his stepfather King Sigurd's, and came there one day very early. As Olaf was coming near to the house, some of the servants ran beforehand to the house, and into the room. Olaf's mother, Asta, was sitting in the room, and around her some of her girls. When the servants told her of King Olaf's approach, and that he might soon be expected, Asta stood up directly, and ordered the men and girls to put everything in the best order. She ordered four girls to bring out all that belonged to the decoration of the room and put it in order with hangings and benches. Two fellows brought straw for the floor, two brought forward four-cornered tables and the drinking-jugs, two bore out victuals and placed the meat on the table, two she sent away from the house to procure in the greatest haste all that was needed, and two carried in the ale; and all the other serving men and girls went outside of the house. Messengers went to seek King Sigurd wherever he might be, and brought to him his dress-clothes, and his horse with gilt saddle, and his bridle, which was gilt and set with precious stones. Four men she sent off to the four quarters of the country to invite all the great people to a feast, which she prepared as a rejoicing for her son's return. All who were before in the house she made to dress themselves with the best they had, and lent clothes to those who had none suitable.

31. KING SIGURD'S DRESS.

King Sigurd Syr was standing in his corn-field when the messengers came to him and brought him the news, and also told him all that Asta was doing at home in the house. He had many people on his farm. Some were then shearing corn, some bound it together, some drove it to the building, some unloaded it and put it in stack or barn; but the king, and two men with him, went sometimes into the field, sometimes to the place where the corn was put into the barn. His dress, it is told, was this:–he had a blue kirtle and blue breeches; shoes which were laced about the legs; a grey cloak, and a grey wide-brimmed hat; a veil before his face; a staff in his hand with a gilt-silver head on it and a silver ring around it. Of Sigurd's living and disposition it is related that he was a very gain-making man who attended carefully to his cattle and husbandry, and managed his housekeeping himself. He was nowise given to pomp, and was rather taciturn. But he was a man of the best understanding in Norway, and also excessively wealthy in movable property. Peaceful he was, and nowise haughty. His wife Asta was generous and high-minded. Their children were, Guthorm, the eldest; then Gunhild; the next Halfdan, Ingerid, and Harald. The messengers said to Sigurd, "Asta told us to bring thee word how much it lay at her heart that thou shouldst on this occasion comport thyself in the fashion of great men, and show a disposition more akin to Harald Harfager's race than to thy mother's father's, Hrane Thin-nose, or Earl Nereid the Old, although they too were very wise men." The king replies, "The news ye bring me is weighty, and ye bring it forward in great heat. Already before now Asta has been taken up much with people who were not so near to her; and I see she is still of the same disposition. She takes this up with great warmth; but can she lead her son out of the business with the same splendour she is leading him into it? If it is to proceed so methinks they who mix themselves up in it regard little property or life. For this man, King Olaf, goes against a great superiority of power; and the wrath of the Danish and Swedish kings lies at the foot of his determination, if he ventures to go against them."

32. OF THE FEAST.

When the king had said this he sat down, and made them take off his shoes, and put corduvan boots on, to which he bound his gold spurs. Then he put off his cloak and coat, and dressed himself in his finest clothes, with a scarlet cloak over all; girded on his sword, set a gilded helmet upon his head, and mounted his horse. He sent his labouring people out to the neighbourhood, and gathered to him thirty well-clothed men, and rode home with them. As they rode up to the house, and were near the room, they saw on the other side of the house the banners of Olaf coming waving; and there was he himself, with about 100 men all well equipped. People were gathered over all upon the house-tops. King Sigurd immediately saluted his stepson from horseback in a friendly way, and invited him and his men to come in and drink a cup with him. Asta, on the contrary, went up and kissed her son, and invited him to stay with her; and land, and people, and all the good she could do for him stood at his service. King Olaf thanked her kindly for her invitation. Then she took him by the hand, and led him into the room to the high-seat. King Sigurd got men to take charge of their clothes, and give their horses corn; and then he himself went to his high-seat, and the feast was made with the greatest splendour.

33. CONVERSATION OF OLAF AND SIGURD.

King Olaf had not been long here before he one day called his stepfather King Sigurd, his mother Asta, and his foster-father Hrane to a conference and consultation. Olaf began thus: "It has so happened," said he, "as is well known to you, that I have returned to this country after a very long sojourn in foreign parts, during all which time I and my men have had nothing for our support but what we captured in war, for which we have often hazarded both life and soul: for many an innocent man have we deprived of his property, and some of their lives; and foreigners are now sitting in the possessions which my father, his father, and their forefathers for a long series of generations owned, and to which I have udal right. They have not been content with this, but have taken to themselves also the properties of all our relations who are descended from Harald Harfager. To some they have left little, to others nothing at all. Now I will disclose to you what I have long concealed in my own mind, that I intend to take the heritage of my forefathers; but I will not wait upon the Danish or Swedish king to supplicate the least thing from them, although they for the time call that their property which was Harald Harfager's heritage. To say the truth, I intend rather to seek my patrimony with battle-axe and sword, and that with the help of all my friends and relations, and of those who in this business will take my side. And in this matter I will so lay hand to the work that one of two things shall happen,–either I shall lay all this kingdom under my rule which they got into their hands by the slaughter of my kinsman Olaf Trygvason, or I shall fall here upon my inheritance in the land of my fathers. Now I expect of thee, Sigurd, my stepfather, as well as other men here in the country who have udal right of succession to the kingdom, according to the law made by King Harald Harfager, that nothing shall be of such importance to you as to prevent you from throwing off the disgrace from our family of being slow at supporting the man who comes forward to raise up again our race. But whether ye show any manhood in this affair or not, I know the inclination of the people well,–that all want to be free from the slavery of foreign masters, and will give aid and strength to the attempt. I have not proposed this matter to any before thee, because I know thou art a man of understanding, and can best judge how this my purpose shall be brought forward in the beginning, and whether we shall, in all quietness, talk about it to a few persons, or instantly declare it to the people at large. I have already shown my teeth by taking prisoner the Earl Hakon, who has now left the country, and given me, under oath, the part of the kingdom which he had before; and I think it will be easier to have Earl Svein alone to deal with, than if both were defending the country against us."

King Sigurd answers, "It is no small affair, King Olaf, thou hast in thy mind; and thy purpose comes more, methinks, from hasty pride than from prudence. But it may be there is a wide difference between my humble ways and the high thoughts thou hast; for whilst yet in thy childhood thou wast full always of ambition and desire of command, and now thou art experienced in battles, and hast formed thyself upon the manner of foreign chiefs. I know therefore well, that as thou hast taken this into thy head, it is useless to dissuade thee from it; and also it is not to be denied that it goes to the heart of all who have courage in them, that the whole Harfager race and kingdom should go to the ground. But I will not bind myself by any promise, before I know the views and intentions of other Upland kings; but thou hast done well in letting me know thy purpose, before declaring it publicly to the people. I will promise thee, however, my interest with the kings, and other chiefs, and country people; and also, King Olaf, all my property stands to thy aid, and to strengthen thee. But we will only produce the matter to the community so soon as we see some progress, and expect some strength to this undertaking; for thou canst easily perceive that it is a daring measure to enter into strife with Olaf the Swedish king, and Canute, who is king both of Denmark and England; and thou requirest great support under thee, if it is to succeed. It is not unlikely, in my opinion, that thou wilt get good support from the people, as the commonalty always loves what is new; and it went so before, when Olaf Trygvason came here to the country, that all rejoiced at it, although he did not long enjoy the kingdom."

When the consultation had proceeded so far, Asta took up the word. "For my part, my son, I am rejoiced at thy arrival, but much more at thy advancing thy honour. I will spare nothing for that purpose that stands in my power, although it be but little help that can be expected from me. But if a choice could be made, I would rather that thou shouldst be the supreme king of Norway, even if thou shouldst not sit longer in thy kingdom than Olaf Trygvason did, than that thou shouldst not be a greater king than Sigurd Syr is, and die the death of old age." With this the conference closed. King Olaf remained here a while with all his men. King Sigurd entertained them, day about, the one day with fish and milk, the other day with flesh-meat and ale.

34. KINGS IN THE UPLAND DISTRICTS.

At that time there were many kings in the Uplands who had districts to rule over, and the most of them were descended from Harald Harfager. In Hedemark two brothers ruled–Hrorek and Ring; in Gudbrandsdal, Gudrod; and there was also a king in Raumarike; and one had Hadaland and Thoten; and in Valders also there was a king. With these district-kings Sigurd had a meeting up in Hadaland, and Olaf Haraldson also met with them. To these district-kings whom Sigurd had assembled he set forth his stepson Olaf's purpose, and asked their aid, both of men and in counsel and consent; and represented to them how necessary it was to cast off the yoke which the Danes and Swedes had laid upon them. He said that there was now a man before them who could head such an enterprise; and he recounted the many brave actions which Olaf had achieved upon his war-expeditions.

Then King Hrorek says, "True it is that Harald Harfager's kingdom has gone to decay, none of his race being supreme king over Norway. But the people here in the country have experienced many things. When King Hakon, Athelstan's foster-son, was king, all were content; but when Gunhild's sons ruled over the country, all were so weary of their tyranny and injustice that they would rather have foreign men as kings, and be themselves more their own rulers; for the foreign kings were usually abroad and cared little about the customs of the people if the scat they laid on the country was paid. When enmity arose between the Danish king Harald and Earl Hakon, the Jomsborg vikings made an expedition against Norway; then the whole people arose, and threw the hostilities from themselves; and thereafter the people encouraged Earl Hakon to keep the country, and defend it with sword and spear against the Danish king. But when he had set himself fast in the kingdom with the help of the people, he became so hard and overbearing towards the country-folks, that they would no longer suffer him. The Throndhjem people killed him, and raised to the kingly power Olaf Trygvason, who was of the udal succession to the kingdom, and in all respects well fitted to be a chief. The whole country's desire was to make him supreme king, and raise again the kingdom which Harald Harfager had made for himself. But when King Olaf thought himself quite firmly seated in his kingdom, no man could rule his own concerns for him. With us small kings he was so unreasonable, as to take to himself not only all the scat and duties which Harald Harfager had levied from us, but a great deal more. The people at last had so little freedom under him, that it was not allowed to every man to believe in what god he pleased. Now since he has been taken away we have kept friendly with the Danish king; have received great help from him when we have had any occasion for it; and have been allowed to rule ourselves, and live in peace and quiet in the inland country, and without any overburden. I am therefore content that things be as they are, for I do not see what better rights I am to enjoy by one of my relations ruling over the country; and if I am to be no better off, I will take no part in the affair."

Then said King Ring, his brother, "I will also declare my opinion that it is better for me, if I hold the same power and property as now, that my relative is king over Norway, rather than a foreign chief, so that our family may again raise its head in the land. It is, besides, my opinion about this man Olaf, that his fate and luck must determine whether he is to obtain the kingdom or not; and if he succeed in making himself supreme king, then he will be the best off who has best deserved his friendship. At present he has in no respect greater power than any of us; nay, indeed, he has less; as we have lands and kingdoms to rule over, and he has nothing, and we are equally entitled by the udal right to the kingdom as he is himself. Now, if we will be his men, give him our aid, allow him to take the highest dignity in the country, and stand by him with our strength, how should he not reward us well, and hold it in remembrance to our great advantage, if he be the honourable man I believe him to be, and all say he is? Therefore let us join the adventure, say I, and bind ourselves in friendship with him."

Then the others, one after the other, stood up and spoke; and the conclusion was, that the most of them determined to enter into a league with

King Olaf. He promised them his perfect friendship, and that he would hold by and improve the country's laws and rights, if he became supreme king of Norway. This league was confirmed by oath.

35. OLAF GETS THE TITLE OF KING FROM THE THING.

THEREAFTER THE KINGS SUMMONED a Thing, and there King Olaf set forth this determination to all the people, and his demand on the kingly power. He desires that the bondes should receive him as king; and promises, on the other hand, to allow them to retain their ancient laws, and to defend the land from foreign masters and chiefs. On this point he spoke well, and long; and he got great praise for his speech. Then the kings rose and spoke, the one after the other, and supported his cause, and this message to the people. At last it came to this, that King Olaf was proclaimed king over the whole country, and the kingdom adjudged to him according to law in the Uplands (A.D. 1014).

36. KING OLAF TRAVELS IN THE UPLANDS.

KING OLAF BEGAN IMMEDIATELY his progress through the country, appointing feasts before him wherever there were royal farms. First he travelled round in Hadaland, and then he proceeded north to Gudbrandsdal. And now it went as King Sigurd Syr had foretold, that people streamed to him from all quarters; and he did not appear to have need for half of them, for he had nearly 300 men. But the entertainments bespoken did not half serve; for it had been the custom that kings went about in guest-quarters in the Uplands with 60 or 70 men only, and never with more than 100 men. The king therefore hastened over the country, only stopping one night at the same place. When he came north to Dovrefield, he arranged his journey so that he came over the mountain and down upon the north side of it, and then came to Opdal, where he remained all night. Afterwards he proceeded through Opdal forest, and came out at Medaldal, where he proclaimed a Thing, and summoned the bondes to meet him at it. The king made a speech to the Thing, and asked the bondes to accept him as king; and promised, on his part, the laws and rights which King Olaf Trygvason had offered them. The bondes had no strength to make opposition to the king; so the result was that they received him as king, and confirmed it by oath: but they sent word to Orkadal and Skaun of all that they knew concerning Olaf's proceedings.

37. LEVY AGAINST OLAF IN THRONDHJEM.

Einar Tambaskelfer had a farm and house at Husaby in Skaun; and now when he got news of Olaf's proceedings, he immediately split up a war-arrow, and sent it out as a token to the four quarters–north, south, east, west,–to call together all free and unfree men in full equipment of war: therewith the message, that they were to defend the land against King Olaf. The message-stick went to Orkadal, and thence to Gaulardal, where the whole war-force was to assemble.

38. OLAF'S PROGRESS IN THRONDHJEM.

King Olaf proceeded with his men down into Orkadal, and advanced in peace and with all gentleness; but when he came to Griotar he met the assembled bondes, amounting to more than 700 men. Then the king arrayed his army, for he thought the bondes were to give battle. When the bondes saw this, they also began to put their men in order; but it went on very slowly, for they had not agreed beforehand who among them should be commander. Now when King Olaf saw there was confusion among the bondes, he sent to them Thorer Gudbrandson; and when he came he told them King Olaf did not want to fight them, but named twelve of the ablest men in their flock of people, who were desired to come to King Olaf. The bondes agreed to this; and the twelve men went over a rising ground which is there, and came to the place where the king's army stood in array. The king said to them, "Ye bondes have done well to give me an opportunity to speak with you, for now I will explain to you my errand here to the Throndhjem country. First I must tell you, what ye already must have heard, that Earl Hakon and I met in summer; and the issue of our meeting was, that he gave me the whole kingdom he possessed in the Throndhjem country, which, as ye know, consists of Orkadal, Gaulardal, Strind, and Eyna district. As a proof of this, I have here with me the very men who were present, and saw the earl's and my own hands given upon it, and heard the word and oath, and witnessed the agreement the earl made with me. Now I offer you peace and law, the same as King Olaf Trygvason offered before me."

The king spoke well, and long; and ended by proposing to the bondes two conditions–either to go into his service and be subject to him, or to fight him. Thereupon the twelve bondes went back to their people, and told the issue of their errand, and considered with the people what they should resolve upon. Although they discussed the matter backwards and forwards for a while, they preferred at last to submit to the king; and it was confirmed by the oath of the bondes. The king now proceeded on his journey, and the bondes made feasts for him. The king then proceeded to the sea-coast, and got ships; and among others he got a long-ship of twenty benches of rowers from Gunnar of Gelmin; another ship of twenty benches he got from Loden of Viggia; and three ships of twenty benches from the farm of Angrar on the ness which farm Earl Hakon had possessed, but a steward managed it for him, by name Bard White. The king had, besides, four or five boats; and with these vessels he went in all haste into the fjord of Throndhjem.

39. OF EARL SVEIN'S PROCEEDINGS.

Earl Svein was at that time far up in the Throndhjem fjord at Steinker, which at that time was a merchant town, and was there preparing for the yule festival (A.D. 1015). When Einar Tambaskelfer heard that the Orkadal people had submitted to King Olaf, he sent men to Earl Svein to bring him the tidings. They went first to Nidaros, and took a rowing-boat which belonged to Einar, with which they went out into the fjord, and came one day late in the evening to Steinker, where they brought to the earl the news about all King Olaf's proceedings. The earl owned a long-ship, which was lying afloat and rigged just outside the town: and immediately, in the evening, he ordered all his movable goods, his people's clothes, and also meat and drink, as much as the vessel could carry, to be put on board, rowed immediately out in the night-time, and came with daybreak to Skarnsund. There he saw King Olaf rowing in with his fleet into the fjord. The earl turned towards the land within Masarvik, where there was a thick wood, and lay so near the rocks that the leaves and branches hung over the vessel. They cut down some large trees, which they laid over the quarter on the sea-side, so that the ship could not be seen for leaves, especially as it was scarcely clear daylight when the king came rowing past them. The weather was calm, and the king rowed in among the islands; and when the king's fleet was out of sight the earl rowed out of the fjord, and on to Frosta, where his kingdom lay, and there he landed.

40. EARL SVEIN'S AND EINAR'S CONSULTATIONS.

Earl Svein sent men out to Gaulardal to his brother-in-law, Einar Tambaskelfer; and when Einar came the earl told him how it had been with him and King Olaf, and that now he would assemble men to go out against King Olaf, and fight him.

Einar answers, "We should go to work cautiously, and find out what King Olaf intends doing; and not let him hear anything concerning us but that we are quiet. It may happen that if he hears nothing about our assembling people, he may sit quietly where he is in Steinker all the Yule; for there is plenty prepared for him for the Yule feast: but if he hears we are assembling men, he will set right out of the fjord with his vessels, and we shall not get hold of him." Einar's advice was taken; and the earl went to Stjoradal, into guest-quarters among the bondes.

When King Olaf came to Steinker he collected all the meat prepared for the Yule feast, and made it be put on board, procured some transport vessels, took meat and drink with him, and got ready to sail as fast as possible, and went out all the way to Nidaros. Here King Olaf Trygvason had laid the foundation of a merchant town, and had built a king's house: but before that Nidaros was only a single house, as before related. When Earl Eirik came to the country, he applied all his attention to his house of Lade, where his father had had his main residence, and he neglected the houses which Olaf had erected at the Nid; so that some were fallen down, and those which stood were scarcely habitable. King Olaf went now with his ships up the Nid, made all the houses to be put in order directly that were still standing, and built anew those that had fallen down, and employed in this work a great many people. Then he had all the meat and drink brought on shore to the houses, and prepared to hold Yule there; so Earl Svein and Einar had to fall upon some other plan.

41. OF SIGVAT THE SKALD.

There was an Iceland man called Thord Sigvaldaskald, who had been long with Earl Sigvalde, and afterwards with the earl's brother, Thorkel the Tall; but after the earl's death Thord had become a merchant. He met King Olaf on his viking cruise in the west, and entered into his service, and followed him afterwards. He was with the king when the incidents above related took place. Thord had a son called Sigvat fostered in the house of Thorkel at Apavatn, in Iceland. When he was nearly a grown man he went out of the country with some merchants; and the ship came in autumn to the Throndhjem country, and the crew lodged in the hered (district). The same winter King Olaf came to Throndhjem, as just now related by us. Now when Sigvat heard that his father Thord was with the king, he went to him, and stayed a while with him. Sigvat was a good skald at an early age. He made a lay in honour of King Olaf, and asked the king to listen to it. The king said he did not want poems composed about him, and said he did not understand the skald's craft. Then Sigvat sang:–

"Rider of dark-blue ocean's steeds!
Allow one skald to sing thy deeds;
And listen to the song of one
Who can sing well, if any can.
For should the king despise all others,
And show no favour to my brothers,
Yet I may all men's favour claim,
Who sing, still of our great king's fame."

King Olaf gave Sigvat as a reward for his verse a gold ring that weighed half a mark, and Sigvat was made one of King Olaf's court-men. Then Sigvat sang:–

"I willingly receive this sword–
By land or sea, on shore, on board,
I trust that I shall ever be
Worthy the sword received from thee.
A faithful follower thou hast bound–
A generous master I have found;
Master and servant both have made
Just what best suits them by this trade."

Earl Svein had, according to custom, taken one half of the harbour-dues from the Iceland ship-traders about autumn (A.D. 1014); for the Earls Eirik and Hakon had always taken one half of these and all other revenues in the Throndhjem country. Now when King Olaf came there, he sent his men to demand that half of the tax from the Iceland traders; and they went up to the king's house and asked Sigvat to help them. He went to the king, and sang:–

"My prayer, I trust, will not be vain–
No gold by it have I to gain:

All that the king himself here wins
Is not red gold, but a few skins.
it is not right that these poor men
Their harbour-dues should pay again.
That they paid once I know is true;
Remit, great king, what scarce is due."

42. OF EARL SVEIN.

Earl Svein and Einar Tambaskelfer gathered a large armed force, with which they came by the upper road into Gaulardal, and so down to Nidaros, with nearly 2000 men. King Olaf's men were out upon the Gaular ridge, and had a guard on horseback. They became aware that a force was coming down the Gaulardal, and they brought word of it to the king about midnight. The king got up immediately, ordered the people to be wakened, and they went on board of the ships, bearing all their clothes and arms on board, and all that they could take with them, and then rowed out of the river. Then came the earl's men to the town at the same moment, took all the Christmas provision, and set fire to the houses. King Olaf went out of the fjord down to Orkadal, and there landed the men from their ships. From Orkadal they went up to the mountains, and over the mountains eastwards into Gudbrandsdal. In the lines composed about Kleng Brusason, it is said that Earl Eirik burned the town of Nidaros:–

"The king's half-finished hall,
Rafters, root, and all,
Is burned down by the river's side;
The flame spreads o'er the city wide."

43. OF KING OLAF.

King Olaf went southwards through Gudbrandsdal, and thence out to Hedemark. In the depth of winter (A.D. 1015) he went about in guest-quarters; but when spring returned he collected men, and went to Viken. He had with him many people from Hedemark, whom the kings had given him; and also many powerful people from among the bondes joined him, among whom Ketil Kalf from Ringanes. He had also people from Raumarike. His stepfather, Sigurd Syr, gave him the help also of a great body of men. They went down from thence to the coast, and made ready to put to sea from Viken. The fleet, which was manned with many fine fellows, went out then to Tunsberg.

44. OF EARL SVEIN'S FORCES.

After Yule (A.D. 1015) Earl Svein gathers all the men of the Throndhjem country, proclaims a levy for an expedition, and fits out ships. At that time there were in the Throndhjem country a great number of lendermen; and many of them were so powerful and well-born, that they descended from earls, or even from the royal race, which in a short course of generations reckoned to Harald Harfager, and they were also very rich. These lendermen were of great help to the kings or earls who ruled the land; for it was as if the lenderman had the bonde-people of each district in his power. Earl Svein being a good friend of the lendermen, it was easy for him to collect people. His brother-in-law, Einar Tambaskelfer, was on his side, and with him many other lendermen; and among them many, both lendermen and bondes, who the winter before had taken the oath of fidelity to King Olaf. When they were ready for sea they went directly out of the fjord, steering south along the land, and drawing men from every district. When they came farther south, abreast of Rogaland, Erling Skialgson came to meet them, with many people and many lendermen with him. Now they steered eastward with their whole fleet to Viken, and Earl Svein ran in there towards the end of Easter. The earl steered his fleet to Grenmar, and ran into Nesjar (A.D. 1015).

45. KING OLAF S FORCES.

King Olaf steered his fleet out from Viken, until the two fleets were not far from each other, and they got news of each other the Saturday before Palm Sunday. King Olaf himself had a ship called the Carl's Head, on the bow of which a king's head was carved out, and he himself had carved it. This head was used long after in Norway on ships which kings steered themselves.

46. KING OLAF'S SPEECH.

As soon as day dawned on Sunday morning, King Olaf got up, put on his clothes, went to the land, and ordered to sound the signal for the whole army to come on shore. Then he made a speech to the troops, and told the whole assembly that he had heard there was but a short distance between them and Earl Svein. "Now," said he, "we shall make ready; for it can be but a short time until we meet. Let the people arm, and every man be at the post that has been appointed him, so that all may be ready when I order the signal to sound for casting off from the land. Then let us row off at once; and so that none go on before the rest of the ships, and none lag behind when I row out of the harbour: for we cannot tell if we shall find the earl where he was lying, or if he has come out to meet us. When we do meet, and the battle begins, let people be alert to bring all our ships in close order, and ready to bind them together. Let us spare ourselves in the beginning, and take care of our weapons, that we do not cast them into the sea, or shoot them away in the air to no purpose. But when the fight becomes hot and the ships are bound together, then let each man show what is in him of manly spirit."

47. OF THE BATTLE AT NESJAR.

KING OLAF HAD IN his ship 100 men armed in coats of ring-mail, and in foreign helmets. The most of his men had white shields, on which the holy cross was gilt; but some had painted it in blue or red. He had also had the cross painted in front on all the helmets, in a pale colour. He had a white banner on which was a serpent figured. He ordered a mass to be read before him, went on board ship, and ordered his people to refresh themselves with meat and drink. He then ordered the war-horns to sound to battle, to leave the harbour, and row off to seek the earl. Now when they came to the harbour where the earl had lain, the earl's men were armed, and beginning to row out of the harbour; but when they saw the king's fleet coming they began to bind the ships together, to set up their banners, and to make ready for the fight. When King Olaf saw this he hastened the rowing, laid his ship alongside the earl's, and the battle began. So says Sigvat the skald:–

"Boldly the king did then pursue
Earl Svein, nor let him out of view.
The blood ran down the reindeer's flank
Of each sea-king–his vessel's plank.
Nor did the earl's stout warriors spare

In battle-brunt the sword and spear.
Earl Svein his ships of war pushed on,
And lashed their stout stems one to one."

It is said that King Olaf brought his ships into battle while Svein was still lying in the harbour. Sigvat the skald was himself in the fight; and in summer, just after the battle, he composed a lay, which is called the "Nesjar Song", in which he tells particularly the circumstances:–

"In the fierce fight 'tis known how near
The scorner of the ice-cold spear
Laid the Charles' head the earl on board,
All eastward of the Agder fjord."

Then was the conflict exceedingly sharp, and it was long before it could be seen how it was to go in the end. Many fell on both sides, and many were the wounded. So says Sigvat:–

"No urging did the earl require,
Midst spear and sword–the battle's fire;
No urging did the brave king need
The ravens in this shield-storm to feed.
Of limb-lopping enough was there,
And ghastly wounds of sword and spear.
Never, I think, was rougher play
Than both the armies had that day."

The earl had most men, but the king had a chosen crew in his ship, who had followed him in all his wars; and, besides, they were so excellently equipped, as before related, that each man had a coat of ring-mail, so that he could not be wounded. So says Sigvat:–

"Our lads, broad-shouldered, tall, and hale,
Drew on their cold shirts of ring-mail.
Soon sword on sword was shrilly ringing,
And in the air the spears were singing.
Under our helms we hid our hair,
For thick flew arrows through the air.
Right glad was I our gallant crew,
Steel-clad from head to foot, to view."

48. EARL SVEIN'S FLIGHT.

When the men began to fall on board the earl's ships, and many appeared wounded, so that the sides of the vessels were but thinly beset with men, the crew of King Olaf prepared to board. Their banner was brought up to the ship that was nearest the earl's, and the king himself followed the banner. So says Sigvat:–

"'On with the king!' his banners waving:
'On with the king!' the spears he's braving!
'On, steel-clad men! and storm the deck,
Slippery with blood and strewed with wreck.
A different work ye have to share,
His banner in war-storm to bear,
From your fair girl's, who round the hall
Brings the full mead-bowl to us all.'"

Now was the severest fighting. Many of Svein's men fell, and some sprang overboard. So says Sigvat:–

"Into the ship our brave lads spring,–
On shield and helm their red blades ring;
The air resounds with stroke on stroke,–
The shields are cleft, the helms are broke.
The wounded bonde o'er the side
Falls shrieking in the blood-stained tide–
The deck is cleared with wild uproar–
The dead crew float about the shore."

And also these lines:–

"The shields we brought from home were white,
Now they are red-stained in the fight:
This work was fit for those who wore
Ringed coats-of-mail their breasts before.
Where for the foe blunted the best sword
I saw our young king climb on board.
He stormed the first; we followed him–
The war-birds now in blood may swim."

Now defeat began to come down upon the earl's men. The king's men pressed upon the earl's ship and entered it; but when the earl saw how it was going, he called out to his forecastle-men to cut the cables and cast the ship loose, which they did. Then the king's men threw grapplings over the timber heads of the ship, and so held her fast to their own; but the earl ordered the timber heads to be cut away, which was done. So says Sigvat:–

"The earl, his noble ship to save,
To cut the posts loud order gave.
The ship escaped: our greedy eyes
Had looked on her as a clear prize.
The earl escaped; but ere he fled
We feasted Odin's fowls with dead:–
With many a goodly corpse that floated
Round our ship's stern his birds were bloated."

Einar Tambaskelfer had laid his ship right alongside the earl's. They threw an anchor over the bows of the earl's ship, and thus towed her away, and they slipped out of the fjord together. Thereafter the whole of the earl's fleet took to flight, and rowed out of the fjord. The skald Berse Torfason was on the forecastle of the earl's ship; and as it was gliding past the king's fleet, King Olaf called out to him–for he knew Berse, who was distinguished as a remarkably handsome man, always well equipped in clothes and arms–"Farewell, Berse!" He replied, "Farewell, king!" So says Berse himself, in a poem he composed when he fell into King Olaf's power, and was laid in prison and in fetters on board a ship:–

"Olaf the Brave
A 'farewell' gave,
(No time was there to parley long,)
To me who knows the art of song.
    The skald was fain
    'Farewell' again
In the same terms back to send–
The rule in arms to foe or friend.
    Earl Svein's distress
    I well can guess,
When flight he was compelled to take:
His fortunes I will ne'er forsake,

Though I lie here
In chains a year,
In thy great vessel all forlorn,
To crouch to thee I still will scorn:
I still will say,
No milder sway
Than from thy foe this land e'er knew:
To him, my early friend, I'm true."

49. EARL SVEIN LEAVES THE COUNTRY.

Now some of the earl's men fled up the country, some surrendered at discretion; but Svein and his followers rowed out of the fjord, and the chiefs laid their vessels together to talk with each other, for the earl wanted counsel from his lendermen. Erling Skialgson advised that they should sail north, collect people, and fight King Olaf again; but as they had lost many people, the most were of opinion that the earl should leave the country, and repair to his brother-in-law the Swedish King, and strengthen himself there with men. Einar Tambaskelfer approved also of that advice, as they had no power to hold battle against Olaf. So they discharged their fleet. The earl sailed across Folden, and with him Einar Tambaskelfer. Erling Skialgson again, and likewise many other lendermen who would not abandon their udal possessions, went north to their homes; and Erling had many people that summer about him.

50. OLAF'S AND SIGURD'S CONSULTATION.

When King Olaf and his men saw that the earl had gathered his ships together, Sigurd Syr was in haste for pursuing the earl, and letting steel decide their cause. But King Olaf replies, that he would first see what the earl intended doing–whether he would keep his force together or discharge his fleet. Sigurd Syr said, "It is for thee, king, to command; but," he adds, "I fear, from thy disposition and wilfulness, that thou wilt some day be betrayed by trusting to those great people, for they are accustomed of old to bid defiance to their sovereigns." There was no attack made, for it was soon seen that the earl's fleet was dispersing. Then King Olaf ransacked the slain, and remained there some days to divide the booty. At that time Sigvat made these verses:–

"The tale I tell is true
To their homes returned but few
Of Svein's men who came to meet
King Olaf's gallant fleet.
From the North these warmen came
To try the bloody game,–
On the waves their corpses borne
Show the game that Sunday morn.
The Throndhjem girls so fair
Their jeers, I think, will spare,
For the king's force was but small
That emptied Throndhjem's hall.
But if they will have their jeer,
They may ask their sweethearts dear,
Why they have returned shorn
Who went to shear that Sunday morn."

And also these:–

"Now will the king's power rise,
For the Upland men still prize
The king who o'er the sea
Steers to bloody victory.
Earl Svein! thou now wilt know
That our lads can make blood flow–
That the Hedemarkers hale
Can do more than tap good ale."

King Olaf gave his stepfather King Sigurd Syr, and the other chiefs who had assisted him, handsome presents at parting. He gave Ketil of Ringanes a yacht of fifteen benches of rowers, which Ketil brought up the Raum river and into the Mjosen lake.

51. OF KING OLAF.

King Olaf sent spies out to trace the earl's doings (A.D. 1015); and when he found that the earl had left the country he sailed out west, and to Viken, where many people came to him. At the Thing there he was taken as king, and so he proceeded all the way to the Naze; and when he heard that Erling Skialgson had gathered a large force, he did not tarry in North Agder, but sailed with a steady fair wind to the Throndhjem country; for there it appeared to him was the greatest strength of the land, if he could subdue it for himself while the earl was abroad. When Olaf came to Throndhjem there was no opposition, and he was elected there to be king. In harvest (A.D. 1015) he took his seat in the town of Nidaros, and collected the needful winter provision (A.D. 1016). He built a king's house, and raised Clement's church on the spot on which it now stands. He parcelled out building ground, which he gave to bondes, merchants, or others who he thought would build. There he sat down with many men-at-arms around him; for he put no great confidence in the Throndhjem people, if the earl should return to the country. The people of the interior of the Throndhjem country showed this clearly, for he got no land-scat from them.

52. PLAN OF SVEIN AND THE SWEDISH KING.

Earl Svein went first to Svithjod to his brother-in-law Olaf the Swedish king, told him all that had happened between him and Olaf the Thick, and asked his advice about what he should now undertake. The king said that the earl should stay with him if he liked, and get such a portion of his kingdom to rule over as should seem to him sufficient; "or otherwise," says he, "I will give thee help of forces to conquer the country again from Olaf." The earl chose the latter; for all those among his men who had great possessions in Norway, which was the case with many who were with him, were anxious to get back; and in the council they held about this, it was resolved that in winter they should take the land-way over Helsingjaland and Jamtaland, and so down into the Throndhjem land; for the earl reckoned most upon the faithful help and strength of the Throndhjem people of the interior as soon as he should appear there. In the meantime, however, it was determined to take a cruise in summer in the Baltic to gather property.

53. EARL SVEIN'S DEATH.

Earl Svein went eastward with his forces to Russia, and passed the summer (A.D. 1015) in marauding there; but on the approach of autumn returned with his ships to Svithjod. There he fell into a sickness, which proved fatal. After the earl's death some of the people who had followed him remained in Svithjod; others went to Helsingjaland, thence to Jamtaland, and so from the east over the dividing ridge of the country to the Throndhjem district, where they told all that had happened upon their journey: and thus the truth of Earl Svein's death was known (A.D. 1016).

54. OF THE THRONDHJEM PEOPLE.

Einar Tambaskelfer, and the people who had followed him went in winter to the Swedish king, and were received in a friendly manner. There were also among them many who had followed the earl. The Swedish king took it much amiss that Olaf the Thick had set himself down in his scat-lands, and driven the earl out of them, and therefore he threatened the king with his heaviest vengeance when opportunity offered. He said that Olaf ought not to have had the presumption to take the dominions which the earl had held of him; and all the Swedish king's men agreed with him. But the Throndhjem people, when they heard for certain that the earl was dead. and could not be expected back to Norway, turned all to obedience to King Olaf. Many came from the interior of the Throndhjem country, and became King Olaf's men; others sent word and tokens that they would service him. Then, in autumn, he went into the interior of Throndhjem, and held Things with the bondes, and was received as king in each district. He returned to Nidaros, and brought there all the king's scat and revenue, and had his winter-seat provided there (A.D. 1016).

55. OF KING OLAF'S HOUSEHOLD.

King Olaf built a king's house in Nidaros, and in it was a large room for his court, with doors at both ends. The king's high-seat was in the middle of the room; and within sat his court-bishop, Grimkel, and next him his other priests; without them sat his counsellors; and in the other high-seat opposite to the king sat his marshal, Bjorn, and next to him his pursuivants. When people of importance came to him, they also had a seat of honour. The ale was drunk by the fire-light. He divided the service among his men after the fashion of other kings. He had in his house sixty court-men and thirty pursuivants; and to them he gave pay and certain regulations. He had also thirty house-servants to do the needful work about the house, and procure what was required. He had, besides, many slaves. At the house were many outbuildings, in which the court-men slept. There was also a large room, in which the king held his court-meetings.

56. OF KING OLAF'S HABITS.

It was King Olaf's custom to rise betimes in the morning, put on his clothes, wash his hands, and then go to the church and hear the matins and morning mass. Thereafter he went to the Thing-meeting, to bring people to agreement with each other, or to talk of one or the other matter that appeared to him necessary. He invited to him great and small who were known to be men of understanding. He often made them recite to him the laws which Hakon Athelstan's foster-son had made for Throndhjem; and after considering them with those men of understanding, he ordered laws adding to or taking from those established before. But Christian privileges he settled according to the advice of Bishop Grimbel and other learned priests; and bent his whole mind to uprooting heathenism, and old customs which he thought contrary to Christianity. And he succeeded so far that the bondes accepted of the laws which the king proposed. So says Sigvat:–

"The king, who at the helm guides
His warlike ship through clashing tides,
Now gives one law for all the land–
A heavenly law, which long will stand."

King Olaf was a good and very gentle man, of little speech, and open-handed although greedy of money. Sigvat the skald, as before related, was in King Olaf's house, and several Iceland men. The king asked particularly how Christianity was observed in Iceland, and it appeared to him to be very far from where it ought to be; for, as to observing Christian practices, it was told the king that it was permitted there to eat horse-flesh, to expose infants as heathens do, besides many other things contrary to Christianity. They also told the king about many principal men who were then in Iceland. Skapte Thorodson was then the lagman of the country. He inquired also of those who were best acquainted with it about the state of people in other distant countries; and his inquiries turned principally on how Christianity was observed in the Orkney, Shetland, and Farey Islands: and, as far as he could learn, it was far from being as he could have wished. Such conversation was usually carried on by him; or else he spoke about the laws and rights of the country.

57. KING OLAF'S MESSENGERS.

The same winter (A.D. 1016) came messengers from the Swedish king, Olaf the Swede, out of Svithjod: and their leaders were two brothers, Thorgaut Skarde and Asgaut the bailiff; and they, had twenty-four men with them, when they came from the eastward, over the ridge of the country down into Veradal, they summoned a Thing of the bondes, talked to them, and demanded of them scat and duties upon account of the king of Sweden. But the bondes, after consulting with each other, determined only to pay the scat which the Swedish king required in so far as King Olaf required none upon his account, but refused to pay scat to both. The messengers proceeded farther down the valley; but received at every Thing they held the same answer, and no money. They went forward to Skaun, held a Thing there, and demanded scat; but it went there as before. Then they came to Stjoradal, and summoned a Thing, but the bondes would not come to it. Now the messengers saw that their business was a failure; and Thorgaut proposed that they should turn about, and go eastward again. "I do not think," says Asgaut, "that we have performed the king's errand unless we go to King Olaf the Thick, since the bondes refer the matter to him." He was their commander; so they proceeded to the town (Nidaros), and took lodging there. The day after they presented themselves to the king, just as he was seated at table, saluted him, and said they came with a message of the Swedish king. The king told them to come to him next day. Next day the king, having heard mass, went to his Thing-house, ordered the messengers of the Swedish king to be called, and told them to produce their message. Then Thorgaut spoke, and told first what his errand was, and next how the Throndhjem people of the interior had replied to it; and asked the king's decision on the business, that they might know what result their errand there was to have. The king answers, "While the earls ruled over the country, it was not to be wondered at if the country people thought themselves bound to obey them, as they were at least of the royal race of the kingdom. But it would have been more just if those earls had given assistance and service to the kings who had a right to the country, rather than to foreign kings, or to stir up opposition to their lawful kings, depriving them of their land and kingdom. With regard to Olaf the Swede, who calls himself entitled to the kingdom of Norway, I, who in fact am so entitled, can see no ground for his claim; but well remember the skaith and damage we have suffered from him and his relations."

Then says Asgaut. "It is not wonderful that thou art called Olaf the Thick, seeing thou answerest so haughtily to such a prince's message, and canst not see clearly how heavy the king's wrath will be for thee to support, as many have experienced who had greater strength than thou appearest to have. But if thou wishest to keep hold of thy kingdom, it will be best for thee to come to the king, and be his man; and we shall beg him to give thee this kingdom in fief under him."

The king replies with all gentleness, "I will give thee an advice, Asgaut, in return. Go back to the east again to thy king, and tell him that early in spring I will make myself ready, and will proceed eastward to the ancient frontier that divided formerly the kingdom of the kings of Norway from Sweden. There he may come if he likes, that we may conclude a peace with each other; and each of us will retain the kingdom to which he is born."

Now the messengers turned back to their lodging, and prepared for their departure, and the king went to table. The messengers came back soon after to the king's house; but the doorkeepers saw it, and reported it to the king, who told them not to let the messengers in. "I will not speak with them," said he. Then the messengers went off, and Thorgaut said he would now return home with his men; but Asgaut insisted still that he would go forward with the king's errand: so they separated. Thorgaut proceeded accordingly through Strind; but Asgaut went into Gaulardal and Orkadal, and intended proceeding southwards to More, to deliver his king's message. When King Olaf came to the knowledge of this he sent out his pursuivants after them, who found them at the ness in Stein, bound their hands behind their backs, and led them down to the point called Gaularas, where they raised a gallows, and hanged them so that they could be seen by those who travelled the usual sea-way out of the fjord. Thorgaut heard this news before he had travelled far on his way home through the Throndhjem country; and he hastened on his journey until he came to the Swedish king, and told him how it had gone with them. The king was highly enraged when he heard the account of it; and he had no lack of high words.

58. OLAF AND ERLING RECONCILED.

The spring thereafter (A.D. 1016) King Olaf Haraldson calls out an army from the Throndhjem land, and makes ready to proceed eastward. Some of the Iceland traders were then ready to sail from Norway. With them King Olaf sent word and token to Hjalte Skeggjason, and summoned him to come to him, and at the same time sent a verbal message to Skapte the lagman, and other men who principally took part in the lawgiving of Iceland, to take out of the law whatever appeared contrary to Christianity. He sent, besides, a message of friendship to the people in general. The king then proceeded southwards himself along the coast, stopping at every district, and holding Things with the bondes; and in each Thing he ordered the Christian law to be read, together with the message of salvation thereunto belonging, and with which many ill customs and much heathenism were swept away at once among the common people: for the earls had kept well the old laws and rights of the country; but with respect to keeping Christianity, they had allowed every man to do as he liked. It was thus come so far that the people were baptized in the most places on the sea-coast, but the most of them were ignorant of Christian law. In the upper ends of the valleys, and in the habitations among the mountains, the greater part of the people were heathen; for when the common man is left to himself, the faith he has been taught in his childhood is that which has the strongest hold over his inclination. But the king threatened the most violent proceedings against great or small, who, after the king's message, would not adopt Christianity. In the meantime Olaf was proclaimed king in every Law Thing in the country, and no man spoke against him. While he lay in Karmtsund messengers went between him and Erling Skjalgson, who endeavoured to make peace between them; and the meeting was appointed in Whitings Isle. When they met they spoke with each other about agreement together; but Erling found something else than he expected in the conversation: for when he insisted on having all the fiefs which Olaf Trygvason, and afterwards the Earls Svein and Hakon, had given him, and on that condition would be his man and dutiful friend, the king answered, "It appears to me, Erling, that it would be no bad bargain for thee to get as great fiefs from me for thy aid and friendship as thou hadst from Earl Eirik, a man who had done thee the greatest injury by the bloodshed of thy men; but even if I let thee remain the greatest lenderman in Norway, I will bestow my fiefs according to my own will, and not act as if ye lendermen had udal right to my ancestor's heritage, and I was obliged to buy your services with manifold rewards." Erling had no disposition to sue for even the smallest thing; and he saw that the king was not easily dealt with. He saw also that he had only two conditions before him: the one was to make no agreement with the king, and stand by the consequences; the other to leave it entirely to the king's pleasure. Although it was much against his inclination, he chose the latter, and merely said to the king, "The service will be the most useful to thee which I give with a free will." And thus their conference ended. Erling's relations and friends came to him afterwards, and advised him to give way, and proceed with more prudence and less pride. "Thou wilt still," they said, "be the most important and most respected lenderman in Norway, both on account of thy own and thy relations' abilities and great wealth." Erling found that this was prudent advice, and that they who gave it did so with a good intention, and he followed it accordingly. Erling went into the king's service on such conditions as the king himself should determine and please. Thereafter they separated in some shape reconciled, and Olaf went his way eastward along the coast (A.D. 1016).

59. EILIF OF GAUTLAND'S MURDER.

As soon as it was reported that Olaf had come to Viken, the Danes who had offices under the Danish king set off for Denmark, without waiting for King Olaf. But King Olaf sailed in along Viken, holding Things with the bondes. All the people of the country submitted to him, and thereafter he took all the king's taxes, and remained the summer (A.D. 1016) in Viken. He then sailed east from Tunsberg across the fjord, and all the way east to Svinasund. There the Swedish king's dominions begin, and he had set officers over this country; namely, Eilif Gautske over the north part, and Hroe Skialge over the east part, all the way to the Gaut river. Hroe had family friends on both sides of the river, and also great farms on Hising Island, and was besides a mighty and very rich man. Eilif was also of great family, and very wealthy. Now when King Olaf came to Ranrike he summoned the people to a Thing, and all who dwelt on the sea-coast or in the out-islands came to him. Now when the Thing was seated the king's marshal, Bjorn, held a speech to them, in which he told the bondes to receive Olaf as their king, in the same way as had been done in all other parts of Norway. Then stood up a bold bonde by name Brynjolf Ulfalde, and said, "We bondes know where the division-boundaries between the Norway and Danish and Swedish kings' lands have stood by rights in old times; namely, that the Gaut river divided their lands between the Vener lake and the sea; but towards the north the forests until Eid forest, and from thence the ridge of the country all north to Finmark. We know, also, that by turns they have made inroads upon each other's territories, and that the Swedes have long had power all the way to Svinasund. But, sooth to say, I know that it is the inclination of many rather to serve the king of Norway, but they dare not; for the Swedish king's dominions surround us, both eastward, southwards, and also up the country; and besides, it may be expected that the king of Norway must soon go to the north, where the strength of his kingdom lies, and then we have no power to withstand the Gautlanders. Now it is for the king to give us good counsel, for we have great desire to be his men." After the Thing, in the evening, Brynjolf was in the king's tent, and the day after likewise, and they had much private conversation together. Then the king proceeded eastwards along Viken. Now when Eilif heard of his arrival, he sent out spies to discover what he was about; but he himself, with thirty men, kept himself high up in the habitations among the hills, where he had gathered together bondes. Many of the bondes came to King Olaf, but some sent friendly messages to him. People went between King Olaf and Eilif, and they entreated each separately to hold a Thing-meeting between themselves, and make peace in one way or another. They told Eilif that they might expect violent treatment from King Olaf if they opposed his orders; but promised Eilif he should not want men. It was determined that they should come down from the high country, and hold a thing with the bondes and the king. King Olaf thereupon sent the chief of his pursuivants, Thorer Lange, with six men, to Brynjolf. They were equipped with their coats-of-mail under their cloaks, and their hats over their helmets. The following day the bondes came in crowds down with Eilif; and in his suite was Brynjolf, and with him Thorer. The king laid his ships close to a rocky knoll that stuck out into the sea, and upon it the king went with his people, and sat down. Below was a flat field, on which the bondes' force was; but Eilif's men were drawn up, forming a shield-fence before him. Bjorn the marshal spoke long and cleverly upon the king's account, and when he sat down Eilif arose to speak; but at the same moment Thorer Lange rose, drew his sword, and struck Eilif on the neck, so that his head flew off. Then the whole bonde-force started up; but the Gautland men set off in full flight and Thorer with his people killed several of them. Now when the crowd was settled again, and the noise over the king stood up, and told the bondes to seat themselves. They did so, and then much was spoken. The end of it was that they submitted to the king, and promised fidelity to him; and he, on the other hand, promised not to desert them, but to remain at hand until the discord between him and the Swedish Olaf was settled in one way or other. King Olaf then brought the whole northern district under his power, and went in summer eastward as far as the Gaut river, and got all the king's scat among the islands. But when summer (A.D. 1016) was drawing towards an end he returned north to Viken, and sailed up the Raum river to a waterfall called Sarp. On the north side of the fall, a point of land juts out into the river. There the king ordered a rampart to be built right across the ness, of stone, turf, and wood, and a ditch to be dug in front of it; so that it was a large earthen fort or burgh, which he made a merchant town of. He had a king's house put up, and ordered the building of Mary church. He also laid out plans for other houses, and got people to build on them. In harvest (A.D. 1016) he let everything be gathered there that was useful for his winter residence (A.D. 1017), and sat there with a great many people, and the rest he quartered in the neighbouring districts. The king prohibited all exports from Viken to Gautland of herrings and salt, which the Gautland people could ill do without. This year the king held a great Yule feast, to which he invited many great bondes.

60. THE HISTORY OF EYVIND URARHORN.

There was a man called Eyvind Urarhorn, who was a great man, of high birth, who had his descent from the East Agder country. Every summer he went out on a viking cruise, sometimes to the West sea, sometimes to the Baltic, sometimes south to Flanders, and had a well-armed cutter (snekkia) of twenty benches of rowers. He had been also at Nesjar, and given his aid to the king; and when they separated the king promised him his favour, and Eyvind, again, promised to come to the king's aid whenever he was required. This winter (A.D. 1017) Eyvind was at the Yule feast of the king, and received goodly gifts from him. Brynjolf Ulfalde was also with the king, and he received a Yule present from the king of a gold-mounted sword, and also a farm called Vettaland, which is a very large head-farm of the district. Brynjolf composed a song about these gifts, of which the refrain was–

"The song-famed hero to my hand
Gave a good sword, and Vettaland."

The king afterwards gave him the title of Lenderman, and Brynjolf was ever after the king's greatest friend.

61. THRAND WHITE'S MURDER.

This winter (A.D. 1017) Thrand White from Throndhjem went east to Jamtaland, to take up scat upon account of King Olaf. But when he had collected the scat he was surprised by men of the Swedish king, who killed him and his men, twelve in all, and brought the scat to the Swedish king. King Olaf was very ill-pleased when he heard this news.

62. CHRISTIANITY PROCLAIMED IN VIKEN.

King Olaf made Christian law to be proclaimed in Viken, in the same way as in the North country. It succeeded well, because the people of Viken were better acquainted with the Christian customs than the people in the north; for, both winter and summer, there were many merchants in Viken, both Danish and Saxon. The people of Viken, also, had much trading intercourse with England, and Saxony, and Flanders, and Denmark; and some had been on viking expeditions, and had had their winter abode in Christian lands.

63. HROE'S FALL.

About spring-time (A.D. 1017) King Olaf sent a message that Eyvind Urarhorn should come to him; and they spake together in private for a long time. Thereafter Eyvind made himself ready for a viking cruise. He sailed south towards Viken, and brought up at the Eikreys Isles without Hising Isle. There he heard that Hroe Skialge had gone northwards towards Ordost, and had there made a levy of men and goods on account of the Swedish king, and was expected from the north. Eyvind rowed in by Haugasund, and Hroe came rowing from the north, and they met in the sound and fought. Hroe fell there, with nearly thirty men; and Eyvind took all the goods Hroe had with him. Eyvind then proceeded to the Baltic, and was all summer on a viking cruise.

64. FALL OF GUDLEIK AND THORGAUT.

There was a man called Gudleik Gerske, who came originally from Agder. He was a great merchant, who went far and wide by sea, was very rich, and drove a trade with various countries. He often went east to Gardarike (Russia), and therefore was called Gudleik Gerske (the Russian). This spring (A.D. 1017) Gudleik fitted out his ship, and intended to go east in summer to Russia. King Olaf sent a message to him that he wanted to speak to him; and when Gudleik came to the king he told him he would go in partnership with him, and told him to purchase some costly articles which were difficult to be had in this country. Gudleik said that it should be according to the king's desire. The king ordered as much money to be delivered to Gudleik as he thought sufficient, and then Gudleik set out for the Baltic. They lay in a sound in Gotland; and there it happened, as it often does, that people cannot keep their own secrets, and the people of the country came to know that in this ship was Olaf the Thick's partner. Gudleik went in summer eastwards to Novgorod, where he bought fine and costly clothes, which he intended for the king as a state dress; and also precious furs, and remarkably splendid table utensils. In autumn (A.D. 1017), as Gudleik was returning from the east, he met a contrary wind, and lay for a long time at the island Eyland. There came Thorgaut Skarde, who in autumn had heard of Gudleik's course, in a long-ship against him, and gave him battle. They fought long, and Gudleik and his people defended themselves for a long time; but the numbers against them were great, and Gudleik and many of his ship's crew fell, and a great many of them were wounded. Thorgaut took all their goods, and King Olaf's, and he and his comrades divided the booty among them equally; but he said the Swedish king ought to have the precious articles of King Olaf, as these, he said, should be considered as part of the scat due to him from Norway. Thereafter Thorgaut proceeded east to Svithjod. These tidings were soon known; and as Eyvind Urarhorn came soon after to Eyland, he heard the news, and sailed east after Thorgaut and his troop, and overtook them among the Swedish isles on the coast, and gave battle. There Thorgaut and the most of his men were killed, and the rest sprang overboard. Eyvind took all the goods and all the costly articles of King Olaf which they had captured from Gudleik, and went with these back to Norway in autumn, and delivered to King Olaf his precious wares. The king thanked him in the most friendly way for his proceeding, and promised him anew his favour and friendship. At this time Olaf had been three years king over Norway (A.D. 1015-1017).

65. MEETING OF OLAF AND RAGNVALD.

The same summer (A.D. 1017) King Olaf ordered a levy, and went out eastwards to the Gaut river, where he lay a great part of the summer. Messages were passing between King Olaf, Earl Ragnvald, and the earl's wife, Ingebjorg, the daughter of Trygve. She was very zealous about giving King Olaf of Norway every kind of help, and made it a matter of her deepest interest. For this there were two causes. She had a great friendship for King Olaf; and also she could never forget that the Swedish king had been one at the death of her brother, Olaf Trygvason; and also that he, on that account only, had any presence to rule over Norway. The earl, by her persuasion, turned much towards friendship with King Olaf; and it proceeded so far that the earl and the king appointed a meeting, and met at the Gaut river. They talked together of many things, but especially of the Norwegian and Swedish kings' relations with each other; both agreeing, as was the truth also, that it was the greatest loss, both to the people of Viken and of Gautland, that there was no peace for trade between the two countries; and at last both agreed upon a peace, and stillstand of arms between them until next summer; and they parted with mutual gifts and friendly speeches.

66. KING OLAF THE SWEDE.

THE KING THEREUPON RETURNED north to Viken, and had all the royal revenues up to the Gaut river; and all the people of the country there had submitted to him. King Olaf the Swede had so great a hatred of Olaf Haraldson, that no man dared to call him by his right name in the king's hearing. They called him the thick man; and never named him without some hard by-name.

67. ACCOUNT OF THEIR RECONCILIATION.

THE BONDES IN VIKEN spoke with each other about there being nothing for it but that the kings should make peace and a league with each other, and insisted upon it that they were badly used by the kings going to war; but nobody was so bold as to bring these murmurs before the king. At last they begged Bjorn the marshal to bring this matter before the king, and entreat him to send messengers to the Swedish king to offer peace on his side. Bjorn was disinclined to do this, and put it off from himself with excuses; but on the entreaties of many of his friends, he promised at last to speak of it to the king; but declared, at the same time, that he knew it would be taken very ill by the king to propose that he should give way in anything to the Swedish king. The same summer (A.D. 1017) Hjalte Skeggjason came over to Norway from Iceland, according to the message sent him by King Olaf, and went directly to the king. He was well received by the king, who told him to lodge in his house, and gave him a seat beside Bjorn the marshal, and Hjalte became his comrade at table. There was good-fellowship immediately between them.

Once, when King Olaf had assembled the people and bondes to consult upon the good of the country, Bjorn the marshal said, "What think you, king, of the strife that is between the Swedish king and you? Many people have fallen on both sides, without its being at all more determined than before what each of you shall have of the kingdom. You have now been sitting in Viken one winter and two summers, and the whole country to the north is lying behind your back unseen; and the men who have property or udal rights in the north are weary of sitting here. Now it is the wish of the lendermen, of your other people, and of the bondes that this should come to an end. There is now a truce, agreement, and peace with the earl, and the West Gautland people who are nearest to us; and it appears to the people it would be best that you sent messengers to the Swedish king to offer a reconciliation on your side; and, without doubt, many who are about the Swedish king will support the proposal, for it is a common gain for those who dwell in both countries, both here and there." This speech of Bjorn's received great applause.

Then the king said, "It is fair, Bjorn, that the advice thou hast given should be carried out by thyself. Thou shalt undertake this embassy thyself, and enjoy the good of it, if thou hast advised well; and if it involve any man in danger, thou hast involved thyself in it. Moreover, it belongs to thy office to declare to the multitude what I wish to have told." Then the king stood up, went to the church, and had high mass sung before him; and thereafter went to table.

The following day Hjalte said to Bjorn, "Why art thou so melancholy, man? Art thou sick, or art thou angry at any one?" Bjorn tells Hjalte his conversation with the king, and says it is a very dangerous errand.

Hjalte says, "It is their lot who follow kings that they enjoy high honours, and are more respected than other men, but stand often in danger of their lives: and they must understand how to bear both parts of their lot. The king's luck is great; and much honour will be gained by this business, if it succeed."

Bjorn answered, "Since thou makest so light of this business in thy speech, wilt thou go with me? The king has promised that I shall have companions with me on the journey."

"Certainly," says Hjalte; "I will follow thee, if thou wilt: for never again shall I fall in with such a comrade if we part."

68. JOURNEY OF BJORN THE MARSHAL.

A FEW DAYS AFTERWARDS, when the king was at a Thing-meeting, Bjorn came with eleven others. He says to the king that they were now ready to proceed on their mission, and that their horses stood saddled at the door. "And now," says he, "I would know with what errand I am to go, or what orders thou givest us."

The king replies, "Ye shall carry these my words to the Swedish king–that I will establish peace between our countries up to the frontier which Olaf Trygvason had before me; and each shall bind himself faithfully not to trespass over it. But with regard to the loss of people, no man must mention it if peace there is to be; for the Swedish king cannot with money pay for the men the Swedes have deprived us of." Thereupon the king rose, and went out with Bjorn and his followers; and he took a gold-mounted sword and a gold ring, and said, in handing over the sword to Bjorn, "This I give thee: it was given to me in summer by Earl Ragnvald. To him ye shall go; and bring him word from me to advance your errand with his counsel and strength. This thy errand I will think well fulfilled if thou hearest the Swedish king's own words, be they yea or nay: and this gold ring thou shalt give Earl Ragnvald. These are tokens[36] he must know well."

Hjalte went up to the king, saluted him, and said, "We need much, king, that thy luck attend us;" and wished that they might meet again in good health.

The king asked where Hjalte was going.

"With Bjorn," said he.

The king said, "It will assist much to the good success of the journey that thou goest too, for thy good fortune has often been proved; and be assured that I shall wish that all my luck, if that be of any weight, may attend thee and thy company."

Bjorn and his followers rode their way, and came to Earl Ragnvald's court, where they were well received. Bjorn was a celebrated and generally known man,–known by sight and speech to all who had ever seen King Olaf; for at every Thing, Bjorn stood up and told the king's message. Ingebjorg, the earl's wife, went up to Hjalte and looked at him. She recognized him, for she was living with her brother Olaf Trygvason when Hjalte was there: and she knew how to reckon up the relationship be-

36 Before writing was a common accomplishment in courts, the only way of accrediting a special messenger between kings and great men was by giving the messenger a token; that is. some article well known by the person receiving the message to be the property of and valued by the person sending it.

tween King Olaf and Vilborg, the wife of Hjalte; for Eirik Bjodaskalle father of Astrid, King Olaf Trygvason's mother, and Bodvar father of Olaf, mother of Gissur White the father of Vilborg, were brother's sons of the lenderman Vikingakare of Vors.

They enjoyed here good entertainment. One day Bjorn entered into conversation with the earl and Ingebjorg, in which he set forth his errand, and produced to the earl his tokens.

The earl replies, "What hast thou done, Bjorn, that the king wishes thy death? For, so far from thy errand having any success, I do not think a man can be found who could speak these words to the Swedish king without incurring wrath and punishment. King Olaf, king of Sweden, is too proud for any man to speak to him on anything he is angry at."

Then Bjorn says, "Nothing has happened to me that King Olaf is offended at; but many of his disposition act both for themselves and others, in a way that only men who are daring can succeed in. But as yet all his plans have had good success, and I think this will turn out well too; so I assure you, earl, that I will actually travel to the Swedish king, and not turn back before I have brought to his ears every word that King Olaf told me to say to him, unless death prevent me, or that I am in bonds, and cannot perform my errand; and this I must do, whether you give any aid or no aid to me in fulfilling the king's wishes."

Then said IngebJorg, "I will soon declare my opinion. I think, earl, thou must turn all thy attention to supporting King Olaf the king of Norway's desire that this message be laid before the Swedish king, in whatever way he may answer it. Although the Swedish king's anger should be incurred, and our power and property be at stake, yet will I rather run the risk, than that it should be said the message of King Olaf was neglected from fear of the Swedish king. Thou hast that birth, strength of relations, and other means, that here in the Swedish land it is free to thee to tell thy mind, if it be right and worthy of being heard, whether it be listened to by few or many, great or little people, or by the king himself."

The earl replies, "It is known to every one how thou urgest me: it may be, according to thy counsel, that I should promise the king's men to follow them, so that they may get their errand laid before the Swedish king, whether he take it ill or take it well. But I will have my own counsel followed, and will not run hastily into Bjorn's or any other man's measures, in such a highly important matter. It is my will that ye all remain here with me, so long as I think it necessary for the purpose of rightly forwarding this mission." Now as the earl had thus given them to understand that he would support them in the business, Bjorn thanked him most kindly, and with the assurance that his advice should rule them altogether. Thereafter Bjorn and his fellow-travellers remained very long in the earl's house.

69. CONVERSATION OF BJORN AND INGEBJORG.

Ingebjorg was particularly kind to them; and Bjorn often spoke with her about the matter, and was ill at ease that their journey was so long delayed. Hjalte and the others often spoke together also about the matter; and Hjalte said; "I will go to the king if ye like; for I am not a man of Norway, and the Swedes can have nothing to say to me. I have heard that there are Iceland men in the king's house who are my acquaintances, and are well treated; namely, the skalds Gissur Black and Ottar Black. From them I shall get out what I can about the Swedish king; and if the business will really be so difficult as it now appears, or if there be any other way of promoting it, I can easily devise some errand that may appear suitable for me."

This counsel appeared to Bjorn and Ingebjorg to be the wisest, and they resolved upon it among themselves. Ingebjorg put Hjalte in a position to travel; gave him two Gautland men with him, and ordered them to follow him, and assist him with their service, and also to go wherever he might have occasion to send them. Besides, Ingebjorg gave him twenty marks of weighed silver money for travelling expenses, and sent word and token by him to the Swedish king Olaf's daughter, Ingegerd, that she should give all her assistance to Hjalte's business, whenever he should find himself under the necessity of craving her help. Hjalte set off as soon as he was ready. When he came to King Olaf he soon found the skalds Gissur and Ottar, and they were very glad at his coming. Without delay they went to the king, and told him that a man was come who was their countryman, and one of the most considerable in their native land, and requested the king to receive him well. The king told them to take Hjalte and his fellow-travellers into their company and quarters. Now when Hjalte had resided there a short time, and got acquainted with people, he was much respected by everybody. The skalds were often in the king's house, for they were well-spoken men; and often in the daytime they sat in front of the king's high-seat, and Hjalte, to whom they paid the highest respect in all things, by their side. He became thus known to the king, who willingly entered into conversation with him, and heard from him news about Iceland.

70. OF SIGVAT THE SKALD.

It happened that before Bjorn set out from home he asked Sigvat the skald, who at that time was with King Olaf, to accompany him on his journey. It was a journey for which people had no great inclination. There was, however, great friendship between Bjorn and Sigvat. Then Sigvat sang:–

"With the king's marshals all have I,
In days gone by,
Lived joyously,–
With all who on the king attend,
And knee before him humbly bend,
Bjorn, thou oft hast ta'en my part–
Pleaded with art,
And touched the heart.
Bjorn! brave stainer of the sword,
Thou art my friend–I trust thy word."

While they were riding up to Gautland, Sigvat made these verses:–

"Down the Fjord sweep wind and rain,
Our stout ship's sails and tackle strain;
Wet to the skin.
We're sound within,
And gaily o'er the waves are dancing,
Our sea-steed o'er the waves high prancing!
Through Lister sea
Flying all free;
Off from the wind with swelling sail,
We merrily scud before the gale,
And reach the sound
Where we were bound.
And now our ship, so gay and grand,
Glides past the green and lovely land,
And at the isle
Moors for a while.
Our horse-hoofs now leave hasty print;
We ride–of ease there's scanty stint–
In heat and haste
O'er Gautland's waste:

Though in a hurry to be married,
The king can't say that we have tarried."

One evening late they were riding through Gautland, and Sigvat made these verses:–

"The weary horse will at nightfall
Gallop right well to reach his stall;
When night meets day, with hasty hoof
He plies the road to reach a roof.
Far from the Danes, we now may ride
Safely by stream or mountain-side;
But, in this twilight, in some ditch
The horse and rider both may pitch."

They rode through the merchant town of Skara, and down the street to the earl's house. He sang:–

"The shy sweet girls, from window high
In wonder peep at the sparks that fly
From our horses heels, as down the street
Of the earl's town we ride so fleet.
Spur on!–that every pretty lass
May hear our horse-hoofs as we pass
Clatter upon the stones so hard,
And echo round the paved court-yard."

71. HJALTE SKEGGJASON WHILE HE WAS IN SVITHIOD.

One day Hjalte, and the skalds with him, went before the king, and he began thus:–"It has so happened, king, as is known to you, that I have come here after a long and difficult journey; but when I had once crossed the ocean and heard of your greatness, it appeared to me unwise to go back without having seen you in your splendour and glory. Now it is a law between Iceland and Norway, that Iceland men pay landing due when they come into Norway, but while I was coming across the sea I took myself all the landing dues from my ship's people; but knowing that thou have the greatest right to all the power in Norway, I hastened hither to deliver to you the landing dues." With this he showed the silver to the king, and laid ten marks of silver in Gissur Black's lap.

The king replies, "Few have brought us any such dues from Norway for some time; and now, Hjalte, I will return you my warmest thanks for having given yourself so much trouble to bring us the landing dues, rather than pay them to our enemies. But I will that thou shouldst take this money from me as a gift, and with it my friendship."

Hjalte thanked the king with many words, and from that day set himself in great favour with the king, and often spoke with him; for the king thought, what was true, that he was a man of much understanding and eloquence. Now Hjalte told Gissur and Ottar that he was sent with tokens to the king's daughter Ingegerd, to obtain her protection and friendship; and he begged of them to procure him some opportunity to speak with her. They answered, that this was an easy thing to do; and went one day to her house, where she sat at the drinking table with many men. She received the skalds in a friendly manner, for they were known to her. Hjalte brought her a salutation from the earl's wife, Ingebjorg; and said she had sent him here to obtain friendly help and succour from her, and in proof whereof produced his tokens. The king's daughter received him also kindly, and said he should be welcome to her friendship. They sat there till late in the day drinking. The king's daughter made Hjalte tell her much news, and invited him to come often and converse with her. He did so: came there often, and spoke with the king's daughter; and at last entrusted her with the purpose of Bjorn's and his comrade's journey, and asked her how she thought the Swedish king would receive the proposal that there should be a reconciliation between the kings. The king's daughter replied, that, in her opinion, it would be a useless attempt to propose to the king any reconciliation with Olaf the Thick; for the king was so enraged against him, that he would not suffer his name to be mentioned before him. It happened one day that Hjalte was sitting with the king and talking to him, and the king was very merry and drunk. Then Hjalte said, "Manifold splendour and grandeur have I seen here; and I have now witnessed with my eyes what I have often heard of, that no monarch in the north is so magnificent: but it is very vexatious that we who come so far to visit it have a road so long and troublesome, both on account of the great ocean, but more especially because it is not safe to travel through Norway for those who are coming here in a friendly disposition. But why is there no one to bring proposals for a peace between you and King Olaf the Thick? I heard much in Norway, and in west Gautland, of the general desire that this peace should have taken place;

and it has been told me for truth, as the Norway king's words, that he earnestly desires to be reconciled to you; and the reason I know is, that he feels how much less his power is than yours. It is even said that he intends to pay his court to your daughter Ingegerd; and that would lead to a useful peace, for I have heard from people of credit that he is a remarkably distinguished man."

The king answers. "Thou must not speak thus, Hjalte; but for this time I will not take it amiss of thee, as thou dost not know what people have to avoid here. That fat fellow shall not be called king in my court, and there is by no means the stuff in him that people talk of: and thou must see thyself that such a connection is not suitable; for I am the tenth king in Upsala who, relation after relation, has been sole monarch over the Swedish, and many other great lands, and all have been the superior kings over other kings in the northern countries. But Norway is little inhabited, and the inhabitants are scattered. There have only been small kings there; and although Harald Harfager was the greatest king in that country, and strove against the small kings, and subdued them, yet he knew so well his position that he did not covet the Swedish dominions, and therefore the Swedish kings let him sit in peace, especially as there was relationship between them. Thereafter, while Hakon Athelstan's foster-son was in Norway he sat in peace, until he began to maraud in Gautland and Denmark; on which a war-force came upon him, and took from him both life and land. Gunhild's sons also were cut off when they became disobedient to the Danish kings; and Harald Gormson joined Norway to his own dominions, and made it subject to scat to him. And we reckon Harald Gormson to be of less power and consideration than the Upsala kings, for our relation Styrbjorn subdued him, and Harald became his man; and yet Eirik the Victorious, my father, rose over Styrbjorn's head when it came to a trial between them. When Olaf Trygvason came to Norway and proclaimed himself king, we would not permit it, but we went with King Svein, and cut him off; and thus we have appropriated Norway, as thou hast not heard, and with no less right than if I had gained it in battle, and by conquering the kings who ruled it before. Now thou canst well suppose, as a man of sense, that I will not let slip the kingdom of Norway for this thick fellow. It is wonderful he does not remember how narrowly he made his escape, when we had penned him in in the Malar lake. Although he slipped away with life from thence, he ought, methinks, to have something else in his mind than to hold out against us Swedes. Now, Hjalte, thou must never again open thy mouth in my presence on such a subject."

Hjalte saw sufficiently that there was no hope of the king's listening to any proposal of a peace, and desisted from speaking of it, and turned the conversation to something else. When Hjalte, afterwards, came into discourse with the king's daughter Ingegerd, he tells her his conversation with the king. She told him she expected such an answer from the king. Hjalte begged of her to say a good word to the king about the matter, but she thought the king would listen as little to what she said: "But speak about it I will, if thou requirest it." Hjalte assured her he would be thankful for the attempt. One day the king's daughter Ingegerd had a conversation with her father Olaf; and as she found her father was in a particularly good humour, she said, "What is now thy intention with regard to the strife with Olaf the Thick? There are many who complain about it, having lost their property by it; others have lost their relations by the Northmen, and all their peace and quiet; so that none of your men see any harm that can be done to Norway. It would be a bad counsel if thou sought the dominion over Norway; for it is a poor country, difficult to come at, and the people dangerous: for the men there will rather have any other for their king than thee. If I might advise, thou wouldst let go all thoughts about Norway, and not desire Olaf's heritage; and rather turn thyself to the kingdoms in the East country, which thy forefathers the former Swedish kings had, and which our relation Styrbjorn lately subdued, and let the thick Olaf possess the heritage of his forefathers and make peace with him."

The king replies in a rage, "It is thy counsel, Ingegerd, that I should let slip the kingdom of Norway, and give thee in marriage to this thick Olaf."–"No," says he, "something else shall first take place. Rather than that, I shall, at the Upsala Thing in winter, issue a proclamation to all Swedes, that the whole people shall assemble for an expedition, and go to their ships before the ice is off the waters; and I will proceed to Norway, and lay waste the land with fire and sword, and burn everything, to punish them for their want of fidelity."

The king was so mad with rage that nobody ventured to say a word, and she went away. Hjalte, who was watching for her, immediately went to her and asked how her errand to the king had turned out. She answered, it turned out as she had expected; that none could venture to put in a word with the king; but, on the contrary, he had used threats; and she begged Hjalte never to speak of the matter again before the king. As Hjalte and Ingegerd spoke together often, Olaf the Thick was often the subject, and he told her about him and his manners; and Hjalte praised the king of Norway what he could, but said no more than was the truth, and she could well perceive it. Once, in a conversation,

Hjalte said to her, "May I be permitted, daughter of the king, to tell thee what lies in my mind?"

"Speak freely," says she; "but so that I alone can hear it."

"Then," said Hjalte, "what would be thy answer, if the Norway king Olaf sent messengers to thee with the errand to propose marriage to thee?"

She blushed, and answered slowly but gently, "I have not made up my mind to answer to that; but if Olaf be in all respects so perfect as thou tellest me, I could wish for no other husband; unless, indeed, thou hast gilded him over with thy praise more than sufficiently."

Hjalte replied, that he had in no respect spoken better of the king than was true. They often spoke together on the same subject. Ingegerd begged Hjalte to be cautious not to mention it to any other person, for the king would be enraged against him if it came to his knowledge. Hjalte only spoke of it to the skalds Gissur and Ottar, who thought it was the most happy plan, if it could but be carried into effect. Ottar, who was a man of great power of conversation, and much beloved in the court, soon brought up the subject before the king's daughter, and recounted to her, as Hjalte had done, all King Olaf's excellent qualities. Often spoke Hjalte and the others about him; and now that Hjalte knew the result of his mission, he sent those Gautland men away who had accompanied him, and let them return to the earl with letters[37] which the king's daughter Ingegerd sent to the earl and Ingebjorg. Hjalte also let them give a hint to the earl about the conversation he had had with Ingegerd, and her answer thereto: and the messengers came with it to the earl a little before Yule.

72. OLAF'S JOURNEY TO THE UPLANDS.

When King Olaf had despatched Bjorn and his followers to Gautland, he sent other people also to the Uplands, with the errand that they should have guest-quarters prepared for him, as he intended that winter (A.D. 1018) to live as guest in the Uplands; for it had been the custom of former kings to make a progress in guest-quarters every third year in the Uplands. In autumn he began his progress from Sarpsborg, and went first to Vingulmark. He ordered his progress so that he came first to lodge in the neighbourhood of the forest habitations, and summoned

37 This seems the first notice we have in the sagas of written letters being sent instead of tokens and verbal messages. –L.

to him all the men of the habitations who dwelt at the greatest distance from the head-habitations of the district; and he inquired particularly how it stood with their Christianity, and, where improvement was needful, he taught them the right customs. If any there were who would not renounce heathen ways, he took the matter so zealously that he drove some out of the country, mutilated others of hands or feet, or stung their eyes out; hung up some, cut down some with the sword; but let none go unpunished who would not serve God. He went thus through the whole district, sparing neither great nor small. He gave them teachers, and placed these as thickly in the country as he saw needful. In this manner he went about in that district, and had 300 deadly men-at-arms with him; and then proceeded to Raumarike. He soon perceived that Christianity was thriving less the farther he proceeded into the interior of the country. He went forward everywhere in the same way, converting all the people to the right faith, and severely punishing all who would not listen to his word.

73. TREACHERY OF THE UPLAND KINGS.

Now when the king who at that time ruled in Raumarike heard of this, he thought it was a very bad affair; for every day came men to him, both great and small, who told him what was doing. Therefore this king resolved to go up to Hedemark, and consult King Hrorek, who was the most eminent for understanding of the kings who at that time were in the country. Now when these kings spoke with each other, they agreed to send a message to Gudrod, the valley-king north in the Gudbrandsdal, and likewise to the king who was in Hadaland, and bid them to come to Hedemark, to meet Hrorek and the other kings there. They did not spare their travelling; for five kings met in Hedemark, at a place called Ringsaker. Ring, King Hrorek's brother, was the fifth of these kings. The kings had first a private conference together, in which he who came from Raumarike first took up the word, and told of King Olaf's proceedings, and of the disturbance he was causing both by killing and mutilating people. Some he drove out of the country, some he deprived of their offices or property if they spoke anything against him; and, besides, he was travelling over the country with a great army, not with the number of people fixed by law for a royal progress in guest-quarters. He added, that he had fled hither upon account of this disturbance, and many powerful people with him had fled from their udal properties in Raumarike. "But although as yet the evil is nearest to us, it will be but a short time before ye will also be exposed to it; therefore it is best that we all consider together what resolution we shall take." When he had ended his speech, Hrorek was desired to speak; and he said, "Now is the day come that I foretold when we had had our meeting at Hadaland, and ye were all so eager to raise Olaf over our heads; namely, that as soon as he was the supreme master of the country we would find it hard to hold him by the horns. We have but two things now to do: the one is, to go all of us to him, and let him do with us as he likes, which I think is the best thing we can do; or the other is, to rise against him before he has gone farther through the country. Although he has 300 or 400 men, that is not too great a force for us to meet, if we are only all in movement together: but, in general, there is less success and advantage to be gained when several of equal strength are joined together, than when one alone stands at the head of his own force; therefore it is my advice, that we do not venture to try our luck against Olaf Haraldson."

Thereafter each of the kings spoke according to his own mind some dissuading from going out against King Olaf, others urging it; and no determination was come to, as each had his own reasons to produce.

Then Gudrod, the valley-king, took up the word, and spoke:–"It appears wonderful to me, that ye make such a long roundabout in coming to a resolution; and probably ye are frightened for him. We are here five kings, and none of less high birth than Olaf. We gave him the strength to fight with Earl Svein, and with our forces he has brought the country under his power. But if he grudges each of us the little kingdom he had before, and threatens us with tortures, or gives us ill words, then, say I for myself, that I will withdraw myself from the king's slavery; and I do not call him a man among you who is afraid to cut him off, if he come into your hands here up in Hedemark. And this I can tell you, that we shall never bear our heads in safety while Olaf is in life." After this encouragement they all agreed to his determination.

Then said Hrorek, "With regard to this determination, it appears to me necessary to make our agreement so strong that no one shall fail in his promise to the other. Therefore, if ye determine upon attacking Olaf at a fixed time, when he comes here to Hedemark, I will not trust much to you if some are north in the valleys, others up in Hedemark; but if our resolution is to come to anything, we must remain here assembled together day and night."

This the kings agreed to, and kept themselves there all assembled, ordering a feast to be provided for them at Ringsaker, and drank there a cup to success; sending out spies to Raumarike, and when one set came in sending out others, so that day and night they had intelligence of Olaf's proceedings, and of the numbers of his men. King Olaf went about in Raumarike in guest-quarters, and altogether in the way before related; but as the provision of the guest-quarter was not always sufficient, upon account of his numerous followers, he laid it upon the bondes to give additional contributions wherever he found it necessary to stay. In some places he stayed longer, in others, shorter than was fixed; and his journey down to the lake Miosen was shorter than had been fixed on. The kings, after taking their resolution, sent out message-tokens, and summoned all the lendermen and powerful bondes from all the districts thereabout; and when they had assembled the kings had a private meeting with them, and made their determination known, setting a day for gathering together and carrying it into effect; and it was settled among them that each of the kings should have 300[38] men. Then they sent away the lendermen to gather the people, and meet all at the appointed place. The most approved of the measure; but it happened here, as it usually does, that every one has some friend even among his enemies.

74. MUTILATING OF THE UPLAND KINGS.

Ketil of Ringanes was at this meeting. Now when he came home in the evening he took his supper, put on his clothes, and went down with his house-servants to the lake; took a light vessel which he had, the same that King Olaf had made him a present of, and launched it on the water. They found in the boat-house everything ready to their hands; betook themselves to their oars, and rowed out into the lake. Ketil had forty well-armed men with him, and came early in the morning to the end of the lake. He set off immediately with twenty men, leaving the other twenty to look after the ship. King Olaf was at that time at Eid, in the upper end of Raumarike. Thither Ketil arrived just as the king was coming from matins. The king received Ketil kindly. He said he must speak with the king in all haste; and they had a private conference together. There Ketil tells the king the resolution which the kings had taken, and their agreement, which he had come to the certain knowledge of. When the king learnt this he called his people together, and sent some out to collect riding-horses in the country; others he sent down to the lake to take all the rowing-vessels they could lay hold of, and keep them for his

38 I.e., 360.

use. Thereafter he went to the church, had mass sung before him, and then sat down to table. After his meal he got ready, and hastened down to the lake, where the vessels were coming to meet him. He himself went on board the light vessel, and as many men with him as it could stow, and all the rest of his followers took such boats as they could get hold of; and when it was getting late in the evening they set out from the land, in still and calm weather. He rowed up the water with 400 men, and came with them to Ringsaker before day dawned; and the watchmen were not aware of the army before they were come into the very court. Ketil knew well in what houses the kings slept, and the king had all these houses surrounded and guarded, so that nobody could get out; and so they stood till daylight. The kings had not people enough to make resistance, but were all taken prisoners, and led before the king. Hrorek was an able but obstinate man, whose fidelity the king could not trust to if he made peace with him; therefore he ordered both his eyes to be punched out, and took him in that condition about with him. He ordered Gudrod's tongue to be cut out; but Ring and two others he banished from Norway, under oath never to return. Of the lendermen and bondes who had actually taken part in the traitorous design, some he drove out of the country, some he mutilated, and with others he made peace. Ottar Black tells of this:–

"The giver of rings of gold,
The army leader bold,
In vengeance springs
On the Hedemark kings.
Olaf the bold and great,
Repays their foul deceit–
In full repays
Their treacherous ways.
He drives with steel-clad hand
The small kings from the land,–
Greater by far
In deed of war.
The king who dwelt most north
Tongueless must wander forth:
All fly away
In great dismay.
King Olaf now rules o'er
What five kings ruled before.
To Eid's old bound

Extends his ground.
No kings in days of yore
E'er won so much before:
That this is so
All Norsemen know."

King Olaf took possession of the land these five kings had possessed, and took hostages from the lendermen and bondes in it. He took money instead of guest-quarters from the country north of the valley district, and from Hedemark; and then returned to Raumarike, and so west to Hadaland. This winter (A.D. 1018) his stepfather Sigurd Syr died; and King Olaf went to Ringerike, where his mother Asta made a great feast for him. Olaf alone bore the title of king now in Norway.

75. KING OLAF'S HALF-BROTHERS.

It is told that when King Olaf was on his visit to his mother Asta, she brought out her children, and showed them to him. The king took his brother Guthorm on the one knee, and his brother Halfdan on the other. The king looked at Guthorm, made a wry face, and pretended to be angry at them: at which the boys were afraid. Then Asta brought her youngest son, called Harald, who was three years old, to him. The king made a wry face at him also; but he looked the king in the face without regarding it. The king took the boy by the hair, and plucked it; but the boy seized the king's whiskers, and gave them a tug. "Then," said the king, "thou wilt be revengeful, my friend, some day." The following day the king was walking with his mother about the farm, and they came to a playground, where Asta's sons, Guthorm and Halfdan, were amusing themselves. They were building great houses and barns in their play, and were supposing them full of cattle and sheep; and close beside them, in a clay pool, Harald was busy with chips of wood, sailing them, in his sport along the edge. The king asked him what these were; and he answered, these were his ships of war. The king laughed, and said, "The time may come, friend, when thou wilt command ships."

Then the king called to him Halfdan and Guthorm; and first he asked Guthorm, "What wouldst thou like best to have?"

"Corn land," replied he.

"And how great wouldst thou like thy corn land to be?"

"I would have the whole ness that goes out into the lake sown with corn every summer." On that ness there are ten farms.

The king replies, "There would be a great deal of corn there." And, turning to Halfdan, he asked, "And what wouldst thou like best to have?"

"Cows," he replied.

"How many wouldst thou like to have?"

"When they went to the lake to be watered I would have so many, that they stood as tight round the lake as they could stand."

"That would be a great housekeeping," said the king; "and therein ye take after your father."

Then the king says to Harald, "And what wouldst thou like best to have?"

"House-servants."

"And how many wouldst thou have?"

"Oh! so many I would like to have as would eat up my brother Halfdan's cows at a single meal."

The king laughed, and said to Asta, "Here, mother, thou art bringing up a king." And more is not related of them on this occasion.

76. THE DIVISION OF THE COUNTRY.

In Svithjod it was the old custom, as long as heathenism prevailed, that the chief sacrifice took place in Goe month at Upsala. Then sacrifice was offered for peace, and victory to the king; and thither came people from all parts of Svithjod. All the Things of the Swedes, also, were held there, and markets, and meetings for buying, which continued for a week: and after Christianity was introduced into Svithjod, the Things and fairs were held there as before. After Christianity had taken root in Svithjod, and the kings would no longer dwell in Upsala, the market-time was moved to Candlemas, and it has since continued so, and it lasts only three days. There is then the Swedish Thing also, and people from all quarters come there. Svithjod is divided into many parts. One part is West Gautland, Vermaland, and the Marks, with what belongs to them; and this part of the kingdom is so large, that the bishop who is set over it has 1100 churches under him. The other part is East Gautland, where there is also a bishop's seat, to which the islands of Gotland and Eyland belong; and forming all together a still greater bishopric. In Svithjod itself there is a part of the country called Sudermanland, where there is also a bishopric. Then comes Westmanland, or Fiathrundaland, which is also a bishopric. The third portion of Svithjod proper is called Tiundaland; the fourth Attandaland; the fifth Sialand, and what belongs to it lies eastward along the coast. Tiundaland is the best and most inhabited part of Svithjod, under which the other kingdoms stand. There Upsala is situated, the seat of the king and archbishop; and from it Upsala-audr, or the domain of the Swedish kings, takes its name. Each of these divisions of the country has its Lag-thing, and its own laws in many parts. Over each is a lagman, who rules principally in affairs of the bondes: for that becomes law which he, by his speech, determines them to make law: and if king, earl, or bishop goes through the country, and holds a Thing with the bondes, the lagmen reply on account of the bondes, and they all follow their lagmen; so that even the most powerful men scarcely dare to come to their Al-thing without regarding the bondes' and lagmen's law. And in all matters in which the laws differ from each other, Upsala-law is the directing law; and the other lagmen are under the lagman who dwells in Tiundaland.

77. OF THE LAGMAN THORGNY.

In Tiundaland there was a lagman who was called Thorgny, whose father was called Thorgny Thorgnyson. His forefathers had for a long course of years, and during many kings' times, been lagmen of Tiundaland. At this time Thorgny was old, and had a great court about him. He was considered one of the wisest men in Sweden, and was Earl Ragnvald's relation and foster-father.

78. MEETING OF RAGNVALD AND INGEGERD.

Now we must go back in our story to the time when the men whom the king's daughter Ingegerd and Hjalte had sent from the east came to Earl Ragnvald. They relate their errand to the earl and his wife Ingebjorg, and tell how the king's daughter had oft spoken to the Swedish king about a peace between him and King Olaf the Thick, and that she was a great friend of King Olaf; but that the Swedish king flew into a passion every time she named Olaf, so that she had no hopes of any peace. The Earl told Bjorn the news he had received from the east; but Bjorn gave the same reply, that he would not turn back until he had met the Swedish king, and said the earl had promised to go with him. Now the winter was passing fast, and immediately after Yule the earl made himself ready to travel with sixty men, among whom where the marshal Bjorn and his companions. The earl proceeded eastward all the way to Svithjod; but when he came a little way into the country he sent his men before him to Upsala with a message to Ingegerd the king's daughter to come out to meet him at Ullaraker, where she had a large farm. When the king's daughter got the earl's message she made herself ready immediately to travel with a large attendance, and Hjalte accompanied her. But before he took his departure he went to King Olaf, and said, "Continue always to be the most fortunate of monarchs! Such splendour as I have seen about thee I have in truth never witnessed elsewhere, and wheresoever I come it shall not be concealed. Now, king, may I entreat thy favour and friendship in time to come?"

The king replies, "Why art thou in so great a haste, and where art thou going?"

Hjalte replies, "I am to ride out to Ullaraker with Ingegerd thy daughter."

The king says, "Farewell, then: a man thou art of understanding and politeness, and well suited to live with people of rank."

Thereupon Hjalte withdrew.

The king's daughter Ingegerd rode to her farm in Ullaraker, and ordered a great feast to be prepared for the earl. When the earl arrived he was welcomed with gladness, and he remained there several days. The earl and the king's daughter talked much, and of many things, but most about the Swedish and Norwegian kings; and she told the earl that in her opinion there was no hope of peace between them.

Then said the earl, "How wouldst thou like it, my cousin, if Olaf king of Norway were to pay his addresses to thee? It appears to us that it would contribute most towards a settled peace if there was relationship established between the kings; but I would not support such a matter if it were against thy inclination."

She replies, "My father disposes of my hand; but among all my other relations thou art he whose advice I would rather follow in weighty affairs. Dost thou think it would be advisable?" The earl recommended it to her strongly, and reckoned up many excellent achievements of King Olaf's. He told her, in particular, about what had lately been done; that King Olaf in an hours time one morning had taken five kings prisoners, deprived them all of their governments, and laid their kingdoms and properties under his own power. Much they talked about the business, and in all their conversations they perfectly agreed with each other. When the earl was ready he took leave, and proceeded on his way, taking Hjalte with him.

79. RAGNVALD AND THORGNY.

Earl Ragnvald came towards evening one day to the house of Lagman Thorgny. It was a great and stately mansion, and many people stood outside, who received the earl kindly, and took care of the horses and baggage. The earl went into the room, where there was a number of people. In the high-seat sat an old man; and never had Bjorn or his companions seen a man so stout. His beard was so long that it lay upon his knee, and was spread over his whole breast; and the man, moreover, was handsome and stately in appearance. The earl went forward and saluted him. Thorgny received him joyfully and kindly, and bade him go to the seat he was accustomed to take. The earl seated himself on the other side, opposite Thorgny. They remained there some days before the earl disclosed his errand, and then he asked Thorgny to go with him into the conversing room. Bjorn and his followers went there with the earl. Then the earl began, and told how Olaf king of Norway had sent these men hither to conclude a peaceful agreement. He showed at great length what injury it was of to the West Gautland people, that there was hostility between their country and Norway. He further related that Olaf the king of Norway had sent ambassadors, who were here present, and to whom he had promised he would attend them to the Swedish king; but he added, "The Swedish king takes the matter so grievously, that he has uttered menaces against those who entertain it. Now so it is, my foster-father, that I do not trust to myself in this matter; but am come on a visit to thee to get good counsel and help from thee in the matter."

Now when the earl had done speaking Thorgny sat silent for a while, and then took up the word. "Ye have curious dispositions who are so ambitious of honour and renown, and yet have no prudence or counsel in you when you get into any mischief. Why did you not consider, before you gave your promise to this adventure, that you had no power to stand against King Olaf? In my opinion it is not a less honourable condition to be in the number of bondes and have one's words free, and be able to say what one will, even if the king be present. But I must go to the Upsala Thing, and give thee such help that without fear thou canst speak before the king what thou findest good."

The earl thanked him for the promise, remained with Thorgny, and rode with him to the Upsala Thing. There was a great assemblage of people at the Thing, and King Olaf was there with his court.

80. OF THE UPSALA THING.

The first day the Thing sat, King Olaf was seated on a stool, and his court stood in a circle around him. Right opposite to him sat Earl Ragnvald and Thorgny in the Thing upon one stool, and before them the earl's court and Thorgny's house-people. Behind their stool stood the bonde community, all in a circle around them. Some stood upon hillocks and heights, in order to hear the better. Now when the king's messages, which are usually handled in the Things, were produced and settled, the marshal Bjorn rose beside the earl's stool, and said aloud, "King Olaf sends me here with the message that he will offer to the Swedish king peace, and the frontiers that in old times were fixed between Norway and Svithjod." He spoke so loud that the Swedish king could distinctly hear him; but at first, when he heard King Olaf's name spoken, he thought the speaker had some message or business of his own to execute; but when he heard of peace, and the frontiers between Norway and Svithjod, he saw from what root it came, and sprang up, and called out that the man should be silent, for that such speeches were useless. Thereupon Bjorn sat down; and when the noise had ceased Earl Ragnvald stood up and made a speech.

He spoke of Olaf the Thick's message, and proposal of peace to Olaf the Swedish king; and that all the West Gautland people sent their entreaty to Olaf that he would make peace with the king of Norway. He recounted all the evils the West Gautlanders were suffering under; that they must go without all the things from Norway which were necessary in their households; and, on the other hand, were exposed to attack and hostility whenever the king of Norway gathered an army and made an inroad on them. The earl added, that Olaf the Norway king had sent men hither with the intent to obtain Ingegerd the king's daughter in marriage.

When the earl had done speaking Olaf the Swedish king stood up and replied, and was altogether against listening to any proposals of peace, and made many and heavy reproaches against the earl for his impudence in entering into a peaceful truce with the thick fellow, and making up a peaceful friendship with him, and which in truth he considered treason against himself. He added, that it would be well deserved if Earl Ragnvald were driven out of the kingdom. The earl had, in his opinion, the influence of his wife Ingebjorg to thank for what might happen; and it was the most imprudent fancy he could have fallen upon to take up with such a wife. The king spoke long and bitterly, turning his speech always against Olaf the Thick. When he sat down not a sound was to be heard at first.

81. THORGNY'S SPEECH.

Then Thorgny stood up; and when he arose all the bondes stood up who had before been sitting, and rushed together from all parts to listen to what Lagman Thorgny would say. At first there was a great din of people and weapons; but when the noise was settled into silent listening, Thorguy made his speech. "The disposition of Swedish kings is different now from what it has been formerly. My grandfather Thorgny could well remember the Upsala king Eirik Eymundson, and used to say of him that when he was in his best years he went out every summer on expeditions to different countries, and conquered for himself Finland, Kirjalaland, Courland, Esthonia, and the eastern countries all around; and at the present day the earth-bulwarks, ramparts, and other great works which he made are to be seen. And, more over, he was not so proud that he would not listen to people who had anything to say to him. My father, again, was a long time with King Bjorn, and was well acquainted with his ways and manners. In Bjorn's lifetime his kingdom stood in great power, and no kind of want was felt, and he was gay and sociable with his friends. I also remember King Eirik the Victorious, and was with him on many a war-expedition. He enlarged the Swedish dominion, and defended it manfully; and it was also easy and agreeable to communicate our opinions to him. But the king we have now got allows no man to presume to talk with him, unless it be what he desires to hear. On this alone he applies all his power, while he allows his scat-lands in other countries to go from him through laziness and weakness. He wants to have the Norway kingdom laid under him, which no Swedish king before him ever desired, and therewith brings war and distress on many a man. Now it is our will, we bondes, that thou King Olaf make peace with the Norway king, Olaf the Thick, and marry thy daughter Ingegerd to him. Wilt thou, however, reconquer the kingdoms in the east countries which thy relations and forefathers had there, we will all for that purpose follow thee to the war. But if thou wilt not do as we desire, we will now attack thee, and put thee to death; for we will no longer suffer law and peace to be disturbed. So our forefathers went to work when they drowned five kings in a morass at the Mula-thing, and they were filled with the same insupportable pride thou hast shown towards us. Now tell us, in all haste, what resolution thou wilt take." Then the whole public approved, with clash of arms and shouts, the lagman's speech.

The king stands up and says he will let things go according to the desire of the bondes. "All Swedish kings," he said, "have done so, and have allowed the bondes to rule in all according to their will." The murmur among the bondes then came to an end, and the chiefs, the king, the earl, and Thorgny talked together, and concluded a truce and reconciliation, on the part of the Swedish king, according to the terms which the king of Norway had proposed by his ambassadors; and it was resolved at the Thing that Ingegerd, the king's daughter, should be married to Olaf Haraldson. The king left it to the earl to make the contract feast, and gave him full powers to conclude this marriage affair; and after this was settled at the Thing, they separated. When the earl returned homewards, he and the king's daughter Ingegerd had a meeting, at which they talked between themselves over this matter. She sent Olaf a long cloak of fine linen richly embroidered with gold, and with silk points. The earl returned to Gautland, and Bjorn with him; and after staying with him a short time, Bjorn and his company returned to Norway. When he came to King Olaf he told him the result of his errand, and the king returned him many thanks for his conduct, and said Bjorn had had great success in bringing his errand to so favourabie a conclusion against such animosity.

82. OF KING HROREK'S TREACHERY.

On the approach of spring (A.D. 1018) King Olaf went down to the coast, had his ships rigged out, summoned troops to him, and proceeded in spring out from Viken to the Naze, and so north to Hordaland. He then sent messages to all the lendermen, selected the most considerable men in each district, and made the most splendid preparations to meet his bride. The wedding-feast was to be in autumn, at the Gaut river, on the frontiers of the two countries. King Olaf had with him the blind king Hrorek. When his wound was healed, the king gave him two men to serve him, let him sit in the high-seat by his side, and kept him in meat and clothes in no respect Norse than he had kept himself before. Hrorek was taciturn, and answered short and cross when any one spoke to him. It was his custom to make his footboy, when he went out in the daytime, lead him away from people, and then to beat the lad until he ran away. He would then complain to King Olaf that the lad would not serve him. The king changed his servants, but it was as before; no servant would hold it out with King Hrorek. Then the king appointed a man called Svein to wait upon and serve King Hrorek. He was Hrorek's relation, and had formerly been in his service. Hrorek continued with his habits of moroseness, and of solitary walks; but when he and Svein were alone together, he was merry and talkative. He used to bring up many things which had happened in former days when he was king. He alluded, too, to the man who had, in his former days, torn him from his kingdom and happiness, and made him live on alms. "It is hardest of all," says he, "that thou and my other relations, who ought to be men of bravery, are so degenerated that thou wilt not avenge the shame and disgrace brought upon our race." Such discourse he often brought out. Svein said, they had too great a power to deal with, while they themselves had but little means. Hrorek said, "Why should we live longer as mutilated men with disgrace? I, a blind man, may conquer them as well as they conquered me when I was asleep. Come then, let us kill this thick Olaf. He is not afraid for himself at present. I will lay the plan, and would not spare my hands if I could use them, but that I cannot by reason of my blindness; therefore thou must use the weapons against him, and as soon as Olaf is killed I can see well enough that his power must come into the hands of his enemies, and it may well be that I shall be king, and thou shalt be my earl." So much persuasion he used that Svein at last agreed to join in the deed. The plan was so laid that when the king was ready to go to vespers, Svein stood on the threshold with a drawn dagger under his cloak. Now when the king came out of the room, it so happened that he walked quicker than Svein expected; and when he looked the king in the face he grew pale, and then white as a corpse, and his hand sank down. The king observed his terror and said, "What is this, Svein? Wilt thou betray me?" Svein threw down his cloak and dagger, and fell at the king's feet, saying, "All is in Gods hands and thine, king!" The king ordered his men to seize Svein, and he was put in irons. The king ordered Hrorek's seat to be moved to another bench. He gave Svein his life, and he left the country. The king appointed a different lodging for Hrorek to sleep in from that in which he slept himself, and in which many of his court-people slept. He set two of his court-men, who had been long with him, and whose fidelity he had proof of, to attend Hrorek day and night; but it is not said whether they were people of high birth or not. King Hrorek's mood was very different at different times. Sometimes he would sit silent for days together, so that no man could get a word out of him; and sometimes he was so merry and gay, that people found a joke in every word he said. Sometimes his words were very bitter. He was sometimes in a mood that he would drink them all under the benches, and made all his neighbours drunk; but in general he drank but little. King Olaf gave him plenty of pocket-money. When he went to his lodgings he would often, before going to bed, have some stoups of mead brought in, which he gave to all the men in the house to drink, so that he was much liked.

83. OF LITTLE FIN.

THERE WAS A MAN from the Uplands called Fin the Little, and some said of him that he was of Finnish[39] race. He was a remarkable little man, but so swift of foot that no horse could overtake him. He was a particularly well-excercised runner with snow-shoes, and shooter with the bow. He had long been in the service of King Hrorek, and often employed in errands of trust. He knew the roads in all the Upland hills, and was well known to all the great people. Now when King Hrorek was set under guards on the journey Fin would often slip in among the men of the guard, and followed, in general, with the lads and serving-men; but as often as he could he waited upon Hrorek, and entered into conversation with him. The king, however, only spoke a word or two with him at a time, to prevent suspicion. In spring, when they came a little way beyond Viken, Fin disappeared from the army for some days, but came back, and stayed with them a while. This happened often, without anyone observing it particularly; for there were many such hangers-on with the army.

84. MURDER OF OLAF'S COURT-MEN.

KING OLAF CAME TO Tunsberg before Easter (A.D. 1018), and remained there late in spring. Many merchant vessels came to the town, both from Saxon-land and Denmark, and from Viken, and from the north parts of the country. There was a great assemblage of people; and as the times were good, there was many a drinking meeting. It happened one evening that King Hrorek came rather late to his lodging; and as he had drunk a great deal, he was remarkably merry. Little Fin came to him with a stoup of mead with herbs in it, and very strong. The king made every one in the house drunk, until they fell asleep each in his berth. Fin had gone away, and a light was burning in the lodging. Hrorek waked the men who usually followed him, and told them he wanted to go out into the yard. They had a lantern with them, for outside it was pitch dark. Out in the yard there was a large privy standing upon pillars, and a stair to go up to it. While Hrorek and his guards were in the yard they heard a man say, "Cut down that devil;" and presently a crash, as if somebody fell. Hrorek said, "These fellows must be dead drunk to be fighting with each other so: run and

39 The Laplanders are called Fins In Norway and Sweden.–L.

separate them." They rushed out; but when they came out upon the steps both of them were killed: the man who went out the last was the first killed. There were twelve of Hrorek's men there, and among them Sigurd Hit, who had been his banner-man, and also little Fin. They drew the dead bodies up between the houses, took the king with them, ran out to a boat they had in readiness, and rowed away. Sigvat the skald slept in King Olaf's lodgings. He got up in the night, and his footboy with him, and went to the privy. But as they were returning, on going down the stairs Sigvat's foot slipped, and he fell on his knee; and when he put out his hands he felt the stairs wet. "I think," said he, laughing, "the king must have given many of us tottering legs tonight." When they came into the house in which light was burning the footboy said, "Have you hurt yourself that you are all over so bloody?" He replied, "I am not wounded, but something must have happened here." Thereupon he wakened Thord Folason, who was standard-bearer, and his bedfellow. They went out with a light, and soon found the blood. They traced it, and found the corpses, and knew them. They saw also a great stump of a tree in which clearly a gash had been cut, which, as was afterwards known, had been done as a stratagem to entice those out who had been killed. Sigvat and Thord spoke together and agreed it was highly necessary to let the king know of this without delay. They immediately sent a lad to the lodging where Hrorek had been. All the men in it were asleep; but the king was gone. He wakened the men who were in the house, and told them what had happened. The men arose, and ran out to the yard where the bodies were; but, however needful it appeared to be that the king should know it, nobody dared to waken him.

Then said Sigvat to Thord, "What wilt thou rather do, comrade, waken the king, or tell him the tidings?"

Thord replies, "I do not dare to waken him, and I would rather tell him the news."

Then said Sigvat, "There is minch of the night still to pass, and before morning Hrorek may get himself concealed in such a way that it may be difficult to find him; but as yet he cannot be very far off, for the bodies are still warm. We must never let the disgrace rest upon us of concealing this treason from the king. Go thou, up to the lodging, and wait for me there."

Sigvat then went to the church, and told the bell-ringer to toll for the souls of the king's court-men, naming the men who were killed. The-bell-ringer did as he was told. The king awoke at the ringing, sat up in his bed, and asked if it was already the hours of matins.

Thord replies, "It is worse than that, for there has occurred a very important affair. Hrorek is fled, and two of the court-men are killed."

The king asked how this had taken place, and Thord told him all he knew. The king got up immediately, ordered to sound the call for a meeting of the court, and when the people were assembled he named men to go out to every quarter from the town, by sea and land, to search for Hrorek. Thorer Lange took a boat, and set off with thirty men; and when day dawned they saw two small boats before them in the channel, and when they saw each other both parties rowed as hard as they could. King Hrorek was there with thirty men. When they came quite close to each other Hrorek and his men turned towards the land, and all sprang on shore except the king, who sat on the aft seat. He bade them farewell, and wished they might meet each other again in better luck. At the same moment Thorer with his company rowed to the land. Fin the Little shot off an arrow, which hit Thorer in the middle of the body, and was his death; and Sigurd Hit, with his men, ran up into the forest. Thorer's men took his body, and transported it, together with Hrorek, to Tunsberg. King Olaf undertook himself thereafter to look after King Hrorek, made him be carefully guarded, and took good care of his treason, for which reason he had a watch over him night and day. King Hrorek thereafter was very gay, and nobody could observe but that he was in every way well satisfied.

85. OF HROREK'S ASSAULT.

It happened on Ascension-day that King Olaf went to high mass, and the bishop went in procession around the church, and conducted the king; and when they came back to the church the bishop led the king to his seat on the north side of the choir. There Hrorek sat next to the king, and concealed his countenance in his upper cloak. When Olaf had seated himself Hrorek laid his hand on the king's shoulder, and felt it.

"Thou hast fine clothes on, cousin, today," said he.

King Olaf replies, "It is a festival today, in remembrance that Jesus Christ ascended to heaven from earth."

King Hrorek says, "I understand nothing about it so as to hold in my mind what ye tell me about Christ. Much of what ye tell me appears to me incredible, although many wonderful things may have come to pass in old times."

When the mass was finished Olaf stood up, held his hands up over his head, and bowed down before the altar, so that his cloak hung down behind his shoulders. Then King Hrorek started up hastily and sharply, and struck at the king with a long knife of the kind called ryting; but the blow was received in the upper cloak at the shoulder, because the king was bending himself forwards. The clothes were much cut, but the king was not wounded. When the king perceived the attack he sprang upon the floor; and Hrorek struck at him again with the knife, but did not reach him, and said, "Art thou flying, Olaf, from me, a blind men?" The king ordered his men to seize him and lead him out of the church, which was done. After this attempt many hastened to King Olaf, and advised that King Hrorek should be killed. "It is," said they, "tempting your luck in the highest degree, king, to keep him with you, and protect him, whatever mischief he may undertake; for night and day he thinks upon taking your life. And if you send him away, we know no one who can watch him so that he will not in all probability escape; and if once he gets loose he will assemble a great multitude, and do much evil."

The king replies, "You say truly that many a one has suffered death for less offence than Hrorek's; but willingly I would not darken the victory I gained over the Upland kings, when in one morning hour I took five kings prisoners, and got all their kingdoms: but yet, as they were my relations, I should not be their murderer but upon need. As yet I can scarcely see whether Hrorek puts me in the necessity of killing him or not."

It was to feel if King Olaf had armour on or not that Hrorek had laid his hand on the king's shoulder.

86. KING HROREK'S JOURNEY TO ICELAND.

THERE WAS AN ICELAND man, by name Thorarin Nefiulfson, who had his relations in the north of the country. He was not of high birth, but particularly prudent, eloquent, and agreeable in conversation with people of distinction. He was also a far-travelled man, who had been long in foreign parts. Thorarin was a remarkably ugly man, principally because he had very ungainly limbs. He had great ugly hands, and his feet were still uglier. Thorarin was in Tunsberg when this event happened which has just been related, and he was known to King Olaf by their having had conversations together. Thorarin was just then done with rigging out a merchant vessel which he owned, and with which he intended to go to Iceland in summer. King Olaf had Thorarin with him as a guest for some days, and conversed much with him; and Thorarin even slept in the king's lodgings. One morning early the king awoke while the others were still sleeping. The sun had newly risen in the sky, and there was much light within. The king saw that Thorarin had stretched out one of his feet from under the bed-clothes, and he looked at the foot a while. In the meantime the others in the lodging awoke; and the king said to Thorarin, "I have been awake for a while, and have seen a sight which was worth seeing; and that is a man's foot so ugly that I do not think an uglier can be found in this merchant town." Thereupon he told the others to look at it, and see if it was not so; and all agreed with the king. When Thorarin observed what they were talking about, he said, "There are few things for which you cannot find a match, and that may be the case here."

The king says, "I would rather say that such another ugly foot cannot be found in the town, and I would lay any wager upon it."

Then said Thorarin, "I am willing to bet that I shall find an uglier foot still in the town."

The king–"Then he who wins shall have the right to get any demand from the other he chooses to make."

"Be it so," said Thorarin. Thereupon he stretches out his other foot from under the bed-clothes, and it was in no way handsomer than the other, and moreover, wanted the little toe. "There," said Thorarin, "see now, king, my other foot, which is so much uglier; and, besides, has no little toe. Now I have won."

The king replies, "That other foot was so much uglier than this one by having five ugly toes upon it, and this has only four; and now I have won the choice of asking something from thee."

"The sovereign's decision must be right," says Thorarin; "but what does the king require of me?"

"To take Hrorek," said the king, "to Greenland, and deliver him to Leif Eirikson."

Thorarin replies, "I have never been in Greenland."

The king–"Thou, who art a far-travelled man, wilt now have an opportunity of seeing Greenland, if thou hast never been there before."

At first Thorarin did not say much about it; but as the king insisted on his wish he did not entirely decline, but said, "I will let you hear, king, what my desire would have been had I gained the wager. It would have been to be received into your body of court-men; and if you will grant me that, I will be the more zealous now in fulfilling your pleasure." The king gave his consent, and Thorarin was made one of the court-men. Then Thorarin rigged out his vessel, and when he was ready he took on board King Hrorek. When Thorarin took leave of King Olaf, he said, "Should it now turn out, king, as is not improbable, and often happens, that we cannot effect the voyage to Greenland, but must run for Iceland or other countries, how shall I get rid of this king in a way that will be satisfactory to you?"

The king–"If thou comest to Iceland, deliver him into the hands of Gudmund Eyolfson, or of Skapte, the lagman, or of some other chief who will receive my tokens and message of friendship. But if thou comest to other countries nearer to this, do so with him that thou canst know with certainty that King Hrorek never again shall appear in Norway; but do so only when thou seest no other way of doing whatsoever."

When Thorarin was ready for sea, and got a wind, he sailed outside of all the rocks and islands, and when he was to the north of the Naze set right out into the ocean. He did not immediately get a good wind, but he avoided coming near the land. He sailed until he made land which he knew, in the south part of Iceland, and sailed west around the land out into the Greenland ocean.

There he encountered heavy storms, and drove long about upon the ocean; but when summer was coming to an end he landed again in Iceland in Breidafjord. Thorgils Arason[40] was the first man of any consequence who came to him. Thorarin brings him the king's salutation, message, and tokens, with which was the desire about King Hrorek's reception. Thorgils received these in a friendly way, and invited King Hrorek to his house, where he stayed all winter. But he did not like being there, and begged that Thorgils would let him go to Gudmund; saying he had heard some time or other that there in Gudmund's house, was the most sumptuous way of living in Iceland, and that it was intended he should be in Gudmund's hands. Thorgils let him have his desire, and conducted him with some men to Gudmund at Modruveller. Gudmund received Hrorek kindly on account of the king's message, and he stayed there the next winter. He did not like being there either; and then Gudmund gave him a habitation upon a small farm called Kalfskin, where there were but few neighbours. There Hrorek passed the third winter, and said that since he had laid down his kingdom he thought himself most comfortably situated here; for here he was most respected by all. The summer after Hrorek fell sick, and died; and it is said he is the only king whose bones rest in Iceland. Thorarin Nefiulfson was afterwards for a long time upon voyages; but sometimes he was with King Olaf.

40 Thorgils was the son of Are Marson, who visited America (Vindland). Thorgils, who was still alive in the year 1024, was noted for his kindness toward all persecuted persons.

87. BATTLE IN ULFREKS-FJORD.

The summer that Thorarin went with Hrorek to Iceland, Hjalte Skeggjason went also to Iceland, and King Olaf gave him many friendly gifts with him when they parted. The same summer Eyvind Urarhorn went on an expedition to the west sea, and came in autumn to Ireland, to the Irish king Konofogor[41]. In autumn Einar earl of Orkney and this Irish king met in Ulfreks-fjord, and there was a great battle, in which Konofogor gained the victory, having many more people. The earl fled with a single ship and came back about autumn to Orkney, after losing most of his men and all the booty they had made. The earl was much displeased with his expedition, and threw the blame upon the Northmen, who had been in the battle on the side of the Irish king, for making him lose the victory.

88. OLAF PREPARES FOR HIS BRIDAL JOURNEY.

Now we begin again our story where we let it slip–at King Olaf's travelling to his bridal, to receive his betrothed Ingegerd the king's daughter. The king had a great body of men with him, and so chosen a body that all the great people he could lay hold of followed him; and every man of consequence had a chosen band of men with him distinguished by birth or other qualifications. The whole were well appointed, and equipped in ships, weapons, and clothes. They steered the fleet eastwards to Konungahella; but when they arrived there they heard nothing of the Swedish king and none of his men had come there. King Olaf remained a long time in summer (A.D. 1018) at Konungahella, and endeavored carefully to make out what people said of the Swedish king's movements, or what were his designs; but no person could tell him anything for certain about it. Then he sent men up to Gautland to Earl Ragnvald, to ask him if he knew how it came to pass that the Swedish king did not come to the meeting agreed on. The earl replies, that he did not know. "But as soon," said he, "as I hear, I shall send some of my men to King Olaf, to let him know if there be any other cause for the delay than the multitude of affairs; as it often happens that the Swedish king's movements are delayed by this more than he could have expected."

41 Konofogor's Irish name was Connor.

89. OF THE SWEDISH KING'S CHILDREN.

This Swedish king, Olaf Eirikson, had first a concubine who was called Edla, a daughter of an earl of Vindland, who had been captured in war, and therefore was called the king's slave-girl. Their children were Emund, Astrid, Holmfrid.... They had, besides, a son, who was born the day before St. Jacob's-day. When the boy was to be christened the bishop called him Jacob, which the Swedes did not like, as there never had been a Swedish king called Jacob. All King Olaf's children were handsome in appearance, and clever from childhood. The queen was proud, and did not behave well towards her step-children; therefore the king sent his son Emund to Vindland, to be fostered by his mother's relations, where he for a long time neglected his Christianity. The king's daughter, Astrid, was brought up in West Gautland, in the house of a worthy man called Egil. She was a very lovely girl: her words came well into her conversation; she was merry, but modest, and very generous. When she was grown up she was often in her father's house, and every man thought well of her. King Olaf was haughty and harsh in his speech. He took very ill the uproar and clamour the country people had raised against him at the Upsala Thing, as they had threatened him with violence, for which he laid the chief blame on Earl Ragnvald. He made no preparation for the bridal, according to the agreement to marry his daughter Ingegerd to Olaf the king of Norway, and to meet him on the borders for that purpose. As the summer advanced many of his men were anxious to know what the kings intentions were; whether to keep to the agreement with King Olaf, or break his word, and with it the peace of the country. But no one was so bold as to ask the king, although they complained of it to Ingegerd, and besought her to find out what the king intended. She replied "I have no inclination to speak to the king again about the matters between him and King Olaf; for he answered me ill enough once before when I brought forward Olaf's name." In the meantime Ingegerd, the king's daughter, took it to heart, became melancholy and sorrowful and yet very curious to know what the king intended. She had much suspicion that he would not keep his word and promise to King Olaf; for he appeared quite enraged whenever Olaf the Thick's name was in any way mentioned.

90. OF THE SWEDISH KING OLAF'S HUNTING.

One morning early the king rode out with his dogs and falcons, and his men around him. When they let slip the falcons the king's falcon killed two black-cocks in one flight, and three in another. The dogs ran and brought the birds when they had fallen to the ground. The king ran after them, took the game from them himself, was delighted with his sport, and said, "It will be long before the most of you have such success." They agreed in this; adding, that in their opinion no king had such luck in hunting as he had. Then the king rode home with his followers in high spirits. Ingegerd, the king's daughter, was just going out of her lodging when the king came riding into the yard, and she turned round and saluted him. He saluted her in return, laughing; produced the birds, and told her the success of his chase.

"Dost thou know of any king," said he, "who made so great a capture in so short a time?"

"It is indeed," replied she, "a good morning's hunting, to have got five black-cocks; but it was a still better when, in one morning, the king of Norway, Olaf, took five kings, and subdued all their kingdoms."

When the king heard this he sprang from his horse, turned to Ingegerd, and said, "Thou shalt know, Ingegerd, that however great thy love may be for this man, thou shalt never get him, nor he get thee. I will marry thee to some chief with whom I can be in friendship; but never can I be a friend of the man who has robbed me of my kingdom, and done me great mischief by marauding and killing through the land." With that their conversation broke off, and each went away.

91. OLAF THE NORWAY KING'S COUNSELS.

INGEGERD, THE KING'S DAUGHTER, had now full certainty of King Olaf's intention, and immediately sent men to West Gautland to Earl Ragnvald, and let him know how it stood with the Swedish king, and that the agreement made with the king of Norway was broken; and advising the earl and people of West Gautland to be upon their guard, as no peace from the people of Norway was to be expected. When the earl got this news he sent a message through all his kingdom, and told the people to be cautious, and prepared in case of war or pillage from the side of Norway. He also sent men to King Olaf the Thick, and let him know the message he had received, and likewise that he wished for himself to hold peace and friendship with King Olaf; and therefore he begged him not to pillage in his kingdom. When this message came to King Olaf it made him both angry and sorry; and for some days nobody got a word from him. He then held a House-Thing with his men, and in it Bjorn arose, and first took the word. He began his speech by telling that he had proceeded eastward last winter to establish a peace, and he told how kindly Earl Ragnvald had received him; and, on the other hand, how crossly and heavily the Swedish king had accepted the proposal. "And the agreement," said he, "which was made, was made more by means of the strength of the people, the power of Thorgny, and the aid of the earl, than by the king's good-will. Now, on these grounds, we know for certain that it is the king who has caused the breach of the agreement; therefore we ought by no means to make the earl suffer, for it is proved that he is King Olaf's firm friend." The king wished now to hear from the chiefs and other leaders of troops what course he should adopt. "Whether shall we go against Gautland, and maraud there with such men as we have got; or is there any other course that appears to you more advisable?" He spoke both long and well.

Thereafter many powerful men spoke, and all were at last agreed in dissuading from hostilities. They argued thus:–"Although we are a numerous body of men who are assembled here, yet they are all only people of weight and power; but, for a war expedition, young men who are in quest of property and consideration are more suitable. It is also the custom of people of weight and power, when they go into battle or strife, to have many people with them whom they can send out before them for their defence; for the men do not fight worse who have little property, but even better than those who are brought up in the midst of wealth." After these considerations the king resolved to dismiss this army from any expedition, and to give every man leave to return home; but proclaimed, at the same time, that next summer the people over the whole country would be called out in a general levy, to march immediately against the Swedish king, and punish him for his want of faith. All thought well of this plan. Then the king returned northwards to Viken, and took his abode at Sarpsborg in autumn, and ordered all things necessary for winter provision to be collected there; and he remained there all winter (A.D. 1019) with a great retinue.

92. SIGVAT THE SKALD'S JOURNEY EASTWARDS.

People talked variously about Earl Ragnvald; some said he was King Olaf's sincere friend; others did not think this likely, and thought it stood in his power to warn the Swedish king to keep his word, and the agreement concluded on between him and King Olaf. Sigvat the poet often expressed himself in conversation as Earl Ragnvald's great friend, and often spoke of him to King Olaf; and he offered to the king to travel to Earl Ragnvald's and spy after the Swedish kings doings, and to attempt, if possible, to get the settlement of the agreement. The king thought well of this plan; for he oft, and with pleasure, spoke to his confidential friends about Ingegerd, the king's daughter. Early in winter (A.D. 1019) Sigvat the skald, with two companions, left Sarpsborg, and proceeded eastwards over the moors to Gautland. Before Sigvat and King Olaf parted he composed these verses:–

"Sit happy in thy hall, O king!
Till I come back, and good news bring:
The skald will bid thee now farewell,
Till he brings news well worth to tell.
He wishes to the helmed hero
Health, and long life, and a tull flow
Of honour, riches, and success–
And, parting, ends his song with this.
The farewell word is spoken now __
The word that to the heart lies nearest;
And yet, O king! before I go,
One word on what I hold the dearest,
I fain would say, "O! may God save
To thee the bravest of the brave,
The land, which is thy right by birth!"
This is my dearest with on earth."

Then they proceeded eastwards towards Eid, and had difficulty in crossing the river in a little cobble; but they escaped, though with danger: and Sigvat sang:–

"On shore the crazy boat I drew,
Wet to the skin, and frightened too;
For truly there was danger then;
The mocking hill elves laughed again.
To see us in this cobble sailing,
And all our sea-skill unavailing.
But better did it end, you see,
Than any of us could foresee."

Then they went through the Eid forest, and Sigvat sang:–

"A hundred miles through Eid's old wood,
And devil an alehouse, bad or good,–

A hundred miles, and tree and sky
Were all that met the weary eye.
With many a grumble, many a groan.
A hundred miles we trudged right on;
And every king's man of us bore
On each foot-sole a bleeding sore."

They came then through Gautland, and in the evening reached a farm-house called Hof. The door was bolted so that they could not come in; and the servants told them it was a fast-day, and they could not get admittance. Sigvat sang:–

"Now up to Hof in haste I hie,
And round the house and yard I pry.
Doors are fast locked–but yet within,
Methinks, I hear some stir and din.
I peep, with nose close to the ground.
Below the door, but small cheer found.
My trouble with few words was paid–
"'Tis holy time,' the house-folkd said.
Heathens! to shove me thus away!
I' the foul fiend's claws may you all lay."

Then they came to another farm, where the good-wife was standing at the door, and told them not to come in, for they were busy with a sacrifice to the elves. Sigvat sang of it thus:–

"'My poor lad, enter not, I pray!'
Thus to me did the old wife say;
'For all of us are heathens here,
And I for Odin's wrath do fear.'
The ugly witch drove me away,
Like scared wolf sneaking from his prey.
When she told me that there within
Was sacrifice to foul Odin."

Another evening, they came to three bondes, all of them of the name of Olver, who drove them away. Sigvat sang:–

"Three of one name,
To their great shame,

The traveller late
Drove from their gate!
Travellers may come
From our viking-home,
Unbidden guests
At these Olvers' feasts."

They went on farther that evening, and came to a fourth bonde, who was considered the most hospitable man in the country; but he drove them away also. Then Sigvat sang:–

"Then on I went to seek night's rest
From one who was said to be the best,
The kindest host in the land around,
And there I hoped to have quarters found.
But, faith,'twas little use to try;
For not so much as raise an eye
Would this huge wielder of the spade:
If he's the hest, it must be said
Bad is the best, and the skald's praise
Cannot be given to churls like these.
I almost wished that Asta's son
In the Eid forest had been one
When we, his men, were even put
Lodging to crave in a heathen's hut.
I knew not where the earl to find;
Four times driven off by men unkind,
I wandered now the whole night o'er,
Driven like a dog from door to door."

Now when they came to Earl Ragnvald's the earl said they must have had a severe journey. Then Sigvat sang:–

"The message-bearers of the king
From Norway came his words to bring;
And truly for their master they
Hard work have done before to-day.
We did not loiter on the road,
But on we pushed for thy abode:
Thy folk, in sooth, were not so kind
That we cared much to lag hehind.

But Eid to rest safe we found,
From robbers free to the eastern bound:
This praise to thee, great earl, is due–
The skald says only what is true."

Earl Ragnvald gave Sigvat a gold arm-ring, and a woman said "he had not made the journey with his black eyes for nothing." Sigvat sang:–

"My coal-black eyes
Dost thou despise?
They have lighted me
Across the sea
To gain this golden prize:
They have lighted me,
Thy eyes to see,
O'er Iceland's main,
O'er hill and plain:
Where Nanna's lad would fear to be
They have lighted me."

Sigvat was long entertained kindly and well in the house of Earl Ragnvald. The earl heard by letters, sent by Ingegerd the king's daughter, that ambassadors from King Jarisleif were come from Russia to King Olaf of Svithjod to ask his daughter Ingegerd in marriage, and that King Olaf had given them hopes that he would agree to it. About the same time King Olaf's daughter Astrid came to Earl Ragnvald's court, and a great feast was made for her. Sigvat soon became acquainted by conversation with the king's daughter, and she knew him by name and family, for Ottar the skald, Sigvat's sister's son, had long intimate acquaintance with King Olaf, the Swedish king. Among other things talked of, Earl Ragnvald asked Sigvat if the king of Norway would not marry the king's daughter Astrid. "If he would do that," said he, "I think we need not ask the Swedish king for his consent." Astrid, the kings daughter, said exactly the same. Soon after Sigvat returns home, and comes to King Olaf at Sarpsborg a little before Yule.

When Sigvat came home to King Olaf he went into the hall, and, looking around on the walls, he sang:–

"When our men their arms are taking
The raven's wings with greed are shaking;
When they come back to drink in hall

Brave spoil they bring to deck the wall–
Shield, helms, and panzers[42]*, all in row,*
Stripped in the field from lifeless fow.
In truth no royal nail comes near
Thy splendid hall in precious gear."

Afterwards Sigvat told of his journey, and sang these verses:–

"The king's court-guards desire to hear
About our journey and our cheer,
Our ships in autumn reach the sound,
But long the way to Swedish ground.
With joyless weather, wind and raind,
And pinching cold, and feet in pain–
With sleep, fatigue, and want oppressed,
No songs had we–we scarce had rest."

And when he came into conversation with the king he sang:–

"When first I met the earl I told
How our king loved a friend so bold;
How in his heart he loved a man
With hand to do, and head to plan.
Thou generous king! with zeal and care
I sought to advance thy great affair;
For messengers from Russian land
Had come to ask Ingegerd's hand.
The earl, thy friend, bids thee, who art
So mild and generous of heart,
His servants all who here may come
To cherish in thy royal home;
And thine who may come to the east
In Ragnvald's hall shall find a feast–
In Ragnvald's house shall find a home–
At Ragnvald's court be still welcome.
When first I came the people's mind
Incensed by Eirik's son I find;
And he refused the wish to meet,
Alleging treachery and deceit.

42 The Pantzer–a complete suit of plate-armour.

But I explained how it was here,
For earl and king, advantage clear
With thee to hold the strictest peace,
And make all force and foray cease.
The earl is wise, and understands
The need of peace for both the lands;
And he entreats thee not to break
The present peace for vengeance's sake!"

He immediately tells King Olaf the news he had heard; and at first the king was much cast down when he heard of King Jarisleif's suit, and he said he expected nothing but evil from King Olaf; but wished he might be able to return it in such a way as Olaf should remember. A while afterwards the king asks Sigvat about various news from Gautland. Sigvat spoke a great deal about Astrid, the kings daughter; how beautiful she was, how agreeable in her conversation; and that all declared she was in no respect behind her sister Ingegerd. The king listened with pleasure to this. Then Sigvat told him the conversation he and Astrid had had between themselves, and the king was delighted at the idea. "The Swedish king," said he, "will scarcely think that I will dare to marry a daughter of his without his consent." But this speech of his was not known generally. King Olaf and Sigvat the skald often spoke about it. The king inquired particularly of Sigvat what he knew about Earl Ragnvald, and "if he be truly our friend," said the king. Sigvat said that the earl was King Olaf's best friend, and sang these verses:–

"The mighty Olaf should not cease
With him to hold good terms and peace;
For this good earl unwearied shows
He is thy friend where all are foes.
Of all who dwell by the East Sea
So friendly no man is as he:
At all their Things he takes thy part,
And is thy firm friend, hand and heart."

93. RAGNVALD AND ASTRA'S JOURNEY.

After Yule (A.D. 1019), Thord Skotakol, a sister's son of Sigvat, attended by one of Sigvat's footboys, who had been with Sigvat the autumn before in Gautland, went quite secretly from the court, and proceeded to Gautland. When they came to Earl Ragnvald's court, they produced the tokens which Olaf himself had sent to the earl, that he might place confidence in Thord. Without delay the earl made himself ready for a journey, as did Astrid, the king's daughter; and the earl took with him 120 men, who were chosen both from among his courtmen and the sons of great bondes, and who were carefully equipped in all things, clothes, weapons, and horses. Then they rode northwards to Sarpsborg, and came there at Candlemas.

94. OF KING OLAF'S MARRIAGE.

King Olaf had put all things in order in the best style. There were all sorts of liquors of the best that could be got, and all other preparations of the same quality. Many people of consequence were summoned in from their residences. When the earl arrived with his retinue the king received him particularly well; and the earl was shown to a large, good, and remarkably well-furnished house for his lodging; and serving-men and others were appointed to wait on him; and nothing was wanting, in any respect, that could grace a feast. Now when the entertainment had lasted some days, the king, the earl, and Astrid had a conference together; and the result of it was, that Earl Ragnvald contracted Astrid, daughter of the Swedish king Olaf, to Olaf king of Norway, with the same dowry which had before been settled that her sister Ingegerd should have from home. King Olaf, on his part, should give Astrid the same bride-gift that had been intended for her sister Ingegerd. Thereupon an eke was made to the feast, and King Olaf and Queen Astrid's wedding was drunk in great festivity. Earl Ragnvald then returned to Gautland, and the king gave the earl many great and good gifts at parting; and they parted the dearest of friends, which they continued to be while they lived.

95. THE AGREEMENT BROKEN BY OLAF.

The spring (A.D. 1019) thereafter came ambassadors from King Jarisleif in Novgorod to Svithjod, to treat more particularly about the promise given by King Olaf the preceding summer to marry his daughter Ingegerd to King Jarisleif. King Olaf tallied about the business with Ingegerd, and told her it was his pleasure that she should marry King Jarisleif. She replied. "If I marry King Jarisleif, I must have as my bride-gift the town and earldom of Ladoga." The Russian ambassadors agreed to this, on the part of their sovereign. Then said Ingegerd, "If I go east to Russia, I must choose the man in Svithjod whom I think most suitable to accompany me; and I must stipulate that he shall not have any less title, or in any respect less dignity, privilege, and consideration there, than he has, here." This the king and the ambassadors agreed to, and gave their hands upon it in confirmation of the condition.

"And who," asked the king, "is the man thou wilt take with thee as thy attendant?"

"That man," she replied, "is my relation Earl Ragnvald."

The king replies, "I have resolved to reward Earl Ragnvald in a different manner for his treason against his master in going to Norway with my daughter, and giving her as a concubine to that fellow, who he knew was my greatest enemy. I shall hang him up this summer."

Then Ingegerd begged her father to be true to the promise he had made her, and had confirmed by giving his hand upon it. By her entreaties it was at last agreed that the king should promise to let Earl Ragnvald go in peace from Svithjod, but that he should never again appear in the king's presence, or come back to Svithjod while Olaf reigned. Ingegerd then sent messengers to the earl to bring him these tidings, and to appoint a place of meeting. The earl immediately prepared for his journey; rode up to East Gautland; procured there a vessel, and, with his retinue, joined Ingegerd, and they proceeded together eastward to Russia. There Ingegerd was married to King Jarisleif; and their children were Valdemar, Vissivald, and Holte the Bold. Queen Ingegerd gave Earl Ragnvald the town of Ladoga, and earldom belonging to it. Earl Ragnvald was there a long time, and was a celebrated man. His sons and Ingebjorg's were Earl Ulf and Earl Eilif.

96. HISTORY OF THE LAGMAN EMUND.

There was a man called Emund of Skara, who was lagman of west Gautland, and was a man of great understanding and eloquence, and of high birth, great connection, and very wealthy; but was considered deceitful, and not to be trusted. He was the most powerful man in West Gautland after the earl was gone. The same spring (A.D. 1019) that Earl Ragnvald left Gautland the Gautland people held a Thing among themselves, and often expressed their anxiety to each other about what the Swedish king might do. They heard he was incensed because they had rather held in friendship with the king of Norway than striven against him; and he was also enraged against those who had attended his daughter Astrid to Norway. Some proposed to seek help and support from the king of Norway, and to offer him their services; others dissuaded from this measure, as West Gautland had no strength to oppose to the Swedes. "And the king of Norway," said they, "is far from us, the chief strength of his country very distant; and therefore let us first send men to the Swedish king to attempt to come to some reconciliation with him. If that fail, we can still turn to the king of Norway." Then the bondes asked Emund to undertake this mission, to which he agreed; and he proceeded with thirty men to East Gautland, where there were many of his relations and friends, who received him hospitably. He conversed there with the most prudent men about this difficult business; and they were all unanimous on one point,–that the king's treatment of them was against law and reason. From thence Emund went into Svithjod, and conversed with many men of consequence, who all expressed themselves in the same way. Emund continued his journey thus, until one day, towards evening, he arrived at Upsala, where he and his retinue took a good lodging, and stayed there all night. The next day Emund waited upon the king, who was just then sitting in the Thing surrounded by many people. Emund went before him, bent his knee, and saluted him. The king looked at him, saluted him, and asked him what news he brought.

Emund replies, "There is little news among us Gautlanders; but it appears to us a piece of remarkable news that the proud, stupid Atte, in Vermaland, whom we look upon as a great sportsman, went up to the forest in winter with his snow-shoes and his bow. After he had got as many furs in the mountains as filled his hand-sledge so full that he could scarcely drag it, he returned home from the woods. But on the way he saw a squirrel in the trees, and shot at it, but did not hit; at which he was so angry, that he left the sledge to run after the squirrel: but still the squirrel sprang where the wood was thickest, sometimes among the roots of the trees, sometimes in the branches, sometimes among the arms that stretch from tree to tree. When Atte shot at it the arrows flew too high or too low, and the squirrel never jumped so that Atte could get a fair aim at him. He was so eager upon this chase that he ran the whole day after the squirrel, and yet could not get hold of it. It was now getting dark; so he threw himself down upon the snow, as he was wont, and lay there all night in a heavy snow-storm. Next day Atte got up to look after his sledge, but never did he find it again; and so he returned home. And this is the only news, king, I have to tell."

The king says, "This is news of but little importance, if it be all thou hast to tell."

Ernund replies, "Lately something happened which may well be called news. Gaute Tofason went with five warships out of the Gaut river, and when he was lying at the Eikrey Isles there came five large Danish merchant-ships there. Gaute and his men immediately took four of the great vessels, and made a great booty without the loss of a man: but the fifth vessel slipped out to sea, and sailed away. Gaute gave chase with one ship, and at first came nearer to them; but as the wind increased, the Danes got away. Then Gaute wanted to turn back; but a storm came on so that he lost his ship at Hlesey, with all the goods, and the greater part of his crew. In the meantime his people were waiting for him at the Eikrey Isles: but the Danes came over in fifteen merchant-ships, killed them all, and took all the booty they had made. So but little luck had they with their greed of plunder."

The king replied. "That is great news, and worth being told; but what now is thy errand here?"

Emund replies, "I travel, sire, to obtain your judgment in a difficult case, in which our law and the Upsala law do not agree."

The king asks, "What is thy appeal case?"

Emund replies, "There were two noble-born men of equal birth, but unequal in property and disposition. They quarrelled about some land, and did each other much damage; but most was done to him who was the more powerful of the two. This quarrel, however, was settled, and judged of at a General Thing; and the judgment was, that the most powerful should pay a compensation. But at the first payment, instead of paying a goose, he paid a gosling; for an old swine he paid a sucking pig; and for a mark of stamped gold only a half-mark, and for the other half-mark nothing but clay and dirt; and, moreover, threatened, in the most violent way, the people whom he forced to receive such goods in payment. Now, sire, what is your judgment?"

The king replies, "He shall pay the full equivalent whom the judgment ordered to do so, and that faithfully; and further, threefold to his king: and if payment be not made within a year and a day, he shall be cut off from all his property, his goods confiscated, and half go the king's house, and half to the other party."

Emund took witnesses to this judgment among the most considerable of the men who were present, according to the laws which were held in the Upsala Thing. He then saluted the king, and went his way; and other men brought their cases before the king, and he sat late in the day upon the cases of the people. Now when the king came to table, he asked where Lagman Emund was. It was answered, he was home at his lodgings. "Then," said the king, "go after him, and tell him to be my guest to-day." Thereafter the dishes were borne in; then came the musicians with harps, fiddles, and musical instruments; and lastly, the cup-bearers. The king was particularly merry, and had many great people at table with him, so that he thought little of Emund. The king drank the whole day, and slept all the night after; but in the morning the king awoke, and recollected what Emund had said the day before: and when he had put on his clothes, he let his wise men be summoned to him; for he had always twelve of the wisest men who sat in judgment with him, and treated the more difficult cases; and that was no easy business, for the king was ill-pleased if the judgment was not according to justice, and yet it was of no use to contradict him. In this meeting the king ordered Lagman Emund to be called before them. The messenger returned, and said, "Sire, Lagman Emund rode away yesterday as soon as he had dined." "Then," said the king, "tell me, ye good chiefs, what may have been the meaning of that law-case which Emund laid before us yesterday?"

They replied, "You must have considered it yourself, if you think there was any other meaning under it than what he said."

The king replied, "By the two noble-born men whom he spoke of, who were at variance, and of whom one was more powerful than the other, and who did each other damage, he must have meant us and Olaf the Thick."

They answered, "It is, sire, as you say."

The king–"Our case was judged at the Upsala Thing. But what was his meaning when he said that bad payment was made; namely, a gosling for a goose, a pig for a swine, and clay and dirt for half of the money instead of gold?"

Arnvid the Blind replied, "Sire, red gold and clay are things very unlike; but the difference is still greater between king and slave. You promised Olaf the Thick your daughter Ingegerd, who, in all branches of her descent, is born of kings, and of the Upland Swedish race of kings, which is the most noble in the North; for it is traced up to the gods themselves. But now Olaf has got Astrid; and although she is a king's child, her mother was but a slave-woman, and, besides, of Vindish race. Great difference, indeed, must there be between these kings, when the one takes thankfully such a match; and now it is evident, as might be expected, that no Northman is to be placed by the side of the Upsala kings. Let us all give thanks that it has so turned out; for the gods have long protected their descendants, although many now neglect this faith."

There were three brothers:–Arnvid the Blind, who had a great understanding, but was so weak-sighted that he was scarcely fit for war; the second was Thorvid the Stammerer, who could not utter two words together at one time, but was remarkably bold and courageous; the third was Freyvid the Deaf, who was hard of hearing. All these brothers were rich and powerful men, of noble birth, great wisdom, and all very dear to the king.

Then said King Olaf, "What means that which Emund said about Atte the Dull?"

None made any reply, but the one looked at the other.

"Speak freely," said the king.

Then said Thorvid the Stammerer, "Atte–quarrel–some–greedy–jealous–deceitful–dull."

Then said the king, "To whom are these words of reproach and mockery applied?"

Freyvid the Deaf replied, "We will speak more clearly if we have your permission."

The king–"Speak freely, Freyvid, what you will."

Freyvid took up the word, and spoke. "My brother Thorvid, who is considered to be the wisest of us brothers, holds the words 'quarrelsome, greedy, jealous, dull,' to be one and the same thing; for it applies to him who is weary of peace, longs for small things without attaining them, while he lets great and useful things pass away as they came. I am deaf; yet so loud have many spoken out, that I can perceive that all men, both great and small, take it ill that you have not kept your promise to the king of Norway; and, worse than that, that you broke the decision of the community as it was delivered at Upsala Thing. You need not fear either the king of Norway, or the king of Denmark, or any other, so long as the Swedish army will follow you; but if the people of the country unanimously turn against you, we, your friends, see no counsel that can be of advantage to you."

The king asks, "Who is the chief who dares to betray the country and me?"

Freyvid replies, "All Swedes desire to have the ancient laws, and their full rights. Look but here, sire, how many chiefs are sitting in council with you. I think, in truth, we are but six whom you call your councillors: all the others, so far as I know, have ridden forth through the districts to hold Things with the people; and we will not conceal it from you, that the message-token has gone forth to assemble a Retributionthing[43]. All of us brothers have been invited to take part in the decisions of this council, but none of us will bear the name of traitor to the sovereign; for that our father never was."

Then the king said, "What council shall we take in this dangerous affair that is in our hands? Good chiefs give me council, that I may keep my kingdom, and the heritage of my forefathers; for I cannot enter into strife against the whole Swedish force."

Arnvid the Blind replies, "Sire, it is my advice that you ride down to Aros with such men as will follow you; take your ship there and go out into the Maeler lake; summon all people to meet you; proceed no longer with haughtiness, but promise every man the law and rights of old established in the country; keep back in this way the message-token, for it cannot as yet, in so short a time have travelled far through the land. Send, then those of your men in whom you have the most confidence to those who have this business on hand, and try if this uproar can be appeased."

The king says that he will adopt this advice. "I will," says he, "that ye brothers undertake this business; for I trust to you the most among my men."

Thorvid the Stammerer said, "I remain behind. Let Jacob, your son, go with them, for that is necessary."

Then said Freyvid, "Let us do as Thorvid says: he will not leave you, and I and Arnvid must travel."

This counsel was followed. Olaf went to his ships, and set out into the Maelar lake, and many people came to him. The brothers Arnvid and Freyvid rode out to Ullaraker, and had with them the king's son Jacob; but they kept it a secret that he was there. The brothers observed that there was a great concourse and war-gathering, for the bondes held the Thing night and day. When Arnvid and Freyvid met their relations and friends, they said they would join with the people; and many agreed to leave the management of the business in the hands of the brothers. But all, as one man, declared they would no longer have King Olaf over them, and no longer suffer his unlawful proceedings, and over-weening pride which would not listen to any man's remonstrances, even when the great chiefs spoke the truth to him. When Freyvid observed the heat of the people, he saw in what a bad situation the king's cause was. He summoned the chiefs of the land to a meeting with him and addressed them thus:–"It appears to me, that if we are to depose Olaf Eirikson

43 Refsithing–a Thing for punishment by penalty or death for crimes and misdemeanours.–L.

from his kingdom, we Swedes of the Uplands should be the leading men in it: for so it has always been, that the counsel which the Upland chiefs have resolved among themselves has always been followed by the men of the rest of the country. Our forefathers did not need to take advice from the West Gautlanders about the government of the Swedes. Now we will not be so degenerate as to need Emund to give us counsel; but let us, friends and relations, unite ourselves for the purpose of coming to a determination." All agreed to this, and thought it was well said. Thereafter the people joined this union which the Upland chiefs made among themselves, and Freyvid and Arnvid were chiefs of the whole assemblage. When Emund heard this he suspected how the matter would end, and went to both the brothers to have a conversation with them. Then Freyvid asked Emund, "Who, in your opinion, should we take for king, in case Olaf Eirikson's days are at an end?"

Emund–"He whom we think best suited to it, whether he be of the race of chiefs or not."

Freyvid answers, "We Uplanders will not, in our time, have the kingdom go out of the old race of our ancestors, which has given us kings for a long course of generations, so long as we have so good a choice as now. King Olaf has two sons, one of whom we will choose for king, although there is a great difference between them. The one is noble-born, and of Swedish race on both sides; the other is a slave-woman's son, and of Vindish race on the mother's side."

This decision was received with loud applause, and all would have Jacob for king.

Then said Emund. "Ye Upland Swedes have the power this time to determinate the matter; but I will tell you what will happen:–some of those who now will listen to nothing but that the kingdom remain in the old race will live to see the day when they will wish the kingdom in another race, as being of more advantage."

Thereupon the brothers Freyvid and Arnvid led the king's son Jacob into the Thing, and saluted him with the title of king; and the Swedes gave him the name of Onund, which he afterwards retained as long as he lived. He was then ten or twelve years old. Thereafter King Onund took a court, and chose chiefs to be around him; and they had as many attendants in their suite as were thought necessary, so that he gave the whole assemblage of bondes leave to return home. After that ambassadors went between the two kings; and at last they had a meeting, and came to an agreement. Olaf was to remain king over the country as long as he lived; but should hold peace and be reconciled with King Olaf of Norway, and also with all who had taken part in this business. Onund should also be king, and have a part of the land, such as the father and son should agree upon; but should be bound to support the bondes in case King Olaf did anything which the bondes would not suffer.

97. MEETING OF RECONCILIATION BETWEEN THE KINGS, AND THEIR GAME AT DICE.

THEREAFTER AMBASSADORS WERE sent to Norway to King Olaf, with the errand that he should come with his retinue to a meeting at Konungahella with the Swedish kings, and that the Swedish kings would there confirm their reconciliation. When King Olaf heard this message, he was willing, now as formerly, to enter into the agreement, and proceeded to the appointed place. There the Swedish kings also came; and the relations, when they met, bound themselves mutually to peace and agreement. Olaf the Swedish king was then remarkably mild in manner, and agreeable to talk with. Thorstein Frode relates of this meeting, that there was an inhabited district in Hising which had sometimes belonged to Norway, and sometimes to Gautland. The kings came to the agreement between themselves that they would cast lots by the dice to determine who should have this property, and that he who threw the highest should have the district. The Swedish king threw two sixes, and said King Olaf need scarcely throw. He replied, while shaking the dice in his hand, "Although there be two sixes on the dice, it would be easy, sire, for God Almighty to let them turn up in my favour." Then he threw, and had sixes also. Now the Swedish king threw again, and had again two sixes. Olaf king of Norway then threw, and had six upon one dice, and the other split in two, so as to make seven eyes in all upon it; and the district was adjudged to the king of Norway. We have heard nothing else of any interest that took place at this meeting; and the kings separated the dearest of friends with each other.

98. OF OLAF OF NORWAY, AFTER THE MEETING.

AFTER THE EVENTS NOW related Olaf returned with his people to Viken. He went first to Tunsberg, and remained there a short time, and then proceeded to the north of the country. In harvest-time he sailed north to Throndhjem, and had winter provision laid in there, and remained there all winter (A.D. 1090). Olaf Haraldson was now sole and supreme king of Norway, and the whole of that sovereignty, as Harald Harfager had possessed it, and had the advantage over that monarch of being the only king in the land. By a peaceful agreement he had also recovered that part of the country which Olaf the Swedish king had before occupied; and that part of the country which the Danish king had got he retook by force, and ruled over it as elsewhere in the country. The Danish king Canute ruled at that time both over Denmark and England; but he himself was in England for the most part, and set chiefs over the country in Denmark, without at that time making any claim upon Norway.

99. HISTORY OF THE EARLS OF ORKNEY.

It is related that in the days of Harald Harfager, the king of Norway, the islands of Orkney, which before had been only a resort for vikings, were settled. The first earl in the Orkney Islands was called Sigurd, who was a son of Eystein Giumra, and brother of Ragnvald earl of More. After Sigurd his son Guthorm was earl for one year. After him Torf-Einar, a son of Ragnvald, took the earldom, and was long earl, and was a man of great power. Halfdan Haleg, a son of Harald Harfager, assaulted Torf-Einar, and drove him from the Orkney Islands; but Einar came back and killed Halfdan in the island Ronaldsha. Thereafter King Harald came with an army to the Orkney Islands. Einar fled to Scotland, and King Harald made the people of the Orkney Islands give up their udal properties, and hold them under oath from him. Thereafter the king and earl were reconciled, so that the earl became the king's man, and took the country as a fief from him; but that it should pay no scat or feu-duty, as it was at that time much plundered by vikings. The earl paid the king sixty marks of gold; and then King Harald went to plunder in Scotland, as related in the "Glym Drapa". After Torf-Einar, his sons Arnkel, Erlend, and Thorfin Hausakljufer[44] ruled over these lands. In their days came Eirik Blood-axe from Norway, and subdued these earls. Arnkel and Erlend fell in a war expedition; but Thorfin ruled the country long, and became an old man. His sons were Arnfin, Havard, Hlodver, Liot, and Skule. Their mother was Grelad, a daughter of Earl Dungad of Caithness. Her mother was Groa, a daughter of Thorstein Raud. In the latter days of Earl Thorfin came Eirik Blood-axe's sons, who had

44 Hausakljufer–the splitter of skulls.–L.

fled from Earl Hakon out of Norway, and committed great excesses in Orkney. Earl Thorfin died on a bed of sickness, and his sons after him ruled over the country, and there are many stories concerning them. Hlodver lived the longest of them, and ruled alone over this country. His son was Sigurd the Thick, who took the earldom after him, and became a powerful man and a great warrior. In his days came Olaf Trygvason from his viking expedition in the western ocean, with his troops, landed in Orkney and took Earl Sigurd prisoner in South Ronaldsha, where he lay with one ship. King Olaf allowed the earl to ransom his life by letting himself be baptized, adopting the true faith, becoming his man, and introducing Christianity into all the Orkney Islands. As a hostage, King Olaf took his son, who was called Hunde or Whelp. Then Olaf went to Norway, and became king; and Hunde was several years with King Olaf in Norway, and died there. After his death Earl Sigurd showed no obedience or fealty to King Olaf. He married a daughter of the Scottish king Malcolm, and their son was called Thorfin. Earl Sigurd had, besides, older sons; namely, Sumarlide, Bruse, and Einar Rangmund. Four or five years after Olaf Tryrgvason's fall Earl Sigurd went to Ireland, leaving his eldest sons to rule the country, and sending Thorfin to his mother's father, the Scottish king. On this expedition Earl Sigurd fell in Brian's battle[45]. When the news was received in Orkney, the brothers Sumarlide, Bruse, and Einar were chosen earls, and the country was divided into three parts among them. Thorfin Sigurdson was five years old when Earl Sigurd fell. When the Scottish king heard of the earl's death he gave his relation Thorfin Caithness and Sutherland, with the title of earl, and appointed good men to rule the land for him. Earl Thorfin was ripe in all ways as soon as he was grown up: he was stout and strong, but ugly; and as soon as he was a grown man it was easy to see that he was a severe and cruel but a very clever man. So says Arnor, the earls' skald:–

"Under the rim of heaven no other,
So young in years as Einar's brother,
In battle had a braver hand,
Or stouter, to defend the land."

45 Brian's battle is supposed to have taken place on the 23rd April 1014, at Clontart, near Dublin; and is known in Irish history as the battle of Clontarf, and was one of the bloodiest of the age. It was fought between a viking called Sigtryg and Brian king of Munster, who gained the victory, but lost his life.–L.

100. OF THE EARLS EINAR AND BRUSE.

The brothers Einar and Bruse were very unlike in disposition. Bruse was a soft-minded, peaceable man,-sociable, eloquent, and of good understanding. Einar was obstinate, taciturn, and dull; but ambitious, greedy of money, and withal a great warrior. Sumarlide, the eldest of the brothers, was in disposition like Bruse, and lived not long, but died in his bed. After his death Thorfin claimed his share of the Orkney Islands. Einar replied, that Thorfin had the dominions which their father Sigurd had possessed, namely, Caithness and Sutherland, which he insisted were much larger than a third part of Orkney; therefore he would not consent to Thorfin's having any share. Bruse, on the other hand, was willing, he said, to divide with him. "I do not-desire," he said, "more than the third part of the land, and which of right belongs to me." Then Einar took possession of two parts of the country, by which he became a powerful man, surrounded by many followers. He was often in summer out on marauding expeditions, and called out great numbers of the people to join him; but it went always unpleasantly with the division of the booty made on his viking cruises. Then the bondes grew weary of all these burdens; but Earl Einar held fast by them with severity, calling in all services laid upon the people, and allowing no opposition from any man; for he was excessively proud and overbearing. And now there came dearth and scarcity in his lands, in consequence of the services and money outlay exacted from the bondes; while in the part of the country belonging to Bruse there were peace and plenty, and therefore he was the best beloved by the bondes.

101. OF THORKEL AMUNDASON.

There was a rich and powerful man who was called Amunde, who dwelt in Hrossey at Sandvik, in Hlaupandanes. His son, called Thorkel, was one of the ablest men in the islands. Amunde was a man of the best understanding, and most respected in Orkney. One spring Earl Einar proclaimed a levy for an expedition, as usual. The bondes murmured greatly against it, and applied to Amunde with the entreaty that he would intercede with the earl for them. He replied, that the earl was not a man who would listen to other people, and insisted that it was of no use to make any entreaty to the earl about it. "As things now stand, there is a good understanding between me and the earl; but, in my opinion, there would be much danger of our quarrelling, on account of our different dispositions and views on both sides; therefore I will have nothing to do with it." They then applied to Thorkel, who was also very loath to interfere, but promised at last to do so, in consequence of the great entreaty of the people. Amunde thought he had given his promise too hastily. Now when the earl held a Thing, Thorkel spoke on account of the people, and entreated the earl to spare the people from such heavy burdens, recounting their necessitous condition. The earl replies favourably, saying that he would take Thorkel's advice. "I had intended to go out from the country with six ships, but now I will only take three with me; but thou must not come again, Thorkel, with any such request." The bondes thanked Thorkel for his assistance, and the earl set out on a viking cruise, and came back in autumn. The spring after, the earl made the same levy as usual, and held a Thing with the bondes. Then Thorkel again made a speech, in which he entreated the earl to spare the people. The earl now was angry, and said the lot of the bondes should be made worse in consequence of his intercession; and worked himself up into such a rage, that he vowed they should not both come next spring to the Thing in a whole skin. Then the Thing was closed. When Amunde heard what the earl and Thorkel had said at the Thing, he told Thorkel to leave the country, and he went over to Caithness to Earl Thorfin. Thorkel was afterwards a long time there, and brought up the earl in his youth, and was on that account called Thorkel the Fosterer; and he became a very celebrated man.

102. THE AGREEMENT OF THE EARLS.

There were many powerful men who fled from their udal properties in Orkney on account of Earl Einar's violence, and the most fled over to Caithness to Earl Thorfin: but some fled from the Orkney Islands to Norway, and some to other countries. When Earl Thorfin was grown up he sent a message to his brother Einar, and demanded the part of the dominion which he thought belonged to him in Orkney; namely, a third of the islands. Einar was nowise inclined to diminish his possessions. When Thorfin found this he collected a warforce in Caithness, and proceeded to the islands. As soon as Earl Einar heard of this he collected people, and resolved to defend his country. Earl Bruse also collected men, and went out to meet them, and bring about some agreement between them. An agreement was at last concluded, that Thorfin should have a third part of the islands, as of right belonging to him, but that Bruse and Einar should lay their two parts together, and

Einar alone should rule over them; but if the one died before the other, the longest liver should inherit the whole. This agreement seemed reasonable, as Bruse had a son called Ragnvald, but Einar had no son. Earl Thorfin set men to rule over his land in Orkney, but he himself was generally in Caithness. Earl Einar was generally on viking expeditions to Ireland, Scotland, and Bretland.

103. EYVIND URARHORN'S MURDER.

One summer (A.D. 1018) that Earl Einar marauded in Ireland, he fought in Ulfreks-fjord with the Irish king Konofogor, as has been related before, and suffered there a great defeat. The summer after this (A.D. 1019) Eyvind Urarhorn was coming from the west from Ireland, intending to go to Norway; but the weather was boisterous, and the current against him, so he ran into Osmundwall, and lay there wind-bound for some time. When Earl Einar heard of this, he hastened thither with many people, took Eyvind prisoner, and ordered him to be put to death, but spared the lives of most of his people. In autumn they proceeded to Norway to King Olaf, and told him Eyvind was killed. The king said little about it, but one could see that he considered it a great and vexatious loss; for he did not usually say much if anything turned out contrary to his wishes. Earl Thorfin sent Thorkel Fosterer to the islands to gather in his scat. Now, as Einar gave Thorkel the greatest blame for the dispute in which Thorfin had made claim to the islands, Thorkel came suddenly back to Caithness from Orkney, and told Earl Thorfin that he had learnt that Earl Einar would have murdered him if his friends and relations had not given him notice to escape. "Now," says he, "it is come so far between the earl and me, that either some thing decisive between us must take place if we meet, or I must remove to such a distance that his power will not reach me." The earl encouraged Thorkel much to go east to Norway to King Olaf. "Thou wilt be highly respected," says he, "wherever thou comest among honourable men; and I know so well thy disposition and the earl's, that it will not be long before ye come to extremities." Thereupon Thorkel made himself ready, and proceeded in autumn to Norway, and then to King Olaf, with whom he stayed the whole winter (A.D. 1020), and was in high favour. The king often entered into conversation with him, and he thought, what was true, that Thorkel was a high-minded man, of good understanding. In his conversations with Thorkel, the king found a great difference in his description of the two earls; for

Thorkel was a great friend of Earl Thorfin, but had much to say against Einar. Early in spring (A.D. 1020) the king sent a ship west over the sea to Earl Thorfin, with the invitation to come east and visit him in Norway. The earl did not decline the invitation, for it was accompanied by assurances of friendship.

104. EARL EINAR'S MURDER.

Earl Thorfin went east to Norway, and came to King Olaf, from whom he received a kind reception, and stayed till late in the summer. When he was preparing to return westwards again, King Olaf made him a present of a large and fully-rigged long-ship. Thorkel the Fosterer joined company with the earl, who gave him the ship which he brought with him from the west. The king and the earl took leave of each other tenderly. In autumn Earl Thorfin came to Orkney, and when Earl Einar heard of it he went on board his ships with a numerous band of men. Earl Bruse came up to his two brothers, and endeavoured to mediate between them, and a peace was concluded and confirmed by oath. Thorkel Fosterer was to be in peace and friendship with Earl Einar; and it was agreed that each of them should give a feast to the other, and that the earl should first be Thorkel's guest at Sandwick. When the earl came to the feast he was entertained in the best manner; but the earl was not cheerful. There was a great room, in which there were doors at each end. The day the earl should depart Thorkel was to accompany him to the other feast; and Thorkel sent men before, who should examine the road they had to travel that day. The spies came back, and said to Thorkel they had discovered three ambushes. "And we think," said they, "there is deceit on foot." When Thorkel heard this he lengthened out his preparations for the journey, and gathered people about him. The earl told him to get ready, as it was time to be on horseback. Thorkel answered, that he had many things to put in order first, and went out and in frequently. There was a fire upon the floor. At last he went in at one door, followed by an Iceland man from Eastfjord, called Halvard, who locked the door after him. Thorkel went in between the fire and the place where the earl was sitting. The earl asked, "Art thou ready at last, Thorkel?"

Thorkel answers, "Now I am ready;" and struck the earl upon the head so that he fell upon the floor.

Then said the Icelander, "I never saw people so foolish as not to drag the earl out of the fire;" and took a stick, which he set under the earl's neck, and put him upright on the bench. Thorkel and his two comrades then went in all haste out of the other door opposite to that by which they went in, and Thorkel's men were standing without fully armed. The earl's men now went in, and took hold of the earl. He was already dead, so nobody thought of avenging him: and also the whole was done so quickly; for nobody expected such a deed from Thorkel, and all supposed that there really was, as before related, a friendship fixed between the earl and Thorkel. The most who were within were unarmed, and they were partly Thorkel's good friends; and to this may be added, that fate had decreed a longer life to Thorkel. When Thorkel came out he had not fewer men with him than the earl's troop. Thorkel went to his ship, and the earl's men went their way. The same day Thorkel sailed out eastwards into the sea. This happened after winter; but he came safely to Norway, went as fast as he could to Olaf, and was well received by him. The king expressed his satisfaction at this deed, and Thorkel was with him all winter (A.D. 1091).

105. AGREEMENT BETWEEN KING OLAF AND EARL BRUSE.

After Earl Einar's fall Bruse took the part of the country which he had possessed; for it was known to many men on what conditions Einar and Bruse had entered into a partnership. Although Thorfin thought it would be more just that each of them had half of the islands, Bruse retained the two-thirds of the country that winter (A.D. 1021). In spring, however, Thorfin produced his claim, and demanded the half of the country; but Bruse would not consent. They held Things and meetings about the business; and although their friends endeavoured to settle it, Thorfin would not be content with less than the half of the islands, and insisted that Bruse, with his disposition, would have enough even with a third part. Bruse replies, "When I took my heritage after my father I was well satisfied with a third part of the country, and there was nobody to dispute it with me; and now I have succeeded to another third in heritage after my brother, according to a lawful agreement between us; and although I am not powerful enough to maintain a feud against thee, my brother, I will seek some other way, rather than willingly renounce my property." With this their meeting ended. But Bruse saw that he had no strength to contend against Thorfin, because Thorfin had both a greater dominion and also could have aid from his mother's brother, the Scottish king. He resolved, therefore, to go out of the country; and he went eastward to King Olaf, and had with him his son Ragnvald, then ten years old. When the earl came to the king he was well received. The earl now declared his errand, and told the king the circumstances of the whole dispute between him and his brother, and asked help to defend his kingdom of Orkney; promising, in return, the fullest friendship towards King Olaf. In his answer, the king began with showing how Harald Harfager had appropriated to himself all udal rights in Orkney, and that the earls, since that time, have constantly held the country as a fief, not as their udal property. "As a sufficient proof of which," said he, "when Eirik Blood-axe and his sons were in Orkney the earls were subject to them; and also when my relation Olaf Trygvason came there thy father, Earl Sigurd, became his man. Now I have taken heritage after King Olaf, and I will give thee the condition to become my man and then I will give thee the islands as a fief; and we shall try if I cannot give thee aid that will be more to the purpose than Thorfin can get from the Scottish king. If thou wilt not accept of these terms, then will I win back my udal property there in the West, as our forefathers and relations of old possessed it."

The earl carefully considered this speech, laid it before his friends, and demanded their advice if he should agree to it, and enter into such terms with King Olaf and become his vassal. "But I do not see what my lot will be at my departure if I say no; for the king has clearly enough declared his claim upon Orkney; and from his great power, and our being in his hands, it is easy for him to make our destiny what he pleases."

Although the earl saw that there was much to be considered for and against it he chose the condition to deliver himself and his dominion into the king's power. Thereupon the king took the earl's power, and the government over all the earl's lands, and the earl became his vassal under oath of fealty.

106. THE EARL'S AGREEMENT TO THE KING'S TERMS.

Thorfin the earl heard that his brother Bruse had gone east to King Olaf to seek support from him; but as Thorfin had been on a visit to King Olaf before, and had concluded a friendship with him, he thought his case would stand well with the king, and that many would support it; but he believed that many more would do so if he went there himself. Earl Thorfin resolved, therefore, to go east himself without delay; and he thought there would be so little difference between the time of his arrival and Bruse's, that Bruse's errand could not be accomplished before he came to King Olaf. But it went otherwise than Earl Thorfin had expected; for when he came to the king the agreement between the king and Bruse was already concluded and settled, and Earl Thorfin did not know a word about Bruse's having surrendered his udal domains until he came to King Olaf. As soon as Earl Thorfin and King Olaf met, the king made the same demand upon the kingdom of Orkney that he had done to Earl Bruse, and required that Thorfin should voluntarily deliver over to the king that part of the country which he had possessed hitherto. The earl answered in a friendly and respectful way, that the king's friendship lay near to his heart: "And if you think, sire, that my help against other chiefs can be of use, you have already every claim to it; but I cannot be your vessel for service, as I am an earl of the Scottish king, and owe fealty to him."

As the king found that the earl, by his answer, declined fulfilling the demand he had made, he said, "Earl, if thou wilt not become my vassal, there is another condition; namely, that I will place over the Orkney Islands the man I please, and require thy oath that thou wilt make no claim upon these lands, but allow whoever I place over them to sit in peace. If thou wilt not accept of either of these conditions, he who is to rule over these lands may expect hostility from thee, and thou must not think it strange if like meet like in this business."

The earl begged of the king some time to consider the matter. The king did so, and gave the earl time to take the counsel of his friends on the choosing one or other of these conditions. Then the earl requested a delay until next summer, that he might go over the sea to the west, for his proper counsellors were all at home, and he himself was but a child in respect of age; but the king required that he should now make his election of one or other of the conditions. Thorkel Fosterer was then with the king, and he privately sent a person to Earl Thorfin, and told him, whatever his intentions might be, not to think of leaving Olaf without being reconciled with him, as he stood entirely in Olaf's power. From such hints the earl saw there was no other way than to let the king have his own will. It was no doubt a hard condition to have no hope of ever regaining his paternal heritage, and moreover to bind himself by oath to allow those to enjoy in peace his domain who had no hereditary right to it; but seeing it was uncertain how he could get away, he resolved to submit to the king and become his vassal, as Bruse had done. The king observed that Thorfin was more high-minded, and less disposed to suffer subjection than Bruse, and therefore he trusted less to Thorfin than to Bruse; and he considered also that Thorfin would trust to the aid of the Scottish king, if he broke the agreement. The king also had discernment enough to perceive that Bruse, although slow to enter into an agreement, would promise nothing but what he intended to keep; but as to Thorfin when he had once made up his mind he went readily into every proposal and made no attempt to obtain any alteration of the king's first conditions: therefore the king had his suspicions that the earl would infringe the agreement.

107. EARL THORFIN'S DEPARTURE, AND RECONCILIATION WITH THORKEL.

When the king had carefully considered the whole matter by himself, he ordered the signal to sound for a General Thing, to which he called in the earls. Then said the king, "I will now make known to the public our agreement with the Orkney earls. They have now acknowledged my right of property to Orkney and Shetland, and have both become my vassals, all which they have confirmed by oath; and now I will invest them with these lands as a fief: namely, Bruse with one third part and Thorfin with one third, as they formerly enjoyed them; but the other third which Einar Rangmund had, I adjudge as fallen to my domain, because he killed Eyvind Urarhorn, my court-man, partner, and dear friend; and that part of the land I will manage as I think proper. I have also my earls, to tell you it is my pleasure that ye enter into an agreement with Thorkel Amundason for the murder of your brother Einar, for I will take that business, if ye agree thereto, within my own jurisdiction." The earls agreed to this, as to everything else that the king proposed. Thorkel came forward, and surrendered to the king's judgment of the case, and the Thing concluded. King Olaf awarded as great a penalty for Earl Einar's murder as for three lendermen; but as Einar himself was the cause of the act, one third of the mulct fell to the ground. Thereafter Earl Thorfin asked the king's leave to depart, and as soon as he obtained it made ready for sea with all speed. It happened one day, when all was ready for the voyage, the earl sat in his ship drinking; and Thorkel Amundason came unexpectedly to him, laid his head upon the earl's knee, and bade him do with him what he pleased. The earl asked why he did so. "We are, you know, reconciled men, according to the king's decision; so stand up, Thorkel."

Thorkel replied, "The agreement which the king made as between me and Bruse stands good; but what regards the agreement with thee thou alone must determine. Although the king made conditions for my property and safe residence in Orkney, yet I know so well thy disposition that there is no going to the islands for me, unless I go there in peace with thee, Earl Thorfin; and therefore I am willing to promise never to return to Orkney, whatever the king may desire."

The earl remained silent; and first, after a long pause, he said, "If thou wilt rather, Thorkel, that I shall judge between us than trust to the king's judgment, then let the beginning of our reconciliation be, that you go with me to the Orkney Islands, live with me, and never leave me but with my will, and be bound to defend my land, and execute all that I want done, as long as we both are in life."

Thorkel replies, "This shall be entirely at thy pleasure, earl, as well as everything else in my power." Then Thorkel went on, and solemnly ratified this agreement. The earl said he would talk afterwards about the mulct of money, but took Thorkel's oath upon the conditions. Thorkel immediately made ready to accompany the earl on his voyage. The earl set off as soon as all was ready, and never again were King Olaf and Thorfin together.

108. EARL BRUSE'S DEPARTURE.

Earl Bruse remained behind, and took his time to get ready. Before his departure the king sent for him, and said, "It appears to me, earl, that in thee I have a man on the west side of the sea on whose fidelity I can depend; therefore I intend to give thee the two parts of the country which thou formerly hadst to rule over; for I will not that thou shouldst be a less powerful man after entering into my service than before: but I will secure thy fidelity by keeping thy son Ragnvald with me. I see well enough that with two parts of the country and my help, thou wilt be able to defend what is thy own against thy brother Thorfin." Bruse was thankful for getting two thirds instead of one third of the country, and soon after he set out, and came about autumn to Orkney; but Ragnvald, Bruse's son, remained behind in the East with King Olaf. Ragnvald was one of the handsomest men that could be seen,–his hair long, and yellow as silk; and he soon grew up, stout and tall, and he was a very able and superb man, both of great understanding and polite manners. He was long with King Olaf. Otter Svarte speaks of these affairs in the poem he composed about King Olaf:–

"From Shetland, far off in the cold North Sea,
Come chiefs who desire to be subject to thee:
No king so well known for his will, and his might,
To defend his own people from scaith or unright.
These isles of the West midst the ocean's wild roar,
Scarcely heard the voice of their sovereign before;
Our bravest of sovereigns before could scarce bring
These islesmen so proud to acknowledge their king."

109. OF THE EARLS THORFIN AND BRUSE.

THE BROTHERS THORFIN AND Bruse came west to Orkney; and Bruse took the two parts of the country under his rule, and Thorfin the third part. Thorfin was usually in Caithness and elsewhere in Scotland; but placed men of his own over the islands. It was left to Bruse alone to defend the islands, which at that time were severely scourged by vikings; for the Northmen and Danes went much on viking cruises in the west sea, and frequently touched at Orkney on the way to or from the west, and plundered, and took provisions and cattle from the coast. Bruse often complained of his brother Thorfin, that he made no equipment of war for the defence of Orkney and Shetland, yet levied his share of the scat and duties. Then Thorfin offered to him to exchange, and that Bruse should have one third and Thorfin two thirds of the land, but should undertake the defence of the land, for the whole. Although this exchange did not take place immediately, it is related in the saga of the earls that it was agreed upon at last; and that Thorfin had two parts and Bruse only one, when Canute the Great subdued Norway and King Olaf fled the country. Earl Thorfin Sigurdson has been the ablest earl of these islands, and has had the greatest dominion of all the Orkney earls; for he had under him Orkney, Shetland, and the Hebudes, besides very great possessions in Scotland and Ireland. Arnor, the earls' skald, tells of his possessions:–

"From Thurso-skerry to Dublin,
All people hold with good Thorfin–
All people love his sway,
And the generous chief obey."

Thorfin was a very great warrior. He came to the earldom at five years of age, ruled more than sixty years, and died in his bed about the last days of Harald Sigurdson. But Bruse died in the days of Canute the Great, a short time after the fall of Saint Olaf.

110. OF HAREK OF THJOTTA.

Having now gone through this second story, we shall return to that which we left,–at King Olaf Haraldson having concluded peace with King Olaf the Swedish king, and having the same summer gone north to Throndhjem (1019). He had then been king in Norway five years (A.D. 1015-1019). In harvest time he prepared to take his winter residence at Nidaros, and he remained all winter there (A.D. 1020). Thorkel the Fosterer, Amunde's son, as before related, was all that winter with him. King Olaf inquired very carefully how it stood with Christianity throughout the land, and learnt that it was not observed at all to the north of Halogaland, and was far from being observed as it should be in Naumudal, and the interior of Throndhjem. There was a man by name Harek, a son of Eyvind Skaldaspiller, who dwelt in an island called Thjotta in Halogaland. Eyvind had not been a rich man, but was of high family and high mind. In Thjotta, at first, there dwelt many small bondes; but Harek began with buying a farm not very large and lived on it, and in a few years he had got all the bondes that were there before out of the way; so that he had the whole island, and built a large head-mansion. He soon became very rich; for he was a very prudent man, and very successful. He had long been greatly respected by the chiefs; and being related to the kings of Norway, had been raised by them to high dignities. Harek's father's mother Gunhild was a daughter of Earl Halfdan, and Ingebjorg, Harald Harfager's daughter. At the time the circumstance happened which we are going to relate he was somewhat advanced in years. Harek was the most respected man in Halogaland, and for a long time had the Lapland trade, and did the king's business in Lapland; sometimes alone, sometimes with others joined to him. He had not himself been to wait on King Olaf, but messages had passed between them, and all was on the most friendly footing. This winter (A.D. 1020) that Olaf was in Nidaros, messengers passed between the king and Harek of Thjotta. Then the king made it known that he intended going north to Halogaland, and as far north as the land's end; but the people of Halogaland expected no good from this expedition.

111. OF THE PEOPLE OF HALOGALAND.

Olaf rigged out five ships in spring (A.D. 1020), and had with him about 300 men. When he was ready for sea he set northwards along the land; and when he came to Naumudal district he summoned the bondes to a Thing, and at every Thing was accepted as king. He also made the laws to be read there as elsewhere, by which the people are commanded to observe Christianity; and he threatened every man with loss of life, and limbs, and property who would not subject himself to Christian law. He inflicted severe punishments on many men, great as well as small, and left no district until the people had consented to adopt the holy faith. The most of the men of power and of the great bondes made feasts for the king, and so he proceeded all the way north to Halogaland. Harek of Thjotta also made a feast for the king, at which there was a great multitude of guests, and the feast was very splendid. Harek was made lenderman, and got the same privileges he had enjoyed under the former chiefs of the country.

112. OF ASMUND GRANKELSON.

There was a man called Grankel, or Granketil, who was a rich bonde, and at this time rather advanced in age. In his youth he had been on viking cruises, and had been a powerful fighter; for he possessed great readiness in all sorts of bodily exercises. His son Asmund was equal to his father in all these, and in some, indeed, he excelled him. There were many who said that with respect to comeliness, strength, and bodily expertness, he might be considered the third remarkably distinguished for these that Norway had ever produced. The first was Hakon Athelstan's foster-son; the second, Olaf Trygvason. Grankel invited King Olaf to a feast, which was very magnificent; and at parting Grankel presented the king with many honourable gifts and tokens of friendship. The king invited Asmund, with many persuasions, to follow him; and as Asmund could not decline the honours offered him, he got ready to travel with the king, became his man, and stood in high favour with him. The king remained in Halogaland the greater part of the summer, went to all the Things, and baptized all the people. Thorer Hund dwelt at that time in the island Bjarkey. He was the most powerful man in the North, and also became one of Olaf's lendermen. Many sons of great bondes resolved also to follow King Olaf from Halogaland. Towards the end of summer King Olaf left the North, and sailed back to Throndhjem, and landed at Nidaros, where he passed the winter (A.D. 1021). It was then that Thorkel the Fosterer came from the West from Orkney, after killing Einar Rangmumd, as before related. This autumn corn was dear in Throndhjem, after a long course of good seasons, and the farther north the dearer was the corn; but there was corn enough in the East country, and in the Uplands, and it was of great help to the people of Throndhjem that many had old corn remaining beside them.

113. OF THE SACRIFICES OF THE THRONDHJEM PEOPLE.

In autumn the news was brought to King Olaf that the bondes had had a great feast on the first winter-day's eve, at which there was a numerous attendance and much drinking; and it was told the king that all the remembrance-cups to the Asas, or old gods, were blessed according to the old heathen forms; and it was added, that cattle and horses had been slain, and the altars sprinkled with their blood, and the sacrifices accompanied with the prayer that was made to obtain good seasons. It was also reported that all men saw clearly that the gods were offended at the Halogaland people turning Christian. Now when the king heard this news he sent men into the Throndhjem country, and ordered several bondes, whose names he gave, to appear before him. There was a man called Olver of Eggja, so called after his farm on which he lived. He was powerful, of great family, and the head-man of those who on account of the bondes appeared before the king. Now, when they came to the king, he told them these accusations; to which Olver, on behalf of the bondes, replied, that they had had no other feasts that harvest than their usual entertainments, and social meetings, and friendly drinking parties. "But as to what may have been told you of the words which may have fallen from us Throndhjem people in our drinking parties, men of understanding would take good care not to use such language; but I cannot hinder drunken or foolish people's talk." Olver was a man of clever speech, and bold in what he said, and defended the bondes against such accusations. In the end, the king said the people of the interior of Thorndhjem must themselves give the best testimony to their being in the right faith. The bondes got leave to return home, and set off as soon as they were ready.

114. OF THE SACRIFICES BY THE PEOPLE OF THE INTERIOR OF THE THRONDHJEM DISTRICT.

Afterwards, when winter was advanced, it was told the king that the people of the interior of Throndhjem had assembled in great number at Maerin, and that there was a great sacrifice in the middle of winter, at which they sacrificed offerings for peace and a good season. Now when the king knew this on good authority to be true, he sent men and messages into the interior, and summoned the bondes whom he thought of most understanding into the town. The bondes held a council among themselves about this message; and all those who had been upon the same occasion in the beginning of winter were now very unwilling to make the journey. Olver, however, at the desire of all the bondes, allowed himself to be persuaded. When he came to the town he went immediately before the king, and they talked together. The king made the same accusation against the bondes, that they had held a mid-winter sacrifice. Olver replies, that this accusation against the bondes was false. "We had," said he, "Yule feasts and drinking feasts wide around in the districts; and the bondes do not prepare their feasts so sparingly, sire, that there is not much left over, which people consume long afterwards. At Maerin there is a great farm, with a large house on it, and a great neighbourhood all around it, and it is the great delight of the people to drink many together in company." The king said little in reply, but looked angry, as he thought he knew the truth of the matter better than it was now represented. He ordered the bondes to return home. "I shall some time or other," said he, "come to the truth of what you are now concealing, and in such a way that ye shall not be able to contradict it. But, however, that may be, do not try such things again." The bondes returned home, and told the result of their journey, and that the king was altogether enraged.

115. MURDER OF OLVER OF EGGJA.

At Easter (A.D. 1021) the king held a feast, to which he had invited many of the townspeople as well as bondes. After Easter he ordered his ships to be launched into the water, oars and tackle to be put on board, decks to be laid in the ships, and tilts[46] and rigging to be set

46 The ships appear to have been decked fore and aft only; and in the

up, and to be laid ready for sea at the piers. Immediately after Easter he sent men into Veradal. There was a man called Thoralde, who was the king's bailiff, and who managed the king's farm there at Haug; and to him the king sent a message to come to him as quickly as possible. Thoralde did not decline the journey, but went immediately to the town with the messenger. The king called him in and in a private conversation asked him what truth there was in what had been told him of the principles and living of the people of the interior of Throndhjem, and if it really was so that they practised sacrifices to heathen gods. "I will," says the king, "that thou declare to me the things as they are, and as thou knowest to be true; for it is thy duty to tell me the truth, as thou art my man."

Thoralde replies, "Sire, I will first tell you that I have brought here to the town my two children, my wife, and all my loose property that I could take with me, and if thou desirest to know the truth it shall be told according to thy command; but if I declare it, thou must take care of me and mine."

The king replies, "Say only what is true on what I ask thee, and I will take care that no evil befall thee."

Then said Thoralde, "If I must say the truth, king, as it is, I must declare that in the interior of the Throndhjem land almost all the people are heathen in faith, although some of them are baptized. It is their custom to offer sacrifice in autumn for a good winter, a second at midwinter, and a third in summer. In this the people of Eyna, Sparby, Veradal, and Skaun partake. There are twelve men who preside over these sacrifice-feasts; and in spring it is Olver who has to get the feast in order, and he is now busy transporting to Maerin everything needful for it." Now when the king had got to the truth with a certainty, he ordered the signal to be sounded for his men to assemble, and for the men-at-arms to go on board ship. He appointed men to steer the ships, and leaders for the people, and ordered how the people should be divided among the vessels. All was got ready in haste, and with five ships and 300 men he steered up the fjord. The wind was favourable, the ships sailed briskly before it, and nobody could have thought that the king would be so soon there. The king came in the night time to Maerin, and immediately surrounded the house with a ring of armed men. Olver was taken, and the king ordered him to be put to death, and many other men besides. Then the king took all the provision for the feast, and had

middle, where the rowers sat, to have had tilts or tents set up at night to sleep under.–L.

it brought to his ships; and also all the goods, both furniture, clothes, and valuables, which the people had brought there, and divided the booty among his men. The king also let all the bondes he thought had the greatest part in the business be plundered by his men-at-arms. Some were taken prisoners and laid in irons, some ran away, and many were robbed of their goods. Thereafter the bondes were summoned to a Thing; but because he had taken many powerful men prisoners, and held them in his power, their friends and relations resolved to promise obedience to the king, so that there was no insurrection against the king on this occasion. He thus brought the whole people back to the right faith, gave them teachers, and built and consecrated churches. The king let Olver lie without fine paid for his bloodshed, and all that he possessed was adjudged to the king; and of the men he judged the most guilty, some he ordered to be executed, some he maimed, some he drove out of the country, and took fines from others. The king then returned to Nidaros.

116. OF THE SONS OF ARNE.

THERE WAS A MAN called Arne Arnmodson, who was married to Thora, Thorstein Galge's daughter. Their children were Kalf, Fin, Thorberg, Amunde, Kolbjorn, Arnbjorn, and Arne. Their daughter, who was called Ragnhild, was married to Harek of Thjotta. Arne was a lenderman, powerful, and of ability, and a great friend of King Olaf. At that time his sons Kalf and Fin were with the king, and in great favour. The wife whom Olver of Eggja had left was young and handsome, of great family, and rich, so that he who got her might be considered to have made an excellent marriage; and her land was in the gift of the king. She and Olver had two sons, who were still in infancy. Kalf Arneson begged of the king that he would give him to wife the widow of Olver; and out of friendship the king agreed to it, and with her he got all the property Olver had possessed. The king at the same time made him his lenderman, and gave him an office in the interior of the Throndhjem country. Kalf became a great chief, and was a man of very great understanding.

117. KING OLAF'S JOURNEY TO THE UPLANDS.

WHEN KING OLAF HAD been seven years (A.D. 1015-1021) in Norway the earls Thorfin and Bruse came to him, as before related, in the summer, from Orkney, and he became master of their land. The same summer Olaf went to North and South More, and in autumn to Raumsdal. He left his ships there, and came to the Uplands, and to Lesjar. Here he laid hold of all the best men, and forced them, both at Lesjar and Dovre, either to receive Christianity or suffer death, if they were not so lucky as to escape. After they received Christianity, the king took their sons in his hands as hostages for their fidelity. The king stayed several nights at a farm in Lesjar called Boar, where he placed priests. Then he proceeded over Orkadal and Lorodal, and came down from the Uplands at a place called Stafabrekka. There a river runs along the valley, called the Otta, and a beautiful hamlet, by name Loar, lies on both sides of the river, and the king could see far down over the whole neighbourhood. "A pity it is," said the king, "so beautiful a hamlet should be burnt." And he proceeded down the valley with his people, and was all night on a farm called Nes. The king took his lodging in a loft, where he slept himself; and it stands to the present day, without anything in it having been altered since. The king was five days there, and summoned by message-token the people to a Thing, both for the districts of Vagar, Lear, and Hedal; and gave out the message along with the token, that they must either receive Christianity and give their sons as hostages, or see their habitations burnt. They came before the king, and submitted to his pleasure; but some fled south down the valley.

118. THE STORY OF DALE-GUDBRAND.

There was a man called Dale-Gudbrand, who was like a king in the valley (Gudbrandsdal), but was only herse in title. Sigvat the skald compared him for wealth and landed property to Erling Skjalgson. Sigvat sang thus concerning Erling:–

"I know but one who can compare
With Erling for broad lands and gear–
Gudbrand is he, whose wide domains
Are most like where some small king reigns.
These two great bondes, I would say,
Equal each other every way.
He lies who says that he can find
One by the other left behind."

Gudbrand had a son, who is here spoken of. Now when Gudbrand received the tidings that King Olaf was come to Lear, and obliged people to accept Christianity, he sent out a message-token, and summoned all the men in the valley to meet him at a farm called Hundthorp. All came, so that the number could not be told; for there is a lake in the neighbourhood called Laugen, so that people could come to the place both by land and by water. There Gudbrand held a Thing with them, and said, "A man is come to Loar who is called Olaf, and will force upon us another faith than what we had before, and will break in pieces all our gods. He says that he has a much greater and more powerful god; and it is wonderful that the earth does not burst asunder under him, or that our god lets him go about unpunished when he dares to talk such things. I know this for certain, that if we carry Thor, who has always stood by us, out of our temple that is standing upon this farm, Olaf's god will melt away, and he and his men be made nothing so soon as Thor looks upon them." Then the bondes all shouted as one person that Olaf should never get away with life if he came to them; and they thought he would never dare to come farther south through the valley. They chose out 700 men to go northwards to Breida, to watch his movements. The leader of this band was Gudbrand's son, eighteen years of age, and with him were many other men of importance. When they came to a farm called Hof they heard of the king; and they remained three nights there. People streamed to them from all parts, from Lesjar, Loar, and Vagar, who did not wish to receive Christianity. The king and Bishop Sigurd fixed teachers in Loaf and in Vagar. From thence they went round Vagarost, and came down into the valley at Sil, where they stayed all night, and heard the news that a great force of men were assembled against them. The bondes who were in Breida heard also of the king's arrival, and prepared for battle. As soon as the king arose in the morning he put on his armour, and went southwards over the Sil plains, and did not halt until he came to Breida, where he saw a great army ready for battle. Then the king drew up his troops, rode himself at the head of them, and began a speech to the bondes, in which he invited them to adopt Christianity. They replied, "We shall give thee something else to do to-day than to be mocking us;" and raised a general shout, striking also upon their shields with their weapons. Then the king's men ran forward and threw their spears; but the bondes turned round instantly and fled, so that only few men remained behind. Gudbrand's son was taken prisoner; but the king gave him his life, and took him with him. The king was four days here. Then the king said to Gudbrand's son, "Go home now to thy father, and tell him I expect to be with him soon."

He went accordingly, and told his father the news, that they had fallen in with the king, and fought with him; but that their whole army, in the very beginning, took flight. "I was taken prisoner," said he, "but the king gave me my life and liberty, and told me to say to thee that he will soon be here. And now we have not 200 men of the force we raised against him; therefore I advise thee, father, not to give battle to that man."

Says Gudbrand, "It is easy to see that all courage has left thee, and it was an unlucky hour ye went out to the field. Thy proceeding will live long in the remembrance of people, and I see that thy fastening thy faith on the folly that man is going about with has brought upon thee and thy men so great a disgrace."

But the night after, Gudbrand dreamt that there came to him a man surrounded by light, who brought great terror with him, and said to him, "Thy son made no glorious expedition against King Olaf; but still less honour wilt thou gather for thyself by holding a battle with him. Thou with all thy people wilt fall; wolves will drag thee, and all thine, away; ravens wilt tear thee in stripes." At this dreadful vision he was much afraid, and tells it to Thord Istermage, who was chief over the valley. He replies, "The very same vision came to me." In the morning they ordered the signal to sound for a Thing, and said that it appeared to them advisable to hold a Thing with the man who had come from the north with this new teaching, to know if there was any truth in it. Gudbrand then said to his son, "Go thou, and twelve men with thee, to the king who gave thee thy life." He went straightway, and found the king, and laid before him their errand; namely, that the bondes would hold a Thing with him, and make a truce between them and him. The king was content; and they bound themselves by faith and law mutually to hold the peace so long as the Thing lasted. After this was settled the men returned to Gudbrand and Thord, and told them there was made a firm agreement for a truce. The king, after the battle with the son of Gudbrand, had proceeded to Lidstad, and remained there for five days: afterwards he went out to meet the bondes, and hold a Thing with them. On that day there fell a heavy rain. When the Thing was seated, the king stood up and said that the people in Lesjar, Loaf, and Vagar had received Christianity, broken down their houses of sacrifice, and believed now in the true God who had made heaven and earth and knows all things.

Thereupon the king sat down, and Gudbrand replies, "We know nothing of him whom thou speakest about. Dost thou call him God, whom neither thou nor any one else can see? But we have a god who call be seen every day, although he is not out to-day, because the weather is wet, and he will appear to thee terrible and very grand; and

I expect that fear will mix with your very blood when he comes into the Thing. But since thou sayest thy God is so great, let him make it so that to-morrow we have a cloudy day but without rain, and then let us meet again."

The king accordingly returned home to his lodging, taking Gudbrand's son as a hostage; but he gave them a man as hostage in exchange. In the evening the king asked Gudbrand's son what like their god was. He replied, that he bore the likeness of Thor; had a hammer in his hand; was of great size, but hollow within; and had a high stand, upon which he stood when he was out. "Neither gold nor silver are wanting about him, and every day he receives four cakes of bread, besides meat." They then went to bed, but the king watched all night in prayer. When day dawned the king went to mass, then to table, and from thence to the Thing. The weather was such as Gudbrand desired. Now the bishop stood up in his choir-robes, with bishop's coif upon his head, and bishop's staff in his hands. He spoke to the bondes of the true faith, told the many wonderful acts of God, and concluded his speech well.

Thord Istermage replies, "Many things we are told of by this horned man with the staff in his hand crooked at the top like a ram's horn; but since ye say, comrades, that your god is so powerful, and can do so many wonders, tell him to make it clear sunshine to-morrow forenoon, and then we shall meet here again, and do one of two things,– either agree with you about this business, or fight you." And they separated for the day.

119. DALE-GUDBRAND IS BAPTIZED.

There was a man with King Olaf called Kolbein Sterke (the strong), who came from a family in the Fjord district. Usually he was so equipped that he was girt with a sword, and besides carried a great stake, otherwise called a club, in his hands. The king told Kolbein to stand nearest to him in the morning; and gave orders to his people to go down in the night to where the ships of the bondes lay and bore holes in them, and to set loose their horses on the farms where they were; all which was done. Now the king was in prayer all the night, beseeching God of His goodness and mercy to release him from evil. When mass was ended, and morning was grey, the king went to the Thing. When he came there some bondes had already arrived, and they saw a great crowd coming along, and bearing among them a huge man's image glancing with gold and silver. When the bondes who were at the Thing saw it they started up, and bowed themselves down before the ugly idol. Thereupon it was set down upon the Thing-field; and on the one side of it sat the bondes, and on the other the king and his people.

Then Dale-Gudbrand stood up, and said, "Where now, king, is thy god? I think he will now carry his head lower; and neither thou, nor the man with the horn whom ye call bishop, and sits there beside thee, are so bold to-day as on the former days; for now our god, who rules over all, is come, and looks on you with an angry eye; and now I see well enough that ye are terrified, and scarcely dare to raise your eyes. Throw away now all your opposition, and believe in the god who has all your fate in his hands."

The king now whispers to Kolbein Sterke, without the bondes perceiving it, "If it come so in the course of my speech that the bondes look another way than towards their idol, strike him as hard as thou canst with thy club."

The king then stood up and spoke. "Much hast thou talked to us this morning, and greatly hast thou wondered that thou canst not see our God; but we expect that he will soon come to us. Thou wouldst frighten us with thy god, who is both blind and deaf, and can neither save himself nor others, and cannot even move about without being carried; but now I expect it will be but a short time before he meets his fate: for turn your eyes towards the east,–behold our God advancing in great light."

The sun was rising, and all turned to look. At that moment Kolbein gave their god a stroke, so that the idol burst asunder; and there ran out of it mice as big almost as cats, and reptiles, and adders. The bondes were so terrified that some fled to their ships; but when they sprang out upon them they filled with water, and could not get away. Others ran to their horses, but could not find them. The king then ordered the bondes to be called together, saying he wanted to speak with them; on which the bondes came back, and the Thing was again seated.

The king rose up and said, "I do not understand what your noise and running mean. Ye see yourselves what your god can do,–the idol ye adorned with gold and silver, and brought meat and provisions to. Ye see now that the protecting powers who used it were the mice and adders, reptiles and paddocks; and they do ill who trust to such, and will not abandon this folly. Take now your gold and ornaments that are lying strewed about on the grass, and give them to your wives and daughters; but never hang them hereafter upon stock or stone. Here are now two conditions between us to choose upon,–either accept Christianity, or fight this very day; and the victory be to them to whom the God we worship gives it."

Then Dale-Gudbrand stood up and said, "We have sustained great damage upon our god; but since he will not help us, we will believe in the God thou believest in."

Then all received Christianity. The bishop baptized Gudbrand and his son. King Olaf and Bishop Sigurd left behind them teachers, and they who met as enemies parted as friends; and Gudbrand built a church in the valley.

120. HEDEMARK BAPTIZED.

King Olaf proceeded from thence to Hedemark, and baptized there; but as he had formerly carried away their kings as prisoners, he did not venture himself, after such a deed, to go far into the country with few people at that time, but a small part of Hedemark was baptized; but the king did not desist from his expedition before he had introduced Christianity over all Hedemark, consecrated churches, and placed teachers. He then went to Hadaland and Thoten, improving the customs of the people, and persisting until all the country was baptized. He then went to Ringerike, where also all people went over to Christianity. The people of Raumarike then heard that Olaf intended coming to them, and they gathered a great force. They said among themselves that the journey Olaf had made among them the last time was not to be forgotten, and he should never proceed so again. The king, notwithstanding, prepared for the journey. Now when the king went up into Raumarike with his forces, the multitude of bondes came against him at a river called Nitja; and the bondes had a strong army, and began the battle as soon as they met; but they soon fell short, and took to flight. They were forced by this battle into a better disposition, and immediately received Christianity; and the king scoured the whole district, and did not leave it until all the people were made Christians. He then went east to Soleys, and baptized that neighbourhood. The skald Ottar Black came to him there, and begged to be received among his men. Olaf the Swedish king had died the winter before (A.D. 1021), and Onund, the son of Olaf, was now the sole king over all Sweden. King Olaf returned, when the winter (A.D. 1022) was far advanced, to Raumarike. There he assembled a numerous Thing, at a place where the Eidsvold Things have since been held. He made a law, that the Upland people should resort to this Thing, and that Eidsvold laws should be good through all the districts of the Uplands, and wide around in other quarters, which also has taken place. As spring was advancing, he rigged his ships, and went by sea to Tunsberg. He remained there during the spring, and the time the town was most frequented, and goods from other countries were brought to the town for sale. There had been a good year in Viken, and tolerable as far north as Stad; but it was a very dear time in all the country north of there.

121. RECONCILIATION OF THE KING AND EINAR.

In spring (A.D. 1022) King Olaf sent a message west to Agder, and north all the way to Hordaland and Rogaland, prohibiting the exporting or selling of corn, malt, or meal; adding, that he, as usual, would come there with his people in guest-quarters. The message went round all the districts; but the king remained in Viken all summer, and went east to the boundary of the country. Einar Tambaskelfer had been with the Swedish king Olaf since the death of his relation Earl Svein, and had, as the khag's man, received great fiefs from him. Now that the king was dead, Einar had a great desire to come into friendship agreement with Olaf; and the same spring messages passed between them about it. While the king was lying in the Gaut river, Einar Tambaskelfer came there with some men; and after treating about an agreement, it was settled that Einar should go north to Throndhjem, and there take possession of all the lands and property which Bergliot had received in dower. Thereupon Einar took his way north; but the king remained behind in Viken, and remained long in Sarpsborg in autumn (A.D. 1022), and during the first part of winter.

122. RECONCILIATION OF THE KING AND ERLING.

Erling Skjalgson held his dominion so, that all north from Sogn Lake, and east to the Naze, the bondes stood under him; and although he had much smaller royal fiefs than formerly, still so great a dread of him prevailed that nobody dared to do anything against his will, so that the king thought his power too great. There was a man called Aslak Fitiaskalle, who was powerful and of high birth. Erling's father Skjalg, and Aslak's father Askel, were brother's sons. Aslak was a great friend of King Olaf, and the king settled him in South Hordaland, where he gave him a great fief, and great income, and ordered him in no respect to give way to Erling. But this came to nothing when the king was not in the neighbourhood; for then Erling would reign as he used to do, and was not more humble because Aslak would thrust himself forward as his equal. At last the strife went so far that Aslak could not keep his place, but hastened to King Olaf, and told him the circumstances between him and Erling. The king told Aslak to remain with him until he should meet Erling; and sent a message to Erling that he should come to him in spring at Tunsberg. When they all arrived there they held a meeting at which the king said to him, "It is told me concerning thy government, Erling, that no man from Sogn Lake to the Naze can enjoy his freedom for thee; although there are many men there who consider themselves born to udal rights, and have their privileges like others born as they are. Now, here is your relation Aslak, who appears to have suffered great inconvenience from your conduct; and I do not know whether he himself is in fault, or whether he suffers because I have placed him to defend what is mine; and although I name him, there are many others who have brought the same complaint before us, both among those who are placed in office in our districts, and among the bailiffs who have our farms to manage, and are obliged to entertain me and my people."

Erling replies to this, "I will answer at once. I deny altogether that I have ever injured Aslak, or any one else, for being in your service; but this I will not deny, that it is now, as it has long been, that each of us relations will willingly be greater than the other: and, moreover, I freely acknowledge that I am ready to bow my neck to thee, King Olaf; but it is more difficult for me to stoop before one who is of slave descent in all his generation, although he is now your bailiff, or before others who are but equal to him in descent, although you bestow honours on them."

Now the friends of both interfered, and entreated that they would be reconciled; saying, that the king never could have such powerful aid as from Erling, "if he was your friend entirely." On the other hand, they represent to Erling that he should give up to the king; for if he was in friendship with the king, it would be easy to do with all the others what he pleased. The meeting accordingly ended so that Erling should retain the fiefs he formerly had, and every complaint the king had against Erling should be dropped; but Skjalg, Erling's son, should come to the king, and remain in his power. Then Aslak returned to his dominions, and the two were in some sort reconciled. Erling returned home also to his domains, and followed his own way of ruling them.

123. HERE BEGINS THE STORY OF ASBJORN SELSBANE.

There was a man named Sigurd Thoreson, a brother of Thorer Hund of Bjarkey Island. Sigurd was married to Sigrid Skjalg's daughter, a sister of Erling. Their son, called Asbjorn, became as he grew up a very able man. Sigurd dwelt at Omd in Thrandarnes, and was a very rich and respected man. He had not gone into the king's service; and Thorer in so far had attained higher dignity than his brother, that he was the king's lenderman. But at home, on his farm, Sigurd stood in no respect behind his brother in splendour and magnificence. As long as heathenism prevailed, Sigurd usually had three sacrifices every year: one on winter-night's eve, one on mid-winter's eve, and the third in summer. Although he had adopted Christianity, he continued the same custom with his feasts: he had, namely, a great friendly entertainment at harvest time; a Yule feast in winter, to which he invited many; the third feast he had about Easter, to which also he invited many guests. He continued this fashion as long as he lived. Sigurd died on a bed of sickness when Asbjorn was eighteen years old. He was the only heir of his father, and he followed his father's custom of holding three festivals every year. Soon after Asbjorn came to his heritage the course of seasons began to grow worse, and the corn harvests of the people to fail; but Asbjorn held his usual feasts, and helped himself by having old corn, and an old provision laid up of all that was useful. But when one year had passed and another came, and the crops were no better than the year before, Sigrid wished that some if not all of the feasts should be given up. That Asbjorn would not consent to, but went round in harvest among his friends, buying corn where he could get it, and some he received in presents. He thus kept his feasts this winter also; but the spring after people got but little seed into the ground, for they had to buy the seed-corn. Then Sigurd spoke of diminishing the number of their house-servants. That Asbjorn would not consent to, but held by the old fashion of the house in all things. In summer (A.D. 1022) it appeared again that there would be a bad year for corn; and to this came the report from the south that King Olaf prohibited all export of corn, malt, or meal from the southern to the northern parts of the country. Then Asbjorn perceived that it would be difficult to procure what was necessary for a house-keeping, and resolved to put into the water a vessel for carrying goods which he had, and which was large enough to go to sea with. The ship was good, all that belonged to her was of the best, and in the sails were stripes of cloth of various colours. Asbjorn made himself ready for a voyage, and put to sea with twenty men. They sailed from the north in summer; and nothing is told of their voyage until one day, about the time the days begin to shorten, they came to Karmtsund, and landed at Augvaldsnes. Up in the island Karmt there is a large farm, not far from the sea, and a large house upon it called Augvaldsnes, which was a king's house, with an excellent farm, which Thorer Sel, who was the king's bailiff, had under his management. Thorer was a man of low birth, but had swung himself up in the world as an active man; and he was polite in speech, showy in clothes, and fond of distinction, and not apt to give way to others, in which he was supported by the favour of the king. He was besides quick in speech, straightforward, and free in conversation. Asbjorn, with his company, brought up there for the night; and in the morning, when it was light, Thorer went down to the vessel with some men, and inquired who commanded the splendid ship. Asbjorn named his own and his father's name. Thorer asks where the voyage was intended for, and what was the errand.

Asbjorn replies, that he wanted to buy corn and malt; saying, as was true, that it was a very dear time north in the country. "But we are told that here the seasons are good; and wilt thou, farmer, sell us corn? I see that here are great corn stacks, and it would be very convenient if we had not to travel farther."

Thorer replies, "I will give thee the information that thou needst not go farther to buy corn, or travel about here in Rogaland; for I can tell thee that thou must turn about, and not travel farther, for the king forbids carrying corn out of this to the north of the country. Sail back again, Halogalander, for that will be thy safest course."

Asbjorn replies, "If it be so, bonde, as thou sayest, that we can get no corn here to buy, I will, notwithstanding, go forward upon my errand, and visit my family in Sole, and see my relation Erling's habitation."

Thorer: "How near is thy relationship to Erling?"

Asbjorn: "My mother is his sister."

Thorer: "It may be that I have spoken heedlessly, if so be that thou art sister's son of Erling."

Thereupon Asbjorn and his crew struck their tents, and turned the ship to sea. Thorer called after them. "A good voyage, and come here again on your way back." Asbjorn promised to do so, sailed away, and came in the evening to Jadar. Asbjorn went on shore with ten men; the other ten men watched the ship. When Asbjorn came to the house he was very well received, and Erling was very glad to see him, placed him beside himself, and asked him all the news in the north of the country. Asbjorn concealed nothing of his business from him; and Erling said it happened unfortunately that the king had just forbid the sale of corn. "And I know no man here." says he, "who has courage to break the king's order, and I find it difficult to keep well with the king, so many are trying to break our friendship."

Asbjorn replies, "It is late before we learn the truth. In my childhood I was taught that my mother was freeborn throughout her whole descent, and that Erling of Sole was her boldest relation; and now I hear thee say that thou hast not the freedom, for the king's slaves here in Jadar, to do with thy own corn what thou pleasest."

Erling looked at him, smiled through his teeth, and said, "Ye Halogalanders know less of the king's power than we do here; but a bold man thou mayst be at home in thy conversation. Let us now drink, my friend, and we shall see tomorrow what can be done in thy business."

They did so, and were very merry all the evening. The following day Erling and Asbjorn talked over the matter again, and Erling said. "I have found out a way for you to purchase corn, Asbjorn. It is the same thing to you whoever is the seller." He answered that he did not care of whom he bought the corn, if he got a good right to his purchase. Erling said. "It appears to me probable that my slaves have quite as much corn as you require to buy; and they are not subject to law, or land regulation, like other men." Asbjorn agreed to the proposal. The slaves were now spoken to about the purchase, and they brought forward corn and malt, which they sold to Asbjorn, so that he loaded his vessel with what he wanted. When he was ready for sea Erling followed him on the road, made him presents of friendship, and they took a kind farewell of each other. Asbjorn got a good breeze, landed in the evening at Karmtsund, near to Augvaldsnes, and remained there for the night. Thorer Sel had heard of Asbjorn's voyage, and also that his vessel was deeply laden. Thorer summoned people to him in the night, so that before daylight he had sixty men; and with these he went against Asbjorn as soon as it was light, and went out to the ship just as Asbjorn and his men were putting on their clothes. Asbjorn saluted Thorer, and Thorer asked what kind of goods Asbjorn had in the vessel.

He replied, "Corn and malt."

Thorer said, "Then Erling is doing as he usually does, and despising the king's orders, and is unwearied in opposing him in all things, insomuch that it is wonderful the king suffers it."

Thorer went on scolding in this way, and when he was silent Asbjorn said that Erling's slaves had owned the corn.

Thorer replied hastily, that he did not regard Erling's tricks. "And now, Asbjorn, there is no help for it; ye must either go on shore, or we will throw you overboard; for we will not be troubled with you while we are discharging the cargo."

Asbjorn saw that he had not men enough to resist Thorer; therefore he and his people landed, and Thorer took the whole cargo out of the vessel. When the vessel was discharged Thorer went through the ship, and observed. "Ye Halogalanders have good sails: take the old sail of our vessel and give it them; it is good enough for those who are sailing in a light vessel." Thus the sails were exchanged. When this was done Asbjorn and his comrades sailed away north along the coast, and did not stop until they reached home early in whiter. This expedition was talked of far and wide, and Asbjorn had no trouble that winter in making feasts at home. Thorer Hund invited Asbjorn and his mother, and also all whom they pleased to take along with him, to a Yule feast; but Asbjorn sat at home, and would not travel, and it was to be seen that Thorer thought Asbjorn despised his invitation, since he would not come. Thorer scoffed much at Asbjorn's voyage. "Now," said he, "it is evident that Asbjorn makes a great difference in his respect towards his relations; for in summer he took the greatest trouble to visit his relation Erling in Jadar, and now will not take the trouble to come to me in the next house. I don't know if he thinks there may be a Thorer Sel in his way upon every holm." Such words, and the like sarcasms, Asbjorn heard of; and very ill satisfied he was with his voyage, which had thus made him a laughing-stock to the country, and he remained at home all winter, and went to no feasts.

124. MURDER OF THORER SEL.

ASBJORN HAD A LONG-ship standing in the noust (shipshed), and it was a snekke (cutter) of twenty benches; and after Candlemas (February 2, 1023), he had the vessel put in the water, brought out all his furniture, and rigged her out. He then summoned to him his friends and people, so that he had nearly ninety men all well armed. When he was ready for sea, and got a wind, he sailed south along the coast, but as the wind did not suit, they advanced but slowly. When they came farther south they steered outside the rocks, without the usual ships' channel, keeping to sea as much as it was possible to do so. Nothing is related of his voyage before the fifth day of Easter (April 18, 1023), when, about evening, they came on the outside of Karmt Island. This island is so shaped that it is very long, but not broad at its widest part; and without it lies the usual ships' channel. It is thickly inhabited; but where the island is exposed to the ocean great tracts of it are uncultivated. Asbjorn and his men landed at a place in the island that was uninhabited. After they had set up their ship-tents Asbjorn said, "Now ye must remain here and wait for me. I will go on land in the isle, and spy what news there may be which we know nothing of." Asbjorn had on mean clothes, a broadbrimmed hat, a fork in his hand, but had girt on his sword under his clothes. He went up to the land, and in through the island; and when he came upon a hillock, from which he could see the house on Augvaldsnes, and on as far as Karmtsund, he saw people in all quarters flocking together by land and by sea, and all going up to the house of Augvaldsnes. This seemed to him extraordinary; and therefore he went up quietly to a house close by, in which servants were cooking meat. From their conversation he discovered immediately that the king Olaf had come there to a feast, and that he had just sat down to table. Asbjorn turned then to the feasting-room, and when he came into the ante-room one was going in and another coming out; but nobody took notice of him. The hall-door was open, and he saw that Thorer Sel stood before the table of the high-seat. It was getting late in the evening, and Asbjorn heard people ask Thorer what had taken place between him and Asbjorn; and Thorer had a long story about it, in which he evidently departed from the truth. Among other things he heard a man say, "How did Asbjorn behave when you discharged his vessel?" Thorer replied, "When we were taking out the cargo he bore it tolerably, but not well; and when we took the sail from him he wept." When Asbjorn heard this he suddenly drew his sword, rushed into the hall, and cut at Thorer. The stroke took him in the neck, so that the head fell upon the table before the king, and the body at his feet, and the tablecloth was soiled with blood from top to bottom. The king ordered him to be seized and taken out. This was done. They laid hands on Asbjorn, and took him from the hall. The table-furniture and table-cloths were removed, and also Thorer's corpse, and all the blood wiped up. The king was enraged to the highest; but remained quiet in speech, as he always was when in anger.

125. OF SKJALG, THE SON OF ERLING SKJALGSON.

Skjalg Erlingson stood up, went before the king, and said, "Now may it go, as it often does, that every case will admit of alleviation. I will pay thee the mulct for the bloodshed on account of this man, so that he may retain life and limbs. All the rest determine and do, king, according to thy pleasure."

The king replies, "Is it not a matter of death, Skjalg, that a man break the Easter peace; and in the next place that he kills a man in the king's lodging; and in the third that he makes my feet his execution-block, although that may appear a small matter to thee and thy father?"

Skjalg replies, "It is ill done, king, in as far as it displeases thee; but the deed is, otherwise, done excellently well. But if the deed appear to thee so important, and be so contrary to thy will, yet may I expect something for my services from thee; and certainly there are many who will say that thou didst well."

The king replies, "Although thou hast made me greatly indebted to thee, Skjalg, for thy services, yet I will not for thy sake break the law, or cast away my own dignity."

Then Skjalg turned round, and went out of the hall. Twelve men who had come with Skjalg all followed him, and many others went out with him. Skjalg said to Thorarin Nefiulfson, "If thou wilt have me for a friend, take care that this man be not killed before Sunday." Thereupon Skjalg and his men set off, took a rowing boat which he had, and rowed south as fast as they could, and came to Jadar with the first glimpse of morning. They went up instantly to the house, and to the loft in which Erling slept. Skjalg rushed so hard against the door that it burst asunder at the nails. Erling and the others who were within started up. He was in one spring upon his legs, grasped his shield and sword, and rushed to the door, demanding who was there. Skjalg named himself, and begs him to open the door. Erling replies, "It was most likely to be thee who hast behaved so foolishly; or is there any one who is pursuing thee?" Thereupon the door was unlocked. Then said Skjalg, "Although it appears to thee that I am so hasty, I suppose our relation Asbjorn will not think my proceedings too quick; for he sits in chains there in the north at Augvaldsnes, and it would be but manly to hasten back and stand by him." The father and son then had a conversation together, and Skjalg related the whole circumstances of Thorer Sel's murder.

126. OF THORARIN NEFIULFSON.

King Olaf took his seat again when everything in the hall was put in order, and was enraged beyond measure. He asked how it was with the murderer. He was answered, that he was sitting out upon the doorstep under guard.

The king says, "Why is he not put to death?"

Thorarin Nefiulfson replies, "Sire, would you not call it murder to kill a man in the night-time?"

The king answers, "Put him in irons then, and kill him in the morning."

Then Asbjorn was laid in chains, and locked up in a house for the night. The day after the king heard the morning mass, and then went to the Thing, where he sat till high mass. As he was going to mass he said to Thorarin, "Is not the sun high enough now in the heavens that your friend Asbjorn may be hanged?"

Thorarin bowed before the king, and said, "Sire, it was said by Bishop Sigurd on Friday last, that the King who has all things in his power had to endure great temptation of spirit; and blessed is he who rather imitates him, than those who condemned the man to death, or those who caused his slaughter. It is not long till tomorrow, and that is a working day."

The king looked at him, and said, "Thou must take care then that he is not put to death to-day; but take him under thy charge, and know for certain that thy own life shall answer for it if he escape in any way."

Then the king went away. Thorarin went also to where Asbjorn lay in irons, took off his chains, and brought him to a small room, where he had meat and drink set before him, and told him what the king had determined in case Asbjorn ran away. Asbjorn replies, that Thorarin need not be afraid of him. Thorarin sat a long while with him during the day, and slept there all night. On Saturday the king arose and went to the early mass, and from thence he went to the Thing, where a great many bondes were assembled, who had many complaints to be determined. The king sat there long in the day, and it was late before the people went to high mass. Thereafter the king went to table. When he had got meat he sat drinking for a while, so that the tables were not removed. Thorarin went out to the priest who had the church under his care, and gave him two marks of silver to ring in the Sabbath as soon as the king's table was taken away. When the king had drunk as much as he wished the tables were removed. Then said the king, that it was now time for the slaves to go to the murderer and put him to death. In the same moment the bell rang in the Sabbath.

Then Thorarin went before the king, and said, "The Sabbath-peace this man must have, although he has done evil."

The king said, "Do thou take care, Thorarin, that he do not escape."

The king then went to the church, and attended the vesper service, and Thorarin sat the whole day with Asbjorn. On Sunday the bishop visited

Asbjorn, confessed him, and gave him orders to hear high mass. Thorarin then went to the king, and asked him to appoint men to guard the murderer. "I will now," he said, "be free of this charge." The king thanked him for his care, and ordered men to watch over Asbjorn, who was again laid in chains. When the people went to high mass Asbjorn was led to the church, and he stood outside of the church with his guard; but the king and all the people stood in the church at mass.

127. ERLING'S RECONCILIATION WITH KING OLAF.

Now we must again take up our story where we left it,–that Erling and his son Skjalg held a council on this affair, and according to the resolution of Erling, and of Skjalg and his other sons, it was determined to assemble a force and send out message-tokens. A great multitude of people accordingly came together. They got ready with all speed, rigged their ships, and when they reckoned upon their force they found they had nearly 1500 men. With this war-force they set off, and came on Sunday to Augvaldsnes on Karmt Island. They went straight up to the house with all the men, and arrived just as the Scripture lesson was read. They went directly to the church, took Asbjorn, and broke off his chains. At the tumult and clash of arms all who were outside of the church ran into it; but they who were in the church looked all towards them, except the king, who stood still, without looking around him. Erling and his sons drew up their men on each side of the path which led from the church to the hall, and Erling with his sons stood next to the hall. When high mass was finished the king went immediately out of the church, and first went through the open space between the ranks drawn up, and then his retinue, man by man; and as he came to the door Erling placed himself before the door, bowed to the king, and saluted him. The king saluted him in return, and prayed God to help him. Erling took up the word first, and said, "My relation, Asbjorn, it is reported to me, has been guilty of misdemeanor, king; and it is a great one, if he has done anything that incurs your displeasure. Now I am come to entreat for him peace, and such penalties as you yourself may determine; but that thereby he redeem life and limb, and his remaining here in his native land."

The king replies, "It appears to me, Erling, that thou thinkest the case of Asbjorn is now in thy own power, and I do not therefore know why thou speakest now as if thou wouldst offer terms for him. I think thou hast drawn together these forces because thou are determined to settle what is between us."

Erling replies, "Thou only, king, shalt determine, and determine so that we shall be reconciled."

The king: "Thinkest thou, Erling, to make me afraid? And art thou come here in such force with that expectation? No, that shall not be; and if that be thy thought, I must in no way turn and fly."

Erling replies, "Thou hast no occasion to remind me how often I have come to meet thee with fewer men than thou hadst. But now I shall not conceal what lies in my mind, namely, that it is my will that we now enter into a reconciliation; for otherwise I expect we shall never meet again." Erling was then as red as blood in the face.

Now Bishop Sigurd came forward to the king and said, "Sire, I entreat you on God Almighty's account to be reconciled with Erling according to his offer,–that the man shall retain life and limb, but that thou shalt determine according to thy pleasure all the other conditions."

The king replies, "You will determine."

Then said the bishop, "Erling, do thou give security for Asbjorn, such as the king thinks sufficient, and then leave the conditions to the mercy of the king, and leave all in his power."

Erling gave a surety to the king on his part, which he accepted.

Thereupon Asbjorn received his life and safety, and delivered himself into the king's power, and kissed his hand.

Erling then withdrew with his forces, without exchanging salutation with the king; and the king went into the hall, followed by Asbjorn. The king thereafter made known the terms of reconciliation to be these:–"In the first place, Asbjorn, thou must submit to the law of the land, which commands that the man who kills a servant of the king must undertake his service, if the king will. Now I will that thou shalt undertake the office of bailiff which Thorer Sel had, and manage my estate here in Augvaldsnes." Asbjorn replies, that it should be according to the king's will; "but I must first go home to my farm, and put things in order there." The king was satisfied with this, and proceeded to another guest-quarter. Asbjorn made himself ready with his comrades, who all kept themselves concealed in a quiet creek during the time Asbjorn was away from them. They had had their spies out to learn how it went with him, and would not depart without having some certain news of him.

128. OF THORER HUND AND ASBJORN SELSBANE.

Asbjorn then set out on his voyage, and about spring (A.D. 1023) got home to his farm. After this exploit he was always called Asbjorn

Selsbane. Asbjorn had not been long at home before he and his relation Thorer met and conversed together, and Thorer asked Asbjorn particularly all about his journey, and about all the circumstances which had happened on the course of it. Asbjorn told everything as it had taken place.

Then said Thorer, "Thou thinkest that thou hast well rubbed out the disgrace of having been plundered in last harvest."

"I think so," replies Asbjorn; "and what is thy opinion, cousin?"

"That I will soon tell thee," said Thorer. "Thy first expedition to the south of the country was indeed very disgraceful, and that disgrace has been redeemed; but this expedition is both a disgrace to thee and to thy family, if it end in thy becoming the king's slave, and being put on a footing with that worst of men, Thorer Sel. Show that thou art manly enough to sit here on thy own property, and we thy relations shall so support thee that thou wilt never more come into such trouble."

Asbjorn found this advice much to his mind; and before they parted it was firmly, determined that Asbjorn should remain on his farm, and not go back to the king or enter into his service. And he did so, and sat quietly at home on his farm.

129. KING OLAF BAPTIZES IN VORS AND VALDERS.

After King Olaf and Erling Skjalgson had this meeting at Augvaldsnes, new differences arose between them, and increased so much that they ended in perfect enmity. In spring (A.D. 1023) the king proceeded to guest-quarters in Hordaland, and went up also to Vors, because he heard there was but little of the true faith among the people there. He held a Thing with the bondes at a place called Vang, and a number of bondes came to it fully armed. The king ordered them to adopt Christianity; but they challenged him to battle, and it proceeded so far that the men were drawn up on both sides. But when it came to the point such a fear entered into the blood of the bondes that none would advance or command, and they chose the part which was most to their advantage; namely, to obey the king and receive Christianity; and before the king left them they were all baptized. One day it happened that the king was riding on his way a singing of psalms, and when he came right opposite some hills he halted and said, "Man after man shall relate these my words, that I think it not advisable for any king of Norway to travel hereafter between these hills." And it is a saying among the people that the most kings since that time have avoided it. The king proceeded to

Ostrarfjord, and came to his ships, with which he went north to Sogn, and had his living in guest-quarters there in summer (A.D. 1023); when autumn approached he turned in towards the Fjord district, and went from thence to Valders, where the people were still heathen. The king hastened up to the lake in Valders, came unexpectedly on the bondes, seized their vessels, and went on board of them with all his men. He then sent out message-tokens, and appointed a Thing so near the lake that he could use the vessels if he found he required them. The bondes resorted to the Thing in a great and well-armed host; and when he commanded them to accept Christianity the bondes shouted against him, told him to be silent, and made a great uproar and clashing of weapons. But when the king saw that they would not listen to what he would teach them, and also that they had too great a force to contend with, he turned his discourse, and asked if there were people at the Thing who had disputes with each other which they wished him to settle. It was soon found by the conversation of the bondes that they had many quarrels among themselves, although they had all joined in speaking against Christianity. When the bondes began to set forth their own cases, each endeavored to get some upon his side to support him; and this lasted the whole day long until evening, when the Thing was concluded. When the bondes had heard that the king had travelled to Valders, and was come into their neighborhood, they had sent out message-tokens summoning the free and the unfree to meet in arms, and with this force they had advanced against the king; so that the neighbourhood all around was left without people. When the Thing was concluded the bondes still remained assembled; and when the king observed this he went on board his ships, rowed in the night right across the water, landed in the country there, and began to plunder and burn. The day after the king's men rowed from one point of land to another, and over all the king ordered the habitations to be set on fire. Now when the bondes who were assembled saw what the king was doing, namely, plundering and burning, and saw the smoke and flame of their houses, they dispersed, and each hastened to his own home to see if he could find those he had left. As soon as there came a dispersion among the crowd, the one slipped away after the other, until the whole multitude was dissolved. Then the king rowed across the lake again, burning also on that side of the country. Now came the bondes to him begging for mercy, and offering to submit to him. He gave every man who came to him peace if he desired it, and restored to him his goods; and nobody refused to adopt Christianity. The king then had the people christened, and took hostages from the bondes. He ordered churches to be built and consecrated, and placed teachers in them. He remained a long time here in autumn, and had his ships drawn across the neck of land between the two lakes. The king did not go far from the sides of the lakes into the country, for he did not much trust the bondes. When the king thought that frost might be expected, he went further up the country, and came to Thoten. Arnor, the earl's skald, tells how King Olaf burnt in the Uplands, in the poem he composed concerning the king's brother King Harald:–

"Against the Upland people wroth,
Olaf, to most so mild, went forth:
The houses burning,
All people mourning;
Who could not fly
Hung on gallows high.
It was, I think, in Olaf's race
The Upland people to oppress."

Afterwards King Olaf went north through the valleys to Dovrefield, and did not halt until he reached the Throndhjem district and arrived at Nidaros, where he had ordered winter provision to be collected, and remained all winter (A.D. 1024). This was the tenth year of his reign.

130. OF EINAR TAMBASKELFER.

THE SUMMER BEFORE Einar Tambaskelfer left the country, and went westward to England (A.D. 1023). There he met his relative Earl Hakon, and stayed some time with him. He then visited King Canute, from whom he received great presents. Einar then went south all the way to Rome, and came back the following summer (A.D. 1024), and returned to his house and land. King Olaf and Einar did not meet this time.

131. THE BIRTH OF KING MAGNUS.

THERE WAS A GIRL whose name was Alfhild, and who was usually called the king's slave-woman, although she was of good descent. She was a remarkably handsome girl, and lived in King Olaf's court. It was reported this spring that Alfhild was with child, and the king's confidential friends knew that he was father of the child. It happened one night that Alfhild was taken ill, and only few people were at hand; namely, some women, priests, Sigvat the skald, and a few others. Alfhild was so ill that she was nearly dead; and when she was delivered of a man-child, it was some time before they could discover whether the child was in life. But when the infant drew breath, although very weak, the priest told Sigvat to hasten to the king, and tell him of the event.

He replies, "I dare not on any account waken the king; for he has forbid that any man should break his sleep until he awakens of himself."

The priest replies, "It is of necessity that this child be immediately baptized, for it appears to me there is but little life in it."

Sigvat said, "I would rather venture to take upon me to let thee baptize the child, than to awaken the king; and I will take it upon myself if anything be amiss, and will give the child a name."

They did so; and the child was baptized, and got the name of Magnus. The next morning, when the king awoke and had dressed himself, the circumstance was told him. He ordered Sigvat to be called, and said. "How camest thou to be so bold as to have my child baptized before I knew anything about it?"

Sigvat replies, "Because I would rather give two men to God than one to the devil."

The king–"What meanest thou?"

Sigvat–"The child was near death, and must have been the devil's if it had died as a heathen, and now it is God's. And I knew besides that if thou shouldst be so angry on this account that it affected my life, I would be God's also."

The king asked, "But why didst thou call him Magnus, which is not a name of our race?"

Sigvat–"I called him after King Carl Magnus, who, I knew, had been the best man in the world."

Then said the king, "Thou art a very lucky man, Sigvat; but it is not wonderful that luck should accompany understanding. It is only wonderful how it sometimes happens that luck attends ignorant men, and that foolish counsel turns out lucky." The king was overjoyed at the circumstance. The boy grew up, and gave good promise as he advanced in age.

132. THE MURDER OF ASBJORN SELSBANE.

The same spring (A.D. 1024) the king gave into the hands of Asmund Grankelson the half of the sheriffdom of the district of Halogaland, which Harek of Thjotta had formerly held, partly in fief, partly for defraying the king's entertainment in guest-quarters. Asmund had a ship manned with nearly thirty well-armed men. When Asmund came north he met Harek, and told him what the king had determined with regard to the district, and produced to him the tokens of the king's full powers. Harek said, "The king had the right to give the sheriffdom to whom he pleased; but the former sovereigns had not been in use to diminish our rights who are entitled by birth to hold powers from the king, and to give them into the hands of the peasants who never before held such offices." But although it was evident that it was against Harek's inclination, he allowed Asmund to take the sheriffdom according to the king's order. Then Asmund proceeded home to his father, stayed there a short time, and then went north to Halogaland to his sheriffdom; and he came north to Langey Island, where there dwelt two brothers called Gunstein and Karle, both very rich and respectable men. Gunstein, the eldest of the brothers, was a good husbandman. Karle was a handsome man in appearance, and splendid in his dress; and both were, in many respects, expert in all feats. Asmund was well received by them, remained with them a while, and collected such revenues of his sheriffdom as he could get. Karle spoke with Asmund of his wish to go south with him and take service in the court of King Olaf, to which Asmund encouraged him much, promising his influence with the king for obtaining for Karle such a situation as he desired; and Karle accordingly accompanied Asmund. Asmund heard that Asbjorn, who had killed Thorer Sel, had gone to the market-meeting of Vagar with a large ship of burden manned with nearly twenty men, and that he was now expected from the south. Asmund and his retinue proceeded on their way southwards along the coast with a contrary wind, but there was little of it. They saw some of the fleet for Vagar sailing towards them; and they privately inquired of them about Asbjorn, and were told he was upon the way coming from the south. Asmund and Karle were bedfellows, and excellent friends. One day, as Asmund and his people were rowing through a sound, a ship of burden came sailing towards them. The ship was easily known, having high bulwarks, was painted with white and red colours, and coloured cloth was woven in the sail. Karle said to Asmund, "Thou hast often said thou wast curious to see Asbjorn who killed Thorer Sel; and if I know one ship from another, that is his which is coming sailing along."

Asmund replies, "Be so good, comrade, and tell me which is he when thou seest him."

When the ships came alongside of each other, "That is Asbjorn," said Karle; "the man sitting at the helm in a blue cloak."

Asmund replies, "I shall make his blue cloak red;" threw a spear at Asbjorn, and hit him in the middle of the body, so that it flew through and through him, and stuck fast in the upper part of the stern-post; and Asbjorn fell down dead from the helm. Then each vessel sailed on its course, and Asbjorn's body was carried north to Thrandarnes. Then Sigrid sent a message to Bjarkey Isle to Thorer Hund, who came to her while they were, in the usual way, dressing the corpse of Asbjorn. When he returned Sigrid gave presents to all her friends, and followed Thorer to his ship; but before they parted she said, "It has so fallen out, Thorer, that my son has suffered by thy friendly counsel, but he did not retain life to reward thee for it; but although I have not his ability yet will I show my good will. Here is a gift I give thee, which I expect thou wilt use. Here is the spear which went through Asbjorn my son, and there is still blood upon it, to remind thee that it fits the wound thou hast seen on the corpse of thy brother's son Asbjorn. It would be a manly deed, if thou shouldst throw this spear from thy hand so that it stood in Olaf's breast; and this I can tell thee, that thou wilt be named coward in every man's mouth, if thou dost not avenge Asbjorn." Thereupon she turned about, and went her way.

Thorer was so enraged at her words that he could not speak. He neither thought of casting the spear from him, nor took notice of the gangway; so that he would have fallen into the sea, if his men had not laid hold of him as he was going on board his ship. It was a feathered spear; not large, but the handle was gold-mounted. Now Thorer rowed away with his people, and went home to Bjarkey Isle. Asmund and his companions also proceeded on their way until they came south to Throndhjem, where they waited on King Olaf; and Asmund related to the king all that had happened on the voyage. Karle became one of the king's court-men, and the friendship continued between him and Asmund. They did not keep secret the words that had passed between Asmund and Karle before Asbjorn was killed; for they even told them to the king. But then it happened, according to the proverb, that every one has a friend in the midst of his enemies. There were some present who took notice of the words, and they reached Thorer Hund's ears.

133. OF KING OLAF.

When spring (A.D. 1024) was advanced King Olaf rigged out his ships, and sailed southwards in summer along the land. He held Things with the bondes on the way, settled the law business of the people, put to rights the faith of the country, and collected the king's taxes wherever he came. In autumn he proceeded south to the frontier of the country; and King Olaf had now made the people Christians in all the great districts, and everywhere, by laws, had introduced order into the country. He had also, as before related, brought the Orkney Islands under his power, and by messages had made many friends in Iceland, Greenland, and the Farey Islands. King Olaf had sent timber for building a church to Iceland, of which a church was built upon the Thing-field where the General Thing is held, and had sent a bell for it, which is still there. This was after the Iceland people had altered their laws, and introduced Christianity, according to the word King Olaf had sent them. After that time, many considerable persons came from Iceland, and entered into King Olaf's service; as Thorkel Eyjolfson, and Thorleif Bollason, Thord Kolbeinson, Thord Barkarson, Thorgeir Havarson, Thormod Kalbrunar-skald. King Olaf had sent many friendly presents to chief people in Iceland; and they in return sent him such things as they had which they thought most acceptable. Under this show of friendship which the king gave Iceland were concealed many things which afterwards appeared.

134. KING OLAF'S MESSAGE TO ICELAND, AND THE COUNSELS OF THE ICELANDERS.

King Olaf this summer (A.D. 1024) sent Thorarin Nefiulfson to Iceland on his errands; and Thorarin went out of Throndhjem fjord along with the king, and followed him south to More. From thence Thorarin went out to sea, and got such a favourable breeze that after four days sail he landed at the Westman Isles, in Iceland. He proceeded immediately to the Althing, and came just as the people were upon the Lawhillock, to which he repaired. When the cases of the people before the Thing had been determined according to law, Thorarin Nefiulfson took up the word as follows:–"We parted four days ago from King Olaf Haraldson, who sends God Almighty's and his own salutation to all the chiefs and principal men of the land; as also to all the people in general, men and women, young and old, rich and poor. He also lets you know that he will be your sovereign if ye will become his subjects, so that he and you will be friends, assisting each other in all that is good."

The people replied in a friendly way, that they would gladly be the king's friends, if he would be a friend of the people of their country.

Then Thorarin again took up the word:–"This follows in addition to the king's message, that he will in friendship desire of the people of the north district that they give him the island, or out-rock, which lies at the mouth of Eyfjord, and is called Grimsey, for which he will give you from his country whatever good the people of the district may desire. He sends this message particularly to Gudmund of Modruvellir to support this matter, because he understands that Gudmund has most influence in that quarter."

Gudmund replies, "My inclination is greatly for King Olaf's friendship, and that I consider much more useful than the out-rock he desires. But the king has not heard rightly if he think I have more power in this matter than any other, for the island is a common. We, however, who have the most use of the isle, will hold a meeting among ourselves about it."

Then the people went to their tent-houses; and the Northland people had a meeting among themselves, and talked over the business, and every one spoke according to his judgment. Gudmund supported the matter, and many others formed their opinions by his. Then some asked why his brother Einar did not speak on the subject. "We think he has the clearest insight into most things."

Einar answers, "I have said so little about the matter because nobody has asked me about it; but if I may give my opinion, our countrymen might just as well make themselves at once liable to land-scat to King Olaf, and submit to all his exactions as he has them among his people in Norway; and this heavy burden we will lay not only upon ourselves, but on our sons, and their sons, and all our race, and on all the community dwelling and living in this land, which never after will be free from this slavery. Now although this king is a good man, as I well believe him to be, yet it must be hereafter, when kings succeed each other, that some will be good, and some bad. Therefore if the people of this country will preserve the freedom they have enjoyed since the land was first inhabited, it is not advisable to give the king the smallest spot to fasten himself upon the country by, and not to give him any kind of scat or service that can have the appearance of a duty. On the other hand, I think it very proper that the people send the king such friendly presents of hawks or horses, tents or sails, or such things which are suitable gifts; and these are well applied if they are repaid with friendship. But as to Grimsey Isle, I have to say, that although nothing is drawn from it that can serve for food, yet it could support a great war-force cruising from thence in long-ships; and then, I doubt not, there would be distress enough at every poor peasant's door."

When Einar had thus explained the proper connection of the matter, the whole community were of one mind that such a thing should not be permitted; and Thorarin saw sufficiently well what the result of his errand was to be.

135. THE ANSWER OF THE ICELANDERS.

The day following, Thorarin went again to the Lawhill, and brought forward his errand in the following words:–"King Olaf sends his message to his friends here in the country, among whom he reckons Gudmund Eyjolfson, Snorre Gode, Thorkel Eyjolfson, Skapte the lagman, and Thorstein Halson, and desires them by me to come to him on a friendly visit; and adds, that ye must not excuse yourselves, if you regard his friendship as worth anything." In their answer they thanked the king for his message and added, that they would afterwards give a reply to it by Thorarin when they had more closely considered the matter with their friends. The chiefs now weighed the matter among themselves, and each gave his own opinion about the journey. Snorre and Skapte dissuaded from such a dangerous proceeding with the people of Norway; namely, that all the men who had the most to say in the country should at once leave Iceland. They added, that from this message, and from what Einar had said, they had the suspicion that the king intended to use force and strong measures against the Icelanders if he ruled in the country. Gudmund and Thorkel Eyjolfson insisted much that they should follow King Olaf's invitation, and called it a journey of honour. But when they had considered the matter on all sides, it was at last resolved that they should not travel themselves, but that each of them should send in his place a man whom they thought best suited for it. After this determination the Thing was closed, and there was no journey that summer. Thorarin made two voyages that summer, and about harvest was back again at King Olaf's, and reported the result of his mission, and that some of the chiefs, or their sons, would come from Iceland according to his message.

136. OF THE PEOPLE OF THE FAREY ISLANDS.

The same summer (A.D. 1024) there came from the Farey Islands to Norway, on the king's invitation, Gille the lagman, Leif Ossurson, Thoralf of Dimun, and many other bondes' sons. Thord of Gata made himself ready for the voyage; but just as he was setting out he got a stroke of palsy, and could not come, so he remained behind. Now when the people from the Farey Isles arrived at King Olaf's, he called them to him to a conference, and explained the purpose of the journey he had made them take, namely, that he would have scat from the Farey Islands, and also that the people there should be subject to the laws which the king should give them. In that meeting it appeared from the king's words that he would make the Farey people who had come answerable, and would bind them by oath to conclude this union. He also offered to the men whom he thought the ablest to take them into his service, and bestow honour and friendship on them. These Farey men understood the king's words so, that they must dread the turn the matter might take if they did not submit to all that the king desired. Although they held several meetings about the business before it ended, the king's desire at last prevailed. Leif, Gille, and Thoralf went into the king's service, and became his courtmen; and they, with all their travelling companions, swore the oath to King Olaf, that the law and land privilege which he set them should be observed in the Farey Islands, and also the scat be levied that he laid upon them. Thereafter the Farey people prepared for their return home, and at their departure the king gave those who had entered into his service presents in testimony of his friendship, and they went their way. Now the king ordered a ship to be rigged, manned it, and sent men to the Farey Islands to receive the scat from the inhabitants which they should pay him. It was late before they were ready; but they set off at last: and of their journey all that is to be told is, that they did not come back, and no scat either, the following summer; for nobody had come to the Farey Isles, and no man had demanded scat there.

137. OF THE MARRIAGE OF KETIL AND OF THORD TO THE KING'S SISTERS.

King Olaf proceeded about harvest time to Viken, and sent a message before him to the Uplands that they should prepare guest-quarters for him, as he intended to be there in winter. Afterwards he made ready for his journey, and went to the Uplands, and remained the winter there; going about in guest-quarters, and putting things to rights where he saw it needful, advancing also the cause of Christianity wheresoever it was requisite. It happened while King Olaf was in Hedemark that

Ketil Kalf of Ringanes courted Gunhild, a daughter of Sigurd Syr and of King Olaf's mother Asta. Gunhild was a sister of King Olaf, and therefore it belonged to the king to give consent and determination to the business. He took it in a friendly way; for he know Ketil, that he was of high birth, wealthy, and of good understanding, and a great chief; and also he had long been a great friend of King Olaf, as before related. All these circumstances induced the king to approve of the match, and so it was that Ketil got Gunhild. King Olaf was present at the wedding. From thence the king went north to Gudbrandsdal, where he was entertained in guest-quarters. There dwelt a man, by name Thord Guthormson, on a farm called Steig; and he was the most powerful man in the north end of the valley. When Thord and the king met, Thord made proposals for Isrid, the daughter of Gudbrand, and the sister of King Olaf's mother, as it belonged to the king to give consent. After the matter was considered, it was determined that the marriage should proceed, and Thord got Isrid. Afterwards Thord was the king's faithful friend, and also many of Thord's relations and friends, who followed his footsteps. From thence King Olaf returned south through Thoten and Hadaland, from thence to Ringerike, and so to Viken. In spring (A.D. 1025) he went to Tunsberg, and stayed there while there was the market-meeting, and a great resort of people. He then had his vessels rigged out, and had many people about him.

138. OF THE ICELANDERS.

THE SAME SUMMER (A.D. 1025) came Stein, a son of the lagman Skapte, from Iceland, in compliance with King Olaf's message; and with him Thorod, a son of Snorre the gode, and Geller, a son of Thorkel Eyjolfson, and Egil, a son of Hal of Sida, brother of Thorstein Hal. Gudmund Eyjolfson had died the winter before. These Iceland men repaired to King Olaf as soon as they had opportunity; and when they met the king they were well received, and all were in his house. The same summer King Olaf heard that the ship was missing which he had sent the summer before to the Farey Islands after the scat, and nobody knew what had become of it. The king fitted out another ship, manned it, and sent it to the Farey Islands for the scat. They got under weigh, and proceeded to sea; but as little was ever heard of this vessel as of the former one, and many conjectures were made about what had become of them.

139. HERE BEGINS THE STORY OF CANUTE THE GREAT.

During this time Canute the Great, called by some Canute the Old, was king of England and Denmark. Canute the Great was a son of Svein Haraldson Forkedbeard, whose forefathers, for a long course of generations, had ruled over Denmark. Harald Gormson, Canute's grandfather, had conquered Norway after the fall of Harald Grafeld, Gunhild's son, had taken scat from it, and had placed Earl Hakon the Great to defend the country. The Danish King, Svein Haraldson, ruled also over Norway, and placed his son-in-law Earl Eirik, the son of Earl Hakon, to defend the country. The brothers Eirik and Svein, Earl Hakon's sons, ruled the land until Earl Eirik went west to England, on the invitation of his brother-in-law Canute the Great, when he left behind his son Earl Hakon, sister's son of Canute the Great, to govern Norway. But when Olaf the Thick came first to Norway, as before related, he took prisoner Earl Hakon the son of Eirik, and deposed him from the kingdom. Then Hakon proceeded to his mother's brother, Canute the Great, and had been with him constantly until the time to which here in our saga we have now come. Canute the Great had conquered England by blows and weapons, and had a long struggle before the people of the land were subdued. But when he had set himself perfectly firm in the government of the country, he remembered that he also had right to a kingdom which he had not brought under his authority; and that was Norway. He thought he had hereditary right to all Norway; and his sister's son Hakon, who had held a part of it, appeared to him to have lost it with disgrace. The reason why Canute and Hakon had remained quiet with respect to their claims upon Norway was, that when King Olaf Haraldson landed in Norway the people and commonalty ran together in crowds, and would hear of nothing but that Olaf should be king over all the country, although some afterwards, who thought that the people upon account of his power had no self-government left to them, went out of the country. Many powerful men, or rich bondes sons, had therefore gone to Canute the Great, and pretended various errands; and every one who came to Canute and desired his friendship was loaded with presents. With Canute, too, could be seen greater splendour and pomp than elsewhere, both with regard to the multitude of people who were daily in attendance, and also to the other magnificent things about the houses he owned and dwelt in himself. Canute the Great drew scat and revenue from the people who were the richest of all in northern lands; and in the same proportion as he had greater revenues than other kings, he also made greater presents than other kings. In his whole kingdom peace was so well established, that no man dared break it. The people of the country kept the peace towards each other, and had their old country law: and for this he was greatly celebrated in all countries. And many of those who came from Norway represented their hardships to Earl Hakon, and some even to King Canute himself; and that the Norway people were ready to turn back to the government of King Canute, or Earl Hakon, and receive deliverance from them. This conversation suited well the earl's inclination, and he carried it to the king, and begged of him to try if King Olaf would not surrender the kingdom, or at least come to an agreement to divide it; and many supported the earl's views.

140. CANUTE'S MESSAGE TO KING OLAF.

Canute the Great sent men from the West, from England, to Norway, and equipped them magnificently for the journey. They were bearers of the English king Canute's letter and seal. They came about spring (A.D. 1025) to the king of Norway, Olaf Haraldson, in Tunsberg. Now when it was told the king that ambassadors had arrived from Canute the Great he was ill at ease, and said that Canute had not sent messengers hither with any messages that could be of advantage to him or his people; and it was some days before the ambassadors could come before the king. But when they got permission to speak to him they appeared before the king, and made known King Canute's letter, and their errand which accompanied it; namely, "that King Canute considers all Norway as his property, and insists that his forefathers before him have possessed that kingdom; but as King Canute offers peace to all countries, he will also offer peace to all here, if it can be so settled, and will not invade Norway with his army if it can be avoided. Now if King Olaf Haraldson wishes to remain king of Norway, he will come to King Canute, and receive his kingdom as a fief from him, become his vassal, and pay the scat which the earls before him formerly paid." Thereupon they presented their letters, which contained precisely the same conditions.

Then King Olaf replies, "I have heard say, by old stories, that the Danish king Gorm was considered but a small king of a few people, for he ruled over Denmark alone; but the kings who succeeded him thought that was too little. It has since come so far that King Canute rules over Denmark and England, and has conquered for himself a great part of Scotland. Now he claims also my paternal heritage, and will then show some moderation in his covetousness. Does he wish to rule over all the countries of the North? Will he eat up all the kail in England? He shall do so, and reduce that country to a desert, before I lay my head in his hands, or show him any other kind of vassalage. Now ye shall tell him these my words,–I will defend Norway with battle-axe and sword as long as life is given me, and will pay scat to no man for my kingdom."

After this answer King Canute's ambassadors made themselves ready for their journey home, and were by no means rejoiced at the success of their errand.

Sigvat the skald had been with King Canute, who had given him a gold ring that weighed half a mark. The skald Berse Skaldtorfason was also there, and to him King Canute gave two gold rings, each weighing two marks, and besides a sword inlaid with gold. Sigvat made this song about it:–

"When we came o'er the wave, you cub,
When we came o'er the wave,
To me one ring, to thee two rings,
The mighty Canute gave:
One mark to me,
Four marks to thee,–
A sword too, fine and brave.
Now God knows well,
And skalds can tell,
What justice here would crave."

SIGVAT THE SKALD WAS very intimate with King Canute's messengers, and asked them many questions. They answered all his inquiries about their conversation with King Olaf, and the result of their message. They said the king listened unwillingly to their proposals. "And we do not know," say they, "to what he is trusting when he refuses becoming King Canute's vassal, and going to him, which would be the best thing he could do; for King Canute is so mild that however much a chief may have done against him, he is pardoned if he only show himself obedient. It is but lately that two kings came to him from the North, from Fife in Scotland, and he gave up his wrath against them, and allowed them to retain all the lands they had possessed before, and gave them besides very valuable gifts." Then Sigvat sang:–

"From the North land, the midst of Fife,
Two kings came begging peace and life;
Craving from Canute life and peace,–
May Olaf's good luck never cease!
May he, our gallant Norse king, never
Be brought, like these, his head to offer
As ransom to a living man
For the broad lands his sword has won."

King Canute's ambassadors proceeded on their way back, and had a favourable breeze across the sea. They came to King Canute, and told him the result of their errand, and King Olaf's last words. King Canute replies, "King Olaf guesses wrong, if he thinks I shall eat up all the kail in England; for I will let him see that there is something else than kail under my ribs, and cold kail it shall be for him." The same summer (A.D. 1025) Aslak and Skjalg, the sons of Erling of Jadar, came from Norway to King Canute, and were well received; for Aslak was married to Sigrid, a daughter of Earl Svein Hakonson, and she and Earl Hakon Eirikson were brothers' children. King Canute gave these brothers great fiefs over there, and they stood in great favour.

141. KING OLAF'S ALLIANCE WITH ONUND THE KING OF SVITHJOD.

King Olaf summoned to him all the lendermen, and had a great many people about him this summer (A.D. 1025), for a report was abroad that King Canute would come from England. People had heard from merchant vessels that Canute was assembling a great army in England. When summer was advanced, some affirmed and others denied that the army would come. King Olaf was all summer in Viken, and had spies out to learn if Canute was come to Denmark. In autumn (A.D. 1025) he sent messengers eastward to Svithjod to his brother-in-law King Onund, and let him know King Canute's demand upon Norway; adding, that, in his opinion, if Canute subdued Norway, King Onund would not long enjoy the Swedish dominions in peace. He thought it advisable, therefore, that they should unite for their defence. "And then," said he, "we will have strength enough to hold out against Canute." King Onund received King Olaf's message favourably, and replied to it, that he for his part would make common cause with King Olaf, so that each of them should stand by the one who first required help with all the strength of his kingdom. In these messages between them it was also determined that they should have a meeting, and consult with each other. The following winter (A.D. 1026) King Onund intended to travel across West Gautland, and King Olaf made preparations for taking his winter abode at Sarpsborg.

142. KING CANUTE'S AMBASSADORS TO ONUND OF SVITHJOD.

In autumn King Canute the Great came to Denmark, and remained there all winter (A.D. 1026) with a numerous army. It was told him that ambassadors with messages had been passing between the Swedish and Norwegian kings, and that some great plans must be concerting between them. In winter King Canute sent messengers to Svithjod, to King Onund, with great gifts and messages of friendship. He also told Onund that he might sit altogether quiet in this strife between him and Olaf the Thick; "for thou, Onund," says he, "and thy kingdom, shall be in peace as far as I am concerned." When the ambassadors came to King Onund they presented the gifts which King Canute sent him, together with the friendly message. King Onund did not hear their speech very willingly, and the ambassadors could observe that King Onund was most inclined to a friendship with King Olaf. They returned accordingly, and told King Canute the result of their errand, and told him not to depend much upon the friendship of King Onund.

143. THE EXPEDITION TO BJARMALAND.

This winter (A.D. 1026) King Olaf sat in Sarpsborg, and was surrounded by a very great army of people. He sent the Halogalander Karle to the north country upon his business. Karle went first to the Uplands, then across the Dovrefield, and came down to Nidaros, where he received as much money as he had the king's order for, together with a good ship, such as he thought suitable for the voyage which the king had ordered him upon; and that was to proceed north to Bjarmaland. It was settled that the king should be in partnership with Karle, and each of them have the half of the profit. Early in spring Karle directed his course to Halogaland, where his brother Gunstein prepared to accompany him, having his own merchant goods with him. There were about twenty-five men in the ship; and in spring they sailed north to Finmark. When Thorer Hund heard this, he sent a man to the brothers with the verbal message that he intended in summer to go to Bjarmaland, and that he would sail with them, and that they should divide what booty they made equally between them. Karle sent him back the message that Thorer must have twenty-five men as they had, and they were willing to divide the booty that might be taken equally, but not the merchant goods which each had for himself. When Thorer's messenger came back he had put a stout long-ship he owned into the water, and rigged it, and he had put eighty men on board of his house-servants. Thorer alone had the command over this crew, and he alone had all the goods they might acquire on the cruise. When Thorer was ready for sea he set out northwards along the coast, and found Karle a little north of Sandver. They then proceeded with good wind. Gunstein said to his brother, as soon as they met Thorer, that in his opinion Thorer was strongly manned. "I think," said he, "we had better turn back than sail so entirely in Thorer's power, for I do not trust him." Karle replies, "I will not turn back, although if I had known when we were at home on Langey Isle that Thorer Hund would join us on this voyage with so large a crew as he has, I would have taken more hands with us." The brothers spoke about it to Thorer, and asked what was the meaning of his taking more people with him than was agreed upon between them. He replies, "We have a large ship which requires many hands, and methinks there cannot be too many brave lads for so dangerous a cruise." They went in summer as fast in general as the vessels could go. When the wind was light the ship of the brothers sailed fastest, and they separated; but when the wind freshened Thorer overtook them. They were seldom together, but always in sight of each other. When they came to Bjarmaland they went straight to the merchant town, and the market began. All who had money to pay with got filled up with goods. Thorer also got a number of furs, and of beaver and sable skins. Karle had a considerable sum of money with him, with which he purchased skins and furs. When the fair was at an end they went out of the Vina river, and then the truce of the country people was also at an end. When they came out of the river they held a seaman's council, and Thorer asked the crews if they would like to go on the land and get booty.

They replied, that they would like it well enough, if they saw the booty before their eyes.

Thorer replies, that there was booty to be got, if the voyage proved fortunate; but that in all probability there would be danger in the attempt.

All said they would try, if there was any chance of booty. Thorer explained, that it was so established in this land, that when a rich man died all his movable goods were divided between the dead man and his heirs. He got the half part, or the third part, or sometimes less, and that part was carried out into the forest and buried,–sometimes under a mound, sometimes in the earth, and sometimes even a house was built over it. He tells them at the same time to get ready for this expedition at the fall of day. It was resolved that one should not desert the other, and none should hold back when the commander ordered them to come on board again. They now left people behind to take care of the ships, and went on land, where they found flat fields at first, and then great forests. Thorer went first, and the brothers Karle and Gunstein in rear. Thorer commanded the people to observe the utmost silence. "And let us peel the bark off the trees," says he, "so that one tree-mark can be seen from the other." They came to a large cleared opening, where there was a high fence upon which there was a gate that was locked. Six men of the country people held watch every night at this fence, two at a time keeping guard, each two for a third part of the night, when Thorer and his men came to the fence the guard had gone home, and those who should relieve them had not yet come upon guard. Thorer went to the fence, stuck his axe up in it above his head, hauled himself up by it, and so came over the fence, and inside the gate. Karle had also come over the fence, and to the inside of the gate; so that both came at once to the port, took the bar away, and opened the port; and then the people got in within the fence. Then said Thorer, "Within this fence there is a mound in which gold, and silver, and earth are all mixed together: seize that. But within here stands the Bjarmaland people's god Jomala: let no one be so presumptuous as to rob him." Thereupon they went to the mound and took as much of the money as they could carry away in their clothes, with which, as might be expected, much earth was mixed. Thereafter Thorer said that the people now should retreat. "And ye brothers, Karle and Gunstein," says he, "do ye lead the way, and I will go last." They all went accordingly out of the gate: but Thorer went back to Jomala, and took a silver bowl that stood upon his knee full of silver money. He put the silver in his purse, and put his arm within the handle of the bowl, and so went out of the gate. The whole troop had come without the fence; but when they perceived that Thorer had stayed behind, Karle returned to trace him, and when they met upon the path Thorer had the silver bowl with him. Thereupon Karle immediately ran to Jomala; and observing he had a thick gold ornament hanging around his neck, he lifted his axe, cut the string with which the ornament was tied behind his neck, and the stroke was so strong that the head of Jomala rang with such a great sound that they were all astonished. Karle seized the ornament, and they all hastened away. But the moment the sound was made the watchmen came forward upon the cleared space, and blew their horns. Immediately the sound of the loor[47] was heard all around from every quarter, calling the people together. They hastened to the forest, and rushed into it; and heard the shouts and cries on the other side of the Bjarmaland people in pursuit. Thorer Hund went the last of the whole troop; and before him went two men carrying a great sack between them, in which was something that was like ashes. Thorer took this in his hand, and strewed it upon the footpath, and sometimes over the people. They came thus out of the woods, and upon the fields, but heard incessantly the Bjarmaland people pursuing with shouts and dreadful yells. The army of the Bjarmaland people rushed out after them upon the field, and on both sides of them; but neither the people nor their weapons came so near as to do them any harm: from which they perceived that the Bjarmaland people did not see them. Now when they reached their ships Karle and his brother went on board; for they were the foremost, and Thorer was far behind on the land. As soon as Karle and his men were on board they struck their tents, cast loose their land ropes, hoisted their sails, and their ship in all haste went to sea. Thorer and his people, on the other hand, did not get on so quickly, as their vessel was heavier to manage; so that when they got under sail, Karle and his people were far off from land. Both vessels sailed across the White sea (Gandvik). The nights were clear, so that both ships sailed night and day; until one day, towards the time the day turns to shorten, Karle and his people took up the land near an island, let down the sail, cast anchor, and waited until the slack-tide set in, for there was a strong rost before them. Now Thorer came up, and lay at anchor there also. Thorer and his people then put out a boat, went into it, and rowed to Karle's ship. Thorer came on board, and the brothers saluted him. Thorer told Karle to give him the ornament. "I think," said he, "that I have best earned the ornaments that have been taken, for methinks ye have to thank me for getting away without any loss of men; and also I think thou, Karle, set us in the greatest fright."

Karle replies, "King Olaf has the half part of all the goods I gather on this voyage, and I intend the ornament for him. Go to him, if you like, and it is possible he will give thee the ornament, although I took it from Jomala."

47 Ludr–the loor–is a long tube or roll of birch-bark used as a horn by the herdboys in the mountains in Norway. –L.

Then Thorer insisted that they should go upon the island, and divide the booty.

Gunstein says, "It is now the turn of the tide, and it is time to sail." Whereupon they began to raise their anchor.

When Thorer saw that, he returned to his boat and rowed to his own ship. Karle and his men had hoisted sail, and were come a long way before Thorer got under way. They now sailed so that the brothers were always in advance, and both vessels made all the haste they could. They sailed thus until they came to Geirsver, which is the first roadstead of the traders to the North. They both came there towards evening, and lay in the harbour near the landing-place. Thorer's ship lay inside, and the brothers' the outside vessel in the port. When Thorer had set up his tents he went on shore, and many of his men with him. They went to Karle's ship, which was well provided. Thorer hailed the ship, and told the commanders to come on shore; on which the brothers, and some men with them, went on the land. Now Thorer began the same discourse, and told them to bring the goods they got in booty to the land to have them divided. The brothers thought that was not necessary, until they had arrived at their own neighbourhood. Thorer said it was unusual not to divide booty but at their own home, and thus to be left to the honour of other people. They spoke some words about it, but could not agree. Then Thorer turned away; but had not gone far before he came back, and tells his comrades to wait there. Thereupon he calls to Karle, and says he wants to speak with him alone. Karle went to meet him; and when he came near, Thorer struck at him with a spear, so that it went through him. "There," said Thorer, "now thou hast learnt to know a Bjarkey Island man. I thought thou shouldst feel Asbjorn's spear." Karle died instantly, and Thorer with his people went immediately on board their ship. When Gunstein and his men saw Karle fall they ran instantly to him, took his body and carried it on board their ship, struck their tents, and cast off from the pier, and left the land. When Thorer and his men saw this, they took down their tents and made preparations to follow. But as they were hoisting the sail the fastenings to the mast broke in two, and the sail fell down across the ship, which caused a great delay before they could hoist the sail again. Gunstein had already got a long way ahead before Thorer's ship fetched way, and now they used both sails and oars. Gunstein did the same. On both sides they made great way day and night; but so that they did not gain much on each other, although when they came to the small sounds among the islands Gunstein's vessel was lighter in turning. But Thorer's ship made way upon them, so that when they came up to Lengjuvik, Gunstein turned towards the land, and with all his men ran up into the country, and left his ship. A little after Thorer came there with his ship, sprang upon the land after them, and pursued them. There was a woman who helped Gunstein to conceal himself, and it is told that she was much acquainted with witchcraft. Thorer and his men returned to the vessels, and took all the goods out of Gunstein's vessel, and put on board stones in place of the cargo, and then hauled the ship out into the fjord, cut a hole in its bottom, and sank it to the bottom. Thereafter Thorer, with his people, returned home to Bjarkey Isle. Gunstein and his people proceeded in small boats at first, and lay concealed by day, until they had passed Bjarkey, and had got beyond Thorer's district. Gunstein went home first to Langey Isle for a short time, and then proceeded south without any halt, until he came south to Throndhjem, and there found King Olaf, to whom he told all that had happened on this Bjarmaland expedition. The king was ill-pleased with the voyage, but told Gunstein to remain with him, promising to assist him when opportunity offered. Gunstein took the invitation with thanks, and stayed with King Olaf.

144. MEETING OF KING OLAF AND KING ONUND.

King Olaf was, as before related, in Sarpsborg the winter (A.D. 1026) that King Canute was in Denmark. The Swedish king Onund rode across West Gautland the same winter, and had thirty hundred (3600) men with him. Men and messages passed between them; and they agreed to meet in spring at Konungahella. The meeting had been postponed, because they wished to know before they met what King Canute intended doing. As it was now approaching towards winter, King Canute made ready to go over to England with his forces, and left his son Hardaknut to rule in Denmark, and with him Earl Ulf, a son of Thorgils Sprakaleg. Ulf was married to Astrid, King Svein's daughter, and sister of Canute the Great. Their son Svein was afterwards king of Denmark. Earl Ulf was a very distinguished man. When the kings Olaf and Onund heard that Canute the Great had gone west to England, they hastened to hold their conference, and met at Konungahella, on the Gaut river. They had a joyful meeting, and had many friendly conversations, of which something might become known to the public; but they also spake often a great deal between themselves, with none but themselves two present, of which only some things afterwards were carried into effect, and thus became known to every one. At parting the kings presented each other with gifts, and parted the best of friends. King Onund went up into Gautland, and Olaf northwards to Viken, and afterwards to Agder, and thence northwards along the coast, but lay a long time at Egersund waiting a wind. Here he heard that Erling Skjalgson, and the inhabitants of Jadar with him, had assembled a large force. One day the king's people were talking among themselves whether the wind was south or south-west, and whether with that wind they could sail past Jadar or not. The most said it was impossible to fetch round. Then answers Haldor Brynjolfson, "I am of opinion that we would go round Jadar with this wind fast enough if Erling Skjalgson had prepared a feast for us at Sole." Then King Olaf ordered the tents to be struck, and the vessels to be hauled out, which was done. They sailed the same day past Jadar with the best wind, and in the evening reached Hirtingsey, from whence the king proceeded to Hordaland, and was entertained there in guest-quarters.

145. THORALF'S MURDER.

The same summer (A.D. 1026) a ship sailed from Norway to the Farey Islands, with messengers carrying a verbal message from King Olaf, that one of his court-men, Leif Ossurson, or Lagman Gille, or Thoralf of Dimun, should come over to him from the Farey Islands. Now when this message came to the Farey Islands, and was delivered to those whom it concerned, they held a meeting among themselves, to consider what might lie under this message, and they were all of opinion that the king wanted to inquire into the real state of the event which some said had taken place upon the islands; namely, the failure and disappearance of the former messengers of the king, and the loss of the two ships, of which not a man had been saved. It was resolved that Thoralf should undertake the journey. He got himself ready, and rigged out a merchant-vessel belonging to himself, manned with ten or twelve men. When it was ready, waiting a wind, it happened, at Austrey, in the house of Thrand of Gata, that he went one fine day into the room where his brother's two sons, Sigurd and Thord, sons of Thorlak, were lying upon the benches in the room. Gaut the Red was also there, who was one of their relations and a man of distinction. Sigurd was the oldest, and their leader in all things. Thord had a distinguished name, and was called Thord the Low, although in reality he was uncommonly tall, and yet in proportion more strong than large. Then Thrand said, "How many things are changed in the course of a man's life! When we were young, it was rare for young people who were able to do anything to sit or lie still upon a fine day, and our forefathers would scarcely have believed that Thoralf of Dimun would be bolder and more active than ye are. I believe the vessel I have standing here in the boat-house will be so old that it will rot under its coat of tar. Here are all the houses full of wool, which is neither used nor sold. It should not be so if I were a few winters younger." Sigurd sprang up, called upon Gaut and Thord, and said he would not endure Thrand's scoffs. They went out to the houseservants, and launched the vessel upon the water, brought down a cargo, and loaded the ship. They had no want of a cargo at home, and the vessel's rigging was in good order, so that in a few days they were ready for sea. There were ten or twelve men in the vessel. Thoralf's ship and theirs had the same wind, and they were generally in sight of each other. They came to the land at Herna in the evening, and Sigurd with his vessel lay outside on the strand, but so that there was not much distance between the two ships. It happened towards evening, when it was dark, that just as Thoralf and his people were preparing to go to bed, Thoralf and another went on shore for a certain purpose. When they were ready, they prepared to return on board. The man who had accompanied Thoralf related afterwards this story,–that a cloth was thrown over his head, and that he was lifted up from the ground, and he heard a great bustle. He was taken away, and thrown head foremost down; but there was sea under him, and he sank under the water. When he got to land, he went to the place where he and Thoralf had been parted, and there he found Thoralf with his head cloven down to his shoulders, and dead. When the ship's people heard of it they carried the body out to the ship, and let it remain there all night. King Olaf was at that time in guest-quarters at Lygra, and thither they sent a message. Now a Thing was called by message-token, and the king came to the Thing. He had also ordered the Farey people of both vessels to be summoned, and they appeared at the Thing. Now when the Thing was seated, the king stood up and said, "Here an event has happened which (and it is well that it is so) is very seldom heard of. Here has a good man been put to death, without any cause. Is there any man upon the Thing who can say who has done it?"

Nobody could answer.

"Then," said the king, "I cannot conceal my suspicion that this deed has been done by the Farey people themselves. It appears to me that it has been done in this way,–that Sigurd Thorlakson has killed the man, and Thord the Low has cast his comrade into the sea. I think, too, that the motives to this must have been to hinder Thoralf from telling about the misdeed of which he had information; namely, the murder which I suspect was committed upon my messengers."

When he had ended his speech, Sigurd Thorlakson stood up, and desired to be heard. "I have never before," said he, "spoken at a Thing, and I do not expect to be looked upon as a man of ready words. But I think there is sufficient necessity before me to reply something to this. I will venture to make a guess that the speech the king has made comes from some man's tongue who is of far less understanding and goodness than he is, and has evidently proceeded from those who are our enemies. It is speaking improbabilities to say that I could be Thoralf's murderer; for he was my foster-brother and good friend. Had the case been otherwise, and had there been anything outstanding between me and Thoralf, yet I am surely born with sufficient understanding to have done this deed in the Farey Islands, rather than here between your hands, sire. But I am ready to clear myself, and my whole ship's crew, of this act, and to make oath according to what stands in your laws. Or, if ye find it more satisfactory, I offer to clear myself by the ordeal of hot iron; and I wish, sire, that you may be present yourself at the proof."

When Sigurd had ceased to speak there were many who supported his case, and begged the king that Sigurd might be allowed to clear himself of this accusation. They thought that Sigurd had spoken well, and that the accusation against him might be untrue.

The king replies, "It may be with regard to this man very differently, and if he is belied in any respect he must be a good man; and if not, he is the boldest I have ever met with: and I believe this is the case, and that he will bear witness to it himself."

At the desire of the people, the king took Sigurd's obligation to take the iron ordeal; he should come the following day to Lygra, where the bishop should preside at the ordeal; and so the Thing closed. The king went back to Lygra, and Sigurd and his comrades to their ship.

As soon as it began to be dark at night Sigurd said to his ship's people. "To say the truth, we have come into a great misfortune; for a great lie is got up against us, and this king is a deceitful, crafty man. Our fate is easy to be foreseen where he rules; for first he made Thoralf be slain, and then made us the misdoers, without benefit of redemption by fine. For him it is an easy matter to manage the iron ordeal, so that I fear he will come ill off who tries it against him. Now there is coming a brisk mountain breeze, blowing right out of the sound and off the land; and it is my advice that we hoist our sail, and set out to sea. Let Thrand himself come with his wool to market another summer; but if I get away, it is my opinion I shall never think of coming to Norway again."

His comrades thought the advice good, hoisted their sail, and in the night-time took to the open sea with all speed. They did not stop until they came to Farey, and home to Gata. Thrand was ill-pleased with their voyage, and they did not answer him in a very friendly way; but they remained at home, however, with Thrand. The morning after, King Olaf heard of Sigurd's departure, and heavy reports went round about this case; and there were many who believed that the accusation against Sigurd was true, although they had denied and opposed it before the king. King Olaf spoke but little about the matter, but seemed to know of a certainty that the suspicion he had taken up was founded in truth. The king afterwards proceeded in his progress, taking up his abode where it was provided for him.

146. OF THE ICELANDERS.

King Olaf called before him the men who had come from Iceland, Thorod Snorrason, Geller Thorkelson, Stein Skaptason, and Egil Halson, and spoke to them thus:–"Ye have spoken to me much in summer about making yourselves ready to return to Iceland, and I have never given you a distinct answer. Now I will tell you what my intention is. Thee, Geller, I propose to allow to return, if thou wilt carry my message there; but none of the other Icelanders who are now here may go to Iceland before I have heard how the message which thou, Geller, shalt bring thither has been received."

When the king had made this resolution known, it appeared to those who had a great desire to return, and were thus forbidden, that they were unreasonably and hardly dealt with, and that they were placed in the condition of unfree men. In the meantime Geller got ready for his journey, and sailed in summer (A.D. 1026) to Iceland, taking with him the message he was to bring before the Thing the following summer (A.D. 1027). The king's message was, that he required the Icelanders to adopt the laws which he had set in Norway, also to pay him thane-tax and nose-tax[48]; namely, a penny for every nose, and the penny at the rate of ten pennies to the yard of wadmal[49]. At the same time he prom-

48 Nefgildi (nef=nose), a nose-tax or poll-tax payable to the king. This ancient "nose-tax" was also imposed by the Norsemen on conquered countries, the penalty for defaulters being the loss of their nose.

49 Wadmal was the coarse woollen cloth made in Iceland, and so generally used for clothing that it was a measure of value in the North, like money, for other commodities.–L.

ised them his friendship if they accepted, and threatened them with all his vengeance if they refused his proposals.

The people sat long in deliberation on this business; but at last they were unanimous in refusing all the taxes and burdens which were demanded of them. That summer Geller returned back from Iceland to Norway to King Olaf, and found him in autumn in the east in Viken, just as he had come from Gautland; of which I shall speak hereafter in this story of King Olaf. Towards the end of autumn King Olaf repaired north to Throndhjem, and went with his people to Nidaros, where he ordered a winter residence to be prepared for him. The winter (A.D. 1027) that he passed here in the merchant-town of Nidaros was the thirteenth year of his reign.

147. OF THE JAMTALAND PEOPLE.

There was once a man called Ketil Jamte, a son of Earl Onund of Sparby, in the Throndhjem district. He fled over the ridge of mountains from Eystein Illrade, cleared the forest, and settled the country now called the province of Jamtaland. A great many people joined him from the Throndhjem land, on account of the disturbances there; for this King Eystein had laid taxes on the Throndhjem people, and set his dog, called Saur, to be king over them. Thorer Helsing was Ketil's grandson, and he colonised the province called Helsingjaland, which is named after him. When Harald Harfager subdued the kingdom by force, many people fled out of the country from him, both Throndhjem people and Naumudal people, and thus new settlements were added to Jamtaland; and some settlers went even eastwards to Helsingjaland and down to the Baltic coast, and all became subjects of the Swedish king. While Hakon Athelstan's foster-son was over Norway there was peace, and merchant traffic from Throndhjem to Jamtaland; and, as he was an excellent king, the Jamtalanders came from the east to him, paid him scat, and he gave them laws and administered justice. They would rather submit to his government than to the Swedish king's, because they were of Norwegian race; and all the Helsingjaland people, who had their descent from the north side of the mountain ridge, did the same. This continued long after those times, until Olaf the Thick and the Swedish king Olaf quarrelled about the boundaries. Then the Jamtaland and Helsingjaland people went back to the Swedish king; and then the forest of Eid was the eastern boundary of the land, and the mountain ridge, or keel of the country, the northern: and the Swedish king took scat of Helsingjaland,

and also of Jamtaland. Now, thought the king of Norway, Olaf, in consequence of the agreement between him and the Swedish king, the scat of Jamtaland should be paid differently than before; although it had long been established that the Jamtaland people paid their scat to the Swedish king, and that he appointed officers over the country. The Swedes would listen to nothing, but that all the land to the east of the keel of the country belonged to the Swedish king. Now this went so, as it often happens, that although the kings were brothers-in-law and relations, each would hold fast the dominions which he thought he had a right to. King Olaf had sent a message round in Jamtaland, declaring it to be his will that the Jamtaland people should be subject to him, threatening them with violence if they refused; but the Jamtaland people preferred being subjects of the Swedish king.

148. STEIN'S STORY.

THE ICELANDERS, Thorod Snorrason and Stein Skaptason, were ill-pleased at not being allowed to do as they liked. Stein was a remarkably handsome man, dexterous at all feats, a great poet, splendid in his apparel, and very ambitious of distinction. His father, Skapte, had composed a poem on King Olaf, which he had taught Stein, with the intention that he should bring it to King Olaf. Stein could not now restrain himself from making the king reproaches in word and speech, both in verse and prose. Both he and Thorod were imprudent in their conversation, and said the king would be looked upon as a worse man than those who, under faith and law, had sent their sons to him, as he now treated them as men without liberty. The king was angry at this. One day Stein stood before the king, and asked if he would listen to the poem which his father Skapte had composed about him. The king replies, "Thou must first repeat that, Stein, which thou hast composed about me." Stein replies, that it was not the case that he had composed any. "I am no skald, sire," said he; "and if I even could compose anything, it, and all that concerns me, would appear to thee of little value." Stein then went out, but thought he perceived what the king alluded to. Thorgeir, one of the king's land-bailiffs, who managed one of his farms in Orkadal, happened to be present, and heard the conversation of the king and Stein, and soon afterwards Thorgeir returned home. One night Stein left the city, and his footboy with him. They went up Gaularas and into Orkadal. One evening they came to one of the king's farms which Thorgeir had the management of, and Thorgeir invited

Stein to pass the night there, and asked where he was travelling to. Stein begged the loan of a horse and sledge, for he saw they were just driving home corn.

Thorgeir replies, "I do not exactly see how it stands with thy journey, and if thou art travelling with the king's leave. The other day, methinks, the words were not very sweet that passed between the king and thee."

Stein said, "If it be so that I am not my own master for the king, yet I will not submit to such treatment from his slaves;" and, drawing his sword, he killed the landbailiff. Then he took the horse, put the boy upon him, and sat himself in the sledge, and so drove the whole night. They travelled until they came to Surnadal in More. There they had themselves ferried across the fjord, and proceeded onwards as fast as they could. They told nobody about the murder, but wherever they came called themselves king's men, and met good entertainment everywhere. One day at last they came towards evening to Giske Isle, to Thorberg Arnason's house. He was not at home himself, but his wife Ragnhild, a daughter of Erling Skjalgson, was. There Stein was well received, because formerly there had been great friendship between them. It had once happened, namely, that Stein, on his voyage from Iceland with his own vessel, had come to Giske from sea, and had anchored at the island. At that time Ragnhild was in the pains of childbirth, and very ill, and there was no priest on the island, or in the neighbourhood of it. There came a message to the merchant-vessel to inquire if, by chance, there was a priest on board. There happened to be a priest in the vessel, who was called Bard; but he was a young man from Westfjord, who had little learning. The messengers begged the priest to go with them, but he thought it was a difficult matter: for he knew his own ignorance, and would not go. Stein added his word to persuade the priest. The priest replies, "I will go if thou wilt go with me; for then I will have confidence, if I should require advice." Stein said he was willing; and they went forthwith to the house, and to where Ragnhild was in labour. Soon after she brought forth a female child, which appeared to be rather weak. Then the priest baptized the infant, and Stein held it at the baptism, at which it got the name of Thora; and Stein gave it a gold ring. Ragnhild promised Stein her perfect friendship, and bade him come to her whenever he thought he required her help. Stein replied that he would hold no other female child at baptism, and then they parted. Now it was come to the time when Stein required this kind promise of Ragnhild to be fulfilled, and he told her what had happened, and that the king's wrath had fallen upon him. She answered, that all the aid she could give should stand at his service; but bade him wait for Thorberg's arrival. She then showed him to a seat beside her son Eystein Orre, who was then twelve years old. Stein presented gifts to Ragnhild and Eystein. Thorberg had already heard how Stein had conducted himself before he got home, and was rather vexed at it. Ragnhild went to him, and told him how matters stood with Stein, and begged Thorberg to receive him, and take care of him.

Thorberg replies, "I have heard that the king, after sending out a message-token, held a Thing concerning the murder of Thorgeir, and has condemned Stein as having fled the country, and likewise that the king is highly incensed: and I have too much sense to take the cause of a foreigner in hand, and draw upon myself the king's wrath. Let Stein, therefore, withdraw from hence as quickly as thou canst."

Ragnhild replied, that they should either both go or both stay.

Thorberg told her to go where she pleased. "For I expect," said he, "that wherever thou goest thou wilt soon come back, for here is thy importance greatest."

Her son Eystein Orre then stood forward, and said he would not stay behind if Ragnhild goes.

Thorberg said that they showed themselves very stiff and obstinate in this matter. "And it appears that ye must have your way in it, since ye take it so near to heart; but thou art reckoning too much, Ragnhild, upon thy descent, in paying so little regard to King Olaf's word."

Ragnhild replied, "If thou art so much afraid to keep Stein with thee here, go with him to my father Erling, or give him attendants, so that he may get there in safety." Thorberg said he would not send Stein there; "for there are enough of things besides to enrage the king against Erling." Stein thus remained there all winter (A.D. 1027).

After Yule a king's messenger came to Thorberg, with the order that Thorberg should come to him before midsummer; and the order was serious and severe. Thorberg laid it before his friends, and asked their advice if he should venture to go to the king after what had taken place. The greater number dissuaded him, and thought it more advisable to let Stein slip out of his hands than to venture within the king's power: but Thorberg himself had rather more inclination not to decline the journey. Soon after Thorberg went to his brother Fin, told him the circumstances, and asked him to accompany him. Fin replied, that he thought it foolish to be so completely under woman's influence that he dared not, on account of his wife, keep the fealty and law of his sovereign.

"Thou art free," replied Thorberg, "to go with me or not; but I believe it is more fear of the king than love to him that keeps thee back." And so they parted in anger.

Then Thorberg went to his brother Arne Arnason, and asked him to go with him to the king. Arne says, "It appears to me wonderful that such a sensible, prudent man, should fall into such a misfortune, without necessity, as to incur the king's indignation. It might be excused if it were thy relation or foster-brother whom thou hadst thus sheltered; but not at all that thou shouldst take up an Iceland man, and harbour the king's outlaw, to the injury of thyself and all thy relations."

Thorberg replies, "It stands good, according to the proverb,–a rotten branch will be found in every tree. My father's greatest misfortune evidently was that he had such ill luck in producing sons that at last he produced one incapable of acting, and without any resemblance to our race, and whom in truth I never would have called brother, if it were not that it would have been to my mother's shame to have refused."

Thorberg turned away in a gloomy temper, and went home. Thereafter he sent a message to his brother Kalf in the Throndhjem district, and begged him to meet him at Agdanes; and when the messengers found Kalf he promised, without more ado, to make the journey. Ragnhild sent men east to Jadar to her father Erling, and begged him to send people. Erling's sons, Sigurd and Thord, came out, each with a ship of twenty benches of rowers and ninety men. When they came north Thorberg received them joyfully, entertained them well, and prepared for the voyage with them. Thorberg had also a vessel with twenty benches, and they steered their course northwards. When they came to the mouth of the Throndhjem fjord Thorberg's two brothers, Fin and Arne, were there already, with two ships each of twenty benches. Thorberg met his brothers with joy, and observed that his whetstone had taken effect; and Fin replied he seldom needed sharpening for such work. Then they proceeded north with all their forces to Throndhjem, and Stein was along with them. When they came to Agdanes, Kaff Arnason was there before them; and he also had a wellmanned ship of twenty benches. With this war-force they sailed up to Nidaros, where they lay all night. The morning after they had a consultation with each other. Kalf and Erling's sons were for attacking the town with all their forces, and leaving the event to fate; but Thorberg wished that they should first proceed with moderation, and make an offer; in which opinion Fin and Arne also concurred. It was accordingly resolved that Fin and Arne, with a few men, should first wait upon the king. The king had previously heard that they had come so strong in men, and was therefore very sharp in his speech. Fin offered to pay mulct for Thorberg, and also for Stein, and bade the king to fix what the penalties should be, however large; stipulating only for Thorberg safety and his fiefs, and for Stein life and limb.

The king replies, "It appears to me that ye come from home so equipped that ye can determine half as much as I can myself, or more; but this I expected least of all from you brothers, that ye should come against me with an army; and this counsel, I can observe, has its origin from the people of Jadar; but ye have no occasion to offer me money in mulct."

Fin replies, "We brothers have collected men, not to offer hostility to you, sire, but to offer rather our services; but if you will bear down Thorberg altogether, we must all go to King Canute the Great with such forces as we have."

Then the king looked at him, and said, "If ye brothers will give your oaths that ye will follow me in the country and out of the country, and not part from me without my leave and permission, and shall not conceal from me any treasonable design that may come to your knowledge against me, then will I agree to a peace with you brothers."

Then Fin returned to his forces, and told the conditions which the king had proposed to them. Now they held a council upon it, and Thorberg, for his part, said he would accept the terms offered. "I have no wish," says he, "to fly from my property, and seek foreign masters; but, on the contrary, will always consider it an honour to follow King Olaf, and be where he is." Then says Kalf, "I will make no oath to King Olaf, but will be with him always, so long as I retain my fiefs and dignities, and so long as the king will be my friend; and my opinion is that we should all do the same." Fin says, "we will venture to let King Olaf himself determine in this matter." Arne Arnason says, "I was resolved to follow thee, brother Thorberg, even if thou hadst given battle to King Olaf, and I shall certainly not leave thee for listening to better counsel; so I intend to follow thee and Fin, and accept the conditions ye have taken."

Thereupon the brothers Thorberg, Fin, and Arne, went on board a vessel, rowed into the fjord, and waited upon the king. The agreement went accordingly into fulfillment, so that the brothers gave their oaths to the king. Then Thorberg endeavored to make peace for Stein with the king; but the king replied that Stein might for him depart in safety, and go where he pleased, but "in my house he can never be again." Then Thorberg and his brothers went back to their men. Kalf went to Eggja, and Fin to the king; and Thorberg, with the other men, went south to their homes. Stein went with Erling's sons; but early in the spring (A.D. 1027) he went west to England into the service of Canute the Great, and was long with him, and was treated with great distinction.

149. FIN ARNASON'S EXPEDITION TO HALOGALAND.

Now when Fin Arnason had been a short time with King Olaf, the king called him to a conference, along with some other persons he usually held consultation with; and in this conference the king spoke to this effect:–"The decision remains fixed in my mind that in spring I should raise the whole country to a levy both of men and ships, and then proceed, with all the force I can muster, against King Canute the Great: for I know for certain that he does not intend to treat as a jest the claim he has awakened upon my kingdom. Now I let thee know my will, Fin Arnason, that thou proceed on my errand to Halogaland, and raise the people there to an expedition, men and ships, and summon that force to meet me at Agdanes." Then the king named other men whom he sent to Throndhjem, and some southwards in the country, and he commanded that this order should be circulated through the whole land. Of Fin's voyage we have to relate that he had with him a ship with about thirty men, and when he was ready for sea he prosecuted his journey until he came to Halogaland. There he summoned the bondes to a Thing, laid before them his errand, and craved a levy. The bondes in that district had large vessels, suited to a levy expedition, and they obeyed the king's message, and rigged their ships. Now when Fin came farther north in Halogaland he held a Thing again, and sent some of his men from him to crave a levy where he thought it necessary. He sent also men to Bjarkey Island to Thorer Hund, and there, as elsewhere, craved the quota to the levy. When the message came to Thorer he made himself ready, and manned with his house-servants the same vessel he had sailed with on his cruise to Bjarmaland, and which he equipped at his own expense. Fin summoned all the people of Halogaland who were to the north to meet at Vagar. There came a great fleet together in spring, and they waited there until Fin returned from the North. Thorer Hund had also come there. When Fin arrived he ordered the signal to sound for all the people of the levy to attend a House-Thing; and at it all the men produced their weapons, and also the fighting men from each ship-district were mustered. When that was all finished Fin said, "I have also to bring thee a salutation, Thorer Hund, from King Olaf, and to ask thee what thou wilt offer him for the murder of his court-man Karle, or for the robbery in taking the king's goods north in Lengjuvik. I have the king's orders to settle that business, and I wait thy answer to it."

Thorer looked about him, and saw standing on both sides many fully armed men, among whom were Gunstein and others of Karle's kindred. Then said Thorer, "My proposal is soon made. I will refer altogether to the king's pleasure the matter he thinks he has against me."

Fin replies, "Thou must put up with a less honour; for thou must refer the matter altogether to my decision, if any agreement is to take place."

Thorer replies, "And even then I think it will stand well with my case, and therefore I will not decline referring it to thee."

Thereupon Thorer came forward, and confirmed what he said by giving his hand upon it; and Fin repeated first all the words he should say.

Fin now pronounced his decision upon the agreement,–that Thorer should pay to the king ten marks of gold, and to Gunstein and the other kindred ten marks, and for the robbery and loss of goods ten marks more; and all which should be paid immediately.

Thorer says, "This is a heavy money mulct."

"Without it," replies Fin, "there will be no agreement."

Thorer says, there must time be allowed to gather so much in loan from his followers; but Fin told him to pay immediately on the spot; and besides, Thorer should lay down the great ornament which he took from Karle when he was dead. Thorer asserted that he had not got the ornament. Then Gunstein pressed forward, and said that Karle had the ornament around his neck when they parted, but it was gone when they took up his corpse. Thorer said he had not observed any ornament; but if there was any such thing, it must be lying at home in Bjarkey. Then Fin put the point of his spear to Thorer's breast, and said that he must instantly produce the ornament; on which Thorer took the ornament from his neck and gave it to Fin. Thereafter Thorer turned away, and went on board his ship. Fin, with many other men, followed him, went through the whole vessel, and took up the hatches. At the mast they saw two very large casks; and Fin asked, "What are these puncheons?"

Thorer replies, "It is my liquor."

Fin says, "Why don't you give us something to drink then, comrade, since you have so much liquor?"

Thorer ordered his men to run off a bowlfull from the puncheons, from which Fin and his people got liquor of the best quality. Now Fin ordered Thorer to pay the mulcts. Thorer went backwards and forwards through the ship, speaking now to the one, now to the other, and Fin calling out to produce the pence. Thorer begged him to go to the shore, and said he would bring the money there, and Fin with his men went on shore. Then Thorer came and paid silver; of which, from one purse, there were weighed ten marks. Thereafter Thorer brought many knotted nightcaps; and in some was one mark, in others half a mark, and in others some small money. "This is money my friends and other good people have lent me," said he; "for I think all my travelling money is gone." Then Thorer went back again to his ship, and returned, and paid the silver by little and little; and this lasted so long that the day was drawing towards evening. When the Thing had closed the people had gone to their vessels, and made ready to depart; and as fast as they were ready they hoisted sail and set out, so that most of them were under sail. When Fin saw that they were most of them under sail, he ordered his men to get ready too; but as yet little more than a third part of the mulct had been paid. Then Fin said, "This goes on very slowly, Thorer, with the payment. I see it costs thee a great deal to pay money. I shall now let it stand for the present, and what remains thou shalt pay to the king himself." Fin then got up and went away.

Thorer replies, "I am well enough pleased, Fin, to part now; but the good will is not wanting to pay this debt, so that both thou and the king shall say it is not unpaid."

Then Fin went on board his ship, and followed the rest of his fleet. Thorer was late before he was ready to come out of the harbour. When the sails were hoisted he steered out over Westfjord, and went to sea, keeping south along the land so far off that the hill-tops were half sunk, and soon the land altogether was sunk from view by the sea. Thorer held this course until he got into the English sea, and landed in England. He betook himself to King Canute forthwith, and was well received by him. It then came out that Thorer had with him a great deal of property; and, with other things, all the money he and Karle had taken in Bjarmaland. In the great liquor-casks there were sides within the outer sides, and the liquor was between them. The rest of the casks were filled with furs, and beaver and sable skins. Thorer was then with King Canute. Fin came with his forces to King Olaf, and related to him how all had gone upon his voyage, and told at the same time his suspicion that Thorer had left the country, and gone west to England to King Canute. "And there I fear he will cause as much trouble."

The king replies, "I believe that Thorer must be our enemy, and it appears to me always better to have him at a distance than near."

150. DISPUTE BETWEEN HAREK AND ASMUND.

ASMUND GRANKELSON HAD BEEN this winter (A.D. 1027) in Halogaland in his sheriffdom, and was at home with his father Grankel. There lies a rock out in the sea, on which there is both seal and bird catching, and a fishing ground, and egg-gathering; and from old times it had been an appendage to the farm which Grankel owned, but now Harek of Thjotta laid claim to it. It had gone so far, that some years he had taken by force all the gain of this rock; but Asmund and his father thought that they might expect the king's help in all cases in which the right was upon their side. Both father and son went therefore in spring to Harek, and brought him a message and tokens from King Olaf that he should drop his claim. Harek answered Asmund crossly, because he had gone to the king with such insinuations–"for the just right is upon my side. Thou shouldst learn moderation, Asmund, although thou hast so much confidence in the king's favour. It has succeeded with thee to kill some chiefs, and leave their slaughter unpaid for by any mulct; and also to plunder us, although we thought ourselves at least equal to all of equal birth, and thou art far from being my equal in family."

Asmund replies, "Many have experienced from thee, Harek, that thou art of great connections, and too great power; and many in consequence have suffered loss in their property through thee. But it is likely that now thou must turn thyself elsewhere, and not against us with thy violence, and not go altogether against law, as thou art now doing." Then they separated.

Harek sent ten or twelve of his house-servants with a large rowing boat, with which they rowed to the rock, took all that was to be got upon it, and loaded their boat. But when they were ready to return home, Asmund Grankelson came with thirty men, and ordered them to give up all they had taken. Harek's house-servants were not quick in complying, so that Asmund attacked them. Some of Harek's men were cudgelled, some wounded, some thrown into the sea, and all they had caught was taken from on board of their boat, and Asmund and his people took it along with them. Then Harek's servants came home, and told him the event. Harek replies, "That is called news indeed that seldom happens; never before has it happened that my people have been beaten."

The matter dropped. Harek never spoke about it, but was very cheerful. In spring, however, Harek rigged out a cutter of twenty seats of rowers, and manned it with his house-servants, and the ship was remarkably well fitted out both with people and all necessary equipment; and Harek went to the levy; but when he came to King Olaf, Asmund was there before him. The king summoned Harek and Asmund to him, and reconciled them so that they left the matter entirely to him. Asmund then produced witnesses to prove that Grankel had owned the rock, and the king gave judgment accordingly. The case had a one-sided result. No mulct was paid for Harek's house-servants, and the rock was declared to be Grankel's. Harek observed it was no disgrace to obey the king's decision, whatever way the case itself was decided.

151. THOROD'S STORY.

Thorod Snorrason had remained in Norway, according to King Olaf's commands, when Geller Thorkelson got leave to go to Iceland, as before related. He remained there (A.D. 1027) with King Olaf, but was ill pleased that he was not free to travel where he pleased. Early in winter, King Olaf, when he was in Nidaros, made it known that he would send people to Jamtaland to collect the scat; but nobody had any great desire to go on this business, after the fate of those whom King Olaf had sent before, namely, Thrand White and others, twelve in number, who lost their lives, as before related; and the Jamtalanders had ever since been subject to the Swedish king. Thorod Snorrason now offered to undertake this journey, for he cared little what became of him if he could but become his own master again. The king consented, and Thorod set out with eleven men in company. They came east to Jamtaland, and went to a man called Thorar, who was lagman, and a person in high estimation. They met with a hospitable reception; and when they had been there a while, they explained their business to Thorar. He replied, that other men and chiefs of the country had in all respects as much power and right to give an answer as he had, and for that purpose he would call together a Thing. It was so done; the message-token was sent out, and a numerous Thing assembled. Thorar went to the Thing, but the messengers in the meantime remained at home. At the Thing, Thorar laid the business before the people, but all were unanimous that no scat should be paid to the king of Norway; and some were for hanging the messengers, others for sacrificing them to the gods. At last it was resolved to hold them fast until the king of Sweden's sheriffs arrived, and they could treat them as they pleased with consent of the people; and that, in the meantime, this decision should be concealed, and the messengers treated well, and detained under pretext that they must wait until the scat is collected; and that they should be separated, and placed two and two, as if for the convenience of boarding them. Thorod and another remained in Thorar's house. There was a great Yule feast and ale-drinking, to which each brought his own liquor; for there were many peasants in the village, who all drank in company together at Yule. There was another village not far distant, where Thorar's brother-in-law dwelt, who was a rich and powerful man, and had a grown-up son. The brothers-in-law intended to pass the Yule in drinking feasts, half of it at the house of the one and half with the other; and the feast began at Thorar's house. The brothers-in-law drank together, and Thorod and the sons of the peasants by themselves; and it was a drinking match. In the evening words arose, and comparisons between the men of Sweden and of Norway, and then between their kings both of former times and at the present, and of the manslaughters and robberies that had taken place between the countries. Then said the peasants sons, "If our king has lost most people, his sheriffs will make it even with the lives of twelve men when they come from the south after Yule; and ye little know, ye silly fools, why ye are kept here." Thorod took notice of these words, and many made jest about it, and scoffed at them and their king. When the ale began to talk out of the hearts of the Jamtalanders, what Thorod had before long suspected became evident. The day after Thorod and his comrade took all their clothes and weapons, and laid them ready; and at night, when the people were all asleep, they fled to the forest. The next morning, when the Jamtalanders were aware of their flight, men set out after them with dogs to trace them, and found them in a wood in which they had concealed themselves. They brought them home to a room in which there was a deep cellar, into which they were thrown, and the door locked upon them. They had little meat, and only the clothes they had on them. In the middle of Yule, Thorar, with all his freeborn men, went to his brother's-in-law, where he was to be a guest until the last of Yule. Thorar's slaves were to keep guard upon the cellar, and they were provided with plenty of liquor; but as they observed no moderation in drinking, they became towards evening confused in the head with the ale. As they were quite drunk, those who had to bring meat to the prisoners in the cellar said among themselves that they should want for nothing. Thorod amused the slaves by singing to them. They said he was a clever man, and gave him a large candle that was lighted; and the slaves who were in went to call the others to come in; but they were all so confused with the ale, that in going out they neither locked the cellar nor the room after them. Now Thorod and his comrades tore up their skin clothes in strips, knotted them together, made a noose at one end, and threw up the rope on the floor of the room. It fastened itself around a chest, by which they tried to haul themselves up. Thorod lifted up his comrade until he stood on his shoulders, and from thence scrambled up through the hatchhole. There was no want of ropes in the chamber, and he threw a rope down to Thorod; but when he tried to draw him up, he could not move him from the spot. Then Thorod told him to cast the rope over a cross-beam that was in the house, make a loop in it, and place as much wood and stones in the loop as would outweigh him; and the heavy weight went down into the cellar, and Thorod was drawn up by it. Now they took as much clothes as they required in the room; and among other things they took some reindeer hides, out of which they cut sandals, and bound them under their feet, with the hoofs of the reindeer feet trailing behind. But before they set off they set fire to a large corn barn which was close by, and then ran out into the pitch-dark night. The barn blazed, and set fire to many other houses in the village. Thorod and his comrade travelled the whole night until they came to a lonely wood, where they concealed themselves when it was daylight. In the morning they were missed. There was chase made with dogs to trace the footsteps all round the house; but the hounds always came back to the house, for they had the smell of the reindeer hoofs, and followed the scent back on the road that the hoofs had left, and therefore could not find the right direction. Thorod and his comrade wandered long about in the desert forest, and came one evening to a small house, and went in. A man and a woman were sitting by the fire. The man called himself Thorer, and said it was his wife who was sitting there, and the hut belonged to them. The peasant asked them to stop there, at which they were well pleased. He told them that he had come to this place, because he had fled from the inhabited district on account of a murder. Thorod and his comrade were well received, and they all got their supper at the fireside; and then the benches were cleared for them, and they lay down to sleep, but the fire was still burning with a clear light. Thorod saw a man come in from another house, and never had he seen so stout a man. He was dressed in a scarlet cloak beset with gold clasps, and was of very handsome appearance. Thorod heard him scold them for taking guests, when they had scarcely food for themselves. The housewife said, "Be not angry, brother; seldom such a thing happens; and rather do them some good too, for thou hast better opportunity to do so than we." Thorod heard also the stout man named by the name of Arnliot Gelline, and observed that the woman of the house was his sister. Thorod had heard speak of Arnliot as the greatest-of robbers and malefactors. Thorod and his companion slept the first part of the night, for they were wearied with walking; but when a third of the night was still to come, Arnliot awoke them, told them to get up, and make ready to depart. They arose immediately, put on their clothes, and some breakfast was given them; and Arnliot gave each of them also a pair of skees. Arnliot made himself ready to accompany them, and got upon his skees, which were both broad and long; but scarcely had he swung his skee-staff before he was a long way past them. He waited for them, and said they would make no progress in this way, and told them to stand upon the edge of his skees beside him. They did so. Thorod stood nearest to him, and held by Arnliot's belt, and his comrade held by him. Arnliot strode on as quickly with them both, as if he was alone and without any weight. The following day they came, towards night, to a lodge for travellers, struck fire, and prepared some food; but Arnliot told them to throw away nothing of their food, neither bones nor crumbs. Arnliot took a silver plate out of the pocket of his cloak, and ate from it. When they were done eating, Arnliot gathered up the remains of their meal, and they prepared to go to sleep. In the other end of the house there was a loft upon cross-beams, and Arnliot and the others went up, and laid themselves down to sleep. Arnliot had a large halberd, of which the upper part was mounted with gold, and the shaft was so long that with his arm stretched out he could scarcely touch the top of it; and he was girt with a sword. They had both their weapons and their clothes up in the loft beside them. Arnliot, who lay outermost in the loft, told them to be perfectly quiet. Soon after twelve men came to the house, who were merchants going with their wares to Jamtaland; and when they came into the house they made a great disturbance, were merry, and made a great fire before them; and when they took their supper they cast away all the bones around them. They then prepared to go to sleep, and laid themselves down upon the benches around the fire. When they, had been asleep a short time, a huge witch came into the house; and when she came in, she carefully swept together all the bones and whatever was of food kind into a heap, and threw it into her mouth. Then she gripped the man who was nearest to her, riving and tearing him asunder, and threw him upon the fire. The others awoke in dreadful fright, and sprang up, but she took them, and put them one by one to death, so that only one remained in life. He ran under the loft calling for help, and if there was any one on the loft to help him. Arnliot reached down his hand, seized him by the shoulder, and drew him up into the loft. The witch-wife had turned towards the fire, and began to eat the men who were roasting.

Now Arnliot stood up, took his halberd, and struck her between the shoulders, so that the point came out at her breast. She writhed with it, gave a dreadful shriek, and sprang up. The halberd slipped from Arnliot's hands, and she ran out with it. Arnliot then went in; cleared away the dead corpses out of the house; set the door and the door-posts up, for she had torn them down in going out; and they slept the rest of the night. When the day broke they got up; and first they took their breakfast. When they had got food, Arnliot said, "Now we must part here. Ye can proceed upon the new-traced path the merchants have made in coming here yesterday. In the meantime I will seek after my halberd, and in reward for my labour I will take so much of the goods these men had with them as I find useful to me. Thou, Thorod, must take my salutation to King Olaf; and say to him that he is the man I am most desirous to see, although my salutation may appear to him of little worth." Then he took his silver plate, wiped it dry with a cloth, and said, "Give King Olaf this plate; salute him, and say it is from me." Then they made themselves ready for their journey, and parted. Thorod went on with his comrade and the man of the merchants company who had escaped. He proceeded until he came to King Olaf in the town (Nidaros); told the king all that had happened, and presented to him the silver plate. The king said it was wrong that Arnliot himself had not come to him; "for it is a pity so brave a hero, and so distinguished a man, should have given himself up to misdeeds."

Thorod remained the rest of the winter with the king, and in summer got leave to return to Iceland; and he and King Olaf parted the best of friends.

152. KING OLAF'S LEVY OF MEN.

King Olaf made ready in spring (A.D. 1027) to leave Nidaros, and many people were assembled about him, both from Throndhjem and the Northern country; and when he was ready he proceeded first with his men to More, where he gathered the men of the levy, and did the same at Raumsdal. He went from thence to South More. He lay a long time at the Herey Isles waiting for his forces; and he often held House-things, as many reports came to his ears about which he thought it necessary to hold councils. In one of these Things he made a speech, in which he spoke of the loss he suffered from the Farey islanders. "The scat which they promised me," he said, "is not forthcoming; and I now intend to send men thither after it." Then he proposed to different men to undertake this expedition; but the answer was, that all declined the adventure.

Then there stood up a stout and very remarkable looking man in the Thing. He was clad in a red kirtle, had a helmet on his head, a sword in his belt, and a large halberd in his hands. He took up the word and said, "In truth here is a great want of men. Ye have a good king; but ye are bad servants who say no to this expedition he offers you, although ye have received many gifts of friendship and tokens of honour from him. I have hitherto been no friend of the king, and he has been my enemy, and says, besides, that he has good grounds for being so. Now, I offer, sire, to go upon this expedition, if no better will undertake it."

The king answers, "Who is this brave man who replies to my offer? Thou showest thyself different from the other men here present, in offering thyself for this expedition from which they excuse themselves, although I expected they would willingly have undertaken it; but I do not know thee in the least, and do not know thy name."

He replies, "My name, sire, is not difficult to know, and I think thou hast heard my name before. I am Karl Morske."

The king–"So this is Karl! I have indeed heard thy name before; and, to say the truth, there was a time when our meeting must have been such, if I had had my will; that thou shouldst not have had to tell it now. But I will not show myself worse than thou, but will join my thanks and my favour to the side of the help thou hast offered me. Now thou shalt come to me, Karl, and be my guest to-day; and then we shall consult together about this business." Karl said it should be so.

153. KARL MORSKE'S STORY.

Karl Morske had been a viking, and a celebrated robber. Often had the king sent out men against him, and wished to make an end of him; but Karl, who was a man of high connection, was quick in all his doing's, and besides a man of great dexterity, and expert in all feats. Now when Karl had undertaken this business the king was reconciled to him, gave him his friendship, and let him be fitted out in the best manner for this expedition. There were about twenty men in the ship; and the king sent messages to his friends in the Farey Islands, and recommended him also to Leif Ossurson and Lagman Gille, for aid and defence; and for this purpose furnished Karl with tokens of the full powers given him. Karl set out as soon as he was ready; and as he got a favourable breeze soon came to the Farey Islands, and landed at Thorshavn, in the island Straumey. A

Thing was called, to which there came a great number of people. Thrand of Gata came with a great retinue, and Leif and Gille came there also, with many in their following. After they had set up their tents, and put themselves in order, they went to Karl Morske, and saluted each other on both sides in a friendly way. Then Karl produced King Olaf's words, tokens, and friendly message to Leif and Gille, who received them in a friendly manner, invited Karl to come to them, and promised him to support his errand, and give him all the aid in their power, for which he thanked them. Soon after came Thrand of Gata, who also received Karl in the most friendly manner, and said he was glad to see so able a man coming to their country on the king's business, which they were all bound to promote. "I will insist, Karl," says he, "on thy taking-up thy winter abode with me, together with all those of thy people who may appear to thee necessary for thy dignity."

Karl replies, that he had already settled to lodge with Leif; "otherwise I would with great pleasure have accepted thy invitation."

"Then fate has given great honour to Leif," says Thrand; "but is there any other way in which I can be of service?"

Karl replies, that he would do him a great service by collecting the scat of the eastern island, and of all the northern islands.

Thrand said it was both his duty and interest to assist in the king's business, and thereupon Thrand returned to his tent; and at that Thing nothing else worth speaking of occurred. Karl took up his abode with Leif Ossurson, and was there all winter (A.D. 1028). Leif collected the scat of Straumey Island, and all the islands south of it. The spring after Thrand of Gata fell ill, and had sore eyes and other complaints; but he prepared to attend the Thing, as was his custom. When he came to the Thing he had his tent put up, and within it another black tent, that the light might not penetrate. After some days of the Thing had passed, Leif and Karl came to Thrand's tent, with a great many people, and found some persons standing outside. They asked if Thrand was in the tent, and were told he was. Leif told them to bid Thrand come out, as he and Karl had some business with him. They came back, and said that Thrand had sore eyes, and could not come out; "but he begs thee, Leif, to come to him within." Leif told his comrades to come carefully into the tent, and not to press forward, and that he who came last in should go out first. Leif went in first, followed by Karl, and then his comrades; and all fully armed as if they were going into battle. Leif went into the black tent and asked if Thrand was there. Thrand answered and saluted Leif. Leif returned his salutation, and asked if he had brought the scat from the northern islands, and if he would pay the scat that had been collected. Thrand replies, that he had not forgotten what had been spoken of between him and Karl, and that he would now pay over the scat. "Here is a purse, Leif, full of silver, which thou canst receive." Leif looked around, and saw but few people in the tent, of whom some were lying upon the benches, and a few were sitting up. Then Leif went to Thrand, and took the purse, and carried it into the outer tent, where it was light, turned out the money on his shield, groped about in it with his hand, and told Karl to look at the silver. When they had looked at it a while, Karl asked Leif what he thought of the silver. He replied, "I am thinking where the bad money that is in the north isles can have come from." Thrand heard this, and said, "Do you not think, Leif, the silver is good?" "No," says he. Thrand replies, "Our relations, then, are rascals not to be trusted. I sent them in spring to collect the scat in the north isles, as I could not myself go anywhere, and they have allowed themselves to be bribed by the bondes to take false money, which nobody looks upon as current and good; it is better, therefore, Leif, to look at this silver which has been paid me as land-rent." Leif thereupon carried back this silver, and received another bag, which he carried to Karl, and they looked over the money together. Karl asked Leif what he thought of this money. He answered, that it appeared to him so bad that it would not be taken in payment, however little hope there might be of getting a debt paid in any other way: "therefore I will not take this money upon the king's account." A man who had been lying on the bench now cast the skin coverlet off which he had drawn over his head, and said, "True is the old word,–he grows worse who grows older: so it is with thee, Thrand, who allowest Karl Morske to handle thy money all the day." This was Gaut the Red. Thrand sprang up at Gaut's words, and reprimanded his relation with many angry words. At last he said that Leif should leave this silver, and take a bag which his own peasants had brought him in spring. "And although I am weak-sighted, yet my own hand is the truest test." Another man who was lying on the bench raised himself now upon his elbow; and this was Thord the Low. He said, "These are no ordinary reproaches we suffer from Karl Morske, and therefore he well deserves a reward for them." Leif in the meantime took the bag, and carried it to Karl; and when they cast their eyes on the money, Leif said, "We need not look long at this silver, for here the one piece of money is better than the other; and this is the money we will have. Let a man come to be present at the counting it out." Thrand says that he thought Leif was the fittest man to do it upon his account. Leif and Karl thereupon went a short way from the tent, sat down, and counted and weighed the silver. Karl took the helmet off his head, and received in it the weighed silver. They saw a man coming to them who had a stick with an axe-head on it in his hand, a hat low upon his head, and a short green cloak. He was bare-legged, and had linen breeches on tied at the knee. He laid his stick down in the field, and went to Karl and said, "Take care, Karl Morske, that thou does not hurt thyself against my axe-stick." Immediately a man came running and calls with great haste to Leif Ossurson, telling him to come as quickly as possible to Lagman Gille's tent; "for," says he, "Sirurd Thorlakson ran in just now into the mouth of the tent, and gave one of Gille's men a desperate wound." Leif rose up instantly, and went off to Gille's tent along with his men. Karl remained sitting, and the Norway people stood around in all corners. Gaut immediately sprang up, and struck with a hand-axe over the heads of the people, and the stroke came on Karl's head; but the wound was slight. Thord the Low seized the stick-axe, which lay in the field at his side, and struck the axe-blade right into Karl's skull. Many people now streamed out of Thrand's tent. Karl was carried away dead. Thrand was much grieved at this event, and offered money-mulcts for his relations; but Leif and Gille, who had to prosecute the business, would accept no mulct. Sigurd was banished the country for having wounded Gille's tent comrade, and Gaut and Thord for the murder of Karl. The Norway people rigged out the vessel which Karl had with him, and sailed eastward to Olaf, and gave him these tidings. He was in no pleasant humour at it, and threatened a speedy vengeance; but it was not allotted by fate to King Olaf to revenge himself on Thrand and his relations, because of the hostilities which had begun in Norway, and which are now to be related. And there is nothing more to be told of what happened after King Olaf sent men to the Farey Islands to take scat of them. But great strife arose after Karl's death in the Farey Islands between the family of Thrand of Gata and Leif Ossurson, and of which there are great sagas.

154. KING OLAF'S EXPEDITION WITH HIS LEVY.

Now we must proceed with the relation we began before,–that King Olaf set out with his men, and raised a levy over the whole country (A.D. 1027). All lendermen in the North followed him excepting Einar Tambaskelfer, who sat quietly at home upon his farm since his return to the country, and did not serve the king. Einar had great estates and wealth, although he held no fiefs from the king, and he lived splendidly. King Olaf sailed with his fleet south around Stad, and many people from the districts around joined him. King Olaf himself had a ship which he had got built the winter before (A.D. 1027), and which was called the Visund[50]. It was a very large ship, with a bison's head gilded all over upon the bow. Sigvat the skald speaks thus of it:–

"Trygvason's Long Serpent bore,
Grim gaping o'er the waves before,
A dragon's head with open throat,
When last the hero was afloat:
His cruise was closed,
As God disposed.
Olaf has raised a bison's head,
Which proudly seems the waves to tread.
While o'er its golden forehead dashing
The waves its glittering horns are washing:
May God dispose
A luckier close."

The king went on to Hordaland; there he heard the news that Erling Skjalgson had left the country with a great force, and four or five ships. He himself had a large war-ship, and his sons had three of twenty rowing-banks each; and they had sailed westward to England to Canute the Great. Then King Olaf sailed eastward along the land with a mighty war-force, and he inquired everywhere if anything was known of Canute's proceedings; and all agreed in saying he was in England but added that he was fitting out a levy, and intended coming to Norway. As Olaf had a large fleet, and could not discover with certainty where he should go to meet King Canute, and as his people were dissatisfied with lying quiet in one place with so large an armament, he resolved to sail with his fleet south to Denmark, and took with him all the men who were best appointed and most warlike; and he gave leave to the others to return home. Now the people whom he thought of little use having gone home, King Olaf had many excellent and stout men-at-arms besides those who, as before related, had fled the country, or sat quietly at home; and most of the chief men and lendermen of Norway were along with him.

50 Visundr is the buffalo; although the modern bison, or American animal of that name, might have been known through the Greenland colonists, who in this reign had visited some parts of America.–L.

155. OF KING OLAF AND KING ONUND.

When King Olaf sailed to Denmark, he set his course for Seeland; and when he came there he made incursions on the land, and began to plunder. The country people were severely treated; some were killed, some bound and dragged to the ships. All who could do so took to flight, and made no opposition. King Olaf committed there the greatest ravages. While Olaf was in Seeland, the news came that King Onund Olafson of Sweden had raised a levy, and fallen upon Scania, and was ravaging there; and then it became known what the resolution had been that the two kings had taken at the Gaut river, where they had concluded a union and friendship, and had bound themselves to oppose King Canute. King Onund continued his march until he met his brother-in-law King Olaf. When they met they made proclamation both to their own people and to the people of the country, that they intended to conquer Denmark; and asked the support of the people of the country for this purpose. And it happened, as we find examples of everywhere, that if hostilities are brought upon the people of a country not strong enough to withstand, the greatest number will submit to the conditions by which peace can be purchased at any rate. So it happened here that many men went into the service of the kings, and agreed to submit to them. Wheresoever they went they laid the country all round subjection to them, and otherwise laid waste all with fire and sword.

Of this foray Sigvat the skald speaks, in a ballad he composed concerning King Canute the Great:–

"'Canute is on the sea!'
The news is told,
And the Norsemen bold
Repeat it with great glee.
And it runs from mouth to mouth–
'On a lucky day
We came away
From Throndhjem to the south.'
Across the cold East sea,
The Swedish king
His host did bring,
To gain great victory.
King Onund came to fight,
In Seeland's plains,
Against the Danes,

With his steel-clad men so bright.
Canute is on the land;
Side to side
His long-ships ride
Along the yellow strand.
Where waves wash the green banks,
Mast to mast,
All bound fast,
His great fleet lies in ranks."

156. OF KING CANUTE THE GREAT.

King Canute had heard in England that King Olaf of Norway had called out a levy, and had gone with his forces to Denmark, and was making great ravages in his dominions there. Canute began to gather people, and he had speedily collected a great army and a numerous fleet. Earl Hakon was second in command over the whole.

Sigvat the skald came this summer (A.D. 1027) from the West, from Ruda (Rouen) in Valland, and with him was a man called Berg. They had made a merchant voyage there the summer before. Sigvat had made a little poem about this journey, called "The Western Traveller's Song," which begins thus:–

"Berg! many a merry morn was pass'd,
When our vessel was made fast,
And we lay on the glittering tide
or Rouen river's western side."

When Sigvat came to England he went directly to King Canute, and asked his leave to proceed to Norway; for King Canute had forbidden all merchant vessels to sail until he himself was ready with his fleet. When Sigvat arrived he went to the house in which the king was lodged; but the doors were locked, and he had to stand a long time outside, but when he got admittance he obtained the permission he desired. He then sang:–

"The way to Jutland's king I sought;
A little patience I was taught.
The doors were shut–all full within;
The udaller could not get in.

But Gorm's great son did condescend
To his own chamber me to send,
And grant my prayer–although I'm one
Whose arms the fetters' weight have known."

When Sigvat became aware that King Canute was equipping an armament against King Olaf, and knew what a mighty force King Canute had, he made these lines:–

"The mighty Canute, and Earl Hakon,
Have leagued themselves, and counsel taken
Against King Olaf's life,
And are ready for the strife.
In spite of king and earl, I say,
'I love him well–may he get away:'
On the Fields, wild and dreary,
With him I'd live, and ne'er be weary."

Sigvat made many other songs concerning this expedition of Canute and Hakon. He made this among others:–

"'Twas not the earl's intention then
'Twixt Olaf and the udalmen
Peace to establish, and the land
Upright to hold with Northman's hand;
But ever with deceit and lies
Eirik's descendant, Hakon, tries
To make ill-will and discontent,
Till all the udalmen are bent
Against King Olaf's rule to rise."

157. OF KING CANUTE'S SHIP THE DRAGON.

CANUTE THE GREAT WAS at last ready with his fleet, and left the land; and a vast number of men he had, and ships frightfully large. He himself had a dragon-ship, so large that it had sixty banks of rowers, and the head was gilt all over. Earl Hakon had another dragon of forty banks, and it also had a gilt figure-head. The sails of both were in stripes of blue, red, and green, and the vessels were painted all above the water-stroke; and all that belonged to their equipment was most splendid. They had also many other huge ships remarkably well fitted out, and grand. Sigvat the skald talks of this in his song on Canute:–

"Canute is out beneath the sky–
Canute of the clear blue eye!
The king is out on the ocean's breast,
Leading his grand fleet from the West.
On to the East the ship-masts glide,
Glancing and bright each long-ship's side.
The conqueror of great Ethelred,
Canute, is there, his foemen's dread:
His dragon with her sails of blue,
All bright and brilliant to the view,
High hoisted on the yard arms wide,
Carries great Canute o'er the tide.
Brave is the royal progress–fast
The proud ship's keel obeys the mast,
Dashes through foam, and gains the land,
Raising a surge on Limfjord's strand."

It is related that King Canute sailed with this vast force from England, and came with all his force safely to Denmark, where he went into Limfjord, and there he found gathered besides a large army of the men of the country.

158. HARDAKNUT TAKEN TO BE KING IN DENMARK.

Earl Ulf Sprakalegson had been set as protector over Denmark when King Canute went to England, and the king had intrusted his son Hardaknut in the earl's hands. This took place the summer before (A.D. 1026), as we related. But the earl immediately gave it out that King Canute had, at parting, made known to him his will and desire that the Danes should take his son Hardaknut as king over the Danish dominions. "On that account," says the earl, "he gave the matter into our hands; as I, and many other chiefs and leading men here in the country, have often complained to King Canute of the evil consequences to the country of being without a king, and that former kings thought it honour and power enough to rule over the Danish kingdom alone; and in the times that are past many kings have ruled over this kingdom. But now there are greater difficulties than have ever been before; for we have been so fortunate hitherto as to live without disturbance from foreign kings, but now we hear the king of Norway is going to attack us, to which is added the fear of the people that the Swedish king will join him; and now King Canute is in England." The earl then produced King Canute's letter and seal, confirming all that the earl asserted. Many other chiefs supported this business; and in consequence of all these persuasions the people resolved to take Hardaknut as king, which was done at the same Thing. The Queen Emma had been principal promoter of this determination; for she had got the letter to be written, and provided with the seal, having cunningly got hold of the king's signet; but from him it was all concealed. Now when Hardaknut and Earl Ulf heard for certain that King Olaf was come from Norway with a large army, they went to Jutland, where the greatest strength of the Danish kingdom lies, sent out message-tokens, and summoned to them a great force; but when they heard the Swedish king was also come with his army, they thought they would not have strength enough to give battle to both, and therefore kept their army together in Jutland, and resolved to defend that country against the kings. The whole of their ships they assembled in Limfjord, and waited thus for King Canute. Now when they heard that King Canute had come from the West to Limfjord they sent men to him, and to Queen Emma, and begged her to find out if the king was angry at them or not, and to let them know. The queen talked over the matter with him, and said, "Your son Hardaknut will pay the full mulct the king may demand, if he has done anything which is thought to be against the king." He replies, that Hardaknut has not done this of his own judgement. "And therefore," says he, "it has turned out as might have been expected, that when he, a child, and without understanding, wanted to be called king, the country, when any evil came and an enemy appeared, must be conquered by foreign princes, if our might had not come to his aid. If he will have any reconciliation with me let him come to me, and lay down the mock title of king he has given himself." The queen sent these very words to Hardaknut, and at the same time she begged him not to decline coming; for, as she truly observed, he had no force to stand against his father. When this message came to Hardaknut he asked the advice of the earl and other chief people who were with him; but it was soon found that when the people heard King Canute the Old was arrived they all streamed to him, and seemed to have no confidence but in him alone. Then Earl Ulf and his fellows saw they had but two roads to take; either to go to the king and leave all to his mercy, or to fly the country. All pressed Hardaknut to go to his father, which advice he followed. When they met he fell at his father's feet, and laid his seal, which accompanied the kingly title, on his knee. King Canute took Hardaknut by the hand, and placed him in as high a seat as he used to sit in before. Earl Ulf sent his son Svein, who was a sister's son of King Canute, and the same age as Hardaknut, to the king. He prayed for grace and reconciliation for his father, and offered himself as hostage for the earl. King Canute ordered him to tell the earl to assemble his men and ships, and come to him, and then they would talk of reconciliation. The earl did so.

159. FORAY IN SCANIA.

WHEN KING OLAF AND King Onund heard that King Canute was come from the West, and also that he had a vast force, they sailed east to Scania, and allowed themselves to ravage and burn in the districts there, and then proceeded eastward along the land to the frontier of Sweden. As soon as the country people heard that King Canute was come from the West, no one thought of going into the service of the two kings.

Now the kings sailed eastward along the coast, and brought up in a river called Helga, and remained there some time. When they heard that King Canute was coming eastward with his forces against them, they held a council; and the result was, that King Olaf with his people went up the country to the forest, and to the lake out of which the river Helga flows. There at the riverhead they made a dam of timber and turf, and dammed in the lake. They also dug a deep ditch, through which they led several waters, so that the lake waxed very high. In the river-bed they laid large logs of timber. They were many days about this work, and King Olaf had the management of this piece of artifice; but King Onund had only to command the fleet and army. When King Canute heard of the proceedings of the two kings, and of the damage they had done to his dominions, he sailed right against them to where they lay in Helga river. He had a War-force which was one half greater than that of both the kings together. Sigvat speaks of these things:–

"The king, who shields
His Jutland fields
From scaith or harm
By foeman's arm,
Will not allow
Wild plundering now:
'The greatest he,
On land or sea.'"

160. BATTLE IN HELGA RIVER.

One day, towards evening, King Onund's spies saw King Canute coming sailing along, and he was not far off. Then King Onund ordered the war-horns to sound; on which his people struck their tents, put on their weapons, rowed out of the harbour and east round the land, bound their ships together, and prepared for battle. King Onund made his spies run up the country to look for King Olaf, and tell him the news. Then King Olaf broke up the dam, and let the river take its course. King Olaf travelled down in the night to his ships. When King Canute came outside the harbour, he saw the forces of the kings ready for battle. He thought that it would be too late in the day to begin the fight by the time his forces could be ready; for his fleet required a great deal of room at sea, and there was a long distance between the foremost of his ships and the hindmost, and between those outside and those nearest the land, and there was but little wind. Now, as Canute saw that the Swedes and Norwegians had quitted the harbour, he went into it with as many ships as it could hold; but the main strength of the fleet lay without the harbour. In the morning, when it was light, a great part of the men went on shore; some for amusement, some to converse with the people of other ships. They observed nothing until the water came rushing over them like a waterfall, carrying huge trees, which drove in among their ships, damaging all they struck; and the water covered all the fields. The men on shore perished, and many who were in the ships. All who could do it cut their cables; so that the ships were loose, and drove before the stream, and were scattered here and there. The great dragon, which King Canute himself was in, drove before the stream; and as it could not so easily be turned with oars, drove out among Olaf's and Onund's ships. As they knew the ship, they laid her on board on all quarters. But the ship was so high in the hull, as if it were a castle, and had besides such a numerous and chosen crew on board, well armed and exercised, that it was not easy to attack her. After a short time also Earl Ulf came up with his fleet; and then the battle began, and King Canute's fleet gathered together from all quarters. But the kings Olaf and Onund, seeing they had for this time got all the victory that fate permitted them to gain, let their ships retreat, cast themselves loose from King Canute's ship, and the fleets separated. But as the attack had not been made as King Canute had determined, he made no further attempt; and the kings on each side arranged their fleets and put their ships in order. When the fleets were parted, and each sailing its course, Olaf and Onund looked over their forces, and found they had suffered no loss of men. In the meantime they saw that if they waited until King Canute got his large fleet in order to attack them, the difference of force was so great that for them there was little chance of victory. It was also evident that if the battle was renewed, they must suffer a great loss of men. They took the resolution, therefore, to row with the whole fleet eastward along the coast. Observing that King Canute did not pursue them, they raised up their masts and set sail. Ottar Svarte tells thus of it in the poem he composed upon King Canute the Great:–

"The king, in battle fray,
Drove the Swedish host away:
The wolf did not miss prey,
Nor the raven on that day.
Great Canute might deride
Two kings if he had pride,
For at Helga river's side
They would not his sword abide."

Thord Sjarekson also sang these lines in his death song of King Olaf:–

"King Olaf, Agder's lord,
Ne'er shunned the Jutland king,
But with his blue-edged sword
Broke many a panzer ring.
King Canute was not slow:
King Onund filled the plain
With dead, killed by his bow:
The wolf howled o'er the slain."

161. KING OLAF AND KING ONUND'S PLANS.

King Olaf and King Onund sailed eastward to the Swedish king's dominions; and one day, towards evening, landed at a place called Barvik, where they lay all night. But then it was observed of the Swedes that they were home-sick; for the greater part of their forces sailed eastward along the land in the night, and did not stop their course until they came home to their houses. Now when King Onund observed this he ordered, as soon as the day dawned, to sound the signal for a House-thing; and the whole people went on shore, and the Thing sat down. Then King Onund took up the word, and spake thus: "So it is, King

Olaf, that, as you know, we have been assembled in summer, and have forayed wide around in Denmark, and have gained much booty, but no land. I had 350 vessels, and now have not above 100 remaining with me. Now it appears to me we can make no greater progress than we have made, although you have still the 60 vessels which have followed you the whole summer. It therefore appears to me best that we come back to my kingdom; for it is always good to drive home with the wagon safe. In this expedition we have won something, and lost nothing. Now I will offer you, King Olaf, to come with me, and we shall remain assembled during the winter. Take as much of my kingdom as you will, so that you and the men who follow you may support yourselves well; and when spring comes let us take such measures as we find serviceable. If you, however, will prefer to travel across our country, and go overland to Norway, it shall be free for you to do so."

King Olaf thanked King Onund for his friendly offer. "But if I may advise," says he, "then we should take another resolution, and keep together the forces we have still remaining. I had in the first of summer, before I left Norway, 350 ships; but when I left the country I chose from among the whole war-levy those I thought to be the best, and with them I manned 60 ships; and these I still have. Now it appears to me that the part of your war-force which has now run away is the most worthless, and of least resistance; but now I see here all your chiefs and leaders, and I know well that the people who belong to the court-troops[51] are by far the best suited to carry arms. We have here chosen men and superb ships, and we can very well lie all winter in our ships, as viking's custom is. But Canute cannot lie long in Helga river; for the harbour will not hold so many vessels as he has. If he steers eastward after us, we can escape from him, and then people will soon gather to us; but if he return to the harbours where his fleet can lie, I know for certain that the desire to return home will not be less in his army than in ours. I think, also, we have ravaged so widely in summer, that the villagers, both in Scania and in Halland, know well whose favour they have to seek. Canute's army will thus be dispersed so widely, that it is uncertain to whom fate may at the last give the victory; but let us first find out what resolution he takes."

Thus King Olaf ended his speech, and it found much applause, and his advice was followed. Spies were sent into King Canute's army, and both the kings Olaf and Onund remained lying where they were.

51 The thingmen, or hired body-guard attending the court.–L.

162. OF KING CANUTE AND EARL ULF.

When King Canute saw that the kings of Norway and Sweden steered eastward with their forces along the coast, he sent men to ride night and day on the land to follow their movements. Some spies went forward, others returned; so that King Canute had news every day of their progress. He had also spies always in their army. Now when he heard that a great part of the fleet had sailed away from the kings, he turned back with his forces to Seeland, and lay with his whole fleet in the Sound; so that a part lay on the Scania side, and a part on the Seeland side. King Canute himself, the day before Michaelmas, rode with a great retinue to Roeskilde. There his brother-in-law, Earl Ulf, had prepared a great feast for him. The earl was the most agreeable host, but the king was silent and sullen. The earl talked to him in every way to make him cheerful, and brought forward everything which he thought would amuse him; but the king remained stern, and speaking little. At last the earl proposed to him a game at chess, which he agreed to; and a chess-board was produced, and they played together. Earl Ulf was hasty in temper, stiff, and in nothing yielding; but everything he managed went on well in his hands; and he was a great warrior, about whom there are many stories. He was the most powerful man in Denmark next to the king. Earl Ulf's sister Gyda was married to Earl Gudin (Godwin) Ulfnadson; and their sons were Harald king of England, and Earl Toste, Earl Valthiof, Earl Morukare, and Earl Svein. Gyda was the name of their daughter, who was married to the English king Edward the Good.

163. OF THE EARL'S MURDER.

When they had played a while the king made a false move, at which the earl took a knight from the king; but the king set the piece again upon the board, and told the earl to make another move; but the earl grew angry, threw over the chess-board, stood up, and went away. The king said, "Runnest thou away, Ulf the coward?" The earl turned round at the door and said, "Thou wouldst have run farther at Helga river, if thou hadst come to battle there. Thou didst not call me Ulf the coward, when I hastened to thy help while the Swedes were beating thee like a dog." The earl then went out, and went to bed. A little later the king also went to bed. The following morning while the king was putting on his clothes he said to his footboy, "Go thou to Earl Ulf, and kill him."

The lad went, was away a while, and then came back.

The king said, "Hast thou killed the earl?"

"I did not kill him, for he was gone to Saint Lucius' church."

There was a man called Ivar White, a Norwegian by birth, who was the king's courtman and chamberlain. The king said to him, "Go thou and kill the earl."

Ivar went to the church, and in at the choir, and thrust his sword through the earl, who died on the spot. Then Ivar went to the king, with the bloody sword in his hand.

The king said, "Hast thou killed the earl?"

"I have killed him," says he.

"Thou didst well."

After the earl was killed the monks closed the church, and locked the doors. When that was told the king he sent a message to the monks, ordering them to open the church and sing high mass. They did as the king ordered; and when the king came to the church he bestowed on it great property, so that it had a large domain, by which that place was raised very high; and these lands have since always belonged to it. King Canute rode down to his ships, and lay there till late in harvest with a very large army.

164. OF KING OLAF AND THE SWEDES.

When King Olaf and King Onund heard that King Canute had sailed to the Sound, and lay there with a great force, the kings held a House-thing, and spoke much about what resolution they should adopt. King Olaf wished they should remain there with all the fleet, and see what King Canute would at last resolve to do. But the Swedes held it to be unadvisable to remain until the frost set in, and so it was determined; and King Onund went home with all his army, and King Olaf remained lying after them.

165. OF EGIL AND TOFE.

While King Olaf lay there, he had frequently conferences and consultations with his people. One night Egil Halson and Tofe Valgautson had the watch upon the king's ship. Tofe came from West Gautland, and was a man of high birth. While they sat on watch they heard much lamentation and crying among the people who had been taken in the war, and who lay bound on the shore at night. Tofe said it made him ill to hear such distress, and asked Egil to go with him, and let loose these people. This work they set about, cut the cords, and let the people escape, and they looked upon it as a piece of great friendship; but the king was so enraged at it, that they themselves were in the greatest danger. When Egil afterwards fell sick the king for a long time would not visit him, until many people entreated it of him. It vexed Egil much to have done anything the king was angry at, and he begged his forgiveness. The king now dismissed his wrath against Egil, laid his hands upon the side on which Egil's pain was, and sang a prayer; upon which the pain ceased instantly, and Egil grew better. Tofe came, after entreaty, into reconciliation with the king, on condition that he should exhort his father Valgaut to come to the king. He was a heathen; but after conversation with the king he went over to Christianity, and died instantly when he was baptized.

166. TREACHERY TOWARDS KING OLAF.

King Olaf had now frequent conferences with his people, and asked advice from them, and from his chiefs, as to what he should determine upon. But there was no unanimity among them–some considering that unadvisable which others considered highly serviceable; and there was much indecision in their councils. King Canute had always spies in King Olaf's army, who entered into conversation with many of his men, offering them presents and favour on account of King Canute. Many allowed themselves to be seduced, and gave promises of fidelity, and to be King Canute's men, and bring the country into his hands if he came to Norway. This was apparent, afterwards, of many who at first kept it concealed. Some took at once money bribes, and others were promised money afterwards; and a great many there were who had got great presents of money from him before: for it may be said with truth of King Canute, that every man who came to him, and who he thought had the spirit of a man and would like his favour, got his hands full of gifts and money. On this account he was very popular, although his generosity was principally shown to foreigners, and was greatest the greater distance they came from.

167. KING OLAF'S CONSULTATIONS.

King Olaf had often conferences and meetings with his people, and asked their counsel; but as he observed they gave different opinions, he had a suspicion that there must be some who spoke differently from what they really thought advisable for him, and he was thus uncertain if all gave him due fidelity in council. Some pressed that with the first fair wind they should sail to the Sound, and so to Norway. They said the Danes would not dare to attack them, although they lay with so great a force right in the way. But the king was a man of too much understanding not to see that this was impracticable. He knew also that Olaf Trygvason had found it quite otherwise, as to the Danes not daring to fight, when he with a few people went into battle against a great body of them. The king also knew that in King Canute's army there were a great many Norwegians; therefore he entertained the suspicion that those who gave this advice were more favourable to King Canute than to him. King Olaf came at last to the determination, from all these considerations, that the people who would follow him should make themselves ready to proceed by land across Gautland, and so to Norway. "But our ships," said he, "and all things that we cannot take with us, I will send eastward to the Swedish king's dominions, and let them be taken care of for us there."

168. HAREK OF THJOTTA'S VOYAGE.

Harek of Thjotta replied thus to the king's speech: "It is evident that I cannot travel on foot to Norway. I am old and heavy, and little accustomed to walking. Besides, I am unwilling to part with my ship; for on that ship and its apparel I have bestowed so much labour, that it would go much against my inclination to put her into the hands of my enemies." The king said, "Come along with us, Harek, and we shall carry thee when thou art tired of walking." Then Harek sang these lines:–

"I'11 mount my ocean steed,
And o'er the sea I'll speed;
Forests and hills are not for me,–
I love the moving sea,
Though Canute block the Sound,
Rather than walk the ground,
And leave my ship, I'll see
What my ship will do for me."

Then King Olaf let everything be put in order for the journey. The people had their walking clothing and weapons, but their other clothes and effects they packed upon such horses as they could get. Then he sent off people to take his ships east to Calmar. There he had the vessels laid up, and the ships' apparel and other goods taken care of. Harek did as he had said, and waited for a wind, and then sailed west to Scania, until, about the decline of the day, he came with a fresh and fair wind to the eastward of Holar. There he let the sail and the vane, and flag and mast be taken down, and let the upper works of the ship be covered over with some grey tilt-canvas, and let a few men sit at the oars in the fore part and aft, but the most were sitting low down in the vessel.

When Canute's watchmen saw the ship, they talked with each other about what ship it might be, and made the guess that it must be one loaded with herrings or salt, as they only saw a few men at the oars; and the ship, besides, appeared to them grey, and wanting tar, as if burnt up by the sun, and they saw also that it was deeply loaded. Now when Harek came farther through the Sound, and past the fleet, he raised the mast, hoisted sail, and set up his gilded vane. The sail was white as snow, and in it were red and blue stripes of cloth interwoven. When the king's men saw the ship sailing in this state, they told the king that probably King Olaf had sailed through them. But King Canute replies, that King Olaf was too prudent a man to sail with a single ship through King Canute's fleet, and thought it more likely to be Harek of Thjotta, or the like of him. Many believed the truth to be that King Canute knew of this expedition of Harek, and that it would not have succeeded so if they had not concluded a friendship beforehand with each other; which seemed likely, after King Canute's and Harek's friendly understanding became generally known.

Harek made this song as he sailed northward round the isle of Vedrey:–

"The widows of Lund may smile through their tears,
The Danish girls may have their jeers;
They may laugh or smile,
But outside their isle
Old Harek still on to his North land steers."

Harek went on his way, and never stopped till he came north to Halogaland, to his own house in Thjotta.

169. KING OLAF'S COURSE FROM SVITHJOD.

When King Olaf began his journey, he came first into Smaland, and then into West Gautland. He marched quietly and peaceably, and the country people gave him all assistance on his journey. Thus he proceeded until he came into Viken, and north through Viken to Sarpsborg, where he remained, and ordered a winter abode to be prepared (A.D. 1028). Then he gave most of the chiefs leave to return home, but kept the lendermen by him whom he thought the most serviceable. There were with him also all the sons of Arne Arnmodson, and they stood in great favour with the king. Geller Thorkelson, who the summer before had come from Iceland, also came there to the king, as before related.

170. OF SIGVAT THE SKALD.

Sigvat the skald had long been in King Olaf's household, as before related, and the king made him his marshal. Sigvat had no talent for speaking in prose; but in skaldcraft he was so practised, that the verses came as readily from his tongue as if he were speaking in usual language. He had made a mercantile journey to Normandy, and in the course of it had come to England, where he met King Canute, and obtained permission from him to sail to Norway, as before related. When he came to Norway he proceeded straight to King Olaf, and found him at Sarpsborg. He presented himself before the king just as he was sitting down to table. Sigvat saluted him. The king looked at Sigvat and was silent. Then Sigvat sang:–

"Great king! thy marshal is come home,
No more by land or sea to roam,
  But by thy side
  Still to abide.
Great king! what seat here shall he take
For the king's honour–not his sake?
  For all seats here
  To me are dear."

Then was verified the old saying, that "many are the ears of a king;" for King Olaf had heard all about Sigvat's journey, and that he had spoken with Canute. He says to Sigvat, "I do not know if thou art my marshal, or hast become one of Canute's men." Sigvat said:–

"Canute, whose golden gifts display
A generous heart, would have me stay,
Service in his great court to take,
And my own Norway king forsake.
Two masters at a time, I said,
Were one too many for men bred
Where truth and virtue, shown to all,
Make all men true in Olaf's hall."

Then King Olaf told Sigvat to take his seat where he before used to sit; and in a short time Sigvat was in as high favour with the king as ever.

171. OF ERLING SKJALGSON AND HIS SONS.

ERLING SKJALGSON AND ALL his sons had been all summer in King Canute's army, in the retinue of Earl Hakon. Thorer Hund was also there, and was in high esteem. Now when King Canute heard that King Olaf had gone overland to Norway, he discharged his army, and gave all men leave to go to their winter abodes. There was then in Denmark a great army of foreigners, both English, Norwegians, and men of other countries, who had joined the expedition in summer. In autumn (A.D. 1027) Erling Skjalgson went to Norway with his men, and received great presents from King Canute at parting; but Thorer Hund remained behind in King Canute's court. With Erling went messengers from King Canute well provided with money; and in winter they travelled through all the country, paying the money which King Canute had promised to many in autumn for their assistance. They gave presents in money, besides, to many whose friendship could be purchased for King Canute. They received much assistance in their travels from Erling. In this way it came to pass that many turned their support to King Canute, promised him their services, and agreed to oppose King Olaf. Some did this openly, but many more concealed it from the public. King Olaf heard this news, for many had something to tell him about it; and the conversation in the court often turned upon it. Sigvat the skald made a song upon it:-

"The base traitors ply
With purses of gold,
Wanting to buy
What is not to be sold,-

The king's life and throne
Wanting to buy:
But our souls are our own,
And to hell we'll not hie.
No pleasure in heaven,
As we know full well,
To the traitor is given,–
His soul is his hell."

Often also the conversation turned upon how ill it beseemed Earl Hakon to raise his hand in arms against King Olaf, who had given him his life when he fell into the king's power; but Sigvat was a particular friend of Earl Hakon, and when he heard the earl spoken against he sang:–

"Our own court people we may blame,
If they take gold to their own shame,
Their king and country to betray.
With those who give it's not the same,
From them we have no faith to claim:
'Tis we are wrong, if we give way."

172. OF KING OLAF'S PRESENTS AT YULE.

King Olaf gave a great feast at Yule, and many great people had come to him. It was the seventh day of Yule, that the king, with a few persons, among whom was Sigvat, who attended him day and night, went to a house in which the king's most precious valuables were kept. He had, according to his custom, collected there with great care the valuable presents he was to make on New Year's eve. There was in the house no small number of gold-mounted swords; and Sigvat sang:–

"The swords stand there,
All bright and fair,–
Those oars that dip in blood:
If I in favour stood,
I too might have a share.
A sword the skald would gladly take,
And use it for his master's sake:
In favour once he stood,
And a sword has stained in blood."

The king took a sword of which the handle was twisted round with gold, and the guard was gold-mounted, and gave it to him. It was a valuable article; but the gift was not seen without envy, as will appear hereafter.

Immediately after Yule (1028) the king began his journey to the Uplands; for he had a great many people about him, but had received no income that autumn from the North country, for there had been an armament in summer, and the king had laid out all the revenues he could command; and also he had no vessels with which he and his people could go to the North. At the same time he had news from the North, from which he could see that there would be no safety for him in that quarter, unless he went with a great force. For these reasons he determined to proceed through the Uplands, although it was not so long a time since he had been there in guest-quarters as the law prescribes, and as the kings usually had the custom of observing in their visits. When he came to the Uplands the lendermen and the richest bondes invited him to be their guest, and thus lightened his expenses.

173. OF BJORN THE BAILIFF.

THERE WAS A MAN called Bjorn who was of Gautland family, and a friend and acquaintance of Queen Astrid, and in some way related to her. She had given him farm-management and other offices in the upper part of Hedemark. He had also the management of Osterdal district. Bjorn was not in esteem with the king, nor liked by the bondes. It happened in a hamlet which Bjorn ruled over, that many swine and cattle were missing: therefore Bjorn ordered a Thing to be called to examine the matter. Such pillage he attributed chiefly to the people settled in forest-farms far from other men; by which he referred particularly to those who dwelt in Osterdal, for that district was very thinly inhabited, and full of lakes and forest-cleanings, and but in few places was any great neighbourhood together.

174. OF RAUD'S SONS.

THERE WAS A MAN called Raud who dwelt in Osterdal. His wife was called Ragnhild; and his sons, Dag and Sigurd, were men of great talent. They were present at the Thing, made a reply in defence of the Osterdal people, and removed the accusation from them. Bjorn thought they were too pert in their answer, and too fine in their clothes and weapons; and therefore turned his speech against these brothers, and said it was not unlikely they may have committed these thefts. They denied it, and the Thing closed. Soon after King Olaf, with his retinue, came to guest-quarters in the house of bailiff Bjorn. The matter which had been before the Thing was then complained of to the king; and Bjorn said that Raud's sons appeared to him to have committed these thefts. A messenger was sent for Raud's sons; and when they appeared before the king he said they had not at all the appearance of thieves, and acquitted them. Thereupon they invited the king, with all his retinue, to a three days' entertainment at their father's; and although Bjorn dissuaded him from it, the king went. At Raud's there was a very excellent feast. The king asked Raud what people he and his wife were. Raud answered that he was originally a Swedish man, rich and of high birth; "but I ran away with the wife I have ever since had, and she is a sister of King Hring Dagson." The king then remembered both their families. He found that father and sons were men of understanding, and asked them what they could do. Sigurd said he could interpret dreams, and determine the time of the day although no heavenly bodies could be seen. The king made trial of his art, and found it was as Sigurd had said. Dag stated, as his accomplishment, that he could see the misdeeds and vices of every man who came under his eye, when he chose to observe him closely. The king told him to declare what faults of disposition he saw in the king himself. Dag mentioned a fault which the king was sensible he really had. Then the king asked what fault the bailiff Bjorn had. Dag said Bjorn was a thief; and told also where Bjorn had concealed on his farm the bones, horns, and hides of the cattle he had stolen in autumn; "for he committed," said Dag, "all the thefts in autumn which he accuses other people of." Dag also told the king the places where the king should go after leaving them. When the king departed from Raud's house he was accompanied on the way, and presented with friendly gifts; and Raud's sons remained with the king. The king went first to Bjorn's, and found there that all Dag had told him was true. Upon which he drove Bjorn out of the country; and he had to thank the queen that he preserved life and limbs.

175. THORER'S DEATH.

Thorer, a son of Olver of Eggja, a stepson of Kalf Arnason, and a sister's son of Thorer Hund, was a remarkably handsome man, stout and strong. He was at this time eighteen years old; had made a good marriage in Hedemark, by which he got great wealth; and was besides one of the most popular of men, and formed to be a chief. He invited the king and his retinue home to him to a feast. The king accepted the invitation, went to Thorer's, and was well received. The entertainment was very splendid; they were excellently treated, and all that was set before the guests was of the best that could be got. The king and his people talked among themselves of the excellence of everything, and knew not what they should admire the most,–whether Thorer's house outside, or the inside furniture, the table service, or the liquors, or the host who gave them such a feast. But Dag said little about it. The king used often to speak to Dag, and ask him about various things; and he had proved the truth of all that Dag had said, both of things that had happened or were to happen, and therefore the king had much confidence in what he said. The king called Dag to him to have a private conversation together, and spoke to him about many things. Afterwards the king turned the conversation on Thorer,–what an excellent man Thorer was, and what a superb feast he had made for them. Dag answered but little to this, but agreed it was true what the king said. The king then asked Dag what disposition or faith he found in Thorer. Dag replied that he must certainly consider Thorer of a good disposition, if he be really what most people believe him to be. The king told him to answer direct what he was asked, and said that it was his duty to do so. Dag replies, "Then thou must allow me to determine the punishment if I disclose his faith." The king replied that he would not submit his decision to another man, but again ordered Dag to reply to what he asked.

Dag replies, "The sovereign's order goes before all. I find this disposition in Thorer, as in so many others, that he is too greedy of money."

The king: "Is he then a thief, or a robber?"

"He is neither."

"What is he then?"

"To win money he is a traitor to his sovereign. He has taken money from King Canute the Great for thy head."

The king asks, "What proof hast thou of the truth of this?"

Dag: "He has upon his right arm, above the elbow, a thick gold ring, which King Canute gave him, and which he lets no man see."

This ended their conference, and the king was very wroth. Now as the king sat at table, and the guests had drunk a while with great mirth, and Thorer went round to see the guests well served, the king ordered Thorer to be called to him. He went up before the table, and laid his hands upon it.

The king asked, "How old a man art thou, Thorer?"

He answered, "I am eighteen years old."

"A stout man thou art for those years, and thou hast been fortunate also."

Then the king took his right hand, and felt it towards the elbow.

Thorer said, "Take care, for I have a boil upon my arm."

The king held his hand there, and felt there was something hard under it. "Hast thou not heard," said he, "that I am a physician? Let me see the boil."

As Thorer saw it was of no use to conceal it longer, he took off the ring and laid it on the table.

The king asked if that was the gift of King Canute.

Thorer replied that he could not deny it was.

The king ordered him to be seized and laid in irons. Kalf came up and entreated for mercy, and offered money for him, which also was seconded by many; but the king was so wroth that nobody could get in a word. He said Thorer should suffer the doom he had prepared for himself. Thereupon he ordered Thorer to be killed. This deed was much detested in the Uplands, and not less in the Throndhjem country, where many of Thorer's connections were. Kalf took the death of this man much to heart, for he had been his foster-son in childhood.

176. THE FALL OF GRJOTGARD.

Grjotgard Olverson, Thorer's brother, and the eldest of the brothers, was a very wealthy man, and had a great troop of people about him. He lived also at this time in Hedemark. When he heard that Thorer had been killed, he made an attack upon the places where the king's goods and men were; but, between whiles, he kept himself in the forest and other secret places. When the king heard of this disturbance, he had inquiry made about Grjotgard's haunts, and found out that he had taken up night-quarters not far from where the king was. King Olaf set out in the night-time, came there about day-dawn, and placed a circle of men round the house in which Grjotgard was sleeping. Grjotgard and his men, roused by the stir of people and clash of arms, ran to their weapons, and Grjotgard himself sprang to the front room. He asked who commanded the troop; and it was answered him, "King Olaf was come there." Grjotgard asked if the king would hear his words. The king, who stood at the door, said that Grjotgard might speak what he pleased, and he would hear his words. Grjotgard said, "I do not beg for mercy;" and at the same moment he rushed out, having his shield over his head, and his drawn sword in his hand. It was not so much light that he could see clearly. He struck his sword at the king; but Arnbjorn ran in, and the thrust pierced him under his armour into his stomach, and Arnbjorn got his deathwound. Grjotgard was killed immediately, and most of his people with him. After this event the king turned back to the south to Viken.

177. KING OLAF SENDS FOR HIS SHIPS AND GOODS.

Now WHEN THE KING came to Tunsberg he sent men out to all the districts, and ordered the people out upon a levy. He had but a small provision of shipping, and there were only bondes' vessels to be got. From the districts in the near neighbourhood many people came to him, but few from any distance; and it was soon found that the people had turned away from the king. King Olaf sent people to Gautland for his ships, and other goods and wares which had been left there in autumn; but the progress of these men was very slow, for it was no better now than in autumn to sail through the Sound, as King Canute had in spring fitted out an army throughout the whole of the Danish dominions, and had no fewer than 1200 vessels.

178. KING OLAF'S COUNSELS.

THE NEWS CAME TO Norway that King Canute had assembled an immense armament through all Denmark, with which he intended to conquer Norway. When this became known the people were less willing to join King Olaf, and he got but little aid from the bondes. The king's men often spoke about this among themselves. Sigvat tells of it thus:–

"Our men are few, our ships are small,
While England's king is strong in all;
But yet our king is not afraid–
O! never be such king betrayed!
'Tis evil counsel to deprive
Our king of countrymen to strive

To save their country, sword in hand:
Tis money that betrays our land."

The king held meetings with the men of the court, and sometimes House-things with all his people, and consulted with them what they should, in their opinion, undertake. "We must not conceal from ourselves," said he, "that Canute will come here this summer; and that he has, as ye all know, a large force, and we have at present but few men to oppose to him; and, as matters now stand, we cannot depend much on the fidelity of the country people." The king's men replied to his speech in various ways; but it is said that Sigvat the skald replied thus, advising flight, as treachery, not cowardice, was the cause of it:–

"We may well fly, when even our foe
Offers us money if we go.
I may be blamed, accused of fear;
But treachery, not faith, rules here.
Men may retire who long have shown
Their faith and love, and now alone
Retire because they cannot save–
This is no treachery in the brave."

179. HAREK OF THJOTTA BURNS GRANKEL AND HIS MEN.

The same spring (A.D. 1028) it happened in Halogaland that Harek of Thjotta remembered how Asmund Grankelson had plundered and beaten his house-servants. A cutter with twenty rowing-benches, which belonged to Harek, was afloat in front of the house, with tent and deck, and he spread the report that he intended to go south to Throndhjem. One evening Harek went on board with his house-servants, about eighty men, who rowed the whole night; and he came towards morning to Grankel's house, and surrounded it with his men. They then made an attack on the house, and set fire to it; and Grankel with his people were burnt, and some were killed outside; and in all about thirty men lost their lives. After this deed Harek returned home, and sat quietly in his farm. Asmund was with King Olaf when he heard of it; therefore there was nobody in Halogaland to sue Harek for mulct for this deed, nor did he offer any satisfaction.

180. KING CANUTE'S EXPEDITION TO NORWAY.

Canute the Great collected his forces, and went to Limfjord. When he was ready with his equipment he sailed from thence with his whole fleet to Norway; made all possible speed, and did not land to the eastward of the Fjords, but crossed Folden, and landed in Agder, where he summoned a Thing. The bondes came down from the upper country to hold a Thing with Canute, who was everywhere in that country accepted as king. Then he placed men over the districts, and took hostages from the bondes, and no man opposed him. King Olaf was in Tunsberg when Canute's fleet sailed across the mouth of the fjord. Canute sailed northwards along the coast, and people came to him from all the districts, and promised him fealty. He lay a while in Egersund, where Erling Skjalgson came to him with many people, and King Canute and Erling renewed their league of friendship. Among other things, Canute promised Erling the whole country between Stad and Rygiarbit to rule over. Then King Canute proceeded; and, to be short in our tale, did not stop until he came to Throndhjem, and landed at Nidaros. In Throndhjem he called together a Thing for the eight districts, at which King Canute was chosen king of all Norway. Thorer Hund, who had come with King Canute from Denmark, was there, and also Harek of Thjotta; and both were made sheriffs of the king, and took the oath of fealty to him. King Canute gave them great fiefs, and also right to the Lapland trade, and presented them besides with great gifts. He enriched all men who were inclined to enter into friendly accord with him both with fiefs and money, and gave them greater power than they had before.

181. OF KING CANUTE.

When King Canute had laid the whole of Norway trader his authority, he called together a numerous Thing, both of his own people and of the people of the country; and at it he made proclamation, that he made his relation Earl Hakon the governor-in-chief of all the land in Norway that he had conquered in this expedition. In like manner he led his son Hardaknut to the high-seat at his side, gave him the title of king, and therewith the whole Danish dominion. King Canute took as hostages from all lendermen and great bondes in Norway either their sons, brothers, or other near connections, or the men who were dearest to them and appeared to him most suitable; by which he, as before observed, secured their fidelity to him. As soon as Earl Hakon had attained this power in Norway his brother-in-law, Einar Tambaskelfer, made an agreement with him, and received back all the fiefs he formerly had possessed while the earls ruled the country. King Canute gave Einar great gifts, and bound him by great kindness to his interests; and promised that Einar should be the greatest and most important man in Norway, among those who did not hold the highest dignity, as long as he had power over the country. He added to this, that Einar appeared to him the most suitable man to hold the highest title of honour in Norway if no earls remained, and his son Eindride also, on account of his high birth. Einar placed a great value on these promises, and, in return, promised the greatest fidelity. Einar's chiefship began anew with this.

182. OF THORARIN LOFTUNGA.

There was a man by name Thorarin Loftunga, an Icelander by birth, and a great skald, who had been much with the kings and other great chiefs. He was now with King Canute the Great, and had composed a flock, or short poem, in his praise. When the king heard of this he was very angry, and ordered him to bring the next day a drapa, or long poem, by the time he went to table; and if he failed to do so, said the king, "he shall be hanged for his impudence in composing such a small poem about King Canute." Thorarin then composed a stave as a refrain, which he inserted in the poem, and also augmented it with several other strophes or verses. This was the refrain:–

"Canute protects his realm, as Jove,
Guardian of Greece, his realm above."

King Canute rewarded him for the poem with fifty marks of silver. The poem was called the "Headransom" ("Hofudlausn"). Thorarin composed another poem about King Canute, which was called the "Campaign Poem" ("Togdrapa"); and therein he tells King Canute's expedition when he sailed from Denmark to Norway; and the following are strophes from one of the parts of this poem:–

"Canute with all his men is out,
Under the heavens in war-ships stout,–
'Out on the sea, from Limfjord's green,
My good, my brave friend's fleet is seen.

The men of Adger on the coast
Tremble to see this mighty host:
The guilty tremble as they spy
The victor's fleet beneath the sky.

"The sight surpasses far the tale,
As glacing in the sun they sail;
The king's ship glittering all with gold,
And splendour there not to be told.
Round Lister many a coal-black mast
Of Canute's fleet is gliding past.
And now through Eger sound they ride,
Upon the gently heaving tide.

"And all the sound is covered o'er
With ships and sails, from shore to shore,
A mighty king, a mighty host,
Hiding the sea on Eger coast.
And peaceful men in haste now hie
Up Hiornagla-hill the fleet to spy,
As round the ness where Stad now lies
Each high-stemmed ship in splendour flies.

"Nor seemed the voyage long, I trow,
To warrior on the high-built bow,
As o'er the ocean-mountains riding
The land and hill seem past him gliding.
With whistling breeze and flashing spray
Past Stein the gay ships dashed away;
In open sea, the southern gale
Filled every wide out-bellying sail.

"Still on they fly, still northward go,
Till he who conquers every foe,
The mighty Canute, came to land,
Far in the north on Throndhjem's strand.
There this great king of Jutland race,
Whose deeds and gifts surpass in grace
All other kings, bestowed the throne
Of Norway on his sister's son.

"To his own son he gave the crown
(This I must add to his renown)
Of Denmark–land of shadowy vales,
In which the white swan trims her sails."

Here it is told that King Canute's expedition was grander than saga can tell; but Thorarin sang thus because he would pride himself upon being one of King Canute's retinue when he came to Norway.

183. OF THE MESSENGERS SENT BY KING OLAF FOR HIS SHIPS.

The men whom King Olaf had sent eastwards to Gautland after his ships took with them the vessels they thought the best, and burnt the rest. The ship-apparel and other goods belonging to the king and his men they also took with them; and when they heard that King Canute had gone to Norway they sailed west through the Sound, and then north to Viken to King Olaf, to whom they delivered his ships. He was then at Tunsberg. When King Olaf learnt that King Canute was sailing north along the coast, King Olaf steered with his fleet into Oslo fjord, and into a branch of it called Drafn, where he lay quiet until King Canute's fleet had sailed southwards again. On this expedition which King Canute made from the North along the coast, he held a Thing in each district, and in every Thing the country was bound by oath in fealty to him, and hostages were given him. He went eastward across the mouths of the fjords to Sarpsborg, and held a Thing there, and, as elsewhere, the country was surrendered to him under oath of fidelity. King Canute then returned south to Denmark, after having conquered Norway without stroke of sword, and he ruled now over three kingdoms. So says Halvard Hareksblese when he sang of King Canute:–

"The warrior-king, whose blood-stain'd shield
Has shone on many a hard-fought field,
England and Denmark now has won,
And o'er three kingdoms rules alone.
Peace now he gives us fast and sure,
Since Norway too is made secure
By him who oft, in days of yore,
Glutted the hawk and wolf with gore."

184. OF KING OLAF IN HIS PROCEEDINGS.

King Olaf sailed with his ships out to Tunsberg, as soon as he heard that King Canute had turned back, and was gone south to Denmark. He then made himself ready with the men who liked to follow him, and had then thirteen ships. Afterwards he sailed out along Viken; but got little money, and few men, as those only followed him who dwelt in islands, or on outlying points of land. The king landed in such places, but got only the money and men that fell in his way; and he soon perceived that the country had abandoned him. He proceeded on according to the winds. This was in the beginning of winter (A.D. 1029). The wind turned very late in the season in their favour, so that they lay long in the Seley islands, where they heard the news from the North, through merchants, who told the king that Erling Skjalgson had collected a great force in Jadar, and that his ship lay fully rigged outside of the land, together with many other vessels belonging to the bondes; namely, skiffs, fisher-yachts, and great row-boats. Then the king sailed with his fleet from the East, and lay a while in Egersund. Both parties heard of each other now, and Erling assembled all the men he could.

185. OF KING OLAF'S VOYAGE.

On Thomasmas, before Yule (Dec. 21), the king left the harbour as soon as day appeared. With a good but rather strong gale he sailed northwards past Jadar. The weather was rainy, with dark flying clouds in the sky. The spies went immediately in through the Jadar country when the king sailed past it; and as soon as Erling heard that the king was sailing past from the East, he let the war-horn call all the people on board, and the whole force hastened to the ships, and prepared for battle. The king's ship passed by Jadar at a great rate; but thereafter turned in towards the land, intending to run up the fjords to gather men and money. Erling Skjalgson perceived this, and sailed after him with a great force and many ships. Swiftly their vessels flew, for they had nothing on board but men and arms: but Erling's ship went much faster than the others; therefore he took in a reef in the sails, and waited for the other vessels. Then the king saw that Erling with his fleet gained upon him fast; for the king's ships were heavily laden, and were besides water-soaked, having been in the sea the whole summer, autumn, and winter, up to this time. He saw also that there would be a great want of men, if he should go against the whole of Erling's fleet when it was assembled. He hailed from ship to ship the orders to let the sails gently sink, and to unship the booms and outriggers, which was done. When Erling saw this he calls out to his people, and orders them to get on more sail. "Ye see," says he, "that their sails are diminishing, and they are getting fast away from our sight." He took the reef out of the sails of his ship, and outsailed all the others immediately; for Erling was very eager in his pursuit of King Olaf.

186. OF ERLING SKJALGSON'S FALL.

King Olaf then steered in towards the Bokn fjord, by which the ships came out of sight of each other. Thereafter the king ordered his men to strike the sails, and row forwards through a narrow sound that was there, and all the ships lay collected within a rocky point. Then all the king's men put on their weapons. Erling sailed in through the sound, and observed nothing until the whole fleet was before him, and he saw the king's men rowing towards him with all their ships at once. Erling and his crew let fall the sails, and seized their weapons; but the king's fleet surrounded his ship on all sides. Then the fight began, and it was of the sharpest; but soon the greatest loss was among Erling's men. Erling stood on the quarter-deck of his ship. He had a helmet on his head, a shield before him, and a sword in his hand. Sigvat the skald had remained behind in Viken, and heard the tidings. He was a great friend of Erling, had received presents from him, and had been at his house. Sigvat composed a poem upon Erling's fall, in which there is the following verse:–

"Erling has set his ship on sea–
Against the king away is he:
He who oft lets the eagle stain
Her yellow feet in blood of slain.
His little war-ship side by side
With the king's fleet, the fray will bide.
Now sword to sword the fight is raging,

Which Erling with the king is waging."

Then Erling's men began to fall, and at the same moment his ship was carried by boarding, and every man of his died in his place. The king himself was amongst the foremost in the fray. So says Sigvat:–

"The king's men hewed with hasty sword,–
The king urged on the ship to board,–
All o'er the decks the wounded lay:
Right fierce and bloody was that fray.
In Tungur sound, on Jadar shore,
The decks were slippery with red gore;
Warm blood was dropping in the sound,
Where the king's sword was gleaming round."

So entirely had Erling's men fallen, that not a man remained standing in his ship but himself alone; for there was none who asked for quarter, or none who got it if he did ask. There was no opening for flight, for there lay ships all around Erling's ship on every side, and it is told for certain that no man attempted to fly; and Sigvat says:–

"All Erling's men fell in the fray,
Off Bokn fjord, this hard-fought day.
The brave king boarded, onward cheered,
And north of Tungur the deck was cleared.
Erling alone, the brave, the stout,
Cut off from all, yet still held out;
High on the stern–a sight to see–
In his lone ship alone stood he."

Then Erling was attacked both from the forecastle and from the other ships. There was a large space upon the poop which stood high above the other ships, and which nobody could reach but by arrow-shot, or partly with the thrust of spear, but which he always struck from him by parrying. Erling defended himself so manfully, that no example is known of one man having sustained the attack of so many men so long. Yet he never tried to get away, nor asked for quarter. So says Sigvat:–

"Skjalg's brave son no mercy craves,–
The battle's fury still he braves;
The spear-storm, through the air sharp singing,
Against his shield was ever ringing.
So Erling stood; but fate had willed
His life off Bokn should be spilled.
No braver man has, since his day,
Past Bokn fjord ta'en his way."

When Olaf went back a little upon the fore-deck he saw Erling's behaviour; and the king accosted him thus:–"Thou hast turned against me to-day, Erling."

He replies, "The eagle turns his claws in defence when torn asunder." Sigvat the skald tells thus of these words of Erling:–

"Erling, our best defence of old,–
Erling the brave, the brisk, the bold,–
Stood to his arms, gaily crying,
'Eagles should show their claws, though dying:'
The very words which once before
To Olaf he had said on shore,
At Utstein when they both prepared
To meet the foe, and danger shared."

Then said the king, "Wilt thou enter into my service, Erling?"

"That I will," said he; took the helmet off his head, laid down his sword and shield, and went forward to the forecastle deck.

The king struck him in the chin with the sharp point of his battle-axe, and said, "I shall mark thee as a traitor to thy sovereign."

Then Aslak Fitiaskalle rose up, and struck Erling in the head with an axe, so that it stood fast in his brain, and was instantly his death-wound. Thus Erling lost his life.

The king said to Aslak, "May all ill luck attend thee for that stroke; for thou hast struck Norway out of my hands."

Aslak replied, "It is bad enough if that stroke displease thee, for I thought it was striking Norway into thy hands; and if I have given thee offence, sire, by this stroke, and have thy ill-will for it, it will go badly with me, for I will get so many men's ill-will and enmity for this deed that I would need all your protection and favour."

The king replied that he should have it.

Thereafter the king ordered every man to return to his ship, and to get ready to depart as fast as he could. "We will not plunder the slain," says he, "and each man may keep what he has taken." The men returned to the ships and prepared themselves for the departure as quickly as possible; and scarcely was this done before the vessels of the bondes ran in from the south into the sound. It went with the bonde-army as is often seen, that the men, although many in numbers, know not what to do when they have experienced a check, have lost their chief, and are without leaders. None of Erling's sons were there, and the bondes therefore made no attack, and the king sailed on his way northwards.

But the bondes took Erling's corpse, adorned it, and carried it with them home to Sole, and also the bodies of all who had fallen. There was great lamentation over Erling; and it has been a common observation among people, that Erling Skjalgson was the greatest and worthiest man in Norway of those who had no high title. Sigvat made these verses upon the occasion:–

"Thus Erling fell–and such a gain
To buy with such a loss was vain;
For better man than he ne'er died,
And the king's gain was small beside.
In truth no man I ever knew
Was, in all ways, so firm and true;
Free from servility and pride,
Honoured by all, yet thus he died."

Sigvat also says that Aslak had very unthinkingly committed this murder of his own kinsman:–

"Norway's brave defender's dead!
Aslak has heaped on his own head
The guilt of murdering his own kin:
May few be guilty of such sin!
His kinsman's murder on him lies–
Our forefathers, in sayings wise,
Have said, what is unknown to few,
'Kinsmen to kinsmen should be true.'"

187. OF THE INSURRECTION OF AGDER DISTRICT.

Of Erling's sons some at that time were north in Throndhjem, some in Hordaland, and some in the Fjord district, for the purpose of collecting men. When Erling's death was reported, the news came also that there was a levy raising in Agder, Hordaland, and Rogaland. Forces were raised and a great army assembled, under Erling's sons, to pursue King Olaf.

When King Olaf retired from the battle with Erling he went northward through the sounds, and it was late in the day. It is related that the king then made the following verses:–

"This night, with battle sounds wild ringing,
Small joy to the fair youth is bringing
Who sits in Jadar, little dreaming
O'er what this night the raven's screaming.
The far-descended Erling's life
Too soon has fallen; but, in the strife
He met the luck they well deserve
Who from their faith and fealty swerve."

Afterwards the king sailed with his fleet along the land northwards, and got certain tidings of the bondes assembling an army. There were many chiefs and lendermen at this time with King Olaf, and all the sons of Arne. Of this Bjarne Gullbrarskald speaks in the poem he composed about Kalf Arnason:–

"Kalf! thou hast fought at Bokn well;
Of thy brave doings all men tell:
When Harald's son his men urged on
To the hard strife, thy courage shone.
Thou soon hadst made a good Yule feast
For greedy wolf there in the East:
Where stone and spear were flying round,
There thou wast still the foremost found.
The people suffered in the strife
When noble Erling lost his life,
And north of Utstein many a speck
Of blood lay black upon the deck.
The king, 'tis clear, has been deceived,
By treason of his land bereaved;
And Agder now, whose force is great.
Will rule o'er all parts of the state."

King Olaf continued his voyage until he came north of Stad, and brought up at the Herey Isles. Here he heard the news that Earl Hakon had a great war-force in Throndhjem, and thereupon the king held a council with his people. Kalf Arnason urged much to advance to Throndhjem, and fight Earl Hakon, notwithstanding the difference of numbers. Many others supported this advice, but others dissuaded from it, and the matter was left to the king's judgment.

188. DEATH OF ASLAK FITIASKALLE.

Afterwards the king went into Steinavag, and remained there all night; but Aslak Fitiaskalle ran into Borgund, where he remained the night, and where Vigleik Arnason was before him. In the morning, when Aslak was about returning on board, Vigleik assaulted him, and sought to avenge Erling's murder. Aslak fell there. Some of the king's court-men, who had been home all summer, joined the king here. They came from Frekeysund, and brought the king tidings that Earl Hakon, and many lendermen with him, had come in the morning to Frekeysund with a large force; "and they will end thy days, sire, if they have strength enough." Now the king sent his men up to a hill that was near; and when they came to the top, and looked northwards to Bjarney Island, they perceived that a great armament of many ships was coming from the north, and they hastened back to the king with this intelligence. The king, who was lying there with only twelve ships, ordered the war-horn to sound, the tents to be taken down on his ships, and they took to their oars. When they were quite ready, and were leaving the harbour, the bonde army sailed north around Thiotande with twenty-five ships. The king then steered inside of Nyrfe Island, and inside of Hundsver. Now when King Olaf came right abreast of Borgund, the ship which Aslak had steered came out to meet him, and when they found the king they told him the tidings,–that Vigleik Arnason had killed Aslak Fitiaskalle, because he had killed Erling Skjalgson. The king took this news very angrily, but could not delay his voyage on account of the enemy and he sailed in by Vegsund and Skor. There some of his people left him; among others, Kalf Arnason, with many other lendermen and ship commanders, who all went to meet Earl Hakon. King Olaf, however, proceeded on his way without stopping until he came to Todar fjord, where he brought up at Valdal, and landed from his ship. He had then five ships with him, which he drew up upon the shore, and took care of their sails and materials. Then he set up his land-tent upon a point of land called Sult, where there are pretty flat fields, and set up a cross near to the point of land. A bonde, by name Bruse, who dwelt there in More, and was chief over the valley, came down to King Olaf, together with many other bondes, and received him well, and according to his dignity; and he was friendly, and pleased with their reception of him. Then the king asked if there was a passable road up in the country from the valley to Lesjar; and Bruse replied, that there was an urd in the valley called Skerfsurd not passable for man or beast. King Olaf answers, "That we must try, bonde, and it will go as God pleases. Come here in the morning with your yoke, and come yourself with it, and let us then see. When we come to the sloping precipice, what chance there may be, and if we cannot devise some means of coming over it with horses and people."

189. CLEARING OF THE URD.

Now when day broke the bondes drove down with their yokes, as the king had told them. The clothes and weapons were packed upon horses, but the king and all the people went on foot. He went thus until he came to a place called Krosbrekka, and when he came up upon the hill he rested himself, sat down there a while, looked down over the fjord, and said, "A difficult expedition ye have thrown upon my hands, ye lendermen, who have now changed your fealty, although but a little while ago ye were my friends and faithful to me." There are now two crosses erected upon the bank on which the king sat. Then the king mounted a horse, and rode without stopping up the valley, until he came to the precipice. Then the king asked Bruse if there was no summer hut of cattle-herds in the neighbourhood, where they could remain. He said there was. The king ordered his land-tent to be set up, and remained there all night. In the morning the king ordered them to drive to the urd, and try if they could get across it with the waggons. They drove there, and the king remained in the meantime in his tent. Towards evening the king's court-men and the bondes came back, and told how they had had a very fatiguing labour, without making any progress, and that there never could be a road made that they could get across: so they continued there the second night, during which, for the whole night, the king was occupied in prayer. As soon as he observed day dawning he ordered his men to drive again to the urd, and try once more if they could get across it with the waggons; but they went very unwillingly, saying nothing could be gained by it. When they were gone the man who had charge of the king's kitchen came, and said there were only two carcasses of young cattle remaining of provision: "Although you, sire, have 400 men, and there are 100 bondes besides." Then the king ordered that he should set all the kettles on the fire, and put a little bit of meat in each kettle, which was done. Then the king went there, and made the sign of the cross over each kettle, and told them to make ready the meat. The king then went to the urd called Skerfsurd, where a road should be cleared. When the king came all his people were sitting down, quite worn out with the hard labour. Bruse said, "I told you, sire, but you would not believe me, that we could make nothing of this urd." The king laid aside his cloak, and told them to go to work once more at the urd. They did so, and now twenty men could handle stones which before 100 men could not move from the place; and thus before midday the road was cleared so well that it was as passable for men, and for horses with packs, as a road in the plain fields. The king, after this, went down again to where the meat was, which place is called Olaf's Rock. Near the rock is a spring, at which Olaf washed himself; and therefore at the present day, when the cattle in the valley are sick, their illness is made better by their drinking at this well. Thereafter the king sat down to table with all the others; and when he was satisfied he asked if there was any other sheeling on the other side of the urd, and near the mountains, where they could pass the night. Bruse said there was such a sheeling, called Groningar; but that nobody could pass the night there on account of witchcraft, and evil beings who were in the sheeling. Then the king said they must get ready for their journey, as he wanted to be at the sheeling for the night. Then came the kitchen-master to the king, and tells that there was come an extraordinary supply of provisions, and he did not know where it had come from, or how. The king thanked God for this blessing, and gave the bondes who drove down again to their valley some rations of food, but remained himself all night in the sheeling. In the middle of the night, while the people were asleep, there was heard in the cattle-fold a dreadful cry, and these words: "Now Olaf's prayers are burning me," says the spirit, "so that I can no longer be in my habitation; now must I fly, and never more come to this fold." When the king's people awoke in the morning the king proceeded to the mountains, and said to Bruse, "Here shall now a farm be settled, and the bonde who dwells here shall never want what is needful for the support of life; and never shall his crop be destroyed by frost, although the crops be frozen on the farms both above it and below it." Then the king proceeded over the mountains, and came to a farm called Einby, where he remained for the night. King Olaf had then been fifteen years king of Norway (A.D. 1015-1029), including the year both he and Svein were in the country, and this year we have now been telling about. It was, namely, a little past Yule when the king left his ships and took to the land, as before related. Of this portion of his reign the priest Are Thorgilson the Wise was the first who wrote; and he was both faithful in his story, of a good memory, and so old a man that he could remember the men, and had heard their accounts, who were so old that through their age they could remember these circumstances as he himself wrote them in his books, and he named the men from whom he received his information. Otherwise it is generally said that King Olaf had been fifteen years king of Norway when he fell; but they who say so reckon to Earl Svein's government, the last year he was in the country, for King Olaf lived fifteen years afterwards as king.

190. OLAF'S PROPHECIES.

When the king had been one night at Lesjar he proceeded on his journey with his men, day by day; first into Gudbrandsdal, and from thence out to Redemark. Now it was seen who had been his friends, for they followed him; but those who had served him with less fidelity separated from him, and some showed him even indifference, or even full hostility, which afterwards was apparent; and also it could be seen clearly in many Upland people that they took very ill his putting Thorer to death, as before related. King Olaf gave leave to return home to many of his men who had farms and children to take care of; for it seemed to them uncertain what safety there might be for the families and property of those who left the country with him. Then the king explained to his friends his intention of leaving the country, and going first east into Svithjod, and there taking his determination as to where he should go; but he let his friends know his intention to return to the country, and regain his kingdoms, if God should grant him longer life; and he did not conceal his expectation that the people of Norway would again return to their fealty to him. "I think," says he, "that Earl Hakon will have Norway but a short time under his power, which many will not think an extraordinary expectation, as Earl Hakon has had but little luck against me; but probably few people will trust to my prophecy, that Canute the Great will in the course of a few years die, and his kingdoms vanish; and there will he no risings in favour of his race." When the king had ended his speech, his men prepared themselves for their departure. The king, with the troop that followed him, turned east to Eid forest. And there were along with him the Queen Astrid; their daughter Ulfhild; Magnus, King Olaf's son; Ragnvald Brusason; the three sons of Arne, Thorberg, Fin, and Arne, with many lendermen; and the king's attendants consisted of many chosen men. Bjorn the marshal got leave to go home, and he went to his farm, and many others of the king's friends returned home with his permission to their farms. The king begged them to let him know the events which might happen in the country, and which it might be important for him to know; and now the king proceeded on his way.

191. KING OLAF PROCEEDS TO RUSSIA.

It is to be related of King Olaf's journey, that he went first from Norway eastward through Eid forest to Vermaland, then to Vatnsby, and through the forests in which there are roads, until he came out in Nerike district. There dwelt a rich and powerful man in that part called Sigtryg, who had a son, Ivar, who afterwards became a distinguished person. Olaf stayed with Sigtryg all spring (A.D. 1029); and when summer came he made ready for a journey, procured a ship for himself, and without stopping went on to Russia to King Jarisleif and his queen Ingegerd; but his own queen Astrid, and their daughter Ulfhild, remained behind in Svithjod, and the king took his son Magnus eastward with him. King Jarisleif received King Olaf in the kindest manner, and made him the offer to remain with him, and to have so much land as was necessary for defraying the expense of the entertainment of his followers. King Olaf accepted this offer thankfully, and remained there. It is related that King Olaf was distinguished all his life for pious habits, and zeal in his prayers to God. But afterwards, when he saw his own power diminished, and that of his adversaries augmented, he turned all his mind to God's service; for he was not distracted by other thoughts, or by the labour he formerly had upon his hands, for during all the time he sat upon the throne he was endeavouring to promote what was most useful: and first to free and protect the country from foreign chiefs' oppressions, then to convert the people to the right faith; and also to establish law and the rights of the country, which he did by letting justice have its way, and punishing evil-doers.

192. CAUSES OF THE REVOLT AGAINST KING OLAF.

It had been an old custom in Norway that the sons of lendermen, or other great men, went out in war-ships to gather property, and they marauded both in the country and out of the country. But after King Olaf came to the sovereignty he protected the country, so that he abolished all plundering there; and even if they were the sons of powerful men who committed any depredation, or did what the king considered against law, he did not spare them at all, but they must suffer in life or limbs; and no man's entreaties, and no offer of money-penalties, could help them. So says Sigvat:–

"They who on viking cruises drove
With gifts of red gold often strove
To buy their safety–but our chief
Had no compassion for the thief.
He made the bravest lose his head
Who robbed at sea, and pirates led;
And his just sword gave peace to all,
Sparing no robber, great or small."

And he also says:–

"Great king! whose sword on many a field
Food to the wandering wolf did yield,
And then the thief and pirate band
Swept wholly off by sea and land–
Good king! who for the people's sake
Set hands and feet upon a stake,
When plunderers of great name and bold
Harried the country as of old.
The country's guardian showed his might
When oft he made his just sword bite
Through many a viking's neck and hair,
And never would the guilty spare.
King Magnus' father, I must say,
Did many a good deed in his day.
Olaf the Thick was stern and stout,
Much good his victories brought out."

He punished great and small with equal severity, which appeared to the chief people of the country too severe; and animosity rose to the highest when they lost relatives by the king's just sentence, although they were in reality guilty. This was the origin of the hostility of the great men of the country to King Olaf, that they could not bear his just judgments. He again would rather renounce his dignity than omit righteous judgment. The accusation against him, of being stingy with his money, was not just, for he was a most generous man towards his friends; but that alone was the cause of the discontent raised against him, that he appeared hard and severe in his retributions. Besides, King Canute offered great sums of money, and the great chiefs were corrupted by this, and by his offering them greater dignities than they had possessed before. The inclinations of the people, also, were all in favour of

Earl Hakon, who was much beloved by the country folks when he ruled the country before.

193. OF JOKUL BARDSON.

Earl Hakon had sailed with his fleet from Throndhjem, and gone south to More against King Olaf, as before related. Now when the king bore away, and ran into the fjord, the earl followed him thither; and then Kalf Arnason came to meet him, with many of the men who had deserted King Olaf. Kalf was well received. The earl steered in through Todar fjord to Valdal, where the king had laid up his ships on the strand. He took the ships which belonged to the king, had them put upon the water and rigged, and cast lots, and put commanders in charge of them according to the lots. There was a man called Jokul, who was an Icelander, a son of Bard Jokulson of Vatnsdal; the lot fell upon Jokul to command the Bison, which King Olaf himself had commanded. Jokul made these verses upon it:–

"Mine is the lot to take the helm
Which Olaf owned, who owned the realm;
From Sult King Olaf's ship to steer
(Ill luck I dread on his reindeer).
My girl will never hear the tidings,
Till o'er the wild wave I come riding
In Olaf's ship, who loved his gold,
And lost his ships with wealth untold."

We may here shortly tell what happened a long time after.–that this Jokul fell in with King Olaf's men in the island of Gotland, and the king ordered him to be taken out to be beheaded. A willow twig accordingly was plaited in with his hair, and a man held him fast by it. Jokul sat down upon a bank, and a man swung the axe to execute him; but Jokul hearing the sound, raised his head, and the blow struck him in the head, and made a dreadful wound. As the king saw it would be his death-wound, he ordered them to let him lie with it. Jokul raised himself up, and he sang:–

"My hard fate I mourn,–
Alas! my wounds burn,
My red wounds are gaping,
My life-blood escaping.

My wounds burn sore;
But I suffer still more
From the king's angry word,
Than his sharp-biting sword."

194. OF KALF ARNASON.

Kalf Arnason went with Earl Hakon north to Throndhjem, and the earl invited him to enter into his service. Kalf said he would first go home to his farm at Eggja, and afterwards make his determination; and Kalf did so. When he came home he found his wife Sigrid much irritated; and she reckoned up all the sorrow inflicted on her, as she insisted, by King Olaf. First, he had ordered her first husband Olver to be killed. "And now since," says she, "my two sons; and thou thyself, Kalf, wert present when they were cut off, and which I little expected from thee." Kalf says, it was much against his will that Thorer was killed. "I offered money-penalty for him," says he; "and when Grjotgard was killed I lost my brother Arnbjorn at the same time." She replies, "It is well thou hast suffered this from the king; for thou mayest perhaps avenge him, although thou wilt not avenge my injuries. Thou sawest how thy foster-son Thorer was killed, with all the regard of the king for thee." She frequently brought out such vexatious speeches to Kalf, to which he often answered angrily; but yet he allowed himself to be persuaded by her to enter into the earl's service, on condition of renewing his fiefs to him. Sigrid sent word to the earl how far she had brought the matter with Kalf. As soon as the earl heard of it, he sent a message to Kalf that he should come to the town to him. Kalf did not decline the invitation, but came directly to Nidaros, and waited on the earl, who received him kindly. In their conversation it was fully agreed upon that Kalf should go into the earl's service, and should receive great fiefs. After this Kalf returned home, and had the greater part of the interior of the Throndhjem country under him. As soon as it was spring Kalf rigged out a ship that belonged to him, and when she was ready he put to sea, and sailed west to England; for he had heard that in spring King Canute was to sail from Denmark to England, and that King Canute had given Harald, a son of Thorkel the High, an earldom in Denmark. Kalf Arnason went to King Canute as soon as he arrived in England. Bjarne Gullbrarskald tells of this:–

"King Olaf eastward o'er the sea
To Russia's monarch had to flee;

Our Harald's brother ploughed the main,
And furrowed white its dark-blue plain.
Whilst thou–the truth I still will say,
Nor fear nor favour can me sway–
Thou to King Canute hastened fast,
As soon as Olaf's luck was past."

Now when Kalf came to King Canute the king received him particularly well, and had many conversations with him. Among other things, King Canute, in a conference, asked Kalf to bind himself to raise a warfare against King Olaf, if ever he should return to the country. "And for which," says the king, "I will give thee the earldom, and place thee to rule over Norway; and my relation Hakon shall come to me, which will suit him better, for he is so honourable and trustworthy that I believe he would not even throw a spear against the person of King Olaf if he came back to the country." Kalf lent his ear to what the king proposed, for he had a great desire to attain this high dignity; and this conclusion was settled upon between King Canute and Kalf. Kalf then prepared to return home, and on his departure he received splendid presents from King Canute. Bjarne the skald tells of these circumstances:–

"Sprung from old earls!–to England's lord
Thou owest many a thankful word
For many a gift: if all be true,
Thy interest has been kept in view;
For when thy course was bent for home,
(Although that luck is not yet come,)
'That Norway should be thine,' 'tis said,
The London king a promise made."

Kalf thereafter returned to Norway, and came to his farm.

195. OF THE DEATH OF EARL HAKON.

Earl Hakon left the country this summer (A.D. 1029), and went to England, and when he came there was well received by the king. The earl had a bride in England, and he travelled to conclude this marriage, and as he intended holding his wedding in Norway, he came to procure those things for it in England which it was difficult to get in Norway. In autumn he made ready for his return, but it was somewhat late before he was clear for sea; but at last he set out. Of his voyage all that can be told is, that the vessel was lost, and not a man escaped. Some relate that the vessel was seen north of Caithness in the evening in a heavy storm, and the wind blowing out of Pentland Firth. They who believe this report say the vessel drove out among the breakers of the ocean; but with certainty people knew only that Earl Hakon was missing in the ocean, and nothing belonging to the ship ever came to land. The same autumn some merchants came to Norway, who told the tidings that were going through the country of Earl Hakon being missing; and all men knew that he neither came to Norway nor to England that autumn, so that Norway that winter was without a head.

196. OF BJORN THE MARSHAL.

BJORN THE MARSHAL SAT at home on his farm after his parting from King Olaf. Bjorn was a celebrated man; therefore it was soon reported far and wide that he had set himself down in quietness. Earl Hakon and the other chiefs of the country heard this also, and sent persons with a verbal message to Bjorn. When the messengers arrived Bjorn received them well; and afterwards Bjorn called them to him to a conference, and asked their business. He who was their foreman presented to Bjorn the salutations of King Canute, Earl Hakon, and of several chiefs. "King Canute," says he, "has heard much of thee, and that thou hast been long a follower of King Olaf the Thick, and hast been a great enemy of King Canute; and this he thinks not right, for he will be thy friend, and the friend of all worthy men, if thou wilt turn from thy friendship to King Olaf and become his enemy. And the only thing now thou canst do is to seek friendship and protection there where it is most readily to be found, and which all men in this northern world think it most honourable to be favoured with. Ye who have followed Olaf the Thick should consider how he is now separated from you; and that now ye have no aid against King Canute and his men, whose lands ye plundered last summer, and whose friends ye murdered. Therefore ye ought to accept, with thanks, the friendship which the king offers you; and it would become you better if you offered money even in mulct to obtain it."

When he had ended his speech Bjorn replies, "I wish now to sit quietly at home, and not to enter into the service of any chief."

The messenger answers, "Such men as thou art are just the right men to serve the king; and now I can tell thee there are just two things for thee to choose,–either to depart in peace from thy property, and wander about as thy comrade Olaf is doing; or, which is evidently better, to accept King Canute's and Earl Hakon's friendship, become their man, and take the oaths of fealty to them. Receive now thy reward." And he displayed to him a large bag full of English money.

Bjorn was a man fond of money, and self-interested; and when he saw the silver he was silent, and reflected with himself what resolution he should take. It seemed to him much to abandon his property, as he did not think it probable that King Olaf would ever have a rising in his favour in Norway. Now when the messenger saw that Bjorn's inclinations were turned towards the money, he threw down two thick gold rings, and said, "Take the money at once, Bjorn, and swear the oaths to King Canute; for I can promise thee that this money is but a trifle, compared to what thou wilt receive if thou followest King Canute."

By the heap of money, the fine promises, and the great presents, he was led by covetousness, took the money, went into King Canute's service, and gave the oaths of fealty to King Canute and Earl Hakon, and then the messengers departed.

197. BJORN THE MARSHAL'S JOURNEY.

WHEN BJORN HEARD THE tidings that Earl Hakon was missing he soon altered his mind, and was much vexed with himself for having been a traitor in his fidelity to King Olaf. He thought, now, that he was freed from the oath by which he had bound himself to Earl Hakon. It seemed to Bjorn that now there was some hope that King Olaf might again come to the throne of Norway if he came back, as the country was without a head. Bjorn therefore immediately made himself ready to travel, and took some men with him. He then set out on his journey, travelling night and day, on horseback when he could, and by ship when he found occasion; and never halted until he came, after Yule, east to Russia to King Olaf, who was very glad to see Bjorn. Then the king inquired much about the news from Norway. Bjorn tells him that Earl Hakon was missing, and the kingdom left without a head. At this news the men who had followed King Olaf were very glad,–all who had left property, connections, and friends in Norway; and the longing for home was awakened in them. Bjorn told King Olaf much news from Norway, and very anxious the king was to know, and asked much how his friends had kept their fidelity towards him. Bjorn answered, it had gone differently with different people.

Then Bjorn stood up, fell at the king's feet, held his foot, and said, "All is in your power, sire, and in God's! I have taken money from King Canute's men, and sworn them the oaths of fealty; but now will I follow thee, and not part from thee so long as we both live."

The king replies, "Stand up, Bjorn' thou shalt be reconciled with me; but reconcile thy perjury with God. I can see that but few men in Norway have held fast by their fealty, when such men as thou art could be false to me. But true it is also that people sit in great danger when I am distant, and they are exposed to the wrath of my enemies."

Bjorn then reckoned up those who had principally bound themselves to rise in hostility against the king and his men; and named, among others, Erling's son in Jadar and their connections, Einar Tambaskelfer, Kalf Arnason, Thorer Hund, and Harek of Thjotta.

198. OF KING OLAF.

After King Olaf came to Russia he was very thoughtful, and weighed what counsel he now should follow. King Jarisleif and Queen Ingegerd offered him to remain with them, and receive a kingdom called Vulgaria, which is a part of Russia, and in which land the people were still heathen. King Olaf thought over this offer; but when he proposed it to his men they dissuaded him from settling himself there, and urged the king to betake himself to Norway to his own kingdom: but the king himself had resolved almost in his own mind to lay down his royal dignity, to go out into the world to Jerusalem, or other holy places, and to enter into some order of monks. But yet the thought lay deep in his soul to recover again, if there should be any opportunity for him, his kingdom in Norway. When he thought over this, it recurred to his mind how all things had gone prosperously with him during the first ten years of his reign, and how afterwards every thing he undertook became heavy, difficult, and hard; and that he had been unlucky, on all occasions in which he had tried his luck. On this account he doubted if it would be prudent to depend so much upon his luck, as to go with so little strength into the hands of his enemies, seeing that all the people of the country had taken part with them to oppose King Olaf. Such cares he had often on his mind, and he left his cause to God, praying that He would do what to Him seemed best. These thoughts he turned over in his mind, and knew not what to resolve upon; for he saw how evidently dangerous that was which his inclination was most bent upon.

199. OF KING OLAF'S DREAM.

One night the king lay awake in his bed, thinking with great anxiety about his determination, and at last, being tired of thinking, sleep came over him towards morning; but his sleep was so light that he thought he was awake, and could see all that was doing in the house. Then he saw a great and superb man, in splendid clothes, standing by his bed; and it came into the king's mind that this was King Olaf Trygvason who had come to him. This man said to him, "Thou are very sick of thinking about thy future resolutions; and it appears to me wonderful that these thoughts should be so tumultuous in thy soul that thou shouldst even think of laying down the kingly dignity which God hath given thee, and of remaining here and accepting of a kingdom from foreign and unknown kings. Go back rather to that kingdom which thou hast received in heritage, and rule over it with the strength which God hath given thee, and let not thy inferiors take it from thee. It is the glory of a king to be victorious over his enemies, and it is a glorious death to die in battle. Or art thou doubtful if thou hast right on thy side in the strife with thine enemies? Thou must have no doubts, and must not conceal the truth from thyself. Thou must go back to thy country, and God will give open testimony that the kingdom is thine by property." When the king awoke he thought he saw the man's shoulders going out. From this time the king's courage rose, and he fixed firmly his resolution to return to Norway; to which his inclination also tended most, and which he also found was the desire of all his men. He bethought himself also that the country being without a chief could be easily attacked, from what he had heard, and that after he came himself many would turn back towards him. When the king told his determination to his people they all gave it their approbation joyfully.

200. OF KING OLAF'S HEALING POWERS.

It is related that once upon a time, while King Olaf was in Russia, it happened that the son of an honest widow had a sore boil upon his neck, of which the lad lay very ill; and as he could not swallow any food, there was little hope of his life. The boy's mother went to Queen Ingegerd, with whom she was acquainted, and showed her the lad. The queen said she knew no remedy for it. "Go," said she, "to King Olaf, he is the best physician here; and beg him to lay his hands on thy lad, and bring him my words if he will not otherwise do it." She did as the queen told her; and when she found the king she says to him that her son is dangerously ill of a boil in his neck, and begs him to lay his hand on the boil. The king tells her he is not a physician, and bids her go to where there were physicians. She replies, that the queen had told her to come to him; "and told me to add the request from her, that you would would use the remedy you understood, and she said that thou art the best physician here in the town." Then the king took the lad, laid his hands upon his neck, and felt the boil for a long time, until the boy made a very wry face. Then the king took a piece of bread, laid it in the figure of the cross upon the palm of his hand, and put it into the boy's mouth. He swallowed it down, and from that time all the soreness left his neck, and in a few days he was quite well, to the great joy of his mother and all his relations. Then first came Olaf into the repute of having as much healing power in his hands as is ascribed to men who have been gifted by nature with healing by the touch; and afterwards when his miracles were universally acknowledged, this also was considered one of his miracles.

201. KING OLAF BURNS THE WOOD SHAVINGS ON HIS HAND FOR HIS SABBATH BREACH.

It happened one Sunday that the king sat in his highseat at the dinner table, and had fallen into such deep thought that he did not observe how time went. In one hand he had a knife, and in the other a piece of fir-wood from which he cut splinters from time to time. The table-servant stood before him with a bowl in his hands; and seeing what the king was about, and that he was involved in thought, he said, "It is Monday, sire, to-morrow." The king looked at him when he heard this, and then it came into his mind what he was doing on the Sunday. Then the king ordered a lighted candle to be brought him, swept together all the shavings he had made, set them on fire, and let them burn upon his naked hand; showing thereby that he would hold fast by God's law and commandment, and not trespass without punishment on what he knew to be right.

202. OF KING OLAF.

When King Olaf had resolved on his return home, he made known his intention to King Jarisleif and Queen Ingegerd. They dissuaded him from this expedition, and said he should receive as much power in their dominions as he thought desirable; but begged him not to put himself within the reach of his enemies with so few men as he had. Then King Olaf told them of his dream; adding, that he believed it to be God's will and providence that it should be so. Now when they found he was determined on travelling to Norway, they offered him all the assistance to his journey that he would accept from them. The king thanked them in many fine words for their good will; and said that he accepted from them, with no ordinary pleasure, what might be necessary for his undertaking.

203. OF KING OLAF'S JOURNEY FROM RUSSIA.

Immediately after Yule (A.D. 1080), King Olaf made himself ready; and had about 200 of his men with him. King Jarisleif gave him all the horses, and whatever else he required; and when he was ready he set off. King Jarisleif and Queen Ingegerd parted from him with all honour; and he left his son Magnus behind with the king. The first part of his journey, down to the sea-coast, King Olaf and his men made on the ice; but as spring approached, and the ice broke up, they rigged their vessels, and when they were ready and got a wind they set out to sea, and had a good voyage. When Olaf came to the island of Gotland with his ships he heard the news–which was told as truth, both in Svithjod, Denmark, and over all Norway–that Earl Hakon was missing, and Norway without a head. This gave the king and his men good hope of the issue of their journey. From thence they sailed, when the wind suited, to Svithjod, and went into the Maelar lake, to Aros, and sent men to the Swedish King Onund appointing a meeting. King Onund received his brother-in-law's message in the kindest manner, and went to him according to his invitation. Astrid also came to King Olaf, with the men who had attended her; and great was the joy on all sides at this meeting. The Swedish king also received his brother-in-law King Olaf with great joy when they met.

204. OF THE LENDERMEN IN NORWAY.

Now we must relate what, in the meantime, was going on in Norway. Thorer Hund, in these two winters (A.D. 1029-1030), had made a Lapland journey, and each winter had been a long time on the mountains, and had gathered to himself great wealth by trading in various wares with the Laplanders. He had twelve large coats of reindeer-skin made for him, with so much Lapland witchcraft that no weapon could cut or pierce them any more than if they were armour of ring-mail, nor so much. The spring thereafter Thorer rigged a long-ship which belonged to him, and manned it with his house-servants. He summoned the bondes, demanded a levy from the most northern Thing district, collected in this way a great many people, and proceeded with this force southwards. Harek of Thjotta had also collected a great number of people; and in this expedition many people of consequence took a part, although these two were the most distinguished. They made it known publicly that with this war-force they were going against King Olaf, to defend the country against him, in case he should come from the eastward.

205. OF EINAR TAMBASKELFER.

Einar Tambaskelfer had most influence in the outer part of the Throndhjem country after Earl Hakon's death was no longer doubtful; for he and his son Eindride appeared to be the nearest heirs to the movable property the earl had possessed. Then Einar remembered the promises and offers of friendship which King Canute had made him at parting; and he ordered a good vessel which belonged to him to be got ready, and embarked with a great retinue, and when he was ready sailed southwards along the coast, then set out to sea westwards, and sailed without stopping until he came to England. He immediately waited on King Canute, who received him well and joyfully. Then Einar opened his business to the king, and said he was come there to see the fulfillment of the promises the king had made him; namely, that he, Einar, should have the highest title of honour in Norway if Earl Hakon were no more. King Canute replies, that now the circumstances were altered. "I have now," said he, "sent men and tokens to my son Svein in Denmark, and promised him the kingdom of Norway; but thou shalt retain my friendship, and get the dignity and title which thou art entitled by birth to hold. Thou shalt be lenderman with great fiefs, and be so much more raised above other lendermen as thou art more able than they." Einar saw sufficiently how matters stood with regard to his business, and got ready to return home; but as he now knew the king's intentions, and thought it probable if King Olaf came from the East the country would not be very peaceable, it came into his mind that it would be better to proceed slowly, and not to be hastening his voyage, in order to fight against King Olaf, without his being advanced by it to any higher dignity than he had before. Einar accordingly went to sea when he was ready; but only came to Norway after the events were ended which took place there during that summer.

206. OF THE CHIEF PEOPLE IN NORWAY.

THE CHIEFS IN NORWAY had their spies east in Svithjod, and south in Denmark, to find out if King Olaf had come from Russia. As soon as these men could get across the country, they heard the news that King Olaf was arrived in Svithjod; and as soon as full certainty of this was obtained, the war message-token went round the land. The whole people were called out to a levy, and a great army was collected. The lendermen who were from Agder, Rogaland, and Hordaland, divided themselves, so that some went towards the north, and some towards the east; for they thought they required people on both sides. Erling's sons from Jadar went eastward, with all the men who lived east of them, and over whom they were chiefs; Aslak of Finey, and Erlend of Gerde, with the lendermen north of them, went towards the north. All those now named had sworn an oath to King Canute to deprive Olaf of life, if opportunity should offer.

207. OF HARALD SIGURDSON'S PROCEEDINGS.

NOW WHEN IT WAS reported in Norway that King Olaf was come from the East to Svithjod, his friends gathered together to give him aid. The most distinguished man in this flock was Harald Sigurdson, a brother of King Olaf, who then was fifteen years of age, very stout, and manly of growth as if he were full-grown. Many other brave men were there also; and there were in all 600 men when they proceeded from the uplands, and went eastward with their force through Eid forest to Vermaland. From thence they went eastward through the forests to Svithjod and made inquiry about King Olaf's proceedings.

208. OF KING OLAF'S PROCEEDINGS IN SVITHJOD.

King Olaf was in Svithjod in spring (A.D. 1030), and had sent spies from thence to Norway. All accounts from that quarter agreed that there was no safety for him if he went there, and the people who came from the north dissuaded him much from penetrating into the country. But he had firmly resolved within himself, as before stated, to go into Norway; and he asked King Onund what strength King Onund would give him to conquer his kingdom. King Onund replied, that the Swedes were little inclined to make an expedition against Norway. "We know," says he, "that the Northmen are rough and warlike, and it is dangerous to carry hostility to their doors, but I will not be slow in telling thee what aid I can give. I will give thee 400 chosen men from my court-men, active and warlike, and well equipt for battle; and moreover will give thee leave to go through my country, and gather to thyself as many men as thou canst get to follow thee." King Olaf accepted this offer, and got ready for his march. Queen Astrid, and Ulfhild the king's daughter, remained behind in Svithjod.

209. KING OLAF ADVANCES TO JARNBERALAND.

Just as King Olaf began his journey the men came to him whom the Swedish king had given, in all 400 men, and the king took the road the Swedes showed him. He advanced upwards in the country to the forests, and came to a district called Jarnberaland. Here the people joined him who had come out of Norway to meet him, as before related; and he met here his brother Harald, and many other of his relations, and it was a joyful meeting. They made out together 1200 men.

210. OF DAG HRINGSON.

There was a man called Dag, who is said to have been a son of King Hring, who fled the country from King Olaf. This Hring, it is said further, had been a son of Dag, and grandson of Hring, Harald Harfager's son. Thus was Dag King Olaf's relative. Both Hring the father, and Dag the son, had settled themselves in Svithjod, and got land to rule over. In spring, when Olaf came from the East to Svithjod, he sent a message to his relation Dag, that he should join him in this expedition with all the force he could collect; and if they gained the country of

Norway again, Dag should have no smaller part of the kingdom under him than his forefathers had enjoyed. When this message came to Dag it suited his inclination well, for he had a great desire to go to Norway and get the dominion his family had ruled over. He was not slow, therefore, to reply, and promised to come. Dag was a quick-speaking, quick-resolving man, mixing himself up in everything; eager, but of little understanding. He collected a force of almost 1200 men, with which he joined King Olaf.

211. OF KING OLAF'S JOURNEY.

King Olaf sent a message before him to all the inhabited places he passed through, that the men who wished to get goods and money, and share of booty, and the lands besides which now were in the hands of his enemies, should come to him, and follow him. Thereafter King Olaf led his army through forests, often over desert moors, and often over large lakes; and they dragged, or carried the boats, from lake to lake. On the way a great many followers joined the king, partly forest settlers, partly vagabonds. The places at which he halted for the night are since called Olaf's Booths. He proceeded without any break upon his journey until he came to Jamtaland, from which he marched north over the keel or ridge of the land. The men spread themselves over the hamlets, and proceeded, much scattered, so long as no enemy was expected; but always, when so dispersed, the Northmen accompanied the king. Dag proceeded with his men on another line of march, and the Swedes on a third with their troop.

212. OF VAGABOND-MEN.

There were two men, the one called Gauka-Thorer, the other Afrafaste, who were vagabonds and great robbers, and had a company of thirty men such as themselves. These two men were larger and stronger than other men, and they wanted neither courage nor impudence. These men heard speak of the army that was crossing the country, and said among themselves it would be a clever counsel to go to the king, follow him to his country, and go with him into a regular battle, and try themselves in this work; for they had never been in any battle in which people were regularly drawn up in line, and they were curious to see the king's order of battle. This counsel was approved of by their comrades, and accordingly they went to the road on which King Olaf was to pass. When they came there they presented themselves to the king, with their followers, fully armed. They saluted him, and he asked what people they were. They told their names, and said they were natives of the place; and told their errand, and that they wished to go with the king. The king said, it appeared to him there was good help in such folks. "And I have a great inclination," said he, "to take such; but are ye Christian men?"

Gauka-Thorer replies, that he is neither Christian nor heathen. "I and my comrades have no faith but on ourselves, our strength, and the luck of victory; and with this faith we slip through sufficiently well."

The king replies, "A great pity it is that such brave slaughtering fellows did not believe in Christ their Creator."

Thorer replies, "Is there any Christian man, king, in thy following, who stands so high in the air as we two brothers?"

The king told them to let themselves be baptized, and to accept the true faith. "Follow me then, and I will advance you to great dignities; but if ye will not do so, return to your former vocation."

Afrafaste said he would not take on Christianity, and he turned away.

Then said Gauka-Thorer, "It is a great shame that the king drives us thus away from his army, and I never before came where I was not received into the company of other people, and I shall never return back on this account." They joined accordingly the rear with other forest-men, and followed the troops. Thereafter the king proceeded west up to the keel-ridge of the country.

213. OF KING OLAF'S VISION.

Now when King Olaf, coming from the east, went over the keel-ridge and descended on the west side of the mountain, where it declines towards the sea, he could see from thence far over the country. Many people rode before the king and many after, and he himself rode so that there was a free space around him. He was silent, and nobody spoke to him, and thus he rode a great part of the day without looking much about him. Then the bishop rode up to him, asked him why he was so silent, and what he was thinking of; for, in general, he was very cheerful, and very talkative on a journey to his men, so that all who were near him were merry. The king replied, full of thought, "Wonderful things have come into my mind a while ago. As I just now looked over Norway, out to the west from the mountains, it came into my mind how many happy days I have had in that land. It appeared to me at first as if I saw over all the Throndhjem country, and then over all Norway; and the longer this vision was before my eyes the farther, methought, I saw, until I looked over the whole wide world, both land and sea. Well I know the places at which I have been in former days; some even which I have only heard speak of, and some I saw of which I had never heard, both inhabited and uninhabited, in this wide world." The bishop replied that this was a holy vision, and very remarkable.

214. OF THE MIRACLE ON THE CORN LAND.

WHEN THE KING HAD come lower down on the mountain, there lay a farm before him called Sula, on the highest part of Veradal district; and as they came nearer to the house the corn-land appeared on both sides of the path. The king told his people to proceed carefully, and not destroy the corn to the bondes. The people observed this when the king was near; but the crowd behind paid no attention to it, and the people ran over the corn, so that it was trodden flat to the earth. There dwelt a bonde there called Thorgeir Flek, who had two sons nearly grown up. Thorgeir received the king and his people well, and offered all the assistance in his power. The king was pleased with his offer, and asked Thorgeir what was the news of the country, and if any forces were assembled against him. Thorgeir says that a great army was drawn together in the Throndhjem country, and that there were some lendermen both from the south of the country, and from Halogaland in the north; "but I do not know," says he. "if they are intended against you, or going elsewhere." Then he complained to the king of the damage and waste done him by the people breaking and treading down all his corn fields. The king said it was ill done to bring upon him any loss. Then the king rode to where the corn had stood, and saw it was laid flat on the earth; and he rode round the field, and said, "I expect, bonde, that God will repair thy loss, so that the field, within a week, will be better;" and it proved the best of the corn, as the king had said. The king remained all night there, and in the morning he made himself ready, and told Thorgeir the bonde to accompany him and Thorgear offered his two sons also for the journey; and although the king said that he did not want them with him, the lads would go. As they would not stay behind, the king's court-men were about binding them; but the king seeing it said, "Let them come with us; the lads will come safe back again." And it was with the lads as the king foretold.

215. OF THE BAPTISM OF THE VAGABOND FOREST-MEN.

Thereafter the army advanced to Staf, and when the king reached Staf's moor he halted. There he got the certain information that the bondes were advancing with an army against him, and that he might soon expect to have a battle with them. He mustered his force here, and, after reckoning them up, found there were in the army 900 heathen men, and when he came to know it he ordered them to allow themselves to be baptized, saying that he would have no heathens with him in battle. "We must not," says he, "put our confidence in numbers, but in God alone must we trust; for through his power and favour we must be victorious, and I will not mix heathen people with my own." When the heathens heard this, they held a council among themselves, and at last 400 men agreed to be baptized; but 500 men refused to adopt Christianity, and that body returned home to their land. Then the brothers Gauka-Thorer and Afrafaste presented themselves to the king, and offered again to follow him. The king asked if they had now taken baptism. Gauka-Thorer replied that they had not. Then the king ordered them to accept baptism and the true faith, or otherwise to go away. They stepped aside to talk with each other on what resolution they should take. Afrafaste said, "To give my opinion, I will not turn back, but go into the battle, and take a part on the one side or the other; and I don't care much in which army I am." Gauka-Thorer replies, "If I go into battle I will give my help to the king, for he has most need of help. And if I must believe in a God, why not in the white Christ as well as in any other? Now it is my advice, therefore, that we let ourselves be baptized, since the king insists so much upon it, and then go into the battle with him." They all agreed to this, and went to the king, and said they would receive baptism. Then they were baptized by a priest, and the baptism was confirmed by the bishop. The king then took them into the troop of his court-men, and said they should fight under his banner in the battle.

216. KING OLAF'S SPEECH.

King Olaf got certain intelligence now that it would be but a short time until he had a battle with the bondes; and after he had mustered his men, and reckoned up the force, he had more than 3000 men, which appears to be a great army in one field. Then the king made the following speech to the people: "We have a great army, and excellent troops; and now I will tell you, my men, how I will have our force drawn up. I will let my banner go forward in the middle of the army, and my-court-men, and pursuivants shall follow it, together with the war forces that joined us from the Uplands, and also those who may come to us here in the Throndhjem land. On the right hand of my banner shall be Dag Hringson, with all the men he brought to our aid; and he shall have the second banner. And on the left hand of our line shall the men be whom the Swedish king gave us, together with all the people who came to us in Sweden; and they shall have the third banner. I will also have the people divide themselves into distinct flocks or parcels, so that relations and acquaintances should be together; for thus they defend each other best, and know each other. We will have all our men distinguished by a mark, so as to be a field-token upon their helmets and shields, by painting the holy cross thereupon with white colour. When we come into battle we shall all have one countersign and field-cry,–'Forward, forward, Christian men! cross men! king's men!' We must draw up our meal in thinner ranks, because we have fewer people, and I do not wish to let them surround us with their men. Now let the men divide themselves into separate flocks, and then each flock into ranks; then let each man observe well his proper place, and take notice what banner he is drawn up under. And now we shall remain drawn up in array; and our men shall be fully armed, night and day, until we know where the meeting shall be between us and the bondes." When the king had finished speaking, the army arrayed, and arranged itself according to the king's orders.

217. KING OLAF'S COUNSEL.

THEREAFTER THE KING HAD a meeting with the chiefs of the different divisions, and then the men had returned whom the king had sent out into the neighbouring districts to demand men from the bondes. They brought the tidings from the inhabited places they had gone through, that all around the country was stripped of all men able to carry arms, as all the people had joined the bondes' army; and where they did find any they got but few to follow them, for the most of them answered that they stayed at home because they would not follow either party: they would not go out against the king, nor yet against their own relations. Thus they had got but few people. Now the king asked his men their counsel, and what they now should do. Fin Arnason answered thus to the king's question: "I will say what should be done, if I may advise. We should go with armed hand over all the inhabited places, plunder all the goods, and burn all the habitations, and leave not a hut standing, and thus punish the bondes for their treason against their sovereign. I think many a man will then cast himself loose from the bondes' army, when he sees smoke and flame at home on his farm, and does not know how it is going with children, wives, or old men, fathers, mothers, and other connections. I expect also," he added, "that if we succeed in breaking the assembled host, their ranks will soon be thinned; for so it is with the bondes, that the counsel which is the newest is always the dearest to them all, and most followed." When Fin had ended his speech it met with general applause; for many thought well of such a good occasion to make booty, and all thought the bondes well deserved to suffer damage; and they also thought it probable, what Fin said, that many would in this way be brought to forsake the assembled army of the bondes.

Now when the king heard the warm expressions of his people he told them to listen to him, and said, "The bondes have well deserved that it should be done to them as ye desire. They also know that I have formerly done so, burning their habitations, and punishing them severely in many ways; but then I proceeded against them with fire and sword because they rejected the true faith, betook themselves to sacrifices, and would not obey my commands. We had then God's honour to defend. But this treason against their sovereign is a much less grievous crime, although it does not become men who have any manhood in them to break the faith and vows they have sworn to me. Now, however, it is more in my power to spare those who have dealt ill with me, than those whom God hated. I will, therefore, that my people proceed gently, and commit no ravage. First, I will proceed to meet the bondes; if we can then come to a reconciliation, it is well; but if they will fight with us, then there are two things before us; either we fail in the battle, and then it will be well advised not to have to retire encumbered with spoil and cattle; or we gain the victory, and then ye will be the heirs of all who fight now against us; for some will fall, and others will fly, but both will have forfeited their goods and properties, and then it will be good to enter into full houses and well-stocked farms; but what is burnt is of use to no man, and with pillage and force more is wasted than what turns to use. Now we will spread out far through the inhabited places, and take with us all the men we can find able to carry arms. Then men will also capture cattle for slaughter, or whatever else of provision that can serve for food; but not do any other ravage. But I will see willingly that ye kill any spies of the bonde army ye may fall in with. Dag and his people shall go by the north side down along the valley, and I will go on along the country road, and so we shall meet in the evening, and all have one night quarter."

218. OF KING OLAF'S SKALDS.

It is related that when King Olaf drew up his men in battle order, he made a shield rampart with his troop that should defend him in battle, for which he selected the strongest and boldest. Thereafter he called his skalds, and ordered them to go in within the shield defence. "Ye shall." says the king, "remain here, and see the circumstances which may take place, and then ye will not have to follow the reports of others in what ye afterwards tell or sing concerning it." There were Thormod Kolbrunarskald, Gissur Gulbraskald, a foster-son of Hofgardaref, and Thorfin Mun. Then said Thormod to Gissur, "Let us not stand so close together, brother, that Sigvat the skald should not find room when he comes. He must stand before the king, and the king will not have it otherwise." The king heard this, and said, "Ye need not sneer at Sigvat, because he is not here. Often has he followed me well, and now he is praying for us, and that we greatly need." Thormod replies, "It may be, sire, that ye now require prayers most; but it would be thin around the banner-staff if all thy court-men were now on the way to Rome. True it was what we spoke about, that no man who would speak with you could find room for Sigvat."

Thereafter the skalds talked among themselves that it would be well to compose a few songs of remembrance about the events which would soon be taking place.

Then Gissur sang:–

"From me shall bende girl never hear
A thought of sorrow, care, or fear:
I wish my girl knew how gay
We arm us for our viking fray.
Many and brave they are, we know,
Who come against us there below;
But, life or death, we, one and all,
By Norway's king will stand or fall."

And Thorfin Mun made another song, viz.:–

"Dark is the cloud of men and shields,
Slow moving up through Verdal's fields:
These Verdal folks presume to bring
Their armed force against their king.
On! let us feed the carrion crow,–
Give her a feast in every blow;
And, above all, let Throndhjem's hordes
Feel the sharp edge of true men's swords."

And Thorrood sang:–

"The whistling arrows pipe to battle,
Sword and shield their war-call rattle.
Up! brave men, up! the faint heart here
Finds courage when the danger's near.
Up! brave men, up! with Olaf on!
With heart and hand a field is won.
One viking cheer!–then, stead of words,
We'll speak with our death-dealing swords."

These songs were immediately got by heart by the army.

219. OF KING OLAF'S GIFTS FOR THE SOULS OF THOSE WHO SHOULD BE SLAIN.

Thereafter the king made himself ready, and marched down through the valley. His whole forces took up their night-quarter in one place, and lay down all night under their shields; but as soon as day broke the king again put his army in order, and that being done they proceeded down through the valley. Many bondes then came to the king, of whom the most joined his army; and all, as one man, told the same tale,–that the lendermen had collected an enormous army, with which they intended to give battle to the king.

The king took many marks of silver, and delivered them into the hands of a bonde, and said, "This money thou shalt conceal, and afterwards lay out, some to churches, some to priests, some to alms-men,–as gifts for the life and souls of those who fight against us, and may fall in battle."

The bonde replies, "Should you not rather give this money for the soul-mulct of your own men?"

The king says, "This money shall be given for the souls of those who stand against us in the ranks of the bondes' army, and fall by the weapons of our own men. The men who follow us to battle, and fall therein, will all be saved together with ourself."

220. OF THORMOD KOLBRUNARSKALD.

THIS NIGHT THE KING lay with his army around him on the field, as before related, and lay long awake in prayer to God, and slept but little. Towards morning a slumber fell on him, and when he awoke daylight was shooting up. The king thought it too early to awaken the army, and asked where Thormod the skald was. Thormod was at hand, and asked what was the king's pleasure. "Sing us a song," said the king. Thormod raised himself up, and sang so loud that the whole army could hear him. He began to sing the old "Bjarkamal", of which these are the first verses:–

"The day is breaking,–
The house cock, shaking
His rustling wings,
While priest-bell rings,
Crows up the morn,
And touting horn
Wakes thralls to work and weep;
Ye sons of Adil, cast off sleep,
Wake up! wake up!
Nor wassail cup,
Nor maiden's jeer,
Awaits you here.
Hrolf of the bow!
Har of the blow!
Up in your might! the day is breaking;
'Tis Hild's game[52] *that bides your waking."*

---

52 Hild's game is the battle, from the name of the war-goddess Hild.–L.

Then the troops awoke, and when the song was ended the people thanked him for it; and it pleased many, as it was suitable to the time and occasion, and they called it the house-carle's whet. The king thanked him for the pleasure, and took a gold ring that weighed half a mark and gave it him. Thormod thanked the king for the gift, and said, "We have a good king; but it is not easy to say how long the king's life may be. It is my prayer, sire, that thou shouldst never part from me either in life or death." The king replies, "We shall all go together so long as I rule, and as ye will follow me."

Thormod says, "I hope, sire, that whether in safety or danger I may stand near you as long as I can stand, whatever we may hear of Sigvat travelling with his gold-hilted sword." Then Thormod made these lines:-

"To thee, my king, I'll still be true,
Until another skald I view,
Here in the field with golden sword,
As in thy hall, with flattering word.
Thy skald shall never be a craven,
Though he may feast the croaking raven,
The warrior's fate unmoved I view,-
To thee, my king, I'll still be true."

221. KING OLAF COMES TO STIKLESTAD.

King Olaf led his army farther down through the valley, and Dag and his men went another way, and the king did not halt until he came to Stiklestad. There he saw the bonde army spread out all around; and there were so great numbers that people were going on every footpath, and great crowds were collected far and near. They also saw there a troop which came down from Veradal, and had been out to spy. They came so close to the king's people that they knew each other. It was Hrut of Viggia, with thirty men. The king ordered his pursuivants to go out against Hrut, and make an end of him, to which his men were instantly ready. The king said to the Icelanders, "It is told me that in Iceland it is the custom that the bondes give their house-servants a sheep to slaughter; now I give you a ram to slaughter."[53] The Icelanders were easily invited to this, and went out

53 Hrut means a young ram.–L.

immediately with a few men against Hrut, and killed him and the troop that followed him. When the king came to Stiklestad he made a halt, and made the army stop, and told his people to alight from their horses and get ready for battle; and the people did as the king ordered. Then he placed his army in battle array, and raised his banner. Dag was not yet arrived with his men, so that his wing of the battle array was wanting. Then the king said the Upland men should go forward in their place, and raise their banner there. "It appears to me advisable," says the king, "that Harald my brother should not be in the battle, for he is still in the years of childhood only." Harald replies, "Certainly I shall be in the battle, for I am not so weak that I cannot handle the sword; and as to that, I have a notion of tying the sword-handle to my hand. None is more willing than I am to give the bondes a blow; so I shall go with my comrades." It is said that Harald made these lines:–

"Our army's wing, where I shall stand,
I will hold good with heart and hand;
My mother's eye shall joy to see
A battered, blood-stained shield from me.
The brisk young skald should gaily go
Into the fray, give blow for blow,
Cheer on his men, gain inch by inch,
And from the spear-point never flinch."

Harald got his will, and was allowed to be in the battle.

222. OF THORGILS HALMASON.

A BONDE, by name Thorgils Halmason, father to Grim the Good, dwelt in Stiklestad farm. Thorgils offered the king his assistance, and was ready to go into battle with him. The king thanked him for the offer. "I would rather," says the king, "thou shouldst not be in the fight. Do us rather the service to take care of the people who are wounded, and to bury those who may fall, when the battle is over. Should it happen, bonde, that I fall in this battle, bestow the care on my body that may be necessary, if that be not forbidden thee." Thorgils promised the king what he desired.

223. OLAF'S SPEECH.

Now when King Olaf had drawn up his army in battle array he made a speech, in which he told the people to raise their spirit, and go boldly forward, if it came to a battle. "We have," says he, "many men, and good; and although the bondes may have a somewhat larger force than we, it is fate that rules over victory. This I will make known to you solemnly, that I shall not fly from this battle, but shall either be victorious over the bondes, or fall in the fight. I will pray to God that the lot of the two may befall me which will be most to my advantage. With this we may encourage ourselves, that we have a more just cause than the bondes; and likewise that God must either protect us and our cause in this battle, or give us a far higher recompense for what we may lose here in the world than what we ourselves could ask. Should it be my lot to have anything to say after the battle, then shall I reward each of you according to his service, and to the bravery he displays in the battle; and if we gain the victory, there must be land and movables enough to divide among you, and which are now in the hands of your enemies. Let us at the first make the hardest onset, for then the consequences are soon seen. There being a great difference in the numbers, we have to expect victory from a sharp assault only; and, on the other hand, it will be heavy work for us to fight until we are tired, and unable to fight longer; for we have fewer people to relieve with than they, who can come forward at one time and retreat and rest at another. But if we advance so hard at the first attack that those who are foremost in their ranks must turn round, then the one will fall over the other, and their destruction will be the greater the greater numbers there are together." When the king had ended his speech it was received with loud applause, and the one encouraged the other.

224. OF THORD FOLASON.

Thord Folason carried King Olaf's banner. So says Sigvat the skald, in the death-song which he composed about King Olaf, and put together according to resurrection saga:–

"Thord. I have heard, by Olaf's side,
Where raged the battle's wildest tide,
Moved on, and, as by one accord
Moved with them every heart and sword.

The banner of the king on high,
Floating all splendid in the sky
From golden shaft, aloft he bore,–
The Norsemen's rallying-point of yore."

225. OF KING OLAF'S ARMOUR.

King Olaf was armed thus:–He had a gold-mounted helmet on his head; and had in one hand a white shield, on which the holy cross was inlaid in gold. In his other hand he had a lance, which to the present day stands beside the altar in Christ Church. In his belt he had a sword, which was called Hneiter, which was remarkably sharp, and of which the handle was worked with gold. He had also a strong coat of ring-mail. Sigvat the skald, speaks of this:–

"A greater victory to gain,
Olaf the Stout strode o'er the plain
In strong chain armour, aid to bring
To his brave men on either wing.
High rose the fight and battle-heat,–
the clear blood ran beneath the feet
Of Swedes, who from the East came there,
In Olaf's gain or loss to share."

226. KING OLAF'S DREAM.

Now when King Olaf had drawn up his men the army of the bondes had not yet come near upon any quarter, so the king said the people should sit down and rest themselves. He sat down himself, and the people sat around him in a widespread crowd. He leaned down, and laid his head upon Fin Arnason's knee. There a slumber came upon him, and he slept a little while; but at the same time the bondes' army was seen advancing with raised banners, and the multitude of these was very great.

Then Fin awakened the king, and said that the bonde-army advanced against them.

The king awoke, and said, "Why did you waken me, Fin, and did not allow me to enjoy my dream?"

Fin: "Thou must not be dreaming; but rather thou shouldst be awake, and preparing thyself against the host which is coming down upon us; or, dost thou not see that the whole bonde-crowd is coming?"

The king replies, "They are not yet so near to us, and it would have been better to have let me sleep."

Then said Fin, "What was the dream, sire, of which the loss appears to thee so great that thou wouldst rather have been left to waken of thyself?"

Now the king told his dream,–that he seemed to see a high ladder, upon which he went so high in the air that heaven was open: for so high reached the ladder. "And when you awoke me, I was come to the highest step towards heaven."

Fin replies, "This dream does not appear to me so good as it does to thee. I think it means that thou art fey[54]; unless it be the mere want of sleep that has worked upon thee."

227. OF ARNLJOT GELLINE'S BAPTISM.

When King Olaf was arrived at Stiklestad, it happened, among other circumstances, that a man came to him; and although it was nowise wonderful that there came many men from the districts, yet this must be regarded as unusual, that this man did not appear like the other men who came to him. He was so tall that none stood higher than up to his shoulders: very handsome he was in countenance, and had beautiful fair hair. He was well armed; had a fine helmet, and ring armour; a red shield; a superb sword in his belt; and in his hand a gold-mounted spear, the shaft of it so thick that it was a handful to grasp. The man went before the king, saluted him, and asked if the king would accept his services.

The king asked his name and family, also what countryman he was.

He replies, "My family is in Jamtaland and Helsingjaland, and my name is Arnljot Gelline; but this I must not forget to tell you, that I came to the assistance of those men you sent to Jamtaland to collect scat, and I gave into their hands a silver dish, which I sent you as a token that I would be your friend."

Then the king asked Arnljot if he was a Christian or not. He replied, "My faith has been this, to rely upon my power and strength, and which faith hath hitherto given me satisfaction; but now I intend rather to put my faith, sire, in thee."

54 Fey means doomed to die.

The king replies, "If thou wilt put faith in me thou must also put faith in what I will teach thee. Thou must believe that Jesus Christ has made heaven and earth, and all mankind, and to him shall all those who are good and rightly believing go after death."

Arnljot answers, "I have indeed heard of the white Christ, but neither know what he proposes, nor what he rules over; but now I will believe all that thou sayest to me, and lay down my lot in your hands."

Thereupon Arnljot was baptized. The king taught him so much of the holy faith as appeared to him needful, and placed him in the front rank of the order of battle, in advance of his banner, where also Gauka-Thorer and Afrafaste, with their men, were.

228. CONCERNING THE ARMY COLLECTED IN NORWAY.

Now shall we relate what we have left behind in our tale,–that the lendermen and bondes had collected a vast host as soon as it was reported that King Olaf was come from Russia, and had arrived in Svithjod; but when they heard that he had come to Jamtaland, and intended to proceed westwards over the keel-ridge to Veradal, they brought their forces into the Throndhjem country, where they gathered together the whole people, free and unfree, and proceeded towards Veradal with so great a body of men that there was nobody in Norway at that time who had seen so large a force assembled. But the force, as it usually happens in so great a multitude, consisted of many different sorts of people. There were many lendermen, and a great many powerful bondes; but the great mass consisted of labourers and cottars. The chief strength of this army lay in the Throndhjem land, and it was the most warm in enmity and opposition to the king.

229. OF BISHOP SIGURD.

When King Canute had, as before related, laid all Norway under his power, he set Earl Hakon to manage it, and gave the earl a court-bishop, by name Sigurd, who was of Danish descent, and had been long with King Canute. This bishop was of a very hot temper, and particularly obstinate, and haughty in his speech; but supported King Canute all he could in conversation, and was a great enemy of King Olaf. He was now also in the bondes' army, spoke often before the people, and urged them much to insurrection against King Olaf.

230. BISHOP SIGURD'S SPEECH.

At a House-thing, at which a great many people were assembled, the bishop desired to be heard, and made the following speech: "Here are now assembled a great many men, so that probably there will never be opportunity in this poor country of seeing so great a native army; but it would be desirable if this strength and multitude could be a protection; for it will all be needed, if this Olaf does not give over bringing war and strife upon you. From his very earliest youth he has been accustomed to plunder and kill: for which purposes he drove widely around through all countries, until he turned at last against this, where he began to show hostilities against the men who were the best and most powerful; and even against King Canute, whom all are bound to serve according to their ability, and in whose scat-lands he set himself down. He did the same to Olaf the Swedish king. He drove the earls Svein and Hakon away from their heritages; and was even most tyrannical towards his own connections, as he drove all the kings out of the Uplands: although, indeed, it was but just reward for having been false to their oaths of fealty to King Canute, and having followed this King Olaf in all the folly he could invent; so their friendship ended according to their deserts, by this king mutilating some of them, taking their kingdoms himself, and ruining every man in the country who had an honourable name. Ye know yourselves how he has treated the lendermen, of whom many of the worthlest have been murdered, and many obliged to fly from their country; and how he has roamed far and wide through the land with robber-bands, burning and plundering houses, and killing people. Who is the man among us here of any consideration who has not some great injury from him to avenge? Now he has come hither with a foreign troop, consisting mostly of forest-men, vagabonds, and such marauders. Do ye think he will now be more merciful to you, when he is roaming about with such a bad crew, after committing devastations which all who followed him dissuaded him from? Therefore it is now my advice, that ye remember King Canute's words when he told you, if King Olaf attempted to return to the country ye should defend the liberty King Canute had promised you, and should oppose and drive away such a vile pack. Now the only thing to be done is to advance against them, and cast forth these malefactors to the wolves and eagles, leaving their corpses on the spot they cover, unless ye drag them aside to out-of-the-way corners in the woods or rocks. No man would be so imprudent as to remove them to churches, for they are all robbers and evil-doers." When he had ended his speech it was hailed with the loudest applause, and all unanimously agreed to act according to his recommendation.

231. OF THE LENDERMEN.

THE LENDERMEN WHO HAD come together appointed meetings with each other, and consulted together how they should draw up their troops, and who should be their leader. Kalf Arnason said that Harek of Thjotta was best fitted to be the chief of this army, for he was descended from Harald Harfager's race. "The king also is particularly enraged against him on account of the murder of Grankel, and therefore he would be exposed to the severest fate if Olaf recovered the kingdom; and Harek withal is a man experienced in battles, and a man who does much for honour alone."

Harek replies, that the men are best suited for this who are in the flower of their age. "I am now," says he, "an old and decaying man, not able to do much in battle: besides, there is near relationship between me and King Olaf; and although he seems not to put great value upon that tie, it would not beseem me to go as leader of the hostilities against him, before any other in this meeting. On the other hand, thou, Thorer, art well suited to be our chief in this battle against King Olaf; and thou hast distinct grounds for being so, both because thou hast to avenge the death of thy relation, and also hast been driven by him as an outlaw from thy property. Thou hast also promised King Canute, as well as thy connections, to avenge the murder of thy relative Asbjorn; and dost thou suppose there ever will be a better opportunity than this of taking vengeance on Olaf for all these insults and injuries?"

Thorer replies thus to his speech: "I do not confide in myself so much as to raise the banner against King Olaf, or, as chief, to lead on this army; for the people of Throndhjem have the greatest part in this armament, and I know well their haughty spirit, and that they would not obey me, or any other Halogaland man, although I need not be reminded of my injuries to be roused to vengeance on King Olaf. I remember well my heavy loss when King Olaf slew four men, all distinguished both by birth and personal qualities; namely, my brother's son Asbjorn, my sister's sons Thorer and Grjotgard, and their father Olver; and it is my duty to take vengeance for each man of them. I will not conceal that I have selected eleven of my house-servants for that purpose, and of those who are the most daring; and I do not think we shall be behind others in exchanging blows with King Olaf, should opportunity be given."

232. KALF ARNASON'S SPEECH.

THEN KALF ARNASON DESIRED to speak. "It is highly necessary," says he, "that this business we have on hand do not turn out a mockery and child-work, now that an army is collected. Something else is needful, if we are to stand battle with King Olaf, than that each should shove the danger from himself; for we must recollect that although King Olaf has not many people compared to this army of ours, the leader of them is intrepid, and the whole body of them will be true to him, and obedient in the battle. But if we who should be the leaders of this army show any fear, and will not encourage the army and go at the head of it, it must happen that with the great body of our people the spirit will leave their hearts, and the next thing will be that each will seek his own safety. Although we have now a great force assembled, we shall find our destruction certain, when we meet King Olaf and his troops, if we, the chiefs of the people, are not confident in our cause, and have not the whole army confidently and bravely going along with us. If it cannot be so, we had better not risk a battle; and then it is easy to see that nothing would be left us but to shelter ourselves under King Olaf's mercy, however hard it might be, as then we would be less guilty than we now may appear to him to be. Yet I know there are men in his ranks who would secure my life and peace if I would seek it. Will ye now adopt my proposal–then shalt thou, friend Thorer, and thou, Harek, go under the banner which we will all of us raise up, and then follow. Let us all be speedy and determined in the resolution we have taken, and put ourselves so at the head of the bondes' army that they see no distrust in us; for then will the common man advance with spirit when we go merrily to work in placing the army in battle-order, and in encouraging the people to the strife."

When Kalf had ended they all concurred in what he proposed, and all would do what Kalf thought of advantage. All desired Kalf to be the leader of the army, and to give each what place in it he chose.

233. HOW THE LENDERMEN SET UP THEIR BANNERS.

Kalf Arnason then raised his banner, and drew up his house-servants along with Harek of Thjotta and his men. Thorer Hund, with his troop, was at the head of the order of battle in front of the banner; and on both sides of Thorer was a chosen body of bondes, all of them the most active and best armed in the forces. This part of the array was long and thick, and in it were drawn up the Throndhjem people and the Halogalanders. On the right wing was another array; and on the left of the main array were drawn up the men from Rogaland, Hordaland, the Fjord districts, and Scgn, and they had the third banner.

234. OF THORSTEIN KNARRARSMID.

There was a man called Thorstein Knarrarsmid, who was a merchant and master ship-carpenter, stout and strong, very passionate, and a great manslayer. He had been in enmity against King Olaf, who had taken from him a new and large merchant-vessel he had built, on account of some manslaughter-mulct, incurred in the course of his misdeeds, which he owed to the king. Thorstein, who was with the bondes' army, went forward in front of the line in which Thorer Hund stood, and said, "Here I will be, Thorer, in your ranks; for I think, if I and King Olaf meet, to be the first to strive a weapon at him, if I can get so near, to repay him for the robbery of the ship he took from me, which was the best that ever went on merchant voyage." Thorer and his men received Thorstein, and he went into their ranks.

235. OF THE PREPARATIONS OF THE BONDES.

When the bondes' men and array were drawn up the lendermen addressed the men, and ordered them to take notice of the place to which each man belonged, under which banner each should be, who there were in front of the banner, who were his side-men, and that they should be brisk and quick in taking up their places in the array; for the army had still to go a long way, and the array might be broken in the course of march. Then they encouraged the people; and Kalf invited all the men who had any injury to avenge on King Olaf to place themselves under the banner which was advancing against King Olaf's own banner. They should remember the distress he had brought upon them; and, he said, never was there a better opportunity to avenge their grievances, and to free themselves from the yoke and slavery he had imposed on them. "Let him," says he, "be held a useless coward who does not fight this day boldly; and they are not innocents who are opposed to you, but people who will not spare you if ye spare them."

Kalf's speech was received with loud applause, and shouts of encouragement were heard through the whole army.

236. OF THE KING'S AND THE BONDES' ARMIES.

Thereafter the bondes' army advanced to Stiklestad, where King Olaf was already with his people. Kalf and Harek went in front, at the head of the army under their banners. But the battle did not begin immediately on their meeting; for the bondes delayed the assault, because all their men were not come upon the plain, and they waited for those who came after them. Thorer Hund had come up with his troop the last, for he had to take care that the men did not go off behind when the battlecry was raised, or the armies were closing with each other; and therefore Kalf and Harek waited for Thorer. For the encouragement of their men in the battle the bondes had the field-cry–"Forward, forward, bondemen!" King Olaf also made no attack, for he waited for Dag and the people who followed him. At last the king saw Dag and his men approaching. It is said that the army of the bondes was not less on this day than a hundred times a hundred men. Sigvat the skald speaks thus of the numbers:–

"I grieve to think the king had brought
Too small a force for what he sought:
He held his gold too fast to bring
The numbers that could make him king.
The foemen, more than two to one,
The victory by numbers won;
And this alone, as I've heard say,
Against King Olaf turned the day."

237. MEETING OF THE KING AND THE BONDES.

As the armies on both sides stood so near that people knew each other, the king said, "Why art thou here, Kalf, for we parted good friends south in More? It beseems thee ill to fight against us, or to throw a spear into our army; for here are four of thy brothers."

Kalf replied, "Many things come to pass differently from what may appear seemly. You parted from us so that it was necessary to seek peace with those who were behind in the country. Now each must remain where he stands; but if I might advise, we should be reconciled."

Then Fin, his brother, answered, "This is to be observed of Kalf, that when he speaks fairly he has it in his mind to do ill."

The king answered, "It may be, Kalf, that thou art inclined to reconciliation; but, methinks, the bondes do not appear so peaceful."

Then Thorgeir of Kviststad said, "You shall now have such peace as many formerly have received at your hands, and which you shall now pay for."

The king replies, "Thou hast no occasion to hasten so much to meet us; for fate has not decreed to thee to-day a victory over me, who raised thee to power and dignity from a mean station."

238. BEGINNING OF THE BATTLE OF STIKLESTAD.

Now came Thorer Hund, went forward in front of the banner with his troop, and called out, "Forward, forward, bondemen!" Thereupon the bondemen raised the war-cry, and shot their arrows and spears. The king's men raised also a war-shout; and that done, encouraged each other to advance, crying out, "Forward, forward, Christ-men! cross-men! king's men!" When the bondes who stood outermost on the wings heard it, they repeated the same cry; but when the other bondes heard them they thought these were king's men, turned their arms against them, and they fought together, and many were slain before they knew each other. The weather was beautiful, and the sun shone clear; but when the battle began the heaven and the sun became red, and before the battle ended it became as dark as at night. King Olaf had drawn up his army upon a rising ground, and it rushed down from thence upon the bonde-army with such a fierce assault, that the bondes' array went before it; so that the breast of the king's array came to stand upon the ground on which the rear of the bondes' array had stood, and many of the bondes' army were on the way to fly, but the lendermen and their house-men stood fast, and the battle became very severe. So says Sigvat:–

"Thundered the ground beneath their tread,
As, iron-clad, thick-tramping, sped

The men-at-arms, in row and rank,
Past Stiklestad's sweet grassy bank.
The clank of steel, the bowstrings' twang,
The sounds of battle, loudly rang;
And bowman hurried on advancing,
Their bright helms in the sunshine glancing."

The lendermen urged their men, and forced them to advance. Sigvat speaks of this:–

"Midst in their line their banner flies,
Thither the stoutest bonde hies:
But many a bonde thinks of home,
And many wish they ne'er had come."

Then the bonde-army pushed on from all quarters. They who stood in front hewed down with their swords; they who stood next thrust with their spears; and they who stood hindmost shot arrows, cast spears, or threw stones, hand-axes, or sharp stakes. Soon there was a great fall of men in the battle. Many were down on both sides. In the first onset fell Arnljot Gelline, Gauka-Thorer, and Afrafaste, with all their men, after each had killed a man or two, and some indeed more. Now the ranks in front of the king's banner began to be thinned, and the king ordered Thord to carry the banner forward, and the king himself followed it with the troop he had chosen to stand nearest to him in battle; and these were the best armed men in the field, and the most expert in the use of their weapons. Sigvat the skald tells of this:–

"Loud was the battle-storm there,
Where the king's banner flamed in air.
The king beneath his banner stands,
And there the battle he commands."

Olaf came forth from behind the shield-bulwark, and put himself at the head of the army; and when the bondes looked him in the face they were frightened, and let their hands drop. So says Sigvat:–

"I think I saw them shrink with fear
Who would not shrink from foeman's spear,
When Olaf's lion-eye was cast

On them, and called up all the past.
Clear as the serpent's eye–his look
No Throndhjem man could stand, but shook
Beneath its glance, and skulked away,
Knowing his king, and cursed the day."

The combat became fierce, and the king went forward in the fray. So says Sigvat:–

"When on they came in fierce array,
And round the king arose the fray,
With shield on arm brave Olaf stood,
Dyeing his sword in their best blood.
For vengeance on his Throndhjem foes,
On their best men he dealt his blows;
He who knew well death's iron play,
To his deep vengeance gave full sway."

239. THORGEIR OF KVISTSTAD'S FALL.

King Olaf fought most desperately. He struck the lenderman before mentioned (Thorgeir of Kviststad) across the face, cut off the nose-piece of his helmet, and clove his head down below the eyes so that they almost fell out. When he fell the king said, "Was it not true, Thorgeir, what I told thee, that thou shouldst not be victor in our meeting?" At the same instant Thord stuck the banner-pole so fast in the earth that it remained standing. Thord had got his death-wound, and fell beneath the banner. There also fell Thorfin Mun, and also Gissur Gullbrarskald, who was attacked by two men, of whom he killed one, but only wounded the other before he fell. So says Hofgardaref:–

"Bold in the Iron-storm was he,
Firm and stout as forest tree,
The hero who, 'gainst two at once,
Made Odin's fire from sword-edge glance;
Dealing a death-blow to the one,
Known as a brave and generous man,
Wounding the other, ere he fell,–
His bloody sword his deeds showed well."

It happened then, as before related, that the sun, although the air was clear, withdrew from the sight, and it became dark. Of this Sigvat the skald speaks:–

"No common wonder in the sky
Fell out that day–the sun on high,
And not a cloud to see around,
Shone not, nor warmed Norway's ground.
The day on which fell out this fight
Was marked by dismal dusky light,
This from the East I heard–the end
Of our great king it did portend."

At the same time Dag Hringson came up with his people, and began to put his men in array, and to set up his banner; but on account of the darkness the onset could not go on so briskly, for they could not see exactly whom they had before them. They turned, however, to that quarter where the men of Hordaland and Rogaland stood. Many of these circumstances took place at the same time, and some happened a little earlier, and some a little later.

240. KING OLAF'S FALL.

ON THE ONE SIDE of Kalf Arnason stood his two relations, Olaf and Kalf, with many other brave and stout men. Kalf was a son of Arnfin Arnmodson, and a brother's son of Arne Arnmodson. On the other side of Kalf Arnason stood Thorer Hund. King Olaf hewed at Thorer Hund, and struck him across the shoulders; but the sword would not cut, and it was as if dust flew from his reindeer-skin coat. So says Sigvat:–

"The king himself now proved the power
Of Fin-folk's craft in magic hour,
With magic song; for stroke of steel
Thor's reindeer coat would never feel,
Bewitched by them it turned the stroke
Of the king's sword,–a dust-like smoke
Rose from Thor's shoulders from the blow
Which the king though would end his foe."

Thorer struck at the king, and they exchanged some blows; but the king's sword would not cut where it met the reindeer skin, although Thorer was wounded in the hands. Sigvat sang thus of it:–

"Some say that Thorer's not right bold;
Why never yet have I been told
Of one who did a bolder thing
Than to change blows with his true king.
Against his king his sword to wield,
Leaping across the shield on shield
Which fenced the king round in the fight,
Shows the dog's[55] courage–brave, not bright."

The king said to Bjorn the marshal, "Do thou kill the dog on whom steel will not bite." Bjorn turned round the axe in his hands, and gave Thorer a blow with the hammer of it on the shoulder so hard that he tottered. The king at the same moment turned against Kalf and his relations, and gave Olaf his death-wound. Thorer Hund struck his spear right through the body of Marshal Bjorn, and killed him outright; and Thorer said, "It is thus we hunt the bear."[56] Thorstein Knarrarsmid struck at King Olaf with his axe, and the blow hit his left leg above the knee. Fin Arnason instantly killed Thorstein. The king after the wound staggered towards a stone, threw down his sword, and prayed God to help him. Then Thorer Hund struck at him with his spear, and the stroke went in under his mail-coat and into his belly. Then Kalf struck at him on the left side of the neck. But all are not agreed upon Kalf having been the man who gave him the wound in the neck. These three wounds were King Olaf's death; and after the king's death the greater part of the forces which had advanced with him fell with the king. Bjarne Gullbrarskald sang these verses about Kalf Arnason:–

"Warrior! who Olaf dared withstand,
Who against Olaf held the land,
Thou hast withstood the bravest, best,
Who e'er has gone to his long rest.
At Stiklestad thou wast the head;
With flying banners onwards led

55 Thorer's name was Hund–the dog; and a play upon Thorer Hund's name was intended by the skald.–L.

56 Bjorn, the marshal's name, signifies a bear.–L.

Thy bonde troops, and still fought on,
Until he fell–the much-mourned one."

Sigvat also made these verses on Bjorn:–

"The marshal Bjorn, too, I find,
A great example leaves behind,
How steady courage should stand proof,
Though other servants stand aloof.
To Russia first his steps he bent,
To serve his master still intent;
And now besides his king he fell,–
A noble death for skalds to tell."

241. BEGINNING OF DAG HRINGSON'S ATTACK.

Dag Hringson still kept up the battle, and made in the beginning so fierce an assault that the bondes gave way, and some betook themselves to flight. There a great number of the bondes fell, and these lendermen, Erlend of Gerde and Aslak of Finey; and the banner also which they had stood under was cut down. This onset was particularly hot, and was called Dag's storm. But now Kalf Arnason, Harek of Thjotta, and Thorer Hund turned against Dag, with the array which had followed them, and then Dag was overwhelmed with numbers; so he betook himself to flight with the men still left him. There was a valley through which the main body of the fugitives fled, and men lay scattered in heaps on both sides; and many were severely wounded, and many so fatigued that they were fit for nothing. The bondes pursued only a short way; for their leaders soon returned back to the field of battle, where they had their friends and relations to look after.

242. KING OLAF'S MIRACLE SHOWN TO THORER HUND.

Thorer Hund went to where King Olaf's body lay, took care of it, laid it straight out on the ground, and spread a cloak over it. He told since that when he wiped the blood from the face it was very beautiful; and there was red in the cheeks, as if he only slept, and even much clearer than when he was in life. The king's blood came on Thorer's hand, and ran up between his fingers to where he had been wounded, and the wound grew up so speedily that it did not require to be bound up. This circumstance was testified by Thorer himself when King Olaf's holiness came to be generally known among the people; and Thorer Hund was among the first of the king's powerful opponents who endeavoured to spread abroad the king's sanctity.

243. OF KALF ARNASON'S BROTHERS.

KALF ARNASON SEARCHED FOR his brothers who had fallen, and found Thorberg and Fin. It is related that Fin threw his dagger at him, and wanted to kill him, giving him hard words, and calling him a faithless villain, and a traitor to his king. Kalf did not regard it, but ordered Fin and Thorberg to be carried away from the field. When their wounds were examined they were found not to be deadly, and they had fallen from fatigue, and under the weight of their weapons. Thereafter Kalf tried to bring his brothers down to a ship, and went himself with them. As soon as he was gone the whole bonde-army, having their homes in the neighbourhood, went off also, excepting those who had friends or relations to look after, or the bodies of the slain to take care of. The wounded were taken home to the farms, so that every house was full of them; and tents were erected over some. But wonderful as was the number collected in the bonde-army, no less wonderful was the haste with which this vast body was dispersed when it was once free; and the cause of this was, that the most of the people gathered together from the country places were longing for their homes.

244. OF THE BONDES OF VERADAL.

THE BONDES WHO HAD their homes in Veradal went to the chiefs Harek and Thorer, and complained of their distress, saying, "The fugitives who have escaped from the battle have proceeded up over the valley of Veradal, and are destroying our habitations, and there is no safety for us to travel home so long as they are in the valley. Go after them with war-force, and let no mother's son of them escape with life; for that is what they intended for us if they had got the upper hand in the battle, and the same they would do now if they met us hereafter, and had better luck than we. It may also be that they will linger in the valley if they have nothing to be frightened for, and then they would not proceed very gently in the inhabited country." The bondes made many words about this, urging the chiefs to advance directly, and kill those who had escaped. Now when the chiefs talked over this matter among themselves, they thought there was much truth in what the bondes said. They resolved, therefore, that Thorer Hund should undertake this expedition through Veradal, with 600 men of his own troops. Then, towards evening, he set out with his men; and Thorer continued his march without halt until he came in the night to Sula, where he heard the news that Dag Hringson had come there in the evening, with many other flocks of the king's men, and had halted there until they took supper, but were afterwards gone up to the mountains. Then Thorer said he did not care to pursue them up through the mountains, and he returned down the valley again, and they did not kill many of them this time. The bondes then returned to their homes, and the following day Thorer, with his people, went to their ships. The part of the king's men who were still on their legs concealed themselves in the forests, and some got help from the people.

245. OF THE KING'S BROTHER, HARALD SIGURDSON.

Harald Sigurdson was severely wounded; but Ragnvald Brusason brought him to a bonde's the night after the battle, and the bonde took in Harald, and healed his wound in secret, and afterwards gave him his son to attend him. They went secretly over the mountains, and through the waste forests, and came out in Jamtaland. Harald Sigurdson was fifteen years old when King Olaf fell. In Jamtaland Harald found Ragnvald Brusason; and they went both east to King Jarisleif in Russia, as is related in the Saga of Harald Sigurdson.

246. OF THORMOD KOLBRUNARSKALD.

Thormod Kolbrunarskald was under King Olaf's banner in the battle; but when the king had fallen, the battle was raging so that of the king's men the one fell by the side of the other, and the most of those who stood on their legs were wounded. Thormod was also severely wounded, and retired, as all the others did, back from where there was most danger of life, and some even fled. Now when the onset began which is called Dag's storm, all of the king's men who were able to combat went there; but Thormod did not come into that combat, being unable to fight, both from his wound and from weariness, but he stood by the side of his comrade in the ranks, although he could do nothing. There he was struck by an arrow in the left side; but he broke off the shaft of the arrow, went out of the battle, and up towards the houses, where he came to a barn which was a large building. Thormod had his drawn sword in his hand; and as he went in a man met him, coming out, and said, "It is very bad there with howling and screaming; and a great shame it is that brisk young fellows cannot bear their wounds: it may be that the king's men have done bravely to-day, but they certainly bear their wounds very ill."

Thormod asks. "What is thy name?"
He called himself Kimbe.
Thormod: "Wast thou in the battle, too?"
"I was with the bondes, which was the best side," says he.
"And art thou wounded any way?" says Thormod.
"A little," said Kimbe. "And hast thou been in the battle too?"
Thormod replied, "I was with them who had the best."
"Art thou wounded?" says Kimbe.
"Not much to signify," replies Thormod.

As Kimbe saw that Thormod had a gold ring on his arm, he said, "Thou art certainly a king's man. Give me thy gold ring, and I will hide thee. The bondes will kill thee if thou fallest in their way."

Thormod says, "Take the ring if thou canst get it: I have lost that which is more worth."

Kimbe stretched out his hand, and wanted to take the ring; but Thormod, swinging his sword, cut off his hand; and it is related that Kimbe behaved himself no better under his wound than those he had been blaming just before. Kimbe went off, and Thormod sat down in the barn, and listened to what people were saying. The conversation was mostly about what each had seen in the battle, and about the valour of the combatants. Some praised most King Olaf's courage, and some named others who stood nowise behind him in bravery. Then Thormod sang these verses:–

"Olaf was brave beyond all doubt,–
At Stiklestad was none so stout;
Spattered with blood, the king, unsparing,

Cheered on his men with deed and daring.
But I have heard that some were there
Who in the fight themselves would spare;
Though, in the arrow-storm, the most
Had perils quite enough to boast."

247. THORMOD'S DEATH.

Thormod went out, and entered into a chamber apart, in which there were many wounded men, and with them a woman binding their wounds. There was fire upon the floor, at which she warmed water to wash and clean their wounds. Thormod sat himself down beside the door, and one came in, and another went out, of those who were busy about the wounded men. One of them turned to Thormod, looked at him, and said, "Why art thou so dead-pale? Art thou wounded? Why dost thou not call for the help of the wound-healers?" Thormod then sang these verses:–

"I am not blooming, and the fair
And slender girl loves to care
For blooming youths–few care for me;
With Fenja's meal I cannot fee.
This is the reason why I feel
The slash and thrust of Danish steel;
And pale and faint, and bent with pain,
Return from yonder battle-plain."

Then Thormod stood up and went in towards the fire, and stood there awhile. The young woman said to him, "Go out, man, and bring in some of the split firewood which lies close beside the door." He went out and brought in an armful of wood, which he threw down upon the floor. Then the nurse-girl looked him in the face, and said, "Dreadfully pale is this man–why art thou so?" Then Thormod sang:–

"Thou wonderest, sweet sprig, at me,
A man so hideous to see:
Deep wounds but rarely mend the face,
The crippling blow gives little grace.
The arrow-drift o'ertook me, girl,–
A fine-ground arrow in the whirl

Went through me, and I feel the dart
Sits, lovely girl, too near my heart."

The girl said, "Let me see thy wound, and I will bind it." Thereupon Thormod sat down, cast off his clothes, and the girl saw his wounds, and examined that which was in his side, and felt that a piece of iron was in it, but could not find where the iron had gone in. In a stone pot she had stirred together leeks and other herbs, and boiled them, and gave the wounded men of it to eat, by which she discovered if the wounds had penetrated into the belly; for if the wound had gone so deep, it would smell of leek. She brought some of this now to Thormod, and told him to eat of it. He replied, "Take it away, I have no appetite for my broth." Then she took a large pair of tongs, and tried to pull out the iron; but it sat too fast, and would in no way come, and as the wound was swelled, little of it stood out to lay hold of. Now said Thormod, "Cut so deep in that thou canst get at the iron with the tongs, and give me the tongs and let me pull." She did as he said. Then Thormod took a gold ring from his hand, gave it to the nurse-woman, and told her to do with it what she liked. "It is a good man's gift," said he: "King Olaf gave me the ring this morning." Then Thormod took the tongs, and pulled the iron out; but on the iron there was a hook, at which there hung some morsels of flesh from the heart,–some white, some red. When he saw that, he said, "The king has fed us well. I am fat, even at the heart-roots;" and so saying he leant back, and was dead. And with this ends what we have to say about Thormod.

248. OF SOME CIRCUMSTANCES OF THE BATTLE.

King Olaf fell on Wednesday, the 29th of July (A.D. 1030). It was near mid-day when the two armies met, and the battle began before half-past one, and before three the king fell. The darkness continued from about half-past one to three also. Sigvat the skald speaks thus of the result of the battle:–

"The loss was great to England's foes,
When their chief fell beneath the blows
By his own thoughtless people given,–
When the king's shield in two was riven.
The people's sovereign took the field,
The people clove the sovereign's shield.

Of all the chiefs that bloody day,
Dag only came out of the fray."

And he composed these:–

"Such mighty bonde-power, I ween,
With chiefs or rulers ne'er was seen.
It was the people's mighty power
That struck the king that fatal hour.
When such a king, in such a strife,
By his own people lost his life,
Full many a gallant man must feel
The death-wound from the people's steel."

The bondes did not spoil the slain upon the field of battle, for immediately after the battle there came upon many of them who had been against the king a kind of dread as it were; yet they held by their evil inclination, for they resolved among themselves that all who had fallen with the king should not receive the interment which belongs to good men, but reckoned them all robbers and outlaws. But the men who had power, and had relations on the field, cared little for this, but removed their remains to the churches, and took care of their burial.

249. A MIRACLE ON A BLIND MAN.

Thorgils Halmason and his son Grim went to the field of battle towards evening when it was dusk, took King Olaf's corpse up, and bore it to a little empty houseman's hut which stood on the other side of their farm. They had light and water with them. Then they took the clothes off the body, swathed it in a linen cloth, laid it down in the house, and concealed it under some firewood so that nobody could see it, even if people came into the hut. Thereafter they went home again to the farmhouse. A great many beggars and poor people had followed both armies, who begged for meat; and the evening after the battle many remained there, and sought lodging round about in all the houses, great or small. It is told of a blind man who was poor, that a boy attended him and led him. They went out around the farm to seek a lodging, and came to the same empty house, of which the door was so low that they had almost to creep in. Now when the blind man had come in, he fumbled about the floor seeking a place where he could lay himself down. He had a hat on his head, which fell down over his face when he stooped down. He felt with his hands that there was moisture on the floor, and he put up his wet hand to raise his hat, and in doing so put his fingers on his eyes. There came immediately such an itching in his eyelids, that he wiped the water with his fingers from his eyes, and went out of the hut, saying nobody could lie there, it was so wet. When he came out of the hut he could distinguish his hands, and all that was near him, as far as things can be distinguished by sight in the darkness of light; and he went immediately to the farm-house into the room, and told all the people he had got his sight again, and could see everything, although many knew he had been blind for a long time, for he had been there, before, going about among the houses of the neighbourhood. He said he first got his sight when he was coming out of a little ruinous hut which was all wet inside. "I groped in the water," said he, "and rubbed my eyes with my wet hands." He told where the hut stood. The people who heard him wondered much at this event, and spoke among themselves of what it could be that produced it: but Thorgils the peasant and his son Grim thought they knew how this came to pass; and as they were much afraid the king's enemies might go there and search the hut, they went and took the body out of it, and removed it to a garden, where they concealed it, and then returned to the farm, and slept there all night.

250. OF THORER HUND.

THE FIFTH DAY (Thursday), Thorer Hund came down the valley of Veradal to Stiklestad; and many people, both chiefs and bondes, accompanied him. The field of battle was still being cleared, and people were carrying away the bodies of their friends and relations, and were giving the necessary help to such of the wounded as they wished to save; but many had died since the battle. Thorer Hund went to where the king had fallen, and searched for his body; but not finding it, he inquired if any one could tell him what had become of the corpse, but nobody could tell him where it was. Then he asked the bonde Thorgils, who said, "I was not in the battle, and knew little of what took place there; but many reports are abroad, and among others that King Olaf has been seen in the night up at Staf, and a troop of people with him: but if he fell in the battle, your men must have concealed him in some hole, or under some stone-heap." Now although Thorer Hund knew for certain that the king had fallen, many allowed themselves to believe, and to spread abroad the report, that the king had escaped from the battle, and would in a short time come again upon them with an army. Then Thorer went to his ships, and sailed down the fjord, and the bonde-army dispersed, carrying with them all the wounded men who could bear to be removed.

251. OF KING OLAF'S BODY.

Thorgils Halmason and his son Grim had King Olaf's body, and were anxious about preserving it from falling into the hands of the king's enemies, and being ill-treated; for they heard the bondes speaking about burning it, or sinking it in the sea. The father and son had seen a clear light burning at night over the spot on the battlefield where King Olaf's body lay, and since, while they concealed it, they had always seen at night a light burning over the corpse; therefore they were afraid the king's enemies might seek the body where this signal was visible. They hastened, therefore, to take the body to a place where it would be safe. Thorgils and his son accordingly made a coffin, which they adorned as well as they could, and laid the king's body in it; and afterwards made another coffin in which they laid stones and straw, about as much as the weight of a man, and carefully closed the coffins. As soon as the whole bonde-army had left Stiklestad, Thorgils and his son made themselves ready, got a large rowing-boat, and took with them seven or eight men, who were all Thorgil's relations or friends, and privately took the coffin with the king's body down to the boat, and set it under the foot-boards. They had also with them the coffin containing the stones, and placed it in the boat where all could see it; and then went down the fjord with a good opportunity of wind and weather, and arrived in the dusk of the evening at Nidaros, where they brought up at the king's pier. Then Thorgils sent some of his men up to the town to Bishop Sigurd, to say that they were come with the king's body. As soon as the bishop heard this news, he sent his men down to the pier, and they took a small rowing-boat, came alongside of Thorgil's ship, and demanded the king's body. Thorgils and his people then took the coffin which stood in view, and bore it into the boat; and the bishop's men rowed out into the fjord, and sank the coffin in the sea. It was now quite dark. Thorgils and his people now rowed up into the river past the town, and landed at a place called Saurhlid, above the town. Then they carried the king's body to an empty house standing at a distance from other houses, and watched over it for the night, while Thorgils went down to the town, where he spoke with some of the best friends of King Olaf, and asked them if they would take charge of the king's body; but none of them dared to do so. Then Thorgils and his men went with the body higher up the river, buried it in a sand-hill on the banks, and levelled all around it so that no one could observe that people had been at work there. They were ready with all this before break of day, when they returned to their vessel, went immediately out of the river, and proceeded on their way home to Stiklestad.

252. OF THE BEGINNING OF KING SVEIN ALFIFASON'S GOVERNMENT.

SVEIN, A SON OF King Canute, and of Alfifa, a daughter of Earl Alfrin, had been appointed to govern Jomsborg in Vindland. There came a message to him from his father King Canute, that he should come to Denmark; and likewise that afterwards he should proceed to Norway, and take that kingdom under his charge, and assume, at the same time, the title of king of Norway. Svein repaired to Denmark, and took many people with him from thence, and also Earl Harald and many other people of consequence attended him. Thorarin Loftunga speaks of this in the song he composed about King Svein, called the "Glelogn Song":-

> *"'Tis told by fame,*
> *How grandly came*
> *The Danes to tend*
> *Their young king Svein.*
> *Grandest was he,*
> *That all could see;*
> *Then, one by one,*
> *Each following man*
> *More splendour wore*
> *Than him before."*

Then Svein proceeded to Norway, and his mother Alfifa was with him; and he was taken to be king at every Law-thing in the country. He had already come as far as Viken at the time the battle was fought at Stiklestad, and King Olaf fell. Svein continued his journey until he came north, in autumn, to the Throndhjem country; and there, as elsewhere, he was received as king.

253. OF KING SVEIN'S LAWS.

King Svein introduced new laws in many respects into the country, partly after those which were in Denmark, and in part much more severe. No man must leave the country without the king's permission; or if he did, his property fell to the king. Whoever killed a man outright, should forfeit all his land and movables. If any one was banished the country, and all heritage fell to him, the king took his inheritance. At Yule every man should pay the king a meal of malt from every harvest steading, and a leg of a three-year old ox, which was called a friendly gift, together with a spand of butter; and every house-wife a rock full of unspun lint, as thick as one could span with the longest fingers of the hand. The bondes were bound to build all the houses the king required upon his farms. Of every seven males one should be taken for the service of war, and reckoning from the fifth year of age; and the outfit of ships should be reckoned in the same proportion. Every man who rowed upon the sea to fish should pay the king five fish as a tax, for the land defence, wherever he might come from. Every ship that went out of the country should have stowage reserved open for the king in the middle of the ship. Every man, foreigner or native, who went to Iceland, should pay a tax to the king. And to all this was added, that Danes should enjoy so much consideration in Norway, that one witness of them should invalidate ten of Northmen[57].

When these laws were promulgated the minds of the people were instantly raised against them, and murmurs were heard among them. They who had not taken part against King Olaf said, "Now take your reward and friendship from the Canute race, ye men of the interior Throndhjem who fought against King Olaf, and deprived him of his kingdom. Ye were promised peace and justice, and now ye have got oppression and slavery for your great treachery and crime." Nor was it very easy to contradict them, as all men saw how miserable the change had been. But people had not the boldness to make an insurrection against King Svein, principally because many had given King Canute their sons or other near relations as hostages; and also because no one appeared as leader of an insurrection. They very soon, however, complained of King Svein; and his mother Alfifa got much of the blame of all that was against their desire. Then the truth, with regard to Olaf, became evident to many.

57 This may probably have referred not to witnesses of an act, but to the class of witnesses in the jurisprudence of the Middle Ages called compurgators, who testified not the fact, but their confidence in the statements of the accused; and from which, possibly, our English bail for offenders arose. –L.

254. OF KING OLAF'S SANCTITY.

THIS WINTER (A.D. 1031) many in the Throndhjem land began to declare that Olaf was in reality a holy man, and his sanctity was confirmed by many miracles. Many began to make promises and prayers to King Olaf in the matters in which they thought they required help, and many found great benefit from these invocations. Some in respect of health, others of a journey, or other circumstances in which such help seemed needful.

255. OF EINAR TAMBASKELFER.

EINAR TAMBASKELFER WAS COME home from England to his farm, and had the fiefs which King Canute had given him when they met in Throndhjem, and which were almost an earldom. Einar had not been in the strife against King Olaf, and congratulated himself upon it. He remembered that King Canute had promised him the earldom over Norway, and at the same time remembered that King Canute had not kept his promise. He was accordingly the first great person who looked upon King Olaf as a saint.

256. OF THE SONS OF ARNE.

FIN ARNASON REMAINED BUT a short time at Eggja with his brother Kalf; for he was in the highest degree ill-pleased that Kalf had been in the battle against King Olaf, and always made his brother the bitterest reproaches on this account. Thorberg Arnason was much more temperate in his discourse than Fin; but yet he hastened away, and went home to his farm. Kalf gave the two brothers a good long-ship, with full rigging and other necessaries, and a good retinue. Therefore they went home to their farms, and sat quietly at home. Arne Arnason lay long ill of his wounds, but got well at last without injury of any limb, and in winter he proceeded south to his farm. All the brothers made their peace with King Svein, and sat themselves quietly down in their homes.

257. BISHOP SIGURD'S FLIGHT.

THE SUMMER AFTER (A.D. 1031) there was much talk about King Olaf's sanctity, and there was a great alteration in the expressions of all people concerning him. There were many who now believed that King Olaf must be a saint, even among those who had persecuted him with the greatest animosity, and would never in their conversation allow truth or justice in his favour. People began then to turn their reproaches against the men who had principally excited opposition to the king; and on this account Bishop Sigurd in particular was accused. He got so many enemies, that he found it most advisable to go over to England to King Canute. Then the Throndhjem people sent men with a verbal message to the Uplands, to Bishop Grimkel, desiring him to come north to Throndhjem. King Olaf had sent Bishop Grimkel back to Norway when he went east into Russia, and since that time Grimkel had been in the Uplands. When the message came to the bishop he made ready to go, and it contributed much to this journey that the bishop considered it as true what was told of King Olaf's miracles and sanctity.

258. KING OLAF THE SAINT'S REMAINS DISINTERRED.

Bishop Grimkel went to Einar Tambaskelfer, who received him joyfully. They talked over many things, and, among others, of the important events which had taken place in the country; and concerning these they were perfectly agreed. Then the bishop proceeded to the town (Nidaros), and was well received by all the community. He inquired particularly concerning the miracles of King Olaf that were reported, and received satisfactory accounts of them. Thereupon the bishop sent a verbal message to Stiklestad to Thorgils and his son Grim, inviting them to come to the town to him. They did not decline the invitation, but set out on the road immediately, and came to the town and to the bishop. They related to him all the signs that had presented themselves to them, and also where they had deposited the king's body. The bishop sent a message to Einar Tambaskelfer, who came to the town. Then the bishop and Einar had an audience of the king and Alfifa, in which they asked the king's leave to have King Olaf's body taken up out of the earth. The king gave his permission, and told the bishop to do as he pleased in the matter. At that time there were a great many people in the town. The bishop, Einar, and some men with them, went to the place where the king's body was buried, and had the place dug; but the coffin had already raised itself almost to the surface of the earth. It was then the opinion of many that the bishop should proceed to have the king buried in the earth at Clement's church; and it was so done. Twelve months and five days (Aug. 3, A.D. 1031), after King Olaf's death his holy remains were dug up, and the coffin had raised itself almost entirely to the surface of the earth; and the coffin appeared quite new, as if it had but lately been made. When Bishop Grimkel came to King Olaf's opened coffin, there was a delightful and fresh smell. Thereupon the bishop uncovered the king's face, and his appearance was in no respect altered, and his cheeks were as red as if he had but just fallen asleep. The men who had seen King Olaf when he fell remarked, also, that his hair and nails had grown as much as if he had lived on the earth all the time that had passed since his fall. Thereupon King Svein, and all the chiefs who were at the place, went out to see King Olaf's body. Then said Alfifa, "People buried in sand rot very slowly, and it would not have been so if he had been buried in earth." Afterwards the bishop took scissors, clipped the king's hair, and arranged his beard; for he had had a long beard, according to the fashion of that time. Then said the bishop to the king and Alfifa, "Now the king's hair and beard are such as when he gave up the ghost, and it has grown as much as ye see has been cut off." Alfifa answers, "I will believe in the sanctity of his hair, if it will not burn in the fire; but I have often seen men's hair whole and undamaged after lying longer in the earth than this man's." Then the bishop had live coals put into a pan, blessed it, cast incense upon it, and then laid King Olaf's hair on the fire. When all the incense was burnt the bishop took the hair out of the fire, and showed the king and the other chiefs that it was not consumed. Now Alfifa asked that the hair should be laid upon unconsecrated fire; but Einar Tambaskelfer told her to be silent, and gave her many severe reproaches for her unbelief. After the bishop's recognition, with the king's approbation and the decision of the Thing, it was determined that King Olaf should be considered a man truly holy; whereupon his body was transported into Clement's church, and a place was prepared for it near the high altar. The coffin was covered with costly cloth, and stood under a gold embroidered tent. Many kinds of miracles were soon wrought by King Olaf's holy remains.

259. OF KING OLAF'S MIRACLES.

In the sand-hill where King Olaf's body had lain on the ground a beautiful spring of water came up and many human ailments and infirmities were cured by its waters. Things were put in order around it, and the water ever since has been carefully preserved. There was first a chapel built, and an altar consecrated, where the king's body had lain; but now Christ's church stands upon the spot. Archbishop Eystein had a high altar raised upon the spot where the king's grave had been, when he erected the great temple which now stands there; and it is the same spot on which the altar of the old Christ church had stood. It is said that Olaf's church stands on the spot on which the empty house had stood in which King Olaf's body had been laid for the night. The place over which the holy remains of King Olaf were carried up from the vessel is now called Olaf's Road, and is now in the middle of the town. The bishop adorned King Olaf's holy remains, and cut his nails and hair; for both grew as if he had still been alive. So says Sigvat the skald:–

"I lie not, when I say the king
Seemed as alive in every thing:
His nails, his yellow hair still growing,
And round his ruddy cheek still flowing,
As when, to please the Russian queen,
His yellow locks adorned were seen;
Or to the blind he cured he gave
A tress, their precious sight to save."

Thorarin Loftunga also composed a song upon Svein Alfifason, called the "Glelogn Song", in which are these verses:–

"Svein, king of all,
In Olaf's hall
Now sits on high;
And Olaf's eye
Looks down from heaven,
Where it is given
To him to dwell:
Or here in cell,
As heavenly saint,
To heal men's plaint,
May our gold-giver
Live here for ever!

"King Olaf there
To hold a share
On earth prepared,
Nor labour spared

A seat to win
From heaven's great King;
Which he has won
Next God's own Son.

"His holy form,
Untouched by worm,
Lies at this day
Where good men pray,
And nails and hair
Grow fresh and fair;
His cheek is red,
His flesh not dead.

"Around his bier,
Good people hear
The small bells ring
Over the king,
Or great bell toll;
And living soul
Not one can tell
Who tolls the bell.

"Tapers up there,
(Which Christ holds dear,)
By day and night
The altar light:
Olaf did so,
And all men know
In heaven he
From sin sits free.

"And crowds do come,
The deaf and dumb,
Cripple and blind,
Sick of all kind,
Cured to be
On bended knee;
And off the ground
Rise whole and sound.

"To Olaf pray
To eke thy day,
To save thy land
From spoiler's hand.
God's man is he
To deal to thee
Good crops and peace;
Let not prayer cease.

"Book-prayers prevail,
If, nail for nail[58]*,*
Thou tellest on,
Forgetting none."

Thorarin Loftunga was himself with King Svein, and heard these great testimonials of King Olaf's holiness, that people, by the heavenly power, could hear a sound over his holy remains as if bells were ringing, and that candles were lighted of themselves upon the altar as by a heavenly fire. But when Thorarin says that a multitude of lame, and blind, and other sick, who came to the holy Olaf, went back cured, he means nothing more than that there were a vast number of persons who at the beginning of King Olaf's miraculous working regained their health. King Olaf's greatest miracles are clearly written down, although they occurred somewhat later.

260. OF KING OLAF'S AGE AND REIGN.

It is reckoned by those who have kept an exact account, that Olaf the Saint was king of Norway for fifteen years from the time Earl Svein left the country; but he had received the title of king from the people of the Uplands the winter before. Sigvat the skald tells this:–

"For fifteen winters o'er the land
King Olaf held the chief command,

58 Before the entrance of the temples or churches were posts called Ondveigis-sulor, with nails called Rigin-naglar– the gods' nails–either for ornament, or, as Schoning suggests, to assist the people in reckoning weeks, months, festivals, and in reckoning or keeping tale of prayers repeated, and to recall them to memory, in the same way as beads are used still by the common people in Catholic countries for the same purpose.–L.

Before he fell up in the North:
His fall made known to us his worth.
No worthier prince before his day
In our North land e'er held the sway,
Too short he held it for our good;
All men wish now that he had stood."

Saint Olaf was thirty-five years old when he fell, according to what Are Frode the priest says, and he had been in twenty pitched battles. So says Sigvat the skald:–

"Some leaders trust in God–some not;
Even so their men; but well I wot
God-fearing Olaf fought and won
Twenty pitched battles, one by one,
And always placed upon his right
His Christian men in a hard fight.
May God be merciful, I pray,
To him–for he ne'er shunned his fray."

We have now related a part of King Olaf's story, namely, the events which took place while he ruled over Norway; also his death, and how his holiness was manifested. Now shall we not neglect to mention what it was that most advanced his honour. This was his miracles; but these will come to be treated of afterwards in this book.

261. OF THE THRONDHJEM PEOPLE.

King Svein, the son of Canute the Great, ruled over Norway for some years; but was a child both in age and understanding. His mother Alfifa had most sway in the country; and the people of the country were her great enemies, both then and ever since. Danish people had a great superiority given them within the country, to the great dissatisfaction of the people; and when conversation turned that way, the people of the rest of Norway accused the Throndhjem people of having principally occasioned King Olaf the Holy's fall, and also that the men of Norway were subject, through them, to the ill government by which oppression and slavery had come upon all the people, both great and small; indeed upon the whole community. They insisted that it was the duty of the Throndhjem people to attempt opposition and insurrection, and thus relieve the country from such tyranny; and, in the opinion of the common people, Throndhjem was also the chief seat of the strength of Norway at that time, both on account of the chiefs and of the population of that quarter. When the Throndhjem people heard these remarks of their countrymen, they could not deny that there was much truth in them, and that in depriving King Olaf of life and land they had committed a great crime, and at the same time the misdeed had been ill paid. The chiefs began to hold consultations and conferences with each other, and the leader of these was Einar Tambaskelfer. It was likewise the case with Kalf Arnason, who began to find into what errors he had been drawn by King Canute's persuasion. All the promises which King Canute had made to Kalf had been broken; for he had promised him the earldom and the highest authority in Norway: and although Kalf had been the leader in the battle against King Olaf, and had deprived him of his life and kingdom, Kalf had not got any higher dignity than he had before. He felt that he had been deceived, and therefore messages passed between the brothers Kalf, Fin, Thorberg, and Arne, and they renewed their family friendship.

262. OF KING SVEIN'S LEVY.

When King Svein had been three years in Norway (A.D. 1031-33), the news was received that a force was assembled in the western countries, under a chief who called himself Trygve, and gave out that he was a son of Olaf Trygvason and Queen Gyda of England. Now when King Svein heard that foreign troops had come to the country, he ordered out the people on a levy in the north, and the most of the lendermen hastened to him; but Einar Tambaskelfer remained at home, and would not go out with King Svein. When King Svein's order came to Kalf Arnason at Eggja, that he should go out on a levy with King Svein, he took a twenty-benched ship which he owned, went on board with his house-servants, and in all haste proceeded out of the fjord, without waiting for King Svein, sailed southwards to More, and continued his voyage south until he came to Giske to his brother Thorberg. Then all the brothers, the sons of Arne, held a meeting, and consulted with each other. After this Kalf returned to the north again; but when he came to Frekeysund, King Svein was lying in the sound before him. When Kalf came rowing from the south into the sound they hailed each other, and the king's men ordered Kalf to bring up with his vessel, and follow the king for the defence of the country. Kalf replies, "I have done enough, if not too much, when I fought against my own countrymen to increase the power of the Canute family." Thereupon Kalf rowed away to the north until he came home to Eggja. None of these Arnasons appeared at this levy to accompany the king. He steered with his fleet southwards along the land; but as he could not hear the least news of any fleet having come from the west, he steered south to Rogaland, and all the way to Agder; for many guessed that Trygve would first make his attempt on Viken, because his forefathers had been there, and had most of their strength from that quarter, and he had himself great strength by family connection there.

263. KING TRYGVE OLAFSON'S FALL.

When Trygve came from the west he landed first on the coast of Hordaland, and when he heard King Svein had gone south he went the same way to Rogaland. As soon as Svein got the intelligence that Trygve had come from the west he returned, and steered north with his fleet; and both fleets met within Bokn in Soknarsund, not far from the place where Erling Skjalgson fell. The battle, which took place on a Sunday, was great and severe. People tell that Trygve threw spears with both hands at once. "So my father," said he, "taught me to celebrate mass." His enemies had said that he was the son of a priest; but the praise must be allowed him that he showed himself more like a son of King Olaf Trygvason, for this Trygve was a slaughtering man. In this battle King Trygve fell, and many of his men with him; but some fled, and some received quarter and their lives. It is thus related in the ballad of Trygve:–

"Trygve comes from the northern coast,
King Svein turns round with all his host;
To meet and fight, they both prepare,
And where they met grim death was there.
From the sharp strife I was not far,–
I heard the din and the clang of war;
And the Hordaland men at last gave way,
And their leader fell, and they lost the day."

This battle is also told of in the ballad about King Svein, thus:–

"My girl! it was a Sunday morn,
And many a man ne'er saw its eve,

Though ale and leeks by old wives borne
The bruised and wounded did relieve.
'Twas Sunday morn, when Svein calls out,
'Stem to stem your vessels bind;'
The raven a mid-day feast smells out,
And he comes croaking up the wind."

After this battle King Svein ruled the country for some time, and there was peace in the land. The winter after it (A.D. 1034) he passed in the south parts of the country.

264. OF THE COUNSELS OF EINAR TAMBASKELFER AND KALF ARNASON.

Einar Tambaskelfer and Kalf Arnason had this winter meetings and consultations between themselves in the merchant town[59]. Then there came a messenger from King Canute to Kalf Arnason, with a message to send him three dozen axes, which must be chosen and good. Kalf replies, "I will send no axes to King Canute. Tell him I will bring his son Svein so many, that he shall not think he is in want of any."

265. OF EINAR TAMBASKELFER AND KALF ARNASON'S JOURNEY.

Early in spring (A.D. 1034) Einar Tambaskelfer and Kalf Arnason made themselves ready for a journey, with a great retinue of the best and most select men that could be found in the Throndhjem country. They went in spring eastward over the ridge of the country to Jamtaland, from thence to Helsingjaland, and came to Svithjod, where they procured ships, with which in summer they proceeded east to Russia, and came in autumn to Ladoga. They sent men up to Novgorod to King Jarisleif, with the errand that they offered Magnus, the son of King Olaf the Saint, to take him with them, follow him to Norway, and give him assistance to attain his father's heritage and be made king over

59 Nidaros, or Throndhjem, is usually called merely the merchant town.–L.

the country. When this message came to King Jarisleif he held a consultation with the queen and some chiefs, and they all resolved unanimously to send a message to the Northmen, and ask them to come to King Jarisleif and Magnus; for which journey safe conduct was given them. When they came to Novgorod it was settled among them that the Northmen who had come there should become Magnus's men, and be his subjects; and to this Kalf and the other men who had been against King Olaf at Stiklestad were solemnly bound by oath. On the other hand, King Magnus promised them, under oath, secure peace and full reconciliation; and that he would be true and faithful to them all when he got the dominions and kingdom of Norway. He was to become Kalf Arnason's foster-son; and Kalf should be bound to do all that Magnus might think necessary for extending his dominion, and making it more independent than formerly.

BOOK SEVEN

Saga of Magnus the Good

PRELIMINARY REMARKS.

MAGNUS REIGNED FROM A.D. 1035 to 1047, when he died. During the last year of his reign his half-brother Harald Sigurdson was his co-regent.

The history of Magnus is treated in "Agrip.", ch. 28-32; in "Fagrskinna", ch. 119-146; in "Fornmannasogur", part vi., and in "Knytlinga Saga".

The skalds quoted in this saga are: Arnor the earls' skald (Arnor Jarlaskald), Sigvat, Thjodulf, Bjarne Gullbrarskald, Thorgeir Flek, Od Kikinaskald.

1. MAGNUS OLAFSON'S JOURNEY FROM THE WEST.

AFTER YULE MAGNUS OLAFSON began his journey from the East from Novgorod to Ladoga, where he rigged out his ships as soon as the ice was loosened in spring (A.D. 1035). Arnor, the earls' skald, tells of this in the poem on Magnus:–

"It is no loose report that he,
Who will command on land and sea,
In blood will make his foeman feel
Olaf's sword Hneiter's sharp blue steel.
This generous youth, who scatters gold,
Norway's brave son, but ten years old,

Is rigging ships in Russia's lake,
His crown, with friend's support, to take."

In spring Magnus sailed from the East to Svithjod. So says Arnor:–

"The young sword-stainer called a Thing,
Where all his men should meet their king:
Heroes who find the eagle food
Before their lord in arms stood.
And now the curved plank of the bow
Cleaves the blue sea; the ocean-plough
By grey winds driven across the main,
Reaches Sigtuna's grassy plain."

Here it is related that when King Magnus and his fellow-travellers sailed from the East to Svithjod, they brought up at Sigtuna. Emund Olafson was then king in Svithjod. Queen Astrid, who had been married to King Olaf the Saint, was also there. She received very gladly and well her stepson King Magnus, and summoned immediately a numerous Thing of Swedes at a place called Hangtar. At the Thing Queen Astrid spoke these words: "Here is come to us a son of Olaf the Saint, called Magnus, who intends to make an expedition to Norway to seek his father's heritage. It is my great duty to give him aid towards this expedition; for he is my stepson, as is well known to all, both Swedes and Norwegians. Neither shall he want men or money, in so far as I can procure them or have influence, in order that his strength may be as great as possible; and all the men who will support this cause of his shall have my fullest friendship; and I would have it known that I intend myself to go with him on this attempt, that all may see I will spare nothing that is in my power to help him." She spoke long and cleverly in this strain; but when she had ended many replied thus: "The Swedes made no honourable progress in Norway when they followed King Olaf his father, and now no better success is to be expected, as this man is but in years of boyhood; and therefore we have little inclination for this expedition." Astrid replies, "All men who wish to be thought of true courage must not be deterred by such considerations. If any have lost connections at the side of King Olaf, or been themselves wounded, now is the time to show a man's heart and courage, and go to Norway to take vengeance." Astrid succeeded so far with words and encouragement that many men determined to go with her, and follow King Magnus to Norway. Sigvat the skald speaks of this:–

"Now Astrtd, Olaf's widowed Queen,–
She who so many a change had seen,–
Took all the gifts of happier days,
Jewels and rings, all she could raise,
And at a Thing at Hangrar, where
The Swedes were numerous, did declare
What Olaf's son proposed to do,
And brought her gifts–their pay–in view.

"And with the Swedes no wiser plan,
To bring out every brave bold man,
Could have been found, had Magnus been
The son himself of the good queen.
With help of Christ, she hoped to bring
Magnus to be the land's sole king,
As Harald was, who in his day
Obtained o'er all the upper sway.

"And glad are we so well she sped,–
The people's friend is now their head;
And good King Magnus always shows
How much be to Queen Astrid owes.
Such stepmothers as this good queen
In truth are very rarely seen;
And to this noble woman's praise
The skald with joy his song will raise."

Thiodolf the skald also says in his song of Magnus:–

"When thy brave ship left the land,
The bending yard could scarce withstand
The fury of the whistling gale,
That split thy many-coloured sail;
And many a stout ship, tempest-tost,
Was in that howling storm lost
That brought them safe to Sigtuna's shore,
Far from the sound of ocean's roar."

2. MAGNUS'S EXPEDITION FROM SVITHJOD.

King Magnus set out on his journey from Sigtuna with a great force, which he had gathered in Svithjod. They proceeded through Svithjod on foot to Helsingjaland. So says Arnor, the earl's skald:–

"And many a dark-red Swedish shield
Marched with thee from the Swedish field.
The country people crowded in,
To help Saint Olaf's son to win;
And chosen men by thee were led,
Men who have stained the wolf's tongue red.
Each milk-white shield and polished spear
Came to a splendid gathering there."

Magnus Olafson went from the East through Jamtaland over the keel-ridge of the country and came down upon the Throndhjem district, where all men welcomed the king with joy. But no sooner did the men of King Svein, the son of Alfifa, hear that King Magnus Olafson was come to the country, than they fled on all sides and concealed themselves, so that no opposition was made to King Magnus; for King Svein was in the south part of the country. So says Arnor, the earls' skald:–

"He who the eagle's talons stains
Rushed from the East on Throndhjem's plains;
The terror of his plumed helm
Drove his pale foemen from the realm.
The lightning of thy eye so near,
Great king! thy foemen could not bear,
Scattered they fled–their only care
If thou their wretched lives wilt spare."

3. MAGNUS MADE KING.

Magnus Olafson advanced to the town (Nidaros), where he was joyfully received. He then summoned the people to the Eyra-thing[60]; and

60 Eyra Thing, held on the ayr of the river Nid, that is, on the spit of sand, still called an ayr in the north of Scotland, dividing a lake, pond, or river-mouth from the sea. At the Thing held here the kings of Norway were chosen and proclaimed. It was held to be the proper Thing for settling disputes between

when the bondes met at the Thing, Magnus was taken to be king over the whole land, as far as his father Olaf had possessed it. Then the king selected a court, and named lendermen, and placed bailiffs and officers in all domains and offices. Immediately after harvest King Magnus ordered a levy through all Throndhjem land, and he collected men readily; and thereafter he proceeded southwards along the coast.

4. KING SVEIN'S FLIGHT.

King Svein Alfifason was staying in South Hordaland when he heard this news of war. He immediately sent out war-tokens to four different quarters, summoned the bondes to him, and made it known to all that they should join him with men and ships to defend the country. All the men who were in the neighbourhood of the king presented themselves; and the king formed a Thing, at which in a speech he set forth his business, and said he would advance against Magnus Olafson and have a battle with him, if the bondes would aid his cause. The king's speech was not very long, and was not received with much approbation by the bondes. Afterwards the Danish chiefs who were about the king made long and clever speeches; but the bondes then took up the word, and answered them; and although many said they would follow Svein, and fight on his side, some refused to do so bluntly, some were altogether silent, and some declared they would join King Magnus as soon as they had an opportunity. Then King Svein says, "Methinks very few of the bondes to whom we sent a message have appeared here; and of those who have come, and tell us to our face that they will join King Magnus as soon as they can, we shall have as little benefit as of those who say they will sit at home quietly. It is the same with those who say nothing at all. But as to those who promise to help us, there are not more than every other man; and that force will avail us little against King Magnus. It is my counsel, therefore, that we do not trust to these bondes; but let us rather go to the land where all the people are sure and true to us, and where we will obtain forces to conquer this country again." As soon as the king had made known this resolution all his men followed it, turned their ship's bows, and hoisted sail. King Svein sailed eastward along the land, and then set right over to Denmark without delay, and Hardaknut received his brother Svein very kindly. At their first meeting Hardaknut offered King Svein to divide the kingdom of Denmark with him, which offer King Svein accepted.

---

kings in Norway.–L.

5. KING MAGNUS'S JOURNEY TO NORWAY.

In autumn (A.D. 1035) King Magnus proceeded eastward to the end of the country, and was received as king throughout the whole land, and the country people were rejoiced at his arrival.

6. DEATH OF KING CANUTE THE GREAT AND HIS SON SVEIN.

King Svein, Canute's son, went to Denmark, as before related, and took part in the government with his brother Hardaknut. In the same autumn King Canute the Great died in England, the 13th November, forty years old, and was buried at Winchester. He had been king of Denmark for twenty-seven years, and over Denmark and England together twenty-four years, and also over Norway for seven years. King Canute's son Harald was then made king in England. The same winter (A.D. 1036) King Svein, Alfifa's son, died in Denmark. Thiodolf the skald made these lines concerning King Magnus:-

"Through Sweden's dirty roads the throng
Followed the king in spearmen strong.
Svein doth fly, in truth afraid,
And partly by his men betrayed;
Flying to Denmark o'er the sea,
He leaves the land quite clear to thee."

Bjarne Gullbrarskald composed the following lines concerning Kalf Arnason:-

"By thee the kings got each his own,-
Magnus by thee got Norway's throne;
And Svein in Denmark got a seat,
When out of Norway he was beat.
Kalf! It was you who showed the way
To our young king, the battle-lover,-
From Russia to his father's sway
You showed the way, and brought him over."

King Magnus ruled over Norway this winter (A.D. 1036), and Hardaknut over Denmark.

7. RECONCILIATION BETWEEN HARDAKNUT AND KING MAGNUS.

The following spring (A.D. 1036) the kings on both sides ordered out a levy, and the news was that they would have a battle at the Gaut river; but when the two armies approached each other, the lendermen in the one army sent messengers to their connections and friends in the other; and it came to a proposal for a reconciliation between the two kings, especially as, from both kings being but young and childish, some powerful men, who had been chosen in each of the countries for that purpose, had the rule of the country on their account. It thus was brought about that there was a friendly meeting between the kings, and in this meeting a peace was proposed; and the peace was to be a brotherly union under oath to keep the peace towards each other to the end of their lives; and if one of them should die without leaving a son, the longest liver should succeed to the whole land and people. Twelve of the principal men in each kingdom swore to the kings that this treaty should be observed, so long as any one of them was in life. Then the kings separated, and each returned home to his kingdom; and the treaty was kept as long as both lived.

8. OF QUEEN ASTRID.

Queen Astrid, who had been married to King Olaf the Saint, came to Norway with King Magnus her stepson, as before related, and was held by him deservedly in great honour and esteem. Then came also Alfhild, King Magnus's mother, to the court, and the king received her with the greatest affection, and showed her great respect. But it went with Alfhild, as it does with many who come to power and honour, that pride keeps pace with promotion. She was ill pleased that Queen Astrid was treated with more respect, had a higher seat, and more attention. Alfhild wanted to have a seat next to the king, but Astrid called Alfhild her slave-woman, as indeed she had formerly been when Astrid was queen of Norway and King Olaf ruled the land, and therefore would on no account let her have a seat beside her, and they could not lodge in the same house.

9. OF SIGVAT THE SKALD.

SIGVAT THE SKALD HAD gone to Rome, where he was at the time of the battle of Stiklestad.

He was on his way back from the South when he heard tidings of King Olaf's fall, which gave him great grief. He then sang these lines:–

"One morning early on a hill,
The misty town asleep and still,
Wandering I thought upon the fields.
Strewed o'er with broken mail and shields,
Where our king fell,–our kind good king,
Where now his happy youthful spring?
My father too!–for Thord was then
One of the good king's chosen men."

One day Sigvat went through a village, and heard a husband lamenting grievously over the loss of his wife, striking his breast, tearing his clothes, weeping bitterly, and saying he wanted to die; and Sigvat sang these lines:–

"This poor man mourns a much-loved wife,
Gladly would he be quit of life.
Must love be paid for by our grief?
The price seems great for joy so brief.
But the brave man who knows no fear
Drops for his king a silent tear,
And feels, perhaps, his loss as deep
As those who clamour when they weep."

Sigvat came home to Norway to the Throndhjem country, where he had a farm and children. He came from the South along the coast in a merchant vessel, and as they lay in Hillarsund they saw a great many ravens flying about. Then Sigvat said:–

"I see here many a croaking raven
Flying about the well-known haven:
When Olaf's ship was floating here,
They knew that food for them was near;
When Olaf's ship lay here wind-bound,
Oft screamed the erne o'er Hillar sound,

Impatient for the expected prey,
And wont to follow to the fray."

When Sigvat came north to the town of Throndhjem King Svein was there before him. He invited Sigvat to stay with him, as Sigvat had formerly been with his father King Canute the Great; but Sigvat said he would first go home to his farm. One day, as Sigvat was walking in the street, he saw the king's men at play, and he sang:–

"One day before I passed this way,
When the king's guards were at their play,
Something there was–I need not tell–
That made me pale, and feel unwell.
Perhaps it was I thought, just then,
How noble Olaf with his men,
In former days, I oft have seen
In manly games upon this green."

Sigvat then went to his farm; and as he heard that many men upbraided him with having deserted King Olaf, he made these verses:–

"May Christ condemn me still to burn
In quenchless fire, if I did turn,
And leave King Olaf in his need,–
My soul is free from such base deed.
I was at Rome, as men know well
Who saw me there, and who can tell
That there in danger I was then:
The truth I need not hide from men."

Sigvat was ill at ease in his home. One day he went out and sang:–

"While Olaf lived, how smiled the land!
Mountain and cliff, and pebbly strand.
All Norway then, so fresh, so gay,
On land or sea, where oft I lay.
But now to me all seems so dready,
All black and dull–of life I'm weary;
Cheerless to-day, cheerless to-morrow–
Here in the North we have great sorrow."

Early in winter Sigvat went westward over the ridge of the country to Jamtaland, and onwards to Helsingjaland, and came to Svithjod. He went immediately to Queen Astrid, and was with her a long time, and was a welcome guest. He was also with her brother King Emund, and received from him ten marks of proved silver, as is related in the song of Canute. Sigvat always inquired of the merchants who traded to Novgorod if they could tell him any news of Magnus Olafson. Sigvat composed these lines at that time:–

"I ask the merchant oft who drives
His trade to Russia, 'How he thrives,
Our noble prince? How lives he there?
And still good news–his praise–I hear.
To little birds, which wing their way
Between the lands, I fain would say,
How much we long our prince to see,
They seem to hear a wish from me."

10. OF KING MAGNUS'S FIRST ARRIVAL IN SVITHJOD.

Immediately after Magnus Olafson came to Svithjod from Russia, Sigvat met him at Queen Astrid's house, and glad they all were at meeting. Sigvat then sang:–

"Thou art come here, prince, young and bold!
Thou art come home! With joy behold
Thy land and people. From this hour
I join myself to thy young power.
I could not o'er to Russie hie,–
Thy mother's guardian here was I.
It was my punishment for giving
Magnus his name, while scarcely living."

Afterwards Sigvat travelled with Queen Astrid, and followed Magnus to Norway. Sigvat sang thus:–

"To the crowds streaming to the Thing,
To see and hear Magnus their king,
Loudly, young king, I'll speak my mind–
'God to His people has been kind.'

If He, to whom be all the praise,
Give us a son in all his ways
Like to his sire, no folk on earth
Will bless so much a royal birth."

Now when Magnus became king of Norway Sigvat attended him, and was his dearest friend. Once it happened that Queen Astrid and Alfhild the king's mother had exchanged some sharp words with each other, and Sigvat said:–

"Alfhild! though it was God's will
To raise thee–yet remember still
The queen-born Astrid should not be
Kept out of due respect by thee."

11. KING OLAF'S SHRINE.

King Magnus had a shrine made and mounted with gold and silver, and studded with jewels. This shrine was made so that in shape and size it was like a coffin. Under it was an arched way, and above was a raised roof, with a head and a roof-ridge. Behind were plaited hangings; and before were gratings with padlocks, which could be locked with a key. In this shrine King Magnus had the holy remains of King Olaf deposited, and many were the miracles there wrought. Of this Sigvat speaks:–

"For him a golden shrine is made,
For him whose heart was ne'er afraid
Of mortal man–the holy king,
Whom the Lord God to heaven did bring.
Here many a man shall feel his way,
Stone-blind, unconscious of the day,
And at the shrine where Olaf lies
Give songs of praise for opened eyes."

It was also appointed by law that King Olaf's holy day should be held sacred over all Norway, and that day has been kept ever afterwards as the greatest of Church days. Sigvat speaks of it:–

"To Olaf, Magnus' father, raise,
Within my house, the song of praise!

With joy, yet grief, we'll keep the day
Olaf to heaven was called away.
Well may I keep within my breast
A day for him in holy rest,–
My upraised hands a golden ring
On every branch[61] *bear from that king."*

12. OF THORER HUND.

Thorer Hund left the country immediately after King Olaf's fall. He went all the way to Jerusalem, and many people say he never came back. Thorer Hund had a son called Sigurd, father of Ranveig who was married to Joan, a son of Arne Arnason. Their children were Vidkun of Bjarkey, Sigurd Hund, Erling, and Jardthrud.

13. OF THE MURDER OF HAREK OF THJOTTA.

Harek of Thjotta sat at home on his farm, till King Magnus Olafson came to the country and was made king. Then Harek went south to Throndhjem to King Magnus. At that time Asmund Grankelson was in the king's house. When Harek came to Nidaros, and landed out of the ship, Asmund was standing with the king in the gallery outside the loft, and both the king and Asmund knew Harek when they saw him. "Now," says Asmund to the king, "I will pay Harek for my father's murder." He had in his hand a little thin hatchet. The king looked at him, and said, "Rather take this axe of mine." It was thick, and made like a club. "Thou must know, Asmund," added he, "that there are hard bones in the old fellow." Asmund took the axe, went down, and through the house, and when he came down to the cross-road Harek and his men coming up met him. Asmund struck Harek on the head, so that the axe penetrated to the brains; and that was Harek's death-wound. Asmund turned back directly to the king's house, and the whole edge of the axe was turned with the blow. Then said the king, "What would thy axe have done, for even this one, I think, is spoilt?" King Magnus afterwards gave him a fief and office in Halogaland, and many are the tales about the strife between Asmund and Harek's sons.

61 The fingers, the branches of the hand, bore golden fruits from the generosity of the king.–L.

14. OF THORGEIR FLEK.

Kalf Arnason had at first, for some time, the greatest share of the government of the country under King Magnus; but afterwards there were people who reminded the king of the part Kalf had taken at Stiklestad, and then it became difficult for Kalf to give the king satisfaction in anything. Once it happened there were many men with the king bringing their affairs before him; and Thorgeir Flek from Sula in Veradal, of whom mention is made before in the history of King Olaf the Saint, came to him about some needful business. The king paid no attention to his words, but was listening to people who stood near him. Then Thorgeir said to the king, so loud that all who were around him could hear:–

"Listen, my lord, to my plain word.
I too was there, and had to bear
A bloody head from Stiklestad:
For I was then with Olaf's men.
Listen to me: well did I see
The men you're trusting the dead corpse thrusting
Out of their way, as dead it lay;
And striking o'er your father's gore."

There was instantly a great uproar, and some told Thorgeir to go out; but the king called him, and not only despatched his business to his satisfaction, but promised him favour and friendship.

15. KALF ARNASON FLIES THE COUNTRY

Soon after this the king was at a feast at the farm of Haug in Veradel, and at the dinner-table Kalf Arnason sat upon one side of him, and Einar Tambaskelfer on the other. It was already come so far that the king took little notice of Kalf, but paid most attention to Einar. The king said to Einar, "Let us ride to-day to Stiklestad. I should like to see the memorials of the things which took place there." Einar replies, "I can tell thee nothing about it; but take thy foster-father Kalf with thee; he can give thee information about all that took place." When the tables were removed, the king made himself ready, and said to Kalf, "Thou must go with me to Stiklestad."

Kalf replied, "That is really not my duty."

Then the king stood up in a passion, and said, "Go thou shalt, Kalf!" and thereupon he went out.

Kalf put on his riding clothes in all haste, and said to his foot-boy, "Thou must ride directly to Eggja, and order my house-servants to ship all my property on board my ship before sunset."

King Magnus now rides to Stiklestad, and Kalf with him. They alighted from horseback, and went to the place where the battle had been. Then said the king to Kalf, "Where is the spot at which the king fell?"

Kalf stretched out his spear-shaft, and said, "There he lay when he fell."

The king: "And where wast thou, Kalf?"

Kalf: "Here where I am now standing."

The king turned red as blood in the face, and said, "Then thy axe could well have reached him."

Kalf replied, "My axe did not come near him;" and immediately went to his horse, sprang on horseback, and rode away with all his men; and the king rode back to Haug. Kalf did not stop until he got home in the evening to Eggja. There his ship lay ready at the shore side, and all his effects were on board, and the vessel manned with his house-servants. They set off immediately by night down the fjord, and afterwards proceeded day and night, when the wind suited. He sailed out into the West sea, and was there a long time plundering in Ireland, Scotland, and the Hebudes. Bjarne Gullbrarskald tells of this in the song about Kalf:–

"Brother of Thorberg, who still stood
Well with the king! in angry mood
He is the first to break with thee,
Who well deserves esteemed to be;
He is the first who friendship broke,
For envious men the falsehood spoke;
And he will he the first to rue
The breach of friendship 'twixt you two."

16. OF THE THREATS OF THE BONDES.

King Magnus added to his property Veggia, which Hrut had been owner of, and Kviststad, which had belonged to Thorgeir, and also Eggja, with all the goods which Kalf had left behind him; and thus he confiscated to the king's estate many great farms, which had belonged to those of the bonde-army who had fallen at Stiklestad. In like manner, he laid heavy fined upon many of those who made the greatest opposition to King Olaf. He drove some out of the country, took large sums of money from others, and had the cattle of others slaughtered for his use. Then the bondes began to murmur, and to say among themselves, "Will he go on in the same way as his father and other chiefs, whom we made an end of when their pride and lawless proceedings became insupportable?" This discontent spread widely through the country. The people of Sogn gathered men, and, it was said, were determined to give battle to King Magnus, if he came into the Fjord district. King Magnus was then in Hordaland, where he had remained a long time with a numerous retinue, and was now come to the resolution to proceed north to Sogn. When the king's friends observed this, twelve men had a meeting, and resolved to determine by casting lots which of them should inform the king of the discontent of the people; and it so happened that the lot fell upon Sigvat.

17. OF THE FREE-SPEAKING SONG ("BERSOGLISVISUR").

Sigvat accordingly composed a poem, which he called the "Free-speaking Song", which begins with saying the king had delayed too long to pacify the people, who were threatening to rise in tumult against him. He said:–

"Here in the south, from Sogn is spread
The news that strife draws to a head:
The bondes will the king oppose–
Kings and their folk should ne'er be foes.
Let us take arms, and briskly go
To battle, if it must be so;
Defend our king–but still deplore
His land plunged in such strife once more."

In this song are also these verses:–

"Hakon, who at Fitiar died,–
Hakon the Good, could not abide
The viking rule, or robber train,
And all men's love he thus did gain.

The people since have still in mind
The laws of Hakon, just and kind;
And men will never see the day
When Hakon's laws have passed away.

"The bondes ask but what is fair;
The Olafs and the Earls, when there
Where Magnus sits, confirmed to all
Their lands and gear–to great and small,
Bold Trygve's son, and Harald's heir,
The Olafs, while on earth they were,
Observed the laws themselves had made,
And none was for his own afraid.

"Let not thy counsellors stir thy wrath
Against the man who speaks the truth;
Thy honour lies in thy good sword,
But still more in thy royal word;
And, if the people do not lie,
The new laws turn out not nigh
So Just and mild, as the laws given
At Ulfasund in face of heaven.

"Dread king! who urges thee to break
Thy pledged word, and back to take
Thy promise given? Thou warrior bold;
With thy own people word to hold,
Thy promise fully to maintain,
Is to thyself the greatest gain:
The battle-storm raiser he
Must by his own men trusted be.

"Who urges thee, who seek'st renown,
The bondes' cattle to cut down?
No king before e'er took in hand
Such viking-work in his own land.
Such rapine men will not long bear,
And the king's counsellors will but share
In their ill-will: when once inflamed,
The king himself for all is blamed.

"Do cautious, with this news of treason
Flying about–give them no reason.
We hange the thief, but then we use
Consideration of the excuse.
I think, great king (who wilt rejoice
Eagle and wolf with battle voice),
It would be wise not to oppose
Thy bondes, and make them thy foes.

"A dangerous sign it is, I fear,
That old grey-bearded men appear
In corners whispering at the Thing,
As if they had bad news to bring.
The young sit still,–no laugh, or shout,–
More looks than words passing shout;
And groups of whispering heads are seen,
On buttoned breasts, with lowering mien.

"Among the udalmen, they say
The king, if he could have his way,
Would seize the bondes' udal land,
And free-born men must this withstand.
In truth the man whose udal field,
By any doom that law can yield
From him adjudged the king would take,
Could the king's throne and power shake."

This verse is the last:–

"A holy bond between us still
Makes me wish speedy end to ill:
The sluggard waits till afternoon,–
At once great Magnus! grant our boon.
Then we will serve with heart and hand,
With thee we'll fight by sea or land:
With Olaf's sword take Olaf's mind,
And to thy bondes be more kind."

In this song the king was exhorted to observe the laws which his father had established. This exhortation had a good effect on the king, for many others held the same language to him. So at last the king consulted the most prudent men, who ordered all affairs according to law. Thereafter King Magnus had the law-book composed in writing which is still in use in Throndhjem district, and is called "The Grey Goose"[62]. King Magnus afterwards became very popular, and was beloved by all the country people, and therefore he was called Magnus the Good.

18. OF THE ENGLISH KINGS.

The king of the English, King Harald, died (A.D. 1040) five years after his father King Canute, and was buried beside his father at Winchester. After his death his brother Hardaknut, the second son of the old King Canute, was king of England, and was thus king both of Denmark and England. He ruled these kingdoms two years, and then died of sickness in England, leaving no children. He was buried at Winchester beside his father. After his death Edward the Good, a son of the English king Ethelred (and Emma, a daughter of Richard earl of Rouen), was chosen king in England. King Edward the Good was, on his mother's side, a brother of Harald and Hardaknut, the sons of Canute the Great; and the daughter of Canute and Queen Emma was Gunhild, who was married to the Emperor Henry of Germany, who was called Henry the Mild. Gunhild had been three years in Germamy when she fell sick, and she died five years after the death of her father King Canute the Great.

19. OF KING MAGNUS OLAFSON.

When King Magnus Olafson heard of Hardaknut's death, he immediately sent people south to Denmark, with a message to the men who had bound themselves by oath to the peace and agreement which

62 "The Grey Goose", so called probably from the colour of the parchment on which it is written, is one of the most curious relics of the Middle Ages, and give us an unexpected view of the social condition of the Northmen in the eleventh century. Law appears to have been so far advanced among them that the forms were not merely established, but the slightest breach of the legal forms of proceeding involved the loss of the case. The "Grey Goose" embraces subjects not dealt with probably by any other code in Europe at that period. The provision for the poor, the equality of weights and measures, police of markets and of sea havens, provision for illegitimate children of the poor, inns for travellers, wages of servants and support of them in sickness, protection of pregnant women and even of domestic animals from injury, roads, bridges, vagrants, beggars, are subjects treated of in this code.-"Schlegel."-L.

was made between King Magnus and Hardaknut, and reminded them of their pledge. He added, as a conclusion, that in summer (A.D. 1042.) he would come with his army to Denmark to take possession of his Danish dominions, in terms of the agreement, or to fall in the field with his army. So says Arnor, the earls' skald:–

"Wise were the words, exceeding wise,
Of him who stills the hungriest cries
Of beasts of prey–the earl's lord;
And soon fulfilled will be his word:
'With his good sword he'll Denmark gain,
Or fall upon a bloody plain;
And rather than give up his cause,
Will leave his corpse to raven's claws.'"

20. KING MAGNUS'S ARMAMENT.

Thereafter King Magnus gathered together a great army, and summoned to him all lendermen and powerful bondes, and collected warships. When the army was assembled it was very handsome, and well fitted out. He had seventy large vessels when he sailed from Norway. So says Thiodolf the skald:–

"Brave king! the terror of the foe,
With thee will many a long-ship go.
Full seventy sail are gathered here,
Eastward with their great king to steer.
And southward now the bright keel glides;
O'er the white waves the Bison rides.
Sails swell, yards crack, the highest mast
O'er the wide sea scarce seen at last."

Here it related that King Magnus had the great Bison, which his father King Olaf had built. It had more than thirty banks of rowers; and forward on the bow was a great buffalo head, and aft on the stern-post was its tail. Both the head and the tail, and both sides of the ship, were gilded over. Of this speaks Arnor, the earls' skald:–

"The white foam lashing o'er the deck
Oft made the glided head to shake;

The helm down, the vessel's heel
Oft showed her stem's bright-glacing steel.
Around Stavanger-point careering,
Through the wild sea's white flames steering,
Tackle loud singing to the strain,
The storm-horse flies to Denmark's plain."

King Magnus set out to sea from Agder, and sailed over to Jutland. So says Arnor:–

"I can relate how through the gale
The gallant Bison carried sail.
With her lee gunwale in the wave,
The king on board, Magnus the brave!
The iron-clad Thingmen's chief to see
On Jutland's coast right glad were we,–
Right glad our men to see a king
Who in the fight his sword could swing."

21. KING MAGNUS COMES TO DENMARK.

When King Magnus came to Denmark he was joyfully received. He appointed a Thing without delay, to which he summoned the people of the country, and desired they would take him as king, according to the agreement which had been entered into. As the highest of the chiefs of the country were bound by oath to King Magnus, and were desirous of keeping their word and oath, they endeavoured zealously to promote the cause with the people. It contributed also that King Canute the Great, and all his descendants, were dead; and a third assistance was, that his father King Olaf's sanctity and miracles were become celebrated in all countries.

22. KING MAGNUS CHOSEN KING OF DENMARK.

King Magnus afterwards ordered the people to be summoned to Viborg to a Thing. Both in older and later times, the Danes elected their kings at the Viborg Thing. At this Thing the Danes chose Magnus Olafson to be king of all the Danish dorninions. King Magnus remained long in Denmark during the summer (A.D. 1042); and wherever he came the people received him joyfully, and obeyed him willingly. He divided the country into baronies and districts, and gave fiefs to men of power in the land. Late in autumn he returned with his fleet to Norway, but lay for some time at the Gaut river.

23. OF SVEIN ULFSON.

There was a man, by name Svein, a son of Earl Ulf, and grandson of Thorgils Sprakaleg. Svein's mother was Astrid, a daughter of King Svein Forkbeard. She was a sister of Canute the Great by the father's side, and of the Swedish King Olaf Eirikson by the mother's side; for her mother was Queen Sigrid the Haughty, a daughter of Skoglar Toste. Svein Ulfson had been a long time living with his relation the Swedish king, ever since King Canute had ordered his father Ulf to be killed, as is related in the saga of old King Canute, that he had his brother-in-law, Earl Ulf, murdered in Roskilde; and on which account Svein had not since been in Denmark. Svein Ulfson was one of the handsomest men that could be seen; he was very stout and strong, and very expert in all exercises, and a well-spoken man withal. Every one who knew him said he had every quality which became a good chief. Svein Ulfson waited upon King Magnus while he lay in the Gaut river, as before mentioned, and the king received him kindly, as he was by many advised to do; for Svein was a particularly popular man. He could also speak for himself to the king well and cleverly; so that it came at lasf to Svein's entering into King Magnus's service, and becoming his man. They often talked together afterwards in private concerning many affairs.

24. SVEIN ULFSON CREATED AN EARL.

One day, as King Magnus sat in his high-seat and many people were around him, Svein Ulfson sat upon a footstool before the king. The king then made a speech: "Be it known to you, chiefs, and the people in general, that I have taken the following resolution. Here is a distinguished man, both for family and for his own merits, Svein Ulfson, who has entered into my service, and given me promise of fidelity. Now, as ye know, the Danes have this summer become my men, so that when I am absent from the country it is without a head; and it is not unknown to you how it is ravaged by the people of Vindland, Kurland, and others from the Baltic, as well as by Saxons. Therefore

I promised them a chief who could defend and rule their land; and I know no man better fitted, in all respects, for this than Svein Ulfson, who is of birth to be chief of the country. I will therefore make him my earl, and give him the government of my Danish dominions while I am in Norway; just as King Canute the Great set his father, Earl Ulf, over Denmark while he was in England."

Then Einar Tambaskelfer said, "Too great an earl–too great an earl, my foster-son!"

The king replied in a passion, "Ye have a poor opinion of my judgment, I think. Some consider that ye are too great earls, and others that ye are fit for nothing."

Then the king stood up, took a sword, and girt it on the earl's loins, and took a shield and fastened it on his shoulders, put a helmet upon his head, and gave him the title of earl, with the same fiefs in Denmark which his father Earl Ulf had formerly held. Afterwards a shrine was brought forth containing holy relics, and Svein laid his hand hereon, and swore the oath of fidelity to King Magnus; upon which the king led the earl to the highseat by his side. So says Thiodolf:–

"Twas at the Gaut river's shore,
With hand on shrine Svein Ulfson swore.
King Magnus first said o'er the oath,
With which Svein Ulfson pledged his troth.
The vows by Svein solemnly given,
On holy bones of saints in heaven,
To Magnus seemed both fair and fast;
He found they were too fair to last."

Earl Svein went thereafter to Denmark, and the whole nation received him well. He established a court about him, and soon became a great man. In winter (A.D. 1043), he went much about the country, and made friends among the powerful chiefs; and, indeed, he was beloved by all the people of the land.

25. KING MAGNUS'S FORAY.

King Magnus proceeded northward to Norway with his fleet, and wintered there; but when the spring set in (A.D. 1048) he gathered a large force, with which he sailed south to Demnark, having heard the news from Vindland that the Vindland people in Jomsborg had withdrawn from their submission to him. The Danish kings had formerly had a very large earldom there, and they first founded Jomsborg; and now the place was become a very strong fortress. When King Magnus heard of this, he ordered a large fleet and army to be levied in Denmark, and sailed in summer to Vindland with all his forces, which made a very large army altogether. Arnor, the earls' skald, tells of it thus:–

"Now in this strophe, royal youth!
I tell no more than the plain truth.
Thy armed outfit from the strand
Left many a keel-trace on the sand,
And never did a king before
SO many ships to any shore
Lead on, as thou to Vindland's isle:
The Vindland men in fright recoil."

Now when King Magnus came to Vindland he attacked Jomsborg, and soon took the fortress, killing' many people, burning and destroying both in the town and in the courttry all around, and making the greatest havoc. So says Arnor, the earl's skald:–

"The robbers, hemmed 'twixt death and fire,
Knew not how to escape thy ire;
O'er Jomsborg castle's highest towers
Thy wrath the whirlwind-fire pours.
The heathen on his false gods calls,
And trembles even in their halls;
And by the light from its own flame
The king this viking-hold o'ercame."

Many people in Vindland submitted to King Magnus, but many more got out of the way and fled. King Magnus returned to Denmark, and prepared to take his winter abode there, and sent away the Danish, and also a great many of the Norwegian people he had brought with him.

26. SVEIN RECEIVES THE TITLE OF KING.

THE SAME WINTER (A.D. 1043), in which Svein Ulfson was raised to the government of the whole Danish dominions, and had made friends of a great number of the principal chiefs in Denmark, and obtained the affections of the people, he assumed by the advice of many of the chiefs the title of king. But when in the spring thereafter he heard that King Magnus had come from the north with a great army, Svein went over to Scania, from thence up to Gautland, and so on to Svithjod to his relation, King Emund, where he remained all summer, and sent spies out to Denmark, to inquire about the king's proceedings and the number of his men. Now when Svein heard that King Magnus had let a great part of his army go away, and also that he was south in Jutland, he rode from Svithjod with a great body of peopie which the Swedish king had given him. When Svein came to Scania the people of that country received him well, treated him as their king, and men joined him in crowds. He then went on to Seeland, where he was also well received, and the whole country joined him. He then went to Fyen, and laid all the islands under his power; and as the people also joined him, he collected a great army and many ships of war.

27. OF KING MAGNUS'S MILITARY FORCE.

King Magnus heard this news, and at the same time that the people of Vindland had a large force on foot. He summoned people therefore to come to him, and drew together a great army in Jutland. Otto, also, the Duke of Brunsvik, who had married Ulfhild, King Olaf the Saint's daughter, and the sister of King Magnus, came to him with a great troop. The Danish chiefs pressed King Magnus to advance against the Vindland army, and not allow pagans to march over and lay waste the country; so it was resolved that the king with his army should proceed south to Heidaby. While King Magnus lay at Skotborg river, on Hlyrskog Heath, he got intelligence concerning the Vindland army, and that it was so numerous it could not be counted; whereas King Magnus had so few, that there seemed no chance for him but to fly. The king, however, determined on fighting, if there was any possibility of gaining the victory; but the most dissuaded him from venturing on an engagement, and all, as one man, said that the Vindland people had undoubtedly a prodigious force. Duke Otto, however, pressed much to go to battle. Then the king ordered the whole army to be gathered by the war trumpets into battle array, and ordered all the men to arm, and to lie down for the night under their shields; for he was told the enemy's army had come to the neighbourhood. The king was very thoughtful; for he was vexed that he should be obliged to fly, which fate he had never experienced before. He slept but little all night, and chanted his prayers.

28. OF KING OLAF'S MIRACLE.

The following day was Michaelmas eve. Towards dawn the king slumbered, and dreamt that his father, King Olaf the Saint, appeared to him, and said, "Art thou so melancholy and afraid, because the Vindland people come against thee with a great army? Be not afraid of heathens, although they be many; for I shall be with thee in the battle. Prepare, therefore, to give battle to the Vindlanders, when thou hearest my trumpet." When the king awoke he told his dream to his men, and the day was then dawning. At that moment all the people heard a ringing of bells in the air; and those among King Magnus's men who had been in Nidaros thought that it was the ringing of the bell called Glod, which King Olaf had presented to the church of Saint Clement in the town of Nidaros.

29. BATTLE OF HLYRSKOG HEATH.

Then King Magnus stood up, and ordered the war trumpets to sound, and at that moment the Vindland army advanced from the south across the river against him; on which the whole of the king's army stood up, and advanced against the heathens. King Magnus threw off from him his coat of ring-mail, and had a red silk shirt outside over his clothes, and had in his hands the battle-axe called Hel[63], which had belonged to King Olaf. King Magnus ran on before all his men to the enemy's army, and instantly hewed down with both hands every man who came against him. So says Arnor, the earls' skald:–

"His armour on the ground he flung
His broad axe round his head he swung;
And Norway's king strode on in might,
Through ringing swords, to the wild fight.
His broad axe Hel with both hands wielding,
Shields, helms, and skulls before it yielding,
He seemed with Fate the world to share,
And life or death to deal out there."

This battle was not very long; for the king's men were very fiery, and where they came the Vindland men fell as thick as tangles heaped up by the waves on the strand. They who stood behind betook themselves to

63 Hel–Death: the goddess of Death.–L.

flight, and were hewed down like cattle at a slaughter. The king himself drove the fugitives eastward over the heath, and people fell all over the moor. So says Thiodolf:–

"And foremost he pursued,
And the flying foe down hewed;
An eagle's feast each stroke,
As the Vindland helms he broke.
He drove them o'er the hearth,
And they fly from bloody death;
But the moor, a mile or more,
With the dead was studded o'er."

It is a common saying, that there never was so great a slaughter of men in the northern lands, since the time of Christianity, as took place among the Vindland people on Hlyrskog's Heath. On the other side, not many of King Magnus's people were killed, although many were wounded. After the battle the king ordered the wounds of his men to be bound; but there were not so many doctors in the army as were necessary, so the king himself went round, and felt the hands of those he thought best suited for the business; and when he had thus stroked their palms, he named twelve men, who, he thought, had the softest hands, and told them to bind the wounds of the people; and although none of them had ever tried it before, they all became afterwards the best of doctors. There were two Iceland men among them; the one was Thorkil, a son of Geire, from Lyngar; the other was Atle, father of Bard Svarte of Selardal, from whom many good doctors are descended. After this battle, the report of the miracle which King Olaf the Saint had worked was spread widely through the country; and it was the common saying of the people, that no man could venture to fight against King Magnus Olafson, for his father Saint Olaf stood so near to him that his enemies, on that account, never could do him harm.

30. BATTLE AT RE.

King Magnus immediately turned round with his army against Svein, whom he called his earl, although the Danes called him their king; and he collected ships, and a great force, and on both sides a great strength was assembled. In Svein's army were many chiefs from Scania, Halland, Seeland, and Fyen; while King Magnus, on the other hand, had mostly Norway and Jutland men, and with that war-force he hastened to meet

Svein. They met at Re, near Vestland; and there was a great battle, which ended in King Magnus gaining the victory, and Svein taking flight. After losing many people, Svein fled back to Scania, and from thence to Gautland, which was a safe refuge if he needed it, and stood open to him. King Magnus returned to Jutland, where he remained all winter (A.D. 1044) with many people, and had a guard to watch his ships. Arnor, the earls' skald, speaks of this:–

"At Re our battle-loving lord
In bloody meeting stained his sword,–
At Re upon the western shore,
In Vestland warrior's blood once more."

31. BATTLE AT AROS.

Svein Ulfson went directly to his ships as soon as he heard that King Magnus had left his fleet. He drew to him all the men he could, and went round in winter among the islands, Seeland, Fyen, and others. Towards Yule he sailed to Jutland, and went into Limfjord, where many people submitted to him. He imposed scat upon some, but some joined King Magnus. Now when King Magnus heard what Svein was doing, he betook himself to his ships with all the Northmen then in Denmark, and a part of the Danish troops, and steered south along the land. Svein was then in Aros with a great force; and when he heard of King Magnus he laid his vessels without the town, and prepared for battle. When King Magnus heard for certain where Svein was, and that the distance between them was but short, he held a House-thing, and addressed his people thus: "It is reported to me that the earl and his fleet are lying not far from us, and that he has many people. Now I would let you know that I intend to go out against the earl and fight for it, although, we have fewer people. We will, as formerly, put our trust in God, and Saint Olaf, my father, who has given us victory sometimes when we fought, even though we had fewer men than the enemy. Now I would have you get ready to seek out the enemy, and give battle the moment we find him by rowing all to attack, and being all ready for battle." Thereupon the men put on their weapons, each man making himself and his place ready; and then they stretched themselves to their oars. When they saw the earl's ships they rowed towards them, and made ready to attack. When Svein's men saw the forces they armed themselves, bound their ships together, and then began one of the sharpest of battles. So says Thiodolf, the skald:–

"Shield against shield, the earl and king
Made shields and swords together ring.
The gold-decked heroes made a play
Which Hild's iron-shirt men say
They never saw before or since
On battle-deck; the brave might wince,
As spear and arrow whistling flew,
Point blank, death-bringing, quick and true."

They fought at the bows, so that the men only on the bows could strike; the men on the forecastle thrust with spears: and all who were farther off shot with light spears or javelins, or war-arrows. Some fought with stones or short stakes; and those who were aft of the mast shot with the bow. So Says Thiodolf:–

"Steel-pointed spear, and sharpened stake,
Made the broad shield on arm shake:
The eagle, hovering in the air,
Screamed o'er the prey preparing there.
And stones and arrows quickly flew,
And many a warrior bold they slew.
The bowman never twanged his bow
And drew his shaft so oft as now;
And Throndhjem's bowmen on that day
Were not the first tired of this play:
Arrows and darts so quickly fly,
You could not follow with the eye."

Here it appears how hot the battle was with casting weapons. King Magnus stood in the beginning of the battle within a shield-rampart; but as it appeared to him that matters were going on too slowly, he leaped over the shields, and rushed forward in the ship, encouraging his men with a loud cheer, and springing to the bows, where the battle was going on hand to hand. When his men saw this they urged each other on with mutual cheering, and there was one great hurrah through all the ships. So says Thiodolf:–

"'On with our ships! on to the foe!'
Cry Magnus' men–on, on they go.
Spears against shields in fury rattle,–
Was never seen so fierce a battle."

And now the battle was exceedingly sharp; and in the assault Svein's ship was cleared of all her forecastle men, upon and on both sides of the forecastle. Then Magnus boarded Svein's ship, followed by his men; and one after the other came up, and made so stout an assault that Svein's men gave way, and King Magnus first cleared that ship, and then the rest, one after the other. Svein fled, with a great part of his people; but many fell, and many got life and peace. Thiodolf tells of this:–

"Brave Magnus, from the stern springing
On to the stem, where swords were ringing
From his sea-raven's beak of gold
Deals death around–the brave! the bold!
The earl's housemen now begin
To shrink and fall: their ranks grow thin–
The king's luck thrives–their decks are cleared,
Of fighting men no more appeared.
The earl's ships are driven to flight,
Before the king would stop the fight:
The gold-distributor first then
Gave quarters to the vanquished men."

This battle was fought on the last Sunday before Yule. So says Thiodolf:–

"'Twas on a Sunday morning bright,
Fell out this great and bloody fight,
When men were arming, fighting, dying,
Or on the red decks wounded lying.
And many a man, foredoomed to die,
To save his life o'erboard did fly,
But sank; for swimming could not save,
And dead men rolled in every wave."

Magnus took seven ships from Svein's people. So says Thiodolf:–

"Thick Olaf's son seven vessels cleared,
And with his fleet the prizes steered.
The Norway girls will not be sad
To hear such news–each from her lad."

He also sings:–

"The captured men will grieve the most
Svein and their comrades to have lost;
For it went ill with those who fled,
Their wounded had no easy bed.
A heavy storm that very night
O'ertook them flying from the fight;
And skulls and bones are tumbling round,
Under the sea, on sandy ground."

Svein fled immediately by night to Seeland, with the men who had escaped and were inclined to follow him; but King Magnus brought his ships to the shore, and sent his men up the country in the night-time, and early in the morning they came flown to the strand with a great booty in cattle. Thiodolf tells about it:–

"But yesterday with heavy stones
We crushed their skulls, and broke their bones,
And thinned their ranks; and now to-day
Up through their land we've ta'en our way,
And driven their cattle to the shore,
And filled out ships with food in store.
To save his land from our quick swords,
Svein will need something more than words."

32. SVEIN'S FLIGHT.

King Magnus sailed with his fleet from the south after Svein to Seeland; but as soon as the king came there Svein fled up the country with his men, and Magnus followed them, and pursued the fugitives, killing all that were laid hold of. So says Thiodolf:–

"The Seeland girl asks with fear,
'Whose blood-bespattered shield and spear–
The earl's or king's–up from the shore
Moved on with many a warrior more?'
We scoured through all their muddy lanes,
Woodlands, and fields, and miry plains.

Their hasty footmarks in the clay
Showed that to Ringsted led their way.

"Spattered with mud from heel to head,
Our gallant lord his true men led.
Will Lund's earl halt his hasty flight,
And try on land another fight?
His banner yesterday was seen,
The sand-bills and green trees between,
Through moss and mire to the strand,
In arrow flight, leaving the land."

Then Svein fled over to Fyen Island, and King Magnus carried fire and sword through Seeland, and burnt all round, because their men had joined Svein's troop in harvest. So says Thiodolf:–

"As Svein in winter had destroyed
The royal house, the king employed
No little force to guard the land,
And the earl's forays to withstand.
An armed band one morn he found,
And so beset them round and round,
That Canute's nephew quickly fled,
Or he would have been captive led.

"Our Throndhjem king in his just ire
Laid waste the land with sword and fire,
Burst every house, and over all
Struck terror into great and small.
To the earl's friends he well repaid
Their deadly hate–such wild work made
On them and theirs, that from his fury,
Flying for life, away they hurry."

33. BURNING IN FYEN.

As soon as King Magnus heard that Svein with his troops had gone across to Fyen, he sailed after them; and when Svein heard this news he went on board ship and sailed to Scania, and from thence to Gautland, and at last to the Swedish King. King Magnus landed in Fyen, and plundered and burned over all; and all of Svein's men who came there fled far enough. Thiodolf speaks of it thus:–

> *"Fiona isle, once green and fair,*
> *Lies black and reeking through the air:*
> *The red fog rises, thick and hot,*
> *From burning farm and smouldering cot.*
> *The gaping thralls in terror gaze*
> *On the broad upward-spiring blaze,*
> *From thatched roofs and oak-built walls,*
> *Their murdered masters' stately halls.*
>
> *"Svein's men, my girl, will not forget*
> *That thrice they have the Norsemen met,*
> *By sea, by land, with steel, with fire,*
> *Thrice have they felt the Norse king's ire.*
> *Fiona's maids are slim and fair,*
> *The lovely prizes, lads, we'll share:*
> *Some stand to arms in rank and row,*
> *Some seize, bring off, and fend with blow."*

After this the people of Denmark submitted to King Magnus, and during the rest of the winter, there was peace. King Magnus then appointed some of his men to govern Denmark; and when spring was advanced he sailed northwards with his fleet to Norway, where he remained a great part of the summer.

34. BATTLE AT HELGANES

Now, when Svein heard that King Magnus had gone to Norway he rode straight down, and had many people out of Svithjod with him. The people of Scania received him well, and he again collected an army, with which he first crossed over into Seeland and seized upon it and Fyen, and all the other isles. When King Magnus heard of this he gathered together men and ships, and sailed to Denmark; and as soon as he knew where Svein was lying with his ships King Magnus sailed to meet him. They met at a place called Helganes, and the battle began about the fall of day. King Magnus had fewer men, but larger and better equipt vessels. So says Arnor, the earls' skald:–

"At Helganes–so goes the tale–
The brave wolf-feeder, under sail,
Made many an ocean-elk[64] his prey,
Seized many a ship ere break of day.
When twilight fell he urged the fight,
Close combat–man to man all night;
Through a long harvest night's dark hours,
Down poured the battle's iron showers."

The battle was very hot, and as night advanced the fall of men was great. King Magnus, during the whole night, threw hand-spears. Thiodolf speaks of this:–

"And there at Helganes sunk down,
Sore wounded, men of great renown;
And Svein's retainers lost all heart,
Ducking before the flying dart.
The Norsemen's king let fly his spears,
His death-wounds adding to their fears;
For each spear-blade was wet all o'er,
Up to the shaft in their life-gore."

To make a short tale, King Magnus won the victory in this battle, and Svein fled. His ship was cleared of men from stem to stern; and it went so on board many others of his ships. So says Thiodolf:–

"Earl Svein fled from the empty deck,
His lonely ship an unmann'd wreck;
Magnus the Good, the people's friend,
Pressed to the death on the false Svein.
Hneiter[65], the sword his father bore,
Was edge and point, stained red with gore;
Swords sprinkle blood o'er armour bright,

When kings for land and power fight."

64 Ship.–L.

65 This was the name of Saint Olaf's sword, which Magnus had recovered.–L.

And Arnor says:–

"The cutters of Bjorn's own brother
Soon changed their owner for another;
The king took them and all their gear;
The crews, however, got off clear."

A great number of Svein's men fell, and King Magnus and his men had a vast booty to divide. So says Thiodolf:–

"Where the Norsemen the Danish slew,
A Gautland shield and breast-plate true
Fell to my share of spoil by lot;
And something more i' the south I got:
(There all the summer swords were ringing)
A helm, gay arms, and gear worth bringing,
Home to my quiet lovely one
I sent–with news how we had won."

Svein fled up to Scania with all the men who escaped with him; and King Magnus and his people drove the fugitives up through the country without meeting any opposition either from Svein's men or the bondes. So says Thiodolf:–

"Olaf's brave son then gave command,
All his ships' crews should quickly land:
King Magnus, marching at their head,
A noble band of warriors led.
A foray through the land he makes;
Denmark in every quarter shakes.
Up hill and down the horses scour,
Carrying the Danes from Norsemen's power."

King Magnus drove with fire and sword through the land. So says Thiodolf:–

"And now the Norsemen storm along,
Following their banner in a throng:
King Magnus' banner flames on high,
A star to guide our roaming by.
To Lund, o'er Scania's peaceful field,

My shoulder bore my useless shield;
A fairer land, a better road,
As friend or foe, I never trod."

They began to burn the habitations all around, and the people fled on every side. So says Thiodolf:–

"Our ice-cold iron in great store,
Our arms, beside the king we bore:
The Scanian rogues fly at the view
Of men and steel all sharp and true.
Their timbered houses flame on high,
Red flashing over half the sky;
The blazing town flings forth its light,
Lighting the cowards on their flight."

And he also sang:–

"The king o'er all the Danish land
Roams, with his fire-bringing band:
The house, the hut, the farm, the town,
All where men dwelt is burned down.
O'er Denmark's plains and corn-fields,
Meadows and moors, are seen our shields:
Victorious over all, we chase
Svein's wounded men from place to place.

"Across Fiona's moor again,
The paths late trodden by our men
We tread once more, until quite near,
Through morning mist, the foes appear.
Then up our numerous banners flare
In the cold early morning air;
And they from Magnus' power who fly
Cannot this quick war-work deny."

Then Svein fled eastwards along Scania, and King Magnus returned to his ships, and steered eastwards also along the Scanian coast, having got ready with the greatest haste to sail. Thiodolf sings thus about it:–

"No drink but the salt sea
On board our ships had we,
When, following our king,
On board our ships we spring.
Hard work on the salt sea,
Off Scania's coast, had we;
But we laboured for the king,
To his foemen death to bring."

Svein fled to Gautland, and then sought refuge with the Swedish king, with whom he remained all winter (A.D. 1046), and was treated with great respect.

35. OF KING MAGNUS'S CAMPAIGN.

WHEN KING MAGNUS HAD subdued Scania he turned about, and first went to Falster, where he landed, plundered, and killed many people who had before submitted to Svein. Arnor speaks of this:–

"A bloody vengeance for their guile
King Magnus takes on Falster Isle;
The treacherous Danes his fury feel,
And fall before his purpled steel.
The battle-field is covered o'er,
With eagle's prey from shore to shore;
And the king's courtmen were the first
To quench with blood the raven's thirst."

Thereafter Magnus with his fleet proceeded to the isle of Fyen, went on land, plundered, and made great devastation. So says Arnor, the earls' skald:–

"To fair Fiona's grassy shore
His banner now again he bore:
He who the mail-shirt's linked chains
Severs, and all its lustre stains,–
He will be long remembered there,
The warrior in his twentieth year,
Whom their black ravens from afar
Saluted as he went to war."

36. OF KING MAGNUS'S BATTLES.

King Magnus remained in Denmark all that winter (A.D. 1046), and sat in peace. He had held many battles, and had gained the victory in all. So says Od Kikinaskald:–

"'Fore Michaelmas was struck the blow,
That laid the Vindland vikings low;
And people learned with joy to hear
The clang of arms, and leaders' cheer.
Short before Yule fell out the day,
Southward of Aros, where the fray,
Though not enough the foe to quell,
Was of the bloodiest men can tell."

And Arnor says:–

"Olaf's avenger who can sing?
The skald cannot o'ertake the king,
Who makes the war-bird daily drain
The corpse-blood of his foemen slain.
Four battles won within a year,–
Breaker of shields! with swords and spear,
And hand to hand, exalt thy fame
Above the kings of greatest name."

King Magnus had three battles with Svein Ulfson. So says Thiodolf:–

"To our brave Throndhjem sovereign's praise
The skald may all his skaldcraft raise;
For fortune, and for daring deed,
His song will not the truth exceed.
After three battles to regain
What was his own, unjustly ta'en,
Unjustly kept, and dues denied,
He levied dues in red-blood dyed."

37. OF KING MAGNUS, AND THORFIN AND RAGNVALD, EARLS OF ORKNEY.

WHILE KING MAGNUS THE Good, a son of King Olaf the Saint, ruled over Norway, as before related, the Earl Ragnvald Brusason lived with him. Earl Thorfin Sigurdson, the uncle of Ragnvald, ruled then over Orkney. King Magnus sent Ragnvald west to Orkney, and ordered that Thorfin should let him have his father's heritage. Thorfin let Ragnvald have a third part of the land along with him; for so had Erase, the father of Ragnvald, had it at his dying day. Earl Thorfin was married to Ingebjorg, the earl-mother, who was a daughter of Fin Arnason. Earl Ragnvald thought he should have two-thirds of the land, as Olaf the Saint had promised to his father Bruse, and as Bruse had enjoyed as long as Olaf lived. This was the origin of a great strife between these relations, concerning which we have a long saga. They had a great battle in Pentland Firth, in which Kalf Arnason was with Earl Thorfin. So says Bjarne Gullbrarskald:–

"Thy cutters, dashing through the tide,
Brought aid to Earl Thorfin's side,
Fin's son-in-law, and people say
Thy aid made Bruse's son give way.
Kalf, thou art fond of warlike toil,
Gay in the strife and bloody broil;
But here 'twas hate made thee contend
Against Earl Ragnvald, the king's friend."

38. OF KING MAGNUS'S LETTER TO ENGLAND.

KING MAGNUS RULED THEN both over Denmark and Norway; and when he had got possession of the Danish dominions he sent ambassadors over to England to King Edward, who brought to him King Magnus's letter and seal. And in this letter there stood, along with a salutation from King Magnus, these words:–"Ye must have heard of the agreement which I and Hardaknut made,–that he of us two who survived the other should have all the land and people which the deceased had possessed. Now it has so turned out, as ye have no doubt heard, that I have taken the Danish dominions as my heritage after Hardaknut. But before he departed this life he had England as well as Denmark; therefore I consider myself now, in consequence of my rights by this agreement, to own England also. Now I will therefore that thou deliver to me the kingdom; otherwise I will seek to take it by arms, both from Denmark and Norway; and let him rule the land to whom fate gives the victory."

39. KING EDWARD'S ANSWER TO KING MAGNUS'S LETTER.

Now when King Edward had read this letter, he replied thus: "It is known to all men in this country that King Ethelred, my father, was udal-born to this kingdom, both after the old and new law of inheritance. We were four sons after him; and when he by death left the throne my brother Edmund took the government and kingdom; for he was the oldest of us brothers, and I was well satisfied that it was so. And after him my stepfather, Canute the Great, took the kingdom, and as long as he lived there was no access to it. After him my brother Harald was king as long as he lived; and after him my brother Hardaknut took the kingdoms both of Denmark and England; for he thought that a just brotherly division that he should have both England and Denmark, and that I should have no kingdom at all. Now he died, and then it was the resolution of all the people of the country to take me for king here in England. So long as I had no kingly title I served only superiors in all respects, like those who had no claims by birth to land or kingdom. Now, however, I have received the kingly title, and am consecrated king. I have established my royal dignity and authority, as my father before me; and while I live I will not renounce my title. If King Magnus come here with an army, I will gather no army against him; but he shall only get the opportunity of taking England when he has taken my life. Tell him these words of mine." The ambassadors went back to King Magnus, and told him the answer to their message. King Magnus reflected a while, and answered thus: "I think it wisest, and will succeed best, to let King Edward have his kingdom in peace for me, and that I keep the kingdoms God has put into my hands."

BOOK EIGHT

Saga of Harald Hardrade

PRELIMINARY REMARKS.

HARALD, SON OF SIGURD Syr, was born in the year A.D. 1015, and left Norway A.D. 1030. He was called Hardrade, that is, the severe counsellor, the tyrant, though the Icelanders never applied this epithet to him. Harald helped the Icelanders in the famine of A.D. 1056, and sent them timber for a church at Thingvol. It was the Norwegians who gave him the name tyrant in contrast to the "debonairete" of Magnus. He came to Norway in A.D. 1046, and became sole king in A.D. 1047. He died in A.D. 1066, and his son and successor Magnus died in A.D. 1069.

His saga is to be compared with "Agrip", "Fagrskinna", and "Morkinskinna".

The skalds quoted are: Thiodolf, Bolverk, Illuge Bryndalaskald, Stuf the skald, Thorarin Skeggjason, Valgard o' Val, Od Kikinaskald, Grane Skald, Thorleik the Fair, Stein Herdison, Ulf the Marshal, Arnor the earls' skald, Thorkel Skallason, and King Harald Hardrade himself.

1. HARALD ESCAPES FROM THE BATTLE OF STIKLESTAD.

HARALD, SON OF SIGURD Syr, brother of Olaf the Saint, by the same mother, was at the battle of Stiklestad, and was fifteen years old when King Olaf the Saint fell, as was before related. Harald was wounded, and escaped with other fugitives. So says Thiodolf:–

"At Haug the fire-sparks from his shield
Flew round the king's head on the field,
As blow for blow, for Olaf's sake,
His sword and shield would give and take.
Bulgaria's conqueror, I ween,
Had scarcely fifteen winters seen,
When from his murdered brother's side
His unhelmed head he had to hide."

Ragnvald Brusason led Harald from the battle, and the night after the fray took him to a bonde who dwelt in a forest far from other people. The peasant received Harald, and kept him concealed; and Harald was waited upon until he was quite cured of his wounds. Then the bonde's son attended him on the way east over the ridge of the land, and they went by all the forest paths they could, avoiding the common road. The bonde's son did not know who it was he was attending; and as they were riding together between two uninhabited forests, Harald made these verses:

"My wounds were bleeding as I rode;
And down below the bondes strode,
Killing the wounded with the sword,
The followers of their rightful lord.
From wood to wood I crept along,
Unnoticed by the bonde-throng;
'Who knows,' I thought, 'a day may come
My name will yet be great at home.'"

He went eastward over the ridge through Jamtaland and Helsingjaland, and came to Svithjod, where he found Ragnvald Brusason, and many others of King Olaf's men who had fled from the battle at Stiklestad, and they remained there till winter was over.

2. HARALD'S JOURNEY TO CONSTANTINOPLE.

The spring after (A.D. 1031) Harald and Ragnvald got ships, and went east in summer to Russia to King Jarisleif, and were with him all the following winter. So says the skald Bolverk:–

"The king's sharp sword lies clean and bright,
Prepared in foreign lands to fight:

Our ravens croak to have their fill,
The wolf howls from the distant hill.
Our brave king is to Russia gone,–
Braver than he on earth there's none;
His sharp sword will carve many feast
To wolf and raven in the East."

King Jarisleif gave Harald and Ragnvald a kind reception, and made Harald and Ellif, the son of Earl Ragnvald, chiefs over the land-defence men of the king. So says Thiodolf:–

"Where Ellif was, one heart and hand
The two chiefs had in their command;
In wedge or line their battle order
Was ranged by both without disorder.
The eastern Vindland men they drove
Into a corner; and they move
The Lesians, although ill at ease,
To take the laws their conquerors please."

Harald remained several years in Russia, and travelled far and wide in the Eastern land. Then he began his expedition out to Greece, and had a great suite of men with him; and on he went to Constantinople. So says Bolverk:–

"Before the cold sea-curling blast
The cutter from the land flew past,
Her black yards swinging to and fro,
Her shield-hung gunwale dipping low.
The king saw glancing o'er the bow
Constantinople's metal glow
From tower and roof, and painted sails
Gliding past towns and wooded vales."

3. OF HARALD.

At that time the Greek empire was ruled by the Empress Zoe the Great, and with her Michael Catalactus. Now when Harald came to Constantinople he presented himself to the empress, and went into her pay; and immediately, in autumn, went on board the galleys manned with troops which went out to the Greek sea. Harald had his own men along with him. Now Harald had been but a short time in the army before all the Varings flocked to him, and they all joined together when there was a battle. It thus came to pass that Harald was made chief of the Varings. There was a chief over all the troops who was called Gyrger, and who was a relation of the empress. Gyrger and Harald went round among all the Greek islands, and fought much against the corsairs.

4. OF HARALD AND GYRGER CASTING LOTS.

It happened once that Gyrger and the Varings were going through the country, and they resolved to take their night quarters in a wood; and as the Varings came first to the ground, they chose the place which was best for pitching their tents upon, which was the highest ground; for it is the nature of the land there to be soft when rain falls, and therefore it is bad to choose a low situation for your tents. Now when Gyrger, the chief of the army, came up, and saw where the Varings had set up their tents, he told them to remove, and pitch their tents elsewhere, saying he would himself pitch his tents on their ground. Harald replies, "If ye come first to the night quarter, ye take up your ground, and we must go pitch our tents at some other place where we best can. Now do ye so, in the same way, and find a place where ye will. It is, I think, the privilege of us Varings here in the dominions of the Greek emperor to be free, and independent of all but their own commanders, and bound only to serve the emperor and empress." They disputed long and hotly about this, and both sides armed themselves, and were on the way to fight for it; but men of understanding came between and separated them. They said it would be better to come to an agreement about such questions, so that in future no dispute could arise. It came thus to an arbitration between them, at which the best and most sagacious men should give their judgment in the case. At this arbitration it was determined, with the consent of all parties, that lots should be thrown into a box, and the Greeks and Varings should draw which was first to ride, or to row, or to take place in a harbour, or to choose tent ground; and each side should be satisfied with what the drawing of the lots gave them. Accordingly the lots were made and marked. Harald said to Gyrger, "Let me see what mark thou hast put upon thy lot, that we may not both mark our lots in the same way." He did so. Then Harald marked his lot, and put it into the box along with the other. The man who was to draw out the lots then took up one of the lots between his fingers, held it up in the air, and said, "This lot shall be the first to ride, and to row, and to take place in harbour and on the tent field." Harald seized his band, snatched the die, and threw it into the sea, and called out, "That was our lot!" Gyrger said, "Why did you not let other people see it?" Harald replies, "Look at the one remaining in the box,–there you see your own mark upon it." Accordingly the lot which was left behind was examined, and all men saw that Gyrger's mark was upon it, and accordingly the judgment was given that the Varings had gained the first choice in all they had been quarrelling about. There were many things they quarrelled about, but the end always was that Harald got his own way.

5. HARALD'S EXPEDITION IN THE LAND OF THE SARACENS (SERKLAND).

THEY WENT OUT ALL on a campaign in summer. When the whole army was thus assembled Harald kept his men out of the battle, or wherever he saw the least danger, under pretext of saving his men; but where he was alone with his own men only, he fought so desperately that they must either come off victorious or die. It thus happened often that when he commanded the army he gained victories, while Gyrger could do nothing. The troops observed this, and insisted they would be more successful if Harald alone was chief of the whole army, and upbraided the general with never effecting anything, neither himself, nor his people. Gyrger again said that the Varings would give him no assistance, and ordered Harald to go with his men somewhere else, and he, with the rest of his army, would win what they could. Harald accordingly left the army with the Varings and the Latin men, and Gyrger on his side went off with the Greek troops. Then it was seen what each could do. Harald always gained victories and booty; but the Greeks went home to Constantinople with their army, all except a few brave men, who, to gain booty and money, joined themselves to Harald, and took him for their leader. He then went with his troops westward to Africa, which the Varings call Serkland, where he was strengthened with many men. In Serkland he took eighty castles, some of which surrendered, and others were stormed. He then went to Sicily. So says Thiodolf:–

"The serpent's bed of glowing gold
He hates–the generous king, the bold!
He who four score towers laid low,

Ta'en from the Saracenic foe.
Before upon Sicilian plains,
Shield joined to shield, the fight he gains,
The victory at Hild's war game;
And now the heathens dread his name."

So says also Illuge Bryndala-skald:–

"For Michael's empire Harald fought,
And southern lands to Michael brought;
So Budle's son his friendship showed
When he brought friends to his abode."

Here it is said that Michael was king of the Greeks at that time. Harald remained many years in Africa, where he gathered great wealth in gold, jewels, and all sorts of precious things; and all the wealth he gathered there which he did not need for his expenses, he sent with trusty men of his own north to Novgorod to King Jarisleif's care and keeping. He gathered together there extraordinary treasure, as is reasonable to suppose; for he had the plundering of the part of the world richest in gold and valuable things, and he had done such great deeds as with truth are related, such as taking eighty strongholds by his valour.

6. BATTLE IN SICILY.

Now when Harald came to Sicily he plundered there also, and sat down with his army before a strong and populous castle. He surrounded the castle; but the walls were so thick there was no possibility of breaking into it, and the people of the castle had enough of provisions, and all that was necessary for defence. Then Harald hit upon an expedient. He made his bird-catchers catch the small birds which had their nests within the castle, but flew into the woods by day to get food for their young. He had small splinters of tarred wood bound upon the backs of the birds, smeared these over with wax and sulphur, and set fire to them. As soon as the birds were let loose they all flew at once to the castle to their young, and to their nests, which they had under the house roofs that were covered with reeds or straw. The fire from the birds seized upon the house roofs; and although each bird could only carry a small burden of fire, yet all at once there was a mighty flame, caused by so many birds carrying fire with them and spreading it widely among the house roofs. Thus one house after the other was set on fire, until the castle itself was in flames. Then the people came out of the castle and begged for mercy; the same men who for many days had set at defiance the Greek army and its leader. Harald granted life and safety to all who asked quarter, and made himself master of the place.

7. BATTLE AT ANOTHER CASTLE.

There was another castle before which Harald had come with his army. This castle was both full of people and so strong, that there was no hope of breaking into it. The castle stood upon a flat hard plain. Then Harald undertook to dig a passage from a place where a stream ran in a bed so deep that it could not be seen from the castle. They threw out all the earth into the stream, to be carried away by the water. At this work they laboured day and night, and relieved each other in gangs; while the rest of the army went the whole day against the castle, where the castle people shot through their loop-holes. They shot at each other all day in this way, and at night they slept on both sides. Now when Harald perceived that his underground passage was so long that it must be within the castle walls, he ordered his people to arm themselves. It was towards daybreak that they went into the passage. When they got to the end of it they dug over their heads until they came upon stones laid in lime which was the floor of a stone hall. They broke open the floor and rose into the hall. There sat many of the castle-men eating and drinking, and not in the least expecting such uninvited wolves; for the Varings instantly attacked them sword in hand, and killed some, and those who could get away fled. The Varings pursued them; and some seized the castle gate, and opened it, so that the whole body of the army got in. The people of the castle fled; but many asked quarter from the troops, which was granted to all who surrendered. In this way Harald got possession of the place, and found an immense booty in it.

8. BATTLE AT A THIRD CASTLE.

They came to a third castle, the greatest and strongest of them all, and also the richest in property and the fullest of people. Around this castle there were great ditches, so that it evidently could not be taken by the same device as the former; and they lay a long time before it without doing anything. When the castle-men saw this they became bolder, drew up their array on the castle walls, threw open the castle gates, and shouted to the Varings, urging them, and jeering at them, and telling them to come into the castle, and that they were no more fit for battle than so many poultry. Harald told his men to make as if they did not know what to do, or did not understand what was said. "For," says he, "if we do make an assault we can effect nothing, as they can throw their weapons under their feet among us; and if we get in the castle with a party of our people, they have it in their power to shut them in. and shut out the others; for they have all the castle gates beset with men. We shall therefore show them the same scorn they show us, and let them see we do not fear them. Our men shall go out upon the plain nearest to the castle; taking care, however, to keep out of bow-shot. All our men shall go unarmed, and be playing with each other, so that the castle-men may see we do not regard them or their array." Thus it went on for some days, without anything being done.

9. OF ULF AND HALDOR.

Two Iceland men were then with Harald; the one was Haldor[66], a son of the gode Snorre, who brought this account to Iceland; the other was Ulf Uspakson, a grandson of Usvifer Spake. Both were very strong men, bold under arms, and Harald's best friends; and both were in this play. Now when some days were passed the castle people showed more courage, and would go without weapons upon the castle wall, while the castle gates were standing open. The Varings observing this, went one day to their sports with the sword under their cloaks, and the helmet under their hats. After playing awhile they observed that the castle people were off their guard; and instantly seizing their weapons, they made at the castle gate. When the men of the castle saw this they went against them armed completely, and a battle began in the castle gate. The Varings had no shields, but wrapped their cloaks round their left arms. Some of them were wounded, some killed, and all stood in great danger. Now came Harald with the men who had remained in the camp, to the assistance of his people; and the castle-men had now got out upon the walls, from which they shot and threw stones down upon them; so that there was a severe battle, and those who were in the castle gates thought that help was brought them slower than they could have

66 One of the descendants of this Haldor was Snorre Sturlason, the author of "Heimskringla".

wished. When Harald came to the castle gate his standard-bearer fell, and Harald said to Haldor, "Do thou take up the banner now." Haldor took up the banner, and said foolishly, "Who will carry the banner before thee, if thou followest it so timidly as thou hast done for a while?" But these were words more of anger than of truth; for Harald was one of the boldest of men under arms. Then they pressed in, and had a hard battle in the castle; and the end was that Harald gained the victory and took the castle. Haldor was much wounded in the face, and it gave him great pain as long as he lived.

10. BATTLE AT A FOURTH CASTLE.

The fourth castle which Harald came to was the greatest of all we have been speaking about. It was so strong that there was no possibility of breaking into it. They surrounded the castle, so that no supplies could get into it. When they had remained here a short time Harald fell sick, and he betook himself to his bed. He had his tent put up a little from the camp, for he found quietness and rest out of the clamour and clang of armed men. His men went usually in companies to or from him to hear his orders; and the castle people observing there was something new among the Varings, sent out spies to discover what this might mean. When the spies came back to the castle they had to tell of the illness of the commander of the Varings, and that no assault on that account had been made on the castle. A while after Harald's strength began to fail, at which his men were very melancholy and cast down; all which was news to the castle-men. At last Harald's sickness increased so rapidly that his death was expected through all the army. Thereafter the Varings went to the castle-men; told them, in a parley, of the death of their commander; and begged of the priests to grant him burial in the castle. When the castle people heard this news, there were many among them who ruled over cloisters or other great establishments within the place, and who were very eager to get the corpse for their church, knowing that upon that there would follow very rich presents. A great many priests, therefore, clothed themselves in all their robes, and went out of the castle with cross and shrine and relics and formed a beautiful procession. The Varings also made a great burial. The coffin was borne high in the air, and over it was a tent of costly linen and before it were carried many banners. Now when the corpse was brought within the castle gate the Varings set down the coffin right across the entry, fixed a bar to keep the gates open, and sounded to battle with all their trumpets, and drew their swords. The whole army of the Varings, fully armed, rushed from the camp to the assault of the castle with shout and cry; and the monks and other priests who had gone to meet the corpse and had striven with each other who should be the first to come out and take the offering at the burial, were now striving much more who should first get away from the Varings; for they killed before their feet every one who was nearest, whether clerk or unconsecrated. The Varings rummaged so well this castle that they killed all the men, pillaged everything and made an enormous booty.

11. OF HARALD.

Harald was many years in these campaigns, both in Serkland and in Sicily. Then he came back to Constantinople with his troops and stayed there but a little time before he began his expedition to Jerusalem. There he left the pay he had received from the Greek emperor and all the Varings who accompanied him did the same. It is said that on all these expeditions Harald had fought eighteen regular battles. So says Thiodolf:–

"Harald the Stern ne'er allowed
Peace to his foemen, false and proud;
In eighteen battles, fought and won,
The valour of the Norseman shone.
The king, before his home return,
Oft dyed the bald head of the erne
With bloody specks, and o'er the waste
The sharp-claw'd wolf his footsteps traced."

12. HARALD'S EXPEDITION TO PALESTINE.

Harald went with his men to the land of Jerusalem and then up to the city of Jerusalem, and wheresoever he came in the land all the towns and strongholds were given up to him. So says the skald Stuf, who had heard the king himself relate these tidings:–

"He went, the warrior bold and brave,
Jerusalem, the holy grave,
And the interior of the land,

To bring under the Greeks' command;
And by the terror of his name
Under his power the country came,
Nor needed wasting fire and sword
To yield obediance to his word."

HERE IT IS TOLD that this land came without fire and sword under Harald's command. He then went out to Jordan and bathed therein, according to the custom of other pilgrims. Harald gave great gifts to our Lord's grave, to the Holy Cross, and other holy relics in the land of Jerusalem. He also cleared the whole road all the way out to Jordan, by killing the robbers and other disturbers of the peace. So says the skald Stuf:–

"The Agder king cleared far and wide
Jordan's fair banks on either side;
The robber-bands before him fled,
And his great name was widely spread.
The wicked people of the land
Were punished here by his dread hand,
And they hereafter will not miss
Much worse from Jesus Christ than this."

13. HARALD PUT IN PRISON.

THEREAFTER HE WENT BACK to Constantinople. When Harald returned to Constantinople from Jerusalem he longed to return to the North to his native land; and when he heard that Magnus Olafson, his brother's son, had become king both of Norway and Denmark, he gave up his command in the Greek service. And when the empress Zoe heard of this she became angry and raised an accusation against Harald that he had misapplied the property of the Greek emperor which he had received in the campaigns in which he was commander of the army. There was a young and beautiful girl called Maria, a brother's daughter of the empress Zoe, and Harald had paid his addresses to her; but the empress had given him a refusal. The Varings, who were then in pay in Constantinople, have told here in the North that there went a report among well-informed people that the empress Zoe herself wanted Harald for her husband, and that she chiefly blamed Harald for his determination to leave Constantinople, although another reason was given out to the public. Constantinus

Monomachus was at that time emperor of the Greeks and ruled along with Zoe. On this account the Greek emperor had Harald made prisoner and carried to prison.

14. KING OLAF'S MIRACLE AND BLINDING THE GREEK EMPEROR.

When Harald drew near to the prison King Olaf the Saint stood before him and said he would assist him. On that spot of the street a chapel has since been built and consecrated to Saint Olaf and which chapel has stood there ever since. The prison was so constructed that there was a high tower open above, but a door below to go into it from the street. Through it Harald was thrust in, along with Haldor and Ulf. Next night a lady of distinction with two servants came, by the help of ladders, to the top of the tower, let down a rope into the prison and hauled them up. Saint Olaf had formerly cured this lady of a sickness and he had appeared to her in a vision and told her to deliver his brother. Harald went immediately to the Varings, who all rose from their seats when he came in and received him with joy. The men armed themselves forthwith and went to where the emperor slept. They took the emperor prisoner and put out both the eyes of him. So says Thorarin Skeggjason in his poem:–

"Of glowing gold that decks the hand
The king got plenty in this land;
But it's great emperor in the strife
Was made stone-blind for all his life."

So says Thiodolf, the skald, also:–

"He who the hungry wolf's wild yell
Quiets with prey, the stern, the fell,
Midst the uproar of shriek and shout
Stung tho Greek emperor's eyes both out:
The Norse king's mark will not adorn,
The Norse king's mark gives cause to mourn;
His mark the Eastern king must bear,
Groping his sightless way in fear."

In these two songs, and many others, it is told that Harald himself blinded the Greek emperor; and they would surely have named some duke, count, or other great man, if they had not known this to be the true account; and King Harald himself and other men who were with him spread the account.

15. HARALD'S JOURNEY FROM CONSTANTINOPLE.

THE SAME NIGHT King Harald and his men went to the house where Maria slept and carried her away by force. Then they went down to where the galleys of the Varings lay, took two of them and rowed out into Sjavid sound. When they came to the place where the iron chain is drawn across the sound, Harald told his men to stretch out at their oars in both galleys; but the men who were not rowing to run all to the stern of the galley, each with his luggage in his hand. The galleys thus ran up and lay on the iron chain. As soon as they stood fast on it, and would advance no farther, Harald ordered all the men to run forward into the bow. Then the galley, in which Harald was, balanced forwards and swung down over the chain; but the other, which remained fast athwart the chain, split in two, by which many men were lost; but some were taken up out of the sound. Thus Harald escaped out of Constantinople and sailed thence into the Black Sea; but before he left the land he put the lady ashore and sent her back with a good escort to Constantinople and bade her tell her relation, the Empress Zoe, how little power she had over Harald, and how little the empress could have hindered him from taking the lady. Harald then sailed northwards in the Ellipalta and then all round the Eastern empire. On this voyage Harald composed sixteen songs for amusement and all ending with the same words. This is one of them:–

"Past Sicily's wide plains we flew,
A dauntless, never-wearied crew;
Our viking steed rushed through the sea,
As viking-like fast, fast sailed we.
Never, I think, along this shore
Did Norsemen ever sail before;
Yet to the Russian queen, I fear,
My gold-adorned, I am not dear."

With this he meant Ellisif, daughter of King Jarisleif in Novgorod.

16. OF KING HARALD.

When Harald came to Novgorod King Jarisleif received him in the most friendly way and he remained there all winter (A.D. 1045). Then he took into his own keeping all the gold and the many kinds of precious things which he had sent there from Constantinople and which together made up so vast a treasure that no man in the Northern lands ever saw the like of it in one man's possession. Harald had been three times in the poluta-svarf while he was in Constantinople. It is the custom, namely, there, that every time one of the Greek emperors dies, the Varings are allowed poluta-svarf; that is, they may go through all the emperor's palaces where his treasures are and each may take and keep what he can lay hold of while he is going through them.

17. KING HARALD'S MARRIAGE.

This winter King Jarisleif gave Harald his daughter Elisabeth in marriage. She is called by the Northmen Ellisif. This is related by Stuf the Blind, thus:–

"Agder's chief now got the queen
Who long his secret love had been.
Of gold, no doubt, a mighty store
The princess to her husband bore."

In spring he began his journey from Novgorod and came to Aldeigjuborg, where he took shipping and sailed from the East in summer. He turned first to Svithjod and came to Sigtuna. So says Valgard o' Val:–

"The fairest cargo ship e'er bore,
From Russia's distant eastern shore
The gallant Harald homeward brings–
Gold, and a fame that skald still sings.
The ship through dashing foam he steers,
Through the sea-rain to Svithjod veers,
And at Sigtuna's grassy shores
His gallant vessel safely moors."

18. THE LEAGUE BETWEEN KING HARALD AND SVEIN ULFSON.

HARALD FOUND THERE BEFORE him Svein Ulfson, who the autumn before (A.D. 1045) had fled from King Magnus at Helganes; and when they met they were very friendly on both sides. The Swedish king, Olaf the Swede, was brother of the mother of Ellisif, Harald's wife; and Astrid, the mother of Svein, was King Olaf's sister. Harald and Svein entered into friendship with each other and confirmed it by oath. All the Swedes were friendly to Svein, because he belonged to the greatest family in the country; and thus all the Swedes were Harald's friends and helpers also, for many great men were connected with him by relationship. So says Thiodolf:

"Cross the East sea the vessel flew,–
Her oak-keel a white furrow drew
From Russia's coast to Swedish land.
Where Harald can great help command.
The heavy vessel's leeward side
Was hid beneath the rushing tide;
While the broad sail and gold-tipped mast
Swung to and fro in the hard blast."

19. KING HARALD'S FORAY.

THEN HARALD AND SVEIN fitted out ships and gathered together a great force; and when the troops were ready they sailed from the East towards Denmark. So says Valgard:–

"Brave Yngve! to the land decreed
To thee by fate, with tempest speed
The winds fly with thee o'er the sea–
To thy own udal land with thee.
As past the Scanlan plains they fly,
The gay ships glances 'twixt sea and sky,
And Scanian brides look out, and fear
Some ill to those they hold most dear."

They landed first in Seeland with their men and herried and burned in the land far and wide. Then they went to Fyen, where they also landed and wasted. So says Valgard:–

"Harald! thou hast the isle laid waste,
The Seeland men away hast chased,
And the wild wolf by daylight roams
Through their deserted silent homes.
Fiona too could not withstand
The fury of thy wasting hand.
Helms burst, shields broke,–Fiona's bounds.
Were filled with death's terrific sounds.

"Red flashing in the southern sky,
The clear flame sweeping broad and high,
From fair Roeskilde's lofty towers,
On lowly huts its fire-rain pours;
And shows the housemates' silent train
In terror scouring o'er the plain,
Seeking the forest's deepest glen,
To house with wolves, and 'scape from men.

"Few were they of escape to tell,
For, sorrow-worn, the people fell:
The only captives form the fray
Were lovely maidens led away.
And in wild terror to the strand,
Down to the ships, the linked band
Of fair-haired girls is roughly driven,
Their soft skins by the irons riven."

20. KING MAGNUS'S LEVY.

King Magnus Olafson sailed north to Norway in the autumn after the battle at Helganes (A.D. 1045). There he hears the news that Harald Sigurdson, his relation, was come to Svithjod; and moreover that Svein Ulfson and Harald had entered into a friendly bond with each other and gathered together a great force, intending first to subdue Denmark and then Norway. King Magnus then ordered a general levy over all Norway and he soon collected a great army. He hears then that Harald and Svein were come to Denmark and were burning and laying waste the land and that the country people were everywhere submitting to them. It was also told that King Harald was stronger and stouter than other men, and so wise withal that nothing was impossible to him, and he had always the victory when he fought a battle; and he was also so rich in gold that no man could compare with him in wealth. Thiodolf speaks thus of it:

"Norsemen, who stand the sword of foe
Like forest-stems unmoved by blow!
My hopes are fled, no peace is near,–
People fly here and there in fear.
On either side of Seeland's coast
A fleet appears–a white winged host;
Magnus form Norway takes his course,
Harald from Sweden leads his force.

21. TREATY BETWEEN HARALD AND MAGNUS.

Those of Harald's men who were in his counsel said that it would be a great misfortune if relations like Harald and Magnus should fight and throw a death-spear against each other; and therefore many offered to attempt bringing about some agreement between them, and the kings, by their persuasion, agreed to it. Thereupon some men were sent off in a light boat, in which they sailed south in all haste to Denmark, and got some Danish men, who were proven friends of King Magnus, to propose this matter to Harald. This affair was conducted very secretly. Now when Harald heard that his relation, King Magnus, would offer him a league and partition, so that Harald should have half of Norway with King Magnus, and that they should divide all their movable property into two equal parts, he accepted the proposal, and the people went back to King Magnus with this answer.

22. TREATY BETWEEN HARALD AND SVEIN BROKEN.

A little after this it happened that Harald and Svein one evening were sitting at table drinking and talking together, and Svein asked Harald what valuable piece of all his property he esteemed the most.

He answered, it was his banner Land-waster.

Svein asked what was there remarkable about it, that he valued it so highly.

Harald replied, it was a common saying that he must gain the victory before whom that banner is borne, and it had turned out so ever since he had owned it.

Svein replies, "I will begin to believe there is such virtue in the banner when thou hast held three battles with thy relation Magnus, and hast gained them all."

Then answered Harald with an angry voice, "I know my relationship to King Magnus, without thy reminding me of it; and although we are now going in arms against him, our meeting may be of a better sort."

Svein changed colour, and said, "There are people, Harald, who say that thou hast done as much before as only to hold that part of an agreement which appears to suit thy own interest best."

Harald answers, "It becomes thee ill to say that I have not stood by an agreement, when I know what King Magnus could tell of thy proceedings with him."

Thereupon each went his own way. At night, when Harald went to sleep within the bulwarks of his vessel, he said to his footboy, "I will not sleep in my bed to-night, for I suspect there may be treachery abroad. I observed this evening that my friend Svein was very angry at my free discourse. Thou shalt keep watch, therefore, in case anything happen in the night." Harald then went away to sleep somewhere else, and laid a billet of wood in his place. At midnight a boat rowed alongside to the ship's bulwark; a man went on board, lifted up the cloth of the tent of the bulwarks, went up, and struck in Harald's bed with a great ax, so that it stood fast in the lump of wood. The man instantly ran back to his boat again, and rowed away in the dark night, for the moon was set; but the axe remained sticking in the piece of wood as an evidence. Thereupon Harald waked his men and let them know the treachery intended. "We can now see sufficiently," said he, "that we could never match Svein if he practises such deliberate treachery against us; so it will be best for us to get away from this place while we can. Let us cast loose our vessel and row away as quietly as possible." They did so, and rowed during the night northwards along the land; and then proceeded night and day until they came to King Magnus, where he lay with his army. Harald went to his relation Magnus, and there was a joyful meeting betwixt them. So says Thiodolf:–

"The far-known king the order gave,
In silence o'er the swelling wave,

With noiseless oars, his vessels gay
From Denmark west to row away;
And Olaf's son, with justice rare,
Offers with him the realm to share.
People, no doubt, rejoiced to find
The kings had met in peaceful mind."

Afterwards the two relatives conversed with each other and all was settled by peaceful agreement.

23. KING MAGNUS GIVES HARALD HALF OF NORWAY.

King Magnus lay at the shore and had set up tents upon the land. There he invited his relation, King Harald, to be his guest at table; and Harald went to the entertainment with sixty of his men and was feasted excellently. Towards the end of the day King Magnus went into the tent where Harald sat and with him went men carrying parcels consisting of clothes and arms. Then the king went to the man who sat lowest and gave him a good sword, to the next a shield, to the next a kirtle, and so on,–clothes, or weapons, or gold; to all he gave one or the other valuable gift, and the more costly to the more distinguished men among them. Then he placed himself before his relation Harald, holding two sticks in his hand, and said, "Which of these two sticks wilt thou have, my friend?"

Harald replies, "The one nearest me."

"Then," said King Magnus, "with this stick I give thee half of the Norwegian power, with all the scat and duties, and all the domains thereunto belonging, with the condition that everywhere thou shalt be as lawful king in Norway as I am myself; but when we are both together in one place, I shall be the first man in seat, service and salutation; and if there be three of us together of equal dignity, that I shall sit in the middle, and shall have the royal tent-ground and the royal landing-place. Thou shalt strengthen and advance our kingdom, in return for making thee that man in Norway whom we never expected any man should be so long as our head was above ground." Then Harald stood up, and thanked him for the high title and dignity. Thereupon they both sat down, and were very merry together. The same evening Harald and his men returned to their ships.

24. HARALD GIVES MAGNUS THE HALF OF HIS TREASURES.

The following morning King Magnus ordered the trumpets to sound to a General Thing of the people; and when it was seated, he made known to the whole army the gift he had given to his relation Harald. Thorer of Steig gave Harald the title of King there at the Thing; and the same day King Harald invited King Magnus to table with him, and he went with sixty men to King Harald's land-tent, where he had prepared a feast. The two kings sat together on a high-seat, and the feast was splendid; everything went on with magnificence, and the kings' were merry and glad. Towards the close of the day King Harald ordered many caskets to be brought into the tent, and in like manner people bore in weapons, clothes and other sorts of valuables; and all these King Harald divided among King Magnus's men who were at the feast. Then he had the caskets opened and said to King Magnus, "Yesterday you gave us a large kingdom, which your hand won from your and our enemies, and took us in partnership with you, which was well done; and this has cost you much. Now we on our side have been in foreign parts, and oft in peril of life, to gather together the gold which you here see. Now, King Magnus, I will divide this with you. We shall both own this movable property, and each have his equal share of it, as each has his equal half share of Norway. I know that our dispositions are different, as thou art more liberal than I am; therefore let us divide this property equally between us, so that each may have his share free to do with as he will." Then Harald had a large ox-hide spread out, and turned the gold out of the caskets upon it. Then scales and weights were taken and the gold separated and divided by weight into equal parts; and all people wondered exceedingly that so much gold should have come together in one place in the northern countries. But it was understood that it was the Greek emperor's property and wealth; for, as all people say, there are whole houses there full of red gold. The kings were now very merry. Then there appeared an ingot among the rest as big as a man's hand. Harald took it in his hands and said, "Where is the gold, friend Magnus, that thou canst show against this piece?"

King Magnus replied, "So many disturbances and levies have been in the country that almost all the gold and silver I could lay up is gone. I have no more gold in my possession than this ring." And he took the ring off his hand and gave it to Harald.

Harald looked at it, and said, "That is but little gold, friend, for the king who owns two kingdoms; and yet some may doubt whether thou art rightful owner of even this ring."

Then King Magnus replied, after a little reflection, "If I be not rightful owner of this ring, then I know not what I have got right to; for my father, King Olaf the Saint, gave me this ring at our last parting."

Then said King Harald, laughing, "It is true, King Magnus, what thou sayest. Thy father gave thee this ring, but he took the ring from my father for some trifling cause; and in truth it was not a good time for small kings in Norway when thy father was in full power."

King Harald gave Thorer of Steig at that feast a bowl of mountain birch, that was encircled with a silver ring and had a silver handle, both which parts were gilt; and the bowl was filled with money of pure silver. With that came also two gold rings, which together stood for a mark. He gave him also his cloak of dark purple lined with white skins within, and promised him besides his friendship and great dignity. Thorgils Snorrason, an intelligent man, says he has seen an altar-cloth that was made of this cloak; and Gudrid, a daughter of Guthorm, the son of Thorer of Steig, said, according to Thorgil's account, that she had seen this bowl in her father Guthorm's possession. Bolverk also tells of these matters:–

"Thou, generous king, I have been told,
For the green land hast given gold;
And Magnus got a mighty treasure,
That thou one half might'st rule at pleasure.
The people gained a blessed peace,
Which 'twixt the kings did never cease;
While Svein, disturbed with war's alarms,
Had his folk always under arms."

25. OF KING MAGNUS.

The kings Magnus and Harald both ruled in Norway the winter after their agreement (A.D. 1047), and each had his court. In winter they went around the Upland country in guest-quarters; and sometimes they were both together, sometimes each was for himself. They went all the way north to Throndhjem, to the town of Nidaros. King Magnus had taken special care of the holy remains of King Olaf after he came to the country; had the hair and nails clipped every twelve month, and kept himself the keys that opened the shrine. Many miracles were worked by King Olaf's holy remains. It was not long before there was a breach in the good understanding between the two kings, as many were so mischievous as to promote discord between them.

26. OF SVEIN ULFSON.

Svein Ulfson remained behind in the harbour after Harald had gone away, and inquired about his proceedings. When he heard at last of Magnus and Harald having agreed and joined their forces, he steered with his forces eastward along Scania, and remained there until towards winter, when he heard that King Magnus and King Harald had gone northwards to Norway. Then Svein, with his troops, came south to Denmark and took all the royal income that winter (A.D. 1047).

27. OF THE LEVY OF THE TWO KINGS.

Towards spring (A.D. 1047) King Magnus and his relation, King Harald, ordered a levy in Norway. It happened once that the kings lay all night in the same harbour and next day, King Harald, being first ready, made sail. Towards evening he brought up in the harbour in which Magnus and his retinue had intended to pass the night. Harald laid his vessel in the royal ground, and there set up his tents. King Magnus got under sail later in the day and came into the harbour just as King Harald had done pitching his tents. They saw then that King Harald had taken up the king's ground and intended to lie there. After King Magnus had ordered the sails to be taken in, he said, "The men will now get ready along both sides of the vessel to lay out their oars, and some will open the hatches and bring up the arms and arm themselves; for, if they will not make way for us, we will fight them." Now when King Harald sees that King Magnus will give him battle, he says to his men, "Cut our land-fastenings and back the ship out of the ground, for friend Magnus is in a passion." They did so and laid the vessel out of the ground and King Magnus laid his vessel in it. When they were now ready on both sides with their business, King Harald went with a few men on board of King Magnus's ship. King Magnus received him in a friendly way, and bade him welcome. King Harald answered, "I thought we were come among friends; but just now I was in doubt if ye would have it so. But it is a truth that childhood is hasty, and I will only consider it as a childish freak." Then said King Magnus, "It is no childish whim, but a trait of my family, that I never forget what I have given, or what I have not given. If this trifle had been settled against my will, there would soon have followed' some other discord like it. In all particulars I will hold the agreement between us; but in the same way we will have all that belongs to us by that right." King Harald coolly replied, that it is an old custom for the wisest to give way; and returned to his ship. From such circumstances it was found difficult to preserve good understanding between the kings. King Magnus's men said he was in the right; but others, less wise, thought there was some slight put upon Harald in the business. King Harald's men, besides, insisted that the agreement was only that King Magnus should have the preference of the harbour-ground when they arrived together, but that King Harald was not bound to draw out of his place when he came first. They observed, also, that King Harald had conducted himself well and wisely in the matter. Those who viewed the business in the worst light insisted that King Magnus wanted to break the agreement, and that he had done King Harald injustice, and put an affront on him. Such disputes were talked over so long among foolish people, that the spirit of disagreeing affected the kings themselves. Many other things also occurred, in which the kings appeared determined to have each his own way; but of these little will be set down here.

28. KING MAGNUS THE GOOD'S DEATH.

THE KINGS, Magnus and Harald, sailed with their fleet south to Denmark; and when Svein heard of their approach, he fled away east to Scania. Magnus and Harald remained in Denmark late in summer, and subdued the whole country. In autumn they were in Jutland. One night, as King Magnus lay in his bed, it appeared to him in a dream that he was in the same place as his father, Saint Olaf, and that he spoke to him thus: "Wilt thou choose, my son, to follow me, or to become a mighty king, and have long life; but to commit a crime which thou wilt never be able to expiate?" He thought he made the answer, "Do thou, father, choose for me." Then the king thought the answer was, "Thou shalt follow me." King Magnus told his men this dream. Soon after he fell sick and lay at a place called Sudathorp. When he was near his death he sent his brother, Thorer, with tokens to Svein Ulfson, with the request to give Thorer the aid he might require. In this message King Magnus also gave the Danish dominions to Svein after his death; and said it was just that Harald should rule over Norway and Svein over Denmark. Then King Magnus the Good died (A.D. 1047), and great was the sorrow of all the people at his death. So says Od Kikinaskald:–

"The tears o'er good King Magnus' bier,
The people's tears, were all sincere:
Even they to whom he riches gave
Carried him heavily to the grave.
All hearts were struck at the king's end;
His house-thralls wept as for a friend;
His court-men oft alone would muse,
As pondering o'er unthought of news."

29. KING MAGNUS'S FUNERAL.

After this event King Harald held a Thing of his men-at-arms, and told them his intention to go with the army to Viborg Thing, and make himself be proclaimed king over the whole Danish dominions, to which, he said, he had hereditary right after his relation Magnus, as well as to Norway. He therefore asked his men for their aid, and said he thought the Norway man should show himself always superior to the Dane. Then Einar Tambaskelfer replies that he considered it a greater duty to bring his foster-son King Magnus's corpse to the grave, and lay it beside his father, King Olaf's, north in Throndhjem town, than to be fighting abroad and taking another king's dominions and property. He ended his speech with saying that he would rather follow King Magnus dead than any other king alive. Thereupon he had the body adorned in the most careful way, so that most magnificent preparations were made in the king's ship. Then all the Throndhjem people and all the Northmen made themselves ready to return home with the king's body, and so the army was broken up. King Harald saw then that it was better for him to return to Norway to secure that kingdom first, and to assemble men anew; and so King Harald returned to Norway with all his army. As soon as he came to Norway he held a Thing with the people of the country, and had himself proclaimed king everywhere. He proceeded thus from the East through Viken, and in every district in Norway he was named king. Einar Tambaskelfer, and with him all the Throndhjem troops, went with King Magnus's body and transported it to the town of Nidaros, where it was buried in St. Clement's church, where also was the shrine of King Olaf the Saint. King Magnus was of middle size, of long and clear-complexioned countenance, and light hair, spoke well and hastily, was brisk in his actions, and extremely generous. He was a great warrior, and remarkably bold in arms. He was the most popular of kings, prized even by enemies as well as friends.

30. OF SVEIN ULFSON.

SVEIN ULFSON REMAINED that autumn in Scania (A.D. 1047), and was making ready to travel eastward to Sweden, with the intention of renouncing the title of king he had assumed in Denmark; but just as he was mounting his horse some men came riding to him with the first news that King Magnus was dead, and all the Northmen had left Denmark. Svein answered in haste, "I call God to witness that I shall never again fly from the Danish dominions as long as I live." Then he got on his horse and rode south into Scania, where immediately many people crowded to him. That winter he brought under his power all the Danish dominions, and all the Danes took him for their king. Thorer, King Magnus's brother, came to Svein in autumn with the message of King Magnus, as before related, and was well received; and Thorer remained long with Svein and was well taken care of.

31. OF KING HARALD SIGURDSON.

KING HARALD SIGURDSON took the royal power over all Norway after the death of King Magnus Olafson; and when he had reigned over Norway one winter and spring was come (A.D. 1048), he ordered a levy through all the land of one-half of all men and ships and went south to Jutland. He herried and burned all summer wide around in the land and came into Godnarfjord, where King Harald made these verses:–

"While wives of husbands fondly dream,
Here let us anchor in the stream,
In Godnarfjord; we'll safely moor
Our sea-homes, and sleep quite secure."

Then he spoke to Thiodolf, the skald, and asked him to add to it what it wanted, and he sang:–

"In the next summer, I foresee,
Our anchorage in the South will be;
To hold our sea-homes on the ground,
More cold-tongued anchors will be found."

To this Bolverk alludes in his song also, that Harald went to Denmark the summer after King Magnus's death. Bolverk sings thus:–

"Next summer thou the levy raised,
And seawards all the people gazed,
Where thy sea-steeds in sunshine glancing
Over the waves were gaily prancing;
While the deep ships that plunder bore
Seemed black specks from the distant shore.
The Danes, from banks or hillocks green,
Looked with dismay upon the scene."

32. OF THORKEL GEYSA'S DAUGHTERS.

Then they burned the house of Thorkel Geysa, who was a great lord, and his daughters they carried off bound to their ships. They had made a great mockery the winter before of King Harald's coming with warships against Denmark; and they cut their cheese into the shape of anchors, and said such anchors might hold all the ships of the Norway king. Then this was composed:–

"The Island-girls, we were told,
Made anchors all our fleet to hold:
Their Danish jest cut out in cheese
Did not our stern king's fancy please.
Now many a maiden fair, may be,
Sees iron anchors splash the sea,
Who will not wake a maid next morn
To laugh at Norway's ships in scorn."

It is said that a spy who had seen the fleet of King Harald said to Thorkel Geysa's daughters, "Ye said, Geysa's daughters, that King Harald dared not come to Denmark." Dotta, Thorkel's daughter, replied, "That was yesterday." Thorkel had to ransom his daughters with a great sum. So says Grane:–

"The gold-adorned girl's eye
Through Hornskeg wood was never dry,
As down towards the sandy shore
The men their lovely prizes bore.
The Norway leader kept at bay
The foe who would contest the way,
And Dotta's father had to bring
Treasure to satisfy the king."

KING HARALD PLUNDERED in Denmark all that summer, and made immense booty; but he had not any footing in the land that summer in Denmark. He went to Norway again in autumn and remained there all winter (A.D. 1049).

33. MARRIAGES AND CHILDREN OF HARALD HARDRADE.

THE WINTER AFTER King Magnus the Good died, King Harald took Thora, daughter of Thorberg Arnason, and they had two sons; the oldest called Magnus, and the other Olaf. King Harald and Queen Ellisif had two daughters; the one Maria, the other Ingegerd. The spring after the foray which has just been related King Harald ordered the people out and went with them to Denmark (A.D. 1049), and herried there, and did so summer after summer thereafter. So says Stuf, the skald:–

"Falster lay waste, as people tell,–
The raven in other isles fared well.
The Danes were everywhere in fear,
For the dread foray every year."

34. OF THE ARMAMENTS OF SVEIN ULFSON AND HARALD.

KING SVEIN RULED OVER all the Danish dominions after King Magnus's death. He sat quiet all the winter; but in summer he lay out in his ships with all his people and it was said he would go north to Norway with the Danish army and make not less havoc there than King Harald had made in Denmark. King Svein proposed to King Harald in winter (A.D. 1049) to meet him the following summer at the Gaut river and fight until in the battle-field their differences were ended, or they were settled peacefully. They made ready on both sides all winter with their ships, and called out in summer one-half of all the fighting men. The same summer came Thorleik the Fair out of Iceland, and composed a poem about King Svein Ulfson. He heard, when he arrived in Norway, that King Harald had sailed south to the Gaut river against King Svein. Then Thorleik sang this:–

"The wily Svein, I think, will meet
These inland Norsemen fleet to fleet;
The arrow-storm, and heaving sea,
His vantage-fight and field will be.
God only knows the end of strife,
Or which shall have his land and life;
This strife must come to such an end,
For terms will never bind King Svein."

He also sang these verses:–

"Harald, whose red shield oft has shone
O'er herried coasts, and fields hard won,
Rides in hot wrath, and eager speeds
O'er the blue waves his ocean-steeds.
Svein, who in blood his arrows stains,
Brings o'er the ocean's heaving plains
His gold-beaked ships, which come in view
Out from the Sound with many a hue."

King Harald came with his forces to the appointed meeting-place; but there he heard that King Svein was lying with his fleet at the south side of Seeland. Then King Harald divided his forces; let the greater part of the bonde-troops return home; and took with him his court-men, his lendermen, the best men-at-arms, and all the bonde-troops who lived nearest to the Danish land. They sailed over to Jutland to the south of Vendilskage, and so south to Thioda; and over all they carried fire and sword. So says Stuf, the skald:–

"In haste the men of Thyland fly
From the great monarch's threat'ning eye;

At the stern Harald's angry look
The boldest hearts in Denmark shook."

They went forward all the way south to Heidaby, took the merchant town and burnt it. Then one of Harald's men made the following verses:–

"All Heidaby is burned down!
Strangers will ask where stood the town.
In our wild humour up it blazed,
And Svein looks round him all amazed.
All Heidaby is burned down!
From a far corner of the town
I saw, before the peep of morning,
Roofs, walls, and all in flame high burning."

To this also Thorleik alludes in his verses, when he heard there had been no battle at the Gaut river:–

"The stranger-warrior may inquire
Of Harald's men, why in his ire
On Heidaby his wrath he turns,
And the fair town to ashes burns?
Would that the day had never come
When Harald's ships returned home
From the East Sea, since now the town,
Without his gain, is burned down!"

35. HARALD'S ESCAPE INTO THE JUTLAND SEA.

Then King Harald sailed north and had sixty ships and the most of them large and heavily laden with the booty taken in summer; and as they sailed north past Thioda King Svein came down from the land with a great force and he challenged King Harald to land and fight. King Harald had little more than half the force of King Svein and therefore he challenged Svein to fight at sea. So says Thorleik the Fair:–

"Svein, who of all men under heaven
Has had the luckiest birth-hour given,
Invites his foemen to the field,
There to contest with blood-stained shield.

The king, impatient of delay,
Harald, will with his sea-hawks stay;
On board will fight, and fate decide
If Svein shall by his land abide."

After that King Harald sailed north along Vendilskage; and the wind then came against them, and they brought up under Hlesey, where they lay all night. A thick fog lay upon the sea; and when the morning came and the sun rose they saw upon the other side of the sea as if many lights were burning. This was told to King Harald; and he looked at it, and said immediately, "Strike the tilts down on the ships and take to the oars. The Danish forces are coming upon us, and the fog there where they are must have cleared off, and the sun shines upon the dragon-heads of their ships, which are gilded, and that is what we see." It was so as he had said. Svein had come there with a prodigious armed force. They rowed now on both sides all they could. The Danish ships flew lighter before the oars; for the Northmen's ships were both soaked with water and heavily laden, so that the Danes approached nearer and nearer. Then Harald, whose own dragon-ship was the last of the fleet, saw that he could not get away; so he ordered his men to throw overboard some wood, and lay upon it clothes and other good and valuable articles; and it was so perfectly calm that these drove about with the tide. Now when the Danes saw their own goods driving about on the sea, they who were in advance turned about to save them; for they thought it was easier to take what was floating freely about, than to go on board the Northmen to take it. They dropped rowing and lost ground. Now when King Svein came up to them with his ship, he urged them on, saying it would be a great shame if they, with so great a force, could not overtake and master so small a number. The Danes then began again to stretch out lustily at their oars. When King Harald saw that the Danish ships went faster he ordered his men to lighten their ships, and cast overboard malt, wheat, bacon, and to let their liquor run out, which helped a little. Then Harald ordered the bulwarkscreens, the empty casks and puncheons and the prisoners to be thrown overboard; and when all these were driving about on the sea, Svein ordered help to be given to save the men. This was done; but so much time was lost that they separated from each other. The Danes turned back and the Northmen proceeded on their way. So says Thorleik the Fair:–

"Svein drove his foes from Jutland's coast,–
The Norsemen's ships would have been lost,

But Harald all his vessels saves,
Throwing his booty on the waves.
The Jutlanders saw, as he threw,
Their own goods floating in their view;
His lighten'd ships fly o'er the main
While they pick up their own again."

King Svein returned southwards with his ships to Hlesey, where he found seven ships of the Northmen, with bondes and men of the levy. When King Svein came to them they begged for mercy, and offered ransom for themselves. So says Thorleik the Fair:–

"The stern king's men good offers make,
If Svein will ransom for them take;
Too few to fight, they boldly say
Unequal force makes them give way.
The hasty bondes for a word
Would have betaken them to the sword,
And have prolonged a bloody strife–
Such men can give no price for life."

36. OF HARALD.

King Harald was a great man, who ruled his kingdom well in home-concerns. Very prudent was he, of good understanding; and it is the universal opinion that no chief ever was in northern lands of such deep judgment and ready counsel as Harald. He was a great warrior; bold in arms; strong and expert in the use of his weapons beyond any others, as has been before related, although many of the feats of his manhood are not here written down. This is owing partly to our uncertainty about them, partly to our wish not to put stories into this book for which there is no testimony. Although we have heard, many things talked about, and even circumstantially related, yet we think it better that something may be added to, than that it should be necessary to take something away from our narrative. A great part of his history is put in verse by Iceland men, which poems they presented to him or his sons, and for which reason he was their great friend. He was, indeed, a great friend to all the people of that country; and once, when a very dear time set in, he allowed four ships to transport meal to Iceland, and fixed that the ship-pund should not be dearer than 100 ells of wadmal. He permitted also all poor people, who could find provisions to keep them on the voyage across the sea, to emigrate from Iceland to Norway; and from that time there was better subsistence in the country, and the seasons also turned out better. King Harold also sent from Norway a bell for the church of which Olaf the Saint had sent the timbers to Iceland, and which was erected on the Thing-plain. Such remembrances of King Harald are found here in the country, besides many great gifts which he presented to those who visited him.

37. OF HALDOR SNORRASON.

Haldor Snorrason and Ulf Uspakson, as before related, came to Norway with King Harald. They were, in many respects, of different dispositions. Haldor was very stout and strong, and remarkably handsome in appearance. King Harald gave him this testimony, that he, among all his men, cared least about doubtful circumstances, whether they betokened danger or pleasure; for, whatever turned up, he was never in higher nor in lower spirits, never slept less nor more on account of them, nor ate or drank but according to his custom. Haldor was not a man of many words, but short in conversation, told his opinion bluntly and was obstinate and hard; and this could not please the king, who had many clever people about him zealous in his service. Haldor remained a short time with the king; and then came to Iceland, where he took up his abode in Hjardarholt, and dwelt in that farm to a very advanced age.

38. OF ULF USPAKSON.

Ulf Uspakson stood in great esteem with King Harald; for he was a man of great understanding, clever in conversation, active and brave, and withal true and sincere. King Harald made Ulf his marshal, and married him to Jorun, Thorberg's daughter, a sister of Harald's wife, Thora. Ulf and Jorun's children were Joan the Strong of Rasvol, and Brigida, mother of Sauda-Ulf, who was father of Peter Byrdar-Svein, father of Ulf Fly and Sigrid. Joan the Strong's son was Erlend Himalde, father of Archbishop Eystein and his brothers. King Harald gave Ulf the marshal the rights of a lenderman and a fief of twelve marks income, besides a half-district in the Throndhjem land. Of this Stein Herdison speaks in his song about Ulf.

39. OF THE BUILDING OF CHURCHES AND HOUSES.

King Magnus Olafson built Olaf's church in the town (Nidaros), on the spot where Olaf's body was set down for the night, and which, at that time, was above the town. He also had the king's house built there. The church was not quite finished when the king died; but King Harald had what was wanting completed. There, beside the house, he began to construct a stone hall, but it was not finished when he died. King Harald had the church called Mary Church built from the foundations up, at the sandhill close to the spot where the king's holy remains were concealed in the earth the first winter after his fall. It was a large temple, and so strongly built with lime that it was difficult to break it when the Archbishop Eystein had it pulled down. Olaf's holy remains were kept in Olaf's church while Mary Church was building. King Harald had the king's house erected below Mary Kirk, at the side of the river, where it now is; and he had the house in which he had made the great hall consecrated and called Gregorius Church.

40. BEGINNING OF HAKON IVARSON'S STORY.

There was a man called Ivar the White, who was a brave lenderman dwelling in the Uplands, and was a daughter's son of Earl Hakon the Great. Ivar was the handsomest man that could be seen. Ivar's son was called Hakon; and of him it was said that he was distinguished above all men then in Norway for beauty, strength and perfection of figure. In his very youth he had been sent out on war expeditions, where he acquired great honour and consideration, and became afterwards one of the most celebrated men.

41. OF EINAR TAMBASKELFER.

Einar Tambaskelfer was the most powerful lenderman in the Throndhjem land. There was but little friendship between him and King Harald, although Einar retained all the fiefs he had held while Magnus the Good lived. Einar had many large estates, and was married to Bergliot, a daughter of Earl Hakon, as related above. Their son Eindride was grown up, and married to Sigrid, a daughter of Ketil Kalf and Gunhild, King Harald's sister's daughter. Eindride had inherited the beauty of his mother's father, Earl Hakon, and his sons; and in size and strength he took after his father,

Einar, and also in all bodily perfections by which Einar had been distinguished above other men. He was, also, as well as his father, the most popular of men, which the sagas, indeed, show sufficiently.

42. OF EARL ORM.

Orm was at that time earl in the Uplands. His mother was Ragnhild, a daughter of Earl Hakon the Great, and Orm was a remarkably clever man. Aslak Erlingson was then in Jadar at Sole, and was married to Sigrid, a daughter of Earl Svein Hakonson. Gunhild, Earl Svein's other daughter, was married to the Danish king, Svein Ulfson. These were the descendants of Earl Hakon at that time in Norway, besides many other distinguished people; and the whole race was remarkable for their very beautiful appearance, and the most of them were gifted with great bodily perfection, and were all distinguished and important men.

43. HARALD'S PRIDE.

King Harald was very proud, and his pride increased after he was established in the country; and it came so far that at last it was not good to speak against him, or to propose anything different from what he desired. So says Thiodolf, the skald:–

"In arms 'tis right the common man
Should follow orders, one by one,–
Should stoop or rise, or run or stand,
As his war-leader may command;
But now to the king who feeds the ravens
The people bend like heartless cravens–
Nothing is left them, but consent
To what the king calls his intent."

44. OF THE QUARREL OF KING HARALD AND EINAR TAMBASKELFER.

Einar Tambaskelfer was the principal man among the bondes all about Throndhjem, and answered for them at the Things even against the king's men. Einar knew well the law, and did not want boldness to bring forward his opinion at Things, even if the king was present; and all the bondes stood by him. The king was very angry at this, and it came so far that they disputed eagerly against each other. Einar said that the bondes would not put up with any unlawful proceedings from him if he broke through the law of the land; and this occurred several times between them. Einar then began to keep people about him at home, and he had many more when he came into the town if the king was there. It once happened that Einar came to the town with a great many men and ships; he had with him eight or nine great war-ships and nearly 500 men. When he came to the town he went up from the strand with his attendants. King Harald was then in his house, standing out in the gallery of the loft; and when he saw Einar's people going on shore, it is said Harald composed these verses:–

"I see great Tambaskelfer go,
With mighty pomp, and pride, and show,
Across the ebb-shore up the land,–
Before, behind, an armed band.
This bonde-leader thinks to rule,
And fill himself the royal stool.
A goodly earl I have known
With fewer followers of his own.
He who strikes fire from the shield,
Einar, may some day make us yield,
Unless our axe-edge quickly ends,
With sudden kiss, what he intends."

Einar remained several days in the town.

45. THE FALL OF EINAR AND EINDRIDE.

ONE DAY THERE WAS a meeting held in the town, at which the king himself was present. A thief had been taken in the town, and he was brought before the Thing. The man had before been in the service of Einar, who had been very well satisfied with him. This was told to Einar, and he well knew the king would not let the man off, and more because he took an interest in the matter. Einar, therefore, let his men get under arms, went to the Thing, and took the man by force. The friends on both sides then came between and endeavoured to effect a reconciliation; and they succeeded so far that a meeting-place was appointed, to which both should come. There was a Thing-room in the king's house at the river Nid, and the king went into it with a few men, while the most of his people were out in the yard. The king ordered the shutters of the loft-opening to be turned, so that there was but a little space left clear. When Einar came into the yard with his people, he told his son Eindride to remain outside with the men, "for there is no danger here for me." Eindride remained standing outside at the room-door. When Einar came into the Thing-room, he said, "It is dark in the king's Thing-room." At that moment some men ran against him and assaulted him, some with spears, some with swords. When Eindride heard this he drew his sword and rushed into the room; but he was instantly killed along with his father. The king's men then ran up and placed themselves before the door, and the bondes lost courage, having no leader. They urged each other on, indeed, and said it was a shame they should not avenge their chief; but it came to nothing with their attack. The king went out to his men, arrayed them in battle order, and set up his standard: but the bondes did not venture to assault. Then the king went with all his men on board of his ships, rowed down the river, and then took his way out of the fjord. When Einar's wife Bergliot, who was in the house which Einar had possessed in the town, heard of Einar's fall, she went immediately to the king's house where the bondes army was and urged them to the attack; but at the same moment the king was rowing out of the river. Then said Bergliot, "Now we want here my relation, Hakon Ivarson: Einar's murderer would not be rowing out of the river if Ivar stood here on the riverbank." Then Bergliot adorned Einar's and Eindride's corpses and buried them in Olaf's church, beside King Magnus Olafson's burial-place. After Einar's murder the king was so much disliked for that deed that there was nothing that prevented the lendermen and bondes from attacking the king, and giving him battle, but the want of some leader to raise the banner in the bonde army.

46. OF KING HARALD AND FIN ARNASON.

Fin Arnason dwelt at Austrat in Yrjar, and was King Harald's lenderman there. Fin was married to Bergliot, a daughter of Halfdan, who was a son of Sigurd Syr, and brother of Olaf the Saint and of King Harald. Thora, King Harald's wife, was Fin Arnason's brother's daughter: and Fin and all his brothers were the king's dearest friends. Fin Arnason had been for some summers on a viking cruise in the

West sea; and Fin, Guthorm Gunhildson and Hakon Ivarson had all been together on that cruise. King Harald now proceeded out of Throndhjem fjord to Austrat, where he was well received. Afterwards the king and Fin conversed with each other about this new event of Einar's and his son's death, and of the murmuring and threatening which the bondes made against the king.

Fin took up the conversation briskly, and said, "Thou art managing ill in two ways: first, in doing all manner of mischief; and next, in being so afraid that thou knowest not what to do."

The king replied, laughing, "I will send thee, friend, into the town to bring about a reconciliation with the bondes; and if that will not do, thou must go to the Uplands and bring matters to such an understanding with Hakon Ivarson that he shall not be my opponent."

Fin replies, "And how wilt thou reward me if I undertake this dangerous errand; for both the people of Throndhjem and the people of Upland are so great enemies to thee that it would not be safe for any of thy messengers to come among them, unless he were one who would be spared for his own sake?"

The king replies, "Go thou on this embassy, for I know thou wilt succeed in it if any man can, and bring about a reconciliation; and then choose whatever favour from us thou wilt."

Fin says, "Hold thou thy word, king, and I will choose my petition. I will desire to have peace and safe residence in the country for my brother Kalf, and all his estates restored; and also that he receive all the dignity and power he had when he left the country."

The king assented to all that Fin laid down, and it was confirmed by witnesses and shake of hand.

Then said Fin, "What shall I offer Hakon, who rules most among his relations in the land, to induce him to agree to a treaty and reconciliation with thee?"

The king replies, "Thou shalt first hear what Hakon on his part requires for making an agreement; then promote my interest as thou art best able; and deny him nothing in the end short of the kingdom."

Then King Harald proceeded southwards to More, and drew together men in considerable numbers.

47. OF FIN ARNASON'S JOURNEY.

Fin Arnason proceeded to the town and had with him his house-servants, nearly eighty men. When he came into the town he held a

Thing with the town's people. Fin spoke long and ably at the Thing; and told the town's people, and bondes, above all things not to have a hatred against their king, or to drive him away. He reminded them of how much evil they had suffered by acting thus against King Olaf the Saint; and added, that the king was willing to pay penalty for this murder, according to the judgment of understanding and good men. The effect of Fin's speech was that the bondes promised to wait quietly until the messengers came back whom Bergliot had sent to the Uplands to her relative, Hakon Ivarson. Fin then went out to Orkadal with the men who had accompanied him to the town. From thence he went up to Dovrefield, and eastwards over the mountains. He went first to his son-in-law, Earl Orm, who was married to Sigrid, Fin's daughter, and told him his business.

48. OF FIN AND HAKON IVARSON.

Then Fin and Earl Orm appointed a meeting with Hakon Ivarson; and when they met Fin explained his errand to Hakon, and the offer which King Harald made him. It was soon seen, from Hakon's speech, that he considered it to be his great duty to avenge the death of his relative, Eindride; and added, that word was come to him from Throndhjem, from which he might expect help in making head against the king. Then Fin represented to Hakon how much better it would be for him to accept of as high a dignity from the king as he himself could desire, rather than to attempt raising a strife against the king to whom he was owing service and duty. He said if he came out of the conflict without victory, he forfeited life and property: "And even if thou hast the victory, thou wilt still be called a traitor to thy sovereign." Earl Orm also supported Fin's speech. After Hakon had reflected upon this he disclosed what lay on his mind, and said, "I will be reconciled with King Harald if he will give me in marriage his relation Ragnhild, King Magnus Olafson's daughter, with such dower as is suitable to her and she will be content with." Fin said he would agree to this on the king's part; and thus it was settled among them. Fin then returned to Throndhjem, and the disturbance and enmity was quashed, so that the king could retain his kingdom in peace at home; and the league was broken which Eindride's relations had made among themselves for opposing King Harald.

49. OF THE COURTSHIP OF HAKON IVARSON.

WHEN THE DAY ARRIVED for the meeting at which this agreement with Harald should be finally concluded, Hakon went to King Harald; and in their conference the king said that he, for his part, would adhere to all that was settled in their agreement. "Thou Hakon," says he, "must thyself settle that which concerns Ragnhild, as to her accepting thee in marriage; for it would not be advisable for thee, or for any one, to marry Ragnhild without her consent." Then Hakon went to Ragnhild, and paid his addresses to her. She answered him thus: "I have often to feel that my father, King Magnus, is dead and gone from me, since I must marry a bonde; although I acknowledge thou art a handsome man, expert in all exercises. But if King Magnus had lived he would not have married me to any man less than a king; so it is not to be expected that I will take a man who has no dignity or title." Then Hakon went to King Harald and told him his conversation with Ragnhild, and also repeated the agreement which was made between him and Fin, who was with him, together with many others of the persons who had been present at the conversation between him and Fin. Hakon takes them all to witness that such was the agreement that the king should give Ragnhild the dower she might desire. "And now since she will have no man who has not a high dignity, thou must give me such a title of honour; and, according to the opinion of the people, I am of birth, family and other qualifications to be called earl."

The king replies, "When my brother, King Olaf, and his son, King Magnus, ruled the kingdom, they allowed only one earl at a time to be in the country, and I have done the same since I came to the kingly title; and I will not take away from Orm the title of honour I had before given him."

Hakon saw now that his business had not advanced, and was very ill pleased; and Fin was outrageously angry. They said the king had broken his word; and thus they all separated.

50. HAKON'S JOURNEY TO DENMARK.

HAKON THEN WENT OUT of the country with a well-manned ship. When he came to Denmark he went immediately to his relative, King Svein, who received him honourably and gave him great fiefs. Hakon became King Svein's commander of the coast defence against the vikings,–the Vindland people, Kurland people, and others from the East countries,–who infested the Danish dominions; and he lay out with his ships of war both winter and summer.

51. MURDER OF ASMUND.

There was a man called Asmund, who is said to have been King Svein's sister's son, and his foster-son. This Asmund was distinguished among all by his boldness and was much disliked by the king. When Asmund came to years, and to age of discretion, he became an ungovernable person given to murder and manslaughter. The king was ill pleased at this, and sent him away, giving him a good fief, which might keep him and his followers well. As soon as Asmund had got this property from the king he drew together a large troop of people; and as the estate he had got from the king was not sufficient for his expenses he took as his own much more which belonged to the king. When the king heard this he summoned Asmund to him, and when they met the king said that Asmund should remain with the court without keeping any retinue of his own; and this took place as the king desired. But when Asmund had been a little time in the king's court he grew weary of being there, and escaped in the night, returned to his former companions and did more mischief than ever. Now when the king was riding through the country he came to the neighbourhood where Asmund was, and he sent out men-at-arms to seize him. The king then had him laid in irons, and kept him so for some time in hope he would reform; but no sooner did Asmund get rid of his chains than he absconded again, gathered together people and men-at-arms and betook himself to plunder, both abroad and at home. Thus he made great forays, killing and plundering all around. When the people who suffered under these disturbances came to the king and complained to him of their losses, he replied, "Why do ye tell me of this? Why don't you go to Hakon Ivarson, who is my officer for the land-defence, placed on purpose to keep the peace for you peasants, and to hold the vikings in check? I was told that Hakon was a gallant and brave man, but I think he is rather shy when any danger of life is in the way." These words of the king were brought to Hakon, with many additions. Then Hakon went with his men in search of Asmund, and when their ships met Hakon gave battle immediately–and the conflict was sharp, and many men were killed. Hakon boarded Asmund's ship and cut down the men before his feet. At last he and Asmund met and exchanged blows until Asmund fell. Hakon cut off his head, went in all haste to King Svein and found him just sitting down to the dinner-table. Hakon presented himself before the table, laid Asmund's head upon the table before the king, and asked if he knew it. The king made no reply, but became as red as blood in the face. Soon after the king sent him a message, ordering him to leave his service immediately. "Tell him I will do him no harm; but I cannot keep watch over all our relations."[67]

52. HAKON IVARSON'S MARRIAGE.

HAKON THEN LEFT DENMARK, and came north to his estates in Norway. His relation Earl Orm was dead. Hakon's relations and friends were glad to see Hakon, and many gallant men gave themselves much trouble to bring about a reconciliation between King Harald and Hakon. It was at last settled in this way, that Hakon got Ragnhild, the king's daughter, and that King Harald gave Hakon the earldom, with the same power Earl Orm had possessed. Hakon swore to King Harald an oath of fidelity to all the services he was liable to fulfill.

53. RECONCILIATION OF KING HARALD AND KALF.

KALF ARNASON HAD BEEN on a viking cruise to the Western countries ever since he had left Norway; but in winter he was often in the Orkney Islands with his relative, Earl Thorfin. Fin Arnason sent a message to his brother Kalf, and told him the agreement which he had made with King Harald, that Kalf should enjoy safety in Norway, and his estates, and all the fiefs he had held from King Magnus. When this message came to Kalf he immediately got ready for his voyage, and went east to Norway to his brother Fin. Then Fin obtained the king's peace for Kalf, and when Kalf and the king met they went into the agreement which Fin and the king had settled upon before. Kalf bound himself to the king in the same way as he had bound himself to serve King Magnus, according to which Kalf should do all that the king desired and considered of advantage to his realm. Thereupon Kalf received all the estates and fiefs he had before.

67 This incident shows how strong, in those ages, was the tie of relationship, and the point of honour of avenging its injuries–the clanship spirit.–L.

54. FALL OF KALF ARNASON.

The summer following (A.D. 1050) King Harald ordered out a levy, and went to Denmark, where he plundered during the summer; but when he came south to Fyen he found a great force assembled against him. Then the king prepared to land his men from the ships and to engage in a land-fight. He drew up his men on board in order of battle; set Kalf Arnason at the head of one division; ordered him to make the first attack, and told him where they should direct their assault, promising that he would soon make a landing with the others, and come to their assistance. When Kalf came to the land with his men a force came down immediately to oppose them, and Kalf without delay engaged in battle, which, however, did not last long; for Kalf was immediately overpowered by numbers, and betook himself to flight with his men. The Danes pursued them vigorously, and many of the Northmen fell, and among them Kalf Arnason. Now King Harald landed with his array; and they soon came on their way to the field of battle, where they found Kalf's body, and bore it down to the ships. But the king penetrated into the country, killing many people and destroying much. So says Arnor:–

"His shining sword with blood he stains,
Upon Fyona's grassy plains;
And in the midst of fire and smoke,
The king Fyona's forces broke."

55. FIN ARNASON'S EXPEDITION OUT OF THE COUNTRY.

After this Fin Arnason thought he had cause to be an enemy of the king upon account of his brother Kalf's death; and said the king had betrayed Kalf to his fall, and had also deceived him by making him entice his brother Kalf to come over from the West and trust to King Harald's faith. When these speeches came out among people, many said that it was very foolish in Fin to have ever supposed that Kalf could obtain the king's sincere friendship and favour; for they thought the king was the man to seek revenge for smaller offences than Kalf had committed against the king. The king let every one say what he chose, and he himself neither said yes or no about the affair;

but people perceived that the king was very well pleased with what had happened. King Harald once made these verses:–

"I have, in all, the death-stroke given
To foes of mine at least eleven;
Two more, perhaps, if I remember,
May yet be added to this number,
I prize myself upon these deeds,
My people such examples needs.
Bright gold itself they would despise,
Or healing leek-herb underprize,
If not still brought before their eyes."

Fin Arnason took the business so much to heart that he left the country and went to Denmark to King Svein, where he met a friendly reception. They spoke together in private for a long time; and the end of the business was that Fin went into King Svein's service, and became his man. King Svein then gave Fin an earldom, and placed him in Halland, where he was long earl and defended the country against the Northmen.

56. OF GUTHORM GUNHILDSON.

Ketil Kalf and Gunhild of Ringanes had a son called Guthorm, and he was a sister's son to King Olaf and Harald Sigurdson. Guthorm was a gallant man, early advanced to manhood. He was often with King Harald, who loved him much, and asked his advice; for he was of good understanding, and very popular. Guthorm had also been engaged early in forays, and had marauded much in the Western countries with a large force. Ireland was for him a land of peace; and he had his winter quarters often in Dublin, and was in great friendship with King Margad.

57. GUTHORM'S JUNCTION WITH THE IRISH KING MARGAD.

The summer after King Margad, and Guthorm with him, went out on an expedition against Bretland, where they made immense booty. But when the king saw the quantity of silver which was gathered he wanted to have the whole booty, and regarded little his friendship for Guthorm. Guthorm was ill pleased that he and his men should be robbed of their share; but the king said, "Thou must choose one of two things,–either to be content with what we determine, or to fight; and they shall have the booty who gain the victory; and likewise thou must give up thy ships, for them I will have." Guthorm thought there were great difficulties on both sides; for it was disgraceful to give up ships and goods without a stroke, and yet it was highly dangerous to fight the king and his force, the king having sixteen ships and Guthorm only five. Then Guthorm desired three days' time to consider the matter with his people, thinking in that time to pacify the king, and come to a better understanding with him through the mediation of others; but he could not obtain from the king what he desired. This was the day before St. Olaf's day. Guthorm chose the condition that they would rather die or conquer like men, than suffer disgrace, contempt and scorn, by submitting to so great a loss. He called upon God, and his uncle Saint Olaf, and entreated their help and aid; promising to give to the holy man's house the tenth of all the booty that fell to their share, if they gained the victory. Then he arranged his men, placed them in battle order against the great force, prepared for battle, and gave the assault. By the help of God, and the holy Saint Olaf, Guthorm won the battle. King Margad fell, and every man, old and young, who followed him; and after that great victor, Guthorm and all his people returned home joyfully with all the booty they had gained by the battle. Every tenth penny of the booty they had made was taken, according to the vow, to King Olaf the Saint's shrine; and there was so much silver that Guthorm had an image made of it, with rays round the head, which was the size of his own, or of his forecastle-man's head; and the image was seven feet high. The image thus produced was given by Guthorm to King Olaf of the Saint's temple, where it has since remained as a memorial of Guthorm's victory and King Olaf the Saint's miracle.

58. MIRACLE OF KING OLAF IN DENMARK.

There was a wicked, evil-minded count in Denmark who had a Norwegian servant-girl whose family belonged to Throndhjem district. She worshipped King Olaf the Saint, and believed firmly in his sanctity. But the above mentioned count doubted all that was told of the holy man's miracles, insisted that it was nothing but nonsense and idle talk, and made a joke and scorn of the esteem and honour which all the country people showed the good king. Now when his holyday came, on which the mild monarch ended his life, and which all Northmen kept sacred, this unreasonable count would not observe it, but ordered his servant-girl to bake and put fire in the oven that day. She knew well the count's mad passion, and that he would revenge himself severely on her if she refused doing as he ordered. She went, therefore, of necessity, and baked in the oven, but wept much at her work; and she threatened King Olaf that she never would believe in him, if he did not avenge this misdeed by some mischance or other. And now shall ye come to hear a well-deserved vengeance, and a true miracle. It happened, namely, in the same hour that the count became blind of both eyes, and the bread which she had shoved into the oven was turned into stone! Of these stones some are now in St. Olaf's temple, and in other places; and since that time Olafsmas has been always held holy in Denmark.

59. KING OLAF'S MIRACLE ON A CRIPPLE.

West in Valland, a man had such bad health that he became a cripple, and went on his knees and elbows. One day he was upon the road, and had fallen asleep. He dreamt that a gallant man came up to him and asked him where he was going. When he named the neighbouring town, the man said to him, "Go to Saint Olaf's church that stands in London, and there thou shalt be cured." There-upon he awoke, and went straightway to inquire the road to Olaf's church in London. At last he came to London Bridge, and asked the men of the castle if they could tell him where Olaf's church was; but they replied, there were so many churches that they could not tell to whom each of them was consecrated. Soon after a man came up and asked him where he wanted to go, and he answered to Olaf's church. Then said the man, "We shall both go together to Olaf's church, for I know the way to it." Thereupon they went over the bridge to the shrine where Olaf's church was; and when they came to the gates of the churchyard the man mounted over the half-door that was in the gate, but the cripple rolled himself in, and rose up immediately sound and strong: when he looked about him his conductor had vanished.

60. KING HARALD'S FORAY IN DENMARK.

King Harald had built a merchant town in the East at Oslo, where he often resided; for there was good supply from the extensive cultivated district wide around. There also he had a convenient station to defend the country against the Danes, or to make an attack upon Denmark, which he was in the custom of doing often, although he kept no great force on foot. One summer King Harald went from thence with a few light ships and a few men. He steered southwards out from Viken, and, when the wind served, stood over to Jutland, and marauded; but the country people collected and defended the country. Then King Harald steered to Limfjord, and went into the fjord. Limfjord is so formed that its entrance is like a narrow river; but when one gets farther into the fjord it spreads out into a wide sea. King Harald marauded on both sides of the land; and when the Danes gathered together on every side to oppose him, he lay at a small island which was uncultivated. They wanted drink on board his ships, and went up into the island to seek water; but finding none, they reported it to the king. He ordered them to look for some long earthworms on the island, and when they found one they brought it to the king. He ordered the people to bring the worm to a fire, and bake it before it, so that it should be thirsty. Then he ordered a thread to be tied round the tail of the worm, and to let it loose. The worm crept away immediately, while thread wound off from the clew as the worm took it away; and the people followed the worm until it sought downwards in the earth. There the king ordered them to dig for water, which they did, and found so much water that they had no want of it. King Harald now heard from his spies that King Svein was come with a large armament to the mouth of the fjord; but that it was too late for him to come into it, as only one ship at a time can come in. King Harald then steered with his fleet in through the fjord to where it was broadest to a place called Lusbreid. In the inmost bight, there is but a narrow neck of land dividing the fjord from the West sea. Thither King Harald rowed with his men towards evening; and at night when it was dark he unloaded his ships, drew them over the neck of land into the West sea, loaded them again, and was ready with all this before day. He then steered northwards along the Jutland coast. People then said that Harald had escaped from the hands of the Danes. Harald said that he would come to Denmark next time with more people and larger vessels. King Harald then proceeded north to Throndhjem.

61. KING HARALD HAD A SHIP BUILT.

King Harald remained all winter at Nidaros (A.D. 1062) and had a vessel built out upon the strand, and it was a buss. The ship was built of the same size as the Long Serpent, and every part of her was finished with the greatest care. On the stem was a dragon-head, and on the stern a dragon-tail, and the sides of the bows of the ship were gilt. The vessel was of thirty-five rowers benches, and was large for that size, and was remarkably handsome; for the king had everything belonging to the ship's equipment of the best, both sails and rigging, anchors and cables. King Harald sent a message in winter south to Denmark to King Svein, that he should come northwards in spring; that they should meet at the Gaut river and fight, and so settle the division of the countries that the one who gained the victory should have both kingdoms.

62. KING HARALD'S CHALLENGE.

King Harald during this winter called out a general levy of all the people of Norway, and assembled a great force towards spring. Then Harald had his great ship drawn down and put into the river Nid, and set up the dragon's head on her. Thiodolf, the skald, sang about it thus:–

"My lovely girl! the sight was grand
When the great war-ships down the strand
Into the river gently slid,
And all below her sides was hid.
Come, lovely girl, and see the show!–
Her sides that on the water glow,
Her serpent-head with golden mane,
All shining back from the Nid again."

Then King Harald rigged out his ship, got ready for sea, and when he had all in order went out of the river. His men rowed very skilfully and beautifully. So says Thiodolf:–

"It was upon a Saturday,
Ship-tilts were struck and stowed away,
And past the town our dragon glides,
That girls might see our glancing sides.
Out from the Nid brave Harald steers;
Westward at first the dragon veers;
Our lads together down with oars,
The splash is echoed round the shores.

"Their oars our king's men handle well,
One stroke is all the eye can tell:
All level o'er the water rise;
The girls look on in sweet surprise.
Such things, they think, can ne'er give way;
The little know the battle day.
The Danish girls, who dread our shout,
Might wish our ship-gear not so stout.

"'Tis in the fight, not on the wave,
That oars may break and fail the brave.
At sea, beneath the ice-cold sky,
Safely our oars o'er ocean ply;
And when at Throndhjem's holy stream
Our seventy cars in distance gleam,
We seem, while rowing from the sea,
An erne with iron wings to be."

King Harald sailed south along the land, and called out the levy everywhere of men and ships. When they came east to Viken they got a strong wind against them and the forces lay dispersed about in the harbour; some in the isles outside, and some in the fjords. So says Thiodolf:–

"The cutters' sea-bleached bows scarce find
A shelter from the furious wind
Under the inland forests' side,
Where the fjord runs its farthest tide.
In all the isles and creeks around
The bondes' ships lie on the ground,
And ships with gunwales hung with shields
Seek the lee-side of the green fields."

In the heavy storm that raged for some time the great ship had need of good ground tackle. So says Thiodolf:–

"With lofty bow above the seas,
Which curl and fly before the breeze,
The gallant vessel rides and reels,
And every plunge her cable feels.
The storm that tries the spar and mast

Tries the main-anchor at the last:
The storm above, below the rock,
Chafe the thick cable with each shock."

When the weather became favourable King Harald sailed eastwards to the Gaut river with his fleet and arrived there in the evening. So says Thiodolf:–

"The gallant Harald now has come
To Gaut, full half way from his home,
And on the river frontier stands,
To fight with Svein for life and lands.
The night passed o'er, the gallant king
Next day at Thumia calls a Thing,
Where Svein is challenged to appear–
A day which ravens wish were near."

63. OF KING HARALD'S FLEET.

WHEN THE DANES HEARD that the Northmen's army was come to the Gaut river they all fled who had opportunity to get away. The Northmen heard that the Danish king had also called out his forces and lay in the south, partly at Fyen and partly about Seeland. When King Harald found that King Svein would not hold a meeting with him, or a fight, according to what had been agreed upon between them, he took the same course as before–letting the bonde troops return home, but manning 150 ships, with which he sailed southwards along Halland, where he herried all round, and then brought up with his fleet in Lofufjord, and laid waste the country. A little afterwards King Svein came upon them with all the Danish fleet, consisting of 300 ships. When the Northmen saw them King Harald ordered a general meeting of the fleet to be called by sound of trumpet; and many there said it was better to fly, as it was not now advisable to fight. The king replied, "Sooner shall all lie dead one upon another than fly." So says Stein Herdison:–

"With falcon eye, and courage bright,
Our king saw glory in the fight;
To fly, he saw, would ruin bring
On them and him–the folk and king.
'Hands up the arms to one and all!'

Cries out the king; 'we'll win or fall!
Sooner than fly, heaped on each other
Each man shall fall across his brother!'"

Then King Harald drew up his ships to attack, and brought forward his great dragon in the middle of his fleet. So says Thiodolf:–

"The brave king through his vessels' throng
His dragon war-ship moves along;
He runs her gaily to the front,
To meet the coming battle's brunt."

The ship was remarkably well equipt, and fully manned. So says Thiodolf:–

"The king had got a chosen crew–
He told his brave lads to stand true.
The ring of shields seemed to enclose
The ship's deck from the boarding foes.
The dragon, on the Nis-river flood,
Beset with men, who thickly stood,
Shield touching shield, was something rare,
That seemed all force of man to dare."

Ulf, the marshal, laid his ship by the side of the king's and ordered his men to bring her well forward. Stein Herdison, who was himself in Ulf's ship, sings of it thus:–

"Our oars were stowed, our lances high,
As the ship moved swung in the sky.
The marshal Ulf went through our ranks,
Drawn up beside the rowers' banks:
The brave friend of our gallant king
Told us our ship well on to bring,
And fight like Norsemen in the cause–
Our Norsemen answered with huzzas."

Hakon Ivarson lay outside on the other wing, and had many ships with him, all well equipt. At the extremity of the other side lay the Throndhjem chiefs, who had also a great and strong force.

64. OF KING SVEIN'S ARMAMENT.

SVEIN, THE DANISH KING, also drew up his fleet, and laid his ship forward in the center against King Harald's ship, and Fin Arnason laid his ship next; and then the Danes laid their ships, according as they were bold or well-equipt. Then, on both sides, they bound the ships together all through the middle of the fleets; but as the fleets were so large, very many ships remained loose, and each laid his ship forward according to his courage, and that was very unequal. Although the difference among the men was great, altogether there was a very great force on both sides. King Svein had six earls among the people following him. So says Stein Herdison:–

"Danger our chief would never shun,
With eight score ships he would not run:
The Danish fleet he would abide,
And give close battle side by side.
From Leire's coast the Danish king
Three hundred ocean steeds could bring,
And o'er the sea-weed plain in haste
Thought Harald's vessels would be chased."

65. BEGINNING OF THE BATTLE OF NIS-RIVER.

AS SOON AS King Harald was ready with his fleet, he orders the war-blast to sound, and the men to row forward to the attack. So says Stein Herdison:–

"Harald and Svein first met as foes,
Where the Nis in the ocean flows;
For Svein would not for peace entreat,
But, strong in ships, would Harald meet.
The Norsemen prove, with sword in hand,
That numbers cannot skill withstand.
Off Halland's coast the blood of Danes
The blue sea's calm smooth surface stains."

Soon the battle began, and became very sharp; both kings urging on their men. So says Stein Herdison:–

"Our king, his broad shield disregarding,
More keen for striking than for warding,
Now tells his lads their spears to throw,–
Now shows them where to strike a blow.
From fleet to fleet so short the way,
That stones and arrows have full play;
And from the keen sword dropped the blood
Of short-lived seamen in the flood."

It was late in the day when the battle began, and it continued the whole night. King Harald shot for a long time with his bow. So says Thiodolf:–

"The Upland king was all the night
Speeding the arrows' deadly flight.
All in the dark his bow-string's twang
Was answered; for some white shield rang,
Or yelling shriek gave certain note
The shaft had pierced some ring-mail coat,
The foemen's shields and bulwarks bore
A Lapland arrow-scat[68] or more."

Earl Hakon, and the people who followed him, did not make fast their ships in the fleet, but rowed against the Danish ships that were loose, and slew the men of all the ships they came up with. When the Danes observed this each drew his ship out of the way of the earl; but he set upon those who were trying to escape, and they were nearly driven to flight. Then a boat came rowing to the earl's ship and hailed him and said that the other wing of King Harald's fleet was giving way and many of their people had fallen. Then the earl rowed thither and gave so severe an assault that the Danes had to retreat before him. The earl went on in this way all the night, coming forward where he was most wanted, and wheresoever he came none could stand against him. Hakon rowed outside around the battle. Towards the end of the night the greatest part of the Danish fleet broke into flight, for then King Harald with his men boarded the vessel of King Svein; and it was so completely cleared that all the crew fell

68 The Laplanders paid their seat, or yearly tax, in bows and arrows; and the meaning of the skald appears to be, that as many as were paid in a year were shot at the foe.–L.

in the ship, except those who sprang overboard. So says Arnor, the earls' skald:–

"Brave Svein did not his vessel leave
Without good cause, as I believe:
Oft on his casque the sword-blade rang,
Before into the sea he sprang.
Upon the wave his vessel drives;
All his brave crew had lost their lives.
O'er dead courtmen into the sea
The Jutland king had now to flee."

And when King Svein's banner was cut down, and his ship cleared of its crew, all his forces took to flight, and some were killed. The ships which were bound together could not be cast loose, so the people who were in them sprang overboard, and some got to the other ships that were loose; and all King Svein's men who could get off rowed away, but a great many of them were slain. Where the king himself fought the ships were mostly bound together, and there were more than seventy left behind of King Svein's vessels. So says Thiodolf:–

"Svein's ships rode proudly o'er the deep,
When, by a single sudden sweep,
Full seventy sail, as we are told,
Were seized by Norway's monarch bold."

King Harald rowed after the Danes and pursued them; but that was not easy, for the ships lay so thick together that they scarcely could move. Earl Fin Arnason would not flee; and being also shortsighted, was taken prisoner. So says Thiodolf:–

"To the six Danish earls who came
To aid his force, and raise his name,
No mighty thanks King Svein is owing
For mighty actions of their doing.
Fin Arnason, in battle known,
With a stout Norse heart of his own,
Would not take flight his life to gain,
And in the foremost ranks was ta'en."

66. KING SVEIN'S FLIGHT.

Earl Hakon lay behind with his ships, while the king and the rest of the forces were pursuing the fugitives; for the earls' ships could not get forward on account of the ships which lay in the way before him. Then a man came rowing in a boat to the earl's ship and lay at the bulwarks. The man was stout and had on a white hat. He hailed the ship, "Where is the earl?" said he.

The earl was in the fore-hold, stopping a man's blood. The earl cast a look at the man in the hat and asked what his name was. He answered, "Here is Vandrad: speak to me, earl."

The earl leant over the ship's side to him. Then the man in the boat said, "Earl, I will accept of my life from thee, if thou wilt give it."

Then the earl raised himself up, called two men who were friends dear to him, and said to them, "Go into the boat; bring Vandrad to the land; attend him to my friend's Karl the bonde; and tell Karl, as a token that these words come from me, that he let Vandrad have the horse which I gave to him yesterday, and also his saddle, and his son to attend him."

Thereupon they went into the boat and took the oars in hand, while Vandrad steered. This took place just about daybreak, while the vessels were in movement, some rowing towards the land, some towards the sea, both small and great. Vandrad steered where he thought there was most room between the vessels; and when they came near to Norway's ships the earl's men gave their names and then they all allowed them to go where they pleased. Vandrad steered along the shore, and only set in towards the land when they had come past the crowd of ships. They then went up to Karl the bonde's farm, and it was then beginning to be light. They went into the room where Karl had just put on his clothes. The earl's men told him their message and Karl said they must first take some food; and he set a table before them and gave them water to wash with.

Then came the housewife into the room and said, "I wonder why we could get no peace or rest all night with the shouting and screaming."

Karl replies, "Dost thou not know that the kings were fighting all night?"

She asked which had the better of it.

Karl answered, "The Northmen gained."

"Then," said she, "our king will have taken flight."

"Nobody knows," says Karl, "whether he has fled or is fallen."

She says, "What a useless sort of king we have! He is both slow and frightened."

Then said Vandrad, "Frightened he is not; but he is not lucky."

Then Vandrad washed his hands; but he took the towel and dried them right in the middle of the cloth. The housewife snatched the towel from him, and said, "Thou hast been taught little good; it is wasteful to wet the whole cloth at one time."

Vandrad replies, "I may yet come so far forward in the world as to be able to dry myself with the middle of the towel."

Thereupon Karl set a table before them and Vandrad sat down between them. They ate for a while and then went out. The horse was saddled and Karl's son ready to follow him with another horse. They rode away to the forest; and the earl's men returned to the boat, rowed to the earl's ship and told the success of their expedition.

67. OF KING HARALD.

King Harald and his men followed the fugitives only a short way, and rowed back to the place where the deserted ships lay. Then the battle-place was ransacked, and in King Svein's ship was found a heap of dead men; but the king's body was not found, although people believed for certain that he had fallen. Then King Harald had the greatest attention paid to the dead of his men, and had the wounds of the living bound up. The dead bodies of Svein's men were brought to the land, and he sent a message to the peasants to come and bury them. Then he let the booty be divided, and this took up some time. The news came now that King Svein had come to Seeland, and that all who had escaped from the battle had joined him, along with many more, and that he had a great force.

68. FIN ARNASON GETS QUARTER.

Earl Fin Arnason was taken prisoner in the battle, as before related; and when he was led before King Harald the king was very merry, and said, "Fin, we meet here now, and we met last in Norway. The Danish court has not stood very firmly by thee; and it will be a troublesome business for Northmen to drag thee, a blind old man, with them, and preserve thy life."

The earl replies, "The Northmen find it very difficult now to conquer, and it is all the worse that thou hast the command of them."

Then said King Harald, "Wilt thou accept of life and safety, although thou hast not deserved it?"

The earl replies, "Not from thee, thou dog."

The king: "Wilt thou, then, if thy relation Magnus gives thee quarter?"

Magnus, King Harald's son, was then steering the ship.

The earl replies, "Can the whelp rule over life and quarter?"

The king laughed, as if he found amusement in vexing him.–"Wilt thou accept thy life, then, from thy she-relation Thorer?"

The earl: "Is she here?"

"She is here," said the king.

Then Earl Fin broke out with the ugly expressions which since have been preserved, as a proof that he was so mad with rage that he could not govern his tongue:–

"No wonder thou hast bit so strongly, if the mare was with thee."

Earl Fin got life and quarter and the king kept him a while about him. But Fin was rather melancholy and obstinate in conversation; and King Harald said, "I see, Fin, that thou dost not live willingly in company with me and thy relations; now I will give thee leave to go to thy friend King Svein."

The earl said, "I accept of the offer willingly, and the more gratefully the sooner I get away from hence."

The king afterwards let Earl Fin be landed and the traders going to Halland received him well. King Harald sailed from thence to Norway with his fleet; and went first to Oslo, where he gave all his people leave to go home who wished to do so.

69. OF KING SVEIN.

King Svein, it is told, sat in Denmark all that winter, and had his kingdom as formerly. In winter he sent men north to Halland for Karl the bonde and his wife. When Karl came the king called him to him and asked him if he knew him, or thought he had ever seen him before.

Karl replies, "I know thee, sire, and knew thee before, the moment I saw thee; and God be praised if the small help I could give was of any use to thee."

The king replies, "I have to reward thee for all the days I have to live. And now, in the first place, I will give thee any farm in Seeland thou wouldst desire to have; and, in the next place, will make thee a great man, if thou knowest how to conduct thyself."

Karl thanked the king for his promise, and said he had now but one thing to ask.

The king asked what that was.

Karl said that he would ask to take his wife with him.

The king said, "I will not let thee do that; but I will provide thee a far better and more sensible wife. But thy wife can keep the bonde-farm ye had before and she will have her living from it."

The king gave Karl a great and valuable farm, and provided him a good marriage; and he became a considerable man. This was reported far and wide and much praised; and thus it came to be told in Norway.

70. OF THE TALK OF THE COURT-MEN.

King Harald stayed in Oslo the winter after the battle at Nis-river (A.D. 1063). In autumn, when the men came from the south, there was much talk and many stories about the battle which they had fought at Nis-river, and every one who had been there thought he could tell something about it. Once some of them sat in a cellar and drank, and were very merry and talkative. They talked about the Nis-river battle, and who had earne'd the greatest praise and renown. They all agreed that no man there had been at all equal to Earl Hakon. He was the boldest in arms, the quickest, and the most lucky; what he did was of the greatest help, and he won the battle. King Harald, in the meantime, was out in the yard, and spoke with some people. He went then to the room-door, and said, "Every one here would willingly be called Hakon;" and then went his way.

71. OF THE ATTEMPT TO TAKE EARL HAKON.

Earl Hakon went in winter to the Uplands, and was all winter in his domains. He was much beloved by all the Uplanders. It happened, towards spring, that some men were sitting drinking in the town, and the conversation turned, as usual, on the Nis-river battle; and some praised Earl Hakon, and some thought others as deserving of praise as he. When they had thus disputed a while, one of them said, "It is possible that others fought as bravely as the earl at Nis-river; but none, I think, has had such luck with him as he."

The others replied, that his best luck was his driving so many Danes to flight along with other men.

The same man replied, "It was greater luck that he gave King Svein quarter."

One of the company said to him, "Thou dost not know what thou art saying."

He replied, "I know it for certain, for the man told me himself who brought the king to the land."

It went, according to the old proverb, that the king has many ears. This was told the king, and he immediately ordered horses to be gathered, and rode away directly with 900 men. He rode all that night and the following day. Then some men met them who were riding to the town with mead and malt. In the king's retinue was a man called Gamal, who rode to one of these bondes who was an acquaintance of his, and spoke to him privately. "I will pay thee," said he, "to ride with the greatest speed, by the shortest private paths that thou knowest, to Earl Hakon, and tell him the king will kill him; for the king has got to the knowledge that Earl Hakon set King Svein on shore at Nis-river." They agreed on the payment. The bonde rode, and came to the earl just as he was sitting drinking, and had not yet gone to bed. When the bonde told his errand, the earl immediately stood up with all his men, had all his loose property removed from the farm to the forest, and all the people left the house in the night. When the king came he halted there all night; but Hakon rode away, and came east to Svithjod to King Steinkel and stayed with him all summer. King Harald returned to the town, travelled northwards to Throndhjem district, and remained there all summer; but in autumn he returned eastwards to Viken.

72. OF EARL HAKON.

As soon as Earl Hakon heard the king had gone north he returned immediately in summer to the Uplands (A.D. 1063), and remained there until the king had returned from the north. Then the earl went east into Vermaland, where he remained during the winter, and where the king, Steinkel, gave him fiefs. For a short time in winter he went west to Raumarike with a great troop of men from Gautland and Vermaland, and received the scat and duties from the Upland people which belonged to him, and then returned to Glutland, and remained there till spring. King Harald had his seat in Oslo all winter (A.D. 1064), and sent his men to the Uplands to demand the scat, together with the king's land dues, and the mulcts of court; but the Uplanders said they would pay all the scat and dues which they had to pay, to Earl Hakon as long as he was in life, and had forfeited his life or his fief; and the king got no dues that winter.

73. AGREEMENT BETWEEN KING HARALD AND KING SVEIN.

THIS WINTER MESSENGERS and ambassadors went between Norway and Denmark, whose errand was that both Northmen and Danes should make peace, and a league with each other, and to ask the kings to agree to it. These messages gave favourable hopes of a peace; and the matter proceeded so far that a meeting for peace was appointed at the Gaut river between King Harald and King Svein. When spring approached, both kings assembled many ships and people for this meeting. So says a skald in a poem on this expedition of the kings, which begins thus:-

"The king, who from the northern sound
His land with war-ships girds around,
The raven-feeder, filled the coast
With his proud ships, a gallant host!
The gold-tipped stems dash through the foam
That shakes the seamen's planked home;
The high wave breaks up to the mast,
As west of Halland on they passed,

"Harald whose word is fixed and sure,
Whose ships his land from foes secure,
And Svein, whose isles maintain is fleet,
Hasten as friends again to meet;
And every creek with vessels teems,-
All Denmark men and shipping seems;
And all rejoice that strife will cease,
And men meet now but to make peace."

Here it is told that the two kings held the meeting that was agreed upon between them, and both came to the frontiers of their kingdoms. So says the skald:-

"To meet (since peace the Dane now craves)
On to the south upon the waves
Sailed forth our gallant northern king,
Peace to the Danes with him to bring.
Svein northward to his frontier hies
To get the peace his people prize,

And meet King Harald, whom he finds
On land hard used by stormy winds."

When the kings found each other, people began at once to talk of their being reconciled. But as soon as peace was proposed, many began to complain of the damage they had sustained by harrying, robbing and killing men; and for a long time it did not look very like peace. It is here related:–

"Before this meeting of the kings
Each bende his own losses brings,
And loudly claims some recompense
From his king's foes, at their expense.
It is not easy to make peace,
Where noise and talking never cease:
The bondes' warmth may quickly spread,
And kings be by the people led.

"When kings are moved, no peace is sure;
For that peace only is secure
Which they who make it fairly make,–
To each side give, from each side take.
The kings will often rule but ill
Who listen to the people's will:
The people often have no view
But their own interests to pursue."

At last the best men, and those who were the wisest, came between the kings, and settled the peace thus:–that Harald should have Norway, and Svein Denmark, according to the boundaries of old established between Denmark and Norway; neither of them should pay to the other for any damage sustained; the war should cease as it now stood, each retaining what he had got; and this peace should endure as long as they were kings. This peace was confirmed by oath. Then the kings parted, having given each other hostages, as is here related:–

"And I have heard that to set fast
The peace God brought about at last,
Svein and stern Harald pledges sent,
Who witnessed to their sworn intent;
And much I wish that they and all

In no such perjury may fall
That this peace ever should be broken,
And oaths should fail before God spoken."

King Harald with his people sailed northwards to Norway, and King Svein southwards to Denmark.

74. KING HARALD'S BATTLE WITH EARL HAKON.

KING HARALD WAS IN Viken in the summer (A.D. 1064), and he sent his men to the Uplands after the scat and duty which belonged to him; but the bondes paid no attention to the demand, but said they would hold all for Earl Hakon until he came for it. Earl Hakon was then up in Gautland with a large armed force. When summer was past King Harald went south to Konungahella. Then he took all the light-sailing vessels he could get hold of and steered up the river. He had the vessels drawn past all the waterfalls and brought them thus into the Wener lake. Then he rowed eastward across the lake to where he heard Earl Hakon was; but when the earl got news of the king's expedition he retreated down the country, and would not let the king plunder the land. Earl Hakon had a large armed force which the Gautland people had raised for him. King Harald lay with his ships up in a river, and made a foray on land, but left some of his men behind to protect the ships. The king himself rode up with a part of the men, but the greater part were on foot. They had to cross a forest, where they found a mire or lake, and close to it a wood; and when they reached the wood they saw the earl's men, but the mire was between them. They drew up their people now on both sides. Then King Harald ordered his men to sit down on the hillside. "We will first see if they will attack us. Earl Hakon does not usually wait to talk." It was frosty weather, with some snow-drift, and Harald's men sat down under their shields; but it was cold for the Gautlanders, who had but little clothing with them. The earl told them to wait until King Harald came nearer, so that all would stand equally high on the ground. Earl Hakon had the same banner which had belonged to King Magnus Olafson.

The lagman of the Gautland people, Thorvid, sat upon a horse, and the bridle was fastened to a stake that stood in the mire. He broke out with these words: "God knows we have many brave and handsome fellows here, and we shall let King Steinkel hear that we stood by the good earl bravely. I am sure of one thing: we shall behave gallantly against these Northmen, if they attack us; but if our young people give way, and should not stand to it, let us not run farther than to that stream; but if they should give way farther, which I am sure they will not do, let it not be farther than to that hill." At that instant the Northmen sprang up, raised the war-cry, and struck on their shields; and the Gautland army began also to shout. The lagman's horse got shy with the war-cry, and backed so hard that the stake flew up and struck the lagman on the head. He said, "Ill luck to thee, Northman, for that arrow!" and away fled the lagman. King Harald had told his people, "If we do make a clash with the weapons, we shall not however, go down from the hill until they come nearer to us;" and they did so. When the war-cry was raised the earl let his banner advance; but when they came under the hill the king's army rushed down upon them, and killed some of the earl's people, and the rest fled. The Northmen did not pursue the fugitives long, for it was the fall of day; but they took Earl Hakon's banner and all the arms and clothes they could get hold of. King Harald had both the banners carried before him as they marched away. They spoke among themselves that the earl had probably fallen. As they were riding through the forest they could only ride singly, one following the other. Suddenly a man came full gallop across the path, struck his spear through him who was carrying the earl's banner, seized the banner-staff, and rode into the forest on the other side with the banner. When this was told the king he said, "Bring me my armour, for the earl is alive." Then the king rode to his ships in the night; and many said that the earl had now taken his revenge. But Thiodolf sang thus:–

"Steinkel's troops, who were so bold,
Who the Earl Hakon would uphold,
Were driven by our horsemen's power
To Hel, death goddess, in an hour;
And the great earl, so men say
Who won't admit he ran away,
Because his men fled from the ground,
Retired, and cannot now be found."

75. DEATH OF HAL, THE MURDERER OF KODRAN.

The rest of the night Harald passed in his ships; but in the morning, when it was daylight, it was found that so thick ice had gathered about the vessels that one could walk around them. The king ordered his men to cut the ice from the ships all the way out to the clear water; on which they all went to break the ice. King Harald's son, Magnus, steered the vessel that lay lowest down the river and nearest the water. When the people had cleared the ice away almost entirely, a man ran out to the ice, and began hewing away at it like a madman. Then said one of the men, "It is going now as usual, that none can do so much as Hal who killed Kodran, when once he lays himself to the work. See how he is hewing away at the ice." There was a man in the crew of Magnus, the king's son, who was called Thormod Eindridason; and when he heard the name of Kodran's murderer he ran up to Hal, and gave him a death-wound. Kodran was a son of Gudmund Eyjolfson; and Valgerd, who was a sister of Gudmund, was the mother of Jorun, and the grandmother by the mother's side of this Thormod. Thormod was a year old when Kodran was killed, and had never seen Hal Utrygson until now. When the ice was broken all the way out to the water, Magnus drew his ship out, set sail directly, and sailed westward across the lake; but the king's ship, which lay farthest up the river, came out the last. Hal had been in the king's retinue, and was very dear to him; so that the king was enraged at his death. The king came the last into the harbour, and Magnus had let the murderer escape into the forest, and offered to pay the mulct for him; and the king had very nearly attacked Magnus and his crew, but their friends came up and reconciled them.

76. OF KING HARALD.

THAT WINTER (A.D. 1065) King Harald went up to Raumarike, and had many people with him; and he accused the bondes there of having kept from him his scat and duties, and of having aided his enemies to raise disturbance against him. He seized on the bondes and maimed some, killed others, and robbed many of all their property. They who could do it fled from him. He burned everything in the districts and laid them altogether waste. So says Thiodolf:–

"He who the island-people drove,
When they against his power strove,
Now bridle's Raumarike's men,
Marching his forces through their glen.
To punish them the fire he lights
That shines afar off in dark nights
From house and yard, and, as he says,
Will warn the man who disobeys."

Thereafter the king went up to Hedemark, burnt the dwellings, and made no less waste and havoc there than in Raumarike. From thence he went to Hadeland and Ringerike, burning and ravaging all the land. So says Thiodolf:–

"The bonde's household goods are seen
Before his door upon the green,
Smoking and singed: and sparks red hot
Glow in the thatched roof of his cot.
In Hedemark the bondes pray
The king his crushing hand to stay;
In Ringerike and Hadeland,
None 'gainst his fiery wrath can stand."

Then the bondes left all to the king's mercy. After the death of King Magnus fifteen years had passed when the battle at Nis-river took place, and afterwards two years elapsed before Harald and Svein made peace. So says Thiodolf:–

"The Hordland king under the land
At anchor lay close to the strand,
At last, prepared with shield and spear
The peace was settled the third year."

After this peace the disturbances with the people of the Upland districts lasted a year and a half. So says Thiodolf:–

"No easy task it is to say
How the king brought beneath his sway
The Upland bondes, and would give
Nought but their ploughs from which to live.
The king in eighteen months brought down
Their bonde power, and raised his own,
And the great honour he has gained
Will still in memory be retained."

77. OF THE KINGS OF ENGLAND.

Edward, Ethelred's son, was king of England after his brother Hardacanute. He was called Edward the Good; and so he was. King Edward's mother was Queen Emma, daughter of Richard, earl of Rouen. Her brother was Earl Robert, whose son was William the Bastard, who at that time was earl at Rouen in Normandy. King Edward's queen was Gyda, a daughter of Earl Godwin, the son of Ulfnad. Gyda's brothers were, Earl Toste, the eldest; Earl Morukare the next; Earl Walter the third; Earl Svein the fourth; and the fifth was Harald, who was the youngest, and he was brought up at King Edward's court, and was his foster-son. The king loved him very much, and kept him as his own son; for he had no children.

78. OF HARALD GODWINSON.

One summer it happened that Harald, the son of Godwin, made an expedition to Bretland with his ships, but when they got to sea they met a contrary wind, and were driven off into the ocean. They landed west in Normandy, after suffering from a dangerous storm. They brought up at Rouen, where they met Earl William, who received Harald and his company gladly. Harald remained there late in harvest, and was hospitably entertained; for the stormy weather continued, and there was no getting to sea, and this continued until winter set in; so the earl and Harald agreed that he should remain there all winter. Harald sat on the high-seat on one side of the earl; and on the other side sat the earl's wife, one of the most beautiful women that could be seen. They often talked together for amusement at the drinking-table; and the earl went generally to bed, but Harald and the earl's wife sat long in the evenings talking together, and so it went on for a great part of the winter. In one of their conversations she said to Harald, "The earl has asked me what it is we have to talk about so much, for he is angry at it." Harald replies, "We shall then at once let him know all our conversation." The following day, Harald asked the earl to a conference, and they went together into the conference-chamber; where also the queen was, and some of the councillors. Then Harald began thus:–"I have to inform you, earl, that there lies more in my visit here than I have let you know. I would ask your daughter in marriage, and have often spoke over this matter with her mother, and she has promised to support my suit with you." As soon as Harald had made known this proposal of his, it was well received by all who were present. They explained the case to the earl; and at last it came so far that the earl was contracted to Harald, but as she was very young, it was resolved that the wedding should be deferred for some years.

79. KING EDWARD'S DEATH.

When spring came Harald rigged his ships and set off; and he and the earl parted with great friendship. Harald sailed over to England to King Edward, but did not return to Valland to fulfill the marriage agreement. Edward was king over England for twenty-three years and died on a bed of sickness in London on the 5th of January, and was buried in Paul's church. Englishmen call him a saint.

80. HARALD GODWINSON MADE KING OF ENGLAND.

The sons of Earl Godwin were the most powerful men in England. Toste was made chief of the English king's army, and was his land-defence man when the king began to grow old; and he was also placed above all the other earls. His brother Harald was always with the court itself, and nearest to the king in all service, and had the charge of the king's treasure-chamber. It is said that when the king was approaching his last hour, Harald and a few others were with him. Harald first leans down over the king, and then said, "I take you all to witness that the king has now given me the kingdom, and all the realm of England:" and then the king was taken dead out of the bed. The same day there was a meeting of the chiefs, at which there was some talk of choosing a king; and then Harald brought forward his witnesses that King Edward had given him the kingdom on his dying day. The meeting ended by choosing Harald as king, and he was consecrated and crowned the 13th day of Yule, in Paul's church. Then all the chiefs and all the people submitted to him. Now when his brother, Earl Toste, heard of this he took it very ill, as he thought himself quite as well entitled to be king. "I want," said he, "that the principal men of the country choose him whom they think best fitted for it." And sharp words passed between the brothers. King Harald says he will not give up his kingly dignity, for he is seated on the throne which kings sat upon, and is anointed and consecrated a king. On his side also was the strength of the people, for he had the king's whole treasure.

81. EARL TOSTE'S EXPEDITION TO DENMARK.

Now when King Harald perceived that his brother Toste wanted to have him deprived of the kingdom he did not trust him; for Toste was a clever man, and a great warrior, and was in friendship with the principal men of the country. He therefore took the command of the army from Toste, and also all the power he had beyond that of the other earls of the country. Earl Toste, again, would not submit to be his own brother's serving man; therefore he went with his people over the sea to Flanders, and stayed there awhile, then went to Friesland, and from thence to Denmark to his relation King Svein. Earl Ulf, King Svein's father, and Gyda, Earl Toste's mother, were brother's and sister's children. The earl now asked King Svein for support and help of men; and King Svein invited him to stay with him, with the promise that he should get so large an earldom in Denmark that he would be an important chief.

The earl replies, "My inclination is to go back to my estate in England; but if I cannot get help from you for that purpose, I will agree to help you with all the power I can command in England, if you will go there with the Danish army, and win the country, as Canute, your mother's brother, did."

The king replied, "So much smaller a man am I than Canute the Great, that I can with difficulty defend my own Danish dominions against the Northmen. King Canute, on the other hand, got the Danish kingdom in heritage, took England by slash and blow, and sometimes was near losing his life in the contest; and Norway he took without slash or blow. Now it suits me much better to be guided by my own slender ability than to imitate my relation, King Canute's, lucky hits."

Then Earl Toste said, "The result of my errand here is less fortunate than I expected of thee who art so gallant a man, seeing that thy relative is in so great need. It may be that I will seek friendly help where it could less be expected; and that I may find a chief who is less afraid, king, than thou art of a great enterprise."

Then the king and the earl parted, not just the best friends.

82. EARL TOSTE'S EXPEDITION TO NORWAY.

Earl Toste turned away then and went to Norway, where he presented himself to King Harald, who was at that time in Viken. When they met the earl explained his errand to the king. He told him all his proceedings since he left England, and asked his aid to recover his dominions in England.

The king replied that the Northmen had no great desire for a campaign in England, and to have English chiefs over them there. "People say," added he, "that the English are not to be trusted."

The earl replied, "Is it true what I have heard people tell in England, that thy relative, King Magnus, sent men to King Edward with the message that King Magnus had right to England as well as to Denmark, and had got that heritage after Hardacanute, in consequence of a regular agreement?"

The king replied, "How came it that he did not get it, if he had a right to it?"

"Why," replied the earl, "hast thou not Denmark, as King Magnus, thy predecessor, had it?"

The king replies, "The Danes have nothing to brag of over us Northmen; for many a place have we laid in ashes to thy relations."

Then said the earl, "If thou wilt not tell me, I will tell thee. Magnus subdued Denmark, because all the chiefs of the country helped him; and thou hast not done it, because all the people of the country were against thee. Therefore, also, King Magnus did not strive for England, because all the nation would have Edward for king. Wilt thou take England now? I will bring the matter so far that most of the principal men in England shall be thy friends, and assist thee; for nothing is wanting to place me at the side of my brother Harald but the king's name. All men allow that there never was such a warrior in the northern lands as thou art; and it appears to me extraordinary that thou hast been fighting for fifteen years for Denmark, and wilt not take England that lies open to thee."

King Harald weighed carefully the earl's words, and perceived at once that there was truth in much of what he said; and he himself had also a great desire to acquire dominions. Then King Harald and the earl talked long and frequently together; and at last he took the resolution to proceed in summer to England, and conquer the country. King Harald sent a message-token through all Norway and ordered out a levy of one-half of all the men in Norway able to carry arms. When this became generally known, there were many guesses about what might be the end of this expedition. Some reckoned up King Harald's great achievements, and thought he was also the man who could accomplish this. Others, again, said that England was difficult to attack; that it was very full of people; and the men-at-arms, who were called Thingmen, were so brave, that one of them was better than two of Harald's best men. Then said Ulf the marshal:–

"I am still ready gold to gain;
But truly it would be in vain,
And the king's marshal in the hall

Might leave his good post once for all,
If two of us in any strife
Must for one Thingman fly for life,
My lovely Norse maid, in my youth
We thought the opposite the truth."

Ulf the marshal died that spring (A.D. 1066). King Harald stood over his grave, and said, as he was leaving it, "There lies now the truest of men, and the most devoted to his king."

Earl Toste sailed in spring west to Flanders, to meet the people who had left England with him, and others besides who had gathered to him both out of England and Flanders.

83. GYRD'S DREAMS.

King Harald's fleet assembled at the Solunds. When King Harald was ready to leave Nidaros he went to King Olaf's shrine, unlocked it, clipped his hair and nails, and locked the shrine again, and threw the keys into the Nid. Some say he threw them overboard outside of Agdanes; and since then the shrine of Saint Olaf, the king, has never been opened. Thirty-five years had passed since he was slain; and he lived thirty-five years here on earth (A.D. 1080-1066). King Harald sailed with his ships he had about him to the south to meet his people, and a great fleet was collected; so that, according to the people's reckoning, King Harald had nearly 200 ships beside provision-ships and small craft.

While they lay at the Solunds a man called Gyrd, on board the king's ship, had a dream. He thought he was standing in the king's ship and saw a great witch-wife standing on the island, with a fork in one hand and a trough in the other. He thought also that he saw over all the fleet, and that a fowl was sitting upon every ship's stern, and that these fowls were all ravens or ernes; and the witch-wife sang this song:–

"From the east I'll 'tice the king,
To the west the king I'll bring;
Many a noble bone will be
Ravens o'er Giuke's ship are fitting,
Eyeing the prey they think most fitting.
Upon the stem I'll sail with them!
Upon the stem I'll sail with them!"

84. THORD'S DREAM.

There was also a man called Thord, in a ship which lay not far from the king's. He dreamt one night that he saw King Harald's fleet coming to land, and he knew the land to be England. He saw a great battle-array on the land; and he thought both sides began to fight, and had many banners flapping in the air. And before the army of the people of the country was riding a huge witch-wife upon a wolf; and the wolf had a man's carcass in his mouth, and the blood was dropping from his jaws; and when he had eaten up one body she threw another into his mouth, and so one after another, and he swallowed them all. And she sang thus:–

"Skade's eagle eyes
The king's ill luck espies:
Though glancing shields
Hide the green fields,
The king's ill luck she spies.
To bode the doom of this great king,
The flesh of bleeding men I fling
To hairy jaw and hungry maw!
To hairy jaw and hungry maw!"

85. KING HARALD'S DREAM.

King Harald also dreamt one night that he was in Nidaros, and met his brother, King Olaf, who sang to him these verses:–

"In many a fight
My name was bright;
Men weep, and tell
How Olaf fell.
Thy death is near;
Thy corpse, I fear,
The crow will feed,
The witch-wife's steed."

Many other dreams and forebodings were then told of, and most of them gloomy. Before King Harald left Throndhjem, he let his son Magnus be proclaimed king and set him as king over Norway while he was absent. Thora, the daughter of Thorberg, also remained behind; but he took with him Queen Ellisif and her two daughters, Maria and Ingegerd. Olaf, King Harald's son, also accompanied his father abroad.

86. BATTLE AT SCARBOROUGH.

When King Harald was clear for sea, and the wind became favourable, he sailed out into the ocean; and he himself landed in Shetland, but a part of his fleet in the Orkney Islands. King Harald stopped but a short time in Shetland before sailing to Orkney, from whence he took with him a great armed force, and the earls Paul and Erlend, the sons of Earl Thorfin; but he left behind him here the Queen Ellisif, and her daughters Maria and Ingegerd. Then he sailed, leaving Scotland and England westward of him, and landed at a place called Klifland. There he went on shore and plundered, and brought the country in subjection to him without opposition. Then he brought up at Skardaburg, and fought with the people of the place. He went up a hill which is there, and made a great pile upon it, which he set on fire; and when the pile was in clear flame, his men took large forks and pitched the burning wood down into the town, so that one house caught fire after the other, and the town surrendered. The Northmen killed many people there and took all the booty they could lay hold of. There was nothing left for the Englishmen now, if they would preserve their lives, but to submit to King Harald; and thus he subdued the country wherever he came. Then the king proceeded south along the land, and brought up at Hellornes, where there came a force that had been assembled to oppose him, with which he had a battle, and gained the victory.

87. OF HARALD'S ORDER OF BATTLE.

Thereafter the king sailed to the Humber, and up along the river, and then he landed. Up in Jorvik were two earls, Earl Morukare, and his brother, Earl Valthiof, and they had an immense army. While the army of the earls was coming down from the upper part of the country, King Harald lay in the Usa. King Harald now went on the land, and drew up his men. The one arm of this line stood at the outer edge of the river, the other turned up towards the land along a ditch; and there was also a morass, deep, broad, and full of water. The earls let their army proceed slowly down along the river, with all their troops in line.

The king's banner was next the river, where the line was thickest. It was thinnest at the ditch, where also the weakest of the men were. When the earls advanced downwards along the ditch, the arm of the Northmen's line which was at the ditch gave way; and the Englishmen followed, thinking the Northmen would fly. The banner of Earl Morukare advanced then bravely.

88. THE BATTLE AT THE HUMBER.

When King Harald saw that the English array had come to the ditch against him, he ordered the charge to be sounded, and urged on his men. He ordered the banner which was called the Land-ravager to be carried before him, and made so severe an assault that all had to give way before it; and there was a great loss among the men of the earls, and they soon broke into flight, some running up the river, some down, and the most leaping into the ditch, which was so filled with dead that the Norsemen could go dry-foot over the fen. There Earl Morukare fell. So says Stein Herdison:–

"The gallant Harald drove along,
Flying but fighting, the whole throng.
At last, confused, they could not fight,
And the whole body took to flight.
Up from the river's silent stream
At once rose desperate splash and scream;
But they who stood like men this fray
Round Morukare's body lay."

This song was composed by Stein Herdison about Olaf, son of King Harald; and he speaks of Olaf being in this battle with King Harald, his father. These things are also spoken of in the song called "Harald's Stave":–

"Earl Valthiof's men
Lay in the fen,
By sword down hewed,
So thickly strewed,
That Norsemen say
They paved a way
Across the fen
For the brave Norsemen."

Earl Valthiof, and the people who escaped, fled up to the castle of York; and there the greatest loss of men had been. This battle took place upon the Wednesday next Mathias' day (A.D. 1066).

89. OF EARL TOSTE.

Earl Toste had come from Flanders to King Harald as soon as he arrived in England, and the earl was present at all these battles. It happened, as he had foretold the king at their first meeting, that in England many people would flock to them, as being friends and relations of Earl Toste, and thus the king's forces were much strengthened. After the battle now told of, all people in the nearest districts submitted to Harald, but some fled. Then the king advanced to take the castle, and laid his army at Stanforda-bryggiur (Stamford Bridge); and as King Harald had gained so great a victory against so great chiefs and so great an army, the people were dismayed, and doubted if they could make any opposition. The men of the castle therefore determined, in a council, to send a message to King Harald, and deliver up the castle into his power. All this was soon settled; so that on Sunday the king proceeded with the whole army to the castle, and appointed a Thing of the people without the castle, at which the people of the castle were to be present. At this Thing all the people accepted the condition of submitting to Harald, and gave him, as hostages, the children of the most considerable persons; for Earl Toste was well acquainted with all the people of that town. In the evening the king returned down to his ships, after this victory achieved with his own force, and was very merry. A Thing was appointed within the castle early on Monday morning, and then King Harald was to name officers to rule over the town, to give out laws, and bestow fiefs. The same evening, after sunset, King Harald Godwinson came from the south to the castle with a numerous army, and rode into the city with the good-will and consent of the people of the castle. All the gates and walls were beset so that the Northmen could receive no intelligence, and the army remained all night in the town.

90. OF KING HARALD'S LANDING.

On Monday, when King Harald Sigurdson had taken breakfast, he ordered the trumpets to sound for going on shore. The army accordingly got ready, and he divided the men into the parties who should go, and who should stay behind. In every division he allowed two men to land, and one to remain behind. Earl Toste and his retinue prepared to land with King Harald; and, for watching the ships, remained behind the king's son Olaf; the earls of Orkney, Paul and Erlend; and also Eystein Orre, a son of Thorberg Arnason, who was the most able and best beloved by the king of all the lendermen, and to whom the king had promised his daughter Maria. The weather was uncommonly fine, and it was hot sunshine. The men therefore laid aside their armour, and went on the land only with their shields, helmets and spears, and girt with swords; and many had also arrows and bows, and all were very merry. Now as they came near the castle a great army seemed coming against them, and they saw a cloud of dust as from horses' feet, and under it shining shields and bright armour. The king halted his people, and called to him Earl Toste, and asked him what army this could be. The earl replied that he thought it most likely to be a hostle army, but possibly it might be some of his relations who were seeking for mercy and friendship, in order to obtain certain peace and safety from the king. Then the king said, "We must all halt, to discover what kind of a force this is." They did so; and the nearer this force came the greater it appeared, and their shining arms were to the sight like glancing ice.

91. OF EARL TOSTE'S COUNSEL.

Then said King Harald, "Let us now fall upon some good sensible counsel; for it is not to be concealed that this is an hostile army and the king himself without doubt is here."

Then said the earl, "The first counsel is to turn about as fast as we can to our ships to get our men and our weapons, and then we will make a defence according to our ability; or otherwise let our ships defend us, for there these horsemen have no power over us."

Then King Harald said, "I have another counsel. Put three of our best horses under three of our briskest lads and let them ride with all speed to tell our people to come quickly to our relief. The Englishmen shall have a hard fray of it before we give ourselves up for lost."

The earl said the king must order in this, as in all things, as he thought best; adding, at the same time, it was by no means his wish to fly. Then King Harald ordered his banner Land-ravager to be set up; and Frirek was the name of him who bore the banner.

92. OF KING HARALD'S ARMY.

THEN KING HARALD ARRANGED his army, and made the line of battle long, but not deep. He bent both wings of it back, so that they met together; and formed a wide ring equally thick all round, shield to shield, both in the front and rear ranks. The king himself and his retinue were within the circle; and there was the banner, and a body of chosen men. Earl Toste, with his retinue, was at another place, and had a different banner. The army was arranged in this way, because the king knew that horsemen were accustomed to ride forwards with great vigour, but to turn back immediately. Now the king ordered that his own and the earl's attendants should ride forwards where it was most required. "And our bowmen," said he, "shall be near to us; and they who stand in the first rank shall set the spear-shaft on the ground, and the spear-point against the horseman's breast, if he rides at them; and those who stand in the second rank shall set the spear-point against the horse's breast."

93. OF KING HARALD GODWINSON.

KING HARALD GODWINSON had come with an immense army, both of cavalry and infantry. Now King Harald Sigurdson rode around his array, to see how every part was drawn up. He was upon a black horse, and the horse stumbled under him, so that the king fell off. He got up in haste and said, "A fall is lucky for a traveller."

The English king Harald said to the Northmen who were with him, "Do ye know the stout man who fell from his horse, with the blue kirtle and the beautiful helmet?"

"That is the king himself." said they.

The English king said, "A great man, and of stately appearance is he; but I think his luck has left him."

94. OF THE TROOP OF THE NOBILITY.

TWENTY HORSEMEN RODE FORWARD from the Thing-men's troops against the Northmen's array; and all of them, and likewise their horses, were clothed in armour.

One of the horsemen said, "Is Earl Toste in this army?"

The earl answered, "It is not to be denied that ye will find him here."

The horseman says, "Thy brother, King Harald, sends thee salutation, with the message that thou shalt have the whole of Northumberland; and rather than thou shouldst not submit to him, he will give thee the third part of his kingdom to rule over along with himself."

The earl replies, "This is something different from the enmity and scorn he offered last winter; and if this had been offered then it would have saved many a man's life who now is dead, and it would have been better for the kingdom of England. But if I accept of this offer, what will he give King Harald Sigurdson for his trouble?"

The horseman replied, "He has also spoken of this; and will give him seven feet of English ground, or as much more as he may be taller than other men."

"Then," said the earl, "go now and tell King Harald to get ready for battle; for never shall the Northmen say with truth that Earl Toste left King Harald Sigurdson to join his enemy's troops, when he came to fight west here in England. We shall rather all take the resolution to die with honour, or to gain England by a victory."

Then the horseman rode back.

King Harald Sigurdson said to the earl, "Who was the man who spoke so well?"

The earl replied, "That was King Harald Godwinson."

Then, said King Harald Sigurdson, "That was by far too long concealed from me; for they had come so near to our army, that this Harald should never have carried back the tidings of our men's slaughter."

Then said the earl, "It was certainly imprudent for such chiefs, and it may be as you say; but I saw he was going to offer me peace and a great dominion, and that, on the other hand, I would be his murderer if I betrayed him; and I would rather he should be my murderer than I his, if one of two be to die."

King Harald Sigurdson observed to his men, "That was but a little man, yet he sat firmly in his stirrups."

It is said that Harald made these verses at this time:–

"Advance! advance!
No helmets glance,
But blue swords play
In our array.
Advance! advance!
No mail-coats glance,
But hearts are here
That ne'er knew fear."

His coat of mail was called Emma; and it was so long that it reached almost to the middle of his leg, and so strong that no weapon ever pierced it. Then said King Harald Sigurdson, "These verses are but ill composed; I must try to make better;" and he composed the following:–

"In battle storm we seek no lee,
With skulking head, and bending knee,
Behind the hollow shield.
With eye and hand we fend the head;
Courage and skill stand in the stead
Of panzer, helm, and shield,
In hild's bloody field."

Thereupon Thiodolf sang:–

"And should our king in battle fall,–
A fate that God may give to all,–
His sons will vengeance take;
And never shone the sun upon
Two nobler eaglet; in his run,
And them we'll never forsake."

95. OF THE BEGINNING OF THE BATTLE.

NOW THE BATTLE BEGAN. The Englishmen made a hot assault upon the Northmen, who sustained it bravely. It was no easy matter for the English to ride against the Northmen on account of their spears; therefore they rode in a circle around them. And the fight at first was but loose and light, as long as the Northmen kept their order of battle; for although the English rode hard against the Northmen, they gave way again immediately, as they could do nothing against them. Now when the Northmen thought they perceived that the enemy were making but weak assaults, they set after them, and would drive them into flight; but when they had broken their shield-rampart the Englishmen rode up from all sides, and threw arrows and spears on them. Now when King Harald Sigurdson saw this, he went into the fray where the greatest crash of weapons was, and there was a sharp conflict, in which many people fell on both sides. King Harald then was in a rage, and ran out in front of the array, and hewed down with both hands; so that neither helmet nor armour could withstand him, and all who were nearest gave way before him. It was then very near with the English that they had taken to flight. So says Arnor, the earls' skald:–

"Where battle-storm was ringing,
Where arrow-cloud was singing,
Harald stood there,
Of armour bare,
His deadly sword still swinging.
The foeman feel its bite;
His Norsemen rush to fight,
Danger to share,
With Harald there,
Where steel on steel was ringing."

96. FALL OF KING HARALD.

King Harald Sigurdson was hit by an arrow in the windpipe, and that was his death-wound. He fell, and all who had advanced with him, except those who retired with the banner. There was afterwards the warmest conflict, and Earl Toste had taken charge of the king's banner. They began on both sides to form their array again, and for a long time there was a pause in fighting. Then Thiodolf sang these verses:–

"The army stands in hushed dismay;
Stilled is the clamour of the fray.
Harald is dead, and with him goes
The spirit to withstand our foes.
A bloody scat the folk must pay
For their king's folly on this day.
He fell; and now, without disguise,
We say this business was not wise."

But before the battle began again Harald Godwinson offered his brother, Earl Toste, peace, and also quarter to the Northmen who were still alive; but the Northmen called out, all of them together, that they would rather fall, one across the other, than accept of quarter from the Englishmen. Then each side set up a war-shout, and the battle began again. So says Arnor, the earls' skald:–

"The king, whose name would ill-doers scare,
The gold-tipped arrow would not spare.
Unhelmed, unpanzered, without shield,
He fell among us in the field.
The gallant men who saw him fall
Would take no quarter; one and all
Resolved to die with their loved king,
Around his corpse in a corpse-ring."

97. SKIRMISH OF ORRE.

EYSTEIN ORRE CAME UP at this moment from the ships with the men who followed him, and all were clad in armour. Then Eystein got King Harald's banner Land-ravager; and now was, for the third time, one of the sharpest of conflicts, in which many Englishmen fell, and they were near to taking flight. This conflict is called Orre's storm. Eystein and his men had hastened so fast from the ships that they were quite exhausted, and scarcely fit to fight before they came into the battle; but afterwards they became so furious, that they did not guard themselves with their shields as long as they could stand upright. At last they threw off their coats of ringmail, and then the Englishmen could easily lay their blows at them; and many fell from weariness, and died without a wound. Thus almost all the chief men fell among the Norway people. This happened towards evening; and then it went, as one might expect, that all had not the same fate, for many fled, and were lucky enough to escape in various ways; and darkness fell before the slaughter was altogether ended.

98. OF STYRKAR THE MARSHAL.

STYRKAR, KING HARALD SIGURDSON's marshal, a gallant man, escaped upon a horse, on which he rode away in the evening. It was blowing a cold wind, and Styrkar had not much other clothing upon him but his shirt, and had a helmet on his head, and a drawn sword in his hand. As soon as his weariness was over, he began to feel cold. A waggoner met him in a lined skin-coat. Styrkar asks him, "Wilt thou sell thy coat, friend?"

"Not to thee," says the peasant: "thou art a Northman; that I can hear by thy tongue."

Styrkar replies, "If I were a Northman, what wouldst thou do?"

"I would kill thee," replied the peasant; "but as ill luck would have it, I have no weapon just now by me that would do it."

Then Styrkar says, "As you can't kill me, friend, I shall try if I can't kill you." And with that he swung his sword, and struck him on the neck, so that his head came off. He then took the skin-coat, sprang on his horse, and rode down to the strand.

Olaf Haraldson had not gone on land with the others, and when he heard of his father's fall he made ready to sail away with the men who remained.

99. OF WILLIAM THE BASTARD.

When the Earl of Rouen, William the Bastard, heard of his relation, King Edward's, death, and also that Harald Godwinson was chosen, crowned, and consecrated king of England, it appeared to him that he had a better right to the kingdom of England than Harald, by reason of the relationship between him and King Edward. He thought, also, that he had grounds for avenging the affront that Harald had put upon him with respect to his daughter. From all these grounds William gathered together a great army in Normandy, and had many men, and sufficient transport-shipping. The day that he rode out of the castle to his ships, and had mounted his horse, his wife came to him, and wanted to speak with him; but when he saw her he struck at her with his heel, and set his spurs so deep into her breast that she fell down dead; and the earl rode on to his ships, and went with his ships over to England. His brother, Archbishop Otto, was with him; and when the earl came to England he began to plunder, and take possession of the land as he came along. Earl William was stouter and stronger than other men; a great horseman and warrior, but somewhat stern; and a very sensible man, but not considered a man to be relied on.

100. FALL OF KING HARALD GODWINSON.

King Harald Godwinson gave King Harald Sigurdson's son Olaf leave to go away, with the men who had followed him and had not fallen in battle; but he himself turned round with his army to go south, for he had heard that William the Bastard was overwhelming the south of England with a vast army, and was subduing the country for himself. With King Harald went his brothers Svein and Gyrd, and Earl Valthiof. King Harald and Earl William met each other south in England at Helsingja-port (Hastings). There was a great battle in which King Harald and his brother Earl Gyrd and a great part of his men fell. This was the nineteenth day after the fall of King Harald Sigurdson. Harald's brother, Earl Valthiof, escaped by flight, and towards evening fell in with a division of William's people, consisting of 100 men; and when they saw Earl Valthiof's troop they fled to a wood. Earl Valthiof set fire to the wood, and they were all burnt. So says Thorkel Skallason in Valthiof's ballad:–

"Earl Valthiof the brave
His foes a warming gave:
Within the blazing grove
A hundred men he drove.
The wolf will soon return,
And the witch's horse will burn
Her sharp claws in the ash,
To taste the Frenchman's flesh."

101. EARL VALTHIOF'S DEATH.

William was proclaimed king of England. He sent a message to Earl Valthiof that they should be reconciled, and gave him assurance of safety to come to the place of meeting. The earl set out with a few men; but when he came to a heath north of Kastala-bryggia, there met him two officers of King William, with many followers, who took him prisoner, put him in fetters, and afterwards he was beheaded; and the English call him a saint. Thorkel tells of this:–

"William came o'er the sea,
With bloody sword came he:
Cold heart and bloody hand
Now rule the English land.
Earl Valthiof he slew,–
Valthiof the brave and true.
Cold heart and bloody hand
Now rule the English land."

William was after this king of England for twenty-one years, and his descendants have been so ever since.

102. OF OLAF HARALDSON'S EXPEDITION TO NORWAY.

Olaf, the son of King Harald Sigurdson, sailed with his fleet from England from Hrafnseyr, and came in autumn to the Orkney Isles, where the event had happened that Maria, a daughter of Harald Sigurdson, died a sudden death the very day and hour her father, King Harald, fell. Olaf remained there all winter; but the summer after he proceeded east to Norway, where he was proclaimed king along with his brother Magnus. Queen Ellisif came from the West, along with her stepson Olaf and her daughter Ingegerd. There came also with Olaf over the West sea Skule, a son of Earl Toste, and who since has been called the king's foster-son, and his brother Ketil Krok. Both were gallant men, of high family in England, and both were very intelligent; and the brothers were much beloved by King Olaf. Ketil Krok went north to Halogaland, where King Olaf procured him a good marriage, and from him are descended many great people. Skule, the king's foster-son, was a very clever man, and the handsomest man that could be seen. He was the commander of King Olaf's court-men, spoke at the Things[69] and took part in all the country affairs with the king. The king offered to give Skule whatever district in Norway he liked, with all the income and duties that belonged to the king in it. Skule thanked him very much for the offer, but said he would rather have something else from him. "For if there came a shift of kings," said he, "the gift might come to nothing. I would rather take some properties lying near to the merchant towns, where you, sire, usually take up your abode, and then I would enjoy your Yule-feasts." The king agreed to this, and conferred on him lands eastward at Konungahella, Oslo, Tunsberg, Sarpsborg, Bergen, and north at Nidaros. These were nearly the best properties at each place, and have since descended to the family branches which came from Skule. King Olaf gave Skule his female relative, Gudrun, the daughter of Nefstein, in marriage. Her mother was Ingerid, a daughter of Sigurd Syr and Asta, King Olaf the Saint's mother. Ingerid was a sister of King Olaf the Saint and of King Harald. Skule and Gudrun's son was Asolf of Reine, who married Thora, a daughter of Skopte Ogmundson; Asolf's and Thora's son was Guthorm of Reine, father of Bard, and grandfather of King Inge and of Duke Skule.

69 Another instance of the old Norse or Icelandic tongue having been generally known in a part of England.

103. OF KING HARALD SIGURDSON.

One year after King Harald's fall his body was transported from England north to Nidaros, and was buried in Mary church, which he had built. It was a common observation that King Harald distinguished himself above all other men by wisdom and resources of mind; whether he had to take a resolution suddenly for himself and others, or after long deliberation. He was, also, above all other men, bold, brave, and lucky, until his dying day, as above related; and bravery is half victory. So says Thiodolf:–

"Harald, who till his dying day
Came off the best in many a fray,
Had one good rule in battle-plain,
In Seeland and elsewhere, to gain–
That, be his foes' strength more or less,
Courage is always half success."

King Herald was a handsome man, of noble appearance; his hair and beard yellow. He had a short beard, and long mustaches. The one eyebrow was somewhat higher than the other. He had large hands[70] and feet; but these were well made. His height was five ells. He was stern and severe to his enemies, and avenged cruelly all opposition or misdeed. So says Thiodolf:–

"Severe alike to friends or foes,
Who dared his royal will oppose;
Severe in discipline to hold
His men-at-arms wild and bold;
Severe the bondes to repress;
Severe to punish all excess;
Severe was Harald–but we call
That just which was alike to all."

70 It is a singular physical circumstance, that in almost all the swords of those ages to be found in the collection of weapons in the Antiquarian Museum at Copenhagen, the handles indicate a size of hand very much smaller than the hands of modern people of any class or rank. No modern dandy, with the most delicate hands, would find room for his hand to grasp or wield with case some of the swords of these Northmen.–L.

King Harald was most greedy of power, and of all distinction and honour. He was bountiful to the friends who suited him. So says Thiodolf:–

"I got from him, in sea-fight strong,
A mark of gold for my ship-song.
Merit in any way
He generously would pay."

King Harald was fifty years old when he fell. We have no particular account of his youth before he was fifteen years old, when he was with his brother, King Olaf, at the battle of Stiklestad. He lived thirty-five years after that, and in all that time was never free from care and war. King Harald never fled from battle, but often tried cunning ways to escape when he had to do with great superiority of forces. All the men who followed King Harald in battle or skirmish said that when he stood in great danger, or anything came suddenly upon him, he always took that course which all afterwards saw gave the best hope of a fortunate issue.

104. KING HARALD AND KING OLAF COMPARED.

When Haldor, a son of Brynjolf Ulfalde the Old, who was a sensible man and a great chief, heard people talk of how unlike the brothers Saint Olaf and King Harald were in disposition, he used to say, "I was in great friendship with both the brothers, and I knew intimately the dispositions of both, and never did I know two men more like in disposition. Both were of the highest understanding, and bold in arms, and greedy of power and property; of great courage, but not acquainted with the way of winning the favour of the people; zealous in governing, and severe in their revenge. King Olaf forced the people into Christianity and good customs, and punished cruelly those who disobeyed. This just and rightful severity the chiefs of the country could not bear, but raised an army against him, and killed him in his own kingdom; and therefore he is held to be a saint. King Harald, again, marauded to obtain glory and power, forced all the people he could under his power, and died in another king's dominions. Both brothers, in daily life, were of a worthy and considerate manner of living; they were of great experience, and very laborious, and were known and celebrated far and wide for these qualities."

105. KING MAGNUS'S DEATH.

King Magnus Haraldson ruled over Norway the first winter after King Harald's death (A.D. 1067), and afterwards two years (A.D. 1068-1069) along with his brother, King Olaf. Thus there were two kings of Norway at that time; and Magnus had the northern and Olaf the eastern part of the country. King Magnus had a son called Hakon, who was fostered by Thorer of Steig in Gudbrandsdal, who was a brother of King Magnus by the mother's side; and Hakon was a most agreeable man.

After King Harald Sigurdson's death the Danish king Svein let it be known that the peace between the Northmen and the Danes was at an end, and insisted that the league between Harald and Svein was not for longer time than their lives. There was a levy in both kingdoms. Harald's sons called out the whole people in Norway for procuring men and ships, and Svein set out from the south with the Danish army. Messengers then went between with proposals for a peace; and the Northmen said they would either have the same league as was concluded between King Harald and Svein, or otherwise give battle instantly on the spot. Verses were made on this occasion, viz.:-

"Ready for war or peace,
King Olaf will not cease
From foeman's hand
To guard his land."

So says also Stein Herdison in his song of Olaf:-

"From Throndhjem town, where in repose
The holy king defies his foes,
Another Olaf will defend
His kingdom from the greedy Svein.
King Olaf had both power and right,
And the Saint's favour in the fight.
The Saint will ne'er his kin forsake,
And let Svein Ulfson Norway take."

In this manner friendship was concluded between the kings and peace between the countries. King Magnus fell ill and died of the ringworm disease, after being ill for some time. He died and was buried at Nidaros. He was an amiable king and bewailed by the people.

BOOK NINE

Saga of Olaf Kyrre

PRELIMINARY REMARKS.

Snorri's account of Olaf Kyrre corresponds with the statements found in "Agrip", "Fagrskinna", and "Morkinskinna".

There are but few events in Olaf's long reign, and hence he is very appropriately called the Quiet (Kyrre). As Hildebrand says, this saga seems to be written simply to fill out the empty space between Harald Hardrade and Magnus Barefoot.

Skalds quoted in this saga are: Stein Herdison and Stuf.

1. OLAF'S PERSONAL APPEARANCE.

Olaf remained sole king of Norway after the death (A.D. 1069) of his brother King Magnus. Olaf was a stout man, well grown in limbs; and every one said a handsomer man could not be seen, nor of a nobler appearance. His hair was yellow as silk, and became him well; his skin was white and fine over all his body; his eyes beautiful, and his limbs well proportioned. He was rather silent in general, and did not speak much even at Things; but he was merry in drinking parties. He loved drinking much, and was talkative enough then; but quite peaceful. He was cheerful in conversation, peacefully inclined during all his reign, and loving gentleness and moderation in all things. Stein Herdison speaks thus of him:–

"Our Throndhjem king is brave and wise,
His love of peace our bondes prize;

By friendly word and ready hand
He holds good peace through every land.
He is for all a lucky star;
England he frightens from a war;
The stiff-necked Danes he drives to peace;
Troubles by his good influence cease."

2. OF KING OLAF'S MANNER OF LIVING.

IT WAS THE FASHION in Norway in old times for the king's high-seat to be on the middle of a long bench, and the ale was handed across the fire[71]; but King Olaf had his high-seat made on a high bench across the room; he also first had chimney-places in the rooms, and the floors strewed both summer and winter. In King Olaf's time many merchant towns arose in Norway, and many new ones were founded. Thus King Olaf founded a merchant town at Bergen, where very soon many wealthy people settled themselves, and it was regularly frequented by merchants from foreign lands. He had the foundations laid for the large Christ church, which was to be a stone church; but in his time there was little done to it. Besides, he completed the old Christ church, which was of wood. King Olaf also had a great feasting-house built in Nidaros, and in many other merchant towns, where before there were only private feasts; and in his time no one could drink in Norway but in these houses, adorned for the purpose with branches and leaves, and which stood under the king's protection. The great guild-bell in Throndhjem, which was called the pride of the town, tolled to call together to these guilds. The guild-brethren built Margaret's church in Nidaros of stone. In King Olaf's time there were general entertainments and hand-in-hand feasts. At this time also much unusual splendour and foreign customs and fashions in the cut of clothes were introduced; as, for instance, costly hose plaited about the legs. Some had gold rings about the legs, and also used coats which had lists down the sides, and arms five ells long, and so narrow that they must be drawn up with ties, and lay in folds all the

71 We may understand the arrangement by supposing the fire in the middle of the room, the smoke escaping by a hole in the roof, and a long bench on each side of the fire; one bench occupied by the high-seat of the king and great guests, the other by the rest of the guests; and the cup handed across the fire, which appears to have had a religious meaning previous to the introduction of Christianity.–L.

way up to the shoulders. The shoes were high, and all edged with silk, or even with gold. Many other kinds of wonderful ornaments were used at that time.

3. FASHION OF KING OLAF'S COURT.

King Olaf used the fashion, which was introduced from the courts of foreign kings, of letting his grand-butler stand at the end of the table, and fill the table-cups for himself and the other distinguished guests who sat at the table. He had also torch-bearers, who held as many candles at the table as there were guests of distinction present. There was also a marshal's bench outside of the table-circle, where the marshal and other persons of distinction sat with their faces towards the high-seat. King Harald, and the kings before him, used to drink out of deer-horn; and the ale was handed from the high-seat to the otherside over the fire, and he drank to the memory of any one he thought of. So says Stuf the skald:–

"He who in battle is the first,
And now in peace is best to trust,
A welcome, hearty and sincere,
Gave to me on my coming here.
He whom the ravens watch with care,
He who the gold rings does not spare,
A golden horn full to the brink
Gave me himself at Haug to drink."

4. ARRANGEMENT OF KING OLAF'S COURT.

King Olaf had 120 courtmen-at-arms, and 60 pursuivants, besides 60 house-servants, who provided what was wanted for the king's house wherever it might be, or did other work required for the king. When the bondes asked why he kept a greater retinue than the law allowed, or former kings kept when they went in guest-quarters or feasts which the bondes had to provide for them, the king answered, "It does not happen that I rule the kingdom better, or produce greater respect for me than ye had for my father, although I have one-half more people than he had. I do not by any means do it merely to plague you, or to make your condition harder than formerly."

5. KING SVEIN ULFSON'S DEATH.

King Svein Ulfson died ten years after the fall of both the Haralds (A.D. 1076). After him his son, Harald Hein, was king for three years (A.D. 1077-1080); then Canute the Holy for seven years (A.D. 1081-1087); afterwards Olaf, King Svein's third son, for eight years (A.D. 1088-1095). Then Eirik the Good, Svein's fourth son, for eight winters (A.D. 1096-1103). Olaf, the king of Norway, was married to Ingerid, a daughter of Svein, the Danish king; and Olaf, the Danish King Svein's son, married Ingegerd, a daughter of King Harald, and sister of King Olaf of Norway. King Olaf Haraldson, who was called by some Olaf Kyrre, but by many Olaf the Bonde, had a son by Thora, Joan's daughter, who was called Magnus, and was one of the handsomest lads that could be seen, and was promising in every respect. He was brought up in the king's court.

6. MIRACLES OF KING OLAF THE SAINT.

King Olaf had a church of stone built in Nidaros, on the spot where King Olaf's body had first been buried, and the altar was placed directly over the spot where the king's grave had been. This church was consecrated and called Christ Church; and King Olaf's shrine was removed to it, and was placed before the altar, and many miracles took place there. The following summer, on the same day of the year as the church was consecrated, which was the day before Olafsmas, there was a great assemblage of people, and then a blind man was restored to sight. And on the mass-day itself, when the shrine and the holy relics were taken out and carried, and the shrine itself, according to custom, was taken and set down in the churchyard, a man who had long been dumb recovered his speech again, and sang with flowing tongue praise-hymns to God, and to the honour of King Olaf the Saint. The third miracle was of a woman who had come from Svithjod, and had suffered much distress on this pilgrimage from her blindness; but trusting in God's mercy, had come travelling to this solemnity. She was led blind into the church to hear mass this day; but before the service was ended she saw with both eyes, and got her sight fully and clearly, although she had been blind fourteen years. She returned with great joy, praising God and King Olaf the Saint.

7. OF THE SHRINE OF KING OLAF THE SAINT.

There happened a circumstance in Nidaros, when King Olaf's coffin was being carried about through the streets, that it became so heavy that people could not lift it from the spot. Now when the coffin was set down, the street was broken up to see what was under it at that spot, and the body of a child was found which had been murdered and concealed there. The body was carried away, the street put in order again as it had been before, and the shrine carried on according to custom.

8. KING OLAF WAS BLESSED WITH PEACE.

In the days of King Olaf there were bountiful harvests in Norway and many good things. In no man's life had times been so good in Norway since the days of Harald Harfager. King Olaf modified for the better many a matter that his father had inaugurated and maintained with severity. He was generous, but a strict ruler, for he was a wise man, and well understood what was of advantage to the kingdom. There are many stories of his good works. How much he loved and how kind he was to the people may be seen from the following words, which he once spoke at a large banquet. He was happy and in the best of spirits, when one of his men said, "It pleases us, sire, to see you so happy." He answered: "I have reason to be glad when I see my subjects sitting happy and free in a guild consecrated to my uncle, the sainted King Olaf. In the days of my father these people were subjected to much terror and fear; the most of them concealed their gold and their precious things, but now I see glittering on his person what each one owns, and your freedom is my gladness." In his reign there was no strife, and he protected himself and his realm against enemies abroad; and his nearest neighbours stood in great awe of him, although he was a most gentle man, as is confirmed by the skald.

9. MEETING OF OLAF KYRRE AND CANUTE THE SAINT.

King Olaf Kyrre was a great friend of his brother-in-law, the Danish king, Canute the holy. They appointed a meeting and met at the Gaut river at Konungahella, where the kings used to have their meetings. There

King Canute made the proposal that they should send an army westward to England on account of the revenge they had to take there; first and foremost King Olaf himself, and also the Danish king. "Do one of two things," said King Canute,–"either take sixty ships, which I will furnish thee with, and be thou the leader; or give me sixty ships, and I shall be the leader." Then said King Olaf, "This speech of thine, King Canute, is altogether according to my mind; but there is this great difference between us; your family has had more luck in conquering England with great glory, and, among others, King Canute the Great; and it is likely that this good fortune follows your race. On the other hand, when King Harald, my father, went westward to England, he got his death there; and at that time the best men in Norway followed him. But Norway was so emptied then of chosen men, that such men have not since been to find in the country; for that expedition there was the most excellent outfit, and you know what was the end of it. Now I know my own capacity, and how little I am suited to be the leader; so I would rather you should go, with my help and assistance."

So King Olaf gave Canute sixty large ships, with excellent equipment and faithful men, and set his lendermen as chiefs over them; and all must allow that this armament was admirably equipt. It is also told in the saga about Canute, that the Northmen alone did not break the levy when the army was assembled, but the Danes would not obey their king's orders. This king Canute acknowledged, and gave them leave to trade in merchandise where they pleased through his country, and at the same time sent the king of Norway costly presents for his assistance. On the other hand he was enraged against the Danes, and laid heavy fines upon them.

10. A BONDE WHO UNDERSTOOD THE LANGUAGE OF BIRDS.

One summer, when King Olaf's men had gone round the country collecting his income and land dues, it happened that the king, on their return home asked them where on their expedition they had been best entertained. They said it was in the house of a bonde in one of the king's districts. "There is an old bonde there who knows many things before they happen. We asked him about many things, which he explained to us; nay, we even believe that he understands perfectly the language of birds." The king replies, "How can ye believe such nonsense?" and insisted that it was wrong to put confidence in such things. It happened soon after that the king was sailing along the coast; and as they sailed through a Sound the king said, "What is that township up in the country?"

They replied, "That is the district, sire, where we told you we were best entertained."

Then said the king, "What house is that which stands up there, not far from the Sound?"

They replied, "That house belongs to the wise old bonde we told you of, sire."

They saw now a horse standing close to the house. Then said the king, "Go there, and take that horse, and kill him."

They replied, "We would not like to do him such harm."

The king: "I will command. Cut off the horse's head; but take care of yourselves that ye let no blood come to the ground, and bear the horse out to my ship. Go then and bring to me the old man; but tell him nothing of what has happened, as ye shall answer for it with your lives."

They did as they were ordered, and then came to the old man, and told him the king's message. When he came before the king, the king asked him, "Who owns the house thou art dwelling in?"

He replies, "Sire, you own it, and take rent for it."

The king: "Show us the way round the ness, for here thou must be a good pilot."

The old man went into his boat and rowed before the king's ship; and when he had rowed a little way a crow came flying over the ship, and croaking hideously. The peasant listens to the crow. The king said, "Do you think, bonde, that betokens anything?"

"Sire, that is certain," said he.

Then another crow flies over the ship, and screeches dreadfully. The bonde was so ill hearing this that he could not row, and the oars hung loose in his hands.

Then said the king, "Thy mind is turned much to these crows, bonde, and to what they say."

The bonde replies, "Now I suspect it is true what they say."

The third time the crow came flying screeching at its very worst, and almost settling on the ship. Now the bonde threw down his oars, regarded them no more, and stood up before the king.

Then the king said, "Thou art taking this much to heart, bonde; what is it they say?"

The peasant–"It is likely that either they or I have misunderstood–"

"Say on," replied the king.

The bonde replied in a song:–

"The 'one-year old'
Mere nonsense told;
The 'two-years' chatter
Seemed senseless matter;
The three-years' croak
Of wonders spoke.
The foul bird said
My old mare's head
I row along;
And, in her song,
She said the thief
Was the land's chief."

The king said, "What is this, bonde! Wilt thou call me a thief?"

Then the king gave him good presents, and remitted all the land-rent of the place he lived on. So says Stein:–

"The pillar of our royal race
Stands forth adorned with every grace.
What king before e'er took such pride
To scatter bounty far and wide?
Hung round with shields that gleam afar;
The merchant ship on one bestows,
With painted streaks in glowing rows.

"The man-at-arms a golden ring
Boasts as the present of his king;
At the king's table sits the guest,
By the king's bounty richly drest.
King Olaf, Norway's royal son,
Who from the English glory won,
Pours out with ready-giving hand
His wealth on children of the land.

"Brave clothes to servants he awards,
Helms and ring-mail coats grace his guards;
Or axe and sword Har's warriors gain,
And heavy armour for the plain.
Gold, too, for service duly paid,

Red gold all pure, and duly weighed,
King Olaf gives–he loves to pay
All service in a royal way."

11. OF KING OLAF KYRRE'S DEATH.

King Olaf lived principally in his domains on his large farms. Once when he was east in Ranrike, on his estate of Haukby, he took the disease which ended in his death. He had then been king of Norway for twenty-six years (A.D. 1068-1093); for he was made king of Norway the year after King Harald's death. King Olaf's body was taken north to Nidaros, and buried in Christ church, which he himself had built there. He was the most amiable king of his time, and Norway was much improved in riches and cultivation during his reign.

BOOK TEN

Magnus Barefoot's Saga

PRELIMINARY REMARKS.

THE GREATER PART OF the contents of this saga is also found in "Agrip", "Fagrskinna", and "Morkinskinna".

Magnus and his cousin Hakon became kings in 1093, but Hakon ruled only two years and died in 1095. King Magnus fell in the year 1103.

Skalds quoted are: Bjorn Krephende, Thorkel Hamarskald, and Eldjarn.

1. BEGINNING OF THE REIGN OF KING MAGNUS AND HIS COUSIN HAKON.

MAGNUS, KING OLAF'S SON, was, immediately after King Olaf's death, proclaimed at Viken king of all Norway; but the Upland people, on hearing of King Olaf's death, chose Hakon, Thorer's foster-son, a cousin of King Magnus, as king. Thereupon Hakon and Thorer went north to the Throndhjem country, and when they came to Nidaros they summoned the Eyrathing; and at that Thing Hakon desired the bondes to give him the kingly title, which was agreed to, and the Throndhjem people proclaimed him king of half of Norway, as his father, King Magnus, had been before. Hakon relieved the Throndhjem people of all harbour duties, and gave them many other privileges. He did away with Yule-gifts, and gained by this the good-will of all the Throndhjem people. Thereafter Hakon formed a court, and then proceeded to the Uplands, where he gave the Upland people the same privileges as the Throndhjem people; so that they also were perfectly well affected to him, and were his friends. The people in Throndhjem sang this ballad about him:–

"Young Hakon was the Norseman's pride,
And Steig-Thorer was on his side.
Young Hakon from the Upland came,
With royal birth, and blood, and name.
Young Hakon from the king demands
His royal birthright, half the lands;
Magnus will not the kingdom break,–
The whole or nothing he will take."

2. HAKON'S DEATH.

King Magnus proceeded north to the merchant town (Nidaros), and on his arrival went straight to the king's house, and there took up his abode. He remained here the first part of the winter (A.D. 1094), and kept seven longships in the open water of the river Nid, abreast of the king's house. Now when King Hakon heard that King Magnus was come to Throndhjem, he came from the East over the Dovrefield, and thence down from Throndhjem to the merchant town, where he took up his abode in the house of Skule, opposite to Clement's church, which had formerly been the king's house. King Magnus was ill pleased with the great gifts which Hakon had given to the bondes to gain their favour, and thought it was so much given out of his own property. This irritated his mind; and he thought he had suffered injustice from his relative in this respect, that he must now put up with less income than his father and his predecessors before him had enjoyed; and he gave Thorer the blame. When King Hakon and Thorer observed this, they were alarmed for what Magnus might do; and they thought it suspicious that Magnus kept long-ships afloat rigged out, and with tents. The following spring, after Candlemas, King Magnus left the town in the night with his ships; the tents up, and lights burning in the tents. They brought up at Hefring, remained there all night, and kindled a fire on the land. Then Hakon and the men in the town thought some treachery was on foot, and he let the trumpets call all the men together out on the Eyrar, where the whole people of the town came to him, and the people were gathering together the whole night. When it was light in the morning, King Magnus saw the people from all districts gathered together on the Eyrar; and he sailed out of the fjord, and proceeded south to where the Gulathing is held. Hakon thanked the people for their support which they had given him, and got ready to travel east to Viken. But he first held a meeting in the town, where, in a speech, he asked the people for their friendship, promising them his; and added, that he had some suspicions of his relation, King Magnus's intentions. Then King Hakon mounted his horse, and was ready to travel. All men promised him their good-will and support whenever he required them, and the people followed him out to the foot of Steinbjorg. From thence King Hakon proceeded up the Dovrefield; but as he was going over the mountains he rode all day after a ptarmigan, which flew up beside him, and in this chase a sickness overfell him, which ended in his death; and he died on the mountains. His body was carried north, and came to the merchant town just half a month after he left it. The whole townspeople went to meet the body, sorrowing, and the most of them weeping; for all people loved him with sincere affection. King Hakon's body was interred in Christ church, and Hakon and Magnus had ruled the country for two years. Hakon was a man full twenty-five years old, and was one of the chiefs the most beloved by all the people. He had made a journey to Bjarmaland, where he had given battle and gained a victory.

3. OF A FORAY IN HALLAND.

King Magnus sailed in winter (A.D. 1095) eastward to Viken; but when spring approached he went southwards to Halland, and plundered far and wide. He laid waste Viskardal and many other districts, and returned with a great booty back to his own kingdom. So says Bjorn Krephende in his song on Magnus:–

"Through Halland wide around
The clang and shriek resound;
The houses burn,
The people mourn,
Through Halland wide around.
The Norse king strides in flame,
Through Viskardal he came;
The fire sweeps,
The widow weeps,
The Norse king strides in flame."

Here it is told that King Magnus made the greatest devastation through Halland.

4. OF THORER OF STEIG.

"There was a man called Svein, a son of Harald Fietter. He was a Danish man by family, a great viking and champion, and a very clever man, and of high birth in his own country. He had been some time with King Hakon Magnuson, and was very dear to him; but after King Hakon's decease Thorer of Steig, his foster-father, had no great confidence in any treaty or friendship with King Magnus, if the whole country came into his power, on account of the position in which Thorer had stood to King Magnus, and the opposition he had made to him. Thereupon Thorer and Svein took counsel with each other, which they afterwards carried into effect,– to raise, with Thorer's assistance, and his men, a troop against Magnus. But as Thorer was old and heavy, Svein took the command, and name of leader of the troop. In this design several chiefs took part, among whom the principal was Egil Aslakson of Aurland. Egil was a lenderman, and married to Ingebjorg, a daughter of Ogmund Thorbergson, a sister of Skopte of Giske. The rich and powerful man, Skjalg Erlingson, also joined their party. Thorkel Hamarskald speaks of this in his ballad of Magnus:

"Thorer and Egil were not wise,
They aimed too high to win a prize:
There was no reason in their plan,
And it hurt many a udalman.
The stone, too great for them to throw,
Fell back, and hurt them with the blow,
And now the udalmen must rue
That to their friends they were so true."

Thorer and Svein collected a troop in the Uplands, and went down through Raumsdal into Sunmore, and there collected vessels, with which they afterwards sailed north to Throndhjem.

5. OF THORER'S ADVENTURES.

The lenderman Sigurd Ulstreng, a son of Lodin Viggiarskalle, collected men by sending round the war-token, as soon as he heard of Thorer and the troop which followed him, and had a rendezvous with all the men he could raise at Viggia. Svein and Thorer also met there with their people, fought with Sigurd, and gained the victory after giving him a great defeat; and Sigurd fled, and joined King Magnus. Thorer and his followers proceeded to the town (Nidaros), and remained there some time in the fjord, where many people joined them. King Magnus hearing this news immediately collected an army, and proceeded north to Throndhjem. And when he came into the fjord Thorer and his party heard of it while they lay at Herring, and they were ready to leave the fjord; and they rowed their ships to the strand at Vagnvik, and left them, and came into Theksdal in Seliuhverfe, and Thorer was carried in a litter over the mountains. Then they got hold of ships and sailed north to Halogaland. As soon as King Magnus was ready for sea, he sailed from Throndhjem in pursuit of them. Thorer and his party went north all the way to Bjarkey; and Jon, with his son Vidkun, fled from thence. Thorer and his men robbed all the movable goods, and burnt the house, and a good long-ship that belonged to Vidkun. While the hull was burning the vessel keeled to one side, and Thorer called out, "Hard to starboard, Vidkun!" Some verses were made about this burning in Bjarkey:–

"The sweetest farm that I have seen
Stood on Bjarkey's island green;
And now, where once this farmhouse stood,
Fire crackles through a pile of wood;
And the clear red flame, burning high,
Flashes across the dark-night sky.
Jon and Vidkun, this dark night,
Will not be wandering without light."

6. DEATH OF THORER AND EGIL.

Jon and Vidkun travelled day and night till they met King Magnus. Svein and Thorer proceeded northwards with their men, and plundered far and wide in Halogaland. But while they lay in a fjord called Harm, Thorer and his party saw King Magnus coming under sail towards them; and thinking they had not men enough to fight him, they rowed away and fled. Thorer and Egil brought up at Hesjutun; but Svein rowed out to sea, and some of their people rowed into the fjords. King Magnus pursued Thorer, and the vessels struck together while they were landing. Thorer stood in the forecastle of his ship, and Sigurd

Ulstreng called out to him, and asked, "Art thou well, Thorer?" Thorer replied, "I am well in hands, but ill on my feet."

Then all Thorer's men fled up the country, and Thorer was taken prisoner. Egil was also taken prisoner, for he would not leave his wife. King Magnus then ordered both of them to be taken out to Vambarholm; and when they were leading Thorer from the ship he tottered on his legs. Then Vidkun called out, "More to the larboard, Thorer!" When he was being led to the gallows he sang:–

"We were four comrades gay,–
Let one by the helm stay."

When he came to the gallows he said, "Bad counsel comes to a bad end." Then Thorer was hanged; but when he was hoisted up the gallows tree he was so heavy that his neck gave way, and the body fell down to the ground; for Thorer was a man exceedingly stout, both high of stature and thick. Egil was also led to the gallows, and when the king's thralls were about hanging him he said, "Ye should not hang me, for in truth each of you deserves much more to be hanged." People sang these verses about it:–

"I hear, my girl, that Egil said,
When to the gallows he was led,
That the king's thralls far more than he
Deserved to hang on gallows-tree.
It might be so; but, death in view,
A man should to himself be true,–
End a stout life by death as stout,
Showing no fear; or care, or doubt."

King Magnus sat near while they were being hanged, and was in such a rage that none of his men was so bold as to ask mercy for them. The king said, when Egil was spinning at the gallows, "Thy great friends help thee but poorly in time of need." From this people supposed that the king only wanted to have been entreated to have spared Egil's life. Bjorn Krephende speaks of these things:–

"King Magnus in the robbers' gore
Dyed red his sword; and round the shore
The wolves howled out their wild delight,
At corpses swinging in their sight.

Have ye not heard how the king's sword
Punished the traitors to their lord?
How the king's thralls hung on the gallows
Old Thorer and his traitor-fellows?"

7. OF THE PUNISHMENT OF THE THRONDHJEM PEOPLE.

After this King Magnus sailed south to Throndhjem, and brought up in the fjord, and punished severely all who had been guilty of treason towards him; killing some, and burning the houses of others. So says Bjorn Krephende:–

"He who despises fence of shields
Drove terror through the Throndhjem fields,
When all the land through which he came
Was swimming in a flood of flame.
The raven-feeder, will I know,
Cut off two chieftans at a blow;
The wolf could scarcely ravenous be,
The ernes flew round the gallows-tree."

Svein Harald Fletter's son, fled out to sea first, and sailed then to Denmark, and remained there; and at last came into great favour with King Eystein, the son of King Magnus, who took so great a liking to Svein that he made him his dish-bearer, and held him in great respect. King Magnus had now alone the whole kingdom, and he kept good peace in the land, and rooted out all vikings and lawless men. He was a man quick, warlike, and able, and more like in all things to his grandfather, King Harald, in disposition and talents than to his father.

8. OF THE BONDE SVEINKE, AND SIGURD ULSTRENG.

There was a man called Sveinke Steinarson, who was very wealthy, and dwelt in Viken at the Gaut river. He had brought up Hakon Magnuson before Thorer of Steig took him. Sveinke had not yet submitted to King

Magnus. King Magnus ordered Sigurd Ulstreng to be called, and told him he would send him to Sveinke with the command that he should quit the king's land and domain. "He has not yet submitted to us, or shown us due honour." He added, that there were some lendermen east in Viken, namely Svein Bryggjufot, Dag Eilifson, and Kolbjorn Klakke, who could bring this matter into right bearing. Then Sigurd said, "I did not know there was the man in Norway against whom three lendermen besides myself were needful." The king replied, "Thou needst not take this help, unless it be necessary." Now Sigurd made himself ready for the journey with a ship, sailed east to Viken, and there summoned the lendermen to him. Then a Thing was appointed to Viken, to which the people were called who dwelt on the Gaut river, besides others; so that it was a numerous assembly. When the Thing was formed they had to wait for Sveinke. They soon after saw a troop of men coming along, so well furnished with weapons that they looked like pieces of shining ice; and now came Sveinke and his people to the Thing, and set themselves down in a circle. All were clad in iron, with glowing arms, and 500 in number. Then Sigurd stood up, and spoke. "My master, King Magnus, sends God's salutation and his own to all friends, lendermen and others, his subjects in the kingdom; also to the powerful bondes, and the people in general, with kind words and offers of friendship; and to all who will obey him he offers his friendship and good will. Now the king will, with all cheerfulness and peace, show himself a gracious master to all who will submit to him, and to all in his dominions. He will be the leader and defender of all the men of Norway; and it will be good for you to accept his gracious speech, and this offer."

Then stood up a man in the troop of the Elfgrims, who was of great stature and grim countenance, clad in a leather cloak, with a halberd on his shoulder, and a great steel hat upon his head. He looked sternly, and said, "Here is no need of wheels, says the fox, when he draws the trap over the ice." He said nothing more, but sat down again.

Soon after Sigurd Ulstreng stood up again, and spoke thus: "But little concern or help have we for the king's affairs from you, Elfgrims, and but little friendship; yet by such means every man shows how much he respects himself. But now I shall produce more clearly the king's errand." Thereupon he demanded land-dues and levy-dues, together with all other rights of the king, from the great bondes. He bade each of them to consider with himself how they had conducted themselves in these matters; and that they should now promote their own honour, and do the king justice, if they had come short hitherto in doing so. And then he sat down.

Then the same man got up in the troop of Elfgrims who had spoken before, lifted his hat a little up, and said, "The lads run well, say the Laplanders, who have skates for nothing." Then he sat himself down again.

Soon after Sigurd arose, after speaking with the lendermen, and said that so weighty a message as the king's ought not to be treated lightly as a jest. He was now somewhat angry; and added, that they ought not to receive the king's message and errand so scornfully, for it was not decent. He was dressed in a red or scarlet coat, and had a blue coat over it. He cast off his upper coat and said, "Now it is come so far that every one must look to himself, and not loiter and jest with others; for by so doing every man will show what he is. We do not require now to be taught by others; for now we can see ourselves how much we are regarded. But this may be borne with; but not that ye treat so scornfully the king's message. Thereby every one shows how highly he considers himself. There is one man called Sveinke Steinarson, who lives east at the Gaut river; and from him the king will have his just land-dues, together with his own land, or will banish him from the country. It is of no use here to seek excuses, or to answer with sharp words; for people are to be found who are his equals in power, although he now receives our speech so unworthily; and it is better now than afterwards to return to the right way, and do himself honour, rather than await disgrace for his obstinancy." He then sat down.

Sveinke then got up, threw back his steel-hat, and gave Sigurd many scornful words, and said, "Tut! tut! 'tis a shame for the dogs, says the proverb, when the fox is allowed to cast their excrements in the peasant's well. Here will be a miracle! Thou useless fellow! with a coat without arms, and a kirtle with skirts, wilt thou drive me out of the country? Thy relation, Sigurd Woolsack, was sent before on this errand, and one called Gille the Backthief, and one who had still a worse name. They were a night in every house, and stole wherever they came. Wilt thou drive me out of the country? Formerly thou wast not so mighty, and thy pride was less when King Hakon, my foster-son, was in life. Then thou wert as frightened for him when he met thee on the road as a mouse in a mousetrap, and hid thyself under a heap of clothes, like a dog on board a ship. Thou wast thrust into a leather-bag like corn in a sack, and driven from house and farm like a year-old colt from the mares; and dost thou dare to drive me from the land? Thou shouldst rather think thyself lucky to escape from hence with life. Let us stand up and attack him."

Then all his men stood up, and made a great clash with their weapons. Then Svein Bryggjufot and the other lendermen saw there was no other chance for Sigurd but to get him on horseback, which was done, and he rode off into the forest. The end was that Sveinke returned home to his farm, and Sigurd Ulstreng came, with great difficulty, by land north to Throndhjem to King Magnus, and told the result of his errand. "Did I not say," said the king, "that the help of my lendermen would be needed?" Sigurd was ill pleased with his journey; insisted that he would be revenged, cost what it will; and urged the king much. The king ordered five ships to be fitted out; and as soon as they were ready for sea he sailed south along the land, and then east to Viken, where he was entertained in excellent guest-quarters by his lendermen. The king told them he would seek out Sveinke. "For I will not conceal my suspicion that he thinks to make himself king of Norway." They said that Sveinke was both a powerful and an ungovernable man. Now the king went from Viken until he came to Sveinke's farm. Then the lendermen desired that they might be put on shore to see how matters stood; and when they came to the land they saw that Sveinke had already come down from the farm, and was on the road with a number of well-armed men. The lendermen held up a white shield in the air, as a peace-token; and when Sveinke saw it he halted his men, and they approached each other. Then said Kolbjorn Klakke, "King Magnus sends thee God's salutation and his own, and bids thee consider what becomes thee, and do him obedience, and not prepare thyself to give him battle." Kolbjorn offered to mediate peace between them, if he could, and told him to halt his troops.

Sveinke said he would wait for them where he was. "We came out to meet you," he said, "that ye might not tread down our corn-fields."

The lendermen returned to the king, and told him all was now at his pleasure.

The king said, "My doom is soon delivered. He shall fly the country, and never come back to Norway as long as the kingdom is mine; and he shall leave all his goods behind."

"But will it not be more for thy honour," said Kolbjorn, "and give thee a higher reputation among other kings, if, in banishing him from the country, thou shouldst allow him to keep his property, and show himself among other people? And we shall take care that he never comes back while we live. Consider of this, sire, by yourself, and have respect for our assurance."

The king replied, "Let him then go forth immediately."

They went back, therefore, to Sveinke, and told him the king's words; and also that the king had ordered him out of the country, and he should show his obedience, since he had forgotten himself towards the king. "It is for the honour of both that thou shouldst show obedience to the king."

Then Sveinke said, "There must be some great change if the king speaks agreeably to me; but why should I fly the country and my properties? Listen now to what I say. It appears to me better to die upon my property than to fly from my udal estates. Tell the king that I will not stir from them even an arrow-flight."

Kolbjorn replied, "This is scarcely prudent, or right; for it is better for one's own honour to give way to the best chief, than to make opposition to one's own loss. A gallant man succeeds wheresoever he goes; and thou wilt be the more respected wheresoever thou art, with men of power, just because thou hast made head so boldly against so powerful a chief. Hear our promises, and pay some attention to our errand. We offer thee to manage thy estates, and take them faithfully under our protection; and also never, against thy will, to pay scat for thy land until thou comest back. We will pledge our lives and properties upon this. Do not throw away good counsel from thee, and avoid thus the ill fortune of other good men."

Then Sveinke was silent for a short time, and said at last, "Your endeavours are wise; but I have my suspicions that ye are changing a little the king's message. In consideration, however, of the great good-will that ye show me, I will hold your advice in such respect that I will go out of the country for the whole winter, if, according to your promises, I can then retain my estates in peace. Tell the king, also, these my words, that I do this on your account, not on his."

Thereupon they returned to the king, and said, that Sveinke left all in the king's hands. "But entreats you to have respect to his honour. He will be away for three years, and then come back, if it be the king's pleasure. Do this; let all things be done according to what is suitable for the royal dignity and according to our entreaty, now that the matter is entirely in thy power, and we shall do all we can to prevent his returning against thy will."

The king replied, "Ye treat this matter like men, and, for your sakes, shall all things be as ye desire. Tell him so."

They thanked the king, and then went to Sveinke, and told him the king's gracious intentions. "We will be glad," said they, "if ye can be reconciled. The king requires, indeed that thy absence shall be for three years; but, if we know the truth rightly, we expect that before that time he will find he cannot do without thee in this part of the country. It will be to thy own future honour, therefore, to agree to this."

Sveinke replies, "What condition is better than this? Tell the king that I shall not vex him longer with my presence here, and accept of my goods and estates on this condition."

Thereupon he went home with his men, and set off directly; for he had prepared everything beforehand. Kolbjorn remains behind, and makes ready a feast for King Magnus, which also was thought of and prepared. Sveinke, on the other hand, rides up to Gautland with all the men he thought proper to take with him. The king let himself be entertained in guest-quarters at his house, returned to Viken, and Sveinke's estates were nominally the king's, but Kolbjorn had them under his charge. The king received guest-quarters in Viken, proceeded from thence northwards, and there was peace for a while; but now that the Elfgrims were without a chief, marauding gangs infested them, and the king saw this eastern part of the kingdom would be laid waste. It appeared to him, therefore, most suitable and advisable to make Sveinke himself oppose the stream, and twice he sent messages to him. But he did not stir until King Magnus himself was south in Denmark, when Sveinke and the king met, and made a full reconciliation; on which Sveinke returned home to his house and estates, and was afterwards King Magnus's best and trustiest friend, who strengthened his kingdom on the eastern border; and their friendship continued as long as they lived.

9. KING MAGNUS MAKES WAR ON THE SOUTHERN HEBUDES.

King Magnus undertook an expedition out of the country, with many fine men and a good assortment of shipping. With this armament he sailed out into the West sea, and first came to the Orkney Islands. There he took the two earls, Paul and Erlend, prisoners, and sent them east to Norway, and placed his son Sigurd as chief over the islands, leaving some counsellors to assist him. From thence King Magnus, with his followers, proceeded to the Southern Hebudes, and when he came there began to burn and lay waste the inhabited places, killing the people and plundering wherever he came with his men; and the country people fled in all directions, some into Scotland-fjord, others south to Cantire, or out to Ireland; some obtained life and safety by entering into his service. So says Bjorn Krephende:–

"In Lewis Isle with fearful blaze
The house-destroying fire plays;
To hills and rocks the people fly,
Fearing all shelter but the sky.
In Uist the king deep crimson made
The lightning of his glancing blade;
The peasant lost his land and life
Who dared to bide the Norseman's strife.
The hunger battle-birds were filled
In Skye with blood of foemen killed,
And wolves on Tyree's lonely shore
Dyed red their hairy jaws in gore.
The men of Mull were tired of flight;
The Scottish foemen would not fight,
And many an island-girl's wail
Was heard as through the isles we strife sail."

10. OF LAGMAN, KING GUDROD'S SON.

King Magnus came with his forces to the Holy Island (Iona), and gave peace and safety to all men there. It is told that the king opened the door of the little Columb's Kirk there, but did not go in, but instantly locked the door again, and said that no man should be so bold as to go into that church hereafter; which has been the case ever since. From thence King Magnus sailed to Islay, where he plundered and burnt; and when he had taken that country he proceeded south around Cantire, marauding on both sides in Scotland and Ireland, and advanced with his foray to Man, where he plundered. So says Bjorn Krephende:–

"On Sandey's plain our shield they spy:
From Isla smoke rose heaven-high,
Whirling up from the flashing blaze
The king's men o'er the island raise.
South of Cantire the people fled,
Scared by our swords in blood dyed red,
And our brave champion onward goes
To meet in Man the Norseman's foes."

Lagman (Lawman) was the name of the son of Gudrod, king of the Hebudes. Lawman was sent to defend the most northerly islands; but when King Magnus and his army came to the Hebudes, Lawman fled here and there about the isles, and at last King Magnus's men took him and his ship's crew as he was flying over to Ireland. The king put him in irons to secure him. So says Bjorn Krephende:–

"To Gudrod's son no rock or cave,
Shore-side or hill, a refuge gave;
Hunted around from isle to isle,
This Lawman found no safe asyle.
From isle to isle, o'er firth and sound,
Close on his track his foe he found.
At Ness the Agder chief at length
Seized him, and iron-chained his strength."

11. OF THE FALL OF EARL HUGE THE BRAVE.

Afterwards King Magnus sailed to Wales; and when he came to the sound of Anglesey there came against him an army from Wales, which was led by two earls–Hugo the brave, and Hugo the Stout. They began immediately to give battle, and there was a severe conflict. King Magnus shot with the bow; but Huge the Brave was all over in armour, so that nothing was bare about him excepting one eye. King Magnus let fly an arrow at him, as also did a Halogaland man who was beside the king. They both shot at once. The one shaft hit the nose-screen of the helmet, which was bent by it to one side, and the other arrow hit the earl's eye, and went through his head; and that was found to be the king's. Earl Huge fell, and the Britons fled with the loss of many people. So says Bjorn Krephende:–

"The swinger of the sword
Stood by Anglesey's ford;
His quick shaft flew,
And Huge slew.
His sword gleamed a while
O'er Anglesey Isle,
And his Norsemen's band
Scoured the Anglesey land."

There was also sung the following verse about it:–

"On the panzers arrows rattle,
Where our Norse king stands in battle;
From the helmets blood-streams flow,
Where our Norse king draws his bow:
His bowstring twangs,–its biting hail
Rattles against the ring-linked mail.
Up in the land in deadly strife
Our Norse king took Earl Huge's life."

King Magnus gained the victory in this battle, and then took Anglesey Isle, which was the farthest south the Norway kings of former days had ever extended their rule. Anglesey is a third part of Wales. After this battle King Magnus turned back with his fleet, and came first to Scotland. Then men went between the Scottish king, Melkolm and King Magnus, and a peace was made between them; so that all the islands lying west of Scotland, between which and the mainland he could pass in a vessel with her rudder shipped, should be held to belong to the king of Norway. Now when King Magnus came north to Cantire, he had a skiff drawn over the strand at Cantire, and shipped the rudder of it. The king himself sat in the stern-sheets, and held the tiller; and thus he appropriated to himself the land that lay on the farboard side. Cantire is a great district, better than the best of the southern isles of the Hebudes, excepting Man; and there is a small neck of land between it and the mainland of Scotland, over which longships are often drawn.

12. DEATH OF THE EARLS OF ORKNEY.

King Magnus was all the winter in the southern isles, and his men went over all the fjords of Scotland, rowing within all the inhabited and uninhabited isles, and took possession for the king of Norway of all the islands west of Scotland. King Magnus contracted in marriage his son Sigurd to Biadmynia, King Myrkjartan's daughter. Myrkjartan was a son of the Irish king Thialfe, and ruled over Connaught. The summer after, King Magnus, with his fleet, returned east to Norway. Earl Erland died of sickness at Nidaros, and is buried there; and Earl Paul died in Bergen.

Skopte Ogmundson, a grandson of Thorberg, was a gallant lenderman, who dwelt at Giske in Sunmore, and was married to Gudrun, a daughter of Thord Folason. Their children were Ogmund, Fin, Thord, and Thora, who was married to Asolf Skulason. Skopte's and Gudrun's sons were the most promising and popular men in their youth.

13. QUARRELS OF KING MAGNUS AND KING INGE.

Steinkel, the Swedish king, died about the same time (A.D. 1066) as the two Haralds fell, and the king who came after him in Svithjod was called Hakon. Afterwards Inge, a son of Steinkel, was king, and was a good and powerful king, strong and stout beyond most men; and he was king of Svithjod when King Magnus was king of Norway. King Magnus insisted that the boundaries of the countries in old times had been so, that the Gaut river divided the kingdoms of the Swedish and Norwegian kings, but afterwards the Vener lake up to Vermaland. Thus King Magnus insisted that he was owner of all the places lying west of the Vener lake up to Vermaland, which are the districts of Sundal, Nordal, Vear, and Vardyniar, with all the woods belonging thereto. But these had for a long time been under the Swedish dominion, and with respect to scat were joined to West Gautland; and, besides, the forest-settlers preferred being under the Swedish king. King Magnus rode from Viken up to Gautland with a great and fine army, and when he came to the forest-settlements he plundered and burnt all round; on which the people submitted, and took the oath of fidelity to him. When he came to the Vener lake, autumn was advanced and he went out to the island Kvaldinsey, and made a stronghold of turf and wood, and dug a ditch around it. When the work was finished, provisions and other necessaries that might be required were brought to it. The king left in it 300 men, who were the chosen of his forces, and Fin Skoptason and Sigurd Ulstreng as their commanders. The king himself returned to Viken.

14. OF THE NORTHMEN.

When the Swedish king heard this he drew together people, and the report came that he would ride against these Northmen; but there was delay about his riding, and the Northmen made these lines:–

"The fat-hipped king, with heavy sides,
Finds he must mount before he rides."

But when the ice set in upon the Vener lake King Inge rode down, and had near 300 men with him. He sent a message to the Northmen who sat in the burgh that they might retire with all the booty they had taken, and go to Norway. When the messengers brought this message, Sigurd Ulstreng replied to it; saying that King Inge must take the trouble to come, if he wished to drive them away like cattle out of a grass field, and said he must come nearer if he wished them to remove. The messengers returned with this answer to the king, who then rode out with all his army to the island, and again sent a message to the Northmen that they might go away, taking with them their weapons, clothes, and horses; but must leave behind all their booty. This they refused. The king made an assault upon them, and they shot at each other. Then the king ordered timber and stones to be collected, and he filled up the ditch; and then he fastened anchors to long spars which were brought up to the timber-walls, and, by the strength of many hands, the walls were broken down. Thereafter a large pile of wood was set on fire, and the lighted brands were flung in among them. Then the Northmen asked for quarter. The king ordered them to go out without weapons or cloaks. As they went out each of them received a stroke with a whip, and then they set off for Norway, and all the forest-men submitted again to King Inge. Sigurd and his people went to King Magnus, and told him their misfortune.

15. KING MAGNUS AND GIPARDE.

When King Magnus was east in Viken, there came to him a foreigner called Giparde. He gave himself out for a good knight, and offered his services to King Magnus; for he understood that in the king's dominions there was something to be done. The king received him well. At that time the king was preparing to go to Gautland, on which country the king had pretensions; and besides he would repay the Gautland people the disgrace they had occasioned him in spring, when he was obliged to fly from them. He had then a great force in arms, and the West Gautlanders in the northern districts submitted to him. He set up his camp on the borders, intending to make a foray from thence. When King Inge heard of this he collected troops, and hastened to oppose King Magnus; and when King Magnus heard of this expedition, many of the chiefs of the people urged him to turn back; but this the king would not listen to, but in the night time went unsuspectedly against the Swedish king. They met at Foxerne; and when he was drawing up his men in battle order he asked, "Where is Giparde?" but he was not to be found. Then the king made these verses:–

"Cannot the foreign knight abide
Our rough array?–where does he hide?"

Then a skald who followed the king replied:–

"The king asks where the foreign knight
In our array rides to the fight:
Giparde the knight rode quite away
When our men joined in bloody fray.
When swords were wet the knight was slow
With his bay horse in front to go;
The foreign knight could not abide
Our rough array, and went to hide."

There was a great slaughter, and after the battle the field was covered with the Swedes slain, and King Inge escaped by flight. King Magnus gained a great victory. Then came Giparde riding down from the country, and people did not speak well of him for not being in the fight. He went away, and proceeded westward to England; and the voyage was stormy, and Giparde lay in bed. There was an Iceland man called Eldjarn, who went to bale out the water in the ship's hold, and when he saw where Giparde was lying he made this verse:–

"Does it beseem a courtman bold
Here to be dozing in the hold?
The bearded knight should danger face:
The leak gains on our ship apace.
Here, ply this bucket! bale who can;
We need the work of every man.
Our sea-horse stands full to the breast,–
Sluggards and cowards must not rest."

When they came west to England, Giparde said the Northmen had slandered him. A meeting was appointed, and a count came to it, and the case was brought before him for trial. He said he was not much acquainted with law cases, as he was but young, and had only been a short time in office; and also, of all things, he said what he least understood to judge about was poetry. "But let us hear what it was." Then Eldjarn sang:–

"I heard that in the bloody fight
Giparde drove all our foes to flight:

Brave Giparde would the foe abide,
While all our men ran off to hide.
At Foxerne the fight was won
By Giparde's valour all alone;
Where Giparde fought, alone was he;
Not one survived to fight or flee."

Then said the count, "Although I know but little about skald-craft, I can hear that this is no slander, but rather the highest praise and honour." Giparde could say nothing against it, yet he felt it was a mockery.

16. BATTLE OF FOXERNE.

THE SPRING AFTER, as soon as the ice broke up, King Magnus, with a great army, sailed eastwards to the Gaut river, and went up the eastern arm of it, laying waste all that belonged to the Swedish dominions. When they came to Foxerne they landed from their vessels; but as they came over a river on their way an army of Gautland people came against them, and there was immediately a great battle, in which the Northmen were overwhelmed by numbers, driven to flight, and many of them killed near to a waterfall. King Magnus fled, and the Gautlanders pursued, and killed those they could get near. King Magnus was easily known. He was a very stout man, and had a red short cloak over him, and bright yellow hair like silk that fell over his shoulders. Ogmund Skoptason, who was a tall and handsome man, rode on one side of the king. He said, "Sire, give me that cloak."

The king said, "What would you do with it?"

"I would like to have it," said Ogmund; "and you have given me greater gifts, sire."

The road was such that there were great and wide plains, so that the Gautlanders and Northmen were always in sight of each other, unless where clumps of wood and bushes concealed them from each other now and then. The king gave Ogmund the cloak and he put it on. When they came out again upon the plain ground, Ogmund and his people rode off right across the road. The Gautlanders, supposing this must be the king, rode all after him, and the king proceeded to the ships. Ogmund escaped with great difficulty; however, he reached the ships at last in safety. King Magnus then sailed down the river, and proceeded north to Viken.

17. MEETING OF THE KINGS AT THE GAUT RIVER.

The following summer a meeting of the kings was agreed upon at Konghelle on the Gaut river; and King Magnus, the Swedish king, Inge, and the Danish king, Eirik Sveinson, all met there, after giving each other safe conduct to the meeting. Now when the Thing had sat down the kings went forward upon the plain, apart from the rest of the people, and they talked with each other a little while. Then they returned to their people, and a treaty was brought about, by which each should possess the dominions his forefathers had held before him; but each should make good to his own men the waste and manslaughter suffered by them, and then they should agree between themselves about settling this with each other. King Magnus should marry King Inge's daughter Margaret, who afterwards was called Peace-offering. This was proclaimed to the people; and thus, within a little hour, the greatest enemies were made the best of friends.

It was observed by the people that none had ever seen men with more of the air of chiefs than these had. King Inge was the largest and stoutest, and, from his age, of the most dignified appearance. King Magnus appeared the most gallant and brisk, and King Eirik the most handsome. But they were all handsome men; stout, gallant, and ready in speech. After this was settled they parted.

18. KING MAGNUS'S MARRIAGE.

King Magnus got Margaret, King Inge's daughter, as above related; and she was sent from Svithjod to Norway with an honourable retinue. King Magnus had some children before, whose names shall here be given. The one of his sons who was of a mean mother was called Eystein; the other, who was a year younger, was called Sigurd, and his mother's name was Thora. Olaf was the name of a third son, who was much younger than the two first mentioned, and whose mother was Sigrid, a daughter of Saxe of Vik, who was a respectable man in the Throndhjem country; she was the king's concubine. People say that when King Magnus came home from his viking cruise to the Western countries, he and many of his people brought with them a great deal of the habits and fashion of clothing of those western parts. They went about on the streets with bare legs, and had short kirtles and over-cloaks; and therefore his men called him Magnus Barefoot or Bareleg. Some called him Magnus the Tall, others Magnus the Strife-lover. He was distinguished among other men by his tall stature. The mark of his height is put down in Mary church, in the merchant town of Nidaros, which King Harald built. In the northern door there were cut into the wall three crosses, one for Harald's stature, one for Olaf's, and one for Magnus's; and which crosses each of them could with the greatest ease kiss. The upper was Harald's cross; the lowest was Magnus's; and Olaf's was in the middle, about equally distant from both.

It is said that Magnus composed the following verses about the emperor's daughter:–

"The ring of arms where blue swords gleam,
The battle-shout, the eagle's scream,
The Joy of war, no more can please:
Matilda is far o'er the seas.
My sword may break, my shield be cleft,
Of land or life I may be reft;
Yet I could sleep, but for one care,–
One, o'er the seas, with light-brown hair."

He also composed the following:–

"The time that breeds delay feels long,
The skald feels weary of his song;
What sweetens, brightens, eases life?
'Tis a sweet-smiling lovely wife.
My time feels long in Thing affairs,
In Things my loved one ne'er appears.
The folk full-dressed, while I am sad,
Talk and oppose–can I be glad?"

When King Magnus heard the friendly words the emperor's daughter had spoken about him–that she had said such a man as King Magnus was appeared to her an excellent man, he composed the following:–

"The lover hears,–across the sea,
A favouring word was breathed to me.
The lovely one with light-brown hair
May trust her thoughts to senseless air;
Her thoughts will find like thoughts in me;
And though my love I cannot see,

Affection's thoughts fly in the wind,
And meet each other, true and kind."

19. OF THE QUARREL OF KING MAGNUS AND SKOPTE.

Skopte Ogmundson came into variance with King Magnus, and they quarrelled about the inheritance of a deceased person which Skopte retained; but the king demanded it with so much earnestness, that it had a dangerous appearance. Many meetings were held about the affair, and Skopte took the resolution that he and his son should never put themselves into the king's power at the same time; and besides there was no necessity to do so. When Skopte was with the king he represented to him that there was relationship between the king and him; and also that he, Skopte, had always been the king's friend, and his father's likewise, and that their friendship had never been shaken. He added, "People might know that I have sense enough not to hold a strife, sire, with you, if I was wrong in what I asked; but it is inherited from my ancestors to defend my rights against any man, without distinction of persons." The king was just the same on this point, and his resolution was by no means softened by such a speech. Then Skopte went home.

20. FIN SKOPTASON'S PROCEEDINGS.

Then Fin Skoptason went to the king, spoke with him, and entreated him to render justice to the father and son in this business. The king answers angrily and sharply. Then said Fin, "I expected something else, sire, from you, than that you would use the law's vexations against me when I took my seat in Kvaldinsey Island, which few of your other friends would do; as they said, what was true, that those who were left there were deserted and doomed to death, if King Inge had not shown greater generosity to us than you did; although many consider that we brought shame and disgrace only from thence." The king was not to be moved by this speech, and Fin returned home.

21. OGMUND SKOPTASON'S PROCEEDINGS.

Then came Ogmund Skoptason to the king; and when he came before him he produced his errand, and begged the king to do what was right and proper towards him and his father. The king insisted that the right was on his side, and said they were "particularly impudent."

Then said Ogmund, "It is a very easy thing for thee, having the power, to do me and my father injustice; and I must say the old proverb is true, that one whose life you save gives none, or a very bad return. This I shall add, that never again shall I come into thy service; nor my father, if I can help it." Then Ogmund went home, and they never saw each other again.

22. SKOPTE OGMUNDSON'S VOYAGE ABROAD.

The spring after, Skopte Ogmundson made ready to travel out of the country. They had five long-ships all well equipped. His sons, Ogmund, Fin, and Thord, accompanied him on this journey. It was very late before they were ready, and in autumn they went over to Flanders, and wintered there. Early in spring they sailed westward to Valland, and stayed there all summer. Then they sailed further, and through Norvasund; and came in autumn to Rome, where Skopte died. All, both father and sons, died on this journey. Thord, who died in Sicily, lived the longest. It is a common saying among the people that Skopte was the first Northman who sailed through Norvasund; and this voyage was much celebrated.

23. MIRACLE OF KING OLAF THE SAINT AT A FIRE.

It happened once in the merchant town (Nidaros) where King Olaf reposes, that there broke out a fire in the town which spread around. Then Olaf's shrine was taken out of the church, and set up opposite the fire. Thereupon came a crazy foolish man, struck the shrine, threatened the holy saint, and said all must be consumed by the flames, both churches and other houses, if he did not save them by his prayers. Now the burning of the church did cease, by the help of Almighty God; but the insane man got sore eyes on the following night, and he lay there until King Olaf entreated God Almighty to be merciful to him; after which he recovered in the same church.

24. MIRACLE OF KING OLAF ON A LAME WOMAN.

It happened once in the merchant town that a woman was brought to the place where the holy King Olaf reposes. She was so miserably shaped, that she was altogether crumpled up; so that both her feet lay in a circle against her loins. But as she was diligent in her prayers, often weeping and making vows to King Olaf, he cured her great infirmities; so that feet, legs, and other limbs straightened, and every limb and part came to the right use for which they were made. Before she could not creep there, and now she went away active and brisk to her family and home.

25. WAR IN IRELAND.

When King Magnus had been nine years king of Norway (A.D. 1094-1102), he equipped himself to go out of the country with a great force. He sailed out into the West sea with the finest men who could be got in Norway. All the powerful men of the country followed him; such as Sigurd Hranason, Vidkun Jonson, Dag Eilifson, Serk of Sogn, Eyvind Olboge, the king's marshal Ulf Hranason, brother of Sigurd, and many other great men. With all this armament the king sailed west to the Orkney Islands, from whence he took with him Earl Erlend's sons, Magnus and Erling, and then sailed to the southern Hebudes. But as he lay under the Scotch land, Magnus Erlendson ran away in the night from the king's ship, swam to the shore, escaped into the woods, and came at last to the Scotch king's court. King Magnus sailed to Ireland with his fleet, and plundered there. King Myrkjartan came to his assistance, and they conquered a great part of the country, both Dublin and Dyflinnarskire (Dublin shire). King Magnus was in winter (A.D. 1102) up in Connaught with King Myrkjartan, but set men to defend the country he had taken. Towards spring both kings went westward with their army all the way to Ulster, where they had many battles, subdued the country, and had conquered the greatest part of Ulster when Myrkjartan returned home to Connaught.

26. KING MAGNUS'S FORAY ON THE LAND.

King Magnus rigged his ships, and intended returning to Norway, but set his men to defend the country of Dublin. He lay at Ulster ready for sea with his whole fleet. As they thought they needed cattle for ship-provision, King Magnus sent a message to King Myrkjartan, telling him to send some cattle for slaughter; and appointed the day before Bartholomew's day as the day they should arrive, if the messengers reached him in safety; but the cattle had not made their appearance the evening before Bartholomew's mass. On the mass-day itself, when the sun rose in the sky, King Magnus went on shore himself with the greater part of his men, to look after his people, and to carry off cattle from the coast. The weather was calm, the sun shone, and the road lay through mires and mosses, and there were paths cut through; but there was brushwood on each side of the road. When they came somewhat farther, they reached a height from which they had a wide view. They saw from it a great dust rising up the country, as of horsemen, and they said to each other, "That must be the Irish army;" but others said, "It was their own men returning with the cattle." They halted there; and Eyvind Olboge said, "How, sire, do you intend to direct the march? The men think we are advancing imprudently. You know the Irish are treacherous; think, therefore, of a good counsel for your men." Then the king said, "Let us draw up our men, and be ready, if there be treachery." This was done, and the king and Eyvind went before the line. King Magnus had a helmet on his head; a red shield, in which was inlaid a gilded lion; and was girt with the sword of Legbit, of which the hilt was of tooth (ivory), and handgrip wound about with gold thread; and the sword was extremely sharp. In his hand he had a short spear, and a red silk short cloak, over his coat, on which, both before and behind, was embroidered a lion in yellow silk; and all men acknowledged that they never had seen a brisker, statelier man. Eyvind had also a red silk cloak like the king's; and he also was a stout, handsome, warlike man.

27. FALL OF KING MAGNUS.

When the dust-cloud approached nearer they knew their own men, who were driving the cattle. The Irish king had been faithful to the promises he had given the king, and had sent them. Thereupon they all turned towards the ships, and it was mid-day. When they came to the mires they went but slowly over the boggy places; and then the Irish started up on every side against them from every bushy point of land, and the battle began instantly. The Northmen were going divided in various heaps, so that many of them fell.

Then said Eyvind to the king, "Unfortunate is this march to our people, and we must instantly hit upon some good plan."

The king answered, "Call all the men together with the war-horns under the banner, and the men who are here shall make a rampart with their shields, and thus we will retreat backwards out of the mires; and we will clear ourselves fast enough when we get upon firm ground."

The Irish shot boldly; and although they fell in crowds, there came always two in the place of one. Now when the king had come to the nearest ditch there was a very difficult crossing, and few places were passable; so that many Northmen fell there. Then the king called to his lenderman Thorgrim Skinhufa, who was an Upland man, and ordered him to go over the ditch with his division. "We shall defend you," said he, "in the meantime, so that no harm shall come to you. Go out then to those holms, and shoot at them from thence; for ye are good bowmen."

When Thorgrim and his men came over the ditch they cast their shields behind their backs, and set off to the ships.

When the king saw this, he said, "Thou art deserting thy king in an unmanly way. I was foolish in making thee a lenderman, and driving Sigurd Hund out of the country; for never would he have behaved so."

King Magnus received a wound, being pierced by a spear through both thighs above the knees. The king laid hold of the shaft between his legs, broke the spear in two, and said, "Thus we break spear-shafts, my lads; let us go briskly on. Nothing hurts me." A little after King Magnus was struck in the neck with an Irish axe, and this was his death-wound. Then those who were behind fled. Vidkun Jonson instantly killed the man who had given the king his death-wound, and fled, after having received three wounds; but brought the king's banner and the sword Legbit to the ships. Vidkun was the last man who fled; the other next to him was Sigurd Hranason, and the third before him, Dag Eilifson. There fell with King Magnus, Eyvind Olboge, Ulf Hranason, and many other great people. Many of the Northmen fell, but many more of the Irish. The Northmen who escaped sailed away immediately in autumn. Erling, Earl Erlend's'son, fell with King Magnus in Ireland; but the men who fled from Ireland came to the Orkney Islands. Now when King Sigurd heard that his father had fallen, he set off immediately, leaving the Irish king's daughter behind, and proceeded in autumn with the whole fleet directly to Norway.

28. OF KING MAGNUS AND VIDKUN JONSON.

KING MAGNUS WAS TEN years king of Norway (A.D. 1094-1105), and in his days there was good peace kept within the country; but the people were sorely oppressed with levies. King Magnus was beloved by his men, but the bondes thought him harsh. The words have been transmitted from him that he said when his friends observed that he proceeded incautiously when he was on his expeditions abroad,–"The kings are made for honour, not for long life." King Magnus was nearly thirty years of age when he fell. Vidkun did not fly until he had killed the man who gave the king his mortal wound, and for this cause King Magnus's sons had him in the most affectionate regard.

BOOK ELEVEN

Saga of Sigurd the Crusader and his Brothers Eystein and Olaf

PRELIMINARY REMARKS.

"AGRIP", "FAGRSKINNA", and "Morkinskinna" more or less complete the story of the sons of Magnus. They contain some things omitted by Snorre, while, on the other hand, some facts related by Snorre are not found in the above sources.

Thjodrek the Monk tells of Sigurd that he made a Journey to Jerusalem, conquered many heathen cities, and among them Sidon; that he captured a cave defended by robbers, received presents from Baldwin, returned to Norway in Eystein's lifetime, and became insane, as a result, as some say, of a poisonous drink.

The three brothers became kings in the year A.D. 1103. Olaf died 1115, Eystein 1122 or 1123, Sigurd 1130.

Skalds quoted in this saga are: Thorarin Stutfeld, Einar Skulason, Haldor Skvaldre, and Arne Fjoruskeif.

1. BEGINNING OF THE REIGN OF KING MAGNUS'S SONS.

AFTER KING MAGNUS BAREFOOT's fall, his sons, Eystein, Sigurd, and Olaf, took the kingdom of Norway. Eystein got the northern, and Sigurd the southern part of the country. King Olaf was then four or five years old, and the third part of the country which he had was under the management of his two brothers. King Sigurd was chosen king when he was thirteen or fourteen years old, and Eystein was a year older. King Sigurd left west of the sea the Irish king's daughter. When King Magnus's sons were chosen kings, the men who had followed Skopte Ogmundson returned home. Some had been to Jerusalem, some to Constantinople; and there they had made themselves renowned, and they had many kinds of novelties to talk about. By these extraordinary tidings many men in Norway were incited to the same expedition; and it was also told that the Northmen who liked to go into the military service at Constantinople found many opportunities of getting property. Then these Northmen desired much that one of the two kings, either Eystein or Sigurd, should go as commander of the troop which was preparing for this expedition. The kings agreed to this, and carried on the equipment at their common expense. Many great men, both of the lendermen and bondes, took part in this enterprise; and when all was ready for the journey it was determined that Sigurd should go, and Eystein in the meantime, should rule the kingdom upon their joint account.

2. OF THE EARLS OF ORKNEY.

A YEAR OR TWO after King Magnus Barefoot's fall, Hakon, a son of Earl Paul, came from Orkney. The kings gave him the earldom and government of the Orkney Islands, as the earls before him, his father Paul or his Uncle Erland, had possessed it; and Earl Hakon then sailed back immediately to Orkney.

3. KING SIGURD'S JOURNEY OUT OF THE COUNTRY.

FOUR YEARS AFTER THE fall of King Magnus (A.D. 1107), King Sigurd sailed with his people from Norway. He had then sixty ships. So says Thorarin Stutfeld:–

> *"A young king just and kind,*
> *People of loyal mind:*
> *Such brave men soon agree,–*

To distant lands they sail with glee.
To the distant Holy Land
A brave and pious band,
Magnificent and gay,
In sixty long-ships glide away."

King Sigurd sailed in autumn to England, where Henry, son of William the Bastard, was then king, and Sigurd remained with him all winter. So says Einar Skulason:-

"The king is on the waves!
The storm he boldly braves.
His ocean-steed,
With winged speed,
O'er the white-flashing surges,
To England's coast he urges;
And there he stays the winter o'er:
More gallant king ne'er trod that shore."

4. OF KING SIGURD'S JOURNEY.

In spring King Sigurd and his fleet sailed westward to Valland (A.D. 1108), and in autumn came to Galicia, where he stayed the second winter (A.D. 1109). So says Einar Skulason:-

"Our king, whose land so wide
No kingdom stands beside,
In Jacob's land next winter spent,
On holy things intent;
And I have heard the royal youth
Cut off an earl who swerved from truth.
Our brave king will endure no ill,-
The hawks with him will get their fill."

It went thus:-The earl who ruled over the land made an agreement with King Sigurd, that he should provide King Sigurd and his men a market at which they could purchase victuals all the winter; but this he did not fulfil longer than to about Yule. It began then to be difficult to get food and necessaries, for it is a poor barren land. Then King Sigurd with a great body of men went against a castle which belonged to the earl; and the earl fled from it, having but few people. King Sigurd took there a great deal of victuals and of other booty, which he put on board of his ships, and then made ready and proceeded westward to Spain. It so fell out, as the king was sailing past Spain, that some vikings who were cruising for plunder met him with a fleet of galleys, and King Sigurd attacked them. This was his first battle with heathen men; and he won it, and took eight galleys from them. So says Haldor Skvaldre:–

"Bold vikings, not slow
To the death-fray to go,
Meet our Norse king by chance,
And their galleys advance.
The bold vikings lost
Many a man of their host,
And eight galleys too,
With cargo and crew."

Thereafter King Sigurd sailed against a castle called Sintre and fought another battle. This castle is in Spain, and was occupied by many heathens, who from thence plundered Christian people. King Sigurd took the castle, and killed every man in it, because they refused to be baptized; and he got there an immense booty. So says Haldor Skvaldre:–

"From Spain I have much news to tell

Of what our generous king befell.
And first he routs the viking crew,
At Cintra next the heathens slew;
The men he treated as God's foes,
Who dared the true faith to oppose.
No man he spared who would not take
The Christian faith for Jesus' sake."

5. LISBON TAKEN.

After this King Sigurd sailed with his fleet to Lisbon, which is a great city in Spain, half Christian and half heathen; for there lies the division between Christian Spain and heathen Spain, and all the districts which lie west of the city are occupied by heathens. There King Sigurd had his third battle with the heathens, and gained the victory, and with it a great booty. So says Haldor Skvaldre:–

"The son of kings on Lisbon's plains
A third and bloody battle gains.
He and his Norsemen boldly land,
Running their stout ships on the strand."

Then King Sigurd sailed westwards along heathen Spain, and brought up at a town called Alkasse; and here he had his fourth battle with the heathens, and took the town, and killed so many people that the town was left empty. They got there also immense booty. So says Haldor Skvaldre:-

"A fourth great battle, I am told,
Our Norse king and his people hold
At Alkasse; and here again
The victory fell to our Norsemen."

And also this verse:-

"I heard that through the town he went,
And heathen widows' wild lament
Resounded in the empty halls;
For every townsman flies or falls."

6. BATTLE IN THE ISLAND FORMINTERRA.

King Sigurd then proceeded on his voyage, and came to Norfasund; and in the sound he was met by a large viking force, and the king gave them battle; and this was his fifth engagement with heathens since the time he left Norway. He gained the victory here also. So says Haldor Skvaldre:-

"Ye moistened your dry swords with blood,
As through Norfasund ye stood;
The screaming raven got a feast,
As ye sailed onward to the East."

King Sigurd then sailed eastward along the coast of Serkland, and came to an island there called Forminterra. There a great many heathen Moors had taken up their dwelling in a cave, and had built a strong stone wall before its mouth. They harried the country all round, and carried all their booty to their cave. King Sigurd landed on this island, and went to the cave; but it lay in a precipice, and there was a high winding path to the stone wall, and the precipice above projected over it. The heathens defended the stone wall, and were not afraid of the Northmen's arms; for they could throw stones, or shoot down upon the Northmen under their feet; neither did the Northmen, under such circumstances, dare to mount up. The heathens took their clothes and other valuable things, carried them out upon the wall, spread them out before the Northmen, shouted, and defied them, and upbraided them as cowards. Then Sigurd fell upon this plan. He had two ship's boats, such as we call barks, drawn up the precipice right above the mouth of the cave; and had thick ropes fastened around the stem, stern, and hull of each. In these boats as many men went as could find room, and then the boats were lowered by the ropes down in front of the mouth of the cave; and the men in the boats shot with stones and missiles into the cave, and the heathens were thus driven from the stone wall. Then Sigurd with his troops climbed up the precipice to the foot of the stone wall, which they succeeded in breaking down, so that they came into the cave. Now the heathens fled within the stone wall that was built across the cave; on which the king ordered large trees to be brought to the cave, made a great pile in the mouth of it, and set fire to the wood. When the fire and smoke got the upper hand, some of the heathens lost their lives in it; some fled; some fell by the hands of the Northmen; and part were killed, part burned; and the Northmen made the greatest booty they had got on all their expeditions. So says Halder Skvaldre:–

"Forminterra lay
In the victor's way;
His ships' stems fly
To victory.
The bluemen there
Must fire bear,
And Norsemen's steel
At their hearts feel."

And also thus:–

"'Twas a feat of renown,–
The boat lowered down,
With a boat's crew brave,
In front of the cave;
While up the rock scaling,

And comrades up trailing,
The Norsemen gain,
And the bluemen are slain."

And also Thorarin Stutfeld says:–

"The king's men up the mountain's side
Drag two boats from the ocean's tide;
The two boats lay,
Like hill-wolves grey.
Now o'er the rock in ropes they're swinging
Well manned, and death to bluemen bringing;
They hang before
The robber's door."

7. OF THE BATTLES OF IVIZA AND MINORCA.

THEREAFTER KING SIGURD PROCEEDED on his expedition, and came to an island called Iviza (Ivica), and had there his seventh battle, and gained a victory. So says Haldor Skvaldre:–

"His ships at Ivica now ride,
The king's, whose fame spreads far and wide;
And hear the bearers of the shield
Their arms again in battle wield."

Thereafter King Sigurd came to an island called Manork (Minorca), and held there his eighth battle with heathen men, and gained the victory. So says Haldor Skvaldre:–

"On green Minorca's plains
The eighth battle now he gains:
Again the heathen foe
Falls at the Norse king's blow."

8. DUKE ROGER MADE A KING.

IN SPRING KING SIGURD came to Sicily (A.D. 1109), and remained a long time there. There was then a Duke Roger in Sicily, who received the king kindly, and invited him to a feast. King Sigurd came to it with a great retinue, and was splendidly entertained. Every day Duke Roger stood at the company's table, doing service to the king; but the seventh day of the feast, when the people had come to table, and had wiped their hands, King Sigurd took the duke by the hand, led him up to the high-seat, and saluted him with the title of king; and gave the right that there should be always a king over the dominion of Sicily, although before there had only been earls or dukes over that country.

9. OF KING ROGER.

KING ROGER OF SICILY was a very great king. He won and subdued all Apulia, and many large islands besides in the Greek sea; and therefore he was called Roger the Great. His son was William, king of Sicily, who for a long time had great hostility with the emperor of Constantinople. King William had three daughters, but no son. One of his daughters he married to the Emperor Henry, a son of the Emperor Frederik; and their son was Frederik, who for a short time after was emperor of Rome. His second daughter was married to the Duke of Kipr. The third daughter, Margaret, was married to the chief of the corsairs; but the Emperor Henry killed both these brothers-in-law. The daughter of Roger the Great, king of Sicily, was married to the Emperor Manuel of Constantinople; and their son was the Emperor Kirjalax.

10. KING SIGURD'S EXPEDITION TO PALESTINE.

IN THE SUMMER (A.D. 1110) King Sigurd sailed across the Greek sea to Palestine, and thereupon went up to Jerusalem, where he met Baldwin, king of Palestine. King Baldwin received him particularly well, and rode with him all the way to the river Jordan, and then back to the city of Jerusalem. Einar Skulason speaks thus of it:–

> *"Good reason has the skald to sing*
> *The generous temper of the king,*
> *Whose sea-cold keel from northern waves*
> *Ploughs the blue sea that green isles laves.*
> *At Acre scarce were we made fast,*
> *In holy ground our anchors cast,*

When the king made a joyful morn
To all who toil with him had borne."

And again he made these lines:–

"To Jerusalem he came,
He who loves war's noble game,
(The skald no greater monarch finds
Beneath the heaven's wide hall of winds)
All sin and evil from him flings
In Jordan's wave: for all his sins
(Which all must praise) he pardon wins."

King Sigurd stayed a long time in the land of Jerusalem (Jorsalaland) in autumn, and in the beginning of winter.

11. SIDON TAKEN.

King Baldwin made a magnificent feast for King Sigurd and many of his people, and gave him many holy relics. By the orders of King Baldwin and the patriarch, there was taken a splinter off the holy cross; and on this holy relic both made oath, that this wood was of the holy cross upon which God Himself had been tortured. Then this holy relic was given to King Sigurd; with the condition that he, and twelve other men with him, should swear to promote Christianity with all his power, and erect an archbishop's seat in Norway if he could; and also that the cross should be kept where the holy King Olaf reposed, and that he should introduce tithes, and also pay them himself. After this King Sigurd returned to his ships at Acre; and then King Baldwin prepared to go to Syria, to a heathen town called Saet. On this expedition King Sigurd accompanied him, and after the kings had besieged the town some time it surrendered, and they took possession of it, and of a great treasure of money; and their men found other booty. King Sigurd made a present of his share to King Baldwin. So say Haldor Skvaldre:–

"He who for wolves provides the feast
Seized on the city in the East,
The heathen nest; and honour drew,
And gold to give, from those he slew."

Einar Skulason also tells of it:–

"The Norsemen's king, the skalds relate,
Has ta'en the heathen town of Saet:
The slinging engine with dread noise
Gables and roofs with stones destroys.
The town wall totters too,–it falls;
The Norsemen mount the blackened walls.
He who stains red the raven's bill
Has won,–the town lies at his will."

Thereafter King Sigurd went to his ships and made ready to leave Palestine. They sailed north to the island Cyprus; and King Sigurd stayed there a while, and then went to the Greek country, and came to the land with all his fleet at Engilsnes. Here he lay still for a fortnight, although every day it blew a breeze for going before the wind to the north; but Sigurd would wait a side wind, so that the sails might stretch fore and aft in the ship; for in all his sails there was silk joined in, before and behind in the sail, and neither those before nor those behind the ships could see the slightest appearance of this, if the vessel was before the wind; so they would rather wait a side wind.

12. SIGURD'S EXPEDITION TO CONSTANTINOPLE.

When King Sigurd sailed into Constantinople, he steered near the land. Over all the land there are burghs, castles, country towns, the one upon the other without interval. There from the land one could see into the bights of the sails; and the sails stood so close beside each other, that they seemed to form one enclosure. All the people turned out to see King Sigurd sailing past. The Emperor Kirjalax had also heard of King Sigurd's expedition, and ordered the city port of Constantinople to be opened, which is called the Gold Tower, through which the emperor rides when he has been long absent from Constantinople, or has made a campaign in which he has been victorious. The emperor had precious cloths spread out from the Gold Tower to Laktjarna, which is the name of the emperor's most splendid hall. King Sigurd ordered his men to ride in great state into the city, and not to regard all the new things they might see; and this they did. King Sigurd and his followers rode with this great splendour into Constantinople, and then came to the magnificent hall, where everything was in the grandest style.

King Sigurd remained here some time. The Emperor Kirjalax sent his men to him to ask if he would rather accept from the emperor six lispund of gold, or would have the emperor give the games in his honour which the emperor was used to have played at the Padreim. King Sigurd preferred the games, and the messengers said the spectacle would not cost the emperor less than the money offered. Then the emperor prepared for the games, which were held in the usual way; but this day everything went on better for the king than for the queen; for the queen has always the half part in the games, and their men, therefore, always strive against each other in all games. The Greeks accordingly think that when the king's men win more games at the Padreim than the queen's, the king will gain the victory when he goes into battle. People who have been in Constantinople tell that the Padreim is thus constructed:–A high wall surrounds a flat plain, which may be compared to a round bare Thing-place, with earthen banks all around at the stone wall, on which banks the spectators sit; but the games themselves are in the flat plain. There are many sorts of old events represented concerning the Asas, Volsungs, and Giukungs, in these games; and all the figures are cast in copper, or metal, with so great art that they appear to be living things; and to the people it appears as if they were really present in the games. The games themselves are so artfully and cleverly managed, that people appear to be riding in the air; and at them also are used shot-fire[72], and all kinds of harp-playing, singing, and music instruments.

13. SIGURD AND THE EMPEROR OF CONSTANTINOPLE.

It is related that King Sigurd one day was to give the emperor a feast, and he ordered his men to provide sumptuously all that was necessary for the entertainment; and when all things were provided which are suitable for an entertainment given by a great personage to persons of high dignity, King Sigurd ordered his men to go to the street in the city where firewood was sold, as they would require a great quantity to prepare the feast. They said the king need not be afraid of wanting firewood, for every day many loads were brought into the town. When it was necessary, however, to have firewood, it was found that it was all sold, which they told the king. He replied, "Go and try if

72 Fireworks, or the Greek fire, probably were used.–L.

you can get walnuts. They will answer as well as wood for fuel." They went and got as many as they needed. Now came the emperor, and his grandees and court, and sat down to table. All was very splendid; and King Sigurd received the emperor with great state, and entertained him magnificently. When the queen and the emperor found that nothing was wanting, she sent some persons to inquire what they had used for firewood; and they came to a house filled with walnuts, and they came back and told the queen. "Truly," said she, "this is a magnificent king, who spares no expense where his honour is concerned." She had contrived this to try what they would do when they could get no firewood to dress their feast with.

14. KING SIGURD THE CRUSADER'S RETURN HOME.

King Sigurd soon after prepared for his return home. He gave the emperor all his ships; and the valuable figureheads which were on the king's ships were set up in Peter's church, where they have since been to be seen. The emperor gave the king many horses and guides to conduct him through all his dominions. Then King Sigurd left Constantinople; but a great many Northmen remained, and went into the emperor's pay. Then King Sigurd traveled from Bulgaria, and through Hungary, Pannonia. Suabia, and Bavaria, where he met the Roman emperor, Lotharius, who received him in the most friendly way, gave him guides through his dominions, and had markets established for him at which he could purchase all he required. When King Sigurd came to Slesvik in Denmark, Earl Eilif made a sumptuous feast for him; and it was then midsummer. In Heidaby he met the Danish king, Nikolas, who received him in the most friendly way, made a great entertainment for him, accompanied him north to Jutland, and gave him a ship provided with everything needful. From thence the king returned to Norway, and was joyfully welcomed on his return to his kingdom (A.D. 1110). It was the common talk among the people, that none had ever made so honourable a journey from Norway as this of King Sigurd. He was twenty years of age, and had been three years on these travels. His brother Olaf was then twelve years old.

15. EYSTEIN'S DOINGS IN THE MEANTIME.

King Eystein had also effected much in the country that was useful while King Sigurd was on his journey. He established a monastery at

Nordnes in Bergen, and endowed it with much property. He also built Michael's church, which is a very splendid stone temple. In the king's house there he also built the Church of the Apostles, and the great hall, which is the most magnificent wooden structure that was ever built in Norway. He also built a church at Agdanes with a parapet; and a harbour, where formerly there had been a barren spot only. In Nidaros he built in the king's street the church of Saint Nikolas, which was particularly ornamented with carved work, and all in wood. He also built a church north in Vagar in Halogaland, and endowed it with property and revenues.

16. OF KING EYSTEIN.

King Eystein sent a verbal message to the most intelligent and powerful of the men of Jamtaland, and invited them to him; received them all as they came with great kindness; accompanied them part of the way home, and gave them presents, and thus enticed them into a friendship with him. Now as many of them became accustomed to visit him and receive gifts from him, and he also sent gifts to some who did not come themselves, he soon gained the favour of all the people who had most influence in the country. Then he spoke to the Jamtaland people, and told them they had done ill in turning away from the kings of Norway, and withdrawing from them their taxes and allegiance. He began by saying how the Jamtaland people had submitted to the reign of Hakon, the foster-son of Athelstane, and had long afterwards been subjected to the kings of Norway, and he represented to them how many useful things they could get from Norway, and how inconvenient it was for them to apply to the Swedish king for what they needed. By these speeches he brought matters so far that the Jamtaland people of their own accord offered to be subject to him, which they said was useful and necessary for them; and thus, on both sides, it was agreed that the Jamtalanders should put their whole country under King Eystein. The first beginning was with the men of consequence, who persuaded the people to take an oath of fidelity to King Eystein; and then they went to King Eystein and confirmed the country to him by oath; and this arrangement has since continued for a long time. King Eystein thus conquered Jamtaland by his wisdom, and not by hostile inroads, as some of his forefathers had done.

17. OF KING EYSTEIN'S PERFECTIONS.

King Eystein was the handsomest man that could be seen. He had blue open eyes; his hair yellow and curling; his stature not tall, but of the middle size. He was wise, intelligent, and acquainted with the laws and history. He had much knowledge of mankind, was quick in counsel, prudent in words, and very eloquent and very generous. He was very merry, yet modest; and was liked and beloved, indeed, by all the people. He was married to Ingebjorg, a daughter of Guthorm, son of Thorer of Steig; and their daughter was Maria, who afterwards married Gudbrand Skafhogson.

18. OF IVAR INGIMUNDSON.

King Eystein had in many ways improved the laws and priveleges of the country people, and kept strictly to the laws; and he made himself acquainted with all the laws of Norway, and showed in everything great prudence and understanding. What a valuable man King Eystein was, how full of friendship, and how much he turned his mind to examining and avoiding everything that could be of disadvantage to his friends, may be seen from his friendship to an Iceland man called Ivar Ingimundson. The man was witty, of great family, and also a poet. The king saw that Ivar was out of spirits, and asked him why he was so melancholy. "Before, when thou wast with us, we had much amusement with thy conversation. I know thou art a man of too good an understanding to believe that I would do anything against thee. Tell me then what it is."

He replied, "I cannot tell thee what it is."

Then said the king, "I will try to guess what it is. Are there any men who displease thee?"

To this he replied, "No."

"Dost thou think thou art held in less esteem by me than thou wouldst like to be?"

To this he also replied, "No."

"Hast thou observed anything whatever that has made an impression on thee at which thou art ill pleased?"

He replied, it was not this either.

The king: "Would you like to go to other chiefs or to other men?"

To this he answered, "No."

The king: "It is difficult now to guess. Is there any girl here, or in any other country, to whom thy affections are engaged?"

He said it was so.

The king said, "Do not be melancholy on that account. Go to Iceland when spring sets in, and I shall give thee money, and presents, and with these my letters and seal to the men who have the principal sway there; and I know no man there who will not obey my persuasions or threats."

Ivar replied, "My fate is heavier, sire; for my own brother has the girl."

Then said the king, "Throw it out of thy mind; and I know a counsel against this. After Yule I will travel in guest-quarters. Thou shalt come along with me, and thou will have an opportunity of seeing many beautiful girls; and, provided they are not of the royal stock, I will get thee one of them in marriage."

Ivar replies, "Sire, my fate is still the heavier; for as oft as I see beautiful and excellent girls I only remember the more that girl, and they increase my misery."

The king: "Then I will give thee property to manage, and estates for thy amusement."

He replied, "For that I have no desire."

The king: "Then I will give thee money, that thou mayest travel in other countries."

He said he did not wish this.

Then said the king, "It is difficult for me to seek farther, for I have proposed everything that occurs to me. There is but one thing else; and that is but little compared to what I have offered thee. Come to me every day after the tables are removed, and, if I am not sitting upon important business, I shall talk with thee about the girl in every way that I can think of; and I shall do so at leisure. It sometimes happens that sorrow is lightened by being brought out openly; and thou shalt never go away without some gift."

He replied, "This I will do, sire, and return thanks for this inquiry."

And now they did so constantly; and when the king was not occupied with weightier affairs he talked with him, and his sorrow by degrees wore away, and he was again in good spirits.

19. OF KING SIGURD.

King Sigurd was a stout and strong man, with brown hair; of a manly appearance, but not handsome; well grown; of little speech, and often not friendly, but good to his friends, and faithful; not very eloquent, but moral and polite. King Sigurd was self-willed, and severe in his revenge;

strict in observing the law; was generous; and withal an able, powerful king. His brother Olaf was a tall, thin man; handsome in countenance; lively, modest, and popular. When all these brothers, Eystein, Sigurd and Olaf were kings of Norway, they did away with many burthens which the Danes had laid upon the people in the time that Svein Alfifason ruled Norway; and on this account they were much beloved, both by the people and the great men of the country.

20. OF KING SIGURD'S DREAM.

ONCE KING SIGURD FELL into low spirits, so that few could get him to converse, and he sat but a short time at the drinking table. This was heavy on his counsellors, friends, and court; and they begged King Eystein to consider how they could discover the cause why the people who came to the king could get no reply to what they laid before him. King Eystein answered them, that it was difficult to speak with the king about this; but at last, on the entreaty of many, he promised to do it. Once, when they were both together, King Eystein brought the matter before his brother, and asked the cause of his melancholy. "It is a great grief, sire, to many to see thee so melancholy; and we would like to know what has occasioned it, or if perchance thou hast heard any news of great weight?"

King Sigurd replies, that it was not so.

"Is it then, brother," says King Eystein, "that you would like to travel out of the country, and augment your dominions as our father did?"

He answered, that it was not that either.

"Is it, then, that any man here in the country has offended?"

To this also the king said "No."

"Then I would like to know if you have dreamt anything that has occasioned this depression of mind?"

The king answered that it was so.

"Tell me, then, brother, thy dream."

King Sigurd said, "I will not tell it, unless thou interpret it as it may turn out; and I shall be quick at perceiving if thy interpretation be right or not."

King Eystein replies, "This is a very difficult matter, sire, on both sides; as I am exposed to thy anger if I cannot interpret it, and to the blame of the public if I can do nothing in the matter; but I will rather fall under your displeasure, even if my interpretation should not be agreeable."

King Sigurd replies, "It appeared to me, in a dream, as if we brothers were all sitting on a bench in front of Christ church in Throndhjem; and it appeared to me as if our relative, King Olaf the Saint, came out of the church adorned with the royal raiment glancing and splendid, and with the most delightful and joyful countenance. He went to our brother King Olaf, took him by the hand, and said cheerfully, to him, 'Come with me, friend.' On which he appeared to stand up and go into the church. Soon after King Olaf the Saint came out of the church, but not so gay and brilliant as before. Now he went to thee, brother, and said to thee that thou shouldst go with him; on which he led thee with him, and ye went into the church. Then I thought, and waited for it, that he would come to me, and meet me; but it was not so. Then I was seized with great sorrow, and great dread and anxiety fell upon me, so that I was altogether without strength; and then I awoke."

King Eystein replies, "Thus I interpret your dream, sire,–That the bench betokens the kingdom we brothers have; and as you thought King Olaf came with so glad a countenance to our brother, King Olaf, he will likely live the shortest time of us brothers, and have all good to expect hereafter; for he is amiable, young in years, and has gone but little into excess, and King Olaf the Saint must help him. But as you thought he came towards me, but not with so much joy, I may possibly live a few years longer, but not become old, and I trust his providence will stand over me; but that he did not come to me with the same splendour and glory as to our brother Olaf, that will be because, in many ways, I have sinned and transgressed his command. If he delayed coming to thee, I think that in no way betokens thy death, but rather a long life; but it may be that some heavy accident may occur to thee, as there was an unaccountable dread overpowering thee; but I foretell that thou will be the oldest of us, and wilt rule the kingdom longest."

Then said Sigurd, "This is well and intelligently interpreted, and it is likely it will be so." And now the king began to be cheerful again.

21. OF KING SIGURD'S MARRIAGE.

King Sigurd married Malmfrid, a daughter of King Harald Valdemarson, eastward in Novgorod. King Harald Valdemarson's mother was Queen Gyda the Old, a daughter of the Swedish king, Inge Steinkelson. Harald Valdemarson's other daughter, sister to Malmfrid, was Ingebjorg, who was married to Canute Lavard, a son of the Danish king, Eirik the Good, and grandson of King Svein Ulfson. Canute's and

Ingebjorg's children were, the Danish king, Valdemar, who came to the Danish kingdom after Svein Eirikson; and daughters Margaret, Christina, and Catherine. Margaret was married to Stig Hvitaled; and their daughter was Christina, married to the Swedish king, Karl Sorkvison, and their son was King Sorkver.

22. OF THE CASES BEFORE THE THING.

The king's relative, Sigurd Hranason, came into strife with King Sigurd. He had had the Lapland collectorship on the king's account, because of their relationship and long friendship, and also of the many services Sigurd Hranason had done to the kings; for he was a very distinguished, popular man. But it happened to him, as it often does to others, that persons more wicked and jealous than upright slandered him to King Sigurd, and whispered in the king's ear that he took more of the Laplander's tribute to himself than was proper. They spoke so long about this, that King Sigurd conceived a dislike and anger to him, and sent a message to him. When he appeared before the king, the king carried these feelings with him, and said, "I did not expect that thou shouldst have repaid me for thy great fiefs and other dignities by taking the king's property, and abstracting a greater portion of it than is allowable."

Sigurd Hranason replies, "It is not true that has been told you; for I have only taken such portion as I had your permission to take."

King Sigurd replies, "Thou shalt not slip away with this; but the matter shall be seriously treated before it comes to an end." With that they parted.

Soon after, by the advice of his friends, the king laid an action against Sigurd Hranason at the Thing-meeting in Bergen, and would have him made an outlaw. Now when the business took this turn, and appeared so dangerous, Sigurd Hranason went to King Eystein, and told him what mischief King Sigurd intended to do him, and entreated his assistance. King Eystein replied, "This is a difficult matter that you propose to me, to speak against my brother; and there is a great difference between defending a cause and pursuing it in law;" and added, that this was a matter which concerned him and Sigurd equally. "But for thy distress, and our relationship, I shall bring in a word for thee."

Soon after Eystein visited King Sigurd, and entreated him to spare the man, reminding him of the relationship between them and Sigurd Hranason, who was married to their aunt, Skialdvor; and said he would pay the penalty for the crime committed against the king, although he could not with truth impute any blame to him in the matter. Besides, he reminded the king of the long friendship with Sigurd Hranason. King Sigurd replied, that it was better government to punish such acts. Then King Eystein replied, "If thou, brother, wilt follow the law, and punish such acts according to the country's privileges, then it would be most correct that Sigurd Hranason produce his witnesses, and that the case be judged at the Thing, but not at a meeting; for the case comes under the law of the land, not under Bjarkey law." Then said Sigurd, "It may possibly be so that the case belongs to it, as thou sayest, King Eystein; and if it be against law what has hitherto been done in this case, then we shall bring it before the Thing." Then the kings parted, and each seemed determined to take his own way. King Sigurd summoned the parties in the case before the Arnarnes Thing, and intended to pursue it there. King Eystein came also to the Thing-place; and when the case was brought forward for judgment, King Eystein went to the Thing before judgment was given upon Sigurd Hranason. Now King Sigurd told the lagmen to pronounce the judgment; but King Eystein replied thus: "I trust there are here men acquainted sufficiently with the laws of Norway, to know that they cannot condemn a lendermen to be outlawed at this Thing." And he then explained how the law was, so that every man clearly understood it. Then said King Sigurd, "Thou art taking up this matter very warmly, King Eystein, and it is likely the case will cost more trouble before it comes to an end than we intended; but nevertheless we shall follow it out. I will have him condemned to be outlawed in his native place." Then said King Eystein, "There are certainly not many things which do not succeed with thee, and especially when there are but few and small folks to oppose one who has carried through such great things." And thus they parted, without anything being concluded in the case. Thereafter King Sigurd called together a Gula Thing, went himself there, and summoned to him many high chiefs. King Eystein came there also with his suite; and many meetings and conferences were held among people of understanding concerning this case, and it was tried and examined before the lagmen. Now King Eystein objected that all the parties summoned in any cases tried here belonged to the Thing-district; but in this case the deed and the parties belonged to Halogaland. The Thing accordingly ended in doing nothing, as King Eystein had thus made it incompetent. The kings parted in great wrath; and King Eystein went north to Throndhjem. King Sigurd, on the other hand, summoned to him all lendermen, and also the house-servants of the lendermen, and named out of every district a number of the bondes from the south parts of the country, so that he had collected a large army about him; and proceeded with all this crowd northwards along the coast to Halogaland, and intended to use all his power to make Sigurd Hranason an outlaw among his own relations. For this purpose he summoned to him the Halogaland and Naumudal people, and appointed a Thing at Hrafnista. King Eystein prepared himself also, and proceeded with many people from the town of Nidaros to the Thing, where he made Sigurd Hranason, by hand-shake before witnesses, deliver over to him the following and defending this case. At this Thing both the kings spoke, each for his own side. Then King Eystein asks the lagmen where that law was made in Norway which gave the bondes the right to judge between the kings of the country, when they had pleas with each other. "I shall bring witnesses to prove that Sigurd has given the case into my hands; and it is with me, not with Sigurd Hranason, that King Sigurd has to do in this case." The lagmen said that disputes between kings must be judged only at the Eyra Thing in Nidaros.

King Eystein said, "So I thought that it should be there, and the cases must be removed there."

Then King Sigurd said, "The more difficulties and inconvenience thou bringest upon me in this matter, the more I will persevere in it." And with that they parted.

Both kings then went south to Nidaros town, where they summoned a Thing from eight districts. King Eystein was in the town with a great many people, but Sigurd was on board his ships. When the Thing was opened, peace and safe conduct was given to all; and when the people were all collected, and the case should be gone into, Bergthor, a son of Svein Bryggjufot, stood up, and gave his evidence that Sigurd Hranason had concealed a part of the Laplanders' taxes.

Then King Eystein stood up and said, "If thy accusation were true, although we do not know what truth there may be in thy testimony, yet this case has already been dismissed from three Things, and a fourth time from a town meeting; and therefore I require that the lagmen acquit Sigurd in this case according to law." And they did so.

Then said King Sigurd, "I see sufficiently, King Eystein, that thou hast carried this case by law-quirks[73], which I do not understand. But now there remains, King Eystein, a way of determining the case which I am more used to, and which I shall now apply."

73 These law-quirks show a singularly advanced state of law. and deference to the Law Things, amidst such social disorder and misdeeds.-L.

He then retired to his ships, had the tents taken down, laid his whole fleet out at the holm, and held a Thing of his people; and told them that early in the morning they should land at Iluvellir, and give battle to King Eystein. But in the evening, as King Sigurd sat at his table in his ship taking his repast, before he was aware of it a man cast himself on the floor of the forehold, and at the king's feet. This was Sigurd Hranason, who begged the king to take what course with regard to him the king himself thought proper. Then came Bishop Magne and Queen Malmfrid, and many other great personages, and entreated forgiveness for Sigurd Hranason; and at their entreaty the king raised him up, took him by the hand, and placed him among his men, and took him along with himself to the south part of the country. In autumn the king gave Sigurd Hranason leave to go north to his farm, gave him an employment, and was always afterward his friend. After this day, however, the brothers were never much together, and there was no cordiality or cheerfulness among them.

23. OF KING OLAF'S DEATH.

King Olaf Magnuson fell into a sickness which ended in his death. He was buried in Christ church in Nidaros, and many were in great grief at his death. After Olaf's death, Eystein and Sigurd ruled the country, the three brothers together having been kings of Norway for twelve years (A.D. 1104-1115); namely, five years after King Sigurd returned home, and seven years before. King Olaf was seventeen years old when he died, and it happened on the 24th of December.

24. MAGNUS THE BLIND; HIS BIRTH.

King Eystein had been about a year in the east part of the country at that time, and King Sigurd was then in the north. King Eystein remained a long time that winter in Sarpsborg. There was once a powerful and rich bonde called Olaf of Dal, who dwelt in Great Dal in Aumord, and had two children,–a son called Hakon Fauk, and a daughter called Borghild, who was a very beautiful girl, and prudent, and well skilled in many things. Olaf and his children were a long time in winter in Sarpsborg, and Borghild conversed very often with King Eystein; so that many reports were spread about their friendship. The following summer King Eystein went north, and King Sigurd came eastward, where he remained all winter, and was long in Konungahella, which town he greatly enlarged and improved. He built there a great castle of turf and stone, dug a great ditch around it, and built a church and several houses within the castle. The holy cross he allowed to remain at Konungahella, and therein did not fulfill the oath he had taken in Palestine; but, on the other hand, he established tithe, and most of the other things to which he had bound himself by oath. The reason of his keeping the cross east at the frontier of the country was, that he thought it would be a protection to all the land; but it proved the greatest misfortune to place this relic within the power of the heathens, as it afterwards turned out.

When Borghild, Olaf's daughter, heard it whispered that people talked ill of her conversations and intimacy with King Eystein, she went to Sarpsborg; and after suitable fasts she carried the iron as proof of her innocence, and cleared herself thereby fully from all offence. When King Sigurd heard this, he rode one day as far as usually was two days' travelling, and came to Dal to Olaf, where he remained all night, made Borghild his concubine, and took her away with him. They had a son, who was called Magnus, and he was sent immediately to Halogaland, to be fostered at Bjarkey by Vidkun Jonson; and he was brought up there. Magnus grew up to be the handsomest man that could be seen, and was very soon stout and strong.

25. COMPARISON BETWEEN THE TWO KINGS.

KING EYSTEIN AND King Sigurd went both in spring to guest-quarters in the Uplands; and each was entertained in a separate house, and the houses were not very distant from each other. The bondes, however, thought it more convenient that both should be entertained together by turns in each house; and thus they were both at first in the house of King Eystein. But in the evening, when the people began to drink, the ale was not good; so that the guests were very quiet and still. Then said King Eystein, "Why are the people so silent? It is more usual in drinking parties that people are merry, so let us fall upon some jest over our ale that will amuse people; for surely, brother Sigurd, all people are well pleased when we talk cheerfully."

Sigurd replies, bluntly, "Do you talk as much as you please, but give me leave to be silent."

Eystein says, "It is a common custom over the ale-table to compare one person with another, and now let us do so." Then Sigurd was silent.

"I see," says King Eystein, "that I must begin this amusement. Now I will take thee, brother, to compare myself with, and will make it appear so as if we had both equal reputation and property, and that there is no difference in our birth and education."

Then King Sigurd replies, "Do you remember that I was always able to throw you when we wrestled, although you are a year older?"

Then King Eystein replied, "But I remember that you was not so good at the games which require agility."

Sigurd: "Do you remember that I could drag you under water, when we swam together, as often as I pleased?"

Eystein: "But I could swim as far as you, and could dive as well as you; and I could run upon snow-skates so well that nobody could beat me, and you could no more do it than an ox."

Sigurd: "Methinks it is a more useful and suitable accomplishment for a chief to be expert at his bow; and I think you could scarcely draw my bow, even if you took your foot to help."

Eystein: "I am not strong at the bow as you are, but there is less difference between our shooting near; and I can use the skees much better than you, and in former times that was held a great accomplishment."

Sigurd: "It appears to me much better for a chief who is to be the superior of other men, that he is conspicuous in a crowd, and strong and powerful in weapons above other men; easily seen, and easily known, where there are many together."

Eystein: "It is not less a distinction and an ornament that a man is of a handsome appearance, so as to be easily known from others on that account; and this appears to me to suit a chief best, because the best ornament is allied to beauty. I am moreover more knowing in the law than you, and on every subject my words flow more easily than yours."

Sigurd: "It may be that you know more law-quirks, for I have had something else to do; neither will any deny you a smooth tongue. But there are many who say that your words are not to be trusted; that what you promise is little to be regarded; and that you talk just according to what those who are about you say, which is not kingly."

Eystein: "This is because, when people bring their cases before me, I wish first to give every man that satisfaction in his affairs which he desires; but afterwards comes the opposite party, and then there is something to be given or taken away very often, in order to mediate between them, so that both may be satisfied. It often happens, too, that I promise whatever is desired of me, that all may be joyful about me. It would be an easy matter for me to do as you do,–to promise evil to all; and I never hear any complain of your not keeping this promise to them."

Sigurd: "It is the conversation of all that the expedition that I made out of the country was a princely expedition, while you in the meantime sat at home like your father's daughter."

Eystein: "Now you touched the tender spot. I would not have brought up this conversation if I had not known what to reply on this point. I can truly say that I equipt you from home like a sister, before you went upon this expedition."

Sigurd: "You must have heard that on this expedition I was in many a battle in the Saracen's land, and gained the victory in all; and you must have heard of the many valuable articles I acquired, the like of which were never seen before in this country, and I was the most respected wherever the most gallant men were; and, on the other hand, you cannot conceal that you have only a home-bred reputation."

Eystein: "I have heard that you had several battles abroad, but it was more useful for the country what I was doing in the meantime here at home. I built five churches from the foundations, and a harbour out at Agdanes, where it before was impossible to land, and where vessels ply north and south along the coast. I set a warping post and iron ring in the sound of Sinholm, and in Bergen I built a royal hall, while you were killing bluemen for the devil in Serkland. This, I think, was of but little advantage to our kingdom."

King Sigurd said: "On this expedition I went all the way to Jordan and swam across the river. On the edge of the river there is a bush of willows, and there I twisted a knot of willows, and said this knot thou shouldst untie, brother, or take the curse thereto attached."

King Eystein said: "I shall not go and untie the knot which you tied for me; but if I had been inclined to tie a knot for thee, thou wouldst not have been king of Norway at thy return to this country, when with a single ship you came sailing into my fleet."

Thereupon both were silent, and there was anger on both sides. More things passed between the brothers, from which it appeared that each of them would be greater than the other; however, peace was preserved between them as long as they lived.

26. OF KING SIGURD'S SICKNESS.

King Sigurd was at a feast in the Upland, and a bath was made ready for him. When the king came to the bath and the tent was raised over the bathing-tub, the king thought there was a fish in the tub beside him; and a great laughter came upon him, so that he was beside himself, and was out of his mind, and often afterwards these fits returned.

Magnus Barefoot's daughter, Ragnhild, was married by her brothers to Harald Kesia, a son of the Danish king, Eirik the Good; and their sons were Magnus, Olaf, Knut and Harald.

27. OF KING EYSTEIN'S DEATH.

King Eystein built a large ship at Nidaros, which, in size and shape, was like the Long Serpent which King Olaf Trygvason had built. At the stem there was a dragon's head, and at the stern a crooked tail, and both were gilded over. The ship was high-sided; but the fore and aft parts appeared less than they should be. He also made in Nidaros many and large dry-docks of the best material, and well timbered.

Six years after King Olaf's death, it happened that King Eystein, at a feast at Hustadir in Stim, was seized with an illness which soon carried him off. He died the 29th of August, 1123, and his body was carried north to Nidaros, and buried in Christ church; and it is generally said that so many mourners never stood over any man's grave in Norway as over King Eystein's, at least since the time Magnus the Good, Saint Olaf's son, died. Eystein had been twenty years (A.D. 1104-1123) king of Norway; and after his decease his brother, King Sigurd, was the sole king of Norway as long as he lived.

28. BAPTIZING THE PEOPLE OF SMALAND.

The Danish king, Nikolas, a son of Svein Ulfson, married afterwards the Queen Margaret, a daughter of King Inge, who had before been married to King Magnus Barefoot; and their sons were Nikolas and Magnus the Strong. King Nikolas sent a message to King Sigurd the Crusader, and asked him if he would go with him with all his might and help him to the east of the Swedish dominion, Smaland, to baptize the inhabitants; for the people who dwelt there had no regard for Christianity, although some of them had allowed themselves to be baptized. At that time there were many people all around in the Swedish dominions who were heathens, and many were bad Christians; for there were some of the kings who renounced Christianity, and continued heathen sacrifices, as Blotsvein, and afterwards Eirik Arsale, had done. King Sigurd promised to undertake this journey, and the kings appointed their meeting at Eyrarsund. King Sigurd then summoned all people in Norway to a levy, both of men and ships; and when the fleet was assembled he had about 300 ships. King Nikolas came very early to the meeting-place, and stayed there a long time; and the bondes murmured much, and said the Northmen did not intend to come. Thereupon the Danish army dispersed, and the king went away with all his fleet. King Sigurd came there soon afterwards, and was ill pleased; but sailed east to Svimraros, and held a House-thing, at which Sigurd spoke about King Nikolas's breach of faith, and the Northmen, on this account, determined to go marauding in his country. They first plundered a village called Tumathorp, which is not far from Lund; and then sailed east to the merchant-town of Calmar, where they plundered, as well as in Smaland, and imposed on the country a tribute of 1500 cattle for ship provision; and the people of Smaland received Christianity. After this King Sigurd turned about with his fleet, and came back to his kingdom with many valuable articles and great booty, which he had gathered on this expedition; and this levy was called the Calmar levy. This was the summer before the eclipse. This was the only levy King Sigurd carried out as long as he was king.

29. OF THORARIN STUTFELD.

It happened once when King Sigurd was going from the drinking-table to vespers, that his men were very drunk and merry; and many of them sat outside the church singing the evening song, but their singing was very irregular. Then the king said, "Who is that fellow I see standing at the church with a skin jacket on?" They answered, that they did not know. Then the king said:–

> *"This skin-clad man, in sorry plight,*
> *Puts all our wisdom here to flight."*

Then the fellow came forward and said:–

> *"I thought that here I might be known,*
> *Although my dress is scanty grown.*
> *'Tis poor, but I must be content:*
> *Unless, great king, it's thy intent*
> *To give me better; for I have seen*
> *When I and rags had strangers been."*

The king answered, "Come to me to-morrow when I am at the drink-table." The night passed away; and the morning after the Icelander, who was afterwards called Thorarin Stutfetd, went into the drinking-room. A man stood outside of the door of the room with a horn in his hand, and said, "Icelander! the king says that if thou wilt deserve any gift from him thou shalt compose a song before going in, and make it about a man whose name is Hakon Serkson, and who is called Morstrut[74]; and speak about that surname in thy song." The man who spoke to him was called Arne Fioruskeif. Then they went into the room; and when Thorarin came before the king's seat he recited these verses:–

"Throndhjem's warrior-king has said
The skald should be by gifts repaid,
If he before this meeting gave
The king's friend Serk a passing stave.
The generous king has let me know
My stave, to please, must be framed so
That my poor verse extol the fame
Of one called Hakon Lump by name."

Then said the king, "I never said so, and somebody has been making a mock of thee. Hakon himself shall determine what punishment thou shalt have. Go into his suite." Hakon said, "He shall be welcome among us, for I can see where the joke came from;" and he placed the Icelander at his side next to himself, and they were very merry. The day was drawing to a close, and the liquor began to get into their heads, when Hakon said, "Dost thou not think, Icelander, that thou owest me some penalty? and dost thou not see that some trick has been played upon thee?"

Thorarin replies, "It is true, indeed, that I owe thee some compensation."

Hakon says, "Then we shall be quits, if thou wilt make me another stave about Arne."

He said he was ready to do so; and they crossed over to the side of the room where Arne was sitting, and Thorarin gave these verses:–

"Fioruskeif has often spread,
With evil heart and idle head,
The eagle's voidings round the land,

74 Morstrut is a short, fat, punchy fellow.–L.

Lampoons and lies, with ready hand.
Yet this landlouper we all know,
In Africa scarce fed a crow,
Of all his arms used in the field,
Those in most use were helm and shield."

Arne sprang up instantly, drew his sword, and was going to fall upon him; but Hakon told him to let it alone and be quiet, and bade him remember that if it came to a quarrel he would come off the worst himself. Thorarin afterwards went up to the king, and said he had composed a poem which he wished the king to hear. The king consented, and the song is known by the name of the Stutfeld poem. The king asked Thorarin what he intended to do. He replied, it was his intention to go to Rome. Then the king gave him much money for his pilgrimage, and told him to visit him on his return, and promised to provide for him.

30. OF SIGURD AND OTTAR BIRTING.

It is told that King Sigurd, one Whitsunday, sat at table with many people, among whom were many of his friends; and when he came to his high-seat, people saw that his countenance was very wild, and as if he had been weeping, so that people were afraid of what might follow. The king rolled his eyes, and looked at those who were seated on the benches. Then he seized the holy book which he had brought with him from abroad, and which was written all over with gilded letters; so that never had such a costly book come to Norway. His queen sat by his side. Then said King Sigurd, "Many are the changes which may take place during a man's lifetime. I had two things which were dear to me above all when I came from abroad, and these were this book and the queen; and now I think the one is only worse and more loathsome than the other, and nothing I have belonging to me that I more detest. The queen does not know herself how hideous she is; for a goat's horn is standing out on her head, and the better I liked her before the worse I like her now." Thereupon he cast the book on the fire which was burning on the hall-floor, and gave the queen a blow with his fist between the eyes. The queen wept; but more at the king's' illness than at the blow, or the affront she had suffered.

Then a man stood up before the king; his name was Ottar Birting; and he was one of the torch-bearers, although a bonde's son, and was on service that day. He was of small stature, but of agreeable appearance;

lively, bold, and full of fun; black haired, and of a dark skin. He ran and snatched the book which the king had cast into the fire, held it out, and said, "Different were the days, sire, when you came with great state and splendour to Norway, and with great fame and honour; for then all your friends came to meet you with joy, and were glad at your coming. All as one man would have you for king, and have you in the highest regard and honour. But now days of sorrow are come over us; for on this holy festival many of your friends have come to you, and cannot be cheerful on account of your melancholy and ill health. It is much to be desired that you would be merry with them; and do, good king, take this saving advice, make peace first with the queen, and make her joyful whom you have so highly affronted, with a friendly word; and then all your chiefs, friends, and servants; that is my advice."

Then said King Sigurd, "Dost thou dare to give me advice, thou great lump of a houseman's lad!" And he sprang up, drew his sword, and swung it with both hands as if going to cut him down.

But Ottar stood quiet and upright; did not stir from the spot, nor show the slightest sign of fear; and the king turned round the sword-blade which he had waved over Ottar's head, and gently touched him on the shoulder with it. Then he sat down in silence on his high-seat.

All were silent who were in the hall, for nobody dared to say a word. Now the king looked around him, milder than before, and said, "It is difficult to know what there is in people. Here sat my friends, and lendermen, marshals and shield-bearers, and all the best men in the land; but none did so well against me as this man, who appears to you of little worth compared to any of you, although now he loves me most. I came here like a madman, and would have destroyed my precious property; but he turned aside my deed, and was not afraid of death for it. Then he made an able speech, ordering his words so that they were honourable to me, and not saying a single word about things which could increase my vexation; but even avoiding what might, with truth, have been said. So excellent was his speech, that no man here, however great his understanding, could have spoken better. Then I sprang up in a pretended rage, and made as if I would have cut him down; but he was courageous as if he had nothing to fear; and seeing that, I let go my purpose; for he was altogether innocent. Now ye shall know, my friends, how I intend to reward him; he was before my torchbearer, and shall now be my lenderman; and there shall follow what is still more, that he shall be the most distinguished of my lendermen. Go thou and sit among the lendermen, and be a servant no longer."

Ottar became one of the most celebrated men in Norway for various good and praiseworthy deeds.

31. OF KING SIGURD'S DREAM.

In King Sigurd's latter days he was once at an entertainment at one of his farms; and in the morning when he was dressed he was silent and still, so that his friends were afraid he was not able to govern himself. Now the farm bailiff, who was a man of good sense and courage, brought him into conversation, and asked if he had heard any news of such importance that it disturbed his mirth; or if the entertainment had not satisfied him; or if there was anything else that people could remedy.

King Sigurd said, that none of the things he had mentioned was the cause. "But it is that I think upon the dream I had in the night."

"Sire," replied he, "may it prove a lucky dream! I would gladly hear it."

The king: "I thought that I was in Jadar, and looked out towards the sea; and that I saw something very black moving itself; and when it came near it appeared to be a large tree, of which the branches stretched far above the water, and the roots were down in the sea. Now when the tree came to the shore it broke into pieces, and drove all about the land, both the mainland and the out-islands, rocks and strands; and it appeared to me as if I saw over all Norway along the sea-coast, and saw pieces of that tree, some small and some large, driven into every bight."

Then said the bailiff, "It is likely that you an best interpret this dream yourself; and I would willingly hear your interpretation of it."

Then said the king, "This dream appears to me to denote the arrival in this country of some man who will fix his seat here, and whose posterity will spread itself over the land; but with unequal power, as the dream shows."

32. OF ASLAK HANE.

It so happened once, that King Sigurd sat in a gloomy mood among many worthy men. It was Friday evening, and the kitchen-master asked what meat should be made ready.

The king replies, "What else but flesh-meat?" And so harsh were his words that nobody dared to contradict him, and all were ill at ease. Now when people prepared to go to table, dishes of warm flesh-meat were carried in; but all were silent, and grieved at the king's illness. Before the blessing was pronounced over the meat, a man called Aslak Hane spoke. He had been a long time with King Sigurd on his journey abroad, and was not a man of any great family; and was small of stature, but fiery. When he perceived how it was, and that none dared to accost the king, he asked, "What is it, sire, that is smoking on the dish before you?"

The king replies, "What do you mean, Aslak? what do you think it is?"

Aslak: "I think it is flesh-meat; and I would it were not so."

The king: "But if it be so, Aslak?"

He replied, "It would be vexatious to know that a gallant king, who has gained so much honour in the world, should so forget himself. When you rose up out of Jordan, after bathing in the same waters as God himself, with palm-leaves in your hands, and the cross upon your breast, it was something else you promised, sire, than to eat flesh-meat on a Friday. If a meaner man were to do so, he would merit a heavy punishment. This royal hall is not so beset as it should be, when it falls upon me, a mean man, to challenge such an act."

The king sat silent, and did not partake of the meat; and when the time for eating was drawing to an end, the king ordered the flesh dishes to be removed and other food was brought in, such as it is permitted to use. When the meal-time was almost past, the king began to be cheerful, and to drink. People advised Aslak to fly, but he said he would not do so. "I do not see how it could help me; and to tell the truth, it is as good to die now that I have got my will, and have prevented the king from committing a sin. It is for him to kill me if he likes."

Towards evening the king called him, and said, "Who set thee on, Aslak Hane, to speak such free words to me in the hearing of so many people?"

"No one, sire, but myself."

The king: "Thou wouldst like, no doubt, to know what thou art to have for such boldness; what thinkest thou it deserves."

He replies, "If it be well rewarded, sire, I shall be glad; but should it be otherwise, then it is your concern."

Then the king said, "Smaller is thy reward than thou hast deserved. I give thee three farms. It has turned out, what could not have been expected, that thou hast prevented me from a great crime,–thou, and not the lendermen, who are indebted to me for so much good." And so it ended.

33. OF A WOMAN BROUGHT TO THE KING.

ONE YULE EVE THE king sat in the hall, and the tables were laid out, and the king said, "Get me flesh-meat."

They answered, "Sire, it is not the custom to eat flesh-meat on Yule eve."

The king said, "If it be not the custom I will make it the custom."

They went out, and brought him a dolphin. The king stuck his knife into it, but did not eat of it. Then the king said, "Bring me a girl here into the hall." They brought him a woman whose head-dress went far down her brows. The king took her hand in his hands, looked at her, and said, "An ill looking girl!"

((LACUNA–The rest of this story is missing))

34. HARALD GILLE COMES TO NORWAY.

HALKEL HUK, a son of Jon Smiorbalte, who was lenderman in More, made a voyage in the West sea, all the way to the South Hebudes. A man came to him out of Ireland called Gillikrist, and gave himself out for a son of King Magnus Barefoot. His mother came with him, and said his other name was Harald. Halkel received the man, brought him to Norway with him, and went immediately to King Sigurd with Harald and his mother. When they had told their story to the king, he talked over the matter with his principal men, and bade them give their opinions upon it. They were of different opinions, and all left it to the king himself, although there were several who opposed this; and the king followed his own counsel. King Sigurd ordered Harald to be called before him, and told him that he would not deny him the proof, by ordeal, of who his father was; but on condition that if he should prove his descent according to his claim, he should not desire the kingdom in the lifetime of King Sigurd, or of King Magnus: and to this he bound himself by oath. King Sigurd said he must tread over hot iron to prove his birth; but this ordeal was thought by many too severe, as he was to undergo it merely to prove his father, and without getting the kingdom; but Harald agreed to it, and fixed on the trial by iron: and this ordeal was the greatest ever made in Norway; for nine glowing plowshares were laid down, and Harald went over them with bare feet, attended by two bishops.

Three days after the iron trial the ordeal was taken to proof, and the feet were found unburnt. Thereafter King Sigurd acknowledged Harald's relationship; but his son Magnus conceived a great hatred of him, and in this many chiefs followed Magnus. King Sigurd trusted so much to his favour with the whole people of the country, that he desired all men, under oath, to promise to accept Magnus after him as their king; and all the people took this oath.

35. RACE BETWEEN MAGNUS AND HARALD GILLE.

Harald Gille was a tall, slender-grown man, of a long neck and face, black eyes, and dark hair, brisk and quick, and wore generally the Irish dress of short light clothes. The Norse language was difficult for Harald, and he brought out words which many laughed at. Harald sat late drinking one evening. He spoke with another man about different things in the west in Ireland; and among other things, said that there were men in Ireland so swift of foot that no horse could overtake them in running. Magnus, the king's son, heard this, and said, "Now he is lying, as he usually does."

Harald replies, "It is true that there are men in Ireland whom no horse in Norway could overtake." They exchanged some words about this, and both were drunk. Then said Magnus, "Thou shalt make a wager with me, and stake thy head if thou canst not run so fast as I ride upon my horse, and I shall stake my gold ring."

Harald replies, "I did not say that I could run so swiftly; but I said that men are to be found in Ireland who will run as fast; and on that I would wager."

The king's son Magnus replies, "I will not go to Ireland about it; we are wagering here, and not there."

Harald on this went to bed, and would not speak to him more about it. This was in Oslo. The following morning, when the early mass was over, Magnus rode up the street, and sent a message to Harald to come to him. When Harald came he was dressed thus. He had on a shirt and trousers which were bound with ribands under his foot-soles, a short cloak, an Irish hat on his head, and a spear-shaft in his hand. Magnus set up a mark for the race. Harald said, "Thou hast made the course too long;" but Magnus made it at once even much longer, and said it was still too short. There were many spectators. They began the race, and Harald followed always the horse's pace; and when they came to the end of the race course, Magnus said, "Thou hadst hold of the saddle-girth, and the horse dragged thee along." Magnus had his swift runner, the Gautland horse. They began the race again, and Harald ran the whole race-course before the horse. When came to the end Harald asked, "Had I hold of the saddle-girths now?"

Magnus replied, "Thou hadst the start at first."

Then Magnus let his horse breathe a while, and when he was ready he put the spurs to him, and set off in full gallop. Harald stood still, and Magnus looked back, and called, "Set off now."

Then Harald ran quickly past the horse, and came to the end of the course so long before him that he lay down, and got up and saluted Magnus as he came in.

Then they went home to the town. In the meantime King Sigurd had been at high mass, and knew nothing of this until after he had dined that day. Then he said to Magnus angrily, "Thou callest Harald useless; but I think thou art a great fool, and knowest nothing of the customs of foreign people. Dost thou not know that men in other countries exercise themselves in other feats than in filling themselves with ale, and making themselves mad, and so unfit for everything that they scarcely know each other? Give Harald his ring, and do not try to make a fool of him again, as long as I am above ground."

36. OF SIGURD'S SWIMMING.

It happened once that Sigurd was out in his ship, which lay in the harbour; and there lay a merchant ship, which was an Iceland trader, at the side of it. Harald Gille was in the forecastle of the king's ship, and Svein Rimhildson, a son of Knut Sveinson of Jadar, had his berth the next before him. There was also Sigurd Sigurdson, a gallant lenderman, who himself commanded a ship. It was a day of beautiful weather and warm sunshine, and many went out to swim, both from the long-ship and the merchant vessel. An Iceland man, who was among the swimmers, amused himself by drawing those under water who could not swim so well as himself; and at that the spectators laughed. When King Sigurd saw and heard this, he cast off his clothes, sprang into the water, and swam to the Icelander, seized him, and pressed him under the water, and held him there; and as soon as the Icelander came up the king pressed him down again, and thus the one time after the other.

Then said Sigurd Sigurdson, "Shall we let the king kill this man?"

Somebody said, "No one has any wish to interfere."

Sigurd replies, that "If Dag Eilifson were here, we should not be without one who dared."

Then Sigurd sprang overboard, swam to the king, took hold of him, and said, "Sire, do not kill the man. Everybody sees that you are a much better swimmer."

The king replies, "Let me loose, Sigurd: I shall be his death, for he will destroy our people under water."

Sigurd says, "Let us first amuse ourselves; and, Icelander, do thou set off to the land," which he did. The king now got loose from Sigurd, and swam to his ship, and Sigurd went his way: but the king ordered that Sigurd should not presume to come into his presence; this was reported to Sigurd, and so he went up into the country.

37. OF HARALD AND SVEIN RIMHILDSON.

In the evening, when people were going to bed, some of the ship's men were still at their games up in the country. Harald was with those who played on the land, and told his footboy to go out to the ship, make his bed, and wait for him there. The lad did as he was ordered. The king had gone to sleep; and as the boy thought Harald late, he laid himself in Harald's berth. Svein Rimhildson said, "It is a shame for brave men to be brought from their farms at home, and to have here serving boys to sleep beside them." The lad said that Harald had ordered him to come there. Svein Rimhildson said, "We do not so much care for Harald himself lying here, if he do not bring here his slaves and beggars;" and seized a riding-whip, and struck the boy on the head until the blood flowed from him. The boy ran immediately up the country, and told Harald what had happened, who went immediately out to the ship, to the aft part of the forecastle, and with a pole-axe struck Svein so that he received a severe wound on his hands; and then Harald went on shore. Svein ran to the land after him, and, gathering his friends, took Harald prisoner, and they were about hanging him. But while they were busy about this, Sigurd Sigurdson went out to the king's ship and awoke him. When the king opened his eyes and recognised Sigurd, he said. "For this reason thou shalt die, that thou hast intruded into my presence; for thou knowest that I forbade thee:" and with these words the king sprang up.

Sigurd replied, "That is in your power as soon as you please; but other business is more urgent. Go to the land as quickly as possible to help thy brother; for the Rogaland people are going to hang him."

Then said the king, "God give us luck, Sigurd! Call my trumpeter, and let him call the people all to land, and to meet me."

The king sprang on the land, and all who knew him followed him to where the gallows was being erected. The king instantly took Harald to him; and all the people gathered to the king in full armour, as they heard the trumpet. Then the king ordered that Svein and all his comrades should depart from the country as outlaws; but by the intercession of good men the king was prevailed on to let them remain and hold their properties, but no mulct should be paid for Svein's wound.

Then Sigurd Sigurdson asked if the king wished that he should go forth out of the country.

"That will I not," said the king; "for I can never be without thee."

38. OF KING OLAF'S MIRACLE.

THERE WAS A YOUNG and poor man called Kolbein; and Thora, King Sigurd the Crusader's mother, had ordered his tongue to be cut out of his mouth, and for no other cause than that this young man had taken a piece of meat out of the king-mother's tub which he said the cook had given him, and which the cook had not ventured to serve up to her. The man had long gone about speechless. So says Einar Skulason in Olaf's ballad:–

"The proud rich dame, for little cause,
Had the lad's tongue cut from his jaws:
The helpless man, of speech deprived,
His dreadful sore wound scarce survived.
A few weeks since at Hild was seen,
As well as ever he had been,
The same poor lad–to speech restored
By Olaf's power, whom he adored."

Afterwards the young man came to Nidaros, and watched in the Christ church; but at the second mass for Olaf before matins he fell asleep, and thought he saw King Olaf the Saint coming to him; and that Olaf talked to him, and took hold with his hands of the stump of his tongue and pulled it. Now when he awoke he found himself restored, and joyfully did he thank our Lord and the holy Saint Olaf, who had pitied and helped him; for he had come there speechless, and had gone to the holy shrine, and went away cured, and with his speech clear and distinct.

39. KING OLAF'S MIRACLE WITH A PRISONER.

The heathens took prisoner a young man of Danish family and carried him to Vindland, where he was in fetters along with other prisoners. In the day-time he was alone in irons, without a guard; but at night a peasant's son was beside him in the chain, that he might not escape from them. This poor man never got sleep or rest from vexation and sorrow, and considered in many ways what could help him; for he had a great dread of slavery, and was pining with hunger and torture. He could not again expect to be ransomed by his friends, as they had already restored him twice from heathen lands with their own money; and he well knew that it would be difficult and expensive for them to submit a third time to this burden. It is well with the man who does not undergo so much in the world as this man knew he had suffered. He saw but one way; and that was to get off and escape if he could. He resolved upon this in the night-time, killed the peasant, and cut his foot off after killing him, and set off to the forest with the chain upon his leg. Now when the people knew this, soon after daylight in the morning, they pursued him with two dogs accustomed to trace any one who escaped, and to find him in the forest however carefully he might be concealed. They got him into their hands and beat him, and did him all kinds of mischief; and dragging him home, left barely alive, and showed him no mercy. They tortured him severely; put him in a dark room, in which there lay already sixteen Christian men; and bound him both with iron and other tyings, as fast as they could. Then he began to think that the misery and pain he had endured before were but shadows to his present sufferings. He saw no man before his eyes in this prison who would beg for mercy for him; no one had compassion on his wretchedness, except the Christian men who lay bound with him, who sorrowed with him, and bemoaned his fate together with their own misfortunes and helplessness. One day they advised him to make a vow to the holy King Olaf, to devote himself to some office in his sacred house, if he, by God's compassion and Saint Olaf's prayers could get away from this prison. He gladly agreed to this, and made a vow and prepared himself for the situation they mentioned to him. The night after he thought in his sleep that he saw a man, not tall, standing at his side, who spoke to him thus, "Here, thou wretched man, why dost thou not get up?"

He replied, "Sir, who are you?"

"I am King Olaf, on whom thou hast called."

"Oh, my good lord! gladly would I raise myself; but I lie bound with iron and with chains on my legs, and also the other men who lie here."

Thereupon the king accosts him with the words, "Stand up at once and be not afraid; for thou art loose."

He awoke immediately, and told his comrades what, had appeared to him in his dream. They told him to stand up, and try if it was true. He stood up, and observed that he was loose. Now said his fellow-prisoners, this would help him but little, for the door was locked both on the inside and on the outside. Then an old man who sat there in a deplorable condition put in his word, and told him not to doubt the mercy of the man who had loosened his chains; "For he has wrought this miracle on thee that thou shouldst enjoy his mercy, and hereafter be free, without suffering more misery and torture. Make haste, then, and seek the door; and if thou are able to slip out, thou art saved."

He did so, found the door open, slipped out, and away to the forest. As soon as the Vindland people were aware of this they set loose the dogs, and pursued him in great haste; and the poor man lay hid, and saw well where they were following him. But now the hounds lost the trace when they came nearer, and all the eyes that sought him were struck with a blindness, so that nobody could find him, although he lay before their feet; and they all returned home, vexed that they could not find him. King Olaf did not permit this man's destruction after he had reached the forest, and restored him also to his health and hearing; for they had so long tortured and beaten him that he had become deaf. At last he came on board of a ship, with two other Christian men who had been long afflicted in that country. All of them worked zealously in this vessel, and so had a successful flight. Then he repaired to the holy man's house, strong and fit to bear arms. Now he was vexed at his vow, went from his promise to the holy king, ran away one day, and came in the evening to a bonde who gave him lodging for God's sake. Then in the night he saw three girls coming to him; and handsome and nobly dressed were they. They spoke to him directly, and sharply reprimanded him for having been so bold as to run from the good king who had shown so much compassion to him, first in freeing him from his irons, and then from the prison; and yet he had deserted the mild master into whose service he had entered. Then he awoke full of terror, got up early, and told the house-father his dream. The good man had nothing so earnest in life as to send him-back to the holy place. This miracle was first written down by a man who himself saw the man, and the marks of the chains upon his body.

40. KING SIGURD MARRIES CECILIA.

In the last period of King Sigurd's life, his new and extraordinary resolution was whispered about, that he would be divorced from his queen, and would take Cecilia, who was a great man's daughter, to wife. He ordered accordingly a great feast to be prepared, and intended to hold his wedding with her in Bergen. Now when Bishop Magne heard this, he was very sorry; and one day the bishop goes to the king's hall, and with him a priest called Sigurd, who was afterwards bishop of Bergen. When they came to the king's hall, the bishop sent the king a message that he would like to meet him; and asked the king to come out to him. He did so, and came out with a drawn sword in his hand. He received the bishop kindly and asked him to go in and sit down to table with him.

The bishop replies, "I have other business now. Is it true, sire, what is told me, that thou hast the intention of marrying, and of driving away thy queen, and taking another wife?"

The king said it was true.

Then the bishop changed countenance, and angrily replied, "How can it come into your mind, sire, to do such an act in our bishopric as to betray God's word and law, and the holy church? It surprises me that you treat with such contempt our episcopal office, and your own royal office. I will now do what is my duty; and in the name of God, of the holy King Olaf, of Peter the apostle, and of the other saints, forbid thee this wickedness."

While he thus spoke he stood straight up, as if stretching out his neck to the blow, as if ready if the king chose to let the sword fall; and the priest Sigurd, who afterwards was bishop, has declared that the sky appeared to him no bigger than a calf's skin, so frightful did the appearance of the king present itself to him. The king returned to the hall, however, without saying a word; and the bishop went to his house and home so cheerful and gay that he laughed, and saluted every child on his way, and was playing with his fingers. Then the priest Sigurd asked him the reason, saying, "Why are you so cheerful, sir? Do you not consider that the king may be exasperated against you? and would it not be better to get out of the way?"

Then said the bishop, "It appears to me more likely that he will not act so; and besides, what death could be better, or more desirable, than to leave life for the honour of God? or to die for the holy cause of Christianity and our own office, by preventing that which is not right? I am so cheerful because I have done what I ought to do."

There was much noise in the town about this. The king got ready for a journey, and took with him corn, malt and honey. He went south to Stavanger, and prepared a feast there for his marriage with Cecilia. When a bishop who ruled there heard of this he went to the king, and asked if it were true that he intended to marry in the lifetime of the queen.

The king said it was so.

The bishop answers, "If it be so, sire, you must know how much such a thing is forbidden to inferior persons. Now it appears as if you thought it was allowable for you, because you have great power, and that it is proper for you, although it is against right and propriety; but I do not know how you will do it in our bishopric, dishonouring thereby God's command, the holy Church, and our episcopal authority. But you must bestow a great amount of gifts and estates on this foundation, and thereby pay the mulct due to God and to us for such transgression."

Then said the king, "Take what thou wilt of our possessions. Thou art far more reasonable than Bishop Magne."

Then the king went away, as well pleased with this bishop as ill pleased with him who had laid a prohibition on him. Thereafter the king married the girl, and loved her tenderly.

41. IMPROVEMENT OF KONUNGAHELLA.

KING SIGURD IMPROVED the town of Konungahella so much, that there was not a greater town in Norway at the time, and he remained there long for the defence of the frontiers. He built a king's house in the castle, and imposed a duty on all the districts in the neighbourhood of the town, as well as on the townspeople, that every person of nine years of age and upwards should bring to the castle five missile stones for weapons, or as many large stakes sharp at one end and five ells long. In the castle the king built a cross-church of timber, and carefully put together, as far as regards the wood and other materials. The cross-church was consecrated in the 24th year of King Sigurd's reign (A.D. 1127). Here the king deposited the piece of the holy cross, and many other holy relics. It was called the castle church; and before the high altar he placed the tables he had got made in the Greek country, which were of copper and silver, all gilt, and beautifully adorned with jewels. Here was also the shrine which the Danish king Eirik Eimune had sent to King Sigurd; and the altar book, written with gold letters, which the patriarch had presented to King Sigurd.

42. KING SIGURD'S DEATH.

Three years after the consecration of the cross-church, when King Sigurd was stopping at Viken, he fell sick (A.D. 1130). He died the night before Mary's-mass (August 15), and was buried in Halvard's church, where he was laid in the stone wall without the choir on the south side. His son Magnus was in the town at the time and took possession of the whole of the king's treasury when King Sigurd died. Sigurd had been king of Norway twenty-seven years (A.D. 1104-1130), and was forty years of age when he died. The time of his reign was good for the country; for there was peace, and crops were good.

BOOK TWELVE

Saga of Magnus the Blind and of Harald Gille

PRELIMINARY REMARKS

An age of conflict now begins in Norway. On his death, in 1130, Sigurd left his son Magnus and his brother Harald. They soon divided the government, and then entered upon a five-years' conflict, until Magnus, in 1135, with eyes picked out, went into a convent.

The next year, 1136, a new pretender appeared in the person of Sigurd Slembe, who took King Harald's life in 1137. Magnus died in 1139.

Other literature in regard to this epoch is "Fagrskinna" and "Morkinskinna". The corresponding part of "Agrip" is lost.

Skalds quoted are: Haldor Skvaldre, Einar Skulason, and Ivar Ingemundson.

1. MAGNUS AND HARALD PROCLAIMED KINGS.

King Sigurd's son Magnus was proclaimed in Oslo king of all the country immediately after his father's death, according to the oath which the whole nation had sworn to King Sigurd; and many went into his service, and many became his lendermen. Magnus was the handsomest man then in Norway; of a passionate temper, and cruel, but distinguished in bodily exercises. The favour of the people he owed most to the respect for his father. He was a great drinker, greedy of money, hard, and obstinate.

Harald Gille, on the other hand, was very pleasing in intercourse, gay, and full of mirth; and so generous that he spared in nothing for the sake of his friends. He willingly listened to good advice, so that he allowed others to consult with him and give counsel. With all this he obtained favour and a good repute, and many men attached themselves as much to him as to King Magnus. Harald was in Tunsberg when he heard of his brother King Sigurd's death. He called together his friends to a meeting, and it was resolved to hold the Hauga Thing[75] there in the town. At this Thing, Harald was chosen king of half the country, and it was called a forced oath which had been taken from him to renounce his paternal heritage. Then Harald formed a court, and appointed lendermen; and very soon he had as many people about him as King Magnus. Then men went between them, and matters stood in this way for seven days; but King Magnus, finding he had fewer people, was obliged to give way, and to divide the kingdom with Harald into two parts. The kingdom accordingly was so divided (October 3, 1130) that each of them should have the half part of the kingdom which King Sigurd had possessed; but that King Magnus alone should inherit the fleet of ships, the table service, the valuable articles and the movable effects which had belonged to his father, King Sigurd. He was notwithstanding the least satisfied with his share. Although they were of such different dispositions, they ruled the country for some time in peace. King Harald had a son called Sigurd, by Thora, a daughter of Guthorm Grabarde. King Harald afterwards married Ingerid, a daughter of Ragnvald, who was a son of the Swedish King Inge Steinkelson. King Magnus was married to a daughter of Knut Lavard, and she was a sister of the Danish King Valdernar; but King Magnus having no affection for her, sent her back to Denmark; and from that day everything went ill with him, and he brought upon himself the enmity of her family.

2. OF THE FORCES OF HARALD AND MAGNUS.

When the two relations, Harald and Magnus, had been about three years kings of Norway (A.D. 1131-1133), they both passed the fourth winter (A.D. 1134) in the town of Nidaros, and invited each other as guests; but their people were always ready for a fight. In spring King Magnus sailed southwards along the land with his fleet, and drew all the

75 Hauga-thing means a Thing held at the tumuli or burial mounds.–L.

men he could obtain out of each district, and sounded his friends if they would strengthen him with their power to take the kingly dignity from Harald, and give him such a portion of the kingdom, as might be suitable; representing to them that King Harald had already renounced the kingdom by oath. King Magnus obtained the consent of many powerful men. The same spring Harald went to the Uplands, and by the upper roads eastwards to Viken; and when he heard what King Magnus was doing, he also drew together men on his side. Wheresoever the two parties went they killed the cattle, or even the people, upon the farms of the adverse party. King Magnus had by far the most people, for the main strength of the country lay open to him for collecting men from it. King Harald was in Viken on the east side of the fjord, and collected men, while they were doing each other damage in property and life. King Harald had with him Kristrod, his brother by his mother's side, and many other lendermen; but King Magnus had many more. King Harald was with his forces at a place called Fors in Ranrike, and went from thence towards the sea. The evening before Saint Lawrence day (August 10), they had their supper at a place called Fyrileif, while the guard kept a watch on horseback all around the house. The watchmen observed King Magnus's army hastening towards the house, and consisting of full 6000 men, while King Harald had but 1500. Now come the watchmen who had to bring the news to King Harald of what was going on and say that King Magnus's army was now very near the town.

The king says, "What will my relation King Magnus Sigurdson have? He wants not surely to fight us."

Thjostolf Alason replies, "You must certainly, sire, make preparation for that, both for yourself and your men. King Magnus has been drawing together an army all the summer for the purpose of giving you battle when he meets you."

Then King Harald stood up, and ordered his men to take their arms. "We shall fight, if our relative King Magnus wants to fight us."

Then the war-horns sounded, and all Harald's men went out from the house to an enclosed field, and set up their banners. King Harald had on two shirts of ring-mail, but his brother Kristrod had no armour on; and a gallant man he was. When King Magnus and his men saw King Harald's troop they drew up and made their array, and made their line so long that they could surround the whole of King Harald's troop. So says Haldor Skvaldre:–

"King Magnus on the battle-plain
From his long troop-line had great gain;

The plain was drenched with warm blood,
Which lay a red and reeking flood."

3. BATTLE AT FYRILEIF.

King Magnus had the holy cross carried before him in this battle, and the battle was great and severe. The king's brother, Kristrod, had penetrated with his troop into the middle of King Magnus's array, and cut down on each side of him, so that people gave way before him everywhere. But a powerful bonde who was in King Harald's array raised his spear with both hands, and drove it through between Kristrod's shoulders, so that it came out at his breast; and thus fell Kristrod. Many who were near asked the bonde why he had done so foul a deed.

The bonde replies, "He knows the consequences now of slaughtering my cattle in summer, and taking all that was in my house, and forcing me to follow him here. I determined to give him some return when the opportunity came."

After this King Harald's army took to flight, and he fled himself, with all his men. Many fell; and Ingemar Sveinson of Ask, a great chief and lenderman, got there his death-wound, and nearly sixty of King Harald's court-men also fell. Harald himself fled eastward to Viken to his ships, and went out of the country to King Eirik Eimune in Denmark, and found him in Seeland and sought aid from him. King Eirik received him well, and principally because they had sworn to each other to be as brothers[76]; and gave him Halland as a fief to rule over, and gave him seven long-ships, but without equipment. Thereafter King Harald went northwards through Halland, and many Northmen came to meet him. After this battle King Magnus subdued the whole country, giving life and safety to all who were wounded, and had them taken care of equally with his own men. He then called the whole country his own, and had a choice of the best men who were in the country. When they held a council among themselves afterwards, Sigurd Sigurdson, Thorer Ingeridson, and all the men of most understanding, advised that they should keep their forces together in Viken, and remain there, in case Harald should return from the south; but King Magnus would take his own way, and went

76 These brotherhoods, by which one man was bound by oath to aid or avenge another, were common in the Middle Ages among all ranks. "Sworn brothers" is still a common expression with us.–L.

north to Bergen. There he sat all winter (A.D. 1135), and allowed his men to leave him; on which the lendermen returned home to their own houses.

4. DEATH OF ASBJORN AND OF NEREID.

King Harald came to Konungahella with the men who had followed him from Denmark. The lendermen and town's burgesses collected a force against him, which they drew up in a thick array above the town. King Harald landed from his ships, and sent a message to the bondes, desiring that they would not deny him his land, as he wanted no more than what of right belonged to him. Then mediators went between them; and it came to this, that the bondes dismissed their troops, and submitted to him. Thereupon he bestowed fiefs and property on the lendermen, that they might stand by him, and paid the bondes who joined him the lawful mulcts for what they had lost. A great body of men attached themselves, therefore, to King Harald; and he proceeded westwards to Viken, where he gave peace to all men, except to King Magnus's people, whom he plundered and killed wherever he found them. And when he came west to Sarpsborg he took prisoners two of King Magnus s lendermen, Asbjorn and his brother Nereid; and gave them the choice that one should be hanged, and the other thrown into the Sarpsborg waterfall, and they might choose as they pleased. Asbjorn chose to be thrown into the cataract, for he was the elder of the two, and this death appeared the most dreadful; and so it was done. Halder Skvaldre tells of this:–

"Asbjorn, who opposed the king,
O'er the wild cataract they fling:
Nereid, who opposed the king,
Must on Hagbard's high tree swing.
The king given food in many a way
To foul-mouthed beasts and birds of prey:
The generous men who dare oppose
Are treated as the worst of foes."

Thereafter King Harald proceeded north to Tunsberg, where he was well received, and a large force gathered to him.

5. OF THE COUNSELS PROPOSED.

When King Magnus, who was in Bergen, heard these tidings, he called together all the chiefs who were in the town, and asked them their counsel, and what they should now do. Then Sigurd Sigurdson said, "Here I can give a good advice. Let a ship be manned with good men, and put me, or any other lenderman, to command it; send it to thy relation, King Harald, and offer him peace according to the conditions upright men may determine upon, and offer him the half of the kingdom. It appears to me probable that King Harald, by the words and counsel of good men, may accept this offer, and thus there may be a peace established between you."

Then King Magnus replied, "This proposal I will not accept of; for of what advantage would it be, after we have gained the whole kingdom in summer to give away the half of it now? Give us some other counsel."

Then Sigurd Sigurdson answered, "It appears to me, sire, that your lendermen who in autumn asked your leave to return home will now sit at home and will not come to you. At that time it was much against my advice that you dispersed so entirely the people we had collected; for I could well suppose that Harald would come back to Viken as soon as he heard that it was without a chief. Now there is still another counsel, and it is but a poor one; but it may turn out useful to us. Send out your pursuivants, and send other people with them, and let them go against the lendermen who will not join you in your necessity, and kill them; and bestow their property on others who will give you help although they may have been of small importance before. Let them drive together the people, the bad as well as the good; and go with the men you can thus assemble against King Harald, and give him battle."

The king replies, "It would be unpopular to put to death people of distinction, and raise up inferior people who often break faith and law, and the country would be still worse off. I would like to hear some other counsel still."

Sigurd replies, "It is difficult for me now to give advice, as you will neither make peace nor give battle. Let us go north to Throndhjem, where the main strength of the country is most inclined to our side; and on the way let us gather all the men we can. It may be that these Elfgrims will be tired of such a long stride after us."

The king replies, "We must not fly from those whom we beat in summer. Give some better counsel still."

Then Sigurd stood up and said, while he was preparing to go out, "I will now give you the counsel which I see you will take, and which must have its course. Sit here in Bergen until Harald comes with his troops, and then you will either suffer death or disgrace."

And Sigurd remained no longer at that meeting.

6. OF HARALD'S FORCE.

King Harald came from the East along the coast with a great army, and this winter (A.D. 1135) is called on that account the Crowd-winter. King Harald came to Bergen on Christmas eve, and landed with his fleet at Floruvagar; but would not fight on account of the sacred time. But King Magnus prepared for defence in the town. He erected a stone-slinging machine out on the holm, and had iron chains and wooden booms laid across over the passage from the king's house to Nordnes, and to the Monks bridge. He had foot-traps made, and thrown into Saint John's field, and did not suspend these works except during the three sacred days of Christmas. The last holyday of Yule, King Harald ordered his war-horns to sound the gathering of his men for going to the town; and, during the Yule holydays, his army had been increased by about 900 men.

7. KING MAGNUS TAKEN PRISONER.

King Harald made a promise to King Olaf the Saint for victory, that he would build an Olaf's church in the town at his own expense. King Magnus drew up his men in the Christ church yard; but King Harald laid his vessels first at Nordnes. Now when King Magnus and his people saw that, they turned round towards the town, and to the end of the shore; but as they passed through the streets many of the burgesses ran into their houses and homes, and those who went across the fields fell into the foot-traps. Then King Magnus and his men perceived that King Harald had rowed with all his men across to Hegravik, and landed there, and had gone from thence the upper road up the hill opposite the town. Now Magnus returned back again through the streets, and then his men fled from him in all directions; some up to the mountains, some up to the neighbourhood of the convent of nuns, some to churches, or hid themselves as they best could. King Magnus fled to his ship; but there was no possibility of getting away, for the iron chains outside prevented the passage of vessels. He had also but few men with him, and therefore could do nothing. Einar Skulason tells of this in the song of Harald:–

"For a whole week an iron chain
Cut off all sailing to the main:
Bergen's blue stable was locked fast,–
Her floating wains could not get past."

Soon after Harald's people came out to the ships, and then King Magnus was made prisoner. He was sitting behind in the forecastle upon the chests of the high-seat, and at his side Hakon Fauk, his mother's brother, who was very popular but was not considered very wise, and Ivar Assurson. They, and many others of King Magnus's friends, were taken, and some of them killed on the spot.

8. KING MAGNUS MUTILATED.

Thereafter King Harald had a meeting of his counsellors, and desired their counsel; and in this meeting the judgment was given that Magnus should be deposed from his dominions, and should no longer be called king. Then he was delivered to the king's slaves, who mutilated him, picked out both his eyes, cut off one foot, and at last castrated him. Ivar Assurson was blinded, and Hakon Fauk killed. The whole country then was reduced to obedience under King Harald. Afterwards it was diligently examined who were King Magnus's best friends, or who knew most of his concealments of treasure or valuables. The holy cross King Magnus had kept beside him since the battle of Fyrileif, but would not tell where it was deposited for preservation. Bishop Reinald of Stavanger, who was an Englishman, was considered very greedy of money. He was a great friend of King Magnus, and it was thought likely that great treasure and valuables had been given into his keeping. Men were sent for him accordingly, and he came to Bergen, where it was insisted against him that he had some knowledge of such treasure; but he denied it altogether, would not admit it, and offered to clear himself by ordeal. King Harald would not have this, but laid on the bishop a money fine of fifteen marks of gold, which he should pay to the king. The bishop declared he would not thus impoverish his bishop's see, but would rather offer his life. On this they hanged the bishop out on the holm, beside the sling machine. As he was going to the gallows he threw the sock from his foot, and said with an oath, "I know no more about King Magnus's treasure than what is in this sock;" and in it there was a gold ring. Bishop Reinald was buried at Nordnes in Michael's church, and this deed was much blamed. After this Harald Gille was sole king of Norway as long as he lived.

9. WONDERFUL OMENS IN KONUNGAHELLA.

Five years after King Sigurd's death remarkable occurrences took place in Konungahella (A.D. 1135). Guthorm, a son of Harald Fletter, and Saemund Husfreyja, were at that time the king's officers there. Saemund was married to Ingebjorg, a daughter of the priest Andres Brunson. Their sons were Paul Flip and Gunne Fis. Saemund's natural son was called Asmund. Andres Brunson was a very remarkable man, who carried on divine service in the Cross church. His wife[77] was called Solveig. Jon Loptson, who was then eleven years old, was in their house to be fostered and educated. The priest Lopt Saemundson, Jon's father, was also in the town at that time. The priest Andres and Solveig had a daughter by name Helga, who was Einar's wife. It happened now in Konungahella, the next Sunday night after Easter week, that there was a great noise in the streets through the whole town as if the king was going through with all his court-men. The dogs were so affected that nobody could hold them, but they slipped loose; and when they came out they ran mad, biting all that came in their way, people and cattle. All who were bitten by them till the blood came turned raging mad; and pregnant women were taken in labour prematurely, and became mad. From Easter to Ascension-day, these portentous circumstances took place almost every night. People were dreadfully alarmed at these wonders; and many made themselves ready to remove, sold their houses, and went out to the country districts, or to other towns. The most intelligent men looked upon it as something extremely remarkable; were in dread of it; and said, as it proved to be, that it was an omen of important events which had not yet taken place. And the priest Andres, on Whit Sunday, made a long and excellent speech, and turned the conclusion of it to the distressing situation of the townspeople; telling them to muster courage, and not lay waste their excellent town by deserting it, but rather to take the utmost care in all things, and use the greatest foresight against all dangers, as of fire or the enemy, and to pray to God to have mercy on them.

10. THE RISE OF WAR IN KONUNGAHELLA.

Thirteen loaded merchant ships made ready to leave the town, intending to proceed to Bergen; but eleven of them were lost, men and

77 The Catholic priests appear to have had wives at that time in Norway, and celibacy to have been confined to the monks. –L.

goods, and all that was in them; the twelfth was lost also, but the people were saved, although the cargo went to the bottom. At that time the priest Lopt went north to Bergen, with all that belonged to him, and arrived safely. The merchant vessels were lost on Saint Lawrence eve (August 10). The Danish king Eirik and the Archbishop Assur, both sent notice to Konungahella to keep watch on their town; and said the Vindland people had a great force on foot with which they made war far around on Christian people, and usually gained the victory. But the townspeople attended very little to this warning, were indifferent, and forgot more and more the dreadful omens the longer it was since they happened. On the holy Saint Lawrence day, while the words of high mass were spoken, came to the Vindland king Rettibur to Konungahella with 550 Vindland cutters, and in each cutter were forty-four men and two horses. The king's sister's son Dunimiz, and Unibur, a chief who ruled over many people, were with him. These two chiefs rowed at once, with a part of their troops, up the east arm of the Gaut river past Hising Isle, and thus came down to the town; but a part of the fleet lay in the western arm, and came so to the town. They made fast their ships at the piles, and landed their horses, and rode over the height of Bratsas, and from thence up around the town. Einar, a relation of priest Andres, brought these tidings up to the Castle church; for there the whole inhabitants of the town were gathered to hear high mass. Einar came just as the priest Andres was holding his discourse; and he told the people that an army was sailing up against the town with a great number of ships of war, and that some people were riding over Bratsas. Many said it must be the Danish king Eirik, and from him they might expect peace. The people ran down into the town to their properties, armed themselves, and went down upon the piers, whence they immediately saw there was an enemy and an immense army. Nine East-country trading vessels belonging to the merchants were afloat in the river at the piers. The Vindland people first directed their course toward these and fought with the merchants, who armed themselves, and defended themselves long, well, and manfully. There was a hard battle, and resistance, before the merchant vessels were cleared of their men; and in this conflict the Vindland people lost 150 of their ships, with all the men on board. When the battle was sharpest the townsmen stood upon the piers, and shot at the heathens. But when the fight slackened the burgesses fled up to the town, and from thence into the castle; and the men took with them all their valuable articles, and such goods as they could carry. Solveig and her daughters, with two other women, went on shore when the Vindlanders took possession of the merchant vessels. Now the Vindlanders landed, and mustered their men, and discovered their loss. Some of them went up into the town, some on board the merchant ships, and took all the goods they pleased; and then they set fire to the town, and burnt it and the ships. They hastened then with all their army to assault the castle.

11. THE SECOND BATTLE.

King Rettibur made an offer to those who were in the castle that they should go out, and he would give them their lives, weapons, clothes, silver, and gold; but all exclaimed against it, and went out on the fortification; some shot, some threw stones, some sharp stakes. It was a great battle, in which many fell on both sides, but by far the most of the Vindlanders. Solveig came up to a large farm called Solbjorg, and brought the news. A message war-token was there split, and sent out to Skurbagar, where there happened to be a joint ale-drinking feast, and many men were assembled. A bonde called Olver Miklimun (Mickle Mouth) was there, who immediately sprang up, took helmet and shield, and a great axe in his hand, and said, "Stand up, brave lads, and take your weapons. Let us go help the townspeople; for it would appear shameful to every man who heard of it, if we sit here sipping our ale, while good men in the town are losing their lives by our neglect."

Many made an objection, and said they would only be losing their own lives, without being of any assistance to the townspeople.

Then said Olver, "Although all of you should hold back, I will go alone; and one or two heathens, at any rate, shall fall before I fall."

He ran down to the town, and a few men after him to see what he would do, and also whether they could assist him in any way. When he came near the castle, and the heathens saw him, they sent out eight men fully armed against him; and when they met, the heathen men ran and surrounded him on all sides. Olver lifted his axe, and struck behind him with the extreme point of it, hitting the neck of the man who was coming up behind him, so that his throat and jawbone were cut through, and he fell dead backwards. Then he heaved his axe forwards, and struck the next man in the head, and clove him down to the shoulders. He then fought with the others, and killed two of them; but was much wounded himself. The four who remained took to flight, but Olver ran after them. There was a ditch before them, and two of the heathens jumped into it, and Olver killed them both; but he stuck fast himself in the ditch, so that two of the eight heathens escaped. The men who had followed Olver took him up, and brought him back to Skurbagar, where his wounds were bound and healed; and it was the talk of the people, that no single man had ever made such a bloody onset. Two lendermen, Sigurd Gyrdson, a brother of Philip, and Sigard, came with 600 men to Skurbagar; on which Sigurd turned back with 400 men. He was but little respected afterwards, and soon died. Sigard, on the other hand, proceeded with 200 men towards the town; and they gave battle to the heathens, and were all slain. While the Vindlanders were storming the castle, their king and his chiefs were out of the battle. At one place there was a man among the Vindlanders shooting with a bow, and killing a man for every arrow; and two men stood before him, and covered him with their shields. Then Saemund Husfreyja said to his son Asmund, that they should both shoot together at this bowman. "But I will shoot at the man who holds the shield before him." He did so, and he knocked the shield down a little before the man; and in the same instant Asmund shot between the shields, and the arrow hit the bowman in the forehead, so that it came out at his neck, and he fell down dead. When the Vindlanders saw it they howled like dogs, or like wolves. Then King Rettibur called to them that he would give them safety and life, but they refused terms. The heathens again made a hard assault. One of the heathens in particular fought so bravely, and ventured so near, that he came quite up to the castle-gate, and pierced the man who stood outside the gate with his sword; and although they used both arrows and stones against him, and he had neither shield nor helmet, nothing could touch him, for he was so skilled in witchcraft that weapon could not wound him. Then priest Andres took consecrated fire; blew upon it; cut tinder in pieces, and laid it on the fire; and then laid the tinder on the arrow-point, and gave it to Asmund. He shot this arrow at the warlock; and the shaft hit so well that it did its business, and the man of witchcraft fell dead. Then the heathens crowded together as before, howling and whining dreadfully; and all gathered about their king, on which the Christians believed that they were holding a council about retreating. The interpreters, who understood the Vindland tongue, heard the chief Unibur make the following speech: "These people are brave, and it is difficult to make anything of them; and even if we took all the goods in their town, we might willingly give as much more that we had never come here, so great has been our loss of men and chiefs. Early in the day, when we began to assault the castle, they defended themselves first with arrows and spears; then they fought against us with stones; and now with sticks and staves, as against dogs. I see from this that they are in want of weapons and means of defense; so we shall make one more hard assault, and try their strength." It was as he said, that they now fought with stakes; because, in the first assault, they had imprudently used up all their missile weapons and stones; and now when the Christians saw the number of their stakes diminishing, they clave each stake in two. The heathens now made a very hot attack, and rested themselves between whiles, and on both sides they were exhausted. During a rest the Vindland king Rettibur again offered terms, and that they should retain the weapons, clothes, and silver they could carry out of the castle. Saemund Husfreyja had fallen, and the men who remained gave the counsel to deliver up the castle and themselves into the power of the heathens; but it was a foolish counsel; for the heathens did not keep their promises, but took all people, men, women, and children, and killed all of them who were wounded or young, or could not easily be carried with them. They took all the goods that were in the castle; went into the Cross church, and plundered it of all its ornaments. The priest Andres gave King Rettibur a silver-mounted gilt sceptre, and to his sister's son Dunimiz he gave a gold ring. They supposed from this that he was a man of great importance in the town, and held him in higher respect than the others. They took away with them the holy cross, and also the tables which stood before the altar, which Sigurd had got made in the Greek country, and had brought home himself. These they took, and laid flat down on the steps before the altar. Then the heathens went out of the church. Rettibur said, "This house has been adorned with great zeal for the God to whom it is dedicated; but, methinks, He has shown little regard for the town or house: so I see their God has been angry at those who defended them." King Rettibur gave the priest Andres the church, the shrine, the holy cross, the Bible, the altar-book, and four clerks (prisoners); but the heathens burnt the Castle church, and all the houses that were in the castle. As the fire they had set to the church went out twice, they hewed the church down, and then it burnt like other houses. Then the heathens went to their ships with the booty; but when they mustered their people and saw their loss, they made prisoners of all the people, and divided them among the vessels. Now priest Andres went on board the king's ship with the holy cross, and there came a great terror over the heathens on account of the portentous circumstance which took place in the king's ship; namely, it became so hot that all thought they were to be burnt up. The king ordered the interpreter to ask the priest why this happened. He replied, that the Almighty God on whom the Christians believed, sent them a proof of His anger, that they who would not believe in their Creator presumed to lay hands on the emblem of His suffering; and that there lay so much power in the cross, that such, and even clearer miracles, happened to heathen men who had taken the cross in their hands. The king had the priest put into the ship's boat, and the priest Andres carried the holy cross in his grasp. They led the boat along past the ship's bow, and then along the side of the next ship, and then shoved it with a boat-hook in beside the pier. Then Andres went with the cross by night to Solbjorg, in rain and dreadful weather; but brought it in good preservation. King Rettibur, and the men he had remaining, went home to Vindland, and many of the people who were taken at Konungahella were long afterwards in slavery in Vindland; and those who were ransomed and came back to Norway to their udal lands and properties, throve worse than before their capture. The merchant town of Konungahella has never since risen to the importance it was of before this event.

12. OF MAGNUS THE BLIND.

King Magnus, after he was deprived of sight, went north to Nidaros, where he went into the cloister on the holm, and assumed the monk's dress. The cloister received the farm of Great Hernes in Frosta for his support. King Harald alone ruled the country the following winter, gave all men peace and pardon who desired it, and took many of the men into his court-service who had been with King Magnus. Einar Skulason says that King Harald had two battles in Denmark; the one at Hvedn Isle, and the other at Hlesey Isle:–

"Unwearied champion! who wast bred
To stain thy blue-edged weapons red!
Beneath high Hvedn's rocky shore,
The faithless felt thy steel once more."

And again, thus:–

"On Hlesey's plain the foe must quail
'Fore him who dyes their shirts of mail.
His storm-stretched banner o'er his head
Flies straight, and fills the foe with dread."

13. OF KING HARALD GILLE AND BISHOP MAGNUS.

King Harald Gille was a very generous man. It is told that in his time Magnus Einarson came from Iceland to be consecrated a bishop, and the king received him well, and showed him much respect. When the bishop was ready to sail for Iceland again, and the ship was rigged out for sea, he went to the hall where the king was drinking, saluted him politely and warmly, and the king received him joyfully. The queen was sitting beside the king.

Then said the king, "Are you ready, bishop, for your voyage?"

He replied that he was.

The king said, "You come to us just now at a bad time; for the tables are just removed, and there is nothing at hand suitable to present to you. What is there to give the bishop?"

The treasurer replies, "Sire, as far as I know, all articles of any value are given away."

The king: "Here is a drinking goblet remaining; take this, bishop; it is not without value."

The bishop expressed his thanks for the honour shown him.

Then said the queen, "Farewell, bishop! and a happy voyage."

The king said to her, "When did you ever hear a noble lady say so to a bishop without giving him something?"

She replies, "Sire, what have I to give him?"

The king: "Thou hast the cushion under thee."

Thereupon this, which was covered with costly cloth, and was a valuable article, was given to the bishop. When the bishop was going away the king took the cushion from under himself and gave it him, saying, "They have long been together." When the bishop arrived in Iceland to his bishop's see, it was talked over what should be done with the goblet that would be serviceable for the king; and when the bishop asked the opinion of other people, many thought it should be sold, and the value bestowed on the poor. Then said the bishop, "I will take another plan. I will have a chalice made of it for this church, and consecrate it, so that all the saints of whom there are relics in this church shall let the king have some good for his gift every time a mass is sung over it." This chalice has since belonged to the bishopric of Skalholt; and of the costly cloth with which the cushions given him by the king were covered, were made the choristers' cloaks which are now in Skalholt. From this the generous spirit of King Harald may be seen, as well as from many other things, of which but a few are set down here.

14. BEGINNING OF SIGURD SLEMBIDJAKN.

There was a man, by name Sigurd, who was brought up in Norway, and was called priest Adalbrikt's son. Sigurd's mother was Thora, a daughter of Saxe of Vik, a sister of Sigrid, who was mother of King Olaf Magnuson, and of Kare, the king's brother who married Borghild, a daughter of Dag Eilifson. Their sons were Sigurd of Austrat and Dag. Sigurd of Austrat's sons were Jon of Austrat, Thorstein, and Andres the Deaf. Jon was married to Sigrid, a sister of King Inge and of Duke Skule. This Sigurd, in his childhood, was kept at his book, became a clerk, and was consecrated a deacon; but as he ripened in years and strength he became a very clever man, stout, strong, distinguished for all perfections and exercises beyond any of his years,–indeed, beyond any man in Norway. Sigurd showed early traces of a haughty ungovernable spirit, and was therefore called Slembidjakn. He was as handsome a man as could be seen, with rather thin but beautiful hair. When it came to Sigurd's ears that his mother said King Magnus was his father, he laid aside all clerkship; and as soon as he was old enough to be his own master, he left the country. He was a long time on his travels, went to Palestine; was at the Jordan river; and visited many holy places, as pilgrims usually do. When he came back, he applied himself to trading expeditions. One winter he was in Orkney with Earl Harald, and was with him when Thorkel Fostre Summarlidason was killed. Sigurd was also in Scotland with the Scottish king David, and was held in great esteem by him. Thereafter Sigurd went to Denmark; and according to the account of himself and his men, he there submitted to the iron ordeal to confirm his paternal descent, and proved by it, in the presence of five bishops, that he was a son of King Magnus Barefoot. So says Ivar Ingemundson, in Sigurd's song:–

"The holiest five
Of men alive,–
Bishops were they,–
Solemnly say,
The iron glowing
Red hot, yet showing
No scaith on skin,
Proves cause and kin."

King Harald Gille's friends, however, said this was only a lie, and deceit of the Danes.

15. SIGURD IN ICELAND.

It is told before of Sigurd that he passed some years in merchant voyages, and he came thus to Iceland one winter, and took up his lodging with Thorgils Odson in Saurby; but very few knew where he was. In autumn, when the sheep were being driven into a fold to be slaughtered, a sheep that was to be caught ran to Sigurd; and as Sigurd thought the sheep ran to him for protection, he stretched out his hands to it and lifted it over the fold dyke, and let it run to the hills, saying, "There are not many who seek help from me, so I may well help this one." It happened the same winter that a woman had committed a theft, and Thorgils, who was angry at her for it, was going to punish her; but she ran to Sigurd to ask his help, and he set her upon the bench by his side. Thorgils told him to give her up, and told him what she had committed; but Sigurd begged forgiveness for her since she had come to him for protection, and that Thorgils would dismiss the complaint against her, but Thorgils insisted that she should receive her punishment. When Sigurd saw that Thorgils would not listen to his entreaty, he started up, drew his sword, and bade him take her if he dared; and Thorgils seeing that Sigurd would defend the woman by force of arms, and observing his commanding mien, guessed who he must be, desisted from pursuing the woman, and pardoned her. There were many foreign men there, and Sigurd made the least appearance among them. One day Sigurd came into the sitting-room, and a Northman who was splendidly clothed was playing chess with one of Thorads house-servants. The Northman called Sigurd, and asked him his advice how to play; but when Sigurd looked at the board, he saw the game was lost. The man who was playing against the Northman had a sore foot, so that one toe was bruised, and matter was coming out of it. Sigurd, who was sitting on the bench, takes a straw, and draws it along the floor, so that some young kittens ran after it. He drew the straw always before them, until they came near the house-servant's foot, who jumping up with a scream, threw the chessmen in disorder on the board; and thus it was a dispute how the game had stood. This is given as a proof of Sigurd's cunning. People did not know that he was a learned clerk until the Saturday before Easter, when he consecrated the holy water with chant; and the longer he stayed there the more he was esteemed. The summer after, Sigurd told Thorgils before they parted, that he might with all confidence address his friends to Sigurd Slembidjakn. Thorgils asked how nearly he was related to him, on which he replies, "I am Sigurd Slembidjakn, a son of King Magnus Barefoot." He then left Iceland.

16. OF SIGURD SLEMBE.

When Harald Gille had been six years (A.D. 1136), king of Norway, Sigurd came to the country and went to his brother King Harald, and found him in Bergen. He placed himself entirely in the king's hands, disclosed who his father was, and asked him to acknowledge their relationship. The king gave him no hasty or distinct reply; but laid the matter before his friends in a conference at a specially appointed meeting. After this conference it became known that the king laid an accusation against Sigurd, because he had been at the killing of Thorkel Fostre in the West. Thorkel had accompanied Harald to Norway when he first came to the country, and had been one of Harald's best friends. This case was followed up so severely, that a capital accusation against Sigurd was made, and, by the advice of the lendermen, was carried so far, that some of the king's pursuivants went one evening late to Sigurd, and called him to them. They then took a boat and rowed away with Sigurd from the town south to Nordnes. Sigurd sat on a chest in the stern of the boat, and had his suspicions that foul play was intended. He was clothed in blue trousers, and over his shirt he had a hood tied with ribands, which served him for a cloak. He sat looking down, and holding his hood-strings; and sometimes moved them over his head, sometimes let them fall again before him. Now when they had passed the ness, they were drunk, and merry, were rowing so eagerly that they were not taking notice of anything. Sigurd stood up, and went on the boat's deck; but the two men who were placed to guard him stood up also, and followed him to the side of the vessel, holding by his cloak, as is the custom in guarding people of distinction. As he was afraid that they would catch hold of more of his clothes, he seized them both, and leaped overboard with them. The boat, in the meantime, had gone on a long way, and it was a long time before those on board could turn the vessel, and long before they could get their own men taken on board again; and Sigurd dived under water, and swam so far away that he reached the land before they could get the boat turned to pursue him. Sigurd, who was very swift of foot, hied up to the mountains, and the king's men travelled about the whole night seeking him without finding him. He lay down in a cleft of the rocks; and as he was very cold he took off his trousers, cut a hole in the seat of them, and stuck his head through it, and put his arms in the legs of them. He escaped with life this time; and the king's men returned, and could not conceal their unsuccessful adventure.

17. TREACHERY TOWARDS KING HARALD.

SIGURD THOUGHT NOW THAT it would be of no use to seek any help from King Harald again; and he kept himself concealed all the autumn and the beginning of the winter. He lay hid in Bergen, in the house of a priest. King Harald was also in the town, and many great people with him. Now Sigurd considered how, with his friends' help, he might take the king by surprise, and make an end of him. Many men took part in this design; and among them some who were King Harald's court-men and chamberlains, but who had formerly been King Magnus's court-men. They stood in great favour with the king, and some of them sat constantly at the king's table. On Saint Lucia's day (December 13), in the evening when they proposed to execute this treason, two men sat at the king's table talking together; and one of them said to the king, "Sire, we two table-companions submit our dispute to your judgment, having made a wager of a basket of honey to him who guesses right. I say that you will sleep this night with your Queen Ingerid; and he says that you will sleep with Thora, Guthorm's daughter."

The king answered laughing, and without suspecting in the least that there lay treachery under the question, that he who had asked had lost his bet.

They knew thus where he was to be found that night; but the main guard was without the house in which most people thought the king would sleep, viz., that which the queen was in.

18. MURDER OF KING HARALD.

SIGURD SLEMBE, and some men who were in his design, came in the night to the lodging in which King Harald was sleeping; killed the watchman first; then broke open the door, and went in with drawn swords. Ivar Kolbeinson made the first attack on King Harald; and as the king had been drunk when he went to bed he slept sound, and awoke only when the men were striking at him. Then he said in his sleep, "Thou art treating me hardly, Thora." She sprang up, saying, "They are treating thee hardly who love thee less than I do." Harald was deprived of life. Then Sigurd went out with his helpers, and ordered the men to be called to him who had promised him their support if he should get King Harald taken out of the way. Sigurd and his men then went on, and took a boat, set themselves to the oars, and rowed out in front of the king's house; and then it was just beginning to be daylight.

Then Sigurd stood up, spoke to those who were standing on the king's pier, made known to them the murder of King Harald by his hand, and desired that they would take him, and choose him as chief according to his birth. Now came many swarming down to the pier from the king's house; and all with one voice replied, that they would never give obedience or service to a man who had murdered his own brother. "And if thou are not his brother, thou hast no claim from descent to be king." They clashed their weapons together, and adjudged all murderers to be banished and outlawed men. Now the king's horn sounded, and all lendermen and courtmen were called together. Sigurd and his companions saw it was best for them to get way; and he went northward to North Hordaland, where he held a Thing with the bondes, who submitted to him, and gave him the title of king. From thence he went to Sogn, and held a Thing there with the bondes and was proclaimed king. Then he went north across the fjords, and most people supported his cause. So says Ivar Ingemundson:–

"On Harald's fall
The bondes all,
In Hord and Sogn,
Took Magnus' son.
The Things swore too
They would be true
To this new head
In Harald's stead."

King Harald was buried in the old Christ church.

BOOK THIRTEEN

Saga of Sigurd, Inge, and Eystein, the Sons of Harald

PRELIMINARY REMARKS.

Sigurd died A.D. 1155, Eystein 1157, and Inge 1161.

Other literature is "Morkinskinna" and "Fagrskinna."

Sigurd Slembe is the subject of a drama by Bjornstjerne Bjornson, translated into English by William Morton Payne, and published by Houghton, Mifflin & Co., Boston, 1888.

Skalds quoted are: Kolle, Einar Skulason, and Thorbjorn Skakkaskald.

1. HISTORY OF KINGS SIGURD AND INGE.

Queen Ingerid, and with her the lendermen and the court which had been with King Harald, resolved to send a fast-sailing vessel to Throndhjem to make known King Harald's death, and also to desire the Throndhjem people to take King Harald's son Sigurd for king. He was then in the north, and was fostered by Sadagyrd Bardson. Queen Ingerid herself proceeded eastward immediately to Viken. Inge was the name of her son by King Harald, and he was then fostered by Amunde Gyrdson, a grandson of Logberse. When they came to Viken a Borgar-thing was immediately called together, at which Inge, who was in the second year of his age, was chosen king. This resolution was supported by Amunde and Thjostolf Alason, together with many other great chiefs. Now when the tidings came north to Throndhjem that King Harald was murdered, the Throndhjem people took Sigurd, King Harald's son, to be the king; and this resolution was supported by Ottar Birting, Peter Saudaulfson, the brothers Guthorm of Reine, and Ottar Balle, sons of Asolf and many other great chiefs. Afterwards the whole nation almost submitted to the brothers, and principally because their father was considered holy; and the country took the oath to them, that the kingly power should not go to any other man as long as any of King Harald's sons were alive.

2. OF SIGURD SLEMBIDJAKN.

Sigurd Slembe sailed north around Stad; and when he came to North More, he found that letters and full powers had arrived before him from the leaders who had given in their allegiance to Harald's sons; so that there he got no welcome or help. As Sigurd himself had but few people with him, he resolved to go with them to Throndhjem, and seek out Magnus the Blind; for he had already sent a message before him to Magnus's friends. Now when they came to the town, they rowed up the river Nid to meet King Magnus, and fastened their land-ropes on the shore at the king's house; but were obliged to set off immediately, for all the people rose against them. They then landed at Monkholm, and took Magnus the Blind out of the cloister against the will of the monks; for he had been consecrated a monk. It is said by some that Magnus willingly went with them; although it was differently reported, in order to make his cause appear better. Sigurd, immediately after Yule (January, A.D. 1137), went forth with his suite, expecting aid from his relations and Magnus's friends, and which they also got. Sigurd sailed with his men out of the fjord, and was joined afterwards by Bjorn Egilson, Gunnar of Gimsar, Haldor Sigurdson, Aslak Hakonson, the brothers Bendikt and Eirik, and also the court which had before been with King Magnus, and many others. With this troop they went south to More, and down to the mouth of Raumsdal fjord. Here Sigurd and Magnus divided their forces, and Sigurd went immediately westwards across the sea. King Magnus again proceeded to the Uplands, where he expected much help and strength, and which he obtained. He remained there the winter and all the summer (A.D. 1137), and had many people with him; but King Inge proceeded against him with all his forces, and they met at a place called Mynne. There was a great battle, at which King Magnus had the most people. It is related that Thjostolf Alason carried King Inge in his belt as long as the battle lasted, and stood under the banner; but Thjostolf was hard pressed by fatigue and fighting; and it is commonly said that King Inge got his ill health there, and which he retained as long as he lived, so that his back was knotted into a hump, and the one foot was shorter than the other; and he was besides so infirm that he could scarcely walk as long as he lived. The defeat began to turn upon Magnus and his men; and in the front rank of his array fell Haldor Sigurdson, Bjorn Egilson, Gunnar of Gimsar, and a great number of his men, before he himself would take to his horse and fly. So says Kolle:–

> *"Thy arrow-storm on Mynne's banks*
> *Fast thinn'd the foemen's strongest ranks;*
> *Thy good sword hewed the raven's feast*
> *On Mynne's banks up in the East.*
> *Shield clashed on shield, and bucklers broke*
> *Under thy battle-axe's stroke;*
> *While thou, uncovered, urged the fray,*
> *Thy shield and mail-coat thrown away."*

And also this:–

> *"The king to heaven belonging fled,*
> *When thou, in war's quick death-game bred,*
> *Unpanzered, shieldless on the plain*
> *His heavy steel-clad guards hadst slain.*
> *The painted shield, and steel-plate mail,*
> *Before thy fierce attack soon fail,*
> *To Magnus who belongs to heaven,*
>
> *Was no such fame in battle given."*

Magnus fled eastward to Gautland, and then to Denmark. At that time there was in Gautland an earl, Karl Sonason, who was a great and ambitious man. Magnus the Blind and his men said, wherever they happened to meet with chiefs, that Norway lay quite open to any great chieftain who would attack it; for it might well be said there was no king in the country, and the kingdom was only ruled by lendermen, and, among those who had most sway, there was, from mutual jealousy, most discord. Now Karl, being ambitious of power, listens willingly to such speeches; collects men, and rides west to Viken, where many people, out of fear, submit to him. When Thjostolf Alason and Amunde heard of this, they went with the men they could get together, and took King Inge with them. They met Earl Karl and the Gautland army eastward in Krokaskog, where there was a great battle and a great defeat, King Inge gaining the victory. Munan Ogmundson, Earl Karl's mother's brother, fell there. Ogmund, the father of Munan, was a son of Earl Orm Eilifson, and Sigrid, a daughter of Earl Fin Arnason. Astrid, Ogrnund's daughter, was the mother of Earl Karl. Many others of the Gautland people fell at Krokaskog; and the earl fled eastward through the forest. King Inge pursued them all the way out of the kingdom; and this expedition turned out a great disgrace to them. So says Kolle:–

"I must proclaim how our great lord
Coloured deep red his ice-cold sword;
And ravens played with Gautland bones,
And wolves heard Gautlanders' last groans.
Their silly jests were well repaid,–
In Krokaskog their laugh was laid:
Thy battle power was then well tried,
And they who won may now deride."

3. KING EIRIK'S EXPEDITION TO NORWAY.

Magnus the Blind then went to Denmark to King Eirik Eimune, where he was well received. He offered the king to follow him if he would invade Norway with a Danish army, and subdue the country; saying, that if he came to Norway with his army, no man in Norway would venture to throw a spear against him. The king allowed himself to be moved by Magnus's persuasions, ordered a levy, and went north to Norway with 200 ships; and Magnus and his men were with him on this expedition. When they came to Viken, they proceeded peacefully and gently on the east side of the fjord; but when the fleet came westward to Tunsberg, a great number of King Inge's lendermen came against them. Their leader was Vatnorm Dagson, a brother of Gregorius. The Danes could not land to get water without many of them being killed; and therefore they went in through the fjord to Oslo, where Thjostolf Alason opposed them. It is told that some people wanted to carry the holy Halvard's coffin out of the town in the evening when the fleet was first observed, and as many as could took hold of it; but the coffin became so heavy that they could not carry it over the church floor. The morning after, however, when they saw the fleet sailing in past the Hofud Isle, four men carried the coffin out of the town, and Thjostolf and all the townspeople followed it.

4. THE TOWN OF OSLO BURNT.

King Eirik and his army advanced against the town; and some of his men hastened after Thjostolf and his troop. Thjostolf threw a spear at a man named Askel, which hit him under the throat, so that the spear point went through his neck; and Thjostolf thought he had never made a better spear-cast, for, except the place he hit, there was nothing bare to be seen. The shrine of St. Halvard, was taken up to Raumarike, where it remained for three months. Thjostolf went up to Raumarike, and collected men during the night, with whom he returned towards the town in the morning. In the meantime King Eirik set fire to Halvard's church, and to the town, which was entirely burnt. Thjostolf came soon after to the town with the men he had assembled, and Eirik sailed off with his fleet; but could not land anywhere on that side of the fjord, on account of the troops of the lendermen who came down against them; and wherever they attempted a landing, they left five or six men or more upon the strand. King Inge lay with a great number of people into Hornborusund, but when he learned this, he turned about southwards to Denmark again. King Inge pursued him, and took from him all the ships he could get hold of; and it was a common observation among people, that never was so poor an expedition made with so great an armament in another king's dominions. King Eirik was ill pleased at it, and thought King Magnus and his men had been making a fool of him by encouraging him to undertake this expedition, and he declared he would never again besuch friends with them as before.

5. OF SIGURD SLEMBIDJAKN.

Sigurd Slembidjakn came that summer from the West sea to Norway, where he heard of his relation King Magnus's unlucky expedition; so he expected no welcome in Norway, but sailed south, outside the rocks, past the land, and set over to Denmark, and went into the Sound. He fell in with some Vindland cutters south of the islands, gave them battle, and gained the victory. He cleared eight ships, killing many of the men, and he hanged the others.

He also had a battle off the Island Mon with the Vindland men, and gained a victory. He then sailed from the south and came to the eastern arm of the Gaut river, and took three ships of the fleet of Thorer Hvinantorde, and Olaf, the son of Harald Kesia, who was Sigurd's own sister's son; for Ragnhild, the mother of Olaf, was a daughter of King Magnus Barefoot. He drove Olaf up the country.

Thjostolf was at this time in Konungahella, and had collected people to defend the country, and Sigurd steered thither with his fleet. They shot at each other, but he could not effect a landing; and, on both sides, many were killed and many wounded. Ulfhedin Saxolfson, Sigurd's forecastle man, fell there. He was an Icelander, from the north quarter. Sigurd continued his course northwards to Viken and plundered far and wide around. Now when Sigurd lay in a harbour called Portyrja on Limgard's coast, and watched the ships going to or coming from Viken to plunder them, the Tunsberg men collected an armed force against him, and came unexpectedly upon them while Sigurd and his men were on shore dividing their booty. Some of the men came down from the land, but some of the other party laid themselves with their ships right across the harbour outside of them. Sigurd ran up into his ship, and rowed out against them. Vatnorm's ship was the nearest, and he let his ship fall behind the line, and Sigurd rowed clear past, and thus escaped with one ship and the loss of many men. This verse was made upon Vatnorm[78]:–

"The water serpent, people say,
From Portyrja slipped away."

6. THE MURDER OF BEINTEIN.

Sigurd Slembidjakn sailed from thence to Denmark; and at that time a man was lost in his ship, whose name was Kolbein Thorliotson of Batald. He was sitting in a boat which was made fast to the vessel, and upset because she was sailing quickly. When they came south to Denmark, Sigurd's ship itself was cast away; but he got to Alaborg, and was there in winter. The summer after (A.D. 1138) Magnus and Sigurd sailed together from the south with seven ships, and came unexpect-

78 Vatnorm, the name of this man, means the water-serpent, and appears to have been a favourite name for war-ships also; hence the pun in the lines upon Vatnorm.–L.

edly in the night to Lister, where they laid their ships on the land. Beintein Kolbeinson, a court-man of King Inge, and a very brave man, was there. Sigurd and his men jumped on shore at daylight, came unexpectedly on the people, surrounded the house, and were setting fire to the buildings; but Beintein came out of a store-house with his weapons, well armed, and stood within the door with drawn sword, his shield before him, helmet on, and ready to defend himself. The door was somewhat low. Sigurd asked which of his lads had most desire to go in against Beintein, which he called brave man's work; but none was very hurried to make ready for it. While they were discussing this matter Sigurd rushed into the house, past Beintein. Beintein struck at him, but missed him. Sigurd turned instantly on Beintein; and after exchanging blows, Sigurd gave him his death-stroke, and came out presently bearing his head in his hands.

They took all the goods that were in the farm-house, carried the booty to their ships, and sailed away. When King Inge and his friends, and also Kolbein's sons, Sigurd and Gyrd, the brothers of Beintein, heard of Beintein's murder, the king sent a great force against Sigurd Slembe and his followers; and also travelled himself, and took a ship from Hakon Paulson Pungelta, who was a daughter's son of Aslak, a son of Erling Skjalgson of Sole, and cousin of Hakon Mage. King Inge drove Hakon and his followers up the country, and took all their gear. Sigurd Stork, a son of Eindride of Gautdal, and his brother, Eirik Hael, and Andres Kelduskit, son of Grim of Vist, all fled away into the fjords. But Sigurd Slembe, Magnus the Blind and Thorieif Skiappa sailed outside the isles with three ships north to Halogaland; and Magnus was in winter (A.D. 1139) north in Bjarkey Isle with Vidkun Jonson. But Sigurd had the stem and stern-post of his ship cut out, made a hole in her, and sank her in the inner part of Egisfjord, and thereafter he passed the winter at Tialdasund by Gljufrafjord in Hin. Far up the fjord there is a cave in the rock; in that place Sigurd sat with his followers, who were above twenty men, secretly, and hung a grey cloth before the mouth of the hole, so that no person could see them from the strand. Thorleif Skiappa, and Einar, son of Ogmund of Sand, and of Gudrun, daughter of Einar Arason of Reikiaholar, procured food for Sigurd during the winter. It is said that Sigurd made the Laplanders construct two boats for him during the winter up in the fjord; and they were fastened together with deer sinews, without nails, and with twigs of willow instead of knees, and each boat could carry twelve men. Sigurd was with the Laplanders while they were making the boats; and the Laplanders had good ale, with which they entertained Sigurd. Sigurd made these lines on it:–

"In the Lapland tent
Brave days we spent.
Under the grey birch tree;
In bed or on bank
We knew no rank,
And a merry crew were we.

"Good ale went round
As we sat on the ground,
Under the grey birch tree;
And up with the smoke
Flew laugh and joke,
And a merry crew were we."

These boats were so light that no ship could overtake them in the water, according to what was sung at the time:–

"Our skin-sewed Fin-boats lightly swim,
Over the sea like wind they skim.
Our ships are built without a nail;
Few ships like ours can row or sail."

In spring Sigurd and Magnus went south along the coast with the two boats which the Laplanders had made; and when they came to Vagar they killed Svein the priest and his two sons.

7. OF SIGURD'S SLEMBE'S CAMPAIGN.

Thereafter Sigurd came south to Vikar, and seized King Sigurd's lendermen, William Skinnare and Thorald Kept, and killed them both. Then Sigurd turned south-wards along the coast, and met Styrkar Glaesirofa south of Byrda, as he was coming from the south from the town of Nidaros, and killed him. Now when Sigurd came south to Valsnes, he met Svinagrim outside of the ness, and cut off his right hand. From thence he went south to More, past the mouth of the Throndhjem fjord, where they took Hedin Hirdmage and Kalf Kringluauge. They let Hedin escape, but killed Kalf. When King Sigurd, and his foster-father, Sadagyrd, heard of Sigurd Slembidjakn's proceedings, and what he was doing, they sent people to search for him; and their leader was Jon Kauda, a son of Kalf Range. Bishop

Ivar's brother, and besides the priest Jon Smyril. They went on board the ship the Reindeer, which had twenty-two rowing benches, and was one of the swiftest sailing vessels, to seek Sigurd; but as they could not find him, they returned north-wards with little glory; for people said that they had got sight of Sigurd and his people, and durst not attack them. Afterwards Sigurd proceeded southwards to Hordaland, and came to Herdla, where Einar, a son of Laxapaul, had a farm; and went into Hamar's fjord, to the Gangdaga-thing. They took all the goods that were at the farm, and a long-ship of twenty-two benches which belonged to Einar; and also his son, four years old, who was living with one of his labouring people. Some wanted to kill the boy, but others took him and carried him with them. The labouring man said, "It will not be lucky for you to kill the child; and it will be of no use to you to carry him away, for it is my son, and not Einar's." And on his word they let the boy remain, and went away. When Einar came home he gave the labourer money to the value of two ore of gold, and thanked him for his clever invention, and promised him his constant friendship. So says Eirik Odson, who first wrote down this relation; and he heard himself Einar Paulson telling these circumstances in Bergen. Sigurd then went southward along the coast all the way east to Viken, and met Fin Saudaulfson east at Kvildar, as he was engaged in drawing in King Inge's rents and duties, and hanged him. Then they sailed south to Denmark.

8. OF KING INGE'S LETTER TO KING SIGURD.

THE PEOPLE OF VIKEN and of Bergen complained that it was wrong for King Sigurd and his friends to be sitting quietly north in the town of Nidaros, while his father's murderer was cruising about in the ordinary passage at the mouth of the Throndhjem fjord; and King Inge and his people, on the other hand, were in Viken in the midst of the danger, defending the country and holding many battles. Then King Inge sent a letter north to the merchant-town Nidaros, in which were these words: "King Inge Haraldson sends his brother King Sigurd, as also Sadagyrd, Ogmund Svipte, Ottar Birting, and all lendermen, court-men, house-people, and all the public, rich and poor, young and old, his own and God's salutation. The misfortune is known to all men that on account of our childhoods–thou being five, and I but three years of age–we can undertake nothing without the counsel of our friends and other good men. Now I and my men think that we stand nearer to the danger and necessity common to us both, than thou and thy friends; therefore make it so that thou, as soon as possible, come to me, and as strong in troops as possible, that we may be assembled to meet whatever may come. He will be our best friend who does all he can that we may be united, and may take an equal part in all things. But if thou refuse, and wilt not come after this message which I send thee in need, as thou hast done before, then thou must expect that I will come against thee with an armament; and let God decide between us; for we are not in a condition to sit here at so great an expense, and with so numerous a body of troops as are necessary here on account of the enemy, and besides many other pressing charges, whilst thou hast half of all the land-tax and other revenues of Norway. Live in the peace of God!"

9. OTTAR BIRTING'S SPEECH.

Then Ottar Birting stood up in the Thing, and first of all answered thus: "This is King Sigurd's reply to his brother King Inge–that God will reward him for his good salutation, and likewise for the trouble and burden which he and his friends have in this kingdom, and in matters of necessity which effect them both. Although now some think there is something sharp in King Inge's message to his brother Sigurd, yet he has in many respects sufficient cause for it. Now I will make known to you my opinion, and we will hear if King Sigurd and the other people of power will agree to it; and it is, that thou, King Sigurd, make thyself ready, with all the people who will follow thee, to defend thy country; and go as strong in men as possible to thy brother King Inge as soon as thou art prepared, in order to assist each other in all things that are for the common good; and may God Almighty strengthen and assist you both! Now, king, we will have thy words."

Peter, a son of Saudaulf, who was afterwards called Peter Byrdarsvein, bore King Sigurd to the Thing. Then the king said, "Ye must know that, if I am to advise, I will go as soon as possible to my brother King Inge." Then others spoke, one after the other; but although each began his speech in his own way, he ended with agreeing to what Ottar Birting had proposed; and it was determined to call together the war-forces, and go to the east part of the country. King Sigurd accordingly went with great armament east to Viken, and there he met his brother King Inge.

10. FALL OF MAGNUS THE BLIND.

THE SAME AUTUMN (A.D. 1139) Sigurd Slembe and Magnus the Blind came from Denmark with thirty ships, manned both with Danes and Northmen. It was near to winter. When the kings heard of this, they set out with their people eastwards to meet them. They met at Hvalar, near Holm the Grey, the day after Martinmas, which was a Sunday. King Inge and King Sigurd had twenty ships, which were all large. There was a great battle; but, after the first assault, the Danes fled home to Denmark with eighteen ships. On this Sigurd's and Magnus's ships were cleared; and as the last was almost entirely bare of men, and Magnus was lying in his bed, Hreidar Griotgardson, who had long followed him, and been his courtman, took King Magnus in his arms, and tried to run with him on board some other ship. But Hreidar was struck by a spear, which went between his shoulders; and people say King Magnus was killed by the same spear. Hreidar fell backwards upon the deck, and Magnus upon him; and every man spoke of how honourably he had followed his master and rightful sovereign. Happy are they who have such praise! There fell, on King Magnus's ship, Lodin Saupprud of Linustadar, Bruse Thormodson; and the forecastle-men to Sigurd Slembidjakn, Ivar Kolbeinson and Halyard Faeger, who had been in Sigurd Slembe's fore-hold. This Ivar had been the first who had gone in, in the night, to King Harald, and had laid hands on him. There fell a great number of the men of King Magnus and Sigurd Slembe, for Inge's men let not a single one escape if they got hold of him; but only a few are named here. They killed upon a holm more than forty men, among whom were two Icelanders–the priest Sigurd Bergthorson, a grandson of Mas; the other Clemet, a son of Are Einarson. But three Icelanders obtained their lives: namely, Ivar Skrauthanke, a son of Kalf Range, and who afterwards was bishop of Throndhjem, and was father of the archbishop Eirik. Ivar had always followed King Magnus, and he escaped into his brother Jon Kauda's ship. Jon was married to Cecilia, a daughter of Gyrd Bardson, and was then in King Inge's and Sigurd's armament. There were three in all who escaped on board of Jon's ship. The second was Arnbjorn Ambe, who afterwards married Thorstein's daughter in Audsholt; the third was Ivar Dynta, a son of Stare, but on the mother's side of a Throndhjem family,–a very agreeable man. When the troops came to know that these three were on board his ship, they took their weapons and assaulted the vessel, and some blows were exchanged, and the whole fleet had nearly come to a fight among themselves; but it came to an agreement, so that Jon ransomed his brothers Ivar and

Arnbjorn for a fixed sum in ransom, which, however, was afterwards remitted. But Ivar Dynta was taken to the shore, and beheaded; for Sigurd and Gyrd, the sons of Kolbein, would not take any mulct for him, as they knew he had been at their brother Beintein's murder. Ivar the bishop said, that never was there anything that touched him so nearly, as Ivar's going to the shore under the axe, and turning to the others with the wish that they might meet in joy here-after. Gudrid Birger's daughter, a sister of Archbishop Jon, told Eirik Odson that she heard Bishop Ivar say this.

11. SIGURD SLEMBE TAKEN PRISONER.

A man called Thrand Gialdkere was the steersman of King Inge's ship. It was come so far, that Inge's men were rowing in small boats between the ships after those who were swimming in the water, and killed those they could get hold of. Sigurd Slembe threw himself overboard after his ship had lost her crew, stripped off his armour under the water, and then swam with his shield over him. Some men from Thrand's vessel took prisoner a man who was swimming, and were about to kill him; but he begged his life, and offered to tell them where Sigurd Slembe was, and they agreed to it. Shields and spears, dead men, weapons, and clothes, were floating all around on the sea about the ships, "Ye can see," said he, "a red shield floating on the water; he is under it." They rowed to it immediately, took him, and brought him on board of Thrand's ship. Thrand then sent a message to Thjostolf, Ottar, and Amunde. Sigurd Slembe had a tinder box on him; and the tinder was in a walnut-shell, around which there was wax. This is related, because it seems an ingenious way of preserving it from ever getting wet. He swam with a shield over him, because nobody could know one shield from another where so many were floating about; and they would never have hit upon him, if they had not been told where he was. When Thrand came to the land with Sigurd, and it was told to the troops that he was taken, the army set up a shout of joy. When Sigurd heard it he said, "Many a bad man will rejoice over my head this day." Then Thjostolf Alason went to where Sigurd was sitting, struck from his head a silk hat with silver fringes, and said. "Why wert thou so impudent, thou son of a slave! to dare to call thyself King Magnus Barefoot's son?"

Sigurd replied, "Presume not to compare my father to a slave; for thy father was of little worth compared to mine."

Hal, a son of the doctor Thorgeir Steinson, King Inge's court-man, was present at this circumstance, and told it to Eirik Odson, who afterwards wrote these relations in a book, which he called "Hryggjarstykke". In this book is told all concerning Harald Gille and his sons, and Magnus the Blind, and Sigurd Slembidjakn, until their deaths. Eirik was a sensible man, who was long in Norway about that time. Some of his narratives he wrote down from Hakon Mage's account; some were from lendermen of Harald's sons, who along with his sons were in all this feud, and in all the councils. Eirik names, moreover, several men of understanding and veracity, who told him these accounts, and were so near that they saw or heard all that happened. Something he wrote from what he himself had heard or seen.

12. TORTURE OF SIGURD SLEMBE.

Hal says that the chiefs wished to have Sigurd killed instantly; but the men who were the most cruel, and thought they had injuries to avenge, advised torturing him; and for this they named Beintein's brothers, Sigurd and Gyrd, the sons of Kolbein. Peter Byrdarsvein would also avenge his brother Fin. But the chiefs and the greater part of the people went away. They broke his shin-bones and arms with an axe-hammer. Then they stripped him, and would flay him alive; but when they tried to take off the skin, they could not do it for the gush of blood. They took leather whips and flogged him so long, that the skin was as much taken off as if he had been flayed. Then they stuck a piece of wood in his back until it broke, dragged him to a tree and hanged him; and then cut off his head, and brought the body and head to a heap of stones and buried them there. All acknowledge, both enemies and friends, that no man in Norway, within memory of the living, was more gifted with all perfections, or more experienced, than Sigurd, but in some respects he was an unlucky man. Hal says that he spoke little, and answered only a few, and in single words, under his tortures, although they spoke to him. Hal says further, that he never moved when they tortured him, more than if they were striking a stock or a stone. This Hal alleged as proof that he was a brave hero, who had courage to endure tortures; for he still held his tongue, and never moved from the spot. And farther he says, that he never altered his voice in the least, but spoke with as much ease as if he was sitting at the ale-table; neither speaking higher nor lower, nor in a more tremulous voice than he was used to do. He spoke until he gave up the ghost, and sang between whiles parts of the Psalm-book, and which Hal considered beyond the powers and strength of ordinary men. And the priest who had the church in the neighbourhood let Sigurd's body be transported thither to the church. This priest was a friend of Harald's sons: but when they heard it they were angry at him, had the body carried back to where it had been, and made the priest pay a fine. Sigurd's friends afterwards came from Denmark with a ship for his body, carried it to Alaborg, and interred it in Mary church in that town. So said Dean Ketil, who officiated as priest at Mary church, to Eirik; and that Sigurd was buried there. Thjostolf Alason transported Magnus the Blind's body to Oslo, and buried it in Halvard's church, beside King Sigurd his father. Lodin Saupprud was transported to Tunsberg; but the others of the slain were buried on the spot.

13. EYSTEIN HARALDSON COMES TO NORWAY.

When the kings Sigurd and Inge had ruled over Norway about six years, Eystein, who was a son of Harald Gille, came in spring from Scotland (A.D. 1142). Arne Sturla, Thorleif Brynjolfson, and Kolbein Hruga had sailed westward over the sea after Eystein, accompanied him to Norway, and sailed immediately with him to Throndhjem. The Throndhjem people received him well; and at the Eyra-thing of Ascension-day he was chosen king, so that he should have the third part of Norway with his brothers Sigurd and Inge. They were at this time in the east part of the country; and men went between the kings who brought about a peace, and that Eystein should have a third part of the kingdom. People believed what he said of his paternal descent, because King Harald himself had testified to it, and he did not resort to the ordeal of iron. King Eystein's mother was called Bjadok, and she followed him to Norway. Magnus was the name of King Harald Gille's fourth son, who was fostered by Kyrpingaorm. He also was chosen king, and got a fourth part of the country; but Magnus was deformed in his feet, lived but a short time, and died in his bed. Einar Skulason speaks of them:–

"The generous Eystein money gave;
Sigurd in fight was quick and brave;
Inge loved well the war-alarm;
Magnus to save his land from harm.
No country boasts a nobler race
The battle-field, or Thing, to grace.

Four brothers of such high pretence
The sun ne'er shone upon at once."

14. MURDER OF OTTAR BIRTING.

After King Harald Gille's death Queen Ingerid married Ottar Birting, who was a lendermen and a great chief, and of a Throndhjem family, who strengthened King Inge's government much while he was in his childhood. King Sigurd was not very friendly to Ottar; because, as he thought, Ottar always took King Inge's side. Ottar Birting was killed north in the merchant town (Nidaros), in an assault upon him in the twilight as he was going to the evening song. When he heard the whistling of the blow he held up his cloak with his hands against it; thinking, no doubt, it was a snowball thrown at him, as young boys do in the streets. Ottar fell by the stroke; but his son, Alf Hrode, who just at the same moment was coming into the churchyard, saw his father's fall, and saw that the man who had killed him ran east about the church. Alf ran after him, and killed him at the corner of the choir; and people said that he had good luck in avenging his father, and afterwards was much more respected than he had been before.

15. BEGINNING OF KING EYSTEIN.

King Eystein Haraldson was in the interior of the Throndhjem district when he heard of Ottar's murder, and summoned to him the bonde-army, with which he proceeded to the town; and he had many men. Ottar's relations and other friends accused King Sigurd, who was in the town, of having instigated this deed; and the bondes were much enraged against him. But the king offered to clear himself by the ordeal of iron, and thereby to establish the truth of his denial; and accordingly a peace was made. King Sigurd went to the south end of the country, and the ordeal was never afterwards heard of.

16. BEGINNING OF ORM THE KING-BROTHER.

Queen Ingerid had a son to Ivar Sneis, and he was called Orm, and got the surname of King-brother. He was a handsome man in appearance, and became a great chief, as shall be told hereafter. Ingerid afterwards married Arne of Stodreim, who was from this called King's-mate; and their children were Inge, Nikolas, Philip of Herdla, and Margaret, who was first married to Bjorn Buk, and afterwards to Simon Karason.

17. JOURNEY OF ERLING SKAKKE AND EARL RAGNVALD.

Kyrpingaorm and Ragnhild, a daughter of Sveinke Steinarson, had a son called Erling. Kyrpingaorm was a son of Svein Sveinson, who was a son of Erling of Gerd. Otto's mother was Ragna, a daughter of Earl Orm Eilifson and Sigrid, a daughter of Earl Fin Arnason. The mother of Earl Orm was Ragnhild, a daughter of Earl Hakon the Great. Erling was a man of understanding, and a great friend of King Inge, by whose assistance and counsel Erling obtained in marriage Christina, a daughter of King Sigurd the Crusader and Queen Malmfrid. Erling possessed a farm at Studla in South Hordaland. Erling left the country; and with him went Eindride Unge and several lendermen, who had chosen men with them. They intended to make a pilgrimage to Jerusalem, and went across the West sea to Orkney. There Earl Ragnvald and Bishop William joined them; and they had in all fifteen ships from Orkney, with which they first sailed to the South Hebrides, from thence west to Valland, and then the same way King Sigurd the Crusader had sailed to Norvasund; and they plundered all around in the heathen part of Spain. Soon after they had sailed through the Norvasund, Eindride Unge and his followers, with six ships, separated from them; and then each was for himself. Earl Ragnvald and Erling Skakke fell in with a large ship of burden at sea called a dromund, and gave battle to it with nine ships. At last they laid their cutters close under the dromund; but the heathens threw both weapons and stones, and pots full of pitch and boiling oil. Erling laid his ship so close under the dromund, that the missiles of the heathens fell without his ship. Then Erling and his men cut a hole in the dromund, some working below and some above the water-mark; and so they boarded the vessel through it. So says Thorbjorn Skakkaskald, in his poem on Erling:–

"The axes of the Northmen bold
A door into the huge ships' hold
Hewed through her high and curved side,
As snug beneath her bulge they ride.

Their spears bring down the astonished foe,
Who cannot see from whence the blow.
The eagle's prey, they, man by man,
Fall by the Northmen's daring plan."

Audunraude, Erling's forecastle-man, was the first man who got into the dromund. Then they carried her, killing an immense number of people; making an extraordinarily valuable booty, and gaining a famous victory. Earl Ragnvald and Erling Skakke came to Palestine in the course of their expedition, and all the way to the river Jordan. From thence they went first to Constantinople, where they left their ships, travelled northwards by land, and arrived in safety in Norway, where their journey was highly praised. Erling Skakke appeared now a much greater man than before, both on account of his journey and of his marriage; besides he was a prudent sensible man, rich, of great family, eloquent, and devoted to King Inge by the strictest friendship more than to the other royal brothers.

18. BIRTH OF HAKON HERDEBREID.

King Sigurd went to a feast east in Viken along with his court, and rode past a house belonging to a great bonde called Simon. While the king was riding past the house, he heard within such beautiful singing that he was quite enchanted with it, and rode up to the house, and saw a lovely girl standing at the handmill and grinding. The king got off his horse, and went to the girl and courted her. When the king went away, the bonde Simon came to know what the object of the king's visit had been. The girl was called Thora, and she was Simon the bonde's servant-girl. Simon took good care of her afterwards, and the girl brought forth a male child (A.D. 1047), who was called Hakon, and was considered King Sigurd's son. Hakon was brought up by Simon Thorbergson and his wife Gunhild. Their own sons also, Onund and Andreas, were brought up with Hakon, and were so dear to him that death only could have parted them.

19. EYSTEIN AND THE PEASANTS OF HISING ISLE.

While King Eystein Haraldson was in Viken, he fell into disputes with the bondes of Reine and the inhabitants of Hising Isle, who assembled to oppose him; but he gave them battle at a place called Leikberg, and afterwards burnt and destroyed all around in Hising; so that the bondes submitted to his will, paid great fines to the king, and he took hostages from them. So says Einar Skulason:–

"The Viken men
Won't strive again,
With words or blows,
The king to oppose.
None safety found
On Viken's ground,
Till all, afraid,
Pledge and scat paid."

And further:–

"The king came near;
He who is dear
To all good men
Came down the glen,
By Leikberg hill.
They who do ill,
The Reine folk, fly
Or quarter cry."

20. WAR EXPEDITION OF KING HARALDSON.

Soon after King Eystein began his journey out of the country over sea to the West (A.D. 1153), and sailed first to Caithness. Here he heard that Earl Harald Maddad's son was in Thursa, to which he sailed directly in three small boats. The earl had a ship of thirty banks of oars, and nearly eighty men in her. But they were not prepared to make resistance, so that King Eystein was able to board the ship with his men; and he took the earl prisoner, and carried him to his own ship, but the earl ransomed himself with three marks of gold: and thus they parted. Einar Skulason tells of it thus:–

"Earl Harald in his stout ship lay
On the bright sand in Thursa bay;
With fourscore men he had no fear,
*

Nor thought the Norse king was so near,
He who provides the eagle's meals
In three small boats along-shore steals;
And Maddad's son must ransom pay
For his bad outlook that fair day."

From thence King Eystein sailed south along the east side of Scotland, and brought up at a merchant-town in Scotland called Aberdeen, where he killed many people, and plundered the town. So says Einar Skulason:–

"At Aberdeen, too, I am told,
Fell many by our Norsemen bold;
Peace was disturbed, and blue swords broke
With many a hard and bloody stroke."

The next battle was at Hartlepool in the south, with a party of horsemen. The king put them to flight, and seized some ships there. So says Einar:–

"At Hartlepool, in rank and row,
The king's court-men attack the foe.
The king's sharp sword in blood was red,
Blood dropped from every Norse spear-head.
Ravens rejoice o'er the warm food
Of English slain, each where he stood;
And in the ships their thirst was quenched:
The decks were in the foe's blood drenched."

Then he went southwards to England, and had his third battle at Whitby, and gained the victory, and burnt the town. So says Einar:–

"The ring of swords, the clash of shields,
Were loud in Whitby's peaceful fields;
For here the king stirred up the strife.–
Man against man, for death or life.
O'er roof and tower, rose on high
The red wrath-fire in the sky;
House after house the red fiend burns;
By blackened walls the poor man mourns."

Thereafter he plundered wide around in England, where Stephen was then the king. After this King Eystein fought with some cavalry at Skarpasker. So says Einar:–

"At Skarpasker the English horse
Retire before the Norse king's force:
The arrow-shower like snow-drift flew,
And the shield-covered foemen slew."

He fought next at Pilavik, and gained the victory. So says Einar:–

"At Pilavik the wild wolf feeds,
Well furnished by the king's brave deeds
He poured upon the grass-green plain
A red shower from the Perthmen slain.
On westwards in the sea he urges,
With fire and sword the country purges:
Langtown he burns; the country rang,
For sword on shield incessant clang."

Here they burnt Langatun, a large village; and people say that the town has never since risen to its former condition. After this King Eystein left England in autumn, and returned to Norway. People spoke in various ways about this expedition.

21. OF HARALD'S SONS.

There was good peace maintained in Norway in the first years of the government of Harald's sons; and as long as their old counsellors were alive, there was some kind of unanimity among them. While Inge and Sigurd were in their childhood, they had a court together; but Eystein, who was come to age of discretion, had a court for himself. But when Inge's and Sigurd's counsellors were dead,–namely, Sadagyrd Bardson, Ottar Birting, Amunde Gyrdson, Thjostolf Alason, Ogmund Svipter, and Ogmund Denger, a brother of Erling Skakke (Erling was not much looked up to while Ogmund lived),–the two kings, Inge and Sigurd divided their courts. King Inge then got great assistance from Gregorius Dagson, a son of Dag Eilifson by Ragnhild a daughter of Skapte Ogmundson. Gregorius had much property, and was himself a thriving, sagacious man. He presided in the governing the country under King

Inge, and the king allowed him to manage his property for him according to his own judgment.

22. HABITS AND MANNERS OF HARALD'S SONS.

WHEN KING SIGURD grew up he was a very ungovernable, restless man in every way; and so was King Eystein, but Eystein was the more reasonable of the two. King Sigurd was a stout and strong man, of a brisk appearance; he had light brown hair, an ugly mouth; but otherwise a well-shaped countenance. He was polite in his conversation beyond any man, and was expert in all exercises. Einar Skulason speaks of this:–

"Sigurd, expert in every way
To wield the sword in bloody fray,
Showed well that to the bold and brave
God always luck and victory gave.
In speech, as well as bloody deeds,
The king all other men exceeds;
And when he speaks we think that none
Has said a word but he alone."

King Eystein was dark and dingy in complexion, of middle height, and a prudent able man; but what deprived him of consideration and popularity with those under him were his avarice and narrowness. He was married to Ragna, a daughter of Nicolas Mase. King Inge was the handsomest among them in countenance. He had yellow but rather thin hair, which was much curled. His stature was small; and he had difficulty in walking alone, because he had one foot withered, and he had a hump both on his back and his breast. He was of cheerful conversation, and friendly towards his friends; was generous, and allowed other chiefs to give him counsel in governing the country. He was popular, therefore, with the public; and all this brought the kingdom and the mass of the people on his side. King Harald Gille's daughter Brigida was first married to the Swedish king Inge Halsteinson, and afterwards to Earl Karl Sonason, and then to the Swedish king Magnus. She and King Inge Haraldson were cousins by the mother's side. At last Brigida married Earl Birger Brose, and they had four sons, namely, Earl Philip, Earl Knut, Folke, and Magnus. Their daughters were Ingegerd, who was married to the Swedish king Sorkver, and their son was King Jon; a second daughter was called Kristin, and a third Margaret. Harald Gille's second daughter was called Maria, who was married to Simon Skalp, a son of Halkel Huk; and their son was called Nikolas. King Harald Gille's third daughter was called Margaret, who was married to Jon Halkelson, a brother of Simon. Now many things occurred between the brothers which occasioned differences and disputes; but I will only relate what appears to me to have produced the more important events.

23. CARDINAL NIKOLAS COMES TO THE COUNTRY.

In the days of Harald's sons Cardinal Nikolas came from Rome to Norway, being sent there by the pope. The cardinal had taken offence at the brothers Sigurd and Eystein, and they were obliged to come to a reconciliation with him; but, on the other hand, he stood on the most affectionate terms with King Inge, whom he called his son. Now when they were all reconciled with him, he moved them to let Jon Birgerson be consecrated archbishop of Throndhjem and gave him a vestment which is called a pallium; and settled moreover that the archbishop's seat should be in Nidaros, in Christ church, where King Olaf the Saint reposes. Before that time there had only been common bishops in Norway. The cardinal introduced also the law, that no man should go unpunished who appeared with arms in the merchant-town, excepting the twelve men who were in attendancce on the king. He improved many of the customs of the Northmen while he was in the country. There never came a foreigner to Norway whom all men respected so highly, or who could govern the people so well as he did. After some time he returned to the South with many friendly presents, and declared ever afterwards that he was the greatest friend of the people of Norway. When he came south to Rome the former pope died suddenly, and all the people of Rome would have Cardinal Nikolas for pope, and he was consecrated under the name of Adrian; and according to the report of men who went to Rome in his days, he had never any business, however important, to settle with other people, but he would break it off to speak with the Northmen who desired to see him. He was not long pope, and is now considered a saint.

24. MIRACLE OF KING OLAF.

In the time of Harald Gille's sons, it happened that a man called Haldor fell into the hands of the Vindland people, who took him and mutilated him, cut open his neck, took out the tongue through the opening, and cut out his tongue root. He afterwards sought out the holy King Olaf, fixed his mind entirely on the holy man, and weeping besought King Olaf to restore his speech and health. Thereupon he immediately recovered his speech by the good king's compassion, went immediately into his service for all his life, and became an excellent trustworthy man. This miracle took place a fortnight before the last Olafsmas, upon the day that Cardinal Nikolas set foot on the land of Norway.

25. MIRACLES OF KING OLAF ON RICHARD.

In the Uplands were two brothers, men of great family, and men of fortune, Einar and Andres, sons of Guthorm Grabard, and brothers of King Sigurd Haraldson's mother; and they had great properties and udal estates in that quarter. They had a sister who was very handsome, but did not pay sufficient regard to the scandal of evil persons, as it afterwards appeared. She was on a friendly footing with an English priest called Richard, who had a welcome to the house of her brothers, and on account of their friendship for him she did many things to please him, and often to his advantage; but the end of all this was, that an ugly report flew about concerning this girl. When this came into the mouth of the public all men threw the blame on the priest. Her brothers did the same, and expressed publicly, as soon as they observed it, that they laid the blame most on him. The great friendship that was between the earl and the priest proved a great misfortune to both, which might have been expected, as the brothers were silent about their secret determination, and let nothing be observed. But one day they called the priest to them, who went, expecting nothing but good from them; enticed him from home with them, saying that they intended to go to another district, where they had some needful business, and inviting him to go with them. They had with them a farm-servant who knew their purpose. They went in a boat along the shore of a lake which is called Rands lake, and landed at a ness called Skiptisand, where they went on shore and amused themselves awhile. Then they went to a retired place, and commanded their servant-man to strike the priest with an axe-hammer. He struck the priest so hard that he swooned; but when he recovered he said, "Why are ye playing so roughly with me?" They replied, "Although nobody has told thee of it before, thou shalt now find the consequence of what thou hast done." They then upbraided him; but he denied their accusations, and besought God and the holy

King Olaf to judge between them. Then they broke his leg-bones, and dragged him bound to the forest with them; and then they put a string around his head, and put a board under his head and shoulders, and made a knot on the string, and bound his head fast to the board. Then the elder brother, Einar, took a wedge, and put it on the priest's eye, and the servant who stood beside him struck upon it with an axe, so that the eye flew out, and fell upon the board. Then he set the pin upon the other eye, and said to the servant, "Strike now more softly." He did so, and the wedge sprang from the eye-stone, and tore the eyelid loose. Then Einar took up the eyelid in his hand, and saw that the eye-stone was still in its place; and he set the wedge on the cheek, and when the servant struck it the eye-stone sprang out upon the cheek-bone. Thereafter they opened his mouth, took his tongue and cut it off, and then untied his hands and his head. As soon as he came to himself, he thought of laying the eye-stones in their place under the eyelids, and pressing then with both hands as much as he could. Then they carried him on board, and went to a farm called Saeheimrud, where they landed. They sent up to the farm to say that a priest was lying in the boat at the shore. While the message was going to the farm, they asked the priest if he could talk; and he made a noise and attempted to speak. Then said Einar to his brother, "If he recover and the stump of his tongue grow, I am afraid he will get his speech again." Thereupon they seized the stump with a pair of tongs, drew it out, cut it twice, and the third time to the very roots, and left him lying half dead. The housewife in the farm was poor; but she hastened to the place with her daughter, and they carried the priest home to their farm in their cloaks. They then brought a priest, and when he arrived he bound all his wounds; and they attended to his comfort as much as they were able. And thus lay the wounded priest grievously handled, but trusting always to God's grace, and never doubting; and although he was speechless, he prayed to God in thought with a sorrowful mind, but with the more confidence the worse he was. He turned his thoughts also to the mild King Olaf the Saint, God's dear favourite, of whose excellent deeds he had heard so much told, and trusted so much more zealously on him with all his heart for help in his necessity. As he lay there lame, and deprived of all strength, he wept bitterly, moaned, and prayed with a sore heart that the dear King Olaf would help him. Now when this wounded priest was sleeping after midnight, he thought he saw a gallant man coming to him, who spoke these words, "Thou art ill off, friend Richard, and thy strength is little." He thought he replied to this assentingly. Then the man accosted him again, "Thou requirest compassion?" The priest replies, "I need the compassion of Almighty God and the holy King Olaf." He answered, "Thou shalt get it." Thereupon he pulled the tongue-stump so hard that it gave the priest pain; then he stroked with his hands his eyes, and legs, and other wounded members. Then the priest asked who he was. He looked at him, and said, "Olaf, come here from Throndhjem;" and then disappeared. But the priest awoke altogether sound, and thus he spoke: "Happy am I, and thanks be to the Almighty God and the holy King Olaf, who have restored me!" Dreadfully mishandled as he had been, yet so quickly was he restored from his misfortune that he scarcely thought he had been wounded or sick. His tongue was entire; both his eyes were in their places, and were clear-sighted; his broken legs and every other wound were healed, or were free from pain; and, in short, he had got perfect health. But as a proof that his eyes had been punched out, there remained a white scar on each eyelid, in order that this dear king's excellence might be manifest on the man who had been so dreadfully misused.

26. KING INGE AND SIGURD HOLD A THING.

King Eystein and King Sigurd had quarrelled, because King Sigurd had killed King Eystein's court-man Harald, the Viken man, who owned a house in Bergen, and also the priest Jon Tapard, a son of Bjarne Sigurdson. On account of this affair, a conference to settle it was appointed in winter in the Uplands. The two sat together in the conference for a long time, and so much was known of their conference that all three brothers were to meet the following summer in Bergen. It was added, that their conference was to the effect that King Inge should have two or three farms, and as much income as would keep thirty men beside him, as he had not health to be a king. When King Inge and Gregorius heard this report, they came to Bergen with many followers. King Sigurd arrived there a little later, and was not nearly so strong in men. Sigurd and Inge had then been nineteen years kings of Norway (A.D. 1155). King Eystein came later still from the south than the other two from the north. Then King Inge ordered the Thing to be called together on the holm by the sound of trumpet; and Sigurd and Inge came to it with a great many people. Gregorius had two long-ships, and at the least ninety men, whom he kept in provisions. He kept his house-men better than other lendermen; for he never took part in any entertainment where each guest brings his liquor, without having all his house-men to drink with him. He went now to the Thing in a gold-mounted helmet, and all his men had helmets on. The King Inge stood up, and told the assembly what he had heard; how his brothers were going to use him, and depose him from his kingdom; and asked for their assistance. The assembled people made a good return to his speech, and declared they would follow him.

27. OF GREGORIUS DAGSON.

Then King Sigurd stood up and said it was a false accusation that King Inge had made against him and his brother, and insisted that Gregorius had invented it; and insinuated that it would not be long, if he had his will, before they should meet so that the golden helmet should be doffed; and ended his speech by hinting that they could not both live. Gregorius replied, that Sigurd need not long so much for this, as he was ready now, if it must be so. A few days after, one of Gregorius's house-men was killed out upon the street, and it was Sigurd's house-men who killed him. Gregorius would then have fallen upon King Sigurd and his people; but King Inge, and many others, kept him back. But one evening, just as Queen Ingerid, King Inge's mother, was coming from vespers, she came past where Sigurd Skrudhyrna, a courtman of King Inge, lay murdered. He was then an old man, and had served many kings. King Sigurd's courtmen, Halyard Gunnarson, and Sigurd, a son of Eystein Trafale, had killed him; and people suspected it was done by order of King Sigurd. She went immediately to King Inge, and told him he would be a little king if he took no concern, but allowed his courtmen to be killed, the one after the other, like swine. The king was angry at her speech; and while they were scolding about it, came Gregorius in helmet and armour, and told the king not to be angry, for she was only saying the truth. "And I am now," says he, "come to thy assistance, if thou wilt attack King Sigurd; and here we are, above 100 men in helmets and armour, and with them we will attack where others think the attack may be worst." But the most dissuaded from this course, thinking that Sigurd would pay the mulct for the slaughter done. Now when Gregorius saw that there would be no assault, he accosted King Inge thus: "Thou wilt frighten thy men from thee in this way; for first they lately killed my house-man, and now thy court-man, and afterwards they will chase me, or some other of thy lendermen whom thou wouldst feel the loss of, when they see that thou art indifferent about such things; and at last, after thy friends are killed, they will take the royal dignity from thee. Whatever thy other lendermen may do, I will not stay here longer to be slaughtered like an ox; but Sigurd the king and I have a business to settle with each other to-night, in whatever way it may turn out. It is true that there is but little help in thee on account of thy ill health, but I should think thy will should not be less to hold thy hand over thy friends, and I am now quite ready to go from hence to meet Sigurd, and my banner is flying in the yard."

Then King Inge stood up, and called for his arms, and ordered every man who wished to follow him to get ready, declaring it was of no use to try to dissuade him; for he had long enough avoided this, but now steel must determine between them.

28. OF KING SIGURD'S FALL.

King Sigurd sat and drank in Sigrid Saeta's house ready for battle, although people thought it would not come to an assault at all. Then came King Inge with his men down the road from the smithy shops, against the house. Arne, the king's brother-in-law, came out from the Sand-bridge, Aslak Erlendson from his own house, and Gregorius from the street where all thought the assault would be worst. King Sigurd and his men made many shots from the holes in the loft, broke down the fireplaces, and threw stones on them. Gregorius and his men cut down the gates of the yard; and there in the port fell Einar, a son of Laxapaul, who was of Sigurd's people, together with Halvard Gunnarson, who was shot in a loft, and nobody lamented his death. They hewed down the houses, and many of King Sigurd's men left him, and surrendered for quarter. Then King Sigurd went up into a loft, and desired to be heard. He had a gilt shield, by which they knew him, but they would not listen to him, and shot arrows at him as thick as snow in a snow-shower, so that he could not stay there. As his men had now left him, and the houses were being hewn down, he went out from thence, and with him his court-man Thord Husfreyja from Viken. They wanted to come where King Inge was to be found, and Sigurd called to his brother King Inge, and begged him to grant him life and safety; but both Thord and Sigurd were instantly killed, and Thord fell with great glory. King Sigurd was interred in the old Christ church out on the holm. King Inge gave Gregorius the ship King Sigurd had owned. There fell many of King Sigurd's and King Inge's men, although I only name a few; but of Gregorius's men there fell four; and also some who belonged to no party, but were shot on the piers, or out in the ships. It was fought on a Friday, and fourteen days before Saint John the Baptist's day (June 10, 1155). Two or three days after King Eystein came from the eastward with thirty ships, and had along with him his brother's son Hakon, a son of King Sigurd. Eystein did not come up to the town, but lay in Floruvagar, and good men went between to get a reconciliation made. But Gregorius wanted that they should go out against him, thinking there never would be a better opportunity; and offered to be himself the leader. "For thou, king, shalt not go, for we have no want of men." But many dissuaded from this course, and it came to nothing. King Eystein returned back to Viken, and King Inge to Throndhjem, and they were in a sort reconciled; but they did not meet each other.

29. OF GREGORIUS DAGSON.

Somewhat later than King Eystein, Gregorius Dagson also set out to the eastward and came to his farm Bratsberg in Hofund; but King Eystein was up in the fjord at Oslo, and had his ships drawn above two miles over the frozen sea, for there was much ice at that time in Viken. King Eystein went up to Hofund to take Gregorius; but he got news of what was on foot, and escaped to Thelemark with ninety men, from thence over the mountains, and came down in Hardanger; and at last to Studla in Etne, to Erling Skakke's farm. Erling himself had gone north to Bergen; but his wife Kristin, a daughter of King Sigurd, was at home, and offered Gregorius all the assistance he wanted; and he was hospitably received. He got a long-ship there which belonged to Erling, and everything else he required. Gregorius thanked her kindly, and allowed that she had behaved nobly, and as might have been expected of her. Gregorius then proceeded to Bergen, where he met Erling, who thought also that his wife had done well.

30. RECONCILIATION OF EYSTEIN AND INGE.

Then Gregorius went north to Throndhjem, and came there before Yule. King Inge was rejoiced at his safety, and told him to use his property as freely as his own, King Eystein having burnt Gregorius's house, and slaughtered his stock of cattle. The ship-docks which King Eystein the Elder had constructed in the merchant town of Nidaros, and which had been exceedingly expensive, were also burnt this winter, together with some good vessels belonging to King Inge. This deed was ascribed to King Eystein and Philip Gyrdson, King Sigurd's foster-brother, and occasioned much displeasure and hatred. The following summer King Inge went south with a very numerous body of men; and King Eystein came northwards, gathering men also. They met in the east (A.D. 1156) at the Seleys, near to the Naze; but King Inge was by far the strongest in men. It was nearly coming to a battle; but at last they were reconciled on these conditions, that King Eystein should be bound to pay forty-five marks of gold, of which King Inge should have thirty marks, because King Eystein had occasioned the burning of the docks and ships; and, besides, that Philip, and all who had been accomplices in the deed, should be outlawed. Also that the men should be banished the country, against whom it could be proved that they gave blow or wound to King Sigurd; for King Eystein accused King Inge of protecting these men; and that Gregorius should have fifteen marks of gold for the value of his property burnt by King Eystein. King Eystein was ill pleased with these terms, and looked upon the treaty as one forced upon him. From that meeting King Inge went eastward to Viken, and King Eystein north to Throndhjem; and they had no intercourse with each other, nor were the messages which passed between them very friendly, and on both sides they killed each other's friends. King Eystein, besides, did not pay the money; and the one accused the other of not fulfilling what was promised. King Inge and Gregorius enticed many people from King Eystein; among others, Bard Standale Brynjolfson, Simon Skalp, a son of Halkel Huk, Halder Brynjolfson, Jon Halkelson, and many other lendermen.

31. OF EYSTEIN AND INGE.

Two years after King Sigurd's fall (A.D. 1157) both kings assembled armaments; namely, King Inge in the east of the country, where he collected eighty ships; and King Eystein in the north, where he had forty-five, and among these the Great Dragon, which King Eystein Magnuson had built after the Long Serpent; and they had on both sides many and excellent troops. King Inge lay with his ships south at Moster Isle, and King Eystein a little to the north in Graeningasund. King Eystein sent the young Aslak Jonson, and Arne Sturla, a son of Snaebjorn, with one ship to meet King Inge; but when the king's men knew them, they assaulted them, killed many of their people, and took all that was in the ship belonging to them. Aslak and Arne and a few more escaped to the land, went to King Eystein, and told him how King Inge had received them. Thereupon King Eystein held a House-thing, and told his followers how ill King Inge had treated his men, and desired the troops to follow him. "I have," said he, "so many, and such excellent men, that I have no intention to fly, if ye will follow me." But this speech was not received with much favour. Halkel Huk was there; but both his sons, Simon and Jon, were with King Inge. Halkel replied, so loud that many heard him, "Let thy chests of gold follow thee, and let them defend thy land."

32. KING EYSTEIN'S DEATH.

In the night many of King Eystein's ships rowed secretly away, some of them joining King Inge, some going to Bergen, or up into the fjords; so that when it was daylight in the morning the king was lying behind with only ten ships. Then he left the Great Dragon, which was heavy to row, and several other vessels behind; and cut and destroyed the Dragon, started out the ale, and destroyed all that they could not take with them. King Eystein went on board of the ship of Eindride, a son of Jon Morner, sailed north into Sogn, and then took the land-road eastwards to Viken. King Inge took the vessels, and sailed with them outside of the isles to Viken. King Eystein had then got east as far as Fold, and had with him 1200 men; but when they saw King Inge's force, they did not think themselves sufficiently strong to oppose him, and they retired to the forest. Every one fled his own way, so that the king was left with but one man. King Inge and his men observed King Eystein's flight, and also that he had but few people with him, and they went immediately to search for him. Simon Skalp met the king just as he was coming out of a willow bush. Simon saluted him. "God save you, sire," said he.

The king replied, "I do not know if thou are not sire here."

Simon replied, "That is as it may happen."

The king begged him to conceal him, and said it was proper to do so. "For there was long friendship between us, although it has now gone differently."

Simon replied, it could not be.

Then the king begged that he might hear mass before he died, which accordingly took place. Then Eystein laid himself down on his face on the grass, stretched out his hands on each side, and told them to cut the sign of the cross between his shoulders, and see whether he could not bear steel as King Inge's followers had asserted of him. Simon told the man who had to put the king to death to do so immediately, for the king had been creeping about upon the grass long enough. He was accordingly slain, and he appears to have suffered manfully. His body was carried to Fors, and lay all night under the hill at the south side of the church. King Eystein was buried in Fors church, and his grave is in the middle of the church-floor, where a fringed canopy is spread over it, and he is considered a saint. Where he was executed, and his blood ran upon the ground, sprang up a fountain, and another under the hill where his body lay all night. From both these waters many think they have received a cure of sickness and pain. It is reported by the Viken people that many miracles were wrought at King Eystein's grave, until his enemies poured upon it soup made of boiled dog's flesh. Simon Skalp was much hated for this deed, which was generally ascribed to him; but some said that when King Eystein was taken Simon sent a message to King Inge, and the king commanded that King Eystein should not come before his face. So King Sverre has caused it to be written; but Einar Skulason tells of it thus:–

"Simon Skalp, the traitor bold,
For deeds of murder known of old,
His king betrayed; and ne'er will he
God's blessed face hereafter see."

BOOK FOURTEEN

Saga of Hakon Herdebreid (Hakon the Broad-Shouldered)[79]

PRELIMINARY REMARKS.

This saga describes the feud between Hakon Sigurdson and his uncle Inge.

The only skald quoted is Einar Skulason.

1. BEGINNING OF HAKON HERDEBREID.

HAKON, KING SIGURD'S SON, was chosen chief of the troop which had followed King Eystein, and his adherents gave him the title of king. He was ten years old. At that time he had with him Sigurd, a son of Halvard Hauld of Reyr, and Andreas and Onund, the sons of Simon, his foster-brothers, and many chiefs, friends of King Sigurd and King Eystein; and they went first up to Gautland. King Inge took possession of all the estates they had left behind, and declared them banished. Thereafter King Inge went to Viken, and was sometimes also in the north of the country. Gregorius Dagson was in Konungahella, where the danger was greatest, and had beside him a strong and handsome body of men, with which he defended the country.

79 The period is from A.D. 1157 to 1161.–L.

2. OF GREGORIUS DAGSON.

The summer after (A.D. 1158) Hakon came with his men, and proceeded to Konungahella with a numerous and handsome troop. Gregorius was then in the town, and summoned the bondes and townspeople to a great Thing, at which he desired their aid; but he thought the people did not hear him with much favour, so he did not much trust them. Gregorius set off with two ships to Viken, and was very much cast down. He expected to meet King Inge there, having heard he was coming with a great army to Viken. Now when Gregorius had come but a short way north he met Simon Skalp, Haldor Brynjolfson, and Gyrd Amundason, King Inge's foster-brothers. Gregorius was much delighted at this meeting, and turned back with them, being all in one body, with eleven ships. As they were rowing up to Konungahella, Hakon, with his followers, was holding a Thing without the town, and saw their approach; and Sigurd of Reyr said, "Gregorius must be fey to be throwing himself with so few men into our hands." Gregorius landed opposite the town to wait for King Inge, for he was expected, but he did not come. King Hakon put himself in order in the town, and appointed Thorliot Skaufaskalle, who was a viking and a robber, to be captain of the men in the merchant ships that were afloat in the river; and King Hakon and Sigurd were within the town, and drew up the men on the piers, for all the townspeople had submitted to King Hakon.

3. KING HAKON'S FLIGHT.

Gregorius rowed up the river, and let the ship drive down with the stream against Thorliot. They shot at each other a while, until Thorliot and his comrades jumped overboard; and some of them were killed, some escaped to the land. Then Gregorius rowed to the piers, and let a gangway be cast on shore at the very feet of Hakon's men. There the man who carried his banner was slain, just as he was going to step on shore. Gregorius ordered Hal, a son of Audun Halson, to take up the banner, which he did, and bore the banner up to the pier. Gregorius followed close after him, held his shield over his head, and protected him as well as himself. As soon as Gregorius came upon the pier, and Hakon's men knew him, they gave way, and made room for him on every side. Afterwards more people landed from the ships, and then Gregorius made a severe assault with his men; and Hakon's men first moved back, and then ran up into the town. Gregorius pursued them eagerly, drove them twice from the town, and killed many of them. By the report of all men, never was there so glorious an affair as this of Gregorius; for Hakon had more than 4000 men, and Gregorius not full 400. After the battle, Gregorius said to Hal Audunson, "Many men, in my opinion, are more agile in battle than ye Icelanders are, for ye are not so exercised as we Norwegians; but none, I think, are so bold under arms as ye are." King Inge came up soon after, and killed many of the men who had taken part with Hakon; made some pay heavy fines, burnt the houses of some, and some he drove out of the country, or treated otherwise very ill. Hakon fled at first up to Gautland with all his men; but the winter after (A.D. 1159), he proceeded by the upper road to Throndhjem, and came there before Easter. The Throndhjem people received him well, for they had always served under that shield. It is said that the Throndhjem people took Hakon as king, on the terms that he should have from Inge the third part of Norway as his paternal heritage. King Inge and Gregorius were in Viken, and Gregorius wanted to make an expedition against the party in the north; but it came to nothing that winter, as many dissuaded from it.

4. FALL OF GYRD AND HAVARD.

King Hakon left Throndhjem in spring with thirty ships nearly; and some of his men sailed before the rest with seven ships, and plundered in North and South More. No man could remember that there ever before had been plundering between the two towns (Bergen and Nidaros). Jon the son of Halkel Huk collected the bondes in arms, and proceeded against them; took Kolbein Ode prisoner, killed every woman's son of them in his ship. Then they searched for the others, found them all assembled in seven ships, and fought with them; but his father Halkel not coming to his assistance as he had promised, many good bondes were killed, and Jon himself was wounded. Hakon proceeded south to Bergen with his forces; but when he came to Stiornvelta, he heard that King Inge and Gregorius had arrived a few nights before from the east at Bergen, and therefore he did not venture to steer thither. They sailed the outer course southwards past Bergen, and met three ships of King Inge's fleet, which had been outsailed on the voyage from the east. On board of them were Gyrd Amundason, King Inge's foster-brother, who was married to Gyrid a sister of Gregorius, and also lagman Gyrd Gunhildson, and Havard Klining. King Hakon had Gyrd Amundason and Havard Klining put to death; but took lagman Gyrd southwards, and then proceeded east to Viken.

5. OF THE CONSULTATIONS OF KING INGE.

When King Inge heard of this he sailed east after them, and they met east in the Gaut river. King Inge went up the north arm of the river, and sent out spies to get news of Hakon and his fleet; but he himself landed at Hising, and waited for his spies. Now when the spies came back they went to the king, and said that they had seen King Hakon's forces, and all his ships which lay at the stakes in the river, and Hakon's men had bound the stems of their vessels to them. They had two great East-country trading vessels, which they had laid outside of the fleet, and on both these were built high wooded stages (castles). When King Inge heard the preparations they had made, he ordered a trumpet to call a House-thing of all the men; and when the Thing was seated he asked his men for counsel, and applied particularly to Gregorius Dagson, his brother-in-law Erling Skakke, and other lendermen and ship-commanders, to whom he related the preparations of Hakon and his men.

Then Gregorius Dagson replied first, and made known his mind in the following words:–"Sometimes we and Hakon have met, and generally they had the most people; but, notwithstanding, they fell short in battle against us. Now, on the other hand, we have by far the greatest force; and it will appear probable to the men who a short time ago lost gallant relations by them, that this will be a good occasion to get vengeance, for they have fled before us the greater part of the summer; and we have often said that if they waited for us, as appears now to be the case, we would have a brush with them. Now I will tell my opinion, which is, that I will engage them, if it be agreeable to the king's pleasure; for I think it will go now as formerly, that they must give way before us if we attack them bravely; and I shall always attack where others may think it most difficult."

The speech was received with much applause, and all declared they were ready to engage in battle against Hakon. Then they rowed with all the ships up the river, until they came in sight of each other, and then King Inge turned off from the river current under the island. Now the king addressed the lendermen again, and told them to get ready for battle. He turned himself especially to Erling Skakke, and said, what was true, that no man in the army had more understanding and knowledge in fighting battles, although some were more hot. The king then addressed himself to several of the lendermen, speaking to them by name; and ended by desiring that each man should make his attack where he thought it would be of advantage, and thereafter all would act together.

6. ERLING'S SPEECH.

ERLING SKAKKE REPLIED THUS to the king's speech: "It is my duty, sire, not to be silent; and I shall give my advice, since it is desired. The resolution now adopted is contrary to my judgment; for I call it foolhardy to fight under these circumstances, although we have so many and such fine men. Supposing we make an attack on them, and row up against this river-current; then one of the three men who are in each half room must be employed in rowing only, and another must be covering with the shield the man who rows; and what have we then to fight with but one third of our men? It appears to me that they can be of little use in the battle who are sitting at their oars with their backs turned to the enemy. Give me now some time for consideration, and I promise you that before three days are over I shall fall upon some plan by which we can come into battle with advantage."

It was evident from Erling's speech that he dissuaded from an attack; but, notwithstanding, it was urged by many who thought that Hakon would now, as before, take to the land. "And then," said they, "we cannot get hold of him; but now they have but few men, and we have their fate in our own hands."

Gregorius said but little; but thought that Erling rather dissuaded from an attack that Gregorius's advice should have no effect, than that he had any better advice to give.

7. OF HAKON'S FLEET.

THEN SAID KING INGE to Erling, "Now we will follow thy advice, brother, with regard to the manner of attacking; but seeing how eager our counsellors are for it, we shall make the attack this day."

Erling replied, "All the boats and light vessels we have should row outside the island, and up the east arm of the river, and then down with the stream upon them, and try if they cannot cut them loose from the piles. Then we, with the large ships, shall row from below here against them; and I cannot tell until it be tried, if those who are now so furiously warm will be much brisker at the attack than I am."

This counsel was approved by all. There was a ness stretched out between their fleet and Hakon's, so that they could not see each other. Now when Hakon and his men, who had taken counsel with each other in a meeting, saw the boat-squadron rowing down the river, some thought King Inge intended to give them battle; but many believed they did not dare, for it looked as if the attack was given up; and they, besides, were very confident, both in their preparations and men. There were many great people with Hakon: there were Sigurd of Reyr, and Simon's sons; Nikolas Skialdvarson; Eindride, a son of Jon Mornef, who was the most gallant and popular man in the Throndhjem country; and many other lendermen and warriors. Now when they saw that King Inge's men with many ships were rowing out of the river, Hakon and his men believed they were going to fly; and therefore they cut their land-ropes with which they lay fast at the piles, seized their oars, and rowed after them in pursuit. The ships ran fast down with the stream; but when they came further down the river, abreast of the ness, they saw King Inge's main strength lying quiet at the island Hising. King Inge's people saw Hakon's ships under way, and believed they were coming to attack them; and now there was great bustle and clash of arms, and they encouraged each other by a great war-shout. Hakon with his fleet turned northwards a little to the land, where there was a turn in the bight of the river, and where there was no current. They made ready for battle, carried land-ropes to the shore, turned the stems of their ships outwards, and bound them all together. They laid the large East-country traders without the other vessels, the one above, the other below, and bound them to the long-ships. In the middle of the fleet lay the king's ship, and next to it Sigurd's; and on the other side of the king's ship lay Nikolas, and next to him Endride Jonson. All the smaller ships lay farther off, and they were all nearly loaded with weapons and stones.

8. SIGURD OF REYR'S SPEECH.

Then Sigurd of Reyr made the following speech: "Now there is hope that the time is come which has been promised us all the summer, that we shall meet King Inge in battle. We have long prepared ourselves for this; and many of our comrades have boasted that they would never fly from or submit to King Inge and Gregorius, and now let them remember their words. But we who have sometimes got the toothache in our conflicts with them, speak less confidently; for it has happened, as all have heard, that we very often have come off without glory. But, nevertheless, it is now necessary to fight manfully, and stand to it with steadiness; for the only escape for us is in victory. Although we have somewhat fewer men than they, yet luck determines which side shall have the advantage, and God knows that the right is on our side. Inge has killed two of his brothers; and it is obvious to all men that the mulct he intends to pay King Hakon for his father's murder is to murder him also, as well as his other relations, which will be seen this day to be his intent. King Hakon desired from the beginning no more of Norway than the third part, which his father had possessed, and which was denied him; and yet, in my opinion, King Hakon has a better right to inherit after his father's brother, King Eystein, than Inge or Simon Skalp, or the other men who killed King Eystein. Many of them who would save their souls, and yet have defiled their hands with such bloody deeds as Inge has done, must think it a presumption before God that he takes the name of king; and I wonder God suffers such monstrous wickedness as his; but it may be God's will that we shall now put him down. Let us fight then manfully, and God will give us victory; and, if we fall, will repay us with joys unspeakable for now allowing the might of the wicked to prevail over us. Go forth then in confidence, and be not afraid when the battle begins. Let each watch over his own and his comrade's safety, and God protect us all." There went a good report abroad of this speech of Sigurd, and all promised fairly, and to do their duty. King Hakon went on board of the great East-country ship, and a shield-bulwark was made around him; but his standard remained on the long-ship in which it had been before.

9. OF KING INGE'S MEN.

Now must we tell about King Inge and his men. When they saw that King Hakon and his people were ready for battle, and the river only was between them, they sent a light vessel to recall the rest of the fleet which had rowed away; and in the meantime the king waited for them, and arranged the troops for the attack. Then the chiefs consulted in presence of the army, and told their opinions; first, which ships should lie nearest to the enemy; and then where each should attack.

Gregorius spoke thus: "We have many and fine men; and it is my advice, King Inge, that you do not go to the assault with us, for everything is preserved if you are safe. And no man knows where an arrow may hit, even from the hands of a bad bowman; and they have prepared themselves so, that missiles and stones can be thrown from the high stages upon the merchant ships, so that there is less danger for those who are farthest from them. They have not more men than we lendermen can very well engage with. I shall lay my ship alongside their largest ship, and I expect the conflict between us will be but short; for it has often been so in our former meetings, although there has been a much greater want of men with us than now." All thought well of the advice that the king himself should not take part in the battle.

Then Erling Skakke said, "I agree also to the counsel that you, sire, should not go into the battle. It appears to me that their preparations are such, that we require all our precaution not to suffer a great defeat from them; and whole limbs are the easiest cured. In the council we held before to-day many opposed what I said, and ye said then that I did not want to fight; but now I think the business has altered its appearance, and greatly to our advantage, since they have hauled off from the piles, and now it stands so that I do not dissuade from giving battle; for I see, what all are sensible of, how necessary it is to put an end to this robber band who have gone over the whole country with pillage and destruction, in order that people may cultivate the land in peace, and serve a king so good and just as King Inge who has long had trouble and anxiety from the haughty unquiet spirit of his relations, although he has been a shield of defence for the whole people, and has been exposed to manifold perils for the peace of the country." Erling spoke well and long, and many other chiefs also; and all to the same purpose–all urging to battle. In the meantime they waited until all the fleet should be assembled. King Inge had the ship Baekisudin; and, at the entreaty of his friends, he did not join the battle, but lay still at the island.

10. BEGINNING OF THE BATTLE.

When the army was ready they rowed briskly against the enemy, and both sides raised a war-shout. Inge's men did not bind their ships together, but let them be loose; for they rowed right across the current, by which the large ships were much swayed. Erling Skakke laid his ship beside King Hakon's ship, and ran the stem between his and Sigurd's ship, by which the battle began. But Gregorius's ship swung upon the ground, and heeled very much over, so that at first she could not come into the battle; and when Hakon's men saw this they laid themselves against her, and attacked Gregorius's ship on all sides. Ivar, Hakon Mage's son, laid his ship so that the stems struck together; and he got a boat-hook fastened on Gregorius, on that part of his body where the waist is smallest, and dragged him to him, by which Gregorius stumbled against the ship's rails; but the hook slipped to one side, or Gregorius would have been dragged over-board. Gregorius, however, was but little wounded, for he had on a plate coat of armour. Ivar called out to him, that he had a "thick bark." Gregorius replied, that if Ivar went on so he would "require it all, and not have too much." It was very near then that Gregorius and his men had sprung overboard; but Aslak Unge threw an anchor into their ship, and dragged them off the ground. Then Gregorius laid himself against Ivar's ship, and they fought a long while; but Gregorius's ship being both higher sided and more strongly manned, many people fell in Ivar's ship, and some jumped overboard. Ivar was so severely wounded that he could not take part in the fight. When his ship was cleared of the men, Gregorius let Ivar be carried to the shore, so that he might escape; and from that time they were constant friends.

11. KING HAKON'S FLIGHT.

When King Inge and his men saw that Gregorius was aground, he encouraged his crew to row to his assistance. "It was," he said, "the most imprudent advice that we should remain lying here, while our friends are in battle; for we have the largest and best ship in all the fleet. But now I see that Gregorius, the man to whom I owe the most, is in need of help; so we must hasten to the fight where it is sharpest. It is also most proper that I should be in the battle; for the victory, if we win it, will belong to me. And if I even knew beforehand that our men were not to gain the battle, yet our place is where our friends are; for I can do nothing if I lose the men who are justly called the defence of the country, who are the bravest, and have long ruled for me and my kingdom." Thereupon he ordered his banner to be set up, which was done; and they rowed across the river. Then the battle raged, and the king could not get room to attack, so close lay the ships before him. First he lay under the East-country trading ship, and from it they threw down upon his vessel spears, iron-shod stakes, and such large stones that it was impossible to hold out longer there, and he had to haul off. Now when the king's people saw that he was come they made place for him, and then he laid alongside of Eindride Jonson's ship. Now King Hakon's men abandoned the small ships, and went on board the large merchant vessels; but some of them sprang on shore. Erling Skakke and his men had a severe conflict. Erling himself was on the forecastle, and called his forecastlemen, and ordered them to board the king's ship; but they answered, this was no easy matter, for there were beams above with an iron comb on them. Then Erling himself went to the bow, and stayed there a while, until they succeeded in getting on board the king's ship: and then the ship was cleared of men on the bows, and the whole army gave way. Many sprang into the water, many fell, but the greater number got to the land. So says Einar Skulason:–

"Men fall upon the slippery deck–
Men roll off from the blood-drenched wreck;
Dead bodies float down with the stream,
And from the shores witch-ravens scream.
The cold blue river now runs red
With the warm blood of warriors dead,
And stains the waves in Karmt Sound
With the last drops of the death-wound.

"All down the stream, with unmann'd prow,
Floats many an empty long-ship now,
Ship after ship, shout after shout,
Tell that Kign Hakon can't hold out.
The bowmen ply their bows of elm,
The red swords flash o'er broken helm:
King Hakon's men rush to the strand,
Out of their ships, up through the land."

Einar composed a song about Gregorius Dagson, which is called the River-song. King Inge granted life and peace to Nikolas Skialdvarson when his ship was deserted, and thereupon he went into King Inge's service, and remained in it as long as the king lived. Eindride Jonson leaped on board of King Inge's ship when his own was cleared of men, and begged for his life. King Inge wished to grant it; but Havard Klining's son ran up, and gave him a mortal wound, which was much blamed; but he said Eindride had been the cause of his father's death. There was much lamentation at Eindride's death, but principally in the Throndhjem district. Many of Hakon's people fell here, but not many chiefs. Few of King Inge's people fell, but many were wounded. King Hakon fled up the country, and King Inge went north to Viken with his troops; and he, as well as Gregorius, remained in Viken all winter (A.D. 1160). When King Inge's men, Bergliot and his brothers, sons of Ivar of Elda, came from the battle to Bergen, they slew Nickolas Skeg, who had been Hakon's treasurer, and then went north to Throndhjem.

King Hakon came north before Yule, and Sigurd was sometimes home at Reyr; for Gregorius, who was nearly related to Sigurd, had obtained for him life and safety from King Inge, so that he retained all his estates. King Hakon was in the merchant-town of Nidaros in Yule;

and one evening in the beginning of Yule his men fought in the room of the court, and in this affray eight men were killed, and many were wounded. The eighth day of Yule, King Hakon's man Alf Rode, son of Ottar Birting, with about eighty men, went to Elda, and came in the night unexpectedly on the people, who were very drunk, and set fire to the room; but they went out, and defended themselves bravely. There fell Bergliot, Ivar's son, and Ogmund, his brother, and many more. They had been nearly thirty altogether in number. In winter died, north in the merchant-town, Andres Simonson, King Hakon's foster-brother; and his death was much deplored. Erling Skakke and Inge's men, who were in Bergen, threatened that in winter they would proceed against Hakon and his men; but it came to nothing. Gregorius sent word from the east, from Konungahella, that if he were so near as Erling and his men, he would not sit quietly in Bergen while Hakon was killing King Inge's friends and their comrades in war north in the Throndhjem country.

12. THE CONFLICT UPON THE PIERS.

King Inge and Gregorius left the east in spring, and came to Bergen; but as soon as Hakon and Sigurd heard that Inge had left Viken, they went there by land. When King Inge and his people came to Bergen, a quarrel arose between Haldor Brynjolfson and Bjorn Nikolason. Bjorn's house-man asked Haldor's when they met at the pier, why he looked so pale.

He replied, because he had been bled.

"I could not look so pale if I tried, at merely being bled."

"I again think," retorted the other, "that thou wouldst have borne it worse, and less manfully." And no other beginning was there for their quarrel than this. Afterwards one word followed another, till from brawling they came to fighting. It was told to Haldor Brynjolfson, who was in the house drinking, that his house-man was wounded down on the pier and he went there immediately. But Bjorn's house-men had come there before, and as Haldor thought his house-man had been badly treated, he went up to them and beat them; and it was told to Bjorn Buk that the people of Viken were beating his house-men on the pier. Then Bjorn and his house-men took their weapons, hurried down to the pier, and would avenge their men; and a bloody strife began. It was told Gregorius that his relation Haldor required assistance, and that his house-men were being cut down in the street; on which Gregorius and his men ran to the place in their armour. Now it was told Erling Skakke that his sister's son Bjorn was fighting with Gregorius and Haldor down on the piers, and that he needed help. Then he proceeded thither with a great force, and exhorted the people to stand by him; saying it would be a great disgrace never to be wiped out, if the Viken people should trample upon them in their own native place. There fell thirteen men, of whom nine were killed on the spot, and four died of their wounds, and many were wounded. When the word came to King Inge that Gregorius and Erling were fighting down on the piers, he hastened there, and tried to separate them; but could do nothing, so mad were they on both sides. Then Gregorius called to Inge, and told him to go away; for it was in vain to attempt coming between them, as matters now stood. He said it would be the greatest misfortune if the king mixed himself up with it; for he could not be certain that there were not people in the fray who would commit some great misdeed if they had opportunity. Then King Inge retired; and when the greatest tumult was over, Gregorius and his men went to Nikolas church, and Erling behind them, calling to each other. Then King Inge came a second time, and pacified them; and both agreed that he should mediate between them.

When King Inge and Gregorius heard that King Hakon was in Viken, they went east with many ships; but when they came King Hakon fled from them, and there was no battle. Then King Inge went to Oslo, and Gregorius was in Konungahella.

13. MUNAN'S DEATH.

Soon after Gregorius heard that Hakon and his men were at a farm called Saurby, which lies up beside the forest. Gregorius hastened there; came in the night; and supposing that King Hakon and Sigurd would be in the largest of the houses, set fire to the buildings there. But Hakon and his men were in the smaller house, and came forth, seeing the fire, to help their people. There Munan fell, a son of Ale Uskeynd, a brother of King Sigurd Hakon's father. Gregorius and his men killed him, because he was helping those whom they were burning within the house. Some escaped, but many were killed. Asbjorn Jalda, who had been a very great viking, escaped from the house, but was grievously wounded. A bonde met him, and he offered the man money to let him get away; but the bonde replied, he would do what he liked best; and, adding that he had often been in fear of his life for him, he slew him. King Hakon and Sigurd escaped, but many of their people were killed. Thereafter Gregorius returned home to Konungahella. Soon after King Hakon and Sigurd went to Haldor Brynjolfson's farm of Vettaland, set fire to the house, and burnt it. Haldor went out, and was cut down instantly with his house-men; and in all there were about twenty men killed. Sigrid, Haldor's wife, was a sister of Gregorius, and they allowed her to escape into the forest in her night-shift only; but they took with them Amunde, who was a son of Gyrd Amundason and of Gyrid Dag's daughter, and a sister's son of Gregorius, and who was then a boy about five years old.

14. OF THE FALL OF GREGORIUS DAGSON.

WHEN GREGORIUS HEARD THE news he took it much to heart, and inquired carefully where they were. Gregorius set out from Konungahella late in Yule, and came to Fors the thirteenth day of Yule, where he remained a night, and heard vespers the last day of Yule, which was a Saturday, and the holy Evangel was read before him. When Gregorius and his followers saw the men of King Hakon and Sigurd, the king's force appeared to them smaller than their own. There was a river called Befia between them, where they met; and there was unsound ice on the river, for there went a stream under the ice from it. King Hakon and his men had cut a rent in the ice, and laid snow over it, so that nobody could see it. When Gregorius came to the ice on the river the ice appeared to him unsound, he said; and he advised the people to go to the bridge, which was close by, to cross the river. The bonde-troops replied, that they did not know why he should be afraid to go across the ice to attack so few people as Hakon had, and the ice was good enough. Gregorius said it was seldom necessary to encourage him to show bravery, and it should not be so now. Then he ordered them to follow him, and not to be standing on the land while he was on the ice, and he said it was their council to go out upon the dangerous ice, but he had no wish to do so, or to be led by them. Then he ordered the banner to be advanced, and immediately went out on the ice with the men. As soon as the bondes found that the ice was unsound they turned back. Gregorius fell through the ice, but not very deep, and he told his men to take care. There were not more than twenty men with him, the others having turned back. A man of King Hakon's troop shot an arrow at Gregorius, which hit him under the throat, and thus ended his life. Gregorius fell, and ten men with him. It is the talk of all men that he had been the most gallant lenderman in Norway that any man then living could remember; and also he behaved the best towards us Icelanders of any chief since King Eystein the Elder's death. Gregorius's body was carried to Hofund, and interred at Gimsey Isle, in a nunnery which is there, of which Gregorius's sister, Baugeid, was then the abbess.

15. KING INGE HEARS OF GREGORIUS'S FALL.

Two bailiffs went to Oslo to bring the tidings to King Inge. When they arrived they desired to speak to the king: and he asked, what news they brought.

"Gregorius Dagson's death," said they.

"How came that misfortune?" asked the king.

When they had told him how it happened, he said, "They gave advice who understood the least."

It is said he took it so much to heart that he cried like a child. When he recovered himself he said, "I wanted to go to Gregorius as soon as I heard of Haldor's murder; for I thought that Gregorius would not sit long before thinking of revenge. But the people here would think nothing so important as their Yule feasts, and nothing could move them away; and I am confident that if I had been there, he would either have proceeded more cautiously, or I and Gregorius would now have shared one lodging. Now he is gone, the man who has been my best friend, and more than any other has kept the kingdom in my hands; and I think it will be but a short space between us. Now I make an oath to go forth against Hakon, and one of two things shall happen: I shall either come to my death, or shall walk over Hakon and his people; and such a man as Gregorius is not avenged, even if all were to pay the penalty of their lives for him."

There was a man present who replied, "Ye need not seek after them, for they intend to seek you."

Kristin, King Sigurd's daughter and King Inge's cousin, was then in Oslo. The king heard that she intended going away. He sent a message to her to inquire why she wished to leave the town.

She thought it was dangerous and unsafe for a female to be there. The king would not let her go. "For if it go well with me, as I hope, you will be well here; and if I fall, my friends may not get leave to dress my body; but you can ask permission, and it will not be denied you, and you will thereby best requite what I have done for you."

16. OF KING INGE.

On Saint Blasius' day (February 3, 1161), in the evening, King Inge's spies brought him the news that King Hakon was coming towards the town. Then King Inge ordered the war-horns to call together all the troops up from the town; and when he drew them up he could reckon them to be nearly 4000 men. The king let the array be long, but not more than five men deep. Then some said that the king should not be himself in the battle, as they thought the risk too great; but that his brother Orm should be the leader of the army. The king replied, "I think if Gregorius were alive and here now, and I had fallen and was to be avenged, he would not lie concealed, but would be in the battle. Now, although I, on account of my ill health, am not fit for the combat as he was, yet will I show as good will as he would have had; and it is not to be thought of that I should not be in the battle."

People say that Gunhild, who was married to Simon, King Hakon's foster-brother, had a witch employed to sit out all night and procure the victory for Hakon; and that the answer was obtained, that they should fight King Inge by night, and never by day, and then the result would be favourable. The witch who, as people say, sat out was called Thordis Skeggia; but what truth there may be in the report I know not.

Simon Skalp had gone to the town, and was gone to sleep, when the war-shouts awoke him. When the night was well advanced, King Inge's spies came to him, and told him that King Hakon and his army were coming over the ice; for the ice lay the whole way from the town to Hofud Isle.

17. KING INGE'S SPEECH.

Thereupon King Inge went with his army out on the ice, and he drew it up in order of battle in front of the town. Simon Skalp was in that wing of the array which was towards Thraelaberg; and on the other wing, which was towards the Nunnery, was Gudrod, the king of the South Hebudes, a son of Olaf Klining, and Jon, a son of Svein Bergthor Buk. When King Hakon and his army came near to King Inge's array, both sides raised a war-shout. Gudrod and Jon gave King Hakon and his men a sign, and let them know where they were in the line; and as soon as Hakon's men in consequence turned thither, Gudrod immediately fled with 1500 men; and Jon, and a great body of men with him, ran over to King Hakon's army, and assisted them in the fight. When this news was told to King Inge, he said, "Such is the difference between my friends. Never would Gregorius have done so in his life!" There were some who advised King Inge to get on horseback, and ride from the battle up to Raumarike; "where," said they, "you would get help enough, even this very day." The king replied, he had no inclination to do so. "I have heard you often say, and I think truly, that it was of little use to my brother, King Eystein, that he took to flight; and yet he was a man distinguished for many qualities which adorn a king. Now I, who labour under so great decrepitude, can see how bad my fate would be, if I betook myself to what proved so unfortunate for him; with so great a difference as there is between our activity, health, and strength. I was in the second year of my age when I was chosen king of Norway, and I am now twenty-five; and I think I have had misfortune and sorrow under my kingly dignity, rather than pleasure and peaceful days. I have had many battles, sometimes with more, sometimes with fewer people; and it is my greatest luck that I have never fled. God will dispose of my life, and of how long it shall be; but I shall never betake myself to flight."

18. KING INGE'S FALL.

Now as Jon and his troop had broken the one wing of King Inge's array, many of those who were nearest to him fled, by which the whole array was dispersed, and fell into disorder. But Hakon and his men went briskly forwards; and now it was near daybreak. An assault was made against King Inge's banner, and in this conflict King Inge fell; but his brother Orm continued the battle, while many of the army fled up into the town. Twice Orm went to the town after the king's fall to encourage the people, and both times returned, and went out again upon the ice to continue the battle. Hakon's men attacked the wing of the array which Simon Skalp led; and in that assault fell of King Inge's men his brother-in-law, Gudbrand Skafhogson. Simon Skalp and Halvard Hikre went against each other with their troops, and fought while they drew aside past Thraelaberg; and in this conflict both Simon and Halvard fell. Orm, the king's brother, gained great reputation in this battle; but he at last fled. Orm the winter before had been contracted with Ragna, a daughter of Nikolas Mase, who had been married before to King Eystein Haraldson; and the wedding was fixed for the Sunday after Saint Blasius's mass, which was on a Friday. Orm fled east to Svithjod, where his brother Magnus was then king; and their brother Ragnvald was an earl there at that time. They were the sons of Queen Ingerid and Henrik Halte, who was a son of the Danish king Svein Sveinson. The princess Kristin took care of King Inge's body, which was laid on the stone wall of Halvard's church, on the south side without the choir. He had then been king for twenty-three years (A.D. 1137-1161). In this battle many fell on both sides, but principally of King Inge's men. Of King Hakon's people fell Arne Frirekson. Hakon's men took all the feast and victuals prepared for the wedding, and a great booty besides.

19. OF KING HAKON AND QUEEN KRISTIN.

Then King Hakon took possession of the whole country, and distributed all the offices among his own friends, both in the towns and in the country. King Hakon and his men had a meeting in Halvard's church, where they had a private conference concerning the management of the country. Kristin the princess gave the priest who kept the church keys a large sum of money to conceal one of her men in the church, so that she might know what Hakon and his counsellors intended. When she learnt what they had said, she sent a man to Bergen to her husband Erling Skakke, with the message that he should never trust Hakon or his men.

20. OF OLAF'S MIRACLE.

It happened at the battle of Stiklestad, as before related, that King Olaf threw from him the sword called Hneiter when he received his wound. A Swedish man, who had broken his own sword, took it up, and fought with it. When this man escaped with the other fugitives he came to Svithjod, and went home to his house. From that time he kept the sword all his days, and afterwards his son, and so relation after relation; and when the sword shifted its owner, the one told to the other the name of the sword and where it came from. A long time after, in the days of Kirjalax the emperor of Constantinople, when there was a great body of Varings in the town, it happened in the summer that the emperor was on a campaign, and lay in the camp with his army. The Varings who had the guard, and watched over the emperor, lay on the open plain without the camp. They changed the watch with each other in the night, and those who had been before on watch lay down and slept; but all completely armed. It was their custom, when they went to sleep, that each should have his helmet on his head, his shield over him, sword under the head, and the right hand on the sword-handle. One of these comrades, whose lot it was to watch the latter part of the night, found, on awakening towards morning, that his sword was gone. He looked after it, and saw it lying on the flat plain at a distance from him. He got up and took the sword, thinking that his comrades who had been on watch had taken the sword from him in a joke; but they all denied it. The same thing happened three nights. Then he wondered at it, as well as they who saw or heard of it; and people began to ask him how it could have happened. He said that his sword was called Hneiter, and had belonged to King Olaf the Saint, who had himself carried it in the battle of Stiklestad; and he also related how the sword since that time had gone from one to another. This was told to the emperor, who called the man before him to whom the sword belonged, and gave him three times as much gold as the sword was worth; and the sword itself he had laid in Saint Olaf's church, which the Varings supported, where it has been ever since over the altar. There was a lenderman of Norway while Harald Gille's sons, Eystein, Inge, and Sigurd lived, who was called Eindride Unge; and he was in Constantinople when these events took place. He told these circumstances in Norway, according to what Einar Skulason says in his song about King Olaf the Saint, in which these events are sung.

21. OLAF'S MIRACLE IN FAVOUR OF THE VARINGS.

It happened once in the Greek country, when Kirjalax was emperor there, that he made an expedition against Blokumannaland. When he came to the Pezina plains, a heathen king came against him with an innumerable host. He brought with him many horsemen, and many large waggons, in which were large loop-holes for shooting through. When they prepared for their night quarters they drew up their waggons, one by the side of the other, without their tents, and dug a great ditch without; and all which made a defence as strong as a castle. The heathen king was blind. Now when the Greek king came, the heathens drew up their array on the plains before their waggon-fortification. The Greeks drew up their array opposite, and they rode on both sides to fight with each other; but it went on so ill and so unfortunately, that the Greeks were compelled to fly after suffering a great defeat, and the heathens gained a victory. Then the king drew up an array of Franks and Flemings, who rode against the heathens, and fought with them; but it went with them as with the others, that many were killed, and all who escaped took to flight. Then the Greek king was greatly incensed at his men-at-arms; and they replied, that he should now take his wine-bags, the Varings. The king says that he would not throw away his jewels, and allow so few men, however bold they might be, to attack so vast an army. Then Thorer Helsifig, who at that time was leader of the Varings replied to the king's words, "If there was burning fire in the way, I and my people would run into it, if I knew the king's advantage required it." Then the king replied, "Call upon your holy King Olaf for help and strength." The Varings, who were 450 men, made a vow with hand and word to build a church in Constantinople, at their own expense and with the aid of other good men, and have the church consecrated to the honour and glory of the holy King Olaf; and thereupon the Varings rushed into the plain. When the heathens saw them, they told their king that there was another troop of the Greek king's army come out upon the plain; but they were only a handful of people. The king says, "Who is that venerable man riding on a white horse at the head of the troop?" They replied, "We do not see him." There was so great a difference of numbers, that there were sixty heathens for every Christian man; but notwithstanding the Varings went boldly to the attack. As soon as they met terror and alarm seized the army of the heathens, and they instantly began to fly; but the Varings pursued, and soon killed a great number of them. When the Greeks and Franks who before had fled from the heathens saw this, they hastened to take part, and pursue the enemy with the others. Then the Varings had reached the waggon-fortification, where the greatest defeat was given to the enemy. The heathen king was taken in the flight of his people, and the Varings brought him along with them; after which the Christians took the camp of the heathens, and their waggon-fortification.

BOOK FIFTEEN

Magnus Erlingson's Saga

PRELIMINARY REMARKS.

WITH THIS SAGA, which describes a series of conflicts, Snorre's "Heimskringla" ends. King Eystein died in 1177, but Magnus Erlingson continued to reign until his death in 1184. The conflicts continued until the opposition party was led to victory by King Sverre.

The only skald quoted is Thorbjorn Skakkaskald.

1. OF MAGNUS ERLINGSON'S BEGINNING.

WHEN ERLING GOT CERTAIN intelligence of the determinations of Hakon and his counsellors, he sent a message to all the chiefs who he knew had been steady friends of King Inge, and also to his courtmen and his retinue, who had saved themselves by flight, and also to all Gregorius's house-men, and called them together to a meeting. When they met, and conversed with each other, they resolved to keep their men together; and which resolution they confirmed by oath and hand-shake to each other. Then they considered whom they should take to be king. Erling Skakke first spoke, and inquired if it was the opinion of the chiefs and other men of power that Simon Skalp's son, the son of the daughter of King Harald Gille, should be chosen king, and Jon Halkelson be taken to lead the army; but Jon refused it. Then it was inquired if Nikolas Skialdvarson, a sister's son of King Magnus Barefoot, would place himself at the head of the army; but he answered thus:–It was his opinion that some one should be chosen king who was of the royal race; and, for leader of the troops, some one from whom help and understanding were to be looked for; and then it would be easier to gather an army. It was now tried whether Arne would let any of his sons, King Inge's brothers, be proclaimed king. Arne replies, that Kristin's son, she was the daughter of King Sigurd the Crusader, was nearest by propinquity of descent to the crown of Norway. "And here is also a man to be his adviser, and whose duty it is to take care of him and of the kingdom; and that man is his father Erling, who is both prudent, brave, experienced in war, and an able man in governing the kingdom; he wants no capability of bringing this counsel into effect, if luck be with him." Many thought well of this advice.

Erling replied to it, "As far as I can see or hear in this meeting, the most will rather be excused from taking upon themselves such a difficult business. Now it appears to me altogether uncertain, provided we begin this work, whether he who puts himself at the head of it will gain any honour; or whether matters will go as they have done before when any one undertakes such great things, that he loses all his property and possibly his life. But if this counsel be adopted, there may be men who will undertake to carry it through; but he who comes under such an obligation must seek, in every way, to prevent any opposition or enmity from those who are now in this council."

All gave assurance that they would enter into this confederacy with perfect fidelity. Then said Erling, "I can say for myself that it would almost be my death to serve King Hakon; and however dangerous it may be, I will rather venture to adopt your advice, and take upon me to lead this force, if that be the will, counsel, and desire of you all, and if you will all bind yourselves to this agreement by oath."

To this they all agreed; and in this meeting it was determined to take Erling's son Magnus to be king. They afterwards held a Thing in the town; and at this Thing Magnus Erlingson, then five years old, was elected king of the whole country. All who had been servants of King Inge went into his service, and each of them retained the office and dignity he had held under King Inge (A.D. 1161).

2. KING MAGNUS GOES TO DENMARK.

Erling Skakke made himself ready to travel, fitted out ships, and had with him King Magnus, together with the household-men who were on the spot. In this expedition were the king's relatives,–Arne;

Ingerid, King Inge's mother, with her two sons; besides Jon Kutiza, a son of Sigurd Stork, and Erling's house-men, as well as those who had been Gregorius's house-men; and they had in all ten ships. They went south to Denmark to King Valdemar and Buriz Heinrekson, King Inge's brother. King Valdemar was King Magnus's blood-relation; for Ingebjorg, mother of King Valdemar, and Malmfrid, mother of Kristin, King Magnus's mother, were cousins. The Danish king received them hospitably, and he and Erling had private meetings and consultations: and so much was known of their counsels, that King Valdemar was to aid King Magnus with such help as might be required from his kingdom to win and retain Norway. On the other hand, King Valdemar should get that domain in Norway which his ancestors Harald Gormson and Svein Forked-beard had possessed; namely, the whole of Viken as far north as Rygiarbit. This agreement was confirmed by oath and a fixed treaty. Then Erling and King Magnus made themselves ready to leave Denmark, and they sailed out of Vendilskage.

3. BATTLE OF TUNSBERG.

King Hakon went in spring, after the Easter week, north to Throndhjem, and had with him the whole fleet that had belonged to King Inge. He held a Thing there in the merchant-town, and was chosen king of the whole country. Then he made Sigurd of Reyr an earl, and gave him an earldom, and afterwards proceeded southwards with his followers all the way to Viken. The king went to Tunsberg; but sent Earl Sigurd east to Konungahella, to defend the country with a part of the forces in case Erling should come from the south. Erling and his fleet came to Agder, and went straight north to Bergen, where they killed Arne Brigdarskalle, King Hakon's officer, and came back immediately against King Hakon. Earl Sigurd, who had not observed the journey of Erling and his followers from the south, was at that time east in the Gaut river, and King Hakon was in Tunsberg. Erling brought up at Hrossanes, and lay there some nights. In the meantime King Hakon made preparations in the town. When Erling and his fleet were coming up to the town, they took a merchant vessel, filled it with wood and straw, and set fire to it; and the wind blowing right towards the town, drove the vessel against the piers. Erling had two cables brought on board the vessel, and made fast to two boats, and made them row along as the vessel drove. Now when the fire was come almost abreast of the town, those who were in the boats held back the vessel by the ropes, so that the town could not be set on fire; but so thick a smoke spread from it over the town, that one could not see from the piers where the king's array was. Then Erling drew the whole fleet in where the wind carried the fire, and shot at the enemy. When the townspeople saw that the fire was approaching their houses, and many were wounded by the bowmen, they resolved to send the priest Hroald, the long-winded speaker, to Erling, to beg him to spare them and the town; and they dissolved the array in favour of Hakon, as soon as Hroald told them their prayer was granted. Now when the array of towns-people had dispersed, the men on the piers were much thinned: however, some urged Hakon's men to make resistance: but Onund Simonson, who had most influence over the army, said, "I will not fight for Earl Sigurd's earldom, since he is not here himself." Then Onund fled, and was followed by all the people, and by the king himself; and they hastened up the country. King Hakon lost many men here; and these verses were made about it:–

"Onund declares he will not go
In battle 'gainst Earl Sigurd's foe,
If Earl Sigurd does not come,
But with his house-men sits at home.
King Magnus' men rush up the street,
Eager with Hakon's troop to meet;
But Hakon's war-hawks, somewhat shy,
Turn quick about, and off they fly."

Thorbjorn Skakkaskald also said:–

"The Tunsberg men would not be slow
In thy good cause to risk a blow;
And well they knew the chief could stain
The wolves' mouths on a battle-plain.
But the town champion rather fears
The sharp bright glance of levelled spears;
Their steel-clad warrior loves no fight
Where bowstring twangs, or fire flies bright."

King Hakon then took the land-road northwards to Throndhjem. When Earl Sigurd heard of this, he proceeded with all the ships he could get the seaway north-wards, to meet King Hakon there.

4. OF ERLING AND HAKON.

Erling Skakke took all the ships in Tunsberg belonging to King Hakon, and there he also took the Baekisudin which had belonged to King Inge. Then Erling proceeded, and reduced the whole of Viken in obedience to King Magnus, and also the whole country north wheresoever he appeared up to Bergen, where he remained all winter. There Erling killed Ingebjorn Sipil, King Hakon's lenderman of the north part of the Fjord district. In winter (A.D. 1162) King Hakon was in Throndhjem; but in the following spring he ordered a levy, and prepared to go against Erling. He had with him Earl Sigurd, Jon Sveinson, Eindride Unge, Onund Simonson, Philip Peterson, Philip Gyrdson, Ragnvald Kunta, Sigurd Kapa, Sigurd Hiupa, Frirek Keina, Asbjorn of Forland, Thorbjorn, a son of Gunnar the treasurer, and Stradbjarne.

5. OF ERLING'S PEOPLE.

Erling was in Bergen with a great armament, and resolved to lay a sailing prohibition on all the merchant vessels which were going north to Nidaros; for he knew that King Hakon would soon get tidings of him, if ships were sailing between the towns. Besides, he gave out that it was better for Bergen to get the goods, even if the owners were obliged to sell them cheaper than they wished than that they should fall into the hands of enemies and thereby strengthen them. And now a great many vessels were assembled at Bergen, for many arrived every day, and none were allowed to go away. Then Erling let some of the lightest of his vessels be laid ashore, and spread the report that he would wait for Hakon, and, with the help of his friends and relations, oppose the enemy there. He then one day called a meeting of the ship-masters, and gave them and all the merchant ships and their steersmen leave to go where they pleased. When the men who had charge of the cargoes, and were all ready to sail away with their goods, some for trade, others on various business, had got leave from Erling Skakke to depart, there was a soft and favourable wind for sailing north along the coast. Before the evening all who were ready had set sail, and hastened on as fast as they could, according to the speed of their vessels, the one vying with the other. When this fleet came north to More, Hakon's fleet had arrived there before them: and he himself was there fully engaged in collecting people, and summoning to him the lendermen, and all liable to serve in the levy, without having for a long time heard any news from Bergen.

Now, however, they heard, as the latest news, that Erling Skakke had laid his ships up in Bergen, and there they would find him; and also that he had a large force with him. King Hakon sailed from thence to Veey, and sent away Earl Sigurd and Onund Simonson to gather people, and sent men also to both the More districts. After King Hakon had remained a few days at the town he sailed farther, and proceeded to the South, thinking that it would both promote his journey and enable new levies to join him sooner.

Erling Skakke had given leave on Sunday to all the merchant vessels to leave Bergen; and on Tuesday, as soon as the early mass was over, he ordered the warhorns to sound, summoned to him the men-at-arms and the townsmen, and let the ships which were laid up on shore be drawn down into the water. Then Erling held a House-Thing with his men and the people of the levy; told them his intentions; named ship commanders; and had the names called over of the men who were to be on board of the king's ship. This Thing ended with Erling's order to every man to make himself ready in his berth wherever a place was appointed him; and declared that he who remained in the town after the Baekisudin was hauled out, should be punished by loss of life or limb. Orm, the king's brother, laid his ships out in the harbour immediately that evening, and many others, and the greater number were afloat before.

6. OF ERLING SKAKKE.

On Wednesday, before mass was sung in the town, Erling sailed from Bergen with all his fleet, consisting of twenty-one ships; and there was a fresh breeze for sailing northwards along the coast. Erling had his son King Magnus with him, and there were many lendermen accompanied by the finest men. When Erling came north, abreast of the Fjord district, he sent a boat on shore to Jon Halkelson's farm, and took Nikolas, a son of Simon Skalp and of Maria, Harald Gille's daughter, and brought him out to the fleet, and put him on board the king's ship. On Friday, immediately after matins, they sailed to Steinavag, and King Hakon, with thirteen ships, was lying in the harbour in the neighbourhood. He himself and his men were up at play upon the island, and the lendermen were sitting on the hill, when they saw a boat rowing from the south with two men in it, who were bending back deep towards the keel, and taking hasty strokes with their oars. When they came to the shore they did not belay the boat, but both ran from it. The great men seeing this, said to each other, "These men must have some news to tell;" and got up to meet them. When they met, Onund Simonson asked, "Have ye any news of Erling Skakke, that ye are running so fast?"

They answered, as soon as they could get out the words, for they had lost their breath, "Here comes Erling against you, sailing from the south, with twenty-one ships, or thereabouts, of which many are great enough; and now ye will soon see their sails."

Then said Eindride Unge, "Too near to the nose, said the peasant, when his eye was knocked out."

They went in haste now to where the games were playing, and immediately the war-horns resounded, and with the battle-call all the people were gathered down to the ships in the greatest haste. It was just the time of day when their meat was nearly cooked. All the men rushed to the ships, and each ran on board the vessel that was nearest to him, so that the ships were unequally manned. Some took to the oars; some raised the masts, turned the heads of the vessels to the north, and steered for Veey, where they expected much assistance from the towns.

7. FALL OF KING HAKON.

Soon after they saw the sails of Erling's fleet, and both fleets came in sight of each other. Eindride Unge had a ship called Draglaun, which was a large buss-like long-ship, but which had but a small crew; for those who belonged to her had run on board of other ships, and she was therefore the hindmost of Hakon's fleet. When Eindride came abreast of the island Sek, the Baekisudin, which Erling Skakke himself commanded, came up with her; and these two ships were bound fast together. King Hakon and his followers had arrived close to Veey; but when they heard the war-horn they turned again to assist Eindride. Now they began the battle on both sides, as the vessels came up. Many of the sails lay midships across the vessels; and the ships were not made fast to each other, but they lay side by side. The conflict was not long before there came disorder in Hakon's ship; and some fell, and others sprang overboard. Hakon threw over him a grey cloak, and jumped on board another ship; but when he had been there a short time he thought he had got among his enemies; and when he looked about him he saw none of his men nor of his ships near him. Then he went into the Baekisudin to the forecastle-men, and begged his life. They took him in their keeping, and gave him quarter. In this conflict there was a great loss of people, but principally of Hakon's men. In the Baekisudin fell Nikolas, Simon Skalp's son; and Erling's men are accused of having killed him themselves. Then there was a pause in the battle, and the vessels separated. It was now told to Erling that Hakon was on board of his ship; that the forecastle-men had taken him, and threatened that they would defend him with arms. Erling sent men forwards in the ship to bring the forecastle-men his orders to guard Hakon well, so that he should not get away. He at the same time let it be understood that he had no objection to giving the king life and safety, if the other chiefs were willing, and a peace could be established. All the forecastle-men gave their chief great credit and honour for these words. Then Erling ordered anew a blast of the war-horns, and that the ships should be attacked which had not lost their men; saying that they would never have such another opportunity of avenging King Inge. Thereupon they all raised a war-shout, encouraged each other, and rushed to the assault. In this tumult King Hakon received his death-wound. When his men knew he had fallen they rowed with all their might against the enemy, threw away their shields, slashed with both hands, and cared not for life. This heat and recklessness, however, proved soon a great loss to them; for Erling's men saw the unprotected parts of their bodies, and where their blows would have effect. The greater part of Hakon's men who remained fell here; and it was principally owing to the want of numbers, as they were not enough to defend themselves. They could not get quarter, also excepting those whom the chiefs took under their protection and bound themselves to pay ransom for. The following of Hakon's people fell: Sigurd Kapa, Sigurd Hiupa, and Ragnvald Kunta; but some ships crews got away, rowed into the fjords, and thus saved their lives. Hakon's body was carried to Raumsdal, and buried there; but afterwards his brother, King Sverre, had the body transported north to the merchant town Nidaros, and laid in the stone wall of Christ church south of the choir.

8. FLIGHT OF THE CHIEFS OF HAKON'S MEN.

Earl Sigurd, Eindride Unge, Onund Simonson, Frirek Keina, and other chiefs kept the troop together, left the ships in Raumsdal, and went up to the Uplands. King Magnus and his father Erling sailed with their troops north to Nidaros in Throndhjem, and subdued the country as they went along. Erling called together an Eyra-thing, at which King Magnus was proclaimed king of all Norway. Erling, however, remained there but a short time; for he thought the Throndhjem people were not well affected towards him and his son. King Magnus was then called king of the whole country.

King Hakon had been a handsome man in appearance, well grown, tall and thin; but rather broad-shouldered, on which account his men called him Herdebreid. As he was young in years, his lendermen ruled for him. He was cheerful and friendly in conversation, playful and youthful in his ways, and was much liked by the people.

9. OF KING SIGURD'S BEGINNING.

There was an Upland man called Markus of Skog, who was a relation of Earl Sigurd. Markus brought up a son of King Sigurd Mun, who was also called Sigurd. This Sigurd was chosen king (A.D. 1162) by the Upland people, by the advice of Earl Sigurd and the other chiefs who had followed King Hakon. They had now a great army, and the troops were divided in two bodies; so that Markus and the king were less exposed where there was anything to do, and Earl Sigurd and his troop, along with the lendermen, were most in the way of danger. They went with their troops mostly through the Uplands, and sometimes eastwards to Viken. Erling Skakke had his son King Magnus always with him, and he had also the whole fleet and the land defence under him. He was a while in Bergen in autumn; but went from thence eastward to Viken, where he settled in Tunsberg for his winter quarters (A.D. 1163), and collected in Viken all the taxes and revenues that belonged to Magnus as king; and he had many and very fine troops. As Earl Sigurd had but a small part of the country, and kept many men on foot, he soon was in want of money; and where there was no chief in the neighbourhood he had to seek money by unlawful ways,–sometimes by unfounded accusations and fines, sometimes by open robbery.

10. EARL SIGURD'S CONDEMNATION.

At that time the realm of Norway was in great prosperity. The bondes were rich and powerful, unaccustomed to hostilities or violence, and the oppression of roving troops; so that there was soon a great noise and scandal when they were despoiled and robbed. The people of Viken were very friendly to Erling and King Magnus, principally from the popularity of the late King Inge Haraldson; for the Viken people had always served under his banner. Erling kept a guard in the town, and twelve men were on watch every night. Erling had Things regularly with the bondes, at which the misdeeds of Sigurd's people were often talked over; and by the representations of Erling and his adherents, the bondes were brought unanimously to consider that it would be a great good fortune if these bands should be rooted out. Arne, the king's relation, spoke well and long on this subject, and at last severely; and required that all who were at the Thing,–men-at-arms, bondes, towns-men, and merchants,–should come to the resolution to sentence according to law Earl Sigurd and all his troop, and deliver them to Satan, both living and dead. From the animosity and hatred of the people, this was agreed to by all; and thus the unheard-of deed was adopted and confirmed by oath, as if a judgment in the case was delivered there by the Thing according to law. The priest Hroald the Long-winded, who was a very eloquent man, spoke in the case; but his speech was to the same purpose as that of others who had spoken before. Erling gave a feast at Yule in Tunsberg, and paid the wages of the men-at-arms at Candlemas.

11. OF ERLING.

Earl Sigurd went with his best troops down to Viken, where many people were obliged to submit to his superior force, and many had to pay money. He drove about thus widely higher up the country, penetrating into different districts. But there were some in his troop who desired privately to make peace with Erling; but they got back the answer, that all who asked for their lives should obtain quarter, but they only should get leave to remain in the country who had not been guilty of any great offenses against Erling. And when Sigurd's adherents heard that they would not get leave to remain in the country, they held together in one body; for there were many among them who knew for certain that Erling would look upon them as guilty of offences against him. Philip Gyrdson made terms with Erling, got his property back, and went home to his farm; but soon after Sigurd's men came there, and killed him. They committed many crimes against each other, and many men were slain in their mutual persecution; but here what was committed by the chiefs only is written down.

12. ERLING GETS NEWS OF EARL SIGURD.

It was in the beginning of Lent that news came to Erling that Earl Sigurd intended to come upon him; and news of him came here and there, sometimes nearer, sometimes farther off. Erling sent out spies in all quarters around to discover where they were. Every evening he assembled all the men-at-arms by the war-horn out of the town; and for a long time in the winter they lay under arms all night, ready to be drawn up in array. At last Erling got intelligence that Sigurd and his followers were not far distant, up at the farm Re. Erling then began his expedition out of the town, and took with him all the towns-people who were able to carry arms and had arms, and likewise all the merchants; and left only twelve men behind to keep watch in the town. Erling went out of the town on Thursday afternoon, in the second week of Lent (February 19); and every man had two days' provisions with him. They marched by night, and it was late before they got out of the town with the men. Two men were with each shield and each horse; and the people, when mustered, were about 1200 men. When they met their spies, they were informed that Sigurd was at Re, in a house called Rafnnes, and had 500 men. Then Erling called together his people; told them the news he had received, and all were eager to hasten their march, fall on them in the houses, or engage them by night.

Erling replied to them thus:–"It is probable that we and Earl Sigurd shall soon meet. There are also many men in this band whose handywork remains in our memories; such as cutting down King Inge, and so many more of our friends, that it would take long to reckon them up. These deeds they did by the power of Satan, by witchcraft, and by villainy; for it stands in our laws and country rights, that however highly a man may have been guilty, it shall be called villainy and cowardly murder to kill him in the night. This band has had its luck hitherto by following the counsel of men acquainted with witchcraft and fighting by night, and not in the light of day; and by this proceeding have they been victorious hitherto over the chiefs whose heads they have laid low on the earth. Now we have often seen, and proved, how unsuitable and improper it is to go into battle in the nighttime; therefore let us rather have before our eyes the example of chiefs better known to us, and who deserve better to be imitated, and fight by open day in regular battle array, and not steal upon sleeping men in the night. We have people enough against them, so few as they are. Let us, therefore, wait for day and daylight, and keep together in our array in case they attack us."

Thereafter the whole army sat down. Some opened up bundles of hay, and made a bed of it for themselves; some sat upon their shields, and thus waited the daydawn. The weather was raw, and there was a wet snowdrift.

13. OF EARL SIGURD'S BATTLE ARRAY.

Earl Sigurd got the first intelligence of Erling's army, when it was already near to the house. His men got up, and armed themselves; but not knowing how many men Erling had with him, some were inclined to fly, but the most determined to stand. Earl Sigurd was a man of understanding, and could talk well, but certainly was not considered brave enough to take a strong resolution; and indeed the earl showed a great inclination to fly, for which he got many stinging words from his men-at-arms. As day dawned, they began on both sides to draw up their battle array. Earl Sigurd placed his men on the edge of a ridge between the river and the house, at a place at which a little stream runs into the river. Erling and his people placed their array on the other side of the river; but at the back of his array were men on horseback well armed, who had the king with them. When Earl Sigurd's men saw that there was so great a want of men on their side, they held a council, and were for taking to the forest. But Earl Sigurd said, "Ye alleged that I had no courage, but it will now be proved; and let each of you take care not to fail, or fly, before I do so. We have a good battle-field. Let them cross the bridge; but as soon as the banner comes over it let us then rush down the hill upon them, and none desert his neighbour."

Earl Sigurd had on a red-brown kirtle, and a red cloak, of which the corners were tied and turned back; shoes on his feet; and a shield and sword called Bastard. The earl said, "God knows that I would rather get at Erling Skakke with a stroke of Bastard, than receive much gold."

14. EARL SIGURD'S FALL.

Erling Skakke's army wished to go on to the bridge; but Erling told them to go up along the river, which was small, and not difficult to cross, as its banks were flat; and they did so. Earl Sigurd's array proceeded up along the ridge right opposite to them; but as the ridge ended, and the ground was good and level over the river, Erling told his men to sing a Paternoster, and beg God to give them the victory who best deserved it. Then they all sang aloud "Kyrie Eleison", and struck with their weapons on their shields. But with this singing 300 men of Erling's people slipped away and fled. Then Erling and his people went across the river, and the earl's men raised the war-shout; but there was no assault from the ridge down upon Erling's array, but the battle began upon the hill itself. They first used spears then edge weapons; and the earl's banner soon retired so far back, that Erling and his men scaled the ridge. The battle lasted but a short time before the earl's men fled to the forest, which they had close behind them. This was told Earl Sigurd, and his men bade him fly; but he replied, "Let us on while we can." And his men went bravely on, and cut down on all sides. In this tumult fell Earl Sigurd and Jon Sveinson, and nearly sixty men. Erling lost few men, and pursued the fugitives to the forest. There Erling halted his troops, and turned back. He came just as the king's slaves were about stripping the clothes off Earl Sigurd, who was not quite lifeless. He had put his sword in the sheath, and it lay by his side. Erling took it, struck the slaves with it, and drove them away. Then Erling, with his troops, returned, and sat down in Tunsberg. Seven days after Earl Sigurd's fall Erling's men took Eindride Unge prisoner, and killed him, with all his ship's crew.

15. MARKUS OF SKOG, AND SIGURD SIGURDSON.

Markus of Skog, and King Sigurd, his foster-son, rode down to Viken towards spring, and there got a ship; but when Erling heard it he went eastwards against them, and they met at Konungahella. Markus fled with his followers to the island Hising; and there the country people of Hising came down in swarms, and placed themselves in Markus's and Sigurd's array. Erling and his men rowed to the shore; but Markus's men shot at them. Then Erling said to his people, "Let us take their ships, but not go up to fight with a land force. The Hisingers are a bad set to quarrel with,–hard, and without understanding. They will keep this troop but a little while among them, for Hising is but a small spot." This was done: they took the ships, and brought them over to Konungahella. Markus and his men went up to the forest district, from which they intended to make assaults, and they had spies out on both sides. Erling had many men-at-arms with him, whom he brought from other districts, and they made attacks on each other in turn.

16. BEGINNING OF ARCHBISHOP EYSTEIN.

Eystein, a son of Erlend Himaide, was selected to be archbishop, after Archbishop Jon's death; and he was consecrated the same year King Inge was killed. Now when Archbishop Eystein came to his see, he made himself beloved by all the country, as an excellent active man of high birth. The Throndhjem people, in particular, received him with pleasure; for most of the great people in the Throndhjem district were connected with the archbishop by relationship or other connection, and all were his friends. The archbishop brought forward a request to the bondes in a speech, in which he set forth the great want of money for the see, and also how much greater improvement of the revenues would be necessary to maintain it suitably, as it was now of much more importance than formerly when the bishop's see was first established. He requested of the bondes that they should give him, for determining lawsuits, an ore of silver value, instead of what they had before paid, which was an ore of judgment money, of that kind which was paid to the king in judging cases; and the difference between the two kinds of ore was, that the ore he desired was a half greater than the other. By help of the archbishop's relations and friends, and his own activity, this was carried; and it was fixed by law in all the Throndhjem district, and in all the districts belonging to his archbishopric.

17. OF MARKUS AND KING SIGURD.

When Sigurd and Markus lost their ships in the Gaut river, and saw they could get no hold on Erling, they went to the Uplands, and proceeded by land north to Throndhjem. Sigurd was received there joyfully, and chosen king at an Eyra-thing; and many gallant men, with their sons, attached themselves to his party. They fitted out ships, rigged them for a voyage, and proceeded when summer came southwards to More, and took up all the royal revenues wheresoever they came. At this time the following lendermen were appointed in Bergen for the defence of the country:–Nikolas Sigurdson, Nokve Palson, and several military leaders; as Thorolf Dryl, Thorbjorn Gjaldkere, and many others. As Markus and Sigurd sailed south, they heard that Erling's men were numerous in Bergen; and therefore they sailed outside the coast-rocks, and southwards past Bergen. It was generally remarked, that Markus's men always got a fair wind, wherever they wished to sail to.

18. MARKUS AND KING SIGURD KILLED.

As soon as Erling Skakke heard that Sigurd and Markus had sailed southwards, he hastened to Viken, and drew together an armed force; and he soon had a great many men, and many stout ships. But when he came farther in Viken, he met with a strong contrary wind, which kept him there in port the whole summer. Now when Sigurd and Markus came east to Lister, they heard that Erling had a great force in Viken; so they turned to the north again. But when they reached Hordaland, with the intention of sailing to Bergen, and came opposite the town, Nikolas and his men rowed out against them, with more men and larger ships than they had. Sigurd and Markus saw no other way of escaping but to row away southwards. Some of them went out to sea, others got south to the sound, and some got into the Fjords. Markus, and some people with him, sprang upon an isle called Skarpa. Nikolas and his men took their ships, gave Jon Halkelson and a few others quarter, but killed the most of them they could get hold of. Some days after Eindride Heidafylja found Sigurd and Markus, and they were brought to Bergen. Sigurd was beheaded outside of Grafdal, and Markus and another man were hanged at Hvarfsnes. This took place on Michaelmas day (September 29, 1163), and the band which had followed them was dispersed.

19. ERLING AND THE PEOPLE OF HISING ISLE.

Frirek Keina and Bjarne the Bad, Onund Simonson and Ornolf Skorpa had rowed out to sea with some ships, and sailed outside along the land to the east. Wheresoever they came to the land they plundered, and killed Erling's friends. Now when Erling heard that Sigurd and Markus were killed, he gave leave to the lendermen and people of the levy to return home; but he himself, with his men, set his course eastward across the Folden fjord, for he heard of Markus's men there. Erling sailed to Konungahella, where he remained the autumn; and in the first week of winter Erling went out to the island Hising with his men, and called the bondes to a Thing. When the Hising people came to the Thing, Erling laid his law-suit against them for having joined the bands of Sigurd and Markus, and having raised men against him. Assur was the name of one of the greatest of the bondes on the island, and he answered Erling on account of the others. The Thing was long assembled; but at the close the bondes gave the case into Erling's own power, and he appointed a meeting in the town within one week, and named fifteen bondes who should appear there. When they came, he condemned them to pay a penalty of 300 head of cattle; and the bondes returned home ill pleased at this sentence. Soon after the Gaut river was frozen, and Erling's ships were fast in the ice; and the bondes kept back the mulct, and lay assembled for some time. Erling made a Yule feast in the town; but the Hising people had joint-feasts with each other, and kept under arms during Yule. The night after the fifth day of Yule Erling went up to Hising, surrounded Assur's house, and burnt him in it. He killed one hundred men in all, burnt three houses, and then returned to Konungahella. The bondes came then, according to agreement, to pay the mulct.

20. DEATH OF FRIREK KEINA AND BJARNE.

Erling Skakke made ready to sail in spring as soon as he could get his ships afloat for ice, and sailed from Konungahella; for he heard that those who had formerly been Markus's friends were marauding in the north of Viken. Erling sent out spies to learn their doings, searched for them, and found them lying in a harbour. Onund Simonson and Ornolf Skorpa escaped, but Frirek Keina and Bjarne the Bad were taken, and many of their followers were killed. Erling had Frirek bound to an anchor and thrown overboard; and for that deed Erling was much detested in the Throndhjem country, for the most powerful men there were relatives of Frirek. Erling ordered Bjarne the Bad to be hanged; and he uttered, according to his custom, many dreadful imprecations during his execution. Thorbjorn Skakkaskald tells of this business:–

"East of the Fjord beyond the land,
Unnoticed by the pirate band,
Erling stole on them ere they knew,
And seized and killed all Keina's crew.
Keina, fast to an anchor bound,
Was thrown into the deep-blue Sound;
And Bjarne swung high on gallows-tree,
A sight all good men loved to see."

Onund and Ornolf, with the band that had escaped, fled to Denmark; but were sometimes in Gautland, or in Viken.

21. CONFERENCE BETWEEN ERLING AND EYSTEIN.

Erling Skakke sailed after this to Tunsberg, and remained there very long in spring (A.D. 1164); but when summer came he proceeded north to Bergen, where at that time a great many people were assembled. There was the legate from Rome, Stephanus; the Archbishop Eystein, and other bishops of the country. There was also Bishop Brand, who was consecrated bishop of Iceland, and Jon Loptson, a daughter's son of King Magnus Barefoot; and on this occasion King Magnus and Jon's other relations acknowledged the relationship with him.

Archbishop Eystein and Erling Skakke often conversed together in private; and, among other things, Erling asked one day, "Is it true, sir, what people tell me, that you have raised the value of the ore upon the people north in Throndhjem, in the law cases in which money-fees are paid you?"

"It is so," said the archbishop, "that the bondes have allowed me an advance on the ore of law casualties; but they did it willingly, and without any kind of compulsion, and have thereby added to their honour for God and the income of the bishopric."

Erling replies, "Is this according to the law of the holy Olaf? or have you gone to work more arbitrarily in this than is written down in the lawbook?"

The archbishop replies, "King Olaf the Holy fixed the laws, to which he received the consent and affirmative of the people; but it will not be found in his laws that it is forbidden to increase God's right."

Erling: "If you augment your right, you must assist us to augment as much the king's right."

The archbishop: "Thou hast already augmented enough thy son's power and dominion; and if I have exceeded the law in taking an increase of the ore from the Throndhjem people, it is, I think, a much greater breach of the law that one is king over the country who is not a king's son, and which has neither any support in the law, nor in any precedent here in the country."

Erling: "When Magnus was chosen king, it was done with your knowledge and consent, and also of all the other bishops here in the country."

Archbishop: "You promised then, Erling, that provided we gave our consent to electing Magnus king, you would, on all occasions, and with all your power, strengthen God's rights."

Erling: "I may well admit that I have promised to preserve and strengthen God's commands and the laws of the land with all my power, and with the king's strength; and now I consider it to be much more advisable, instead of accusing each other of a breach of our promises, to hold firmly by the agreement entered into between us. Do you strengthen Magnus in his dominion, according to what you have promised; and I will, on my part, strengthen your power in all that can be of advantage or honour."

The conversation now took a more friendly turn; and Erling said, "Although Magnus was not chosen king according to what has been the old custom of this country, yet can you with your power give him consecration as king, as God's law prescribes, by anointing the king to sovereignty; and although I be neither a king, nor of kingly race, yet most of the kings, within my recollection, have not known the laws or the constitution of the country so well as I do. Besides, the mother of King Magnus is the daughter of a king and queen born in lawful wedlock, and Magnus is son of a queen and a lawfully married wife. Now if you will give him royal consecration, no man can take royalty from him. William Bastard was not a king's son; but he was consecrated and crowned king of England, and the royalty in England has ever since remained with his race, and all have been crowned. Svein Ulfson was not a king's son in Denmark, and still he was a crowned king, and his sons likewise, and all his descendants have been crowned kings. Now we have here in Norway an archiepiscopal seat, to the glory and honour of the country; let us also have a crowned king, as well as the Danes and Englishmen."

Erling and the archbishop afterwards talked often of this matter, and they were quite agreed. Then the archbishop brought the business before the legate, and got him easily persuaded to give his consent. Thereafter the archbishop called together the bishops, and other learned men, and explained the subject to them. They all replied in the same terms, that they would follow the counsels of the archbishop, and all were eager to promote the consecration as soon as the archbishop pleased.

22. KING MAGNUS'S CONSECRATION.

Erling Skakke then had a great feast prepared in the king's house. The large hall was covered with costly cloth and tapestry, and adorned with great expense. The court-men and all the attendants were there entertained, and there were numerous guests, and many chiefs. Then King Magnus received the royal consecration from the Archbishop Eystein; and at the consecration there were five other bishops and the legate, besides a number of other clergy. Erling Skakke, and with him twelve other lendermen, administered to the king the oath of the law; and the day of the consecration the king and Erling had the legate, the archbishop, and all the other bishops as guests; and the feast was exceedingly magnificent, and the father and son distributed many great presents. King Magnus was then eight years of age, and had been king for three years.

23. KING VALDEMAR'S EMBASSY.

When the Danish king Valdemar heard the news from Norway that Magnus was become king of the whole country, and all the other parties in the country were rooted out, he sent his men with a letter to King Magnus and Erling, and reminded them of the agreement which Erling had entered into, under oath, with King Valdemar, of which we have spoken before; namely, that Viken from the east to Rygiarbit should be ceded to King Valdemar, if Magnus became the sole king of Norway. When the ambassadors came forward and showed Erling the letter of the Danish king, and he heard the Danish king's demand upon Norway, he laid it before the other chiefs by whose counsels he usually covered his acts. All, as one man, replied that the Danes should never hold the slightest portion of Norway; for never had things been worse in the land than when the Danes had power in it. The ambassadors of the Danish king were urgent with Erling for an answer, and desired to have it decided; but Erling begged them to proceed with him east to Viken, and said he would give his final answer when he had met with the men of most understanding and influence in Viken.

24. ERLING AND THE PEOPLE OF VIKEN.

Erling Skakke proceeded in autumn to Viken, and stayed in Tunsberg, from whence he sent people to Sarpsborg to summon a Thing[80] of four districts; and then Erling went there with his people.

When the Thing was seated Erling made a speech in which he explained the resolutions which had been settled upon between him and

80 This reference to a Thing of the people in the affairs of the country is a striking example of the right of the Things being recognised, in theory at least, as fully as the right of our parliaments in later times.–L.

the Danish king, the first time he collected troops against his enemies. "I will," said Erling, "keep faithfully the agreement which we then entered into with the king, if it be your will and consent, bondes, rather to serve the Danish king than the king who is now consecrated and crowned king of this country."

The bondes replied thus to Erling's speech: "Never will we become the Danish king's men, as long as one of us Viken men is in life." And the whole assembly, with shouts and cries, called on Erling to keep the oath he had taken to defend his son's dominions, "should we even all follow thee to battle." And so the Thing was dissolved.

The ambassadors of the Danish king then returned home, and told the issue of their errand. The Danes abused Erling, and all Northmen, and declared that evil only proceeded from them; and the report was spread, that in Spring the Danish king would send out an army and lay waste Norway. Erling returned in autumn north to Bergen, stayed there all winter, and gave their pay to his people.

25. LETTERS OF THE THRONDHJEM PEOPLE.

The same winter (A.D. 1165) some Danish people came by land through the Uplands, saying they were to go, as was then the general practice, to the holy King Olaf's festival. But when they came to the Throndhjem country, they went to many men of influence, and told their business; which was, that the Danish king had sent them to desire their friendship, and consent, if he came to the country, promising them both power and money. With this verbal message came also the Danish king's letter and seal, and a message to the Throndhjem people that they should send back their letters and seals to him. They did so, and the most of them received well the Danish king's message; whereupon the messengers returned back towards Lent. Erling was in Bergen; and towards spring Erling's friends told him the loose reports they had heard by some merchant vessels that had arrived from Throndhjem, that the Throndhjem people were in hostility openly against him; and had declared that if Erling came to Throndhjem, he should never pass Agdanes in life. Erling said this was mere folly and idle talk. Erling now made it known that he would go to Unarheim to the Gangdag-thing; and ordered a cutter of twenty rowing benches to be fitted out, a boat of fifteen benches, and a provision-ship. When the vessels were ready, there came a strong southerly gale. On the Thursday of the Ascension week, Erling called his people by sound of trumpet to their departure; but the men were loath to leave the town, and were ill inclined to row against the wind. Erling brought his vessels to Biskupshafn. "Well," said Erling, "since ye are so unwilling to row against the wind, raise the mast, hoist the sails, and let the ship go north." They did so, and sailed northwards both day and night. On Wednesday, in the evening, they sailed in past Agdanes, where they found a fleet assembled of many merchant vessels, rowing craft, and boats, all going towards the town to the celebration of the festival,– some before them, some behind them–so that the townspeople paid no attention to the long-ships coming.

26. ERLING AND THE PEOPLE OF THRONDHJEM.

ERLING CAME TO THE town just as vespers was being sung in Christ church. He and his men ran into the town, to where it was told them that the lenderman, Alf Rode, a son of Ottar Birting, was still sitting at table, and drinking with his men. Erling fell upon them; and Alf was killed, with almost all his men. Few other men were killed; for they had almost all gone to church, as this was the night before Christ's Ascension-day. In the morning early, Erling called all the people by sound of trumpet to a Thing out upon Evrar. At the Thing Erling laid a charge against the Throndhjem people, accusing them of intending to betray the country, and take it from the king; and named Bard Standale, Pal Andreason, and Razabard, who then presided over the town's affairs, and many others. They, in their defence, denied the accusation; but Erling's writer stood up, produced many letters with seals, and asked if they acknowledged their seals which they had sent to the Danish king; and thereupon the letters were read. There was also a Danish man with Erling who had gone with the letters in winter, and whom Erling for that purpose had taken into his service. He told to these men the very words which each of them had used. "And you, Razabard, spoke, striking your breast; and the very words you used were, 'Out of this breast are all these counsels produced.'" Bard replied, "I was wrong in the head, sirs, when I spoke so." There was now nothing to be done but to submit the case entirely to the sentence Erling might give upon it. He took great sums of money from many as fines, and condemned all those who had been killed as lawless, and their deeds as lawless; making their deaths thereby not subject to mulct. Then Erling returned south to Bergen.

27. KING VALDEMAR'S EXPEDITION TO NORWAY.

The Danish king Valdemar assembled in spring (A.D. 1165) a great army, and proceeded with it north to Viken. As soon as he reached the dominions of the king of Norway, the bondes assembled in a great multitude. The king advanced peacefully; but when they came to the mainland, the people shot at them even when there were only two or three together, from which the ill-will of the country people towards them was evident. When they came to Tunsberg, King Valdemar summoned a Hauga-thing; but nobody attended it from the country parts. Then Valdemar spoke thus to his troops: "It is evident that all the country-people are against us; and now we have two things to choose: the one to go through the country, sword in hand, sparing neither man nor beast; the other is to go back without effecting our object. And it is more my inclination to go with the army to the East against the heathens, of whom we have enough before us in the East country, than to kill Christian people here, although they have well deserved it." All the others had a greater desire for a foray; but the king ruled, and they all returned back to Denmark without effecting their purpose. They pillaged, however, all around in the distant islands, or where the king was not in the neighbourhood. They then returned south to Denmark without doing anything.

28. ERLING'S EXPEDITION TO JUTLAND.

As soon as Erling heard that a Danish force had come to Viken, he ordered a levy through all the land, both of men and ships, so that there was a great assemblage of men in arms; and with this force he proceeded eastward along the coast. But when he came to Lidandisnes, he heard that the Danish army had returned south to Denmark, after plundering all around them in Viken. Then Erling gave all the people of the levy permission to return home; but he himself and some lendermen, with many vessels, sailed to Jutland after the Danes. When they came to a place called Dyrsa, the Danes who had returned from the expedition lay there with many ships. Erling gave them battle, and there was a fight, in which the Danes soon fled with the loss of many people; and Erling and his men plundered the ships and the town, and made a great booty, with which they returned to Norway. Thereafter, for a time, there was hostility between Norway and Denmark.

29. ERLING'S EXPEDITION TO DENMARK.

THE PRINCESS KRISFIN WENT south in autumn (A.D. 1165) to Denmark, to visit her relation King Valdemar, who was her cousin. The king received her kindly, and gave her fiefs in his kingdom, so that she could support her household well. She often conversed with the king, who was remarkably kind towards her. In the spring following (A.D. 1166) Kristin sent to Erling, and begged him to pay a visit to the Danish king, and enter into a peace with him. In summer Erling was in Viken, where he fitted out a long-ship, manned it with his finest lads, and sailed (a single ship) over to Jutland. When he heard that the Danish king Valdemar was in Randaros, Erling sailed thither, and came to the town just as the king sat at the dinner-table, and most of the people were taking their meal. When his people had made themselves ready according to Erling's orders, set up the ship-tents, and made fast the ship, Erling landed with twelve men, all in armour, with hats over their helmets, and swords under their cloaks. They went to the king's lodging, where the doors stood open, and the dishes were being carried in. Erling and his people went in immediately, and drew up in front of the high-seat. Erling said, "Peace and safe conduct we desire, king, both here and to return home."

The king looked at him, and said, "Art thou here, Erling?"

He replies, "Here is Erling; and tell us, at once, if we shall have peace and safe conduct."

There were eighty of the king's men in the room, but all unarmed. The king replies, "Peace ye shall have, Erling, according to thy desire; for I will not use force or villainy against a man who comes to visit me."

Erling then kissed the king's hand, went out, and down to his ship. Erling stayed at Randaros some time with the king, and they talked about terms of peace between them and between the countries. They agreed that Erling should remain as hostage with the Danish king; and that Asbjorn Snara, Bishop Absalon's brother, should go to Norway as hostage on the other part.

30. KING VALDEMAR AND ERLING.

IN A CONFERENCE WHICH King Valdemar and Erling once had together. Erling said, "Sire, it appears to me likely that it might lead to a peace between the countries if you got that part of Norway which was promised you in our agreement; but if it should be so, what chief would you place over it? Would he be a Dane?"

"No," replied the king; "no Danish chief would go to Norway, where he would have to manage an obstinate hard people, when he has it so easy here with me."

Erling: "It was on that very consideration that I came here; for I would not on any account in the world deprive myself of the advantage of your friendship. In days of old other men, Hakon Ivarson and Fin Arnason, came also from Norway to Denmark, and your predecessor, King Svein, made them both earls. Now I am not a man of less power in Norway than they were then, and my influence is not less than theirs; and the king gave them the province of Halland to rule over, which he himself had and owned before. Now it appears to me, sire, that you, if I become your man and vassal, can allow me to hold of you the fief which my son Magnus will not deny me, by which I will be bound in duty, and ready, to undertake all the service belonging to that title."

Erling spoke such things, and much more in the same strain, until it came at last to this, that Erling became Valdemar's man and vassal; and the king led Erling to the earl's seat one day, and gave him the title of earl, and Viken as a fief under his rule. Earl Erling went thereafter to Norway, and was earl afterwards as long as he lived; and also the peace with the Danish king was afterwards always preserved. Earl Erling had four sons by his concubines. The one was called Hreidar, the next Ogmund; and these by two different mothers: the third was called Fin; the fourth Sigurd: these were younger, and their mother was Asa the Fair. The princess Kristin and Earl Erling had a daughter called Ragnhild, who was married to Jon Thorbergson of Randaberg. Kristin went away from the country with a man called Grim Rusle; and they went to Constantinople, where they were for a time, and had some children.

31. BEGINNING OF OLAF.

Olaf, a son of Gudbrand Skafhaug, and Maria, a daughter of King Eystein Magnuson, were brought up in the house of Sigurd Agnhot in the Uplands. While Earl Erling was in Denmark (A.D. 1166), Olaf and his foster-father gathered a troop together, and many Upland people joined them; and Olaf was chosen king by them. They went with their bands through the Uplands, and sometimes down to Viken, and sometimes east to the forest settlements; but never came on board of ships. Now when, Earl Erling got news of this troop, he hastened to Viken with his forces; and was there in summer in his ships, and in Oslo in autumn (A.D. 1167) and kept Yule there. He had spies up the country after this troop, and went himself, along with Orm, the King-brother, up the country to follow them. Now when they came to a lake called.... ....[81] they took all the vessels that were upon the lake.

32. OF ERLING.

THE PRIEST WHO PERFORMED divine service at a place called Rydiokul, close by the lake, invited the earl to a feast at Candlemas. The earl promised to come; and thinking it would be good to hear mass there, he rowed with his attendants over the lake the night before Candlemas day. But the priest had another plan on hand. He sent men to bring Olaf news of Earl Erling's arrival. The priest gave Erling strong drink in the evening, and let him have an excessive quantity of it. When the earl wished to lie down and sleep, the beds were made ready in the drinking-room; but when they had slept a short time the earl awoke, and asked if it was not the hour for matins. The priest replied, that only a small part of the night was gone, and told him to sleep in peace. The earl replied, "I dream of many things to-night, and I sleep ill." He slumbered again, but awoke soon, and told the priest to get up and sing mass. The priest told the earl to sleep, and said it was but midnight. Then the earl again lay down, slept a little while, and, springing out of bed, ordered his men to put on their clothes. They did so; took their weapons, went to the church, and laid their arms outside while the priest was singing matins.

33. BATTLE AT RYDIOKUL.

AS OLAF GOT THE message in the evening, they travelled in the night six miles, which people considered an extraordinarily long march. They arrived at Rydiokul while the priest was still singing mass, and it was pitch-dark. Olaf and his men went into the room, raised a war-shout, and killed some of the earl's men who had not gone to the early mass. Now when Erling and his men heard the war-shout, they ran to their weapons, and hastened down to their ships. Olaf and his men met them at a fence, at which there was a sharp conflict. Erling and his men retreated along the fence, which protected them. Erling had far fewer men, and many of them had fallen, and still more were wounded. What helped Earl Erling and his men the most was, that Olaf's men could not distinguish them, it was so

81 The name of the lake not given.

dark; and the earl's men were always drawing down to their ships. Are Thorgeirson, father of Bishop Gudmund fell there, and many other of Erling's court-men. Erling himself was wounded in the left side; but some say he did it himself in drawing his sword. Orm the King-brother was also severely wounded; and with great difficulty they escaped to their ships, and instantly pushed off from land. It was generally considered as a most unlucky meeting for Olaf's people, as Earl Erling was in a manner sold into their hands, if they had proceeded with common prudence. He was afterwards called Olaf the Unlucky; but others called his people Hat-lads. They went with their bands through the Uplands as before. Erling again went down to Viken to his ships, and remained there all summer. Olaf was in the Uplands, and sometimes east in the forest districts, where he and his troop remained all the next winter (A.D. 1168).

34. BATTLE AT STANGAR.

The following spring the Hat-lads went down to Viken, and raised the king's taxes all around, and remained there long in summer. When Earl Erling heard this, he hastened with his troops to meet them in Viken, and fell in with them east of the Fjord, at a place called Stangar; where they had a great battle, in which Erling was victorious. Sigurd Agnhot, and many others of Olaf's men, fell there; but Olaf escaped by flight, went south to Denmark, and was all winter (A.D. 1169) in Alaborg in Jutland. The following spring Olaf fell into an illness which ended in death, and he was buried in the Maria church; and the Danes call him a saint.

35. HARALD'S DEATH.

King Magnus had a lenderman called Nikolas Kufung, who was a son of Pal Skaptason. He took Harald prisoner, who called himself a son of King Sigurd Haraldson and the princess Kristin, and a brother of King Magnus by the mother's side. Nikolas brought Harald to Bergen, and delivered him into Earl Erling's hands. It was Erling's custom when his enemies came before him, that he either said nothing to them, or very little, and that in all gentleness, when he had determined to put them to death; or rose with furious words against them, when he intended to spare their lives. Erling spoke but little to Harald, and many, therefore, suspected his intentions; and some begged King Magnus to put in a good word for Harald with the earl; and the king did so. The earl replies, "Thy friends advise thee badly. Thou wouldst govern this kingdom but a short time in peace and safety, if thou wert to follow the counsels of the heart only." Earl Erling ordered Harald to be taken to Nordnes, where he was beheaded.

36. EYSTEIN EYSTEINSON AND THE BIRKEBEINS.

There was a man called Eystein, who gave himself out for a son of King Eystein Haraldson. He was at this time young, and not full grown. It is told of him that he one summer appeared in Svithjod, and went to Earl Birger Brosa, who was then married to Brigida, Eystein's aunt, a daughter of King Harald Gille. Eystein explained his business to him, and asked their assistance. Both Earl Birger and his wife listened to him in a friendly way, and promised him their confidence, and he stayed with them a while. Earl Birger gave him some assistance of men, and a good sum for travelling expenses; and both promised him their friendship on his taking leave. Thereafter Eystein proceeded north into Norway (A.D. 1174), and when he came down to Viken people flocked to him in crowds; and Eystein was there proclaimed king, and he remained in Viken in winter. As they were very poor in money, they robbed all around, wherefore the lendermen and bondes raised men against them; and being thus overpowered by numbers, they fled away to the forests and deserted hill grounds, where they lived for a long time. Their clothes being worn out, they wound the bark of the birch-tree about their legs, and thus were called by the bondes Birkebeins. They often rushed down upon the settled districts, pushed on here or there, and made an assault where they did not find many people to oppose them. They had several battles with the bondes with various success; and the Birkebeins held three battles in regular array, and gained the victory in them all. At Krokaskog they had nearly made an unlucky expedition, for a great number of bondes and men-at-arms were assembled there against them; but the Birkebeins felled brushwood across the roads, and retired into the forest. They were two years (A.D. 1175-1176) in Viken before they showed themselves in the northern parts of the country.

37. BIRKEBEINS, KING EYSTEIN, AND SKAKKE.

Magnus had been king for thirteen years when the Birkebeins first made their appearance. They got themselves ships in the third summer (A.D. 1176), with which they sailed along the coast gathering goods and men. They were first in Viken; but when summer advanced they proceeded northwards, and so rapidly that no news preceded them until they came to Throndhjem. The Birkebeins' troop consisted principally of hill-men and Elfgrims, and many were from Thelemark; and all were well armed. Their king, Eystein, was a handsome man, and with a little but good countenance; and he was not of great stature, for his men called him Eystein Meyla. King Magnus and Earl Erling were in Bergen when the Birkebeins sailed past it to the north; but they did not hear of them.

Earl Erling was a man of great understanding and power, an excellent leader in war, and an able and prudent ruler of the country; but he had the character of being cruel and severe. The cause of this was principally that he never allowed his enemies to remain in the country, even when they prayed to him for mercy; and therefore many joined the bands which were collected against him. Erling was a tall strong-made man, somewhat short-necked and high-shouldered; had a long and sharp countenance of a light complexion, and his hair became very grey. He bore his head a little on one side; was free and agreeable in his manners. He wore the old fashion of clothes,–long body-pieces and long arms to his coats, foreign cloak, and high shoes. He made the king wear the same kind of dress in his youth; but when he grew up, and acted for himself, he dressed very sumptuously.

King Magnus was of a light turn of mind, full of jokes; a great lover of mirth, and not less of women.

38. OF NIKOLAS.

Nikolas was a son of Sigurd Hranason and of Skialdvor, a daughter of Brynjolf Ulfalde, and a sister of Haldor Brynjolfson by the father's side, and of King Magnus Barefoot by the mother's side. Nikolas was a distinguished chief, who had a farm at Ongul in Halogaland, which was called Steig. Nikolas had also a house in Nidaros, below Saint Jon's church, where Thorgeir the scribe lately dwelt. Nikolas was often in the town, and was president of the townspeople. Skialdvor, Nikolas's daughter, was married to Eirik Arnason, who was also a lenderman.

39. OF EIRIK AND NIKOLAS.

As the people of the town were coming from matins the last day of Marymas (September 8th), Eirik came up to Nikolas, and said, "Here are some fishermen come from the sea, who report that some long-ships are sailing into the fjord; and people conjecture that these may be the Birkebeins. It would be advisable to call the townspeople together with the war-horns, to meet under arms out on Eyrar."

Nikolas replies, "I don't go after fishermen's reports; but I shall send out spies to the fjord, and in the meantime hold a Thing to-day."

Eirik went home; but when they were ringing to high mass, and Nikolas was going to church, Eirik came to hint again, and said, "I believe the news to be true; for here are men who say they saw them under sail; and I think it would be most advisable to ride out of town, and gather men with arms; for it appears to me the townspeople will be too few."

Nikolas replies, "Thou art mixing everything together; let us first hear mass, and then take our resolution."

Nikolas then went into the church. When the mass was over Eirik went to Nikolas, and said, "My horses are saddled; I will ride away."

Nikolas replies, "Farewell, then: we will hold a Thing to-day on the Eyrar, and examine what force of men there may be in the town."

Eirik rode away, and Nikolas went to his house, and then to dinner.

40. THE FALL OF NIKOLAS.

The meat was scarcely put on the table, when a man came into the house to tell Nikolas that the Birkebeins were roving up the river. Then Nikolas called to his men to take their weapons. When they were armed Nikolas ordered them to go up into the loft. But that was a most imprudent step; for if they had remained in the yard, the townspeople might have come to their assistance; but now the Birkebeins filled the whole yard, and from thence scrambled from all sides up to the loft. They called to Nikolas, and offered him quarter, but he refused it. Then they attacked the loft. Nikolas and his men defended themselves with bow-shot, hand-shot, and stones of the chimney; but the Birkebeins hewed down the houses, broke up the loft, and returned shot for shot from bow or hand. Nikolas had a red shield in which were gilt nails, and about it was a border of stars. The Birkebeins shot so that the arrows went in up to the arrow feather. Then said Nikolas, "My shield deceives me." Nikolas and a number of his people fell, and his death was greatly lamented. The Birkebeins gave all the towns-people their lives.

41. EYSTEIN PROCLAIMED KING.

Eystein was then proclaimed king, and all the people submitted to him. He stayed a while in the town, and then went into the interior of the Throndhjem land, where many joined him, and among them Thorfin Svarte of Snos with a troop of people. When the Birkebeins, in the beginning of winter (A.D. 1177), came again into the town, the sons of Gudrun from Saltnes, Jon Ketling, Sigurd, and William, joined them; and when they proceeded afterwards from Nidaros up Orkadal, they could number nearly 2000 men. They afterwards went to the Uplands, and on to Thoten and Hadaland, and from thence to Ringerike, and subdued the country wheresover they came.

42. THE FALL OF KING EYSTEIN.

King Magnus went eastward to Viken in autumn with a part of his men and with him Orm, the king's brother; but Earl Erling remained behind in Bergen to meet the Berkebeins in case they took the sea route. King Magnus went to Tunsberg, where he and Orm held their Yule (A.D. 1177). When King Magnus heard that the Birkebeins were up in Re, the king and Orm proceeded thither with their men. There was much snow, and it was dreadfully cold. When they came to the farm they left the beaten track on the road, and drew up their array outside of the fence, and trod a path through the snow with their men, who were not quite 1500 in number. The Birkebeins were dispersed here and there in other farms, a few men in each house. When they perceived King Magnus's army they assembled, and drew up in regular order; and as they thought their force was larger than his, which it actually was, they resolved to fight; but when they hurried forward to the road only a few could advance at a time, which broke their array, and the men fell who first advanced upon the beaten way. Then the Birkebeins' banner was cut down; those who were nearest gave way and some took to flight. King Magnus's men pursued them, and killed one after the other as they came up with them. Thus the Birkebeins could never form themselves in array; and being exposed to the weapons of the enemy singly, many of them fell, and many fled. It happened here, as it often does, that although men be brave and gallant, if they have once been defeated and driven to flight, they will not easily be brought to turn round. Now the main body of the Birkebeins began to fly, and many fell; because Magnus's men killed all they could lay hold of, and not one of them got quarter. The whole body became scattered far and wide. Eystein in his flight ran into a house, and begged for his life, and that the bonde would conceal him; but the bonde killed him, and then went to King Magnus, whom he found at Rafnnes, where the king was in a room warming himself by the fire along with many people. Some went for the corpse, and bore it into the room, where the king told the people to come and inspect the body. A man was sitting on a bench in the corner, and he was a Birkebein, but nobody had observed him; and when he saw and recognised his chief's body he sprang up suddenly and actively, rushed out upon the floor, and with an axe he had in his hands made a blow at King Magnus's neck between the shoulders. A man saw the axe swinging, and pulled the king to a side, by which the axe struck lower in the shoulder, and made a large wound. He then raised the axe again, and made a blow at Orm, the King-brother, who was lying on a bench, and the blow was directed at both legs; but Orm seeing the man about to kill him, drew in his feet instantly, threw them over his head, and the blow fell on the bench, in which the axe stuck fast; and then the blows at the Birkebein came so thick that he could scarcely fall to the ground. It was discovered that he had dragged his entrails after him over the floor; and this man's bravery was highly praised. King Magnus's men followed the fugitives, and killed so many that they were tired of it. Thorfin of Snos, and a very great number of Throndhjem people, fell there.

43. OF THE BIRKEBEINS.

The faction which called itself the Birkebeins had gathered together in great numbers. They were a hardy people, and the boldest of men under arms; but wild, and going forward madly when they had a strong force. They had few men in their faction who were good counsellors, or accustomed to rule a country by law, or to head an army; and if there were such men among them who had more knowledge, yet the many would only allow of those measures which they liked, trusting always to their numbers and courage. Of the men who escaped many were wounded, and had lost both their clothes and their arms, and were altogether destitute of money. Some went east to the borders, some went all the way east to Svithjod; but the most of them went to Thelemark, where they had their families. All took flight, as they had no hope of getting their lives from King Magnus or Earl Erling.

44. OF KING MAGNUS ERLINGSON.

King Magnus then returned to Tunsberg, and got great renown by this victory; for it had been an expression in the mouths of all, that Earl Erling was the shield and support of his son and himself. But after gaining a victory over so strong and numerous a force with fewer troops, King Magnus was considered by all as surpassing other leaders, and that he would become a warrior as much greater than his father, Earl Erling, as he was younger.

READ THE MOST POPULAR ROYAL CLASSICS

20,000 Leagues Under the Sea BY JULES VERNE
A Christmas Carol BY CHARLES DICKENS
A Tale of Two Cities BY CHARLES DICKENS
Aesop's Fables BY AESOP
Alice in Wonderland BY LEWIS CARROLL
Anna Karenina BY LEO TOLSTOY
Anne of Green Gables BY LUCY MAUD MONTGOMERY
Around the World in 80 Days BY JULES VERNE
Black Beauty BY ANNA SEWELL
Candide BY VOLTAIRE
Common Sense BY THOMAS PAINE
Crime and Punishment BY FYODOR DOSTOEVSKY
Don Quixote BY MIGUEL DE CERVANTES
Dracula BY BRAM STOKER
Dubliners BY JAMES JOYCE
Emma BY JANE AUSTEN
Frankenstein BY MARY SHELLEY
Great Expectations BY CHARLES DICKENS
Grimm's Fairy Tales BY JAKOB AND WILHELM GRIMM
Gulliver's Travels BY JONATHAN SWIFT
Hamlet BY WILLIAM SHAKESPEARE
Heart of Darkness BY JOSEPH CONRAD
Jane Eyre BY CHARLOTTE BRONTË
Journey to the Center of the Earth BY JULES VERNE
Les Misérables BY VICTOR HUGO
Macbeth BY WILLIAM SHAKESPEARE
Meditations BY MARCUS AURELIUS
Middlemarch BY GEORGE ELIOT
Moby Dick BY HERMAN MELVILLE
Nicomachean Ethics BY ARISTOTLE
North and South BY ELIZABETH GASKELL
Northanger Abbey BY JANE AUSTEN
Notes from the Underground BY FYODOR DOSTOYEVSKY
Oliver Twist BY CHARLES DICKENS
On War BY CARL VON CLAUSEWITZ
Plato: Five Dialogues BY PLATO
Politics BY ARISTOTLE
Pride & Prejudice BY JANE AUSTEN
Robinson Crusoe BY DANIEL DEFOE
Sense & Sensibility BY JANE AUSTEN
Sons and Lovers BY D. H. LAWRENCE

Tarzan of the Apes by Edgar Rice Burroughs
Tess of the d'Urbervilles by Thomas Hardy
The Adventures of Huckleberry Finn by Mark Twain
The Adventures of Sherlock Holmes by A. Conan Doyle
The Adventures of Tom Sawyer by Mark Twain
The Art of War by Sun Tzu
The Brothers Karamazov by Fyodor Dostoevsky
The Call of the Wild by Jack London
The Count of Monte Cristo by Alexandre Dumas
The Hound of the Baskervilles by Arthur Conan Doyle
The Iliad by Homer
The Importance of Being Earnest by Oscar Wilde
The Jungle Book by Rudyard Kipling
The Last of the Mohicans by James Fenimore Cooper
The Lost World by Arthur Conan Doyle
The Metamorphosis by Franz Kafka
The Murder on the Links by Agatha Christie
The Mysterious Affair at Styles by Agatha Christie
The Odyssey by Homer
The Origin of Species by Charles Darwin
The Picture of Dorian Gray by Oscar Wilde
The Portrait of a Lady by Henry James
The Prince by Niccolò Machiavelli
The Prince and the Pauper by Mark Twain
The Prophet by Kahlil Gibran
The Republic by Plato
The Scarlet Letter by Nathaniel Hawthorne
The Secret Garden by Frances Hodgson Burnett
The Strange Case of Dr. Jekyll & Mr. Hyde by Robert Louis Stevenson
The Swiss Family Robinson by Johann David Wyss
The Tale of Peter Rabbit by Beatrix Potter
The Tenant of Wildfell Hall by Anne Brontë
The Three Musketeers by Alexandre Dumas
The Time Machine by H. G. Wells
The Wealth of Nations by Adam Smith
The Wind in the Willows by Kenneth Grahame
The Wizard of Oz by L. Frank Baum
This Side of Paradise by F. Scott Fitzgerald
Treasure Island by Robert Louis Stevenson
Ulysses by James Joyce
Vanity Fair by William Makepeace Thackeray
War and Peace by Leo Tolstoy
Wuthering Heights by Emily Brontë

www.ingramcontent.com/pod-product-compliance
Lightning Source LLC
Chambersburg PA
CBHW020919310726
48980CB00011B/963/J